Because It's Christmas

The Cape Light Titles

CAPE LIGHT

HOME SONG

A GATHERING PLACE

A NEW LEAF

A CHRISTMAS PROMISE

THE CHRISTMAS ANGEL

A CHRISTMAS TO REMEMBER

A CHRISTMAS VISITOR

A CHRISTMAS STAR

A WISH FOR CHRISTMAS

ON CHRISTMAS EVE

CHRISTMAS TREASURES

A SEASON OF ANGELS

SONGS OF CHRISTMAS

ALL IS BRIGHT

TOGETHER FOR CHRISTMAS

BECAUSE IT'S CHRISTMAS

The Angel Island Titles

THE INN AT ANGEL ISLAND

THE WEDDING PROMISE

A WANDERING HEART

THE WAY HOME

HARBOR OF THE HEART

Thomas Kinkade's Cape Light

Because It's Christmas

KATHERINE SPENCER

BERKLEY
New York

BERKLEY
An imprint of Penguin Random House LLC
375 Hudson Street, New York, New York 10014

Copyright © 2016 by The Thomas Kinkade Company and Parachute Publishing, LLC
Penguin Random House supports copyright. Copyright fuels creativity, encourages diverse
voices, promotes free speech, and creates a vibrant culture. Thank you for buying an authorized
edition of this book and for complying with copyright laws by not reproducing, scanning, or
distributing any part of it in any form without permission. You are supporting writers and
allowing Penguin Random House to continue to publish books for every reader.

BERKLEY is a registered trademark and the B colophon is a trademark of
Penguin Random House LLC.

Library of Congress Cataloging-in-Publication Data
Names: Spencer, Katherine, (date-) author.
Title: Because it's Christmas / Katherine Spencer.
Other titles: Because it is Christmas
Description: First edition. | New York : Berkley Books, 2016. | Series:
Thomas Kinkade's Cape Light ; 17
Identifiers: LCCN 2016027519 (print) | LCCN 2016034339 (ebook) | ISBN
9780425282236 (hardcover) | ISBN 9780698198777
Subjects: LCSH: Cape Light (Imaginary place)—Fiction. | City and town
life—New England—Fiction. | Christmas stories. | BISAC: FICTION /
Religious. | FICTION / Christian / Romance. | GSAFD: Christian fiction. |
Love stories.
Classification: LCC PS3553.A489115 B43 2016 (print) | LCC PS3553.A489115
(ebook) | DDC 813/.54—dc23
LC record available at https://lccn.loc.gov/2016027519

First Edition: November 2016

Printed in the United States of America
1   3   5   7   9   10   8   6   4   2

Jacket image: *Christmas Gate* by Thomas Kinkade. Copyright © 2010 Thomas Kinkade.
Jacket design by Lesley Worrell

To my family—with love always

DEAR READER

Every year my daughter sends me a list of items she'd like to find under the Christmas tree. This tradition has probably evolved from the days of writing letters to Santa. Maybe I don't mind because for so many years I was studying those crayoned lists and doing Santa's shopping. Also, I truly enjoy giving everyone on my list something they really want, valuing accuracy above the surprise factor. Some will say that takes the fun out of gift buying and giving. They might even say I'm lazy. These are usually the same people who roam the mall and Internet tirelessly, searching for those unrequested but hopefully perfect presents. I do admire them.

After writing this latest Cape Light story, I've been wondering which category Heaven falls into: Answering our prayers exactly, down to the item number, color, and size? Or delivering a blessing that's absolutely perfect, though we may never have asked for or even imagined it?

As Christmas draws near, Sophie Potter, Emily Warwick, and Zoey Bates each doubt the wishes closest to their hearts will be fulfilled. All Sophie wants is to remain in her home and spend the rest of her days on her beloved orchard. But her children believe she can no longer live alone, despite the unexpected arrival and companionship of her grandson James.

Emily has lost the election to Charlie Bates. Determined to turn the page, she takes up new hobbies and puts her family first. Secretly, she misses the satisfaction she found guiding the citizens of Cape Light. Must she choose one way or the other? Her Christmas wish is to find some other path. One that makes everyone, including herself, happy.

Zoey has been working hard at college and at the diner her family owns. As the fall semester ends, a wonderful career opportunity moves into her sights, and a special relationship grows with James Potter. But family responsibilities come first. Zoey must put her dreams aside, and James must carry through with his plans. Cape Light is only a short stop in his travels. Or so they both believe.

But Sophie, Emily, and Zoey discover that Heaven has read their "wish lists" very carefully and found each of them the perfect gift for Christmas. Maybe not exactly what they asked for or imagined, but something even better.

I hope you find a few perfect surprises under the tree, too.

Wishing you and everyone you hold dear a wonderful holiday season and a happy, healthy New Year.

Katherine Spencer

CHAPTER ONE

LOUR, BUTTER, SUGAR. YOU DON'T NEED MUCH MORE THAN that." Sophie Potter confided the recipe for her delectable piecrust in an unusually serious tone. "Easy, right?"

"Very easy." Zoey Bates nodded, noticing a dash of flour across Sophie's cheek that was a perfect match to the wispy bun at the back of her head.

They were both elbow-deep in ingredients while neat rows of pans on the long wooden table waited to be filled with apple, pumpkin, or pecan. Zoey would deliver most of the pies to church tomorrow, to be tucked into boxes and baskets of Thanksgiving meals and sent out to families facing difficult times.

Sophie would bring one of each to the Potters' family gathering at her daughter Evelyn's house. And Zoey would take one or two home for her family's holiday dinner, too.

"I bet my dad is going to say, 'Why aren't you ever interested in *my* cooking lessons?'" Zoey imitated her father's voice perfectly. "He always wants to teach me stuff at the diner. But I know he gets most of the cakes and pies from a big commercial bakery. Even though the menu says 'homemade.'"

Sophie laughed and swept a knife edge over a heaping cup of flour to level it. "I'm sure your father can teach you a lot about cooking, too. My girls didn't have any patience to learn from me, either. Now they teach me a thing or two. Evelyn barely agreed to let me bring dessert for Thanksgiving. She'd have me sitting in an easy chair all day, watching TV. Or something equally useless. I didn't dare tell her I was baking for the church baskets."

Sophie's daughter Evelyn lived in town with her family and was still a member of the church she had been raised in, the stone church on the village green, where Zoey's family also attended.

"She'll probably hear about it on Sunday. If she hasn't already. You know how Reverend Ben thanks everybody at the service."

"By then the pies will be long baked and eaten. She won't be able to put up too much of a fuss." Sophie wore a mischievous grin as she mixed the dry ingredients. "You can add a dash of cinnamon and nutmeg, to give it some backbone. But not too much."

Sophie slipped on her glasses before carefully tilting each shaker. She added the spices to the first bowl, then held them out to Zoey. "Here, you try."

Zoey was dicing butter with a special hand tool, as instructed, and felt comfortable with that job. Spices seemed much trickier. "Maybe you should do it. I don't want to ruin the dough."

"Nonsense. How can you learn? Cooking is a lot like life, honey.

You're going to make mistakes, but most can be fixed. Start with a light touch, and you'll do fine."

Zoey took the shaker and followed Sophie's advice, sprinkling carefully.

"Perfect." Sophie mixed more flour, and Zoey continued with the butter.

"How many people will be at your daughter's house?"

Sophie squinted a moment. "Let's see . . . With my grandson's fiancée and my nephew's baby, at least twenty-five. We'll need two big tables—and two turkeys—for sure."

The Potter family tree spread far and wide, and Zoey was not familiar with all of Sophie's relatives; just those who lived in and around Cape Light. She did know others by their photographs, which covered nearly every table, ledge, and wall of the old house.

"That's a lot. Even with the Tulleys and Grandma Dooley, we'll only be eight."

"A small gathering is nice. You can have a real conversation at the table. When the Potter clan gets together, it's mayhem."

"We're not that many people, but it's never that quiet. Not if there's a football game on." Zoey was thinking about her two stepbrothers and her father. Loud when they were happy and their team was winning, and loud if the game was going the other way.

Zoey had not grown up in the Bates household. She had been taken in by Lucy and Charlie Bates about five years ago, when she ran away from a foster home and ended up in the Clam Box one rainy, cold winter night. With barely a dollar in her pocket and nowhere to go, she was so sick with the flu, she could hardly stand. Kindhearted Lucy persuaded Zoey to come home with her and Charlie, and what began as a one-night respite from her hard, chaotic life evolved into Zoey finding the loving family and real home she had never known. Lucy and Charlie had adopted her, and Zoey now thought of them as her real parents, and even called them Mom and Dad.

Sophie shook her head. "Football. If they're not watching it, they're all outside, tackling each other. I tried keeping the game off one year. You would think I'd changed the menu to peanut butter and jelly sandwiches."

Sophie rubbed flour on the rolling pin, a good deal of it powdering her soft arms. "Not my call to make this year. I'm not the hostess." She sighed and suddenly looked serious. "This isn't the first time I'm not having the family for Thanksgiving, but for some reason, it feels like it. Other times, it was my choice to let Evelyn or Una take a turn. This year, they all said they wouldn't allow it. That's what makes it different. I'm afraid they're going to try to take Christmas away from me, too."

Zoey met Sophie's glance and found a defeated look. Defeated and frightened. As if the new rules her children had set down about holiday entertaining warned of bigger battles to come.

"They're worried about you, Sophie. They don't want you to run yourself down and get sick again, like last winter."

"Oh, that bug was a fluke. I was never sick a day in my life before that. I'm still working outside in all types of weather."

The declaration had been true for decades, but was actually not as accurate now. "You were in the hospital for weeks and needed a nurse here every day when you got home."

Zoey remembered the Sunday announcements in church last February; Reverend Ben asking for prayers for Sophie, who was in the hospital with double pneumonia, even in critical condition at one point.

But through the grace of God and her own strong will, Sophie had survived. She had required nursing care at home for months, and visits from friends and neighbors as well. That was when Zoey had begun visiting Sophie, first as a member of the church's Care and Concern group and, soon after, as a real friend. Now Zoey cherished Sophie as more than a friend. Her connection to Sophie felt like family.

Zoey did have Grandma Dooley, Lucy's mother, who had been delighted to finally have a granddaughter to shop for. But they weren't nearly as close as she and Sophie, who was so much fun to talk to and made her feel ten feet tall for the smallest accomplishment. An unlikely friend for a college student, it was true, but Zoey often thought of Sophie as her "real" grandmother, though she had never said it aloud.

"It was rough sledding for a while," Sophie finally admitted. "But I bounced back, a hundred percent. Even the doctor says so. Thank goodness I talked them into letting me come home instead of shipping me off to one of those cookie-cutter assisted living places. Bet they wouldn't let me keep Mac in a place like that."

At the sound of his name, Sophie's dog, Macintosh, who was curled up in his dog bed in a corner of the kitchen, lifted his soft, furry head and met Sophie's glance with an alert look.

"It's all right, Mac. I'm not going anywhere without you," Sophie promised. Comforted by her tone, the border-collie mix settled down and closed his eyes again.

Mac was the perfect dog for Sophie, Zoey thought. Medium-sized, with a shaggy, brown and white coat, he was still nimble enough to steal food off the counter in a flash, yet he had the steady, affectionate temperament of a Labrador. Zoey couldn't imagine Sophie's house without him.

Sophie continued kneading the dough with surprising strength for a woman her age. "Or they'd have me move in with Evelyn. It's hard to say if Mac's included in that long-standing invitation, either. My kids want me to sell this place, no secret there. But I'm not leaving this house on my own two feet. They know that, too."

Zoey hated the idea of Sophie selling the orchard, but she could understand how Sophie's family felt. Zoey worried about Sophie, too, and knew that Sophie had resisted hiring help, claiming she had all her friends and family to help her. Especially friends from the church.

Zoey would have liked to visit Sophie even more than she did, but it was difficult juggling her schedule, with college classes and studying and working at the diner in town that her family owned. She also volunteered at an after-school center for children. Never mind fitting in a social life; even hanging out with girlfriends was a treat these days. Never mind finding a boyfriend, either. She did manage to visit Sophie at least once or twice a week, though she knew that wasn't nearly enough to ensure her safety.

"It was easier when Miranda and Eric were here. You weren't alone so much," Zoey reminded her.

"That's true. But they have their own lives. I was grateful for the years Miranda did stay," Sophie added. "She got a great opportunity in North Carolina, working for a big jewelry firm. I would never have wanted her to give that up. But I can't see why the rest of them want me to give up something I love," she reasoned. "Evelyn already talked me into giving up the Christmas Fair. She doesn't want me to be in charge again this year. I agreed after all her pestering. Now what am I supposed to do with myself over the holidays? Sit in the corner and twiddle my thumbs?"

"Of course not." Zoey was surprised to hear about the fair. Sophie had always been the chairperson of the church's biggest fund-raiser.

The fair had been Sophie's idea, over thirty years ago. Giving it up was a big compromise with her daughter. It sounded as if her children were serious this time.

"Miranda was a godsend. My kids were trying to make me move out back then, too, after my dear Gus died."

Zoey already knew the story of how Miranda came to live on the orchard. Unable to gain much traction in her acting career, Sophie's granddaughter Miranda came to visit one winter to rest and regroup, soon after Sophie's husband, Gus, had passed away. Miranda had always loved making jewelry, and Cape Light turned out to be a perfect place to develop her craft—and the perfect place to meet the love of her life, Eric Copeland. After they married, they stayed on to help Sophie run the orchard while pursuing their own careers and raising a family.

But the couple had moved over a year ago, leaving Sophie to manage a staff of seasonal workers on her own. Problems arose that she could no longer handle. Her children, especially her son, Bart, were often called on to step in.

"Maybe you can figure out some solution, Sophie, some plan your kids will agree to. You never know. Anything can happen."

"Can the good Lord send me another miracle like Miranda? Only He knows for sure. I've been praying on it. You can count on that."

"I'll say a prayer, too," Zoey promised.

"Thanks, honey. I know you will." Sophie's bright blue eyes met Zoey's with a warm look. "I'm also praying that the subject doesn't come up at Thanksgiving dinner. I don't want to spoil the party. I'm hoping it will be too hectic for any serious talk."

Sophie had poured a big bowl of flour into the first bowl of butter and tossed in a few spoonfuls of ice water, and was now kneading a ball of pale yellow dough with all the pent-up emotion the conversation had inspired.

"They think they're going to lay down the law and not allow me to have my Christmas party this year. But I'm set on that. And I'll get my way," Sophie promised.

"I hope so," Zoey said sincerely. "I'll be happy to help you."

"Thanks, honey. I'm going to take you up on that." Sophie pushed and patted the dough. "Okay, you've seen how it's done. Now you take that other bowl of flour and knead some. I'm going to mix the pumpkin filling. Don't handle it too much. It will get tough," she warned as she pushed a bowl in Zoey's direction.

"Start with a light touch?" Zoey replied with a grin.

Sophie nodded, looking pleased. "That's right. A light touch will do it. Most of the time."

"OH, DEAR. THIS DOESN'T LOOK RIGHT AT ALL, DOES IT?" WEARING big red kitchen mitts that looked like lobster claws, Emily Warwick carefully carried a pumpkin pie from the oven out to the dining room.

Her daughter Jane sat at the dining room table, concentrating on a textbook and piles of notes, highlighted and underlined. She lifted her head to watch her mother set the pie on a trivet on the sideboard. The corners of her mouth twitched with a smile. "It's not so bad, Mom," she carefully answered.

"It's okay, you can laugh." Emily shrugged, smiling now, too.

"It might be okay if you scrape the burnt part of the crust a little. Is it done in the middle?"

"I was wondering about that myself. But if I poke it again, it will look even more hideous." Emily glanced back at Jane, and they both laughed. "I only have three more in the oven. They look even worse."

"You tried. That's what counts. Sorry I had to bug out on you."

"You have a test. That's more important." Emily glanced at Jane's textbook, Earth Science, opened to a complicated cross-section diagram of a volcano that made her head spin.

Jane had been talking about the midterm for weeks. Emily knew she should have remembered that before volunteering to bake for the church. She had thought she would do it with her daughter, but had ended up baking, quite unsuccessfully, alone.

"At least we have the brownies you made after school. Those are perfect," Emily said. "I'll buy some pies tomorrow at Willoughby's. That will solve it."

"Good plan," Jane agreed with a sly grin.

"How's the studying coming? Ready to taste test the brownies?" Emily asked hopefully.

"I think I can take a break for that." Jane stacked her textbooks and notes, then cleared a space on the table.

Emily returned from the kitchen with two brownies and two glasses of milk. "Hmm. These are good—as good as the bakery's," she said. "I don't know how you learned to cook like this. Your aunt Jessica? I got Grandma's genes for culinary arts."

Jane's eyes went wide. "Give yourself *some* credit, Mom. Grandma doesn't try at all."

"True. But she opts out on principle." Emily's reply was partly sardonic and partly serious. Her mother, Lillian Warwick Elliot, who had been raised in a wealthy Boston family, still felt cooking and most domestic arts were far below her, and barely deigned to heat a can of soup.

Emily had always wanted to learn how to cook, but never had the time. Until now. Cooking classes were definitely on her list. But at the very top was spending more time with Jane. That was an even more important part of her life, and she had shortchanged it lately.

Practically every woman she knew felt torn between her job and her home life, especially when it came to giving their children enough time and attention. But the question struck Emily deeper than most. She had another daughter, Sara, who was grown and married, living in Boston and working as a reporter. Sara had been born just days after the death of Emily's first husband. Now it seemed another lifetime—Emily and Tim Sutton had eloped just as Emily was due to leave for college. Nine months later, Tim was dead and she was the mother of a newborn. With her life in turmoil and her judgment clouded by grief, Emily had been persuaded by her mother to give up her baby for adoption. It was a decision she always regretted.

Emily had made many attempts to find Sara, without success. But through some miracle—and answered prayers—when she was in her early twenties, Sara came to Cape Light and found Emily. After a rocky start, they formed loving bonds, and Emily quickly learned the knack of mothering an adult child. But Emily had deeply regretted missing out on raising Sara and watching her grow, sharing all the special moments of her childhood and adolescence.

Emily and her second husband, Dan, adopted Jane eleven years ago, when she was an infant. With grown children from his first marriage, Dan didn't want to start another family. But Emily had longed for a baby with all her heart, and Heaven had found a way to bring Jane into their lives. Dan soon realized that they had been blessed, and he couldn't love Jane more if he tried. Emily felt blessed with this second chance to cherish and enjoy all the moments of motherhood she had forfeited with Sara.

But had she really valued that blessing and honored that vow? Emily often wondered about that. Her job as mayor of Cape Light had been so demanding, it was always a juggling act. Now here she was, finally free to carry out that promise to her younger daughter and herself. Though, so far, it was not as easy as she had expected.

Jane sniffed the air, then glanced at the kitchen. "Mom . . . didn't you take the rest of the pies out?"

Emily turned quickly. "Oh, blast . . ." She grabbed the mitts and ran to the stove. A black thread seeped from the oven door, and as she pulled it open, a large black cloud floated out, which she fanned with her hand.

"Are they on fire? Should I call Dad?" Jane sounded alarmed.

"It's okay, honey. Got it under control," Emily replied, though she wasn't entirely sure that was true. "Just open the back door and the windows, so the smoke alarm doesn't go off." Holding her breath, she reached into the oven and took out the charred pies.

Jane had wisely turned on the oven fan before running off to the door and windows. She returned to the kitchen and stared down at the products of her mother's labor. "It's just a timing thing, Mom. You'll get the hang of it."

Emily laughed and coughed, then dropped a kiss on her daughter's head. "If you say so. I'm trying."

An hour later, Emily was still cleaning the kitchen. Jane had finished studying and gone to bed. *I'm not only a bad cook but a messy one,* Emily reflected. She scanned the room, sponge in hand, for any splatters of pumpkin or flour she may have missed.

"What happened in here? Did the pot closet explode again?" Dan stood in the kitchen doorway and gazed around in wonder. His glance fell on the pies—*If you could even call them that,* Emily thought.

"You were baking. I should have guessed. I thought the chimney backed up."

"Very funny." Emily tried to sound insulted, but she couldn't help laughing.

"Were those for our Thanksgiving party?"

"Of course not. I already ordered dessert from the bakery. They were supposed to be for church. For the Thanksgiving baskets they're giving out."

"Oh, I see." Emily couldn't tell if Dan was still puzzled by this fit of domesticity—or if he was thinking the results did not bode well for Thursday. The entire family was coming for dinner this year, and Emily was in charge of the kitchen.

"It does make me a little nervous about cooking for our party," she admitted. "But I'm not actually cooking much. Jessica is bringing a few starters and sides, and I'm getting a lot from Willoughby's."

"Don't worry, Em. It's going to be fine. Jane and I will help you." He touched her arm. "It's just a turkey, honey, not brain surgery."

"I know. But I've been doing a little research on the Internet, and there are a surprising number of theories about the way to roast a turkey. Slow, low-heat, or high? Deboned? Stuffed? Or even upside down? Then there's the whole question of brining . . ."

Emily showed him the thick folder on the kitchen counter where she had been collecting articles and recipes.

Dan's smile grew even wider. "I say keep it simple. Don't make yourself crazy. You ran this town for over fifteen years. I'm sure you can pull a turkey dinner together."

"It's just that I haven't taken on a family holiday since . . . Well, I can't remember the last time. I always had the excuse that I was too busy. I feel like I forgot how to do it. If I ever knew in the first place," she admitted. "But I'm getting organized. I found some good ideas for making a centerpiece and interesting table settings."

"That's just what I mean. Let's buy a bouquet of flowers and stick it in a vase. *Simple.*" Dan paused. "Sometimes, you're like a cannon pointed at a mosquito, sweetheart."

Emily stared back at him. "I'm not sure if that's a compliment or . . . not."

"It's a compliment. Most of the time."

"I know, I have one speed. But I'm not used to doing this yet, Dan, all of this at-home stuff. Not as a full-time job." She glanced around at the jumbled kitchen and the misshapen pies.

Dan's look softened. "I know it's hard for you, a real sea change. But just relax. No one is judging you. No one is peeking through the window, trying to get a photo for the *Cape Light Messenger.*" Dan framed an imaginary headline with his hands. "'Mayor Warwick Incinerates Church Pies.'"

Emily laughed. "*Former* Mayor Warwick. If I was still mayor, I wouldn't have volunteered."

"It hasn't been that long. Not even two weeks, right?"

Emily glanced at the clock. "Two weeks exactly. Three minutes from now. It was midnight when we heard the news, remember?"

Dan nodded, looking serious again. "I do. And you took it very well. Like a champion."

The news was that Charlie Bates had narrowly—but definitely—won the election for mayor. Now, after more than fifteen years and eight terms in the post, Emily no longer held that title. Hearing that news was one of the most difficult moments of her life. The memory was still sharp and painful.

"Thanks, honey. But I don't remember feeling like a champion.

For a moment, I thought I might throw up. At least I didn't cry. I mean, not in public."

Hearing the news, Emily had felt as if some unseen hand had landed a heavy blow straight into her heart. She had lost her breath for a moment and couldn't even stand. But, somehow putting her political self on automatic, she had managed a quick recovery and said all the right things that night to her supporters and to the local media. It was a blur in her memory, though she had watched her performance later on the TV news.

"This whole transition will take time," Dan said. "You're doing great. Remember when I handed the newspaper over to Lindsay?" Dan had stepped down as publisher and owner of the *Cape Light Messenger* and put his daughter in charge—just around the time that Dan and Emily's romance had begun. "I was looking forward to being free of the daily grind for so long. I couldn't wait to jump on my boat and sail into the sunset. But when the time came I felt so confused, I was practically walking into walls."

"With a giant cast on your leg, as I recall. From that fall rigging the new sails. You thought you'd make a quick getaway. But God had other plans for you."

Dan laughed and placed his hands on Emily's shoulders. "For us, I'd say. He made me stick around until I finally noticed the most beautiful, intelligent, and accomplished woman in the world was right under my nose."

"It didn't take *too* long." Emily rolled her eyes, and Dan laughed again. "I know what you're trying to say, but that was different. You wanted to leave your job. I didn't. Though I had been thinking of stepping down soon. But not by losing to Charlie Bates."

"I know, Em. I know it still hurts." Dan pulled her close in a warm hug. "All I'm trying to say is, be patient with yourself. You don't have to be perfect at everything you try to do, and you don't have to volunteer for every project that comes along because you're afraid of being bored or unproductive."

"I guess it's my way of dealing with this. And I did think Jane and I could have some fun. I forgot she was booked up tonight, literally. She's getting older. She's so busy with her own life now, I need to be more mindful of her schedule."

"It's almost as complicated as yours used to be."

"The tables have turned," Emily agreed, though it stung a bit to realize that, too.

Jane's after-school hours, filled with music lessons, sports teams, and study groups, had always seemed like a good arrangement to Emily when she was busy in her office, sometimes late into the night. Dan was in charge of the home front, fitting his writing career around their daughter's many commitments. Now it was Emily's turn.

"I thought the upside of leaving Village Hall would be spending more time with her. But so far, that hasn't happened," Emily admitted.

"That will come, too," Dan advised. "Meanwhile, please don't book yourself up with a million random commitments and causes. I'm going to get you a T-shirt for Christmas that says, 'Stop Me from Volunteering.'"

"That would be great. I'll wear it, I promise. But I also want cooking lessons. And I'd like to start learning a language, too. Maybe Spanish?"

"Good idea. We should study a language together. That will come in handy when we travel." He picked up a dishcloth and began to dry the pile of pans and mixing bowls on the drain board. Emily got back to work, wiping down the counters and stove.

"Right now, I think you should take a break—a break from volunteering, and everything. No one will blame you for taking some time to clear your head. You've earned it."

"I know. But I'm glad the holidays are coming. It's a great distraction—doing all this holiday prep and entertaining. Maybe by the New Year, I'll figure out something useful to do. Part-time, I mean; nothing too intense. I do want to spend a lot more time with you and Janie. That's on the top of my list."

"You're always on the top of my list, Emily." Their eyes met in a loving smile. "I know it wasn't the way you wanted to leave office, but now that it's happened, I have to admit, I'm happy to have my wife back. I love having you around, more than you know. And I can't wait until we do all those amazing things we've always talked about— all the trips and adventures. I think we should take a ski trip in Vermont this winter, over Presidents' Day weekend, and then take a bigger trip when Jane has spring break."

"That would be great. Any ideas?"

"Remember how you always say you'd like to go someplace exotic, on one of those ecotourism trips? I was reading a travel magazine today, and I saw an article about it—places in Costa Rica and even the Galápagos Islands. There are inns in the rainforest, built on stilts, with all these exotic birds and monkeys just roaming around. And we can scuba dive and see giant sea turtles . . ."

Emily smiled, watching her husband get carried away with his descriptions. She wasn't sure if he was imitating an exotic bird or a giant turtle. It didn't really matter; his enthusiasm was contagious. Dan loved to experience different cultures and foreign places—one of the many things Emily had always loved about him.

"That sounds wonderful. Jane would love it, too."

"I think she will. We'll have a great time. That's something to look forward to, right?"

"Absolutely."

"Here's an idea," Dan said, a mischievous look in his eye. "This time, we plan the trip *together*. Instead of you just showing up at the airport and grabbing your ticket and itinerary."

"Oh dear, is that what I do?"

"Well . . . more or less. I've given you a pass all these years. But I think it would be more fun if we both work on it."

"I do, too." Emily touched his cheek. She could see it meant a lot to him. "No more volunteering. I have plenty to do here."

"And it's perfectly fine if you do nothing at all," he reminded her. "We love you the same. Even more."

Emily smiled and felt a bit teary. Dan could always read her like a book. It never failed to amaze her. "Thank you, sweetheart. I love you, too. More than you know."

She had never been more sure of that.

Sophie's house was filled with a sweet, buttery scent as Zoey washed the last of the large mixing bowls. She breathed in the cinnamon-spice aroma like a rare perfume. Sophie was in the next room, talking on the phone to her daughter, Evelyn, reviewing their Thanksgiving menu for the umpteenth time.

Sophie thrived on holiday anticipation. Zoey hoped Sophie's children would let her have Christmas at the orchard again this year. Even more than that, Zoey hoped they didn't force Sophie to leave the orchard altogether.

Zoey stared out the big kitchen window and noticed that it was snowing. When did that start? She hadn't heard any forecasts for snow tonight, but that was the weather in this part of New England—unpredictable.

Fat, heavy flakes had piled around the window frame and coated the landscape with a soft white blanket. The orchard looked lovely, the bare branches draped in white lace.

It would be so hard for Sophie to leave here, Zoey thought. *Hard for me, too, to know I could never come back to visit her. To cook and bake, or help with some household chore. Or just have a cup of tea and listen to her stories.*

She wiped her hands on a towel and glanced around the kitchen. She loved the view of the orchard framed by the window over the sink, and the big farm table, a dozen pie pans long tonight. She loved the worn pots that hung from a rack above the stove, like a crazy wind chime, and the open shelves stacked with mismatched china and oddly shaped glasses, with Sophie's prized collection of teapots on the very top.

Sophie's walk-in pantry was almost as big as Zoey's bedroom, filled with jars of honey, jam and preserves made with fruit from the orchard, and vegetables from her garden. Sophie had kept bees most of her life and was known throughout New England as a gifted "bee charmer." She had given up that hobby a few years ago, but people still said the honey from Potter Orchard was the very richest tasting because Sophie's bees were so content.

But Sophie herself was the real reason Zoey loved coming to the orchard. And she loved the stories that Sophie told—how she inherited the orchard and ran it on her own when she was so young, almost the same age Zoey was right now.

Amazing in that day, Zoey thought, when women were barely allowed to work outside of their homes and never allowed to be the boss of anything. Sophie had been an independent, "liberated" woman before the label existed. Sophie knew she was different from other people; she marched to her own drummer. Zoey felt that way, too. Maybe that's why Sophie really listened and took her seriously—unlike her father or even her mother, at times. That's what she loved about Sophie.

"You cleaned up all by yourself? You didn't have to do that." Sophie's tone was partly scolding but mostly pleased. "It's hard to get Evelyn off the phone when she's all wound up. You'd think she was entertaining two hundred people instead of twenty-five."

"I think twenty-five is plenty. I'd be wired."

"Don't be a fretful hostess, Zoey. Promise me? Always remember to enjoy your own parties. Just put the food out and turn up the music. Everyone does fine. Now, I think we should taste those pies and make sure they'll meet with my daughter's approval. What do they call that—product testing?"

"Good idea." Zoey was sure the pies were perfect, but she was dying for a bite.

"I'll set up the teapot and you put the kettle on. There's a lot of snow out there. It snuck up on us." Sophie glanced out the window to take in the white winter scene. "I don't think you should drive. You call your mom and tell her you're going to stay the night."

"Thanks. I think I will." The orchard was not far from Zoey's house, but on the Beach Road at night in bad weather, she would be crawling in her little hatchback, and the trip would take forever.

Zoey set the honey jar and a pitcher of milk on the table as Sophie brought over the teapot. Three slices of pie sat between their places at the table—apple, pumpkin, and pecan. Zoey couldn't wait to taste each one of them.

Sophie sat down first. "Feels good to get off my feet. We've earned our reward, dear."

Zoey was about to agree when a banging noise filled the room. Someone was knocking on the back door. Mac had settled under the table, waiting for tasty crumbs to rain down, but he now ran to the door, barking wildly, reminding everyone of his formidable skills as Sophie's protector. The two women stared at each other.

"Expecting anyone?" Zoey asked.

"No, I'm not. Who could it be in this weather?"

Sophie began to get up, but Zoey touched her arm. "You sit. I'll get it." Before Sophie could reply, she ran over to the door. The knocking had escalated into a pounding sound.

"All right, I'm coming." Zoey held Mac's collar with one hand and unlatched the door with the other, then turned the knob. But the door was stuck, frozen with the snow and cold. This door was finicky, she recalled. She pulled on the knob again with all her might. It didn't budge at first, then suddenly flew open.

A snow-covered form stumbled inside, falling right into her arms. She raised her hands and pushed back. She could tell it was a man, and a big backpack on his shoulders set him off balance. But she couldn't tell much else.

His coat collar was turned up, his head covered by a baseball cap, and a thick scarf was wrapped around his face so that only his eyes showed.

Mac took a few steps back and growled low in his throat. Zoey stepped back as well and held the dog's collar again. The man tried to pull his scarf away, but it was tied, and his hands looked stiff with cold.

Sophie had jumped to her feet, and she quickly walked toward them. "What in heaven's name! . . . Who are you?"

CHAPTER TWO

HE SCARF FINALLY LOOSENED, AND THE MAN TUGGED OFF his hat. Zoey was surprised to see that he was young, about her age. And very good-looking.

"Grandma, it's *me* . . . James."

"James?" Sophie sounded suspicious of this declaration and walked closer, but her wariness quickly melted to delight. "For heaven's sake . . . where did you come from? You look like the Abominable Snowman. Did you walk all the way from New York?"

Before he could answer, Sophie tugged her unexpected visitor into the kitchen and pushed him down in a chair. "Take off those wet clothes. You're going to catch a cold. Get some towels, Zoey, then fill a pail with hot water for his feet. He's soaking wet."

"Grandma, please. I'm okay. It's just a little snow."

Zoey hoped he was really okay, but felt a chill just watching him unbutton his jacket. She ran to the laundry room, glancing back just for a moment. Thick, reddish-brown hair stood out around his head, and dark blue eyes watched her from beneath thick brows. His cheeks were apple red, like those of a boy in a painting by a Dutch master.

That's James? The most recent photo Sophie had of that grandson showed a boy of about nine or ten, with a scrunched-up face and a mouth full of braces. His looks had sure improved, Zoey thought, her pulse still racing.

Racing back to the kitchen, she caught sight of her reflection in the hall mirror. She took a moment to smooth her long, dark ponytail and tuck her shirt into her jeans, then gave up. *You look like a deep-sea troll and smell like pumpkin pulp. Deal with it.*

When she returned with the towels, James was standing with his back to her. He had taken off his coat and draped it on a chair, and had removed his boots and socks as well. She couldn't help noticing his broad shoulders, outlined by his damp denim shirt.

Sophie stood at the counter, fixing tea with lemon and honey—using not one of the dainty china cups they had been using but the biggest mug in her cupboard.

"Here are the towels." Zoey handed them over and he smiled—a very likable grin that made deep dimples appear in his cheeks. His teeth were very straight and white. *Those braces worked out fine,* she wanted to say. But, of course, she didn't.

"I think you need to soak your feet in some hot water," Sophie said. "Zoey will make a pail for you."

"Don't be silly. I'm fine." He rubbed his head roughly with the towel, then draped it around his shoulders. "I couldn't find a cab at the bus station so I hitched a ride. But they had to let me off at the crossroad."

"You walked all that way? And up the road to the house, too?"

Sophie wasn't really asking him to confirm this, just murmuring to herself. "You should have called. I would have picked you up."

"Picked me up? Dad said you aren't driving anymore."

"I don't. Not really. Only for emergencies." Sophie quickly covered her tracks, her expression suddenly sincere.

Zoey glanced at Sophie and then down at the table, trying not to laugh. Sophie had promised her children that she would stop driving, but had never sold her beloved old truck, Bella, reasoning that a truck was needed at the orchard, even if she didn't drive it.

Zoey knew Sophie still took Bella out on short rides, redefining the meaning of emergency. Like, going to church or visiting friends in the village. Zoey tried to chauffeur her as much as she could, but Sophie could be crafty when she had her mind set.

James laughed and patted his grandmother's hand. "You're not fooling me, Grandma." He glanced over at Zoey. "She drives whenever she feels like it, doesn't she?"

Before Zoey could reply, Sophie jumped in. "Don't put Zoey on the spot. That's not polite. Speaking of manners, I've forgotten mine. James, this is my friend Zoey Bates. Zoey, this is my grandson James Potter. He's Bart's son; Miranda's younger brother."

Zoey had already guessed where James sat on the family tree. James offered his hand, and she briefly shook it.

"She helped me make all these pies, and now she's stuck here for the night."

"Believe me, it's a good night to stay put. And good to meet you, Zoey."

"Nice to meet you. That was quite an entrance . . . Are you an actor?" Zoey wasn't sure why she asked him that. It had just popped into her head. He was certainly good-looking and charming enough to be onstage.

He laughed. "It's even worse. I'm a writer."

"Really? What do you write?"

"Different things—book reviews, short stories. I've had a few pieces published this year. I'm working on a novel right now."

Zoey nodded. She didn't know what to say. She was studying art, but didn't consider herself a real artist yet. She had never sold her work or exhibited in a gallery outside of the college she attended.

Sophie peered at her grandson. "Did you eat anything today? You look hungry."

"I had a sandwich on the bus. But I wouldn't mind some pie." He smiled, eyeing the three slices on the table.

Sophie laughed. "Help yourself." She gave him an extra fork, and he selected the pumpkin. Zoey took the apple, and Sophie, the pecan.

"Well, what do you think?" Sophie asked after a moment.

"Only the best apple pie I ever had in my life," Zoey said, which was true.

"Potter Orchard apples. Doesn't get better than that," Sophie agreed.

"The pumpkin is . . . ambrosia, the nectar of the gods, Grandma. My taste buds are doing backflips."

Sophie laughed. "You've got to be a writer, honey. Your head is full of fine words." She took another taste of her pie, and they sat quietly for a moment, savoring the treat. "So, how's it going in the city, James? Is everything all right?"

James looked up at her briefly and nodded. "Absolutely. I just had some extra time and was planning to go up to Connecticut today. I thought I'd come straight up here instead and visit you. I was writing something the other day about my childhood and all the summer visits to the orchard, staying here with you and Grandpa and the cousins. It was like . . . Apple Camp or something."

"Apple Camp?" Sophie smiled. "I like that. Those were wonderful days; some of the best of my life. You kids could be a handful, but I wouldn't trade those times for anything."

"I wouldn't either, Grandma."

Zoey sat, eating her pie. She knew it wasn't smart to make snap judgments about people—especially about a guy you met five minutes ago. But she already liked James Potter. She could see—or at least, thought she could see—that he was a thoughtful, sensitive person. Funny, too. Important ingredients for a writer, she thought. She wondered if he was a good one.

"As long as your father knows you're here and won't be worried, I think it was very sweet of you to surprise me," Sophie told her grandson. "We can talk more tomorrow. And you can drive me to Evelyn's on Thanksgiving Day," she added. Her bold wink made both Zoey and James smile.

"That's a deal, Grandma. Don't worry, your secret is safe with me."

"And with me," Zoey added, exchanging a brief glance with James.

Sophie had finished and pushed her empty dish aside. "I don't know about you two, but I'm going to wrap these pies and get to bed."

"I'll help you," Zoey offered.

"I'll help, too." James came to his feet and picked up the dirty dishes and cups, balancing the pile on his arm with an expert flair. Zoey didn't doubt his claim that he was a writer. But she did wonder if he was earning his living as a waiter, too.

They quickly packed the pies, putting most of them in boxes for Zoey to bring to church.

"Time for bed, everyone," Sophie announced. "Zoey, you take the room upstairs, next to mine. James, you can sleep in the little bedroom down here. The sheets are clean, and there's an extra quilt in the closet. There are also some dry clothes in that chest that should fit you."

"Thanks, Grandma. I'll be fine."

"Sleep tight, dear." Sophie gave him a hug. "I'm glad you came to see me."

"I'm glad I did, too. Good night, Zoey. Nice to have met you."

Zoey glanced over her shoulder as she followed Sophie down the hallway. "Good night . . . nice to meet you, too." The way he watched as she walked away made Zoey feel self-conscious.

Zoey focused on Sophie, helping her up the stairs. Her older friend had been going full steam all night, but now it was apparent that the baking had not been that easy for her.

They parted at Sophie's bedroom. "Good night, dear. You know where everything is. I'll see you in the morning. And we have a strong young man here to shovel us out." Sophie's tone was a gleeful whisper. "See? God provides."

Zoey just smiled. She was used to shoveling snow and digging her own car out. But she still found Sophie's perspective amusing; Sophie rarely missed a chance to remind Zoey of the heavenly hand she believed watched over everyone.

Before Zoey slipped off to sleep, she remembered her promise, but wasn't quite sure how to start off a prayer for her friend.

Well, God, I promised Sophie I'd say a prayer for her, so here goes. I know that more than anything, she wants to have her Christmas gathering here this year. And more than that, to stay in her house, on her land, until her very last days, even though her children don't want her to do either of those things. I know this might be a tough one to manage. And it might be best for Sophie if she doesn't get her wish. But maybe there's some way things can work out for her? Some way we just can't see and you can? If anyone deserves a favor, you know it's Sophie.

Also, thanks for sending James to shovel. I do need to get into the village early tomorrow, come to think of it.

WHEN ZOEY WOKE THE NEXT MORNING, IT TOOK A MOMENT FOR her to remember that she had stayed over at Sophie's house. The soft, hazy light that filled the bedroom reminded her that it had snowed the night before.

She picked up her phone from the bedside table and checked the time. She had overslept and missed the alarm. How had that happened? She had to rush now. There were no classes today, the day before Thanksgiving, thank goodness. But she had to drop off the pies at church and then race home to shower and change and get over to the diner in time for her shift. Ever since her father had been elected mayor, she had to work more hours at the diner, and he was even nuttier about her coming and going *exactly* on time. *You'd think I was in the army or something.*

Charlie always said he was teaching her valuable lessons that would help her in the "real world"—how to be responsible and mature, how to be a good employee. "Someday you'll thank me," he promised. But that wasn't happening anytime soon, as far as Zoey could see.

She splashed her face with water and combed her hair. She had a dark blue pullover in her backpack and pulled it on, stashing the pumpkin-stained T-shirt in her pack. She was glad in a way to be in a rush and not have much time to spend with James. She still looked like a troll—a tired one who needed her hair washed. And what was the point? He was definitely cute. And cool. But he was older than she was, and he lived in New York City. And a guy like that had to have a girlfriend somewhere. More than one, probably.

Five minutes later, when she walked into the kitchen, James sat at the table, sipping a mug of coffee. Sophie stood at the stove, an apron over her long pink bathrobe. Mac stood right beside her, waiting for a morning treat. Zoey saw scrambled eggs and bacon on a platter on the table, which was set for three. She also smelled toast and something even tastier—coffee cake. How early had Sophie gotten up to cook?

"Help yourself to coffee, Zoey. Scrambled eggs okay? I can make a few over easy for you. Oh, and there's coffee cake, fresh out of the oven."

"It all looks delicious. But I'm in a rush. I have to get to work." Zoey sipped her coffee at the counter. She knew if she sat down, she would be tempted to eat some of the tantalizing breakfast and would get to the diner even later.

"That's all right, dear. I understand. But you take something with you. Some coffee cake, okay?"

Before Zoey could answer, Sophie was cutting a wedge of cake and wrapping it for her to go.

James had left the table but now returned, wearing his jacket, scarf, and boots. And carrying a straw broom. "The snow isn't very high. I think you can get out easily. I'll brush off your car."

Zoey was surprised by the offer, despite Sophie's prediction. She hurried to slip on her parka and grab her backpack. "That's all right. I can do it." She tried to take the broom from him, but he held on tight. She tugged a second and felt silly, watching him slowly smile. "Really," she said, "you don't have to leave your breakfast."

"I have plenty of time for breakfast. I have nothing else to do all day. And right after that, I'm sure my grandmother will want to make me lunch." He glanced over his shoulder at Sophie, who laughed to herself. "And after that, but not too long after . . . she'll be cooking dinner. In fact"—he tilted his head at a charming angle, as if a fascinating insight had just struck him—"I'll be eating here *around* the clock. And you would be doing me a great favor to let me burn some calories by cleaning the snow off your car."

Zoey could not argue, not after that recitation. She could barely answer at all, staring into his bold, blue gaze.

"All right. When you put it that way," she mumbled. She gave Sophie a quick hug and wished her a happy Thanksgiving, then slung her backpack over her shoulder and grabbed one of the boxes packed with pies.

"I'll get the other box," James offered as he opened the back door.

"Thanks." She swept past him. *Is he going to make another Shakespearean speech about that?* She hoped not.

They marched to her car, which was parked a short distance from the house, their steps crunching in the snow. Zoey didn't like to talk a lot in the morning, and she felt intimidated by James as well. Though she hated to admit it.

They set the boxes in the trunk. Then James walked to the front of the car and brushed snow off the windshield and hood with the broom. "Why don't you get in and start the heat? I can handle this."

Zoey started the car and turned on the defroster. She found her snow brush on the backseat and started working on the outside of the car, too. The smaller brush wasn't as effective as the broom, but the snow was very light.

Once the back windows were done, she checked the roof. She could almost hear her father: "It's dangerous to leave snow on the car roof, Zoey. It can slide down on the windshield and blind you while you're driving, and you can end up in an accident."

Even though she rolled her eyes at these disaster warnings from her parents, she did remember them. She jumped up on tiptoe and gave the snow a big swipe with the brush, reaching as far as her arm would stretch.

"Hey . . . what was that?" James popped up like a gopher from a hole. He had been brushing the back of the car, and she hadn't noticed him there. Now he was covered from head to toe.

She didn't want to laugh, but it was hard not to. "Oh, my gosh . . . you look almost as bad as you did last night. What is it with you? Can't you stay frost-free for a few hours?"

"Cute." He wasn't wearing his hat and shook his head like a big dog, snow flying everywhere. "It's not so bad. The snow isn't even cold. See?"

The next thing she knew, a cloud of snow was flying her way, courtesy of one swift, neat stroke with the broom.

Zoey sputtered, wiping snow from her face and eyes. She wanted to yell at him, then had to laugh. "Nice move. For a city boy."

The snow she had wiped from her face was still in her hand, and she quickly packed it—then hurled a tight little snowball straight at him.

"Gotcha!" She couldn't suppress her glee as her frosty missile smacked his shoulder.

"Correction . . . I grew up in the wilds of Connecticut. We have snowballs there, too."

He fired one back in an instant, popping out from behind the car and ducking down again.

Zoey squealed and spun, trying to get out of the way, but it caught her directly on her nose. She raised her hands to her face. "Ouch, that hurt! No fair," she moaned. She turned her back, pretending to be hurt, even though it only stung a little. "I think you broke my nose," she mumbled against her gloves.

James rushed from the other side of the car, slipping and sliding in the snow. "I'm so sorry! I didn't mean to throw it that hard. Here, let me see. Are you bleeding?"

He sounded so worried, Zoey had a momentary pang of conscience. Still, he started it, she reasoned, and she could not resist turning slowly and meeting his concerned expression with another heaping handful.

"Only kidding," she said with a shrug as he coughed and sputtered under this latest assault.

"You little weasel. I'll get you for that." His words were harsh, but he was laughing. At least he was a good sport.

She brushed herself off, jumped behind the wheel, then slammed the door. She rolled the window down a crack. "Thanks for helping me clean the car," she said sweetly. "By the way, I have three brothers. I know this stuff."

"Now she tells me."

"Next time, I'll give you fair warning." Zoey suddenly felt repentant for her sneaky maneuvers.

"It's all right. All's fair in love and snowball fights."

"I don't know about the first part, but I do agree with the second."

"Obviously." He smiled at her, a warm smile that made her feel a bit weak at the knees. "Hope to see you again, Zoey. When there isn't any snow around," he teased.

"Sure, see you," Zoey replied with a brief wave. His parting words surprised her. She didn't know how or when she would see him again anytime soon. He was only visiting for Thanksgiving and was probably leaving tomorrow night, or, at the most, over the weekend.

He was just trying to be nice. He didn't mean anything by it, she decided. She steered her car down the bumpy, snow-covered lane that ran from Sophie's house to the main road. In the rearview mirror, she could still see James watching her drive away—to make sure she didn't get stuck in a drift?

When she reached the road, she glanced back. But he was gone. As she fixed her gaze on the road ahead, Zoey could still see him clearly, in her mind's eye, and knew it would take a while for the image to fade.

SOPHIE HAD WHISKED THE PLATE OF EGGS AND BACON INTO THE oven so the food wouldn't get cold, but as soon as James came through the back door, she quickly set it on the table. He took off his jacket and boots and sat in his place again.

"Did Zoey get off all right?"

"No problem."

She poured more coffee in his mug and then sat in her own seat and filled her plate with bacon and eggs. "She's a dear girl. Puts her heart into everything she puts her hand to. She helps me a lot around here. I'm not sure what I would do without her."

"I'm glad you have help around here, Grandma. And companionship. Zoey has a good sense of humor, I noticed."

Sophie had watched the snow fight from the window. Zoey had gotten the best of her grandson, using her brains instead of her brawn. Sophie smiled; some things did not change.

"She's also very smart and creative," Sophie said. "She's studying to be an art therapist. Did she mention that?"

James looked interested and a bit surprised. "We didn't get to it. I can see the arty side. But she doesn't look . . . I don't know . . . serious enough or something to be a psychologist."

"Oh, she's got a serious side. She's a deep girl. She's been through things." James looked curious to hear more, but Zoey's past was not hers to tell. "So, are you going back to the city Thursday night, or heading back to Connecticut with your dad?"

"I'm not sure. I'll have to check work and see what my schedule is."

Sophie nodded. "Still working at the same café? What was it called again?"

"Bistro Cassis. The tips are good," James added with a shrug.

"No shame in hard work while you get your writing off the ground. Isn't that the plan?"

James nodded, but avoided meeting her gaze. She could always tell when one of her children—or grandchildren—wasn't telling her the truth. Or even shading the story.

"What is it, James? Did you lose your job?"

He finally looked up at her. "What gave you that idea?"

Answering a question with a question. Dead giveaway. Sophie knew her guess had hit its mark.

"I know you love me, honey. But when you take a six-hour bus ride and then walk three miles in the snow to visit, something's up. You could have hopped on a train in Grand Central and been at your father's house in less than half that time. Dry as toast in the bargain."

He didn't answer, just stared straight ahead, his cheeks growing red.

"I might be old, but I can still do simple math, and it doesn't add up."

James sighed and cast her a wry smile. "Yes, I lost my job. I had an argument with the boss and he fired me. My roommate moved out a few days later, and since I needed to save money anyway, I sublet the apartment. I've been couch-surfing ever since. That got old fast. I ran out of couches, and I still haven't found a new job."

"I see." Sophie had suspected it was something like that. "How about your parents? Won't they help you? All kids have tight spots like this, here and there."

"Tell that to my dad. If he ever had a 'tight spot,' he doesn't remember it." James sighed and pushed back his plate. "He has helped me, a few times. But he said he won't do it again—not unless I give up on writing and work for one of his friends. Selling insurance or something. I'd rather take poison."

Sophie shook her head. "Don't even say that." The boy had a flair for drama. "What about your mom? Maybe she'll help you."

"She's sympathetic, but always says I have to talk to him."

"Can't you just try—one more time?" Sophie knew her son, Bart, could dig in his heels when he thought he was right, but he wasn't heartless. He was probably worried about James, who still seemed a little lost two years after graduating college. It was only natural for his father to be concerned. And once Bart thought he had a solution to a problem, he didn't have much patience for considering there might be another way. He always thought he knew best. Especially with his children.

"You've only been out of school . . . two years?"

"A year and a half," James corrected her. "That isn't very long to get a writing career going. Some people take decades. Not that I plan on taking that long," he quickly added.

Sophie had to smile. Young people never think success will take long. Which was good, in a way, she reflected. "Of course not. But it's not the same as other careers. I understand."

"I'm glad somebody does. Tell that to Dad. I'm getting published—in a few places, at least. Editors like my writing; readers, too. Things are going pretty well," James insisted. "But nothing short of the front page of the *New York Times* will impress Dad. All he can say is 'Stop playing around. You have to get serious, James.'"

Unfortunately, Sophie could hear her son saying just that.

"What does he call serious?" Sophie asked curiously.

"Going to law school. Or taking some mind-numbing job in a bank or a brokerage house. Anyplace like that. Where you hand over your brain and become a mindless clone. He has a lot of well-connected friends and wants me to go on interviews. I'm dreading facing him tomorrow. Once he finds out I've lost my apartment and my job—"

"You're *in between* jobs, that's all." Sophie met his glance and saw he appreciated her interpretation.

"Even that explanation won't go over well. You won't tell him, will you?"

"It's your news to tell, dear. But I won't lie if he asks me. I don't want to get in between you and your father, but you're welcome to stay here until you can figure out what you want to do. At least through the holidays."

"Thank you, Grandma. Honest." His expression was a portrait of relief.

"Not at all. It's my pleasure. I have my own battles going on now with your father . . . and your aunts. They're trying to persuade me— more like force me, truth be told—to give up this place. But I'm not going without a fight."

James looked concerned. "I hope they don't make you leave. But I do think you need more help. That's where I come in. I'm going to start by shoveling snow and fixing that back door."

"I'm impressed. Quite a to-do list already." Sophie leaned back and laughed, pleased at her grandson's ambition.

"What did you think, Grandma? I would just lie around all day and eat your cooking? I might try to find a job in town, too. Even if it's just for a few weeks, that will be something. I'm definitely not going back to Connecticut, but I don't want to go back to New York, either. Not right now."

"Really?" Sophie was surprised. She thought James loved the big city. "Where do you want to go? Cross-country or something like that?"

"I want to travel. But outside of the U.S. There's a website that posts work on farms all over the world. It's called Worldwide Agricultural Volunteers—WAVE for short. You can find a farming job with room and board in some interesting country and work there awhile. Then, when you're ready, you go to a new place."

"That sounds very adventurous."

"I did it one summer during college. It was awesome. It's what a real writer would do—have adventures, see the world, meet all kinds of people, and have something to write about. Not just give up at the first speed bump."

Sophie was impressed by her grandson's spirit and persistence. And secretly pleased that he wasn't giving in to his caring but strong-willed father.

"That's a good plan, James," she said. "If I can help you without crossing your father, I will. In the meantime, let's stick together at the Thanksgiving dinner tomorrow. Sounds like we'll *both* be thrown into the lion's den."

Sophie rolled her eyes, and her grandson laughed. Though, in her heart, she wasn't really joking.

CHAPTER THREE

*E*VERYTHING IS DELICIOUS, EMILY. THE TURKEY CAME OUT perfectly. And I love that centerpiece. Did you really make it?"

Emily appreciated her sister, Jessica's, praise. Jessica knew Emily was domestically challenged and was trying her best to be encouraging. She was also very grateful that Emily had taken on Thanksgiving this year. She had been promoted at the bank and had almost no spare time now, though Emily was fairly certain Jess and Sam would still want to have the family over for Christmas Eve, as they usually did.

"I hedged my bets with the roasting. Draped it with cheesecloth *and* used a foil tent," Emily admitted. "Jane and I made the centerpiece. We just copied a picture in a magazine."

Her mother, Lillian, glared at them. "Very festive," she grumbled. "Keep fiddling with mini-pumpkins and pinecones while Rome burns. That's just dandy."

Emily decided to ignore the remark, a veiled reference to the goings-on in Village Hall. Which she was not part of any longer. Despite the fact that she had been voted out of office, her mother persisted in acting as if Emily had deserted her post. Or had perhaps been ousted by some sinister scheme and was now in exile, planning her return. Or should have been.

Dan, who never had high tolerance for his mother-in-law's critiques, was clearly annoyed. "Fiddling while Rome burns? What's that supposed to mean?"

Before Lillian could reply, Emily said, "More sweet potatoes, anyone? These are delicious, Jess."

Jessica forced a smile, her gaze darting warily from Lillian to Dan. "Gee . . . thanks."

"I'll have some more." Jessica's husband, Sam, held out his dish. "They came out great, honey."

"I'll have some as well, thank you." Ezra Elliot, Lillian's husband, glanced at his wife. "Some very fine food at this celebration. We appreciate all the work that went into this meal. Don't we, Lillian?"

Lillian shrugged. "Hats off to the cooks. I hope every family in town is sitting down to such a fine dinner. How does that old saying go—the condemned man ate a hearty meal?"

Dan had begun eating again, but now sat back in his chair, ignoring Emily's desperate look. "Honestly, do you need to hijack our entire Thanksgiving dinner with these grim conundrums?"

Lillian gazed back at him. "It's no riddle. You all know what I'm talking about. How can we sit here so complacently, chatting about pumpkin displays and Brussels sprouts, when the election of Charlie Bates as mayor has sounded a death knell to the village? And I don't see anyone trying to do a thing about it." Lillian stared at Emily, a spark of challenge in her eyes. As if Emily were the obvious choice to spring into action.

Emily shook her head. "Mother, really. Let's not talk about this now, all right?"

"Charlie was elected, fair and square," Dan stated firmly. "I can't imagine what you expect anyone to do. I don't think there's anything to talk about, now or later. Or ever."

Emily knew he was being protective. But after all these years, he still didn't understand that confronting her mother head-on was like waving a red flag in front of a bull.

"Fight him," Lillian replied sharply. "That's what can be done. Fight him on this zoning issue."

"Lily, please," Ezra cut in. "Can't you let us eat our dinner in peace? Thankful for *all* that we do enjoy—instead of spinning gloomy disaster scenarios?" Ezra waved his arms in the air and made a face, making his grandchildren laugh. "Believe me, the world won't come to an end because Charlie Bates was elected mayor."

Well said, Emily thought. Though Lillian did not look pleased to be laughed at. Another red flag.

"I will not pipe down. And I'm surprised at you, Dan, of all people. You spend your days glorifying local history in those books you write. But you don't care a whit if the very soul of this village—its historic character—is wiped out? If the streets are filled with condo developments and strip malls?"

Dan stared straight ahead, his mouth in a tight line. Emily could see he was angry but trying to hold his temper.

Sam spoke up. "This will all blow over. I don't think most people want the zoning changed. Charlie just had a lucky night. You didn't lose by much, Em."

Lillian gave her other son-in-law a look. Everyone knew Sam's sunny disposition and perennial optimism annoyed her like a skin rash. "Emily should have asked for a recount. I told her that a hundred times."

"I decided it was best not to drag out the situation. As Dan said, Charlie won, fair and square. It's out of my hands now, Mother."

Emily had campaigned on the side of zoning that would preserve the open spaces and farmland beyond the village center. Charlie was in favor of changing the zoning to allow for more development— housing developments, condos, and even commercial real estate.

Emily had assumed—wrongly perhaps—that most people in town wouldn't want the village to change in such a harsh way, and that she would win the election handily. But Charlie had argued that change would bring more young residents to the town and more revenue for schools and village improvements. In the end, he had managed to get more of his supporters to the polls, and she had not.

"Since there seems no avoiding it, let's set the record straight," Dan said finally. "Emily ran a great campaign and made a very graceful exit. She has nothing to feel ashamed about. But she's done with politics now, and she's the last person who should be held responsible for the fate of the zoning laws. She's championed these causes long enough, Lillian."

Lillian frowned, as if she had just tasted something sour. "So you say. But I haven't heard that from my daughter yet. Will you stand back and watch that witless wonder ruin this town? You ran on this issue, Emily. You seemed sincere. Or was that all just empty campaign talk? I heard that a group is organizing to oppose new zoning. You can fight Charlie. And you can run again. People will remember whether you stood up for what you believe in—or hung back on the sidelines, baking yams."

Emily sighed. Only Lillian could make "baking yams" sound so disreputable. "I'm taking a break from politics, Mother," she explained patiently. "Just like Dan said. I'm going to sit this one out. Maybe *you* should join the group if you feel that strongly."

"There's an idea." Ezra glanced at Emily, looking pleased at how she had turned the tables. "What do you think of that, Lily?"

Lillian snapped her napkin across her lap and sat up straight in her chair. "I've already signed on. I'm not just a talker, like some people around here."

Emily was surprised to hear that and wondered if it was true. Her mother had volunteered quite a bit when she was younger, but except for the board of the Historical Society, she didn't take part in committee work anymore. *She's just baiting me,* Emily decided. *But I'm not going to bite.*

"You've always been a woman of action, dear," Ezra replied smoothly. "Now that we have that sticky wicket out of the way, let's move on to more cheerful topics. Do I spy an apple pie on the sideboard? Or did Charlie Bates ruin that tradition for us, too?"

Everyone laughed except for Lillian. But she couldn't help smiling a little as she poked her husband with her elbow.

Thank goodness that Ezra is in the family, Emily thought, offering up an extra Thanksgiving prayer. *Where would we be without him?*

By the time Zoey sat down to her family's Thanksgiving dinner, she had been facing turkey and the traditional side dishes all day, working at the diner with Charlie from noon until five. Her older adoptive brother, C.J., had gotten home from college late the night before and stayed home to help set up for their own feast. Zoey's younger adoptive brother, Jamie, had come along to bus tables, but it had still been a hectic shift. The number of customers who showed up for the Clam Box "Thanksgiving Dinner Special" had surprised her.

To Charlie's credit, he had created a cheerful atmosphere, with pots of brightly colored mums and pumpkins on the counter and tables. Many of the customers who arrived looked as if they lived alone or weren't able to cook for themselves.

Her father was actually doing a good deed, Zoey decided, though she wasn't sure he realized it. Or maybe he did? The price for the three-course meal was surprisingly low. "Everyone ought to have some turkey on Thanksgiving," he had been grumbling all day. "Who else is going to serve it to them if I don't?" Charlie might be gruff and stubborn, but he had a good heart.

Zoey was glad when they locked up and went home. Her mom's dinner was much more appealing and far tastier than the one at the diner. Lucy was a very good cook, though she let Charlie have all of the glory.

"Charlie, are you done carving?" Lucy called back as she and Zoey carried side dishes out of the kitchen. "I don't want the rest of the food to get cold."

"Hold your horses. I know my way around a turkey by now. I can't go any faster. There's an art to this, Lucy."

Zoey and her mother shared a secret smile. "Okay. But we're waiting. Speed it up, Picasso."

Tucker Tulley, her father's best friend since childhood, chuckled softly, and so did his wife, Fran. Their children were a bit older than Zoey and her brothers and were busy with their own lives. But they would all be home for Christmas, Fran had been telling everyone. "I can hardly wait," she said.

"I can. The house isn't big enough to hold all of us anymore." Tucker rolled his eyes, but Zoey knew that Tucker was happy as a clam when his children visited.

"There's a beautiful colonial on Ivy Lane that just came on the market," Fran said. "Plenty of bedrooms and motivated sellers." Fran was in real estate, and always campaigning for a new house.

"I'm very thankful for the house we have now," Tucker said. "And thankful to see Charlie finally bringing in that turkey."

Her father bustled into the room, carrying the big platter, an apron over his dress shirt and tie. "I picked out a beautiful bird for you this year. It came out perfectly, if I do say so myself."

Zoey knew that Lucy had cooked everything and should have gotten some credit. "Everything looks delicious, Mom," she said. "Nice carving, Dad," she added.

"Thank you, Zoey. Help yourself, everybody," Charlie said.

"While we're passing around the food, I think it would be nice if we each shared something we're truly thankful for this year," her mother added.

Zoey heard her brother C.J. softly groan. She glanced at him, and they both laughed.

Charlie's eyes darted to his oldest son. "C.J., why don't you start?"

"I better think about it, Dad," Charlie Junior said quickly. "Why don't you come back to me?"

"I'm going to think about it, too, Dad," Jamie said.

Lucy's mother, Grandma Dooley, sat at the head of the table, opposite Charlie. She was in her seventies and looked like an older version of Lucy, with a slim build and red hair that had mostly gone white. "I'll start," she said, bailing out her grandsons. "I think when you're older you're likely to appreciate little things. Just getting up in the morning seems like a blessing," she added with a laugh. "I'm thankful for many things—my health and my friendships. But mainly for my family. I love you all," she said simply. "And I'm just happy to share another Thanksgiving at this table."

"Thanks, Mom. We love you, too." Lucy smiled, her eyes a little misty.

"I'm thankful that our children will all be with us at Christmas," Fran offered, "and that our family is growing. Michael's wife is expecting. We're going to be grandparents."

"What wonderful news! We're so happy for you." Lucy leaned forward in her chair. "When's the baby coming?"

"In April. We have plenty of time to prepare . . . and look for a bigger house." Fran glanced at Tucker again, but he focused on spooning cranberry sauce on his plate.

"You're going to be a grandpa, Tucker? That makes me feel old, my friend," Charlie said.

"Maybe so, but I can hardly wait. You being elected mayor made me feel old, so I guess we're even."

Her father laughed. "That's what I'm thankful for this year. In case anyone has a doubt. It took me long enough, but I finally did it." He paused a moment and sighed, as if he had run a long race and just crossed the finish line, Zoey thought. When he looked up again, he fixed his gaze on Zoey and her brothers. "I hope the young people here take a lesson from that. You don't always get what you want at the first try."

"Very true." Tucker nodded.

As Zoey expected, when it was her mother's turn, Lucy was most thankful for her family and for being able to enjoy their dinner together. "When you work in a hospital, you realize not everyone is this lucky or has a real family."

Zoey agreed. Even if she could forget her younger years—bouncing around foster homes—working at the diner today was proof enough that there were a lot of lonely people out there. She thought of her younger brother, Kevin. They had been separated in the foster system but always kept in contact. Kevin had also been adopted by a loving family, a short time after Zoey had been taken in by Lucy and Charlie. He had lived a short distance away and they had seen each other often, until recently, when his adoptive family moved to Minnesota. Zoey missed him, especially at holidays. But they kept in touch with FaceTime and Skype, and most of all, she knew he was growing up in a happy, safe home. And enjoying a Thanksgiving dinner today, just like this one.

"Zoey, would you like to take a turn?" Lucy prompted.

Zoey felt everyone staring at her. She knew most people thought she was brash and would say just about anything. But inside, she often felt very shy.

"Let's see . . . I guess I'm thankful that I finally found something I really want to do when I finish school—work as an art therapist. A job that won't even feel like work to me," she added.

Lucy had been very encouraging, as always, of Zoey's college major and career plans; Charlie, less so. He didn't have a high opinion of her studying psychology, or art. He thought both were frivolous pursuits and never missed a chance to poke fun at therapy, especially one that involved "arts and crafts."

Zoey ignored his objections. He could be narrow-minded about things he didn't understand.

Lucy reached over and gently touched her hand. "Zoey volunteers at a youth center in Salem. It's part of a psychology course, and she's doing some wonderful work there. We're very proud of her."

"I'm glad for you, honey," Grandma said. "But what does an art therapist do . . . if you don't mind my asking?"

"That's okay, Grandma. A lot of people don't know. Basically, you're a psychologist who helps patients work out their issues using drawings or paintings, as well as talking. The center where I volunteer works with children who can't express their feelings well with words," she added. "This method really helps them."

"That makes sense to me," Tucker said. "You're lucky to find something that you can put your whole heart into." He met her glance with a warm look of approval. "I guess you'll need to go to graduate school for a degree in a field like that."

"Whoa there, Tucker." Charlie held up a hand. "One tuition bill at a time. She isn't even done with four years yet. And we've got Jamie coming through the chute soon, too."

Jamie was sixteen, a sophomore in high school. C.J. was a year older than Zoey and attending the University of Vermont on a lacrosse scholarship, which made her parents very proud.

Zoey didn't want to worry about graduate school. She planned to work hard and get good grades. Maybe she would get a scholarship when the time came. She had applied for an internship at the center during her winter break. It would give her hands-on experience in the field, and would help with recommendations later. Zoey really hoped she'd get it, though she hadn't even been called in for an interview yet.

"Good gravy, Lucy," Charlie said as they started eating. "And the stuffing is very tasty, better than mine. Then again, I'm cooking for the masses. It's hard to include the fine touches."

"You do a good job. I bet a lot of people in town would go without a turkey dinner today if you didn't keep the Clam Box open," Lucy said.

"I agree," Zoey added.

Charlie looked surprised at the compliments. "Thank you, ladies. I had second thoughts about staying open again this year on the holiday. But I don't want anyone to think I'm getting too full of myself because I'm mayor. I felt it was my duty, in a way."

"You've got a lot of love and loyalty for this town, Charlie. That's why you were elected," Tucker said. "How's it going at Village Hall? How do you like being in the hot seat?"

"So far, so good," her father reported happily. "I think Cape Light was ready for a change. I'm not going to sit here and criticize Emily Warwick—"

"I hope not," her mother cut in. "The election is long over, and it *is* Thanksgiving."

"I know, Lucy. Don't worry. But we're among friends here. Let's just say a new broom sweeps clean. And there's a lot to sweep after Emily's umpteen years in office."

A new broom? Charlie was full of corny mottos, spouting them night and day. Zoey had no idea what half of them were supposed to mean.

"Speaking of brooms, how do you manage running the diner *and* being mayor? You must run up and down Main Street all day," Fran said.

"Tell me about it. I'm ready for the Boston Marathon. It hasn't been easy, burning the candle at both ends."

Another one. Zoey rolled her eyes, though she knew that was true; Charlie ran in and out of the diner all day and had almost doubled her hours over the last two weeks. She hadn't made a fuss so far but wasn't sure how much longer she could put up with it. She had her own life to take care of. He didn't seem to understand that.

"You need a manager, Charlie," her mother said. "I thought you were going to promote Trudy."

"I'm trying. But Trudy says she doesn't want the job. Can you believe that? I'm still working on her."

Zoey could believe it. Trudy, a longtime employee, probably thought the job was more bother than it was worth. Trudy knew her father well—his good points and his not-so-good points.

"Zoey's been a big help," he continued. "She's really stepped up. She can help me even more during her winter break."

Zoey nearly dropped her fork. "I can't work full-time during the winter break," she said quickly. "I might get an internship at the center. That's a full-time job. And even if I don't get the internship, I promised them at least twenty hours a week in January, as a volunteer."

Charlie nodded and spooned more mashed potatoes onto his plate. "We'll see, honey. We don't have to talk about it now."

Zoey felt Lucy's arm slip around her shoulders. "We'll work it out, honey. Don't worry about it now."

Zoey nodded and sat back in her chair. Her mom would stick up for her; Zoey felt sure of that. Lucy understood that working at the center was important for Zoey's future. She couldn't act all dedicated and then disappear for two months. What kind of impression would that make?

Luckily, Tucker quickly changed the subject, asking her brothers if they had been watching the Patriots. What a question. That was like asking if they liked to breathe or eat food. They both started talking at once, trying to outdo each other, spouting statistics and recounting each play.

Zoey felt relieved to be out of the spotlight. It wasn't right to argue about this with her parents now and ruin a holiday dinner. But no way was she spending winter break at the diner.

Excuse me? It's my life, and I have some say, Zoey answered back silently. She was happy that her father was finally mayor. That was what he had wanted his entire life. But why was it suddenly her problem? *No way am I going to be stuck in the diner all that time. Dad is crazy if he believes that.*

THE HOLIDAY GATHERING AT EVELYN'S HOUSE WENT SMOOTHLY, thanks to the careful planning of Sophie's daughters. Their large family sat at two long tables that were beautifully set. Beyond Sophie's predictions, three turkeys were needed for their feast.

Evelyn was terrified of running out of white meat. "And I hate when there aren't any leftovers. That's what Thanksgiving is all about—turkey sandwiches and turkey hash."

"And turkey chili," Sophie's younger daughter, Una, added as the women bustled around the kitchen after the meal, cleaning up and putting the food away. The men were in the family room, watching football. Every last one of them, Sophie noticed. She knew it wasn't the modern way, but it was still the Potter way, unlikely to change in her lifetime.

She was in charge of putting out the desserts while Evelyn's daughter, Amelia, washed pots and pans, and the others ran about, drying and putting things away.

"Those pies look delicious, Grandma," Amelia said. "Did you bake all three?"

Sophie proudly lifted her head. "Yes, I did. I baked twelve pies all told. A friend and I did it together," she added. "We gave most to the church for their Thanksgiving baskets."

Her daughters exchanged a look. "That's wonderful, Mom," Evelyn said in her most diplomatic tone. "But at your age—twelve pies? You must have been exhausted. Leave it to the young people now. Give someone else at church a chance to do good deeds."

The others laughed, and Sophie did, too. But her silent alarm sounded. She could smell where this conversation was going.

"It was no trouble. I enjoyed it. And I wasn't tired at all. I made the cranberry relish, the string beans, and the butternut squash soup the day after," she reminded them.

It was true, too. Though James had helped her in the kitchen yesterday.

The coffee was almost ready, and the pleasant aroma filled the air. "The pies look delicious," Evelyn said finally. "We've got some rice pudding, cranberry-orange cake, and brownies for the little ones." She placed those dishes on the table, too.

"So many good cooks in this family. Aren't we lucky," Sophie said.

"It's not luck, Mom. You get the credit for that." Una stepped over and put her arm around Sophie's shoulders. "You taught us everything we know."

Sophie smiled at the compliment. "I taught you the basics. But you two outdo me now with your fancy recipes. Like those turnips cooked with curry. Very tasty," Sophie added, praising their adventurous efforts.

Evelyn laughed. "We're not trying to outdo you, Mom. But it's nice to try a few new dishes. We don't have to eat the same thing every year."

"I've already started working on the Christmas menu. I have a few surprises up my sleeve, too," Una said gleefully.

Sophie pinned her younger daughter with a stare. "That sounds like fun, dear. You bring whatever you like. I'm not like Evelyn. You don't have to clear every covered dish with Homeland Security."

Sophie was trying hard to make light of the subject. But the way Una glanced at Evelyn was making her nervous.

"Well, Mom . . . Evelyn and I want to talk to you about Christmas. We thought that since she had Thanksgiving, I'd have the family for Christmas. It seems only fair. We know that you love having us all over," she quickly added, "but honestly, we both feel . . . and Bart, too . . . that it's too much for you now. Way too much work and stress."

"We would all worry about you, Mom, trying to hold a big party like that." Evelyn put a hand on Sophie's shoulder. "You're not up to it. So please don't argue with us."

"I'm not going to argue," Sophie said calmly. "I'm telling you all, point-blank, I'm having Christmas at my house. Just like I always do. If you don't want to come, well, that's your business."

"Oh, Mom, don't be like that," Una said. "Please don't be so stubborn. All the parents of my friends have passed the big holidays on to their children, and a lot are much younger than you."

Sophie shrugged. "To each his own. Maybe they don't enjoy it. But I do. I see no reason why I can't have you all this year, like I always do. Didn't I just bake a dozen pies without batting an eye? What do I need to do to prove I'm well again—jog home in the snow?"

Her son, Bart, walked into the kitchen, obviously lured by the smell of coffee and the dessert table. "Who's running home in the snow? What are you arguing about in here anyway?"

"Evelyn and I decided that I should have Christmas this year. Remember, we told you?" Una's tone was nervous, Sophie noticed. Maybe there was a chink in their armor.

Bart nodded but avoided Sophie's gaze. "Oh right . . . I remember now," he mumbled.

So he's in on this, too? Surprise, surprise.

"Mom doesn't agree. She not being realistic," Evelyn added. Sophie knew her older daughter was very practical, a trait that served her well most of the time. Being "unrealistic" was one of the most severe criticisms Evelyn could level at anyone.

But there are plenty of times when you should be impractical and unrealistic, Sophie knew. When you should bend a bit, like a birch tree. Evelyn, bless her heart, was more like a mighty oak.

Bart stared down at his mother. "I guess I agree. It's high time you passed the holiday-making to the younger generation. We're not even that young anymore." He laughed, glancing at his sisters.

Sophie knew that was true. But they had no idea how young they seemed to her, still in their forties and fifties. She would give a lot to be that age again. Beyond that, they would always be her children. Her babies.

"Very true. But you never know, this could be my last year in that house. I have my heart set on celebrating Christmas there, like we always do. Like we did when your father was alive. He was crazy about Christmas. That was the high point of his entire year," she reminded them.

She could see the expressions on their faces soften. *Thank you, Gus,* she said silently. *I knew you would help me sort this out.*

"Oh, Mom. You don't have to make us teary now," Una said.

"Sorry, dear. Not at all my intention," Sophie said honestly. "But it's true."

"What's this about it being your last year in the house?" Bart leaned against the counter, a mug of coffee in hand. "Does this mean you're ready to sell the place?"

Sophie had expected this question to come up today. But the dinner conversation had gone so smoothly, she had let her guard down and felt unprepared.

"I didn't say that, son. Don't go putting words in my mouth. I only meant you never know what the good Lord has in store. This could be my last slice of pumpkin pie, for all we know." She smiled and continued to cut the pies, though her hands trembled a bit.

"I hope not, Mom," Evelyn said. "But that's our point. You're not getting any younger. We really don't want you to go through another winter like last year, stuck all alone in that house. Even if your health is perfect."

Before Sophie could reply, Bart said, "We've been waiting for your answer on this question, Mom. Waiting since last winter," he reminded her. "You know what we think you should do. In fact, we've been talking about it, and we'd like you to put the place on the market right after the holidays, sometime in January."

"So, you have your own timetable, whether I'm ready or not. Is that what you're telling me?"

"Not exactly," Evelyn said with a sympathetic look. "It's your house and ultimately your decision. But we have to be reasonable. We want you to be reasonable, too. If this winter is anything like the last, it won't be safe for you to be there all alone. Even with visitors and help from the church group."

"Surely you must see that? You were snowed in several times," Bart reminded her.

"We could hardly take care of you, and we were worried sick. And it's already started snowing," Una pointed out. "Maybe you should move in with me, and we'll make Christmas together—at my house?" she suggested in a more cheerful, cajoling tone.

Sophie swept a glance around the room. Her children stared at her, waiting for her answer. The way they did years ago, waiting for permission to stay up late for a favorite TV show, or to ride their bikes to the beach to go swimming on their own.

"My, my. Time changes everything doesn't it?" she said softly, mainly to herself.

"Yes, Mom. It does, whether we like it or not." Evelyn's tone was low but firm. They meant business this time.

Sophie took a breath and brushed a few crumbs from her hands. "I know you all mean well, trying to push me along, out of love and concern. But put yourself in my shoes. An apple doesn't fall from the tree until it's ripe. That's how I feel. I'm just not ready to go."

"Oh, Mom . . . please." Bart sighed and closed his eyes. She could tell he was trying to hold on to his patience.

"You're not an apple, Mom," Evelyn reminded her sternly.

Under any other circumstance, Sophie would have laughed. Instead, she felt stuck, trying to think of some reply.

James walked in, his focus fixed on the desserts, like a bee heading for a rosebush. He picked up a paper plate and began piling on his selections.

"So, Grandma is not an apple. Did you recently notice that? Or have you been considering the possibility for a while?" He glanced at his aunt, looking amused by the conversation.

"We're in the middle of something, James," his father said. "A serious discussion."

"Sorry to interrupt." He glanced at his father and then at his grandmother. She could tell her grandson knew what the serious topic was. James took a fork and sat down at the table next to Sophie. He began eating, as if minding his own business. But she felt as if a loyal watchdog had suddenly appeared and planted himself at her side.

"We know you don't feel ready now, but will you ever?" Evelyn asked.

"Someday I might," Sophie offered honestly. "I'm not sure yet what I should do. Until then, I'm staying put. At least until the new year. I mean it, too," she added, in case there could be any question.

Her children exchanged looks. She sensed she had gained the edge. *Thank you, Lord. Let's close it now, okay?* she asked silently.

"I guess it can wait a month or so," Bart said. "But in the meantime, you have to have some help in the house. Live-in help. And don't say you don't like that idea either, Mom. I won't sleep a wink if you don't agree to that at least."

"Yes, dear. I understand. I've already got that covered. I will have someone with me day and night, and all the help I need." She turned to her grandson, pleased by the surprised looks on the faces of her children. "James is going to stay with me until the new year. Isn't that good news?"

Her daughters looked over at Bart, but he shrugged in a helpless gesture. "James, is that true?"

"Yes, it is. Grandma and I talked it over yesterday. Things weren't working out with my roommate, and I decided to take a break from New York. Too many distractions from my writing."

Sophie knew that wasn't the entire story. Her son seemed to sense that, too, judging from his expression. She had thought that by now, James would have told his father what was going on in his life. Obviously not.

But it wasn't her place to set the record straight. She would encourage James to be honest with his father. That was the important thing.

"Why don't you regroup in Darien? It's quiet there, too. And much closer to the city and your friends," Bart reminded his son.

"Very true. Too close. Too tempting. Besides, Grandma can use some help and some company. Isn't that what you've been talking about?"

"I think it's very good of you to stay at the orchard right now, James," said Evelyn.

"It certainly solves our problem. For now anyway," Una added.

Sophie sighed. Was she suddenly a problem to be solved? She held her tongue, knowing it was not wise to rile up tempers. Not while she seemed to be winning this battle.

Bart glanced at his sisters, who seemed relieved to hear James's plan. "If that's what you want to do, James, and it's all right with your grandmother—"

"Delighted to have him." Sophie met her grandson's bright gaze. "The nicest surprise I've had in ages."

"I guess it's settled, then. For now," Bart said. "We can wait until the holidays are over, if that's what you need, Mother. But not much longer. I don't mean to sound harsh, but it's for your own good."

"Let's talk again after Christmas," Evelyn suggested.

"Which can be at your house. If you let us all help," Una added.

"Agreed. Thank you, children, for being so reasonable. I'm sealing this bargain with a slice of pie. Anyone care to join me?"

"I'll have another," James said. "I think I'll try apple this time." Sophie met her grandson's bright blue eyes and they shared a secret glance. Somehow, they had outfoxed the hounds. For now.

She didn't mean to be stubborn, but she believed she would know when it was time to leave her house and her trees. It was impossible to explain. But in her heart, she would just know.

CHAPTER FOUR

~⤳

*E*MILY ALWAYS ENJOYED CHURCH ON THE FIRST SUNDAY OF Advent. The sanctuary wasn't decked out in all its Christmas finery yet, but there were plenty of touches to set the mood—a centerpiece of pine boughs on the altar, a wreath hanging behind the pulpit, and the large blue Advent candles that would be lit one by one as Christmas drew near.

"Oh drat . . . that candle prayer. I hope it doesn't slow down the service," her mother muttered.

Emily sat between Dan and her mother. Jane was still at a sleepover, and Ezra, who was coming down with a cold, had decided to stay home. Emily had taken her own car to pick up her mother, expecting that they would run errands after the service. Dan had to head in a different direction to pick Jane up after her party.

Emily and her mother had reached church a few minutes late. Dan had saved them seats toward the back of the sanctuary, which was easiest for Lillian, who walked with a cane, but was the last place she liked to sit.

"They say a few short prayers and light the candle," Emily whispered back. "It doesn't take long at all."

"Who's that family? I don't know them," Lillian replied.

"Jeff and Carrie Carlson, and their son, Noah. Jeff has been in the church a long time. Carrie and her son joined about a year ago."

"I remember him. A doctor of some kind? He lost his wife a few years back," Lillian recalled. "I see he found another."

"They're newlyweds, married in September," Emily said. Had they met at church? Emily didn't think so. Carrie's son, Noah, had brought them together in some way, but she couldn't recall the story.

"Well, I don't know them," Lillian mumbled.

Then you should introduce yourself at coffee hour, Emily was about to reply, but Dan gave them a look.

The Carlsons had stepped up to the candles. They took turns reciting the Advent prayers. Noah did very well for a little boy. He read in a loud voice without stumbling at all.

The warm looks the couple exchanged, the way Jeff put his arm around Carrie's shoulders, and how they both helped Noah light the candle, spoke of loving bonds that made Emily's heart glad. Jeff had told Emily that after he lost his wife, he never imagined finding anyone he could love as much. But he had suddenly found two people who meant more to him than anything.

If Carrie's flowing dress and the way Jeff guided her down the steps were any sign, Emily guessed that they were expecting a little sister or brother for Noah soon, too.

She glanced at her mother, who sat reading the church bulletin, clearly bored by the ritual. Reverend Ben walked up before the congregation and thanked the Carlsons, then began the weekly announcements.

"Many thanks to everyone who donated food and who cooked and baked for the Thanksgiving baskets this year. The baskets were very bountiful and much appreciated," he said sincerely. "Now it's time to start our Christmas projects, including the annual Christmas Fair. As I mentioned last Sunday, our longtime chairperson, Sophie Potter, is stepping down. We are thankful for her many years of service and for her inspiration that created this event, so long ago." He smiled in Sophie's direction. "How many years ago was that, Sophie? Do you remember?"

"I know you won't believe it, but it's almost forty," she called back. "I love doing it, as you all know. But I need to rest on my laurels now. That's what my children tell me," she added with a laugh. "I'm happy to offer advice and cover my share of the crafts and whatever needs doing."

"I'm sure you will," Reverend Ben said kindly. "But we need a new chairperson. No one has come forward yet for the job. As you all know, the fair is an important fund-raiser. We count on it to support our church and outreach projects. There will be a meeting for everyone interested in working on the fair right after the service. Perhaps we can elect a new chairperson today?"

He gazed around the congregation. Emily felt her arm stir. She always loved the fair. What if Reverend Ben didn't find anyone? It would be a shame if the church had to abandon that event. It was an important moneymaker, and she had plenty of experience managing people . . .

She felt Dan lean against her, not that hard or in an obvious way. But enough to keep her arm in place. "Don't you dare," he whispered with a hint of amusement. "Someone else will step up. I promise."

"You're right. I wasn't thinking."

Lillian leaned over. "Quiet, please. I can't hear a thing back here in no-man's-land."

"Sorry, Mother," Emily said automatically, but her mind was on her new life. *Maybe I'll help a little,* she told herself, *but I'm not going to run a thing. Not for a long time.*

ZOEY HAD COME TO CHURCH WITH HER MOTHER AND HER BROTHER Jamie. C.J. had a ride back to school today and might even be gone by now. Charlie had left the house early, off to the diner by dawn. She was going to work there after the service, when the lunch shift started. She didn't mind that much; it was never as frantic as Sunday morning breakfast.

She had spotted James sitting next to Sophie a few rows ahead. She was sure James hadn't noticed her. But when the service ended, James quickly turned and waved, and Zoey waved back.

She wasn't sure if he meant hello or good-bye. Did he want her to walk over and talk? Feeling shy, she decided not to and ducked out a side door, then headed for the diner.

She walked quickly across the green. A strong breeze off the harbor lifted her hair and cooled her warm cheeks. So, he had noticed her. That made her happy. *At least I look better today than when we met. And I don't smell of pumpkin.*

She was usually pretty cool about attention from guys. She attracted her share. But something about James Potter intimidated her. He was older, for one thing, and lived in New York. Zoey had only been there once, on a class trip in middle school. Lucy always promised they would go for a girls' weekend someday, to shop and visit museums. So far, they hadn't made it.

Zoey knew she seemed arty and edgy for Cape Light. She had been a bit wild in high school and still had a blue bracelet tattoo around her wrist and a few extra piercings in her ear. She liked to dress in thrift-shop, bohemian style, too. But she guessed that James met a lot of girls like that, truly hip girls who were actresses, painters, or writers. *He'll never be interested in me. I must seem hopelessly quaint, stuck out here in the middle of nowhere.*

Okay, I have a tiny crush on him, she admitted to herself. *Who wouldn't? But he'll be returning to New York any minute. He was probably waving good-bye. I'm surprised he's stayed this long.*

"ANY SPECIAL REASON YOU DIDN'T WANT TO STAY FOR COFFEE HOUR today, Mother?" Emily snapped her seat belt, curious about her mother's rush to leave church. Lillian had forgone her usual chat with Reverend Ben, including her weekly review of his sermon. She had even skipped socializing in Fellowship Hall, where she enjoyed giving her opinion on a range of subjects and gathering bits of gossip like a lint brush.

"We can stop at the market and the drugstore on the way home. I'm sure you need a few things." Emily glanced at her mother as they headed down Main Street. "Unless you think Ezra needs you?"

"Ezra will be fine. He's a doctor. He should be able to take care of himself for a few hours. He doesn't need me to watch him nap." Her mother turned to her. "I don't need any groceries. But you could take me somewhere. To a meeting. And stay with me until it's done, of course. I won't have a ride home otherwise."

"A meeting? What group is this?" If her mother was going to attend any meetings today, Emily thought it would have been back at the church, one of the committees forming for Christmas projects.

"The open-space group. They're meeting today at the Elks Lodge. We'll be just in time." Lillian pulled out a flyer from her purse and waved it at Emily. Of course, Emily couldn't read it while driving, but she got the main idea from the large headline on top. A knot of dread twisted in her stomach. Of all the underhanded tricks . . .

"You told me to get involved," Lillian reminded her before she could protest. "Practically dared me, I recall. I hear there's going to be a very large turnout. Should be quite interesting."

Emily shook her head. "Mother, this tactic is beyond transparent. Beyond even your usual manipulation. You realize that, don't you?"

Lillian feigned an innocent, even injured, look. "I have no idea what you're talking about. Ezra has a cold. You saw him. Otherwise, he would have driven me. That's what I planned. I suppose you can just drop me there. I might find someone to give me a lift back to town, or call a taxi. Either way, I mean to put my shoulder to the wheel, Emily. Not just spout a lot of fine words about the situation."

Her tone made Emily sigh. Her mother knew very well that Emily would never drop her off and drive away. The Elks Lodge was quite a few miles outside of the village. It would be hard to get a taxi to go out there.

"I'll stay and wait for you, but I'm not participating. I'm sitting this one out," Emily reminded her mother.

"You've made yourself perfectly clear. No need to get huffy. You can stay in the car if you like, check your email. But I guess you don't get nearly as much anymore, since you lost the election. That must leave a lot of time free."

"Yes, it does." Emily forced a smile but didn't say more.

A short time later, they pulled into the parking lot of the Elks Lodge. There were more cars than Emily had expected, and she hoped she could stay under the radar, but her hopes were short-lived.

"Mayor Warwick! So glad you could come." A woman at the door beamed as she handed them agendas.

I should have worn a floppy hat and sunglasses. I'll have to remember to keep some in the car.

"Just call me Emily, please. I'm a private citizen now."

"But concerned about this issue, as we well know," a man nearby replied. He stood at a table, handing out copies of news articles about the issue. Emily recognized him—Martin Becker, a history teacher at the high school. She also recognized the headlines, some trumpeting the arguments against new zoning she had made during her campaign.

Emily smiled back and moved her mother along.

"You should have no qualms about keeping your title. Don't they still call former presidents 'Mr. President'?"

"Mother, don't be absurd. This isn't Washington, D.C."

Emily quickly chose seats for them at the back of the room but, of course, her mother preferred to sit up front. "I can't hear a thing otherwise. You know that," she insisted, pushing ahead to the front of the room.

"All right, you sit up there if you like. I'll see you later," Emily countered, determined to keep her distance from this situation, both figuratively and literally.

Lillian looked cross as Emily walked away, but didn't argue.

Emily settled in a distant spot and reviewed the agenda. She was still annoyed about the way her mother had tricked her into coming, but was secretly interested to see what would go on. Could the group organize and block Charlie Bates and the pro-zoning crew? She hoped so. She worried about the future of the village; all of its historic charm and character was at stake. Everything that made Cape Light . . . well, Cape Light.

Martin Becker and Marion Ross, the woman who had greeted everyone at the door, were up front, running the meeting. They sat at a long table, along with three others. Martin Becker introduced himself.

He seemed intelligent and serious. An argyle vest under a tweed jacket gave him an academic air, along with wire-rim glasses and gray brush-cut hair.

"Thank you all for coming. I hope that you're all ready and willing to fight the changes in the zoning laws that our new mayor supports. We believe these changes will ruin our town's charming, unique character. They will also bring down our property values and harm the wildlife that now thrives in this area.

"The question is, how can we block the group that is determined to push through these changes? Unfortunately, they have the new mayor on their side, as well as most of the town council. This issue is at the top of their to-do list. We do not have much time to organize and fight it. We have to strike back fast and efficiently."

Emily knew this was true. A number of tactics came to mind, but she was determined not to speak. She waited to see what others would suggest.

A few hands went up in the audience, and suggestions were offered—from collecting signatures to holding back on real estate taxes. Not bad ideas, Emily thought, but not time-effective.

"Maybe we should dump some fake tea in the harbor . . . as a protest," one man said. "I bet we would get some news coverage." Probably, Emily thought, though she doubted the theatrics would do anything to block the zoning changes.

A woman in the front row stood up. Emily recognized Grace Hegman, who owned Bramble Antiques Shop. "I'm sorry to seem uninformed, but can you please explain how Mayor Bates and the town council can change the zoning? Don't the village residents have to vote on a question this important?"

"That's true," Martin said. "A vote of all residents must be called. But with their majority, they'll easily pass a call for a vote. And likely set a date within a month or two—before we can get the real facts out to everyone who might vote against the change once they know the true consequences. If the vote were held today, Mayor Bates and his group would likely win. Otherwise Bates wouldn't have been elected."

Emily felt her face flush with embarrassment. When she lost the election, it had been more than a personal defeat. She had let the town down. She had left them unprotected from this disastrous possibility.

Martin suddenly realized his faux pas and looked embarrassed. "Sorry, Mayor Warwick. Former mayor, I mean," he mumbled into the microphone. "No slight intended. You had my vote and, I'd guess, the votes of many others in this room."

Everyone turned to look at her, and Emily forced a smile. "No need for a show of hands. I trust you," she called out, making everyone laugh. "Just to clarify, what Mr. Becker said is true. That's the way it will likely go in Village Hall. Starting with the next council meeting on December fifth, I expect this issue will be discussed. The council will decide then to call a vote on zoning changes that will allow more commercial building."

"Yes, that's right, first Monday of every month. I was just getting to that," Martin Becker quickly added. "The meeting is Monday, December fifth, at six thirty in Village Hall, open to everyone. We need a big turnout and need to voice our opposition. Any other suggestions, Mayor Warwick?"

Everyone looked her way again. Emily felt put on the spot, which was exactly what she had *not* wanted to happen. Her mother caught her eye, smiling and nodding, looking very pleased that her plan had worked out after all.

"Should we get T-shirts and signs made?" one woman asked. "I think that makes a big impression. You can really see how many people are united in the same cause. Red, maybe? With white letters— SOS. 'Save Our Open Spaces.'"

It wasn't exactly an acronym. There was an extra *O* in there, Emily noticed. But she didn't bother to point that out.

"That's an idea," she replied, "but you probably want to focus on a fact sheet. Before the meeting, get it into the hands of as many people as you can and urge them to come to the Village Hall meeting. The flyer should state the points against this idea, plain and simple. It takes a long time for information like this to penetrate and sway opinions. You have to make a real push there."

A job my campaign didn't do all that well, she nearly added.

"Excellent points," Martin said. "We need to have volunteers out every day—at the train station, the post office, and the markets— handing out fact sheets and explaining our position. We'll have a sign-up sheet at this table right after the meeting."

A hand popped up, and Martin recognized a new speaker. Emily quietly sighed. *So much for sitting here like a fly on the wall. You were a very noisy one,* she scolded herself.

Now she had the problem of stepping back—gracefully or awk-wardly. She would be disappointing everyone here who thought she was jumping into this effort with them, heart and soul.

Would it be so bad to take part? Just a little?

Dan won't like it. He won't even like knowing that I came here today. But I can blame my mother.

When the meeting ended, Emily managed to snag Lillian and escort her out of the building without anyone stopping them to talk.

Once in the car, Emily felt herself fuming. She took a moment to collect her patience as she carefully steered out of the parking lot.

"I thought it went very well. You gave them some good advice," Lillian said. "Why bother with T-shirts? Silly window dressing. We need to get the word out, get more citizens on board. That's the only way to beat Bates and his crowd." When Emily didn't answer, she added, "I'm glad to see you've come to your senses. I knew you'd never be able to watch from the sidelines, Emily. It's not your style."

Emily gripped the steering wheel hard to keep from raising her voice. "I know you think you've tricked me into joining this group. But you're wrong. I offered a few remarks to help out. Mainly because everyone was staring at me."

"Tish-tosh. You know you enjoyed it. You could have stepped up and taken the microphone from that Bentley fellow and—"

"Becker. His name is Martin Becker."

"Whatever. You could have stepped into his place, and no one would have objected. In fact, I think even he would have been pleased. Will you let them down now? They think you're signed on to fight the good fight. You certainly made that impression. Some part of you at least must want to join in."

"I'm not going back, so don't try this again," Emily said smoothly. "It won't work twice."

"It was a straightforward request, not subterfuge in the least. I resent your accusation. It's most unfair," Lillian complained.

They drove silently for a few minutes, her mother's head turned toward her window in a stiff pose as she stared out at the tall marsh grass that bordered the Beach Road. Mostly brown this time of year, the thick patches of reeds stretched for miles, swaying gently in the wind, breaking here and there to reveal a pool of water or muddy flats.

A flock of birds rose from the brush and swooped gracefully across the clear sky. Emily's gaze followed them, her heart growing lighter at the sight.

Her mother heaved a heavy sigh. "Suit yourself, Emily. You always do. But don't be surprised if by the time you're ready to come back to politics—and I have no doubt that day will arrive—you'll find an outlet mall on this very road, and the nesting grounds for the osprey and snapping turtles and all those fine, delicate creatures out there will be covered with condo units. This is an important moment. Mark my words, people will remember what you do, and don't do, right now."

Emily did not reply, though she knew there was more than a grain of truth in her mother's goading. But she also knew that Lillian had drawn a great deal of pride and status from being the mother of the mayor. She clearly felt a great loss to her own identity with Emily's defeat. If her daughter couldn't be mayor right now, at least she could lead the charge against Charlie Bates.

But what sense would it make to confront her mother about that and open yet another can of worms? Emily was sure her mother would deny those motives, the same way she denied tricking Emily into attending the meeting.

Emily pulled into her mother's driveway. "I'll help you to the door," she said.

Lillian got out of the car, leaning heavily on her cane. "I'm fine. I've kept you away from . . . well, from whatever you'd rather do today . . . for too long. I can see that."

Emily was about to fire back a tart reply, her patience fraying totally, when she spotted Ezra coming down the walk to meet them. "Here's Ezra. He'll help you in," she said simply. "Good-bye, Mother. Enjoy the rest of your day."

Lillian straightened her spine. "I shall. I'm going to make some calls and get some people from church over to the next meeting. I'm with the rabble-rousers now. You know, I've changed my mind. I hope they *do* give out red T-shirts. I'll be proud to wear one."

Emily smiled at the very idea. She had never seen her mother wearing a T-shirt, much less one with a slogan on it. Perhaps if it was made of cashmere or satin? That might work.

"I'm going to the next meeting on Wednesday. If you don't want to drive me, and Ezra is unable, I'll call a cab," Lillian said.

"You should plan on that," Emily agreed. "I'll be busy. Jane has a volleyball game that day. I promised I'd watch her play."

Her mother tilted her head back, looking stung. "Yes, very important. Good luck to you both." She turned and headed to the door, her cane steadying slow steps.

Ezra stood halfway down the walk, waiting for his wife. He waved, and Emily waved back. Normally, she would go inside and say hello, but today she felt relieved to back out of the driveway and head straight home. The meeting had been only an hour, maybe less. But Emily felt as if she'd been out with her mother for days on end.

"Slow today, especially for a Sunday afternoon. I guess everyone's home, eating their turkey leftovers," Charlie said. He wore his reading glasses balanced on the tip of his nose, his gaze fixed on a letter that was typed on Village Hall stationery.

"Maybe we should close early, Dad," Zoey suggested. "I have a ton of studying and papers to work on. Finals are coming soon."

Zoey had noticed that her father had his own pile of homework, stacks of folders and papers he carried around with him, ever since he had started as mayor. He often left them on the counter or in some other inconvenient spot. It was a miracle that his official documents did not end up splattered with ketchup or drowned in coffee.

But what he had said at their Thanksgiving dinner was true. It was hard for him to run the diner and Village Hall, too. He was either flipping burgers or flipping the pages of a building inspector's report.

"We'll see how it goes," he replied in the vague way parents always did. He slipped the letter in a folder and let his glasses hang on the cord around his neck. "Wipe down all the menus and refill the napkin holders, will you, Zoey?" He turned his head and squinted at the busboy. "Scotty, you come back into the kitchen with me once you've emptied that rack. I've got another job for you."

Zoey had already wiped the menus. Charlie had obviously forgotten. Though the order was a good sign. They might close early, after all. She gathered up the menus, along with the napkin holders.

She had been hoping to read a few pages from a textbook she had stashed near the cash register. No luck with that plan. Her father didn't like to see any of his employees idle for even a minute. The mere possibility really got under his skin, even though he stole plenty of downtime now to keep up with his village duties.

She was in the midst of jamming a wad of napkins into a particularly stubborn holder when a customer walked in. Zoey looked up and nearly sprayed napkins all over the diner, but saved herself from complete mortification just in time.

James Potter met her surprised expression and smiled. "Hey, Zoey. You work here?"

"I do," she said lightly. "Sit down anywhere. I'll get a menu." He was alone. Where was Sophie? And why wasn't he on a train or a bus headed to New York by now?

He smiled again, then chose a table near the window. He hung his thick leather jacket on the back of a chair and took a small notebook and his phone out of one of the pockets before he sat down. He wore a nubby gray sweater that was a bit worn but looked just right on him. His thick hair was windblown, and he smoothed it back with his hand.

Zoey walked to the other side of the counter to grab a menu and a glass of ice water. She snuck a tube of lip gloss from her pocket and swiped some on. Not that all the makeup in the world could do anything to hide her geeky uniform—complete with a ruffled apron and the ugly black sneakers she had to wear for kitchen work.

I looked so cute in church, in my black skirt and boots. Why can't I ever run into this guy when I look half decent?

She set the menu and water in front of him. "There are some specials on the board. Not that anything we serve is actually special," she added quietly.

He laughed. "At least that's honest."

"Why would you eat here when you can have Sophie's cooking?"

"My grandmother has been in one meeting after another after church today. I've been wandering around town, and now I'm hungry enough to eat this menu."

"That's about the level of our cuisine. Don't say I didn't warn you."

"Fair enough." He glanced at the menu a moment. "How about a hamburger, medium, with lettuce, tomato, and fries?"

"Good choice. Anything to drink?"

"Just coffee. Black is fine."

Zoey marked his order on her pad. "I should have guessed. Isn't that the way writers always drink coffee?"

He smiled, amused by her observation. "Not always. I don't stay up all night, drinking coffee and chain-smoking, if that's what you think." His smile widened, and dimples appeared in his cheeks. He really was killer cute; she tried not to stare.

"No offense. But I haven't thought that much about it," she replied with a small smile, then feared her nose was going to start growing like Pinocchio's. "I'll put your order in."

"Great, thanks." He didn't seem offended by her quip. He opened his notebook and took out a pen and a pair of glasses. The square, black frames suddenly made him look very intellectual.

He does look like a real writer. And I haven't even served the black coffee yet, she thought wryly.

A short time later, Zoey returned with his food. James was scribbling wildly in his notebook and didn't notice her. "The ketchup is on the table. Can I get you anything else—more coffee?"

He looked up then, down at the food, as if he had just woken from a nap. She could see that he had been off in his own world, not purposely being rude.

"That was fast. Thanks." He met her gaze and pulled off his

glasses, then took a huge bite of the burger. "This isn't so bad," he mumbled around the mouthful. "How long do church meetings last? My grandmother is the only person in the world without a cell phone."

Zoey checked her watch. "The first probably didn't start until at least half past eleven, after coffee hour. The second meeting probably started around twelve thirty, or even one?"

He looked relieved and ate a French fry. "Thanks. I guess I don't have to choke this down, after all."

"You'd better not. I don't know the Heimlich maneuver, and it takes a long time to read that poster." She was teasing. She knew all types of first-aid procedures, but had never needed to use them. She certainly didn't want to start on James. "More coffee?" she asked.

"I'm good. I keep forgetting I'm not in the city. No reason to stay up all night. I've been sleeping like a baby at my grandmother's house. It's so peaceful out there, it's like a Zen retreat or something."

Zoey smiled. She felt the same about Sophie's house and the orchard. "A Zen retreat with apples."

"Exactly."

She liked the way he laughed at her jokes. She watched James inhale more fries, her tray balanced on her hip. "I thought you'd be on your way back to New York by now."

He shook his head, his blue eyes disconcertingly wide. "I'm staying with my grandmother for a few weeks. Through the holidays. She needs the help, and I can use a break from the city."

"Oh, wow . . . that's good!" Zoey blurted out. Then she quickly tried to backtrack. "I mean, it works out well for both of you. I sort of worry about Sophie being alone out there."

She felt her face turning red. So much for acting cool. No matter what she had said to cover up her flub, he knew now she liked him.

Good job, Zoey. That would have been lame even if you were still in middle school.

"I think it's going to work out fine. This village is more interesting than I remembered." He met her gaze again and smiled. Was he really flirting with her? Zoey gave herself a mental shake. *Get a grip. You have to be imagining that.*

Usually, she would have walked away by now, letting a customer take his time with his meal. For some reason, she felt a sudden, uncontrollable urge to rush him along.

"I guess you're in a hurry to pick up your grandmother. Here's your check." She had added the total and quickly tore off the slip and placed it facedown on his table.

James sat back and stared at her. "Thanks."

"You're welcome." She turned and walked away, feeling his eyes on her.

Back at the counter, she attacked the napkin dispensers again and forced herself not to look at him. He had his notebook open and seemed oblivious once more to his surroundings, lifting the last of his French fries mechanically to his mouth.

If he's staying here a few weeks, does that mean he doesn't have a steady relationship in New York? But maybe his girlfriend is going to visit him here. That wouldn't be too hard.

After a few moments, she saw him stand and put some bills on the table. He slipped on his jacket and headed for the door. "So long, Zoey. I'll see you around."

"Sure. See you." She nodded and looked back at the napkins, her very important work.

The door closed. Zoey sighed with relief. So, James Potter wasn't disappearing to New York this weekend. She wasn't sure if that was good news or bad. She already had a little crush on him and got the feeling he liked her, too.

But she could also see that James knew he was attractive and liked to flirt. She guessed he had girls falling all over him. *I shouldn't take him seriously.*

Her attraction seemed just as pointless now as it had when she thought he was on his way back to Manhattan. Maybe even more.

Even if he doesn't have a steady girlfriend, he would never be interested in me. And he's only staying for a few weeks. It's not as if he's moving here. Another reason not to think too much about him.

Zoey strolled over to pick up the check on James's table and take away the dirty dishes. He had left her a generous tip.

Which I don't exactly deserve. Along with the check and the money, she found another slip of paper, folded in half. It looked like it must have been torn from his notebook. She opened it and read:

"Not all those who wander are lost." —*J. R. R. Tolkien*
Glad I wandered in here today and saw you. —*J.*

Zoey was surprised . . . and pleased. She quickly read the note a second time and felt herself blush. *Maybe he does like me—a little? Or he's a terrible flirt. Maybe both things are true,* she realized with a smile. *I guess now I'll have time to find out.*

She tucked the note in the pocket of her uniform and practically skipped to the register with the table check. Just as she was putting the money in the drawer, a huge crash in the kitchen made her jump. She slammed the register drawer and ran toward the kitchen.

"Dad, is everything okay back there?"

The kitchen doors flew open and Scotty ran out. He pulled on a fleece jacket with one hand and pulled off his apron with the other, then tossed the apron on the counter and headed for the door. "Bye, Zoey. Good luck. Your father is crazy. I hope you know that."

Zoey turned to watch his speedy exit, but didn't reply.

She knew Charlie had his difficult moments. But another part of her—a larger part—bristled with indignation at the insult.

She pushed through the doors to find her father standing in a pile of broken pottery. A broom and a dustpan in hand, he didn't seem to know where to start. It looked as if the dishwasher had exploded, but of course, that was not the problem.

"Dad . . . what a mess. What happened?"

"That damn fool kid . . . I told him not to overload that shelving. The bolt came loose from the wall, and I didn't have a chance to fix it yet. Did he listen to me? No, sir. Why listen to me? I'm only the boss around here."

Zoey bent to pick up a piece of a broken plate near her foot, but Charlie shouted at her, "Gloves, Zoey! Heavy ones. Use your head. I don't need a trip to the emergency room today on top of everything."

Good point, she thought, *though he could have said it in a nicer way.* She pulled on some work gloves she found near the utility closet and brought over another broom and trash bag.

"To top it off, the darn kid quits on me. Jumps right over the mess and out the door. Like a scared rabbit." Her father's voice got progressively louder. "Does he think he's going to come back next week, looking for his paycheck? I'm deducting every dish, cup, and saucer. He's going to end up owing me money."

Unlike some other restaurants, Charlie didn't usually charge the help for items that were broken while serving. It's not as if the Clam Box served on fine china and crystal. But she knew some restaurants did charge the help, and this situation was extreme. Though on the other hand, was it really Scott's fault that her father had not fixed the bolt?

"It's too bad you didn't get to fix the shelf, Dad," Zoey said finally. "Anybody could have overloaded it."

"'Anybody' didn't do it. He did. After I warned him." Charlie dumped a scoop of broken glass into the trash barrel. "I can't do everything around here and run the town, too. That's the problem, Zoey. Flip the burgers, fix the bolts, open up, close down. Et cetera and so on . . ."

Zoey could tell he was approaching some meltdown moment. She didn't know what to say. She picked up a few more pieces of broken pottery and tossed them into the pail, too.

"Problem is, I need a manager, someone who knows the diner and can watch over it for me."

"That's a good idea. You should find someone. Did Trudy ever get back to you?"

"She doesn't want to do it. She's made up her mind. I can't persuade her."

"That's too bad." Trudy had been working at the diner as long as Zoey could remember. She wouldn't need any time to be trained.

"It is too bad," her father said. "That's why I need you to step up. As soon as your term is done, I need you to work here during your school break and handle things. I'll give you a nice raise."

Zoey dropped the bits of broken glass in her hand and stared at him. "I told you I can't work here full-time during my break. I've applied for an internship at the center where I volunteer. If I get it, it starts right after Christmas. Even if I don't, I promised them I'd come in extra hours in January, at least twenty hours a week."

Charlie shook his head. "I know, but this is real work I need you to do. Not volunteer stuff. I can't do two jobs at once, honey. It's just not humanly possible."

Zoey felt so upset and angry, she thought she was going to cry. "My stuff is important, too. I'm really happy that you're finally mayor. I know you really wanted that for a long time. But why does that have to mess up my entire life?"

"Mess up your life?" Charlie looked amused now, leaning on his broom and rolling his eyes. "How am I messing up your entire life? You have more than a month off from school and absolutely nothing to do. A lot of college kids are scrabbling for jobs right now, trying to make a little money over their vacation."

"Then put an ad in the newspaper or post it online. You can hire one of them," she retorted.

He squinted at her. "Don't sass me, young lady. You know what I mean. I've already hired you. I'm expanding your responsibilities and your hours. It's not like I'm asking you to do this for free."

Zoey took a breath and tried another tack. "I know I don't get paid at the center. But I need the experience and good recommendations from the people I work with there for my résumé. If I suddenly disappear for two months, they won't think I have a serious commitment."

Her father didn't answer right away, and for a moment she thought she had swayed him.

"I don't know what to do about that," he finally said. "I think you ought to talk to them, tell them you have a family emergency and you have to take a break for a few weeks. It's not a lie, Zoey. This is important. I don't mean for it all to fall on you. But C.J. has to go back to school right after Christmas, to make up some course he needs during intercession. Or I'd have him in here, too. Though I have to add, I wouldn't trust him to run things around here the way I trust you."

Zoey knew her father thought that was a huge compliment. She did feel a bit proud of his trust in her, but she also wished her brother was here to share the job. C.J. worked in the diner as much as she did when he was home from school, and she missed having him around. At least they had some fun together.

"I'm sorry, honey," Charlie said, "but this is more important than your volunteer work right now. We've got a situation here that's urgent."

"But, Dad—"

He shook his head. "Case closed. I'm not talking about this anymore. Now you go out front and turn the sign. We're closing early today."

Zoey pulled off the gloves and pushed through the kitchen doors. She felt her eyes blur with tears of anger and frustration.

Stuck in this diner her entire winter break? No internship. Not even volunteer hours? And what about a social life or any fun things she might want to do during time off from school? It sounded as if her father expected her to sleep in the pantry or something.

She flipped the sign on the door to SORRY, WE'RE CLOSED. SEE YOU SOON! Then she locked the door and started the rest of the routine— the closing-up chores that she knew by heart.

There had to be some way out of this. Some way to change her father's mind. She wondered if her mother knew about this plan. Zoey doubted it.

Mom will speak up for me, Zoey told herself. *She knows I can't be stuck in the diner for my whole winter break. It's great that Dad got to be mayor. Whoopee for him. But why does that mean my entire life has to be screwed up? It's just totally and completely unfair.*

CHAPTER FIVE

⌒

AREFUL ON THESE POTHOLES, HONEY. I'D RATHER WE DIDN'T bust an axle," Sophie gently warned her grandson. "This truck is so old, no one will be able to find the part."

"Good point, Grandma." James didn't own a car and hadn't been driving at all in the city, so he didn't mind driving slowly today. The truck handled like a small armored tank; he had no idea how his grandmother drove it on her own.

It was nearly two p.m., and they were just getting back from the village. Though Sophie had given up running the church Christmas Fair, she had stayed on after the Sunday service to give her successor detailed instructions.

"You ought to get this private road paved, Grandma."

"I know. I never got around to it. I suppose if I ever want to sell the place, it would be a good idea. You don't want prospective buyers to get their teeth shaken loose before they even see the place."

"Why not? That would definitely put them off," he pointed out.

Sophie laughed. "Good idea. Every time your father suggests it, I'll just put him off. Tell him it gives the place a real country feel."

As they rounded a bend in the lane, another car came into view. It was parked alongside the house, and James recognized it immediately—a sleek BMW sedan with a Connecticut license plate. "Looks like you'll get a chance to tell my dad right now."

His grandmother peered out the windshield. "I'll be. That is his car, isn't it? Sneaky to park on the side of the house like that. I didn't even see it."

"Dad isn't exactly sneaky. But he likes to have an edge. A surprise ambush is definitely his style." James came around to the passenger side and helped his grandmother down from her seat. It was a bit of a hop to the ground, but she was surprisingly nimble for an old person.

She stood by the truck a moment, yanked down her knitted hat. and tucked a few strands of hair under the edge.

"Are you all right, Grandma? Need to catch your breath?"

She shook her head. "Not at all. Just straightening myself out to face your father. It can't be a good sign, him coming all the way out here alone. It might be nothing, but"—she swiped some lipstick across her small mouth and dropped the tube back in her bag, then took her grandson's arm—"I think we should be prepared."

James nodded. He felt the same. Just the sight of the sedan made his stomach knot.

As they walked up to the house, the side door swung open. James's father stood there, smiling. Mac jumped up and did a little dance around his grandmother. James imagined the dog was confused, waiting alone with the surprise visitor.

"There you are. I thought you'd never get back. I tried your cell phone, James. Didn't you see my messages?"

"Sorry, the battery died. I couldn't charge it in the truck."

Bart glanced at the old red pickup. "It's surprising that engine still turns over. Charging a phone might have killed the battery."

"Don't talk that way about Bella. She might hear you." Sophie walked past him and took off her heavy coat and muffler but, for some reason, left her hat on. James guessed she thought it made her look more dignified—or perhaps even regal? The hand-crocheted hat did have a bit of a crown shape to it, and some tiny pearls sewn on as well.

"The truck has a name?" Bart followed his mother into the kitchen. "I suppose you've named the trees, too."

Sophie smiled. "Of course I have. I could pick out each one blind-folded, too. Why do you think they've given us such wonderful-tasting fruit all these years? That's no accident, son." She had flipped Mac a biscuit, and he trotted back to his dog bed and crunched on it happily. Then she turned to the sink and started filling the kettle.

"I'll make some tea. Would you like to have dinner with us, Bart? I'm just heating some leftovers Evelyn gave me."

"Thanks, but I've got to get on the road. I had some business in Boston the last two days. I just stopped by to say hello before I head home."

Cape Light was almost two hours north of Boston. Not exactly the most direct route back to Connecticut, James knew.

"Very thoughtful of you, son. But you didn't have to go out of your way like that," his grandmother said.

"I want to make sure the house is ready for the winter," his father replied. "I think you ought to chop more wood and put insulation tape around all the windows. And the basement door. I can feel a draft from here."

"Good idea. I'll make a note," Sophie replied, though she made no move to write it down.

"Buy plenty of Ice Melt and some sand for that private road. We need to get it paved soon, Mom. It's treacherous."

The kettle hissed, and Sophie turned to lower the heat. "James and I were just talking about that road. You do need to take it slow, but it gives the place a real country feeling. People visiting the orchard for pick-your-own just love that." She glanced at James with a mischievous grin.

"I know you like things a certain way, Mom. You're used to the clutter and the inconveniences. But we need to keep this place up. By the time you're finally ready to sell, it will be a falling-down wreck. I was just upstairs. Some of those rooms look like walk-in closets, and every one of them could use a coat of paint."

"Things do accumulate. I can't argue with that." Sophie carried the teapot to the table and set out three mugs, though James had never once seen his father drink tea.

Sophie sat at the table, and, finally, Bart did, too, taking a chair across from James. "Have you had the chimney cleaned lately?" Sophie nodded, mixing a spoonful of honey into her cup. "How about the gutters? Did you ever call the number I gave you?"

"I just get up there with a broom or a big metal spoon and scoop the leaves out around the end of fall, when it's all come down. I can't see paying anyone to do that."

"You climbed a ladder? By *yourself*?"

Sophie shrugged. "It's not a very tall one. If I lost my balance I'd just end up in the hydrangeas. They're big and soft enough to break even *your* fall."

"Good to know," his father replied. He closed his eyes and rubbed his hand over his face, a gesture James knew signaled that he was trying very hard not to lose his patience.

"Are you all right, Bart?" Sophie asked. "You're not getting one of your headaches, are you? I'm not sure you should drive if that's going on."

"It's not a headache. I'm fine." He opened his eyes, looking in control again. "I'll make a list of what needs to be attended to around here and make some calls for you next week."

"All right. Why don't you try Sam Morgan? He might be in between big jobs. He's a very nice fellow," Sophie added.

"Okay, I will." James couldn't tell what his father was thinking; his expression was unreadable. He suddenly turned and looked at James. "Why aren't you going back to the city? I don't really understand."

James knew he was in the hot seat now. Grandma's turn was over.

"Oh, I don't know. There are too many distractions there for my writing, and I wasn't getting along with my roommate."

His father didn't answer for a moment. "You lost your job. Is that it?"

James sighed and stared down at the table. "Well . . . I did. But that really wasn't all of it. I—"

"I knew it," his father cut in.

"It wasn't just that," James insisted. "I could have found another one."

"Sure, another job waiting tables in some dumpy restaurant. I don't doubt that for a minute. When are you going to get serious about your future, James? You wanted some time after you graduated to try out this writing business. Okay, we gave you time. But it's been almost two years. Time enough for you to stop fooling around."

"I'm not fooling around, Dad. I'm writing every day. I've had articles and short stories published." James didn't mean to raise his voice, but he couldn't help it. "I've sent them to you. Did you even read them?"

His father sighed again. "Of course I did. That isn't the point. It's all very nice, but it doesn't pay the rent if you still need to scrape by waiting tables. You need a real job, with a career track. Or even graduate school. I can get you hooked up in five minutes with twenty interviews." His father picked up his phone and waved it around. "There are young men your age who would jump through flaming hoops to get some of the interviews and training programs I can get for you in a heartbeat, James. Be realistic."

James stood up from his chair. "I'm not a circus animal. You can't just crack the whip and see me jump."

"That's not what I meant, and you know it. You can't hide out up here for the rest of your life, behind your grandmother." Bart cast an accusing stare in his mother's direction.

She made an innocent face, and shrugged. "I invited him to stay here for the holidays. He needs to get his bearings. I don't think there's anything wrong with that."

Bart didn't answer but turned back to James. "And what are you going to do after you get your bearings? Run into the woods and build a cabin, like Henry David Thoreau?"

His father must have learned about Thoreau in school, eons ago, but James was surprised he remembered anything like that, especially since Thoreau was a writer.

"It worked out pretty well for Henry," James replied. "But I plan to travel. I'm going to find jobs in other countries on that website WAVE. Remember when I did that one summer in college?"

"Your mother and I thought of that as summer camp for a twenty-year-old. We didn't intend for you to make a career of it."

"Right, you'd rather I wasted away in a cubicle all day, in some mind-numbing job. I want to see the world, Dad. I want to experience other cultures and meet all kinds of people. I want to have something worthwhile to write about."

James watched his father's color rise. He had pale, sandy hair, thinning on top, and there was no way for him to hide his stress and anger.

"Be serious a moment. Be realistic. All those years of college, all the tuition—what was that for? So you can work on a farm in some backward place where they don't even have running water? You won't last a week. You never even liked to mow the lawn."

James didn't answer. He sat back, his arms folded over his chest. His father didn't understand. He never would. He had never wanted to do anything with his life beyond being a trust attorney. That was his choice. He was very good at it and seemed to like it. James didn't think any less of his father for his choices. But why couldn't he realize not everyone wanted to take the well-traveled path? Not everyone was ambitious for the same kind of success?

His father tried again. "I understand if law school or investments don't grab you. I get that. It's not your style. What about social media or public relations? Or advertising? You might like that. You can write all you want in your spare time. I'll find a nice apartment for you in the city, all your own. Anywhere you like," he added, sweetening the bait.

James took a deep breath. He was not tempted. He would never sell his soul for an apartment. His father should know better than that. "Sorry, Dad. I know you don't understand, but this is my plan. I'm sticking with it."

Bart shook his head. "Your plan, huh? Where do you expect to get the money? Will you pick an airline ticket off one of those apple trees out there?"

James ignored his father's sarcasm. "I'm going to look for a job in town."

"Really? Well, better not rush to pack your bag. This could take a while. You'll be lucky to get the minimum wage out here." His father suddenly pinned his grandmother with a stare. "You're not going to give him money, are you?"

"Who, me? Never crossed my mind," she insisted, though James doubted that. "But since James is staying, maybe he should try his hand on that list of repairs. I mean, if he wants to."

"Great idea. I can paint and use a hammer. I was going to fix a few things around here anyway. You don't have to pay me, Grandma."

"Nonsense. We have to pay someone, and it's hard to find a good repairman for small jobs. Especially this time of the year."

Before his father could weigh in on the idea, James quickly replied, "Great, it's a deal. And I won't charge nearly as much as a real carpenter or a painter would."

His father's glance swept from James to his mother and back again. "No need for me to put my two cents in here. I can see that. It's getting late. I'd better go." He picked up his muffler and hat from a chair.

He walked over to Sophie and kissed her cheek. "Good-bye, Mother. Take care of yourself. And please don't overdo it."

"Don't worry, son. I have James to keep an eye on me."

His father pinned James with a look as he stood at the door.

"I know you think you've gotten your way. But this isn't over, James, not by a long shot."

James wasn't sure what to say. "We can talk more sometime, Dad, if you want."

His father nodded curtly, pulling on his hat. "We will, I promise you." His pulled on the door, but it didn't open right away, adding a comical touch to his angry exit. James kept a straight face until his father managed to get outside and close the door behind him.

Sophie hid a small smile behind her hand. "Oh dear. He was madder than a wet hen, wasn't he? He got like that sometimes when he was a boy. He could get all fired up. There was no talking to him. But then, a little while later, he would settle down and forget all about whatever was bothering him."

James sat back and sighed. "I don't know, Grandma. I doubt he's going to settle down and forget about this. You heard him. I don't think he's going to let it go so easily."

"Maybe not," Sophie conceded. "But the best way to convince someone that you mean business is to do what you said you were going to do. All the fine words in the world don't add up to one single act."

"Good advice. The first thing I'm going to do is fix that door." He got up from the table and set off for the toolbox. "I promised you Tuesday night I'd take care of it."

"So you did," Sophie recalled with a smile. "Thank you, James. I'll mark it off our list."

Sophie woke on Monday morning and glanced at the clock. It was still early; sunlight had barely seeped below the edge of her bedroom curtains. She rolled over and closed her eyes again. Mac was curled at her feet, a warm mass weighing down the quilt at the bottom of the bed. He was content to sleep in, too.

She had been an early riser all her life, up with dawn, good weather and bad. But in her later years, especially since the pneumonia, she sometimes found herself sleeping in until Mac's cold nose nudged her cheek. It wasn't as if she had that much to do. Especially when the orchard was in a quiet season.

She had nearly drifted off again when she suddenly smelled coffee. Coffee? How could that be?

She sat up and remembered—James. He must be up, even though it was barely seven. *There's a surprise. There will be coffee all ready for me when I go downstairs this morning.*

That was enough incentive to make her push the covers back and search for her slippers and robe. The drowsy dog woke and yawned, then reluctantly jumped off the bed and trotted downstairs behind her.

"Morning, Grandma," James said as she entered the kitchen. "I hope I didn't wake you up, banging around down here."

"Didn't hear a thing. I did smell the coffee. That got me moving." She walked to the stove and filled a big mug.

James sat at the table, dressed in jeans and a flannel shirt, his hair still damp from a shower. He was writing in a notebook and barely looked up. "I woke up with an idea for a story. I like to get things down while they're fresh in my head."

"You work. I need to be with my own thoughts, too, for a while."

Sophie walked to the back door and let the dog out. James had done a good job fixing it. It opened smooth as butter. She pulled the collar of her bathrobe close against the chill morning air and gazed at the trees. A frosty mist had settled on the land like a magical cloud.

It would probably burn off soon, if the forecast was right. It looked so delicate and mystical now. Sophie wished she had a camera and could take a photograph.

I might need a picture like that someday, if my children have their way and make me leave here.

She smiled out at the trees a moment, greeting them each by name in her mind. As she turned to go in, Mac came scurrying back and ran inside. "Good dog, Mac. Time for your breakfast," Sophie quietly crooned, mindful of James still writing.

By the time she had given Macintosh his kibble and sat at the table with her mug, James had closed his notebook and put it aside. He smiled at her. "What's on the agenda today? I'm at your service."

"Like a genie in a bottle, aren't you? I forgot how nice it is to have someone in the house," she said honestly. "Visits from friends and family just aren't the same."

"No, I guess not."

She knew he didn't really understand. Not at his age. Her children had grown up and gone their own way, as it should be. Her dear husband had passed on, too. The house had once been a noisy place, full of life. But it had grown very quiet with just her and Mac. The kind of quiet people her age knew too well. It was nice to have someone to plan the day with. Or cook for. A young man like James was her ideal customer.

"I think we ought to start upstairs," she replied after considering his question. "Your father is right. Those rooms need cleaning out and painting. I've been meaning to sort out that old stuff. I bet we can bring most of it to a charity or a shelter."

"Sounds like a good plan," he said cheerfully. He looked down at his perfectly flat stomach and gave it a gentle pat. "I don't need breakfast after that big dinner last night."

"Those measly leftovers?" Sophie scoffed. "That was nothing. It's not healthy to miss breakfast. I'll fix oatmeal."

"Okay, oatmeal. A small bowl. I knew I wasn't going to get away with skipping a meal around here."

Sophie laughed and headed for the stove. "Honey, if you want to get along with your new roommate, you'd better forget about that idea right now."

A short time later they were upstairs, trying to sort out the boxes and assorted items in the large bedroom at the front of the house.

"Best to tackle the worst first," Sophie said, leading the way. James hadn't been in the room in a long time. Probably since he was a boy and would stay over in the summer with his cousins, or visit with his family on a holiday.

"This room definitely needs paint, Grandma. That brown spot on the ceiling doesn't look good," he added, noticing a possible leak from . . . somewhere.

"First things first. Let's start on the boxes and make three piles—keep it, donate it, throw it out. We may need to drive the trash to the dump. I noticed in the local paper the trash collectors are unhappy about their new contract and are 'slowing down service.' Whatever that means."

James wasn't sure, either. "I guess we'll have to see. I can bring it to the dump in your truck. That's no problem."

There was a vast assortment of items collected in the room. James felt overwhelmed as his grandmother dived in, tossing books, clothes, and knickknacks in all directions.

"Look at this picture album. People just don't save photographs like they used to. It's all stuck in their telephones or computers," she murmured, turning the brittle pages.

James glanced over her shoulder and saw a black-and-white photo of a young woman posed next to an apple tree. She wore a simple white blouse with a long sash tie at the neck, in the style of the 1940s or 1950s. Her skirt fell just below her knee, billowing out in the breeze. Her long hair was pinned up on one side, the waves framing her pretty face. Her arm was lifted, touching a branch of the tree, which was filled with white blossoms. She almost looked as if she were sitting in a cloud.

"What a beautiful photo. Is that you, Grandma? Wow . . . you were a knockout."

His grandmother lifted her chin and smiled. "You think so? That photo was taken right before I met your grandfather. I was an old maid. That's what people called me, anyway. My fiancé had died in the war, and I didn't think I'd meet anyone to fall in love with and marry after that."

"But then Grandpa came along," James finished for her.

"He did, thank heaven. The good Lord sent your grandpa to me. One sunny day, I was up on a ladder, picking apples. And my brother brought your grandfather home for a visit. They were army pals. I looked down and saw him. He was so handsome, I almost lost my step and fell into his arms."

James smiled at the story, though he had heard it many times before. His grandmother turned the page and there was his grandfather Gus, wearing an Army uniform that hung loose on his tall, rangy body. His dark hair was slicked back, his eyes bright. He had been very handsome, and had remained so in his later years, when James knew him.

"Look at this one. Now, this is old. I ought to enlarge it and hang it up somewhere." Sophie pointed at a sepia-toned photo, a family portrait formally posed in a studio. Dark velvet curtains framed the family in fancy clothes, the many children and the father carefully positioned, with everyone standing except the mother, who sat on a chair with a high back, a toddler on her knee.

"That's my mother, Mary, and my dad, Jim. You were named after him," Sophie added.

"Yes, I know. But I don't think Dad has any pictures of him. I've always wondered what he looked like."

"There aren't too many. He was a shy man, never liked photographs. I don't know how my mother got him to sit for this one. Those boys are my brothers, and that little curly-headed girl on my mother's knee is me. Can you believe it?"

"You were cute," James said.

"Wasn't I?" His grandmother sounded as if she couldn't believe that she'd ever been that young. "We weren't exactly poor, but not wealthy, either. Those aren't our clothes, though. They were rented out for the portrait. Some women even rented their wedding dresses in those days," she confided with a laugh.

James thought that was interesting. "Did your parents grow up around here? How did they start the orchard?"

"My mother's family lived in Salem. Her father had a big clothing store there. They were fairly well-to-do. She met my father at a church social. They liked each other right away. He was from Ireland, recently landed. He was working for a cousin out here, in Cape Light, who owned a poultry farm. The courting wasn't easy. He didn't own a car. But they managed. Obviously," she added with a smile.

"Sounds very romantic. But how did they end up out here?"

"When they married, my grandfather persuaded them to settle in Salem. He rented a nice house for them and gave my father a job in his store. My father tried it, but he didn't like being a salesman, and he didn't care anything about clothes."

"He had to be his own person, march to a different drummer," James guessed.

"That's right." Sophie smiled. "That must be where you get it from."

"So, what did he do? Go back to the poultry farm?"

Sophie laughed. "Good lord, no. My mother couldn't stand that idea. But they both loved Cape Light."

James could easily imagine it. "It must have been beautiful here back then."

"Yes, but much more remote. Harder to get to without the big highways and train service extended to this point."

"So how did your parents jump from chickens to apples?"

"Lucky for my mother, this orchard and house came up for sale. Bank foreclosure—it was nineteen thirty, the start of the Depression. But her father still had money. He bought this property for a song. He loved his daughter, and he approved of apples. He knew my folks would never be millionaires, but they'd do well if they worked hard, took care of the land and the trees, and managed their business properly. He helped my father with that," she added. "My father, to his credit, paid him back every penny. My grandfather respected that."

James slipped the photo from the plastic sheet that covered it. "I could take this someplace and have it enlarged and framed for you, Grandma. Maybe I should make a few copies. You can give them out at Christmas, to the family—to my father and aunts?"

Sophie beamed. "What a nice idea. Is it much trouble for you?"

"Not at all. But I'd like to look at this album more. Maybe I can do something with the pictures so that they aren't stuck in a box somewhere. I'd like to know more about the family's history, too. I love all your stories."

His grandmother patted his shoulder as she came to her feet again. "I thought you might. You've got more than a touch of the poet in your soul, dear."

As James put the album in a safe place, he noticed a photo on the floor. Sophie had noticed it, too. "Pick that up, will you, dear? Let me see. That one looks more recent . . ."

He handed her the photo. It was clearly more recent. A color photo, though not all that modern, with its bright yellow and red tones. A little boy in a baseball uniform, about to swing his bat, a gap showing in his smile where a tooth was missing.

"That's your father. Didn't you recognize him?"

James shook his head. "That's big, bad Bart? That skinny little twerp?"

Sophie laughed. "One and the same. He thought he was headed for the major leagues at that age. He wasn't very good at baseball, but he loved it, and we encouraged him, Grandpa and me."

"Good to know he wasn't always that realistic about his career goals, either," James said, still stinging from the previous night's showdown.

"He also wanted to be an astronaut." She gazed at the photo a moment. "He was a good boy, always had a kind heart, and was protective of his sisters. Though he could be mischievous. Nothing terrible," she added. "He was a little scoundrel; always made us laugh."

"Sorry, Grandma, I find that hard to believe," James said honestly. His father was still kind and protective of the people he loved. But he didn't have much of a sense of humor or even flexibility.

"He hasn't changed that much," she insisted. "When you have words with him, try to remember this picture. It might help."

James thought that was interesting advice. "Okay, I'll try. But you probably should, too."

His grandmother looked up at him. "You got me there. Maybe you should make copies of that one, too," she added with a laugh.

James gathered a pile of clothes his grandmother had tossed in the donation pile and shoveled them into a large black plastic bag. "Are you really leaving here, Grandma?"

He heard her sigh. "I don't know. In my heart, I don't feel as if I am. I just can't picture it. But lately, it does feel like I'm being swept away on a riptide. I'm trying to fight it, but it's just too strong to swim against."

James heard the sad, defeated sound in her voice. "I don't want to do this repair work if it's going to help my dad and aunts push you out. I can find a job somewhere else. I think I need two jobs anyway, to earn the amount of money I need."

"That's good of you to say, dear. But it won't make a difference either way. The cleaning out and repairs need to be done, whether I stay or not. I can't let the place fall down around me. Maybe my time here has come to an end. 'To everything there is a season, and a time for every purpose under the heaven . . .' You know that Scripture, don't you?"

"Yes, I do." James didn't know too much Scripture, but he was familiar with those famous lines.

"Maybe I just have to get my mind . . . and my heart . . . around those words. It's very hard, going through all this old stuff. It doesn't make the question any clearer," Sophie confessed, gazing around. She looked confused and suddenly tired, he thought. "All I can say is, life goes by awful fast. You don't feel that way when you're young. But at my stage, when you look back, it seems like a movie that was running on fast-forward the whole time. Years and years went by in a heart-beat. Inside, I hardly feel any different at all."

James gazed at her with sympathy but couldn't help smiling, too. "That's a good way to describe it . . . Can I use that line in a story sometime?"

She laughed, surprised and suddenly cheerful. "I'd be honored. I never thought I ever said anything worth writing down." She glanced at her watch. "What do you say—ready for lunch?"

"Sure. Let's take a break." He could tell she was ready to leave this room and her memories. And determined to serve him three squares a day.

AFTER LUNCH, JAMES BEGAN TO CARRY THE TRASH OUT FROM THE room they were cleaning. It was a long walk from the upstairs bed-room down through the kitchen and out the side door to the truck. On the second trip, he piled the boxes high—higher than he could see—and Sophie scurried to the door to open it for him.

"Be careful. You're going to fall like that," she warned.

"I'm okay, Grandma. Just point me toward the truck." He could see a little, around the edge of the cartons. But as he swung out of the house and headed for the driveway, he smacked into something solid—that gave out a high-pitched squeal.

"Oh, my gosh. I didn't see you there . . . I'm so sorry."

The boxes tumbled down, the contents spilling all over the drive—old shoes, broken toys, a woman's wide-brimmed hat covered with dusty cloth flowers, and a water-stained roll of Happy Birthday wrapping paper that unfurled like a flag.

At the same time, Zoey dropped the paper bag she had been carrying, and a collection of pie tins poured out and rattled to the ground, rolling around like pinballs until they each spun to a stop.

James stared at Zoey, and she stared back.

"Instant yard sale?" she asked in a small voice. James grinned, and they both started laughing.

"One man's junk is another man's treasure." James began picking up the fallen debris, and Zoey bent down to help him.

"I should have seen you coming. I was in a daze or something." She had actually been so anxious at the possibility of seeing him, she'd been totally distracted, worrying about her hair and her outfit and what she would say. *So now you just look like a complete klutz. Good job.*

"I piled the boxes too high. It was my fault," he said.

Zoey didn't reply. The guys she knew rarely admitted it when they messed up, and never so easily. *That's refreshing,* she wanted to say.

"No harm done," he added, tossing a worn-out sneaker into one of the cartons. "How about those pie tins? Need any help chasing them down?"

"I can manage." Zoey had to go around the truck to get the last tin, which had rolled underneath and come out the other side. Despite her claim that she could handle it, James had come around the truck and they met face-to-face, practically knocking each other over. Zoey slipped a bit on the gravel, but he grabbed her arms just in time. She stared up at him. She could feel his breath and, for some odd reason, couldn't pull her gaze away from his. His face was so close. Was he going to kiss her?

Mac came racing around the truck. He picked up a pie tin in his mouth, circled them quickly, and dashed off toward the barn, gravel flying out from under his paws.

James laughed, stepping back from her. "What in the world was that—Space Dog?"

"Looks like he beat us both to that one. He must think it's a game. He wants us to chase him."

"That dog needs a Frisbee. There must be at least one in this pile of junk. I'll check before I go to the dump."

"Are you helping Sophie clean out closets?"

"I'm helping her clean out everything. And paint and do some other repairs. I fixed the door. It isn't stuck anymore," he reported proudly.

"Really? I didn't know writers could be handy, too." She was teasing him a little. But it was also true. She was surprised he knew his way around a toolbox.

"My dad taught me. He knows carpentry, how to paint, and all that. My grandfather taught him. Running the orchard, he had to do his own repair work most of the time."

Zoey nodded. "That makes sense."

"My father hates to do any of that stuff now. He always hires someone. But I like it. It makes me feel productive, and it's a good way to earn money," he added, tossing a box into the truck bed.

"So you're going to work on Sophie's house while you're staying here?"

"Yes, it all worked out. She needed to hire a handyman and here I was, just hanging out. I would do it for free, but she insists on paying me. And I really need the money. For my trip," he added, tossing another carton in the truck.

"What trip is that?" Did she miss something the last time she spoke to him? She didn't remember him mentioning that he planned to travel.

James glanced at her and smiled. "Oh, sorry. I told my grandmother, but I guess you weren't around. I'll be leaving right after the holidays. I'm not sure where yet. Someplace really interesting—South America, maybe? There's this website called WAVE where you can find agricultural jobs all over the world. You apply and are matched up with a farm. I did it in college over a summer. I went to Spain. It was a great experience."

"It does sound great." Zoey had always wanted to take a trip like that, just backpacking around and going to different countries with no set schedule. Even a semester abroad would have been great. But her parents couldn't afford it. "How much money do you need to save?"

"At least two thousand dollars, for my airfare and expenses until I start working. I don't have much time. I'd like to leave right after New Year's. I'm going to look for another job in town, too, but at least I can save everything while I'm staying with my grandmother."

"I'd love to travel like that someday, too. Maybe after I graduate. I guess you'll see all kinds of interesting things to write about and meet all sorts of people."

"I hope so," he said cheerfully, tossing another box in the pickup. It fell with a soft thud on top of the others. "My grandmother told me that you're an art major?"

"I have a double major, art and psychology. I'm studying to be an art therapist. I'll have to go to grad school, too."

He looked impressed. "What an interesting career choice. When I was a little kid I had a lot of nightmares. My parents brought me to a shrink, and she made me draw pictures."

Zoey smiled. "I want to work with children, too. I volunteer right now in a center where the counselors work with kids. I'm getting good experience there."

"See, I guessed right off you were the type. Artistic . . . but smart and kind," he added. His blue gaze met hers, and she felt herself starting to blush.

Zoey stepped back, hugging the bag of pie tins. "Why were you having nightmares? Did you ever find out?"

He shrugged. "Too many Harry Potter books. My mother kept telling me it was just a story, but I was sure that we were secretly related. Like he was a lost twin, and nobody wanted to tell me the truth."

Zoey laughed. "Did you get teased in school for having the same last name?"

"A little," he said. "But that only convinced me more. They say children with high IQs have very active imaginations."

"Yes, I've read studies about that."

"Did you read Harry Potter books when you were little?"

"I did," Zoey replied. "Hermione was my favorite. I always wished I could have her for a best friend."

"I liked Hermione, too. I had a crush on her," he admitted. "I never understood why Harry didn't." He smiled. "Now that you mention it, you look a little like her."

He was flirting again. She tried to ignore it, but that was hard.

"Did you grow up in Cape Light?" he asked.

Zoey had guessed that question was coming, but she never liked answering it. It was too complicated. "Not really. But I like it here. It's a nice place to live. For now, I mean."

She heard her phone buzz, signaling a text. She thought it was rude when people pulled out their phones in the middle of a conversation, but this time, she felt saved by the interruption. "I'm sorry, I have to see who this is."

"That's all right. I don't mind." James tossed two more cartons onto the pile. Even though it was cold outside, he wore an open flannel shirt with a T-shirt underneath. The shirt flew open each time he tossed the boxes, and Zoey couldn't help noticing his strong chest.

The text was from her dad, who needed her at the diner earlier than her scheduled shift. She quickly texted him an okay.

"My dad. I have to get to work. He needs me there early," Zoey explained as she slipped the phone into her pocket. "Can you give the pie tins to your grandmother? Oh . . . I forgot they fell. I'll take them home and wash them first."

James pulled the bag from her hand. "No problem. Got this covered. You sound like you're busy enough, running to work, to school. Volunteering," he added. "Do you ever just hang out?"

She wasn't sure why he was asking. Did he think she was some sort of totally serious, stressed-out person, rushing around like a lunatic all the time?

"Sure. I hang out."

"Good to know. Would you like to hang out with me sometime? Like, go to a movie or something?"

Did he just ask me out? Zoey had to take a breath before she answered. "Sure. That would be fun."

"How about Friday night? Have any plans?"

She pretended to think about it a moment, trying not to seem so super available. "I have to work, but I get off at five."

"Great. My grandmother has your number. I'll check in, and we can figure it out."

Zoey nodded, not knowing what to say. She was afraid that she would do or say something terrifically dumb. She glanced at her watch without even seeing it. "Got to go. Good luck with the cleanup."

"Thanks. I need it. My grandmother's a real pack rat. Everything she ever owned has some sort of sentimental value."

"Yeah, I know. But that's what makes her so special."

His expression softened. "Very true. So long, Hermione . . . I mean, Zoey."

"So long, Potter," she called over her shoulder as she walked to her car. "Hope nothing too scary pops out of the closets. But I'm sure you can handle it."

She heard him laugh and saw him wave as she started down the drive.

A date with James? Really? Does he actually like me, or is he just bored to death up here?

Steady, Zoey. You don't want to drive into an apple tree. You have plenty of time to think about this later . . . at the boring old Clam Box.

CHAPTER SIX

ON WEDNESDAY AFTERNOON, EMILY PULLED UP TO EMERSON Middle School and parked near the gym. She was already a few minutes late for Jane's game, but hoped it hadn't started on time. There was usually some delay, waiting for refs or the opposing team to arrive.

She ran down the hallway to the gym, not really noticing how quiet the school was. The gym was surprisingly empty—except for two boys playing basketball at the far end of the shiny wooden floor, the sound of the ball and their shouts echoing in the big space.

"Can you help me?" Emily called. "Isn't there a girls' volleyball game here today?"

The boys stopped and glanced at her. One continued bouncing the ball. "I don't think so."

"I think they're away today," the taller boy said. "There's a schedule on the bulletin board," he added, shooting a hook shot over his friend's head.

"Hey, man, that doesn't count," the shorter boy protested.

"Yeah, it does." He grabbed the rebound and stuffed in another.

Emily shouted back a word of thanks but knew they didn't hear her. She ran back out to the hall and checked the bulletin board near the door, filled with schedules for all the school teams.

Finally, she found it: *Wed. 11/30 Girls Volleyball: Away. Simpson Middle School—Beverly.*

She ran back out to her car, jumped in, and drove out of the lot, heading for Route 1A. She wasn't sure she remembered the way to Simpson Middle School. *The talking gadget on your phone, Emily. No-brainer . . .*

She pulled over to the side, set her phone to direct her—even though the robotic voice drove her crazy—and pulled back out on the road.

"Turn left in five hundred feet, at the next light," the voice said.

"Will do, thanks." *Am I the only person in the world who talks back to that thing?* She could only blame her mother for teaching her and her sister to be unfailingly polite at all times.

Emily's phone rang just as she stopped for a red light. She quickly glanced at the screen—her mother again. Emily didn't have to listen to the message. She knew it was another last-minute pitch to get her to the open-space meeting, though Emily had made it perfectly clear that if her mother wanted to go, she needed to arrange her own ride. But it was more than transportation that Lillian was after. Emily knew that, too.

"Proceed on Route 1A, two miles to Hitchcock Lane." *Two more miles. Not so bad.* Emily remembered now that the school was right after that turn. She drove quickly but carefully the rest of the way and arrived a few minutes later. It wasn't hard to find the gym, and she sighed with relief, hearing the sound of a game going on as she jogged the rest of the way to the open doors and quickly found a seat in the bleachers.

She felt as breathless and sweaty as the players on the court and quickly slipped off her jacket. The whistle sounded and parents cheered. Simpson had just scored. The score looked close. Where was Jane? Emily scanned the court but didn't see her.

Then she spotted her daughter on the bench. Jane looked as though she had been out on the court already; she was chugging from a water bottle, her bangs plastered to her forehead.

Oh drat. For once the coach started her and I missed it?

Emily felt like kicking herself. She tried to catch Jane's eye, but her daughter was focused on her team, jumping up and cheering as a friend spiked the ball so hard it bounced off the floor and into the stands.

Emily cheered, too. "Number Five! Way to go!"

The woman next to her beamed. "That's my daughter, Number Five, Tara Bartow," she said proudly.

"She's very good," Emily replied. "I'm here for Number Nine, Jane Forbes. She's on the bench now, but it looks like she played for a while."

"Yes, she scored three points in the first quarter," Tara's mother reported. "She's terrific."

Emily felt her heart drop. "I'm so sorry I missed it. I went to the wrong school and . . . well, maybe she'll be put in again."

"Hope so." The woman gave her a curious look. "Hey, aren't you Emily Warwick, the mayor?"

Emily smiled but shook her head. "Former mayor."

"Oh, that's right. I thought I recognized you. Well, your granddaughter is a super player. Now you have time to cheer her on."

Emily felt the smile on her face freeze. "She's my daughter. But that's my plan. Thanks."

The other woman's face flushed with embarrassment. Emily was grateful when a loud cheer from the stands distracted both of them. The opposing team had scored, and now they were ahead by three points. Before the two teams could set up again, the whistle sounded for halftime. Jane's coach called his girls into a huddle near the bench.

Emily gazed around, wondering if she knew any of the other parents. They all looked so young. *I don't look that old for my age, do I?* She wondered if she should consider a new hairdo.

Poor Dan was the one who got the grandfather tag, ever since Jane had been a baby. His hair had gone prematurely gray in his early forties.

The woman on her other side chatted with her neighbor. They seemed to be good friends, deep in a serious conversation.

"—but I told them I just can't do it right now. Maybe when Max is done with kindergarten."

"I'd like to go more, too. But I'm in the same boat with the twins. Audrey is having trouble with reading. I've got to stay on top of that," the other mother added. "So much after-school stuff. At least I started the Crock-Pot this morning. I barely have time to figure out dinner."

Emily hadn't given a thought to dinner. Dan usually cooked dinner; he made simple meals, but he was quite good at it. She had made some noises about taking over, but hadn't started yet.

Though she had gone through all these stages with Jane, she didn't feel as if she had much in common with these parents—even if she could manage to break into a conversation.

A woman on the bleacher below sat with needles and yarn, stitching away at a feverish pace. *Maybe I should learn how to knit. It would give me something productive to do over the winter.*

The whistle blew and the teams came back on the court. Emily was excited to see Jane take a front-line position.

The plays were fast, the girls on both teams agile and strong. Emily jumped up and down in her seat as Jane made two huge spikes, the second totally confounding a player on the other side; the poor girl fell to her knees, trying to reach it in time. Luckily, they all wore knee and elbow pads.

The second half of the game flew by, with Jane on the court twice. When the final whistle blew, Emerson Middle School was behind by two points. A narrow loss but well played, Emily thought. She was no stranger to that outcome.

She joined the wave of parents heading down to the court to meet the players. She gave Jane a big hug. "You were awesome, honey. What a spike! I'm going to call you Hammer at home."

Jane looked pleased at her praise, and a little embarrassed, too. She was at that age. "Thanks, Mom. Too bad we lost."

"Not by much. You all played really well. Do you have a lot of homework? I thought we could get ice cream or something. You must be starved."

Jane had been a picky eater as a little girl, but now she could eat a large lunch, another full meal after school, and still have an appetite for dinner. And she just got taller and thinner.

"I have to go back to school on the bus with my team, remember?"

"Sure. That's right. I'll meet you there."

Emily had gone to so few games that she had forgotten the routine. *But I'm going to remember from now on. I'm going to put the schedule in my phone and be at every game.*

"I'm going home with another girl on the team—Tara Bartow? Guess I forgot to send you a text. We're doing a project at school together, and we need to work on it tonight."

"What's the project?"

"It's a debate for history class. It's not due for a few weeks, but we need to figure out a question and take sides and all that."

Emily felt excited at the news. "That's something I can help you with. Maybe your friend should come to our house."

Jane looked uncomfortable at the suggestion. "It's all sort of planned. Another girl is coming, too. It's too late to change it, Mom. But thanks."

"I see." Emily suddenly realized that Jane wasn't used to offering their house for after-school meetings. Usually, Emily wasn't home and Dan was writing and needed quiet.

"Sounds like you'll have more meetings about this. Next time, everyone can come to our house. Maybe I can help a little. I've been in a few debates."

Jane had watched Emily debate in the last two elections and grinned at the understatement. "Sure, you can help us next time. I'd better go. Everyone is getting on the bus."

Emily nodded and kissed her forehead. Jane slung her pack over her shoulder and ran to catch up with her friends. Emily watched, feeling wistful. And a little deflated.

We're all in a period of transition now. Not just me, she reminded herself as she headed for her car. *I can hardly blame Jane for not volunteering our house or asking me for help. She's not used to the fact that I'm totally available for her and not stuck in an office until late at night.*

I need to be patient. It will take her a while to get used to all this. But not too long, I hope.

*   *   *

EMILY GOT HOME TO FIND DAN IN THE KITCHEN, TAKING A FRA-grant roast chicken out of the oven. "How was the game?" he asked.

"Emerson lost but fought valiantly. Your daughter has a mean spike. I never realized she was so tough."

"Oh, Jane has a competitive streak. Not always visible, but definitely there. I wonder who she takes after," he said with a sly smile.

"Yes, I wonder." Emily knew that she, too, could be competitive when necessary. "I like to see her jump in and do battle with a team. But I didn't really have anyone to talk to," she admitted. "One mom thought I was Janie's grandmother." Emily rolled her eyes. "Time for that expensive eye cream?"

"A lot of people marry young around here," Dan pointed out. "You wouldn't feel so out of place as an older mom if we lived in Boston."

"I know. I should be used to it by now, being an older-than-average mom. Maybe I should get bangs next time I get my hair cut? They say it takes ten years off."

Dan laughed and put his hand on her cheek. "Honey, you look fine. You're just not used to hanging out with the after-school sports group. Just don't talk about politics or religion. You'll be fine."

"How about Crock-Pots? That seemed to be a hot topic . . . Do we have one?" She bit down on a raw string bean and gazed around the kitchen.

"Somewhere. I've never used it. Hey, there's something you can work on, mastering the art of Crock-Pot cooking. That would let me out of kitchen detail every night, too."

"Good idea. I'll look for some videos online." She was half joking, but half serious, too. She saw plates stacked on the counter and began setting the table.

"Where's Jane? Did she run up for a shower?"

"She went home with a friend. They have a school project to work on. The history class is having a debate."

"A debate? That's right up your alley."

"I noticed. And I plan to help them. Next time," she clarified. The phone rang, and Emily glanced at the number but didn't pick it up.

"Who's that? Don't you want to answer it?"

"Not right now. It's just my mother. I know what she's calling about."

They heard Lillian's voice on the answering machine. "Emily, are you there? I tried your cell phone. You didn't answer. I'd like to speak with you. I went to the meeting and I have some news. It's important."

Dan turned to look at her. Emily was folding napkins and placing forks and knives at each place.

"What's that all about? What meeting? Something at church?"

"No . . . something else. Some group she wants me to—"

The phone rang again. A name flashed on the caller ID—Martin Becker, the chairman of the open-space group. Had she left her home number with them? She didn't think so.

"Your mother again? I think you should get it, Em. She'll give us no peace." Dan was carving the chicken, his hands too slippery to grab the phone.

"It's not her. Let me just listen a minute . . ."

"Hello, Emily. This is Martin, from SOS. Sorry you missed today's meeting. Your mother said it was okay to call. We decided on a strategy, and we need to be ready for the village meeting next Monday evening. We could really use your input on this. We have so many questions and so little time. If you could get back to me soon, I'd greatly appreciate it."

Dan turned, holding his carving knife and fork in the air like a surgeon. "What's SOS? And what sort of meeting is this? I thought you said you weren't going to—"

"I know what I said. I was really trying to stick to it, too. But last Sunday, Mother tricked me into going to a meeting for a group that's fighting the new zoning proposal. I thought I was taking her food shopping after church, but she made me bring her there instead. And I couldn't just leave her there. Sitting in the car seemed childish, too." She paused. "I know I broke my promise, but I hope you're not mad at me?"

"Of course not. I know how Lillian is. And I know this issue is important to you. You were very vocal about it during your campaign, and I know that wasn't just talk."

"I really do care, Dan. It was encouraging to see how many people joined the group. But I don't want it to look as if I'm purposely trying to undermine Charlie—as if I'm a sore loser, out to embarrass him. That's not it at all."

"I know it's not," he assured her. "But it is a slippery slope. If you get involved, some people will see it that way."

"I sat way at the back and didn't even intend to talk," Emily explained. "But some of the ideas people offered would just be a waste of time. I know how zoning gets changed and the ways to block it. I couldn't help giving a little advice."

Dan stood at the sink, washing his hands. "Sounds like they need it." He turned to face her again, drying his hands with a towel. "I just don't want to see you get swept up in another . . . town tornado. Something like this can eat up all your time again, Em. *Our* time."

"I know. I don't want that either, believe me. We're going to have a really nice Christmas. And plan our trip. I'm just going to help them prepare for the council meeting next Monday night. After that, they're on their own. I'm not going to lead a charge down Main Street. Been there, done that."

Dan smiled and rested his hands on her shoulders. "Good plan. I think everyone in this house has been there and done that."

Emily was glad they had talked this out. She had meant to tell Dan that she had gone to the meeting, but somehow, it had ended up a secret. It was a relief that he knew and wasn't upset that she had broken her promise. Not broken it—bent it, just a bit? Just until the council meeting at Village Hall Monday night. *The trick of life is to set limits,* she advised herself.

Dan had set the platter of chicken on the table, and Emily brought over bowls of green beans and noodles. "This looks delicious. Thanks for cooking. My turn tomorrow night."

"You're welcome. And I was hoping you'd say that," he admitted with a grin.

Another promise she had made to her family. She was going to keep it, too. "I may surprise you," Emily replied.

Dan smiled and kissed her. "You always do."

"THERE ARE THE USUAL PRESCRIPTIONS, AND SOME NEW DRUG THE doctor wants me to take for my stomach acid," Emily's mother told her on Friday afternoon. "The drugstore said it would be ready today, but it's not that important. These doctors are rabid to write out prescriptions. They get fancy dinners and vacations from drug companies. Did you know that? I saw it on the news, a special report."

"I never accepted so much as a ballpoint pen from a drug salesman,"

Ezra shouted from the living room. Emily didn't even realize he'd been listening.

"Of course not, dear. You would never stoop so low," Lillian shouted back. "I mean these young doctors, the type we see."

Emily wondered who her mother could be talking about. Lillian and Ezra's youngest physician had to be over fifty. But she didn't contradict her. She had been at the house almost an hour and was eager to leave. Her mother claimed she had caught Ezra's cold and couldn't go out today, so Emily had offered to help. During the many years she had been mayor, she had managed to run over to Providence Street at random breaks in her day or while driving to or from meetings. She had always shared the care of her mother with her sister. But with Jessica's recent promotion and Emily out of a job, the visits and errands were falling her way.

She really didn't mind. Jessica had shouldered most of it for a long time, and it was her turn to step up. She also had her own errands to cover and wanted to be done in time to pick up Jane at school.

"So it's the drugstore, the library, and these items at the market?" Emily met her mother's glance, trying to keep her on track.

"That's right . . . and mail these bills for me, please?" Lillian passed Emily a handful of envelopes. "And I need you to give out a few of these around town. For the open spacers. I promised I would give them out by today."

Her mother picked up a sheaf of papers from the kitchen counter and held them out to her. Emily could see they were flyers advertising the group's mission and the council's meeting on Monday night.

"Mother, are you serious? I'm not walking down Main Street handing out flyers. Don't be ridiculous."

"I don't see why not. What are you ashamed of?"

"I'm not ashamed of anything. I just don't have time to knock on doors and talk people into taking flyers. Did you really volunteer to do that?"

"Yes, I did. I'm very persuasive when I put my mind to it," her mother said proudly. "But I don't feel well enough to march around all afternoon out there. And you can do it so much faster than I can."

That was true. A lot faster, and with far less danger of falling and breaking a hip.

"Why don't you call Martin and tell him the truth? You've got a cold and can't do it. I'm sure he can find someone else."

"The flyers should have been up days ago. How would that look? So irresponsible." When Emily didn't answer, Lillian added, "Is this so much to ask? Aren't people going to see you at the meeting Monday night with the group? Don't you plan on coming? Or will you sneak in and sit at the back again—incognito?"

"Of course I'm coming," Emily said, though she did plan on keeping a low profile. She knew the newspaper might try to play up her role in the group opposing Charlie. She could only imagine what reporters would infer.

Lillian sighed and sat in a kitchen chair. "Just skip it. I'll get dressed later when I feel a bit stronger and give it a go. I can make it to a few stores. If I get dizzy again, I'll stop. I promise."

Emily knew it was an act. Her mother had not mentioned anything about feeling dizzy before this. Still, she felt her resolve melting. "All right, no need to put on a long face. Give me those." Emily reluctantly took the flyers and stuck them in her bag. "I'll see what I can do."

Lillian shrugged, looking suddenly bright and energetic again. "That's all I've ever asked of you, Emily, that you try your best."

A few minutes later, Emily parked at the harbor and stuck the flyers into her big purse. It was a bright day and not too cold, for December. She walked across the green, deciding to stop at Willoughby's Bakery first. She had noticed the Christmas decorations on Main Street but hadn't seen the ones in the village square yet. She passed the big tree, feeling a little wistful. This was the first year in over fifteen that she hadn't presided over the annual tree lighting—announcing Santa's arrival on his fire truck, tossing candy canes and chocolates to all the children. It was hard to believe she would never lead that event again.

But I had a good run, she reminded herself. *And the only thing you can depend on in life is change.* Emily tossed her scarf around her neck and lifted her chin. Time to get cracking on the flyer assignment. Willoughby's should be an easy sell.

Molly Willoughby was family—her brother Sam was married to Jessica—and she greeted Emily with a hug. She had already heard of the open-space group and quickly agreed to hang the sign in the front window.

"Leave some at the counter. We'll hand them out for you. The last thing this town needs is a bunch of ugly condos and big-box stores." Molly had a way of cutting to the point that Emily loved.

"I know you're the busiest person in the world, but it would help so much if you came to the meeting Monday night," Emily said. "People listen to you and respect your opinion."

Molly laughed. "You make it sound like I should run for mayor next. I have a million things to do, but if you think it's important, I'll try to come."

"It is important. Your opinion would make a big impression on people, believe me."

Emily went into the pharmacy next. She needed to pick up her mother's medications. While Frank Dillard checked on the prescriptions, she showed him the flyer. "This is about the council meeting next Monday night, Frank. Can I hang it up on your bulletin board?"

"I'm sorry, Emily. Lost dogs and cats, people renting apartments, or selling cars—that sort of thing is fine. But we can't take sides on political issues. We have to keep the store a welcoming environment for everyone."

"I'm not asking you to take sides, Frank. It's just information. Won't you read it and then decide?"

He ignored the sheet and her question. "Here are your mother's prescriptions. Give her my best."

Emily thanked him and headed toward the Beanery, a coffee shop and café. They already had two flyers in their windows. No question what side Felicity Bean and her husband, Jonathan, were on. Emily dropped off extras to hand out.

Bowman Realty was next on the street. Emily's longtime friend Betty Bowman had stepped away from her realty business years ago to become Molly Willoughby's partner, finding the bakery and café more interesting than buying and selling houses. But she still held an interest in the firm that carried her name.

Fran Tulley, who had worked there for nearly twenty years, held the reins now. Emily liked Fran, but she knew the Tulleys were best friends with Charlie and Lucy Bates. She doubted the flyer would get far with Fran as gatekeeper.

Fran greeted her cheerfully and glanced at the notice, then put it aside on her desk. "Sure, you can leave it. I'll read it later. How's everything, Emily? How are you adjusting to civilian life?"

"It's a change, but a good one. I'm keeping busy."

Fran smiled. "Yes, I can see. You're a busy bee, as usual. It's hard to sit still and not get involved in things, I'll bet." Her smile was friendly but her tone held an ironic edge.

"Thanks, Fran," Emily said, deciding to ignore any hidden meanings in Fran's words. "I'll see you around."

"Busy bee, my foot," she grumbled, heading to the next store, which was Krueger's Hardware and Variety Store. Fran was a piece of cake next to George Krueger. A huge supporter of Charlie's campaign, he still had a "Vote for Bates" poster in the window.

Are you really going in here? You must know it's pointless.

Before she could decide, George Krueger walked up behind her. "Hello, Emily. Going in or coming out?"

She turned and met his glance. He was holding a brown paper bag, which she guessed was his lunch, from the Clam Box. "Just . . . window shopping." She had been staring in the window, trying to decide, so that wasn't a total lie.

"I'd be happy to help you inside. It's a little chilly out today."

"Yes, it is. I'd better get going. Have a good day."

"You as well," he replied with a curious look.

She continued down the street but was not too far away when she heard him call after her. "You dropped something, Emily."

George Krueger held up one of the flyers and waved it, a sour expression on his face.

Emily turned but didn't walk back. "You can keep that. It's about the council meeting Monday night. Hang it in your window," she suggested, knowing he would do no such thing.

"I know all about it. Thank you very much."

His tone had been tart, but Emily acted as if she hadn't noticed. "Good. See you then."

She glanced over her shoulder, and he caught her eye, crunching the flyer into a ball before going inside his store.

CHARLIE HAD SHUT OFF THE RINGER ON HIS CELL PHONE, BUT IT buzzed insistently. He glanced at the screen to check the number. It wasn't Zoey or Trudy with some diner disaster to report. Just George Krueger, down at the hardware store. What did he want? Charlie let voice mail pick up and turned his attention back to the weekly Friday meeting. His new staff circled the table in the conference room that adjoined his office in Village Hall. They all looked grim and nervous.

The pressure was on with Monday's council meeting only three days away now. They didn't seem to understand how crucial this meeting was for him. Or were they just pretending that they didn't?

"So you're telling me you can't get a complete budget for the road-work project ready by Monday, Ed? Or you just don't want to?" Charlie stared at Ed Shaw, head of the town's public works department. Ed was a young man, in his early thirties, with an engineering degree and plenty of other certifications. What Charlie called "college smart"— no common sense and as slow as molasses in January.

"I don't drag my heels," Ed said evenly. "This report takes time to research and cost out."

"I'm not asking for a price down to the penny. Can't you even estimate?" Charlie pressed him. "How long does it take to crunch a bunch of numbers on a calculator?"

"Pull a figure out of thin air, you mean? That would be bogus and irresponsible. We haven't inspected half the roads yet."

"I don't know why not. You've known since the first day I walked into this office that road repair is a top priority—at the top of the agenda for the council meeting Monday night. You have the whole weekend to work on it. I need a budget for roadwork, snow removal, and a new contract with K&B Carting. Is that a surprise to all of you?"

A small voice in Charlie's head—Lucy's, maybe?—reminded him that raising his voice was a bad idea. But he couldn't stop himself, and he quickly noticed he was shouting at a circle of stunned faces.

Ed Shaw came to his feet. "I'm not a waiter in your diner, Charlie. I don't know what you think goes into compiling a budget for a project like this, but it's not like a customer asking for his check."

"It's not brain surgery, either," Charlie told him. "If you walk out of this meeting, consider yourself fired. And don't expect any recommendations out of me, either."

The others shifted uneasily in their seats.

"You can't fire me. I resign. Mayor Warwick was always happy with my work. I can get a recommendation from her, no problem." Ed picked up his laptop. "It was certainly different when she was in charge," he added, marching out of the meeting room.

Charlie watched his staff exchange glances. Was this the beginning of a mutiny? Were they all still loyal to Emily Warwick and just waiting to walk out? Or maybe they *were* dragging their heels, trying to make him look like an incompetent fool?

Well, he was not about to back down. "Anyone else feels that way, there's the door. Things are different now. I'm the no-excuses mayor, and we're going to run this town on a lean, mean budget. Not like your old boss."

Joe Newland, a building inspector, cleared his throat. But no one made a motion to leave. Charlie felt relieved. Then his secretary, Miriam, stood up.

"I'd better go, too. I'm sorry, but this isn't working out for me," she said. "I tried, but . . . I'm really sorry." Head down, clutching a yellow legal pad to her chest, she scurried out the open door.

Charlie heard muffled laughter. He wasn't laughing, not one bit. He could find another secretary sooner or later, but he needed Shaw to work over the weekend and get the figures ready for the meeting. What a time to walk out on him.

Florence Simpson, the newly elected town clerk who had run on his ticket, opened her own pad to a fresh page. "I'll take the minutes, Charlie. Why don't we continue? We have a lot more to cover."

"That's right. We do. Back to work. We need to figure out those trash collectors. What's the latest, Karl?" he asked, turning the floor over to the town attorney, Karl Nelson, who had been negotiating with the company.

Charlie forced himself to focus on the attorney's report. The bitter taste of Shaw quitting and Miriam deserting the ship, too, lingered. For goodness' sake, wasn't this job hard enough without having to deal with all these touchy personalities? In time, he would weed out the deadwood and get his own people in here. *Right now, you have to make do,* he reminded himself. *You have to pull this group together, and look sharp by Monday night. Even if you have to camp out in this office all weekend to do it.*

AFTER HER LITTLE RUN-IN WITH GEORGE KRUEGER, EMILY STOPPED at the Bramble and had a far more encouraging chat with Grace Hegman, who owned the antiques shop. Grace had a quiet but reassuring way about her and gave Emily a cup of hot tea that took the chill off. Browsing the lovely shop, Emily even found a few Christmas gifts. Though it felt odd to be shopping so early . . . early for *her*.

Grace's father, Digger, came down from their apartment upstairs and chatted with her, too. As Emily had expected, the old seaman was strongly opposed to more building, or altering the village in any way.

"I'm coming to the next meeting. I want a front-row seat. Gracie says the excitement is bad for my heart, but what's the sense of having a heart if you don't listen when it speaks to you?"

"Very true. I'm going to remember that," Emily agreed.

Digger—who had often claimed he could hear clams whispering under the sand and could communicate with fish beneath the waves of the sea—had a poetic way of expressing himself, one that went straight to the core of things, Emily always thought.

The Bramble marked the end of the shops on that side of the street, and Emily crossed to visit an art gallery and a toy store. Her last stops, she decided. It was getting late, and she had to pick up Janie soon.

As she headed for the Firefly Gallery, the distinct aroma of burgers and French fries wafted toward her. The Clam Box. How could she have forgotten? It was right next to the toy shop. The idea of offering her flyers there made her smile. She imagined being chased out with a broom—or something worse.

Lost in the amusing, imagined scene, she nearly missed Charlie Bates, headed straight toward her. Head down, hands deep in his jacket pockets, his expression was grim as he marched briskly along.

Had he noticed her? She wasn't sure. He was staring at the sidewalk, deep in thought. She could have easily passed by, but that seemed churlish, as if she held a grudge. Which she didn't.

"Hello, Charlie. How's it going?"

He looked up, his expression friendly at first, then sour when he realized it was her. "Just fine. Like a well-oiled machine. How about you? How's civilian life, Emily?"

"So far, so good. I enjoy being a private citizen again."

He looked surprised. "Really? That's not what I hear. I hear you're going door-to-door stirring up trouble for me."

Emily wasn't surprised. Somebody—probably George Krueger—had alerted Charlie to her walk down Main Street.

"You want to derail my meeting Monday night, don't you? You just can't stand to see someone else run the show. Well, it's not going to happen. No way, no how."

Emily held on to her temper, though it wasn't easy. Charlie was misinformed—and a bit paranoid, as usual.

"That's not my intention at all. I campaigned on this side of the question, in case you've forgotten."

"Guess what?" Charlie replied. "The election is over. I don't have to debate with you anymore. The voters picked me. Maybe *you've* forgotten *that*." Charlie smiled at her smugly, then turned to go. But someone called out to him and he turned around again.

"What's with the trash collectors, Charlie? Any progress on that yet?"

Nina Barnes, the owner of the Toy Barn, emerged from her shop and walked toward them, black trash bags dangling from each hand. "The truck only stopped once last week. I'm tired of driving to the dump."

"I know it's been tough, Nina. I'm in the same boat at the diner," he reminded her. "But they're asking too much. I can bargain them down, but it's going to take time. We're hiring some outside help. They're starting on Monday," he promised.

"All right. But don't take too long."

"I understand completely."

"Do you? Christmas is coming, Charlie. I don't have time for this, too."

"No worries. I'll get it straightened out," Charlie promised.

Nina nodded and glanced at Emily. "Nice to see you, Emily. Stop by sometime. We can catch up."

"I'd like that." Emily was itching to hand Nina a flyer. She had a feeling the toy shop owner would side with the open-space group. But she decided not to start that conversation in front of Charlie.

As Nina tossed the bags in her car and pulled away, Charlie's smile melted. "I've got to go. I've got two businesses to run now," he added, as if to say, *You have none.* "Enjoy the rest of your walk, Emily."

"Thanks. I will."

She crossed the street again and headed for her car, instantly regretting her sarcastic tone. How had their conversation gone so sour so quickly?

That wasn't at all what I intended. I could help him with K&B Carting. I know how difficult they can be, and I know a few tricks for getting around them. But of course, he won't take my advice.

Do I really want to stir up trouble against Charlie? Am I fooling myself, thinking I'm just concerned about this issue and it has nothing to do with losing the election?

Emily hated to face it, but suddenly she wasn't sure if her motives in this fight were so lily white after all.

CHAPTER SEVEN

⁓

*C*HARLIE SWEPT INTO THE DINER AND HEADED STRAIGHT FOR the kitchen. He pulled off his jacket and slipped on an apron in one efficient, well-practiced motion. Trading barbs with Emily Warwick on the street had been bad enough. But did she have to hang around and gloat while Nina Barnes griped about the trash problem? Just his luck to have some unhappy shopkeeper read him the riot act in front of Her Highness. That must have made her day.

Meanwhile, his day was going from bad to worse to a complete crash-and-burn scenario. At least people listened to him at the diner. He didn't have to deal with a lot of back talk.

Tim, the lunch shift cook, was eager to go and had texted twice. So was Trudy, who sat at a back table, counting her tips. He spotted Zoey at a table by the window, taking an order, but she tagged after him and caught up just past the swinging doors.

"Hey, Dad. I thought you were coming back at two."

"Got held up in the office. But it looks like you've been holding down the fort today. It takes a load off my mind to know you're down here watching over things, Zoey. You know I always say it, but it's true."

Zoey clipped her order on the wheel, then gave him that smile, like she didn't really believe him. "You don't *always* say it, Dad. You hardly say it at all."

"I don't? Well, I'm thinking it. All the time. What do you kids say? You're the bomb?"

Zoey rolled her eyes. "Thanks. By the way, nobody says that anymore," she added in a fake whisper.

He nodded, checking the prep area, the stainless steel tubs of garnish the waitstaff added to the dishes before they went out. "Low on pickle spears, honey, and lemon wedges. Some more red onion wouldn't hurt, either."

Zoey made a face. "I hate red onion. I bet it destroys the ozone layer. Red onion is contributing to global warming."

Charlie laughed. "I don't think so. Just keep the wrapping over it. Life isn't a rose garden, you know."

"I know, Dad." Her singsong tone amused him today for some reason.

"Hey, before you do that, I've got some good news and some bad news. Which do you want first?"

Zoey eyed him warily. "Good news, I guess."

"I hired a new busboy. He starts tomorrow. And we still have Lyle on the schedule," he said, mentioning another staffer who bussed and helped in the kitchen.

"That is good news." She looked genuinely happy, and Charlie felt relieved.

"What's the bad news?" She winced, as if bracing herself. Charlie felt guilty already.

"Come on now, honey, it's not that bad. It's just that I can't stay here late tonight, like I thought. I have to get back to Village Hall for another meeting tonight—about that stalled contract. So I need you to close up."

Before he could say more, Zoey's high-pitched squeal made him raise his hands to cover his ears. How in the world did teenage girls do that?

"Da-a-d! You've got to be kidding! I can't stay tonight. I have a date. I told you this morning, remember?"

Charlie didn't doubt it. She probably had told him, but it had gone in one ear and out the other. He had so many more important things on his mind right now.

"I'm sorry. It must have slipped my mind. I'll make it up to you, honey, I will. But this is really important. It's crucial. I have the big council meeting on Monday night. My first time on the chopping block—the whole town will be there. I can't go in without good news about the contract. I just can't."

She sighed, her shoulders sagging. Tim hit the bell behind the counter. "Order up, Zoey . . . Charlie, when are you jumping in here? I've got to get home."

"Keep your shirt on, man. I'm coming," he grumbled without glancing back. Zoey looked like she was going to cry. He hoped not. It killed him when she cried—especially if he was the one who upset her.

"Daddy, *please*. Do I really have to stay?"

He felt bad now, hearing that plaintive tone. He knew how important a date was at that age. Zoey didn't go out that much, either. She wasn't the party type, like some kids he heard about. He was proud of her for sticking with her studies and doing so well in school.

"Honey, I'm sorry . . . but yeah. You do." Before she could answer back he said, "Who is this guy? Do I know him?"

She shook her head, chin down. "He's not from around here. Just visiting for a few weeks, with his family."

"I see. Well . . . if he likes you that much, he'll ask you out again. Don't worry. It's good to play hard to get. You ought to make a boy ask you out at least two or three times before you say yes. Boys like that, believe me."

She rolled her eyes and grabbed a plate that held a cheeseburger deluxe. "Yeah, maybe back in the eighteen hundreds, when you were a kid. Maybe I should wave a fan in front of my face and act like I have fainting spells."

He knew she was sassing him, but sometimes she was so funny, he couldn't help laughing. "Hey, I'm not kidding. Back in the eighteen eighties, I must have asked your mother out about ten times before she said yes. I knew she was the one. I didn't give up."

Zoey sighed. "Lucky for her." She stood over the garnish bar and added the appropriate extras—a pickle spear and the dreaded red onion slice, wrinkling her nose like a rabbit.

He patted her shoulder. "Don't worry. This boy will ask you out again. Or he's a dumbbell and you're well rid of him."

She headed out to the dining room. "I hope you figure out that contract thing. Those trash collectors are ruining my life."

"You and me both, kiddo." Charlie shook his head as the kitchen doors swung closed behind her.

Nothing easy about this day, he reflected. *Everywhere I turn, drama and more drama. I feel like I'm fighting a wildfire, running from one spot to the other with a water pistol.*

Two more years of being mayor? I'm not sure I can make it.

*　*　*

BETWEEN THE KITCHEN DOORS AND HER CUSTOMER'S TABLE, ZOEY somehow conjured a smile. She set down the burger deluxe platter with extra pickle and red onion. "Can I get you anything else?" she asked.

"All set for now, thank you." The customer, a woman about her mother's age who worked in the bank down the street, came in a few times a week for a late lunch. She usually read a book while she ate and was already engrossed. Zoey checked the author's name. She didn't recognize it, but that didn't mean much. She didn't read many novels these days—mostly just textbooks.

Maybe someday I'll look down and see James Potter's name on the cover, she thought. *I can tell everyone I almost had a date with him. That will be a great story for my grandchildren.*

Back at the counter, she slipped out her cell phone and checked for his number. They had been in touch over the week and had made plans to see a movie in Newburyport and have sushi after.

Zoey hated to break their date. She had really been looking forward to it, and had even planned her outfit down to the earrings.

What if James didn't believe her or felt insulted? What if he didn't even care that much?

She did not need dating advice from her father—even though what he said was true. Some guys did seem to like it if you didn't seem so available. But she didn't think James was like that. She certainly wasn't going to wait for him to ask her out ten times more before she agreed. Once seemed like hitting the lottery.

She chickened out on calling and sent a text:

Sorry but I can't go out tonight. My dad just said I have to stay and close up.

She hit send and waited. Should she add a frowny face? That seemed too much. She didn't want him to think she was that disappointed. Though she was.

Should she say more? Like, "Hope we can do it another time"? As in, *Can we reschedule now? I'm available tomorrow night. And the night after that . . .*

That seemed too obvious. And a little pushy.

His answer was already coming back and appeared on the screen:

Bummer. Another time, I guess. Catch you soon.

Zoey sat back. He didn't seem that concerned about it. That made her feel even worse.

I guess it wasn't a big deal for him. He's just bored. He would have asked out any girl his age who could fog a mirror.

Forget about James. He's sweet, but he's out of your league. And leaving for a trek around the world in a few weeks. Duh? Not exactly steady boyfriend material.

As Sophie would say, *Things happen for a reason.*

Zoey was determined to sleep in Saturday morning. She had drawn her curtains tight the night before and made sure her phone alarm was off. She was tired from last night's long shift at the diner and feeling blue about missing her date. And she had stayed up late, watching a dumb romantic comedy she'd seen a hundred times before.

It felt like the middle of the night when someone gently shook her shoulder. "Zoey? You need to get up now. Sorry, honey." Her mom stood beside the bed, her expression sympathetic.

"Get up? What time is it?" Zoey rolled over to check the bedside clock. It was barely seven. "No way." She rolled over with her back to her mother. "I don't have to be at the center until this afternoon. I want to sleep some more."

"I know, sweetie." She felt Lucy sit on the edge of the bed. "But we have to go down to the diner and do breakfast. Trudy and Tim opened, but they need help. Dad didn't get back from his meeting until three o'clock this morning, and he can't move." Her mother sighed and gently pushed Zoey's hair back from her face. "I'm sorry, sweetie, but we've got to do it. So shake those pretty legs."

Zoey finally opened her eyes. "But I'm scheduled to work at the center this afternoon. I can't cancel on the center, Mom. They're counting on me."

"Just do the breakfast rush with me, Zoey, and you can go. I have the day off, and I'll work until Dad comes in." Lucy stood up and headed for the door. "We all need to pull together now, sweetheart. We have to pitch in and help your father until he sorts things out at Village Hall."

Zoey didn't answer. She knew there was no negotiating. At least she didn't have to work all day. It was good of Lucy to stay and let her go, considering that Lucy's nursing job was intense; she worked at least forty hours a week and often worked overtime, and she probably had her own long list of things she wanted to do on a rare day off.

I'll have to thank her later. When I'm conscious.

*   *   *

THE DINER WAS A WILD SCENE WITH ONLY TRUDY ON THE FLOOR waiting tables. Tim, the backup cook, kept running out of the kitchen, trying to cover the counter customers.

Lucy turned to Zoey briefly as they came in, fresh recruits into the battle zone. "Keep your head down, honey. It's a madhouse in here."

They quickly stashed their coats, pulled on aprons, and grabbed their order pads. Lucy took the tables at the back of the room, where impatient customers waved madly to flag her down. Zoey headed for the booths at the front, moving from table to table, scribbling down orders that she hoped Tim could decode.

"And can I have some more coffee please, miss?" A customer held out her mug.

But before Zoey could reply, a hand holding a coffeepot magically appeared and filled the cup.

"Thanks," the woman said, giving her menu back to Zoey.

Zoey turned, expecting to see Lucy, or maybe Trudy. But it was James, standing a few steps back from the table and grinning at her. He wore a white shirt and black pants and carried a big empty tray.

"What are you doing here?" She tried to keep her voice down, but couldn't hide her shock.

"I'm the new busboy. Your dad hired me yesterday."

"I get that part," she said tartly. "Why didn't you tell me?" She headed off to the kitchen to put the orders in, and he followed.

"I should have told you yesterday. But I thought it would be fun to surprise you."

"Was it?" She tried to sound annoyed, but was actually really happy.

"Yeah, it was." His wide grin underscored his reply. "That's why I didn't ask if you were free tonight when you changed our plans. I knew I had to work here."

Zoey was glad to hear that. Luckily, her back was turned toward him as he followed her through the swinging doors to the kitchen, so he couldn't see how happy she was. Maybe Charlie did have a point about acting a little hard to get. "I see," she said simply. She clipped the orders to the metal wheel at the service window.

"Are you working all day, too?"

"Just for breakfast. I'm going to the children's center this afternoon." She glanced at him. He looked unhappy to hear she was leaving so soon.

A plate of eggs and home fries appeared at the window. "Order up!" Tim shouted. Zoey checked the table number.

"How about Sunday? For our date, I mean."

The question surprised her. So he did want to see her. Her first impulse was to do a cartwheel across the kitchen. Then she realized she had to say no—again. *Why is my life such a total disaster?*

"I'm sorry . . . I really want to, but I have finals next week and a ton of papers due. I really have to study."

He looked disappointed but as if he understood. "No worries. I get it. We'll go out when the semester is over and celebrate."

Zoey smiled again, then heard Trudy call out from the kitchen door, "Hey, new guy—get out there and clear those tables." Trudy stared at James, looking very annoyed as she carried in a tub of dirty dishes. She dumped it near the dishwasher, then held the empty tub out to him. "I can't seat people at dirty tables. And you can't stand around all day flirting."

James ran over, grabbed the tub, and headed out to the dining room. Zoey felt her cheeks redden. She placed another plate of eggs and toast on her tray and headed out to the dining room. But not even Trudy's dark look and mortifying comments could tamp down Zoey's bright mood. As Sophie would say, *You never know what's going to happen when you get up in the morning. Expect the best and that's what you'll find.*

Funny how working extra hours at the diner didn't seem like a jail sentence anymore. It didn't seem so bad at all.

"ARE YOU SURE YOU HAVE TO GO? CAN'T SOMEONE ELSE DRIVE YOUR mother and Ezra over?" Dan stared up at Emily, his fork hovering over a bowl of chili with all the trimmings.

Emily had pulled out the Crock-Pot over the weekend and, by Monday, had been armed with enough recipes to cook with it for the rest of the year. She started with chili, which was simple enough even for her. Dan and Jane seemed to like it, though there had not been enough time for Emily to eat with them—not if she was going to get to the meeting at Village Hall on time.

Jane was still eating, too; her expression told Emily she agreed with her father.

"I'm sorry. It's too late to find them a ride and, frankly, I'm curious to see what happens." Emily grabbed her coat and purse from the rack near the side door. It was already six. She barely had time to pick up the seniors and get over to Village Hall by half past.

"All right, whatever." Dan shook his head and took another bite of his dinner.

She knew Dan thought she was back to her old ways, but part of her was sincerely reluctant to go. She had gone to some trouble to plan a nice family dinner and had even made baked apples for dessert. "I won't be back late," she said, tugging on her jacket.

Jane looked up at her. "Are we still going to practice for my debate?" Emily had forgotten that plan, but caught herself. "Absolutely. I'll be home in an hour," she promised, dropping a quick kiss on Jane's hair. "See you later," she said, avoiding Dan's gaze as she headed out the door.

By the time she guided her mother and Ezra into the meeting room at Village Hall, nearly every seat was filled.

"Just my luck. I hate to sit in the back," Lillian grumbled.

"A hot ticket. I had no idea," Ezra said.

Emily had been hoping to sit in the back and found three seats in a distant corner. She had told Dan the truth; she was curious to see what went on tonight but had no intention of getting involved. *You handed out those flyers and gave them some good pointers on drafting their counterproposal. You've done your part,* she reminded herself.

Charlie sat in the middle of a long table at the front of the room, flanked by the town council. They talked quietly together, Charlie with his hand over his microphone.

A podium with a microphone was set up in front. It looked exactly like one of her meetings, except that Charlie held a gavel. Emily didn't like being so formal and rarely had trouble keeping order or getting the crowd's attention. She wasn't surprised by the accessory. It suited his personality.

"Good evening, everybody. Thanks for coming out tonight and taking part in running our beautiful village," Charlie began cheerfully. "First item on the agenda—K&B Carting Company, contract negotiations." His gaze swept over the audience. "Is this settled yet? No, not yet. But trust me when I say that we have been working night and day to come to terms with this company. For reasons I won't go into here, this company thinks we're soft and willing to give them whatever terms they ask. That may have been true in the past, but it's a different ball game now. We have to show them we're not pushovers anymore. Even if it takes a little longer to get the job done right."

Emily felt her mother's pointy elbow dig into her side. "You know who he's talking about, don't you, you soft old pushover?"

Emily ignored her and did her best to ignore Charlie's thinly veiled criticism. He made her regime sound like a candy store for town contractors. Of course he had to make some excuse, and it was easy to blame this situation on her. For now, at least.

"The handout shows you what they're asking and what we want to pay. And the difference is substantial. The floor is open for comments. Two minutes per speaker," he warned.

Nina Barnes was the first to the microphone. "What's the sense of having free parking if shoppers have to climb over trash bags to get to my store? I just want to see this settled, the sooner the better. We don't have to make some big showdown out of this, Charlie."

A chorus of agreement rose up in the audience. Charlie banged the gavel. "Order, please. If you want to talk, line up at the microphone."

Tucker Tulley was up next. "I think we should stay the course, like Charlie says. If all the firms that do business with the town ask for more money, that's going to raise our taxes."

"Just my point. Thank you, Officer Tulley," Charlie said.

"*Officer* Tulley? They've only known each other since kindergarten," Lillian said.

"Longer than that. I delivered them both within days. They were in the infant ward, side by side," Ezra corrected her.

"That must have been a sight," Lillian murmured.

Audience members asked questions—how long was the new contract and could the town call in a professional mediator?—and all the council members had their say.

"I propose the council take a vote on whether to accept the K&B offer or stand tough," said Karl Nelson, the town attorney.

"I second the motion," added Art Hecht, who owned Hecht Insurance and had always been one of Charlie's supporters.

Emily wasn't surprised to see the vote fall in Charlie's favor.

"It's still the honeymoon phase. They haven't gotten tired of him yet," Lillian said with a shrug.

Charlie banged his gavel. "Motion carried. The town will continue negotiations with K&B and hold the line. Item two: New zoning. A draft of the revised zoning is in the handouts. As I've said, I feel certain this change will have a big payoff for Cape Light—mainly increased revenue to repair our roads, improve our schools, and create more housing for young families and seniors. We'll open the floor to comments, with a two-minute limit per speaker."

"He's quite pleased with himself," Lillian grumbled. "But I think the wind will be blown out of his sails pretty soon."

"We can hope," Ezra quietly agreed.

Emily wasn't sure. Charlie seemed to be steering the ship of state with a steady hand so far.

George Krueger jumped up and took the microphone. "Mr. Mayor, I have a petition here signed by over a thousand residents who support the new zoning proposal. This is something long needed in this town. We can no longer pretend we're living in some bygone day.

We may as well rename our town 'Cape Light Historic Restoration Village.'"

His quip brought laughter from the pro-zoning group.

Lillian sniffed. "An obvious plant from the Bates camp."

"Krueger couldn't possibly have thought up that line," Ezra agreed.

Perhaps, Emily thought. She had to admit that Charlie's side was effective. A string of supporters for the new zoning spoke in detail and at length.

Finally, someone from the open-space group shouted out, "Time limit, Charlie? I thought you said two minutes per speaker?"

"Right you are. Thank you. Next speaker please?"

Martin Becker was next in line, presenting his petition of over a thousand signatures. "These citizens strongly oppose any change in the zoning, especially in the outlying areas of the village, the marshes and farmland. This area is home to an abundance of wildlife. Any sort of development will pose a great threat to these beautiful natural habitats, which are—"

"Thank you, Mr. Becker. Your time is up. Please step away and let the next citizen speak."

"I haven't finished my statement," Martin protested. "If you'll just allow me a few—"

"That's the rule, Mr. Becker. Time is up. I'm just trying to keep this meeting fair and let everyone have their say." Charlie banged the gavel and waved his hand, indicating Martin Becker should move along.

"Silence and censor the opposition, a traditional mode of dictators." Lillian didn't even bother to lower her voice.

Grace Hegman was next. She gently leaned toward the microphone. "I allot my time to Mr. Becker," she said in her whispery voice.

"Hear! Hear! I second that. Nice move, Gracie." Grace's father, Digger, applauded.

Charlie leaned into his microphone. "You can't second what she said. It isn't a motion. And you can't give your time to someone else, Grace. That's not allowed, either."

"But we've always done it that way." She turned around and looked at the audience, tucking a wisp of her gray hair behind her ear. "Haven't we?" she asked in an innocent tone.

"That's right, Grace. We've always been allowed to give time to another speaker. You can't rewrite the rules, Charlie."

Molly Willoughby had come to her feet, very certain about the question.

Charlie covered the mike a moment and conferred with the council. He returned and spoke in a more conciliatory tone. "That was true when my predecessor was in office. But we're following *real* parliamentary procedure now, not some mishmash version. This is the right way to do things, believe me."

"I like the way we did it in Mayor Warwick's day. No one was cut off midsentence," Felicity Bean said.

"You ought to put away your rule book and get off your high horse, Charlie," someone else shouted out.

"All right, simmer down!" Charlie tapped his gavel.

Emily stood up. She had not wanted to say anything, but she had been in that hot seat, and it was painful to watch Charlie flounder.

"What Charlie just said is true. We were not following correct procedure by giving each other time to speak." She heard her mother groan, but ignored her. "It was just the way the meetings had been run, back through Mayor Pritchard's day," she added, mentioning her predecessor.

Charlie looked surprised but quickly followed up. "See, the former mayor agrees with me."

Martin Becker took hold of the microphone again. "Typical of Emily, to be honest and straightforward. And typical of you, Charlie, to change the rules in the middle of the game. I remember when you were fighting the parking meters on Main Street. Your group gave you all of their time, and you held the floor for over an hour."

"Touché, Becker. Well done!" Lillian called out.

Emily had forgotten that famous filibuster. It was actually one of many Charlie had staged during his long career opposing her.

"That was then, this is now. You shouldn't have let me have the floor that long. See where it got you?" Charlie laughed, trying to lighten the mood. "As I was saying, Grace, if you don't have anything to add, please step aside and let the next in line have their turn."

Sam Morgan stood up. "I'd still like to hear the rest of what Mr. Becker has to say. Isn't that the point of these meetings?"

Martin Becker stood at his seat and spoke in a voice loud enough for all to hear. "Thank you, Sam. I was going to add that the environmental impact of this development would be—"

Karl Nelson, the town attorney, took the microphone from Charlie. "Didn't you hear the mayor? Your time is done. The council must insist on order in this meeting."

"Simmer down, everybody!" Charlie yelled. He could hardly be heard over the arguments that had broken out all over the room.

"I've seen enough of Mayor Mad Hatter for one night," Lillian said as she and Ezra got to their feet. "Let's head for the door before the rush." Emily grabbed her coat and purse and then her mother's arm as they swiftly left the room.

Ezra and Lillian had a lot to say on the ride home. "I have to get out to these public forums more often," Ezra said, sounding very energized. "It's better than television."

"Anything is better than television," Lillian replied. "I was surprised you tossed him a lifeline, Emily."

"The man is his own worst enemy. It's his pugnacious attitude," Ezra replied. "That's what gets him into trouble. He's smart enough, in a rough-around-the-edges way. But he has no bedside manner."

"I still don't know how he got elected," Lillian said.

Emily was relieved to see they had reached Providence Street and quickly pulled into the driveway. Her mother was on the verge of calling for a recount—or an impeachment.

Ezra got out of the backseat and helped Lillian from the car. "I'll take it from here, dear. Good night," he called to Emily.

"Good night, Ezra. Good night, Mother," she called back.

She rolled up her window and headed home, feeling drained and unsettled. The meeting had only made the situation worse, heating up antagonism. It was exactly the wrong way to solve the problem.

She walked wearily to the house, hoping Dan had cleaned the kitchen. She was ready for a cup of tea and a good book, then realized how late it was.

Jane's project. I promised her we were going to practice.

It was my idea in the first place.

She pulled her phone from her pocket and saw that Jane had sent her a text at nine o'clock, but she had shut her phone off in the meeting. It was already nine thirty.

"Hello? Where is everyone?" Emily came in the front door and looked around the house. Neither Jane nor Dan were in the family room, or the kitchen, though the TV was on, set to the History channel, of course.

"We're upstairs," Dan called back. He stood at the top of the staircase and stared down at her. "I'm helping Jane with her opening statement for the debate."

She could tell by his tone he was annoyed but trying not to show it. Emily took the stairs two at a time.

"I didn't forget. The meeting turned into a madhouse. How's it going, honey?" She brushed past Dan, who stood near the door of Jane's bedroom. Jane was at her desk, frowning over her laptop.

Jane finally turned to her mother. "I'm not sure. It's too wordy or something."

Emily sat on the edge of the bed and gave Jane her full attention. "We can fix that, don't worry. Let's hear what you have so far."

Dan met her gaze, then slipped out of the room. He did have every right to be annoyed. She had promised Jane she would be home over two hours ago. The meeting had been such a kangaroo court, anyone would have gotten distracted. *But you're stretching yourself too thin again, Emily. You've done your part for the open spacers. You have more important things to focus on.*

"THEY'VE GOT ME TARRED AND FEATHERED, TUCKER. WHAT DO YOU expect from a newspaper that's run by Emily Warwick's daughter-in-law?" Charlie tossed the Tuesday morning edition of the *Cape Light Messenger* on the counter.

Tucker Tulley stirred his coffee. "It's not favorable. No doubt about it."

"'Mayor Bates's Debut: Town Meeting Meltdown.'" Charlie read the headline aloud. "And it gets worse. The inside is full of stories and interviews with residents, and there's even an editorial. Didn't anything else happen in this town yesterday?"

"It's one meeting, Charlie. Try to get the big picture. You're just getting out of the gate."

"Out of the gate and flat on my face, two yards down the track." Charlie focused on the grill, pushing the sizzling bacon to one side, then turning two fried eggs. "Maybe they're right. What do I know about being mayor? Maybe I should stick to dishing out chowder and clam rolls."

"You must know something about being mayor. People voted you in," Tucker reminded him.

"And last night those same voters turned on me like a pack of starving coyotes. You saw it. I tried to keep the peace and not lose my cool, but no one would listen."

"You're spinning too many plates at once. If you don't mind a little restaurant humor." Tucker laughed at his own quip, but Charlie didn't. "You should settle with K&B. Show people you can take action and resolve a big problem. Maybe it's not worth it to hold out."

Charlie served Tucker his usual breakfast: two fried eggs, bacon, and toast. "I hate to look soft after everything I said. But maybe we can reach terms I can live with."

"That's the way, Charlie. You've got to compromise."

"In some situations. Not with those open spacers. They're going for the jugular. Did you see who their ringleader is now? Emily Warwick. Becker is just a front. She's pulling the strings."

"I don't know. She was pretty quiet last night. She even stuck up for you a little."

"That was just a trick," Charlie said. "I know for a fact she's in that gang. It's a revenge thing. She can't stand to see me in office."

Tucker spread butter on his toast and took a bite. "Emily Warwick was against zoning changes during the campaign. It's not as if she never mentioned it. Besides, Charlie, you're mayor now. You have to focus on the problems and fix them. That's the way to win confidence and trust. Never mind about Emily. She's old news. A lot of people voted for you. We're counting on you to step up and prove we made the right choice."

Charlie met Tucker's glance. He felt touched. "I won't let you down, Tucker. I won't let anyone down. But it's impossible to run the diner and be a good mayor, too. I've got to get out from behind this counter and focus on Village Hall."

Tucker wiped his mouth with a napkin and brushed a few crumbs from his uniform. "I saw that coming. Why don't you put an ad in the paper for a manager and maybe another cook?"

"I would, but I'm strapped for cash right now. That campaign cost a lot, and I've got tuition bills to cover, too. Trudy doesn't want the job. She's told me flat out. At least I have Zoey. She can cover for me as soon as the semester ends. She'll do a good job, too," he added. "She looks a little kooky with her hairdos and way-out clothes, but she's a smart girl, very responsible."

"I know she is. But how does she feel about the promotion?"

Charlie felt color rise in his face. He cleared Tucker's empty dish and wiped the counter. "I've brought it up, but she just squawks. You know teenagers. She'll fall in line eventually."

Tucker put his police hat on. "If you say so."

Charlie could tell by Tucker's tone that he didn't think it would be so simple. He crossed his arms over his chest. "I'm her father. She has to do what I say."

Tucker laughed as he headed for the door. "Right. Get back to me on that one."

*   *   *

CHARLIE CLOSED THE DINER AT NINE THAT NIGHT. WHEN HE GOT home, he was glad to see Zoey's car in the driveway. Best to get this news off his chest right away.

The living room and dining room were dark, but he followed the light and laughter coming from the family room in the back of the house. Lucy and Zoey were already in pajamas, watching TV together, sipping hot cocoa and eating popcorn.

"I can't believe she said that! Did you see Briana's face?" Zoey bounced on the chair cushions. "Wait . . . I'm going to play it over. Let me just rewind."

"Oh, yes, let's see that one again." Lucy was still laughing as she greeted him. "Hi, honey. Was the diner busy?"

"Quiet night. A few couples out Christmas shopping. What's going on here? Looks like a slumber party."

He had brought a pile of folders in from his truck, paperwork from Village Hall that he had to look over before he went to sleep. He dropped them on the end table and sat on the sofa next to Lucy.

"We're celebrating," Lucy explained. "Zoey had her last final exam today and just sent in her last term paper."

Charlie was glad to hear that, for more reasons than the relieved look on his daughter's face. He took a handful of popcorn from the bowl. "That's good news. So the semester is officially over?"

Zoey wore a rare, wide smile. "That's right. And I just got an email from the youth center. They want to interview me for the internship. They're only talking to three students, so my chances of getting it are really good."

Charlie felt his heart sink but forced a smile. Lucy was beaming with pride. "Isn't that good news?" she said. "There were at least fifty students who applied, and now Zoey is one of three!"

Charlie nodded. "Just getting called in to talk is a feather in your cap. If you don't get this, another chance like this will come along. You'll see."

Zoey had practically been dancing around with happiness but now stood still in the middle of the room. She looked at him curiously.

The picture on the TV screen was frozen—two women in evening gowns and a lot of smeared makeup were in the middle of some sort of fight. That silly housewife reality show they liked to watch, mostly to make fun of it. Everyone was going to need a laugh in a minute or two, he reflected.

Lucy turned to him. He knew that look. Her antenna was up. "Zoey might get this one. We ought to think positively."

Charlie rubbed his hands together, trying to find the right words. "The thing is, I need Zoey to work in the diner during her school vacation. Full-time. I need her to manage the place so I can focus on being mayor. We talked about it a little, honey, remember?"

Zoey's eyes were glistening with tears. "I can't work at the diner full-time, Dad! I already told you. The internship is full-time."

"I know, I know . . . but other opportunities like this will come along for you, honey." Charlie felt awful. He hated to see her cry, but he needed her to understand. "Listen, I only have this one chance to be mayor. I don't see how I can do it otherwise. I just can't find a manager on such short notice and train them and what have you."

He turned to Lucy. She had to back him up. "You saw what happened at the meeting last night, Lucy. They nearly ate me alive."

Lucy looked upset, too. "That meeting was rough," she agreed, but she didn't say more.

"Dad, *please*. I don't want to work in the diner every single day of my life. Even if I don't get the internship, I promised the center I'd do more hours there. It will be good for my résumé and good experience for me."

Charlie tried to keep his tone calm. "I understand what you're saying. But you've got time for that, Zoey, all the time in the world, even though you can't see it that way." He could tell she wasn't listening to him, but kept going. "My situation is different. It's like . . . like the house is on fire. I've got to take care of it right away. Starting tomorrow."

"Tomorrow? I'm not on the schedule tomorrow," she corrected him in a tart tone.

"Well, I am, as the manager. But I'm off the roster now, and you're being called up from the minors." He knew she didn't understand that baseball terminology but didn't stop to explain. "I'm sorry, honey. This is the only way. You've got to step up and help the family. Do you like seeing your father made into the laughingstock of the entire village?"

From Zoey's expression, he realized that had not been a good question to ask her at this moment.

"Of course not," Lucy cut in. She put her arm around Zoey's shoulders. "I didn't realize it was such a crisis for you, Charlie. I guess the meeting last night was an eye-opener."

She turned to Zoey. "I do think, all things considered, your father can use our help right now. You know how long he's waited to be mayor. He deserves a chance to do a good job now. I'll help at the diner when I can and take fewer hours at the hospital next month. C.J. will be home again at Christmas, at least for a week or so. He can help, too. We'll work it out, honey. It won't be so bad."

Zoey still looked forlorn, on the verge of tears. But at least Lucy had calmed her down a little.

"That's right. It won't be so bad," Charlie repeated. "I'm giving you a nice raise—plenty of extra money for clothes shopping. That part is good, right?"

"There's nothing good about this. But I guess I don't have any choice, do I?" Zoey's gaze bounced from her father to her mother and back again.

Lucy looked upset, too. He could tell she wasn't going to field this one for him.

"No, honey. I'm sorry. You don't," he finally replied.

Lucy rubbed Zoey's shoulder. "Want to watch the rest of the show?"

"I'm tired. I'm going to bed."

Lucy didn't seem surprised. "Okay. Good night, honey."

"Good night, sweetheart," Charlie chimed in.

Zoey left the room and headed upstairs, her dark head hanging to her chest.

Charlie stuffed more popcorn in his mouth, though he wasn't hungry. He watched Lucy walk around the room, clearing up the empty mugs and magazines. Picking up an empty bowl, he followed her into the kitchen.

"Do you think she'll ever forgive me? Maybe when she's forty-something and has teenagers of her own?" he asked quietly. "I feel awful forcing her into this. But I don't know what else to do."

"I know. She's disappointed. She's been working hard to get that internship. Maybe she won't even go for the interview now."

"I hope not. What's the point?" Charlie hoped Zoey would decide not to go. If she was picked, he would have to go through this wringer all over again. "Hey, I'm not heartless. I know this is tough for her, but that's the way life is sometimes. Plans don't always work out."

"True enough." Lucy was fixing the coffeemaker for the morning pot. "But I think she had enough of those lessons before she came to live with us," Lucy added quietly. "I was hoping we could show her the other side of that coin."

Charlie didn't answer. He knew what Lucy said was true.

Lucy said good night and went upstairs, leaving him alone with his thoughts and the paperwork from Village Hall. And a sour feeling in the pit of his stomach.

Well, I got my way tonight, he reflected. *But at a high cost. A mighty high cost.*

CHAPTER EIGHT

*Z*OEY'S ALARM WENT OFF AT HALF PAST SIX ON WEDNESDAY morning. She remembered that she didn't have school and shut it off, gratefully sinking back into her pillow. *No,* another voice said, jogging her awake again. *You have to go to the diner—instead of sleeping in and doing whatever you please the first day of winter break.*

A few minutes later, she heard a tap on the door. "Zoey, are you up?" her dad asked.

"Yes!" she called back. She barely spared him a word more as she came downstairs on time and they drove through the quiet side streets toward the village.

When they reached the diner, Tim was already at work, cooking bacon and home fries and mixing pancake batter.

Her father went into the kitchen to talk to him. Tim didn't know Zoey was going to be the new manager, and Charlie had to explain the sudden change and give him a checklist he had written out and all sorts of other instructions that Tim probably already knew. Zoey got along well with Tim. She was sure they would work out any problems easily.

She stowed her jacket and purse, then checked the dining room to make sure the tables were properly set. A list of specials for the day, written in Tim's hand on a white sheet of paper, sat near the register, and Zoey started working on the chalkboard. She had to search for the box of colored chalk she had bought, and finally found it on a shelf under the cups.

Her father came out of the kitchen. "Use the plain, white chalk, and none of those fancy curlicues, please."

"I'm the manager now. I get to decide if the specials are written in color or not, curly or block lettering, or even bubble. One job out of a zillion that I actually like here," she mused as she wrote out the words with artistic flair: *Soup of the Day—Hearty Homemade Minestrone.*

Her father took a white sheet of paper from his clipboard. "I made you a checklist, too. All the little things you need to be mindful of as manager."

"Okay, Dad. But I think I know what to do by now."

"Humor me, will you, Zoey?"

Zoey finally looked at the page. Her father had catalogued the tasks involved in running the diner in the tiniest detail: unlock doors, put on lights, shut off lights, lock doors.

She knew he wouldn't feel comfortable about leaving her there until she read it through. Or at least pretended to. After a few moments, she looked back up at him. "Okay, I'll keep this handy so I don't forget anything."

"Good idea. Keep it right here, by the register." He reached into his pocket and laid the big key ring on the counter. "You take this. Put it in a safe place. I don't have duplicates of some of those."

"The Burning Sword of the Masters? You're actually giving that *to me*?"

He squinted at her. "I'm sure you're making fun again, but guess I have to ask, what that's supposed to mean?"

"Just being silly." Zoey shrugged. "It's from a video game. The boys play it all the time. *Battle of the Masters*."

"Are you mature enough to handle this or not? This isn't one big joke, Zoey."

"I am, Dad. Don't worry." She had gone too far with that last remark. Now he was all nervous again. "I've been doing all that stuff on the list for a long time. You just never paid me for it."

"Now you're getting paid for it, and getting the title, too. I'm counting on you, honey." He reached over and patted her shoulder. "You can take a lot off my back right now if I don't have to worry about this place, too. These last few weeks have just been too much. Too much for me, anyway."

Something about her father's heartfelt tone and vulnerable expression made Zoey forget her annoyance. He was sincerely grateful, and very worried about being able to do his job as mayor.

"Don't worry, I can do this. And I know you're going to be a good mayor, too."

Charlie looked surprised, his eyes suddenly bright. "Thanks, honey. That means a lot to me." He pulled on his Red Sox cap and headed for the door. "Anything comes up, you just call or text."

"I will," she promised for the hundredth time.

The door opened. Zoey expected an early customer, but it was James.

"Look who's here." Charlie paused and checked his watch. "Late again."

"Sorry, Charlie. My grandma's truck wouldn't start, and I hitched a ride."

Zoey was happy to see him but tried not to show it too much. She hadn't gotten a chance to check if he was on the schedule today. There was one bright spot to the day.

"I'm not surprised. Bella has been very moody lately," Zoey said. "I can pick you up if we're on the schedule together."

"No, you can't," Charlie interrupted. "You're the manager, not a taxi service for the staff. You need to be here all the time. They need to find their own transportation."

"You're the manager? Cool." James had pulled off his jacket and was putting on an apron. "Congratulations."

Zoey smiled, feeling the compliment was silly. "It's no big deal, believe me."

Her father seemed ready to argue about that, too, then shook his head. "I'll call you later. Get some Christmas decorations up today, will you? We're the only place in town without holiday cheer. The box is in the basement somewhere."

"Don't worry. By the time you get back, it will look like Santa's Workshop in here."

"Don't overdo it," he called back over his shoulder as he walked out. "We don't want the customers getting dizzy from too many blinking lights. That's not relaxing when you're eating."

The door closed before Zoey could reply, and Charlie finally set off.

"Are you sure he isn't watching on a baby monitor or something?" James whispered.

"I never thought of that. Where would he hide the camera? Maybe in these donuts?" She lifted the glass lid on a cake stand that held a display of donuts and muffins, then looked it over with a serious expression. "Nothing here. Maybe I should check the crumb cake."

James laughed. "Seriously, I don't think your dad likes me very much."

"He's like that with everybody. You just have to get to know him."

"Is he always that . . . intense?"

"Pretty much. Whenever he acts calm, my mom worries he's coming down with something. It's just that he's wanted to be mayor for so long, and he can't believe he's not doing a great job at it."

"That's what I read in the newspaper. People sound pretty unhappy. No offense," James added quickly.

Zoey knew James was just relating what he had read about Monday night's meeting and didn't mean anything by it, but she didn't like hearing anyone criticize her father. Not even James.

"Anybody would get off to a shaky start, trying to deal with all the problems that are going on in the town right now. And trying to run this place. That's why I said I'd help him now that the semester is over. Even though I did have other plans," she added quietly. "I know he can do a great job. If he gets a chance."

"Sure he can," James agreed quickly. "I didn't mean to say he couldn't. A lot of people in town really like your dad and don't blame him at all for the way the meeting went. It's nice of you to help him."

"I didn't exactly have a choice," Zoey admitted. "But he helps me a lot. I mean, we're a family, so we help each other. I'm trying not to make a big deal out of it." *Trying now,* she amended. Last night was another story.

Digger Hegman came in and sat at the counter. Zoey was not

surprised to see him. The old fisherman still rose before dawn most days and sat at the harbor awhile, watching the boats and birds. His daughter, Grace, worried about him wandering off, but everyone in town knew his routine and kept their eye on him.

"Hey, Digger. I'll be right there," Zoey said.

Digger raised his hand in greeting. "Hot tea, with lemon and honey. Toast and jam. You know my weakness by now."

Zoey smiled and nodded, then turned back to James. "We'd better get to work. We can decorate later, after the breakfast rush."

"Sounds like a plan." James grabbed some empty water pitchers. "Can I ask you one question before we start? I mean, since you're the manager now and everything?"

Zoey turned to him, feeling very official. "Sure. What's up?"

"Since you're done with school, want to go out this weekend? Whenever we're both off from work, I guess."

Zoey smiled. "Thanks. I would. And since I'm the manager, I'll work out the schedule, too."

James grinned and ducked into the kitchen. Zoey grabbed a menu and headed for her first customer, her smile so wide her face hurt.

She'd never admit it to her dad, but maybe being manager did have some perks.

"Let's see . . . whose turn is it?" Emily gazed at the girls who sat side by side on the couch in the family room, her daughter Jane among them. It had been Emily's idea for Jane to invite her team over for a debate practice, pizza party, and sleepover, and Friday was the perfect night.

With their long hair, braces, and almost identical sweatshirts and jeans, Emily thought they looked like a flock of pretty birds. Smart birds, too. They had been rehearsing for the debate for almost an hour, and she was impressed with how far they had come.

"It's my turn, Mrs. Forbes," said Jane's best friend, Maddie.

"Please argue in support of the statement that the American Revolution was fought for economic reasons." Emily read from the points Jane had prepared for her. "You have three minutes for your opening statement, starting now."

Emily looked at her watch and gave a signal. Maddie stood up, notes in hand, and began. She was almost done when Dan walked in the side door with a stack of pizza boxes. Emily watched the girls instantly respond to the aroma, sniffing the air like hungry puppies.

"Time's up. Good job, Maddie," Emily said. "You spoke very clearly and in a firm voice, not too fast but not too slow. And she didn't have her head down, reading off her notes the whole time, right, girls?"

They nodded in reply. There were a few more points to cover, but Emily couldn't resist the smell of the pizza, either. "Looks like dinner's here. Anyone hungry?" She was teasing, of course.

The girls giggled and jostled each other, heading for the counter, where Dan had set up paper plates, napkins and cups, a green salad, and the essential pizzas.

"Help yourselves. Don't be shy."

Jane hung back in the family room with Emily, helping her pick up papers and textbooks. "Great rehearsal today, Jane. I think you'll all do great next week at the debate."

"Thanks, Mom. And thanks for helping us."

Emily slipped an arm around Jane's shoulders. "Thanks for letting me. I can hardly wait."

The girls descended on the pizza, talking and laughing. Emily stood back at the counter with Dan, eating their own pizza standing up.

"How's it going?" Dan asked.

"Very well. They've got the facts down. We're working on speaking skills now, and a few tricks for counterarguments. They'll be in great shape by next Friday."

"Will we have another pizza party and sleepover to celebrate?"

"I was thinking of 'Make Your Own Tacos.' But we're on the same track. Sleepovers are what middle school is all about."

It was a good idea. And Emily wanted Jane to know her home was open to friends as a gathering place, that the fun wasn't always happening at some other girl's house. She knew they had not been good about hosting nights like this, but hoped to catch up quickly.

Her cell phone rang, and she quickly checked the number.

"Who's that? Lillian?" Dan asked.

"Nope. She already called five times today, though. It's Martin Becker. The group is having a meeting tonight. I told him I couldn't come, but he needs some information I promised to research for them."

"Emily, I thought you said that after the Monday night meeting, they were on their own."

"Yes, I know. But something big has come up. And I really have to help them. With some research," she added.

Dan gave her a curious look. "Research into what? Filing a lawsuit against the town?"

"Not a lawsuit. Someone heard that a motion will be pushed through to call for an emergency village-wide vote on changing the zoning. The vote will be held in the middle of the winter when fewer voters are likely to come out, especially older residents."

"Because they're the ones who are most interested in preserving the town," Dan said, understanding. "That's a tricky maneuver. It could work." He started on a second slice.

"It definitely could work. But I'm almost certain there's a village bylaw that would let the open-space group freeze the zoning laws for twenty-four months. I mentioned it to them, and now they seem to be pinning all their hopes on it. I have to find it and figure out how they can use it."

"You're right. You're probably one of the few people in town who would even know of an obscure bylaw like that. But now that you've remembered, can't they take it from here? Just pass the ball and let someone else run down the field."

Emily could see Dan was concerned about her sinking too deep into this issue when she had promised to just stick a toe in and jump right out. Her cell phone sounded again then, this time with a long text from another open-space group volunteer. Emily started to read it and barely noticed Jane standing right next to her.

"We threw our plates and stuff away. We're going up to my room now, okay?"

"Sure, go ahead," Dan said, before Emily had even looked up from her phone. By the time she had, Jane was walking out of the room.

"It's fine, honey. Don't wait too long to start your movie," Emily called after her.

Dan walked over to the snack bar and began clearing up the left-over pizza.

"I'll wrap this one up," she said, taking a box that had not been opened. Her phone buzzed again, but she ignored it.

"It's all right. I've got this. I'm guessing you need to get to your computer. Before your phone explodes," he added.

"I guess I should. The sooner I get this over with, the better."

Dan had his back turned to her as he loaded the dishwasher and didn't reply. She went into her office, feeling unsettled. She could see he thought she was slipping back into her old routine.

But now that she did see a tactic that might save the open-space group, she couldn't turn her back on them. If she could find that bylaw and figure out how to use it, it would be a game changer.

Dan will appreciate this later, she consoled herself. *He wants this side to win, too. Even though he doesn't seem very happy right now,* she had to admit as she turned on her computer. *Not happy at all.*

JAMES PICKED UP ZOEY AT HER HOUSE AT SEVEN O'CLOCK IN HIS grandmother's truck. Zoey would have been happy to run right out when she saw him pull up, but Lucy insisted that she wait for him to come to the door.

"I've heard a lot about him, and I'd like to meet him," Lucy said.

Zoey sighed and rolled her eyes. She hated to be treated as if she were in high school, but she knew it was no use arguing with her mother about this. She had talked about James a lot. Too much probably.

The doorbell rang. Zoey felt a flutter of nerves but tried to disguise it by acting annoyed with her mother. "All right, let's get this over with. I'm putting my jacket on right now. Just say hello, and we're out of here."

"That's fine. I'll get the door." Lucy opened the door. "You must be James. I'm Mrs. Bates. It's nice to meet you."

James smiled and held out his hand, looking sincerely pleased to meet her. "It's nice to meet you, Mrs. Bates."

Zoey could tell by Lucy's expression that she thought James was cute. He did look very handsome tonight, she thought, in a thick black sweater, a tweed sports jacket, and jeans. A blue scarf, which brought out the color of his eyes, was slung around his neck.

Zoey was glad she had decided to wear a nicer outfit than jeans and a sweater. She had on a black minidress with a swirly print, black tights, and boots.

"How are you enjoying your visit to Cape Light? Zoey told me that you've been living in New York. It must be a huge change after that."

Great. Remind him how backwoodsy we are out here, Mom. That will help me tons, Zoey fumed.

"Yes, it's a big change but, so far, a good one for me. I thought I would miss the city. But I really don't."

Before her mother could drag out the conversation, Zoey zipped up her leather jacket. "I'm ready. We don't want to be late for the movie."

"Right." James checked his watch. "I think we'll be fine. As long as Bella doesn't act up."

Lucy was already familiar with Sophie's truck and its name. "I hope not. But if you have any trouble, just call me. I'll be in all night."

"Don't worry, we'll be fine." James had opened the door for her, and Zoey glanced over her shoulder as she walked out and gave her mother a small wave. Lucy blew her a little kiss.

In the truck, sitting side by side, Zoey felt suddenly self-conscious. She had spent time with James at the diner and at Sophie's house, but never alone like this. *It's just a date, Zoey. You've been on a zillion dates before. And he's just a guy. So get over it and act like a human .*

"We have plenty of time before the movie," Zoey admitted as James pulled away from the house. "I just said that so my mother wouldn't ask you any more questions. I'm sorry if it felt like she was interrogating you."

"I didn't mind. Your mom seems very nice. I can see her being a nurse," he added.

"She really loves what she does. It's perfect for her. She didn't go to college after high school. She worked in the diner when C.J. and Jamie were young and went back to school about ten years ago. It took her a long time to get her nursing degree, but she finally did."

"Good for her. I guess if you have a real commitment and don't give up, you can do some amazing things in life."

"That's what she always tells me. Though I hope I don't have to wait that long to get going in my career."

"I don't think you will," James said. "You seem very clear on what you want and how to get there."

Zoey was surprised at his observation. How could he know that about her already? They hardly knew each other. "How about you? You seem to be wandering a bit. But maybe you're not lost . . . as the saying goes."

He turned and met her gaze. She smiled at him, feeling her cheeks get a bit warm, and was glad for the darkness in the truck. "I read that in a book somewhere," she added. "No, come to think of it, not a book. A note someone left for me."

He laughed, his eyes back on the road. "One of my favorites. I even have a T-shirt with that saying. I guess I am wandering right now. But I don't feel lost. I know what I want to do with my life— write books. And that's a lot."

"Yes, it is. It's pretty major," Zoey agreed. She wasn't sure how they had gotten into such a serious conversation so quickly. She usually wasn't like this at all on a first date. It felt more like . . . the tenth? James was so easy to talk to. She felt as if she had known him a long time. And that was rare, too.

Still, she felt like it was time for some lighter talk. She didn't want to seem so super serious and freak him out. "I'm glad we're going to a Hitchcock movie tonight. I took a great film study course on him last semester. We had to see all the movies, even the early ones."

"I missed a few of those," he admitted. "*Rear Window* is my favorite. I haven't seen it in a long time."

"That figures. It's about a guy who's always watching people. I guess you identify with Jimmy Stewart?"

James laughed. "Maybe a little. He's stuck in a wheelchair. I don't know what my excuse is."

"It's a great movie, definitely near the top of my list. But my favorite is *Vertigo*. Amazing psychology. The poor detective is totally manipulated. He believes exactly what he's led to believe."

"Poor Jimmy Stewart. Again," James pointed out. "Since you're a psych major, I had a feeling you would like that one best."

"Makes sense, I guess." Zoey shrugged. Maybe he did know her better than she thought.

The theater was crowded, and coming early turned out to be a good thing. She and James chatted more after they found their seats, but once the film started, he was totally focused on the screen. And so was she. She liked that about him. It bugged her when people talked during a movie or poked her at some funny or scary part. She liked to be totally immersed in the film, and, obviously, so did he.

Though, at one point, he slipped his arm around her shoulders. It was a scary moment, when the dog is digging in the garden, and Zoey didn't mind at all.

After the film, they walked down the street to an Indian restaurant Zoey liked. She hoped James liked it, too, and also hoped it helped him see that the area was not as unsophisticated as he may have thought. The cafés in Newburyport offered all sorts of foods, from many cultures—though back in Cape Light one was hard-pressed to find anything more exotic than chowder, clam rolls, or burgers.

"Hmm. This is good." James tasted a bit of the appetizer, a pastry stuffed with a spicy meat mixture. "You know, I was thinking today, I never met anyone with the name Zoey before. I mean, I've heard the name and read it in books. But I don't think I ever had a friend named Zoey."

A friend? Was that all he thought of her? Zoey brushed aside the worry. Maybe he just didn't know what to call their relationship at this point. *At least he thinks of you as a friend,* she told herself.

She also wasn't sure if she should tell him the truth about her name. Where it had really come from.

"It is unusual. That's why I picked it," she finally replied.

"So it's not your real name?"

"It is my real name now," she explained. "But yes, I picked it for myself, back in middle school. My mother named me Elizabeth. I never liked it. I never liked being called Liz or Liza, and definitely not Beth or Betsy."

James smiled and sipped some water. "I can't see you as any of those names, either. But maybe that's because I know you as Zoey."

"Maybe. I just wanted a name that was unusual. And . . . I guess I wanted to put some distance between who I was and my past. I can see that now that I'm older."

He had stopped eating and put his fork down. "Did something happen to you when you were younger?"

Zoey nodded, still not sure how much she wanted to tell him. But now that she had started, it seemed impossible to tell only part of the story. She took a breath and sat back in her seat. "Lucy and Charlie are not my real father and mother. I mean, they feel real to me. But they adopted me about five years ago. That's why I said my real name is Zoey now. It's the name on my adoption certificate. Zoey Bates."

James stared at her wide-eyed. "Wow. I had no idea. I mean, your family seems so close."

So normal, she knew he meant. "We are close. Lucy and Charlie showed me what it's like to be part of a real family, to have parents who care about you. I never knew my real father, and my mother was in and out of our lives. I have a younger brother, Kevin. He used to live around here, but he was adopted by a wonderful family, too, a few years ago. Last year, they moved to Minnesota."

"I see. So you really have three brothers?"

Zoey nodded. "Kevin and I keep in touch over the phone and by Skype. But I'd love to visit him sometime. Anyway, that's pretty much my story. I didn't mean to go on and on," she added, hoping she hadn't bored him. Or worse yet, sounded like a character out of a soap opera.

"You weren't going on and on. I'm really interested to know more, to know all about you," he said. "How did you get connected with Lucy and Charlie? Were they trying to adopt another child?"

Zoey laughed. "No, not at all. I was running away from a foster home and ended up in the diner. My birth mother had died. I didn't have any money or anywhere to go. And I was sick, real sick. I could hardly stand up. Lucy made me come home with her, and she took care of me. I started living there, and after a few bumps in the road, let's say, Lucy and Charlie wanted to adopt me. And I wanted to stay with them and Jamie and C.J."

"Wow, you've had it rough, Zoey." James reached across the table and took her hand. "It's hard for me to believe. You seem so strong and together. Not at all like someone who had such a tough time growing up."

"I was pretty messed up for a while. Angry and all that. But Lucy and Charlie really helped me. I couldn't love them more if they were my real parents. I owe them a lot," she said quietly. "Most of all, they showed me that I could change. I didn't have to be Elizabeth Dugan, in that dark, angry place. I could be Zoey Bates. I could be happy."

"I'm glad you decided to be Zoey Bates. I like her a lot. And I admire her. Greatly." James smiled, and his compliment made her blush again. "Is that why you want to be an art therapist? To help kids who are going through similar things?"

Zoey nodded. "Exactly. I think I'd be good at it, too. At the center where I volunteer, I think I've helped a few kids make some progress. There's an internship there, over the winter break. I have an interview for it on Monday. But I'm probably not going."

She hadn't meant to tell him that. She hadn't meant to tell anyone. But all of her secrets seemed to pour out so easily when James looked at her in his soft, sweet way.

"You're not? But why? You just said how much you love the work. It would be great experience for you."

"I think so, too. It's sort of a long story. I can't work at the center over winter break because I have to work in the diner. Charlie needs a manager so he can run the town. He can't do two jobs at once anymore."

James looked upset by her explanation. "I guess it's hard to run a business and be mayor, too. But that doesn't seem very fair to you."

"I know. But my family really needs my help right now. That's the bottom line here," she said, sorry now that she had brought up the topic. She didn't want to have the same argument with James that she'd had with her parents—with James playing her part.

James sat back, taking a hint from her tone perhaps. "I know it's not my business, but I really think you should go to the interview. Don't cancel it."

"But what's the point? Even if they like me, I can't take the job."

"It will be a good experience for you, if nothing else. And maybe, if you make a good impression, they'll remember you if they need someone later. And you never know, something might happen out of the blue, and you might be able to work there this winter, after all."

Zoey shrugged, still not convinced.

He took her hand again and searched out her gaze with his own. "Just think about it, okay? I'm working at the diner Monday. I'll help you slip out if that's the problem."

That was part of the problem, but now he was taking that excuse away from her, too.

"All right. I'll think about it," she finally agreed.

"Good. That makes me very happy." His tone was sincere. "You're an awesome person, Zoey. I hate to see you hide your light under a bushel."

Zoey grinned. "That sounds like something my dad would say. He's got a lot of old-fashioned expressions."

James laughed. "I don't know where that came from. I've probably been hanging around my grandmother too long."

They enjoyed the rest of their dinner in a lighter mood and decided to walk around the harbor afterward. The streets and shop windows were decorated for Christmas, and the cobblestone lanes and squares seemed magical. So did the feeling of his arm around her shoulders as she asked him more about his own past. He knew so much about her now, it only seemed fair.

James told her how his family had lived in Boston when he was very young and later moved to Connecticut. His parents divorced when he was eleven years old, and his mother now lived in New York. "It was hard for a while," he admitted. "But there was no big drama. My parents made it as easy as possible for me and Miranda."

They had reached the park at the harbor and strolled down the walkway. The water was dark blue, the sky above an even darker shade, dotted by tiny white stars. It looked so beautiful tonight. Zoey tried to memorize the sight so she could use it in her art someday.

"Did you always want to be a writer?" she asked James suddenly.

"I think so. Though I guess I went through the usual stages boys do, wanting to be a pro athlete."

"I'd like to read more of your writing. The piece I read was so good, really interesting and clever." So far, she had only read one of his blog posts, but his talent was clear to her. "Have you had time to write since you came here? You always seem so busy at Sophie's house, and you're working at the diner now, too."

"I've been able to write a lot, usually early in the morning. My grandmother's been telling me family history—about her parents and grandparents. It's given me ideas for some stories that I'm working on now."

Zoey studied the expression in his eyes. "It must be coming out great. You look very . . . inspired." He did look inspired, his eyes bright and a wide smile lighting his face.

"I am inspired. But not by family history right now. I just think I want to kiss you."

Before Zoey could reply, he moved close and surprised her with a kiss. She closed her eyes and kissed him back, holding tight to his broad shoulders. She wasn't sure how long they stood together like that. She felt the world spinning around her. As if the stars in the blue-black sky had drifted down and were spinning inside her head. An absolutely wonderful feeling.

They suddenly heard voices. A big group of teenagers, coming their way. James stepped back, though he kept his arms around her in a loose embrace. "Guess we should head back to Bella now."

Zoey nodded. "Yeah, I guess we should."

"I had a wonderful time tonight. I hope you know that, Zoey. I feel as if . . . well, as if I've known you forever. It's so strange. But in a good way," he quickly added.

"I know what you mean. I feel the same about you," she admitted. "And now you know my first name was Elizabeth. So you know all my secrets."

James laughed and dropped a kiss on her head. "I'm honored. But I suspect there are a few more hidden up there."

With their arms slung around each other, they walked back to the truck without talking at all. Zoey could rarely recall feeling happier.

EMILY HEARD JANE AND HER FRIENDS HOP DOWN THE STAIRS AND take over the kitchen and family room again. Debate practice and pizza feast over, the girls were now in the baking-cupcakes phase of the sleepover. This would be followed by watching a movie and eating the cupcakes. Emily looked in on them as they poured batter into the tins. She trusted Jane in the kitchen more than she trusted herself and knew they didn't need, or want, her supervision. But she still peeked in from time to time, just to make sure the party was going well.

But with all the giggling and chatting—and the loud movie, which seemed to be about gymnastics or cheerleading—Emily ended up putting in earplugs. The noise was so distracting.

She had to wade through pages of tedious, boring legal language in the village constitution and amendments, dating back to the 1800s. But finally, she found the bylaw she had recalled. She read it over to be sure they could use it to block the vote, then printed out copies of the page.

Emily wasn't sure how long she'd been sitting there when she became aware of Dan standing in the doorway. She looked over at him, then pulled out the earplugs so she could hear what he was saying.

"I'm sorry. I had these things in my ears. The girls were getting a little noisy."

"The girls went upstairs over an hour ago. I think they're asleep."

"Really? I thought they were still watching TV." It felt as if Janie had brought her a cupcake just a few minutes ago. The crumpled wrapper was still on her desk, the candy-trimmed treat less than half-eaten. Emily felt a little guilty. She should have checked on them and made sure they had everything they needed before they went to bed. "Are they okay? Why didn't you call me? I would have helped settle them down."

"They're fine. Considering the amount of junk food they ate, I was expecting at least one stomachache."

Emily laughed. "Well, the night isn't over yet."

"We're getting there. Do you have any idea what time it is?"

Emily glanced at the time on her computer. At first she thought it said eleven fifteen, then realized a digit was missing. It was actually a few minutes past one. "Oh my gosh . . . how did it get so late?" She stared at him, honestly surprised.

"The way it usually does, Emily. Once you get hooked by some cause or issue, you zip up to your own planet. You definitely blasted off tonight, and please don't deny it."

"Yes . . . I know. I'm sorry. But I found the bylaw, Dan. Then I got caught up, checking to see if we could really use it and whether it's airtight."

His expression softened. "At least you found it. What is it all about exactly? You never really told me."

"It's very simple, actually. There's a bylaw in the village charter that states if a large enough group of citizens opposes a change to a village law, they can appeal to the county, and the county can then freeze a vote on the change for two years."

"And then what?"

"Well, that two-year freeze creates time for an independent review of the new zoning ideas. So now the open spacers need to give the county a solid reason for why the situation should be studied by an outside group. Impact on the wildlife and environment should be reason enough. But I want to find out if anyone has ever used this tactic before and what the possible pitfalls are."

"That's smart. But isn't there anyone else that can take it from here? There must be a lawyer or someone with good research skills in that group."

"I did think of passing this along. I'm just afraid some other volunteer won't be able to get all the information together as quickly as I can. There's hardly any time at all. I can also call some county officials and sound them out—people who know how these situations work and will talk to me off the record."

When he didn't reply, she said, "Please don't look at me like that. I'm not leading the charge, but I can provide the ammunition. And I want to see it through. I think this strategy can block the effort to overbuild and ruin the town. At least for two years. That should be long enough for people to see reason."

"Maybe," Dan agreed. "Charlie's term as mayor will be over by then."

"Unless he gets reelected or the mayor coming in has the same dumb idea." Emily paused and met her husband's questioning gaze. "I know what you're thinking. But I have no intention of running again—not in two years, not in twenty. No matter what my mother says."

"I believe you. Still, it's good to hear you say it," he admitted. "I just wonder if maybe you do want to jump back in and you don't even realize it." He paused, then finally said, "Is it all for the cause, or partly just to get back at Charlie? I know that's not your nature, but anybody would be tempted, all things considered."

Emily bristled and sat up straight in her chair. "If you can ask me that, then you obviously don't believe me. You, of all people, should know that I'm not doing this for spite."

Dan sighed. "I'm sorry. I shouldn't have put it like that. But you have to admit, from a distance, it does look like you're trying to undermine Charlie. There are a lot of people in town who are going to think you've gotten involved in this issue to undermine him and set yourself up to be reelected."

"I've asked myself that same question," she admitted. "And I'm certain, down to my toes, that this isn't about revenge. I know how it looks and what some people might think. But I learned a long time ago that you can't control what people think or say about you. All you can do is hope that your actions speak louder than anyone's gossip or mistaken judgments. This issue is important to me and to everyone—

to Jane and our grandchildren. Even to Charlie's grandchildren, though he certainly doesn't see it that way."

Dan stood by her desk chair and rested his hands on her shoulders. "That is true, Em. And it's something I've always loved about you—you're your own person. I'm sorry for sounding as if I doubted that. I just worry about what's going to happen. You must see that everyone in town links you to the open-space group now. Many people even think you're their leader. For better or worse, you're going to end up looking responsible for whatever happens. I hope you're ready for that."

She couldn't argue. She had practically been blamed for the melee at Village Hall—just by being there. There was definitely some truth to Dan's words. She just didn't know what to do about it.

CHAPTER NINE

*Y*ou're up early. And you look too pretty to be heading to the diner." Zoey's mother stood at the kitchen counter in her bathrobe, pouring herself a cup of coffee. "That's a cute outfit, honey."

"Thanks." Zoey was wearing a tunic top she had found in a thrift shop, with big, colorful flowers on a black background. The bell sleeves and neckline were very retro, and it went perfectly with her leggings and boots.

She grabbed a yogurt from the fridge and a bag of frozen blueberries. "I'm working at the diner after church. Sophie's truck wasn't working perfectly Friday night. James had to try the ignition a few times before we could get it started to go home. So I'm giving Sophie a ride to the service."

Lucy sat at the table across from her. "Just Sophie? Or is James going, too?"

"James, too." Zoey had sprinkled the yogurt with granola, chia seeds, frozen blueberries, and cinnamon, then stirred it all up. Her brother C.J. called the mixture Blue Health Glop. But what could you expect from a guy whose favorite breakfast was sausage patties smashed between two Pop-Tarts?

"How was your date? Did you have fun?" Lucy had been up when Zoey came in, but they hadn't talked much.

"It was great. James is really funny. And smart," she added. "And he's a really good writer. He showed me one of his articles the other day. It was published online. I'm going to read some of his fiction, too."

"He sounds like an interesting person. You said he plans to travel—anyplace in particular?"

Zoey glanced up. Lucy was trying to play it cool, but Zoey still picked up a distinct Mom-anxiety-vibe.

"Probably South America, to start. He wants to work on a farm for a while, maybe in Peru or Chile."

"How adventurous. Sounds like something a writer would do. When is he leaving, does he know?"

Zoey spooned up the last drop of her Blue Glop. "Mom, you are so obvious. I know what you're trying to say."

"What am I trying to say?"

"You're worried because I like James and he's not staying here very long."

Lucy shifted, holding her mug with both hands. "I can't say I didn't think of that, honey. You do seem to like this young man, more than I've seen you like anyone lately. He seems very nice and charming. But he is older than you, and he definitely has his plans."

Zoey rolled her eyes. "Two years. That's no big deal. And we've only been on one date. I can't believe you're going off on me like this."

"Okay, one date. But you work together now, and you see him at Sophie's house." Lucy's voice softened. "He's graduated college and he's out in the world. And you're still in school. And he isn't going to be here very long, from the sound of it."

"He's staying through the holidays. He thinks he'll have enough money to leave right after New Year's."

"That's less than a month," her mother pointed out.

Zoey shrugged. She picked up her bowl and mug and set them in the sink. "I know when New Year's is."

Lucy took breakfast ingredients out of the refrigerator—eggs, bread, and orange juice. Jamie would be downstairs soon, hungry enough to eat the kitchen table. Zoey planned to be gone by then.

"I just don't want to see you get involved and then feel bad when he leaves. That's all." Lucy set a frying pan on the stove. "I know I'm interfering. But I wouldn't be a very good mother if I didn't say it. I love you, sweetie. You've had a lot of difficult separations in your life. I don't want to see you get your feelings hurt—if you can help it."

Zoey knew that what Lucy said was true. Her life had been a series of painful separations and losses, until Lucy and Charlie had found her. Zoey sometimes wondered how she was still able to trust people and open up to new relationships. It certainly wasn't as easy for her as it was for most people. But she also knew she had to try. She couldn't hang back, afraid to make connections—or open her heart. What was life all about, anyway, if not that?

"I know what you're trying to say. But it's totally cool. I won't get my feelings hurt. I promise." She stood next to her mother and kissed her cheek. "Okay?"

Lucy slipped her arm around Zoey's waist and gave her a quick squeeze. "Okay . . . but it's not the sort of thing you can promise, sweetheart. I wish it was." Her mother gazed at her with a wistful smile. "See you in church, I guess."

"Sure, see you there."

Zoey headed off for the orchard, relieved to be done with the little heart-to-heart. She knew Lucy meant well, but sometimes she just didn't get it. James was different. He wasn't like other guys.

Still, the warning got under her skin. *Maybe I'm not that good with people moving in and out of my life. But I've worked on that. I've gotten a lot better with it. She should give me some credit.*

And maybe James isn't going to be around for very long. That's fine. I'd regret it more if I don't get to know him. And it seems too late to worry about any of this now.

Zoey pulled up to Sophie's big house and then drove around to the side door. It was easier for Sophie to walk down a step or two there instead of the long flight at the front porch. No matter how strong Sophie claimed to be, Zoey knew that since her illness last winter, Sophie wasn't that sure-footed; now she had to take more care on stairs, or even walking out in the orchard.

Zoey jumped out of the car and knocked on the door. She waited, but no one answered. She knocked again and waited, checking her watch. Maybe they were upstairs, still getting dressed.

Mac ran up to her, wagging his tail. He ambled up the steps and scratched the door, then stared at her as if to say, "We both want in, and you can reach the doorknob."

"All right, if you say so," Zoey said to the dog. She opened the door, calling out as she walked through the mudroom. "Sophie? James? I knocked but nobody heard me."

"We're over here, Zoey. My grandma fell . . ."

Zoey ran toward the sound of his voice and found them in the foyer, at the foot of the stairs. Sophie was dressed for church but stretched out on the floor, James kneeling by her side.

"Oh my gosh . . . what happened?" Zoey knelt down on Sophie's other side and caught the hand that was offered. Sophie looked pale and scared but forced a smile.

"I just got clumsy, dear. Lost my footing on that bottom step. I need to throw out these old house slippers . . ."

Mac had run to Sophie's aid also, and now nosed his way into the group and licked Sophie's face. She laughed and stroked his muzzle. "Now, now, don't you get worried, too."

James gently tugged the dog's collar and pushed him aside. "Does it hurt anywhere, Grandma? I want to help you up, but I don't think we should move you if you broke a hip or anything like that."

"Did you call for an ambulance?" Zoey asked.

"Ambulance? I don't need an ambulance," Sophie insisted. "I've fallen out of plenty of trees and off ladders. Even off a roof once. This was nothing, just a step. Help me up, both of you. Grab under my arms and give me a boost."

Zoey looked at James. "Should we get her up or call somebody?"

He sighed, looking as confused as she felt. "She insists that nothing hurts. I guess it will be okay."

"Of course it will be okay. Wouldn't I know by now if my leg or my hip or my big toe was busted? Now come on. I've seen enough of the ceiling. We could use a splash of paint up there, too, by the way."

Reluctantly, and very gently, Zoey and James helped Sophie to a sitting position. "Saints be praised. I thought you were going to leave me there like a giant turtle on her back."

"You're sure nothing hurts, Grandma?" James asked again.

"Give me a minute. Let me get my bearings."

Her upswept hairdo had shifted to one side, quite a few pins and strands dangling. She still looked pale and shaky, Zoey thought, no matter how she tried to hide it.

"I think you need to go to a doctor or a hospital and get checked out," Zoey said. "I know you don't want to, but just to be safe. It's the smart thing to do."

"Why did you go upstairs again? I thought you were ready to leave for church." James sat on the step next to his grandmother and took her pulse, looking grim as he timed it against his watch.

"I forgot my reading glasses. I like to follow along in the Bible when the Scripture is read aloud."

"You should have told me. I would have gotten them," he said.

"I should have a large-print Bible. That would have solved it completely. I wish someone would get me that for Christmas, instead of more sweaters or knickknacks."

"Oh, so that's the problem. We'll have to tell the doctor you fell because you don't have a large-print Bible?" His tone was half serious and half teasing. "Seriously, Grandma, your pulse is fast. I want to take you to the hospital or an urgent care clinic somewhere. And don't argue about it. We don't have to call an ambulance, but you need to be checked out. If anything is wrong with you, I won't forgive myself. I'm supposed to be taking care of you, not letting you fall down the stairs."

Zoey's heart went out to him. He looked very upset, as if Sophie's fall had been his fault.

"Now, now . . . what are you supposed to do? Follow me around like Mac and watch my every step? It's my own fault. I should have been holding tighter to the banister. And I need to give up these old slippers, as comfortable as they are . . ." Sophie's voice trailed off and she sighed. Finally, she nodded. "All right. If you feel that way, we'll go. But it will be a big waste of time. I'd rather go to church."

"I think we have to miss church today," James replied. "And I'm happy to waste my time to make sure you're fine."

"I can take you to a clinic," Zoey offered.

James looked relieved. "That would be great. I was just thinking I should call my aunt Evelyn."

"Evelyn? Don't you dare." Sophie's tone was as sharp as Zoey had ever heard it. "Let's not call Miss Bossy Pants just yet. Then my pulse really will jump the chart."

Sharing a smile, James and Zoey hoisted Sophie up and helped her into the kitchen. Zoey put boots on her feet, and James found her coat. She winced a bit when Zoey slipped her coat on, and Zoey found an ice pack for her left wrist, which seemed to be a little swollen.

A few minutes later they were in Zoey's car, headed for an urgent care clinic that was near the highway. Sophie was in the backseat, her wrist propped up on a pillow.

When they reached the clinic, Zoey pulled up to the front door. James jumped out and came back with a wheelchair. He looked even more worried as they helped Sophie into the chair and wheeled her inside.

"I hope Aunt Evelyn isn't mad at me for not calling her. I'm sure she would want to know that you fell and I took you here, Grandma."

"We'll let her know in due time. No need to make a drama of this," Sophie replied. "I bet I'll be home trimming our tree tonight."

Zoey followed them inside and waited while Sophie told a nurse about her fall and handed over her insurance cards. It was almost eleven, and Zoey was due at the diner at noon. She considered calling Charlie, but decided to call Lucy instead.

"I didn't make it to church after all. Sophie fell and we had to take her to the urgent care clinic. We just got here, and she's talking to a nurse."

"Oh, dear, that isn't good. Is she all right? Did she break anything?"

"I don't think so. She keeps saying nothing hurts. But her wrist might be sprained."

"I hope it's nothing more than that. Poor thing. She must be shaken up. It's hard to take a fall when you're that age."

Zoey had to smile. "She doesn't seem too shaken. We had to talk her into coming here. She can't wait to get home and work on her Christmas tree."

Her mother laughed. "That's Sophie. I hope she goes easy on those doctors. Don't worry about the diner. I'll talk to your father. If he can't get Trudy, I'll go in for a while."

Zoey felt bad that Lucy was covering for her again, especially since Lucy had planned to go shopping today. There were only two weeks left before Christmas.

"Thanks, Mom. I really don't want to just leave Sophie and James here before I know how she is."

"I understand. You stay. And give Sophie a hug from me. I hope it's nothing. Tell her I'll say a prayer, and I'll tell Reverend Ben, too, okay?"

"I will." By the time Zoey ended the call, Sophie was being wheeled out of the admitting area by an orderly. James walked into the waiting area and sat down in the chair next to Zoey.

"They're going to take X-rays and check for a concussion, though I don't think she hit her head. But better safe than sorry," he added.

"Absolutely."

"I nearly freaked when I heard her shout and found her on the floor, right before you came. It was scary," he admitted.

"I know. I got scared when I saw her, too. But I think she'll be fine."

"I hope so." He reached out and took hold of her hand. "Thanks for bringing us, Zoey. I'm just grateful that out of everybody, you're the one here."

His warm look seemed to say much more, and Zoey returned the gentle pressure of his touch. "You don't have to thank me. I'm glad I could help. It was a lucky thing that we were planning to go to church together. You would have had to call an ambulance. Or Evelyn. And Sophie didn't seem to like either of those ideas."

He smiled. "I feel like you were meant to be there this morning, to help us." He shrugged. "I don't know why. I just do."

Zoey didn't know what to say. She met his glance a moment and looked away. They sat quietly for a while, holding hands.

After a bit, James said, "But I did tell my aunt Evelyn. She texted me while Grandma was getting the X-ray. She wanted to know why we weren't in church yet, so I told her what was going on. She should be here any minute. I hope Grandma isn't mad at me, but it was the right thing to do."

"It was," Zoey agreed. "And you can use your aunt's help. Sophie doesn't like to admit it, but she listens to Evelyn."

A nurse came by holding a clipboard. "James Potter?"

James jumped up. "That's me."

"We just examined your grandmother and gave her an EKG. Her blood pressure and heart rate seem fine. We also X-rayed her left wrist, and there are no broken bones, just a mild sprain. But we still need an MRI of her head. So it will be a while longer."

"All right. Thanks for the update. Can I go inside and wait with her?"

"Sure. Just through those doors, you'll see some patient beds, separated by curtains. You can both go back. It's all right," the nurse added, glancing at Zoey.

Zoey followed James and they quickly found Sophie. She was still wearing her dress and sweater, but her feet were bare, her body covered by a thin blanket. The back of the bed was raised so that she could sit up. Her left wrist was wrapped in an elastic bandage and covered with an ice pack.

"There you are. I told the nurse to go and get you," she greeted them. "Can I go home now? Maybe you can ask somebody."

"Not yet, Grandma. They need to give you a few more tests."

"Fiddlesticks. They just like to use all this machinery. How many pictures of my skeleton does the doctor need to see?"

"They want an MRI of your head. To make sure there's no concussion," James explained.

"To make sure I have some brains left. That's the real reason." Sophie sighed and smoothed down the blanket. "I had so much to do today. I've missed the Christmas Fair committee meeting, too. I wanted to start on my crafts. And decorate the tree. I think we can still do the tree later . . . don't you?"

Her glance at James and then Zoey was just as hopeful as a child's. Zoey knew that neither of them had the heart to refuse her. "Maybe tomorrow or another night this week would be best, Grandma," James said gently.

"I think James is right—" Zoey began, but before she could finish her sentence, the curtain was pulled aside with a swishing sound.

"Mom, are you all right? I knew when I didn't see you in church that something must have happened. James said you fell. Why didn't anyone call me?"

"Hello, Evie. Calm down, I'm fine." Sophie stared at James as she answered her daughter. *What's she doing here?* Zoey could almost hear her say aloud.

"Aunt Evelyn sent me a text while you were getting X-rayed," James explained. "I'm sorry we didn't call you sooner, Aunt Evie. We just wanted to get Grandma to a doctor right away. They haven't found anything wrong so far except a sprained wrist."

"I wish you had called an ambulance and gone to the hospital. This is just a clinic. Mom, does your wrist hurt very much?"

"Just a twinge, dear. No need to fret. The doctor said it was just a mild sprain. I'm sure they'll let me go in no time."

"Let's not rush it. We want to be sure you're all right. You never know with a fall." Evelyn leaned over the bed and smoothed the blanket. She looked like Sophie, Zoey reflected. A short woman with fair hair, a round face, and a plump figure. Her skin was smooth and her eyes bright, like her mother's. But she had not inherited Sophie's peaceful, optimistic disposition.

"She had a full physical and a test for her heart. The doctor said everything was fine," James reported.

Evelyn looked over at him. "Where were you when she fell? Did she have to wait very long for you to come?"

"I was right in the kitchen, waiting for her to come downstairs."

"I know what you're driving at, Evelyn, but this isn't James's fault. He's been keeping a good eye on me. It's just that my slippers are too worn and loose. One of them slipped off my foot as I came down. That's what happened, and poor James can't be blamed because I'm too stubborn to give up my comfortable slippers."

Zoey could see that James felt self-conscious, even a bit embarrassed. He felt bad enough about his grandmother's fall without his aunt rubbing it in.

Evelyn sat back in her chair and set her big purse squarely on her lap. "It's more than the slippers, Mom. It's that big old house and everything that goes with it. I'm not blaming James," she added. "But it just goes to show that even with someone else in the house, it's still not a safe place for you."

"Oh, bother. I knew I'd be hearing that old song sooner or later," Sophie grumbled. "Can't you take a tiny bit of pity on me, Evie? At least wait until I'm out of this bed."

A nurse walked into the room with two orderlies. "We're ready to give you the MRI now, Mrs. Potter."

"Great, let's roll. You folks came just in the nick of time," Sophie said to the orderlies, who cranked down the back of the bed and secured her in place with a belt.

The nurse smiled, looking amused. "It won't take long. Your family can wait here."

Evelyn stood up and blocked her path. "I'm Mrs. Stotlemeir, Mrs. Potter's daughter. Can I speak to you a minute about my mother?"

James caught Zoey's eye and tilted his head, signaling to follow him out of the cubicle as Sophie's bed was rolled away. They walked back to the waiting area, leaving Evelyn with the nurse.

"I think this is going to take a while," James said. "Maybe even longer, now that Evie is here. She'll drive me back to the orchard. You don't have to wait."

Zoey had wondered about that; she was feeling a bit intrusive now, since she wasn't family. It seemed that Evelyn wanted to discuss serious family matters—even if Sophie and James didn't.

"I guess I will go if you think you're okay. I'll call you later and see how she's doing."

James looked pleased to hear that. "Call anytime. I'm on the schedule tomorrow at the diner. I'll see you before your interview."

Her interview for the internship . . . With all the excitement about Sophie, she had nearly forgotten. Zoey was still wrestling with second thoughts about keeping the appointment, but she smiled and nodded. "It isn't until the afternoon. I guess I will see you."

"Don't worry. Jot down some questions you think they'll ask and figure out your answers. Speak from your heart. I know you'll do really well."

"I'll try."

"They would be lucky to have you, Zoey. I think they already know that." He leaned over and kissed her lips, a fleeting, intense kiss that caught Zoey by surprise. She held on to his shoulders, feeling her knees go weak for a crazy moment. She stepped away from him, not knowing what to say. "Let me know about Sophie," she murmured, then turned and quickly left the clinic, not daring to look back.

As Zoey headed to the village, she felt as if she were driving on a cloud. The road flew by, the bare branches and brush changing to houses and then shops on Main Street. She didn't see any of it, her mind filled with images of James, his smile, his voice, and his touch. She was feeling closer to him every time they were together. He was so caring and concerned about his grandmother, handling the situation in such a mature way. He didn't need to thank her so profusely for helping. She hadn't done much. But that was sweet of him, too, she thought.

James was different from other guys she had known. It had sounded so dumb and simplistic when she'd tried to explain that to Lucy that morning, but she didn't know any other way to say it. She had never known anyone quite like him before.

Was she starting to feel too much for him too quickly? Zoey wasn't sure. But she couldn't help looking forward to seeing him tomorrow. To seeing him more and more.

SOPHIE WAS IN THE KITCHEN MONDAY MORNING WHEN SHE HEARD a knock on the front door. She called out to James, then remembered that he was in the barn, searching for paint and brushes. He had to be at the diner in a few hours and wanted to get some work done around the house before he left.

The knocking sounded again, and she called out, "I'm coming. Just a minute."

Mac ran ahead, barking so much she wasn't sure her visitor had heard a word. But she couldn't shout any louder or move any faster this morning. She felt even achier than she had last night.

Falls were like that; it took a while for all the sore muscles to check in. She had forced herself to get out of bed and get dressed at her usual time, though the aches urged her to sleep late. But if Evelyn or Una came by unannounced, Sophie knew it wouldn't help her case one bit to be found in her bathrobe.

She knew it wasn't either of her daughters visiting now. They always let themselves in. She opened the door a crack and saw Reverend Ben.

"Hello, Sophie." His warm smile crinkled up the corners of his eyes. "I wanted to see how you're doing. I heard you had a fall?"

"I took a tumble, Reverend. No real damage, thank goodness. I think the angels caught me." She smiled and waved him in. "I'm just having a second cup of coffee. Will you sit with me awhile?"

"I'd like that very much." Reverend Ben followed her inside and down the hallway.

"Don't mind the house. We're in the middle of cleaning up and painting. And Christmas decorating on top of that." Macintosh followed them into the kitchen, where he circled the minister's legs, his tail wagging. "Don't let Mac bother you, either. He just wants attention."

"Don't we all." Reverend Ben leaned over and stroked the dog's thick fur, not caring a whit about his black pants. Sophie thought she would offer a lint brush before he left. A minister had to look tidy when he was out and about his business.

"Can I help you with anything?" the reverend asked. "You shouldn't be serving me with a bandage on your wrist."

"I'm fine. It's my left hand. Another blessing," she added. "But you can grab the coffeepot while I bring you a mug."

They sat at the table together, and Reverend Ben poured the coffee. There were muffins left from breakfast, which she offered him. No matter what he said about watching his waistline, he could never resist Sophie's baking.

"My, these are good. Apple cinnamon, my favorite."

Sophie smiled. All of her baked treats were his favorite, but she didn't bother to remind him. "I'll give you a few to take home. James complains I cook too much for him."

"I'm surprised you're able to cook at all. Does your wrist hurt much?"

"Only when I forget and try to use it. I've picked apples and handled three kids under five years old with a dislocated shoulder— or worse. This is nothing. I can still do everything I need to do for Christmas."

"I hope so. But you aren't having your family here for the holiday, are you?"

She knew Reverend Ben didn't mean anything by it, but the way he worded the question irked her all the same. "I don't see why not. It's almost two weeks away. My wrist will be fine by then. Besides, I struck a deal with my children about having my Christmas get-together here, like I always do. My daughters tried to wriggle out of it yesterday, but I made them stick to their promise."

Sophie felt a little worked up just recalling the conversation. Once Evelyn had brought her home, Una arrived, and both insisted that she couldn't have Christmas after all—despite the deal they all agreed to on Thanksgiving.

"What sort of deal was that?" Reverend Ben sipped his coffee, his eyes curious behind his gold-rimmed glasses.

"My children have been after me to give up this house and the orchard, Reverend. Ever since I was sick last winter, it's just gotten worse and worse."

"Yes, I remember." Reverend Ben had been very attentive to her during her illness, visiting while she was in the hospital and after she came home. Bringing books, flowers, news of the church and village. He had been a good friend and a bright spot during a long, lonely winter.

He had also been privy to visits with her family, and she was sure they had tried to enlist his help in persuading her to their thinking. But the reverend, good friend and fair-minded as he was, had not taken sides. Sophie was grateful to him for that, too.

"Evelyn wouldn't let me have the family here for Thanksgiving," Sophie explained. "She said it was too much work. But I got them to agree I could have Christmas here. In return, I promised to think about putting the place up for sale. The house needs some attention whether I stay or go. That's why James is doing all this painting and repair work. But I'm sure my kids think that's a sign that they're wearing me down. Even though I have no idea what I want to do."

"It's a difficult decision, for everyone," the reverend said gently. "I guess your mishap yesterday brought this all to the surface again."

"Like a big green sea monster rising from the waves." Sophie waved her hands and made a funny face. Reverend Ben laughed, but she could see the understanding in his eyes. "Evelyn wanted me to go home with her after the clinic. Lucky for me, James is here."

"That is fortunate. But how do you feel about selling the property now? Have you given it more thought?"

"Night and day. It's all I can think about. But not even falling down on my bottom has helped me get to the bottom of it. I'm so confused, Reverend. More than I've ever been in my life. On one hand, I'm coming to see their point of view. They do worry so about me, whether I think they ought to or not. They just do. That's only gotten worse, and it's never going to get better. It's starting to feel selfish to stick to my guns like this. Just yesterday at the hospital, Evie said, 'Can't you see we're worried sick about you? Why are you doing this to us?'" Sophie sighed and shook her head. "She looked like she was going to cry. I never thought I was a self-centered mother, but now I'm thinking maybe I am."

Reverend Ben leaned over and patted her hand. "Don't be so hard on yourself, Sophie. You're the least selfish or self-centered person I've ever met. Your children have your welfare at heart, no question. But you have your own needs and concerns, as well. You've lived here your entire life, from the moment you came into the world."

"Right in that back bedroom," Sophie said with a proud smile.

"My mother was late for everything. She left it too long to get to the hospital." She laughed, and Reverend Ben did, too. But once the mirthful moment passed, she felt a wave of doubt come over her again. "I'm just so confused, Reverend. Do you have any suggestions for me? You're probably the one person I'd really listen to."

Reverend Ben smiled kindly, his eyes bright. "That's quite a compliment, coming from you, Sophie. But I'm sorry, I have no suggestions. None I should share, anyway. No one can tell you what to do or when to do it. But I hope you can quiet the voices of your family, and those of your mind, too. And hear the advice that comes from deep in your heart. And feel at peace with whatever decision you arrive at, knowing it's the right thing to do. The right thing for *you* to do."

"I know what you mean, Reverend. I've asked the good Lord for some guidance. But so far, I don't feel that's helped me get any closer to the answer—unless there's some message for me right under my nose that I can't see."

"It happens that way sometimes. Don't give up on your prayers. I'll pray for you, too."

"Thank you, Reverend. I know that you and Carolyn always have your family at the parsonage for Christmas Day, but I hope you can all stop by here and say hello at some point in the day. Whether I'm at peace with it in my heart or not, I have a feeling this could be my last Christmas here."

Reverend Ben looked sad at her statement. "Let's hope and pray for the best in this situation, for all involved. Whatever that may be," he said. "And we'd be delighted to stop by on Christmas, Sophie. We would be honored."

Sophie nodded, feeling suddenly too teary-eyed to speak. But

Reverend Ben was the sort of friend who understood how you felt and what you were thinking before you even said a word. He was a blessing in their church—and in her life.

Zoey felt like a cat captured in a burlap sack as she struggled to change her outfit in the diner's tiny restroom—exchanging her waitress uniform for black wool pants, a light blue tailored blouse, and a gray tweed blazer. Mondays were usually slow, and the lunch rush had passed, too, so few customers would come in before closing. Trudy was not on the schedule today, but James had promised to wait the tables and do his job, too, so that Zoey could slip out for an hour or two.

She certainly hoped Charlie didn't decide to run down from his office for a surprise visit and find his new manager had flown the coop. But she and James had figured out a story to cover that, too.

As Zoey emerged, she felt another bout of cold feet. How crazy was it to interview for a job that you knew you couldn't accept?

James finished taking an order from a table across the room, and headed toward her. "All set to go, I see. You look awesome, Zoey. Do you have an extra copy of your résumé?"

She nodded, battling another wave of nerves as she pulled on her jacket. "I have about ten copies. And copies of the recommendations from my professors. And two pens that write, and everything else I might need. I'm just not sure why I'm doing this," she admitted. "What's the point? Even if I get the job, I can't take it."

His gaze was sympathetic. "Think positive, Zoey. You never know what might happen. Maybe a new manager for the diner will drop out of the sky. Or maybe the diner will burn down," he added, making her laugh. "Maybe another job at the center will open later on, and you'll make such a great impression on them today, they'll call you first." He gently brushed back a strand of hair that had fallen on her cheek. "I know you're scared, and it seems like a huge effort to do this. But in the long run, you might be very happy you made the effort."

Zoey nodded and zipped up her jacket. "Thanks, Coach. I needed that. I'll try not to be too long."

"Take your time. I've got it under control here," James promised. "I was only kidding about the diner burning down."

She laughed at him. "I hope so."

He gave her one of those smiles that seemed to warm her soul. "Good luck, Zoey. Though I'm sure you don't need it. How could anyone resist you?" James leaned over and quickly kissed her. Zoey felt a thrill down to her toes and a lightness of heart that melted her worries.

On the short drive to Beverly, her mind flip-flopped between her anxiety and James's encouraging words. When she reached the center, she parked in the front, near the offices; it was a part of the building where she rarely ventured. Although she had volunteered there for almost a year, she hardly ever walked into the lobby or spoke to the receptionist, who sat at a desk near a waiting area.

"Zoey Bates. I'm here for an interview with Ms. Foster."

"Go right in, Ms. Bates, first office on the left. Ms. Foster is expecting you."

"Thank you." Zoey nodded and forced a smile. All the articles she had read online about interviews said to make sure you smile a lot, even if you don't feel like it, because smiley people are statistically more likely to be hired.

The executive offices were very modest. The door to Ms. Foster's office was open, and Zoey knocked. A woman with dark hair, streaked with gray, sat behind a desk, typing very quickly on her keyboard.

She looked up and met Zoey's glance over the edge of her red-framed glasses. "Come in, please. You must be Zoey Bates."

"Yes, I am. Nice to meet you, Ms. Foster."

"No need to be formal. You can call me Beth. Have a seat. I've seen you around the center. I understand that you've been volunteering here?"

"Yes, for almost a year. I was taking a psych class and our professor offered extra credit if we volunteered twenty hours. But I really like working with the kids, so I continued coming."

"That's great. I have a recommendation here from one of the counselors you've been working with. She's very impressed." Beth took off her glasses and leaned back in her chair. "Tell me, Zoey, why do you want to be an art therapist?"

"I've always loved drawing and painting and making collages. People say I have some talent," she added modestly. "But I don't think I want to be a professional artist and sell my work and all that. I do it for my own enjoyment and because it helps me express my feelings and figure out things. When I was younger and going through a lot of difficult times in my life—a few really dark places—making art really helped me. Now that I've taken a few psychology courses, I think it would be so great to do that as a career. To help kids who are struggling feel better about themselves and about their lives. Art can really help when kids, or even adults, aren't able to talk about what's bothering them."

Beth had been listening with a thoughtful expression. "I see. So your interest in this field comes out of your life experience. That kind of firsthand insight will help you a lot if you ever get your degree in this area."

"I'm definitely going to get my degree. Even if it takes me forever." Zoey realized too late she had totally blurted, not a good move in an interview. All the articles said that. She felt the color rise in her cheeks and she looked down at her lap.

"I hope it doesn't take that long," Beth said with a small smile. "I meant to say, that's a very positive and inspiring story."

"Thanks. But I hope you don't think I told you all that just to get the job?"

"Not at all." Beth looked down at Zoey's résumé again.

Zoey remembered she was supposed to ask questions, too. "Can you tell me a little about the position—what I'd be doing every day?"

"I was just about to. The intern will work with me and Dr. Simpson, assisting us in screening new patients. You'll also sit in on sessions and handle some paperwork."

Zoey knew who Dr. Simpson was, though she didn't have much contact with him as a volunteer. He had a reputation for being amazing with troubled kids. She thought that she would like working with Beth, too. She seemed smart, calm, and easy to talk to—someone Zoey could learn a lot from.

They talked about the courses Zoey had taken so far and those she had scheduled for the spring. A few minutes later, Beth thanked her for coming in. "It's been a pleasure meeting you, Zoey. We're making our decision soon."

Zoey stood up and grabbed her purse, then shook Beth's hand. "Thank you for taking the time to see me today," she said, just as she recalled from her prep articles. "I look forward to hearing from you."

Beth smiled in a warm, kind way. "Thank you, Zoey. I hope to see you around the center either way."

Zoey checked her watch as she walked out to her car. She would be back in the village in fifteen minutes. She had only been gone from the diner an hour. It had all worked out.

Still, Zoey wasn't sure if she had made the right impression. Beth seemed to like her, but she also seemed like a nice person who would act interested in everyone. What did she mean by "Hope to see you around the center either way"? *That could mean she doesn't think I'll get the job,* Zoey thought.

Her head was spinning and it took her a moment to remember that even if she was offered this internship, she couldn't take it. Her father had made up his mind, and he wouldn't budge. With all the pressure he was under right now, it was a terrible time to ask him about it again.

But James had been right; the interview had been a good experience. Of course, she hoped that they chose her. But part of her hoped they chose someone else. She would feel so awful refusing the job, she didn't know if she could face it.

CHAPTER TEN

~~~

*S*O I GUESS WE'RE NOT GOING TO THE MALL AFTER ALL?"
Jane stood in the doorway of Emily's office on Monday
afternoon, a schoolbook tucked under her arm and a frustrated
expression on her pretty face.

Emily had her hand over the telephone, several documents opened
at once on her laptop, and others spread out on her desk. The office
seemed dark. Had the sun gone down already? These winter days . . .
She checked the time and felt a sudden panic. How had it gotten so
late? Jane had been waiting almost two hours?

"I'm so sorry, honey . . . I just can't get off the phone. These documents are a complete mess." She could tell from Jane's expression that
her explanation wasn't cutting it. "Let's go after dinner. I'll make
something fast. Hamburgers," Emily said, suddenly inspired.

All she needed now was the meat, rolls, and everything else that went with it . . . Maybe she could text Dan and ask him to pick up some takeout?

Just like the old days, a little voice chided her. *The old days that you said were over.*

"I have a test tomorrow, Mom. I can't go tonight." Jane didn't usually sigh and pout, but she looked on the verge right now.

A voice on the phone drew her attention. "Emily? Are you still there? I didn't get the changes to page three."

"Can I call you back, Martin? In a minute, I promise." Emily ended the call with Martin Becker without giving him a chance to reply. She turned to Jane with her full attention. "I'm really sorry. They asked me to quickly look over a few documents that are going to the county executive's office. I never thought I would get stuck here all afternoon."

Not to mention for the rest of the night, Emily added silently. *Dan will love that.* But the documents outlining the SOS appeal were a mess. The group had an appointment on Friday at the county office, and all the materials for their appeal had to be hand-delivered by tomorrow noon.

Jane, of course, was not interested in any of those reasons for missing their shopping trip. Emily had promised her a new outfit for the debate on Friday, and she wanted to keep that promise. As usual, she had been walking too fine a line today.

"Let's see. How about tomorrow after school? Or tomorrow night? You usually have Tuesdays free."

"There's a game tomorrow, Mom." Jane's tone suggested Emily should have known. "And I have a study group for the science final after that."

A game? Emily didn't see that on her phone calendar and quickly typed it in. She had already had to miss one game on the weekend and hoped she didn't miss another. The season was almost over, and Jane's team was going into a play-off round.

"I can go to the mall Wednesday if you pick me up at school. But on Thursday I have a presentation for English, so I wanted to work on that Wednesday night."

Emily sighed and put her phone down. "I'm sorry, honey. I have to be someplace on Wednesday. At another meeting," she admitted. "How about Thursday? I know you don't have a game that day."

Jane looked alarmed. "Thursday is so close. What if we don't find anything? And I still have to practice my opening statement that night."

"It won't be hard to find something nice. You look good in everything. We'll come right home, and I'll help you rehearse. You could do that debate tomorrow, Jane. It's only natural to be nervous about getting up in front of an audience, but once you get going, you'll be fine. Remember what we said about picking out a friendly face in the crowd—like me or Dad?" She was teasing a bit now, but hoped her words were reassuring.

"I know." Jane finally smiled. "But I'd rather not be shopping the night before."

Jane was more like Dan, very organized and always prepared well ahead. She had taken on none of Emily's last-minute tendencies, which was something Emily usually admired about her. Though not at the moment.

"We'll go right from school. It won't take long," Emily promised.

The phone rang and Emily checked the number. Martin Becker again. She sighed and let voice mail take the message.

Dan suddenly appeared in the doorway, peeking over Jane's head. "Hi, everybody, what's for dinner?"

He's home already? There goes my plan to have him shop.

"Nothing yet," Emily answered honestly. "Jane and I were just about to go out—"

"About two hours ago," Jane cut in.

"But I got held up. So we never made it."

"Another Lillian emergency? Did she run out of Epsom salts again?"

A silly joke, but it was actually true that her mother had once called late at night, asking Emily to run to a twenty-four-hour store for Epsom salts. She was soaking her feet in hot water for some reason and hoped Emily could bring the necessary salts before the water cooled off.

"I was asked to proofread the appeal documents that the open-space group put together. But it's a mess. And the packet has to go to the county executive tomorrow."

"So you had to revise it?"

"More like rewrite it from scratch. It's still not done. They caught us just as we were walking out the door, right, Jane?"

Jane stood with her arms crossed over her chest, looking unhappy.

Emily got up from her desk, slipping her phone in a pocket. "I'll leave this for now. Let's figure out dinner."

"I'll get the menus." Jane's tone was resigned as she headed to the kitchen for the file of take-out menus they kept handy. They hadn't used them that much lately, Emily reflected.

"Sorry about the takeout. I'm going to try the Crock-Pot again tomorrow. A chicken curry thing," she promised, knowing Dan liked spicy foods.

He was not distracted by her tactic. "Emily, you're doing it again. You know that, right?"

"I know. But this time they really ambushed me, honestly. It's just this one last push. I tried to hand it off, like you said. But I'm the only one who seems to know how to navigate this phase, and what to say to win the appeal. They've got the research about how development would stress the environment. It's enough to show cause for further study—and freeze the new zoning—but it has to be presented clearly. And they don't have much time."

"I know all that, Em. I care about preserving the village as much as anybody. But I care about having a nice Christmas, all three of us together for once, even more. So you missed a shopping trip with Janie. No big deal. I know that will work out. Meanwhile, have we done any Christmas shopping? Have we put up a tree? If it wasn't for the lights I put up outside last week, you wouldn't even know a holiday is coming around here."

"Janie's been very busy, too," Emily pointed out. "She didn't want to put up the tree until the debate was over."

"Like mother, like daughter," Dan said with a reluctant grin. "I just hope you won't be like this all through the holidays. I'm getting worried about that, no matter what you say."

"I'm sorry," she said sincerely. "I know what this looks like, but please don't worry. My part is totally and completely over this week. I'm rewriting this appeal and going with them to see the county executive on Friday, and that's it. I've already told Martin Becker and Marion Ross. And my mother," she added for good measure.

"Jane's debate is Friday, right after school."

"Dan, please. How could you think I'd possibly forget that?" She didn't mean to sound sharp, but she felt hurt. Hadn't she been the one coaching Jane's team?

Jane was in the family room, studying the take-out menus. Emily took some dishes from the cupboard and put them out on the table, though she had no idea what they would be eating.

Dan did not look reassured. "I just hope this meeting doesn't conflict with the debate."

"Absolutely not. It's starting at noon and shouldn't take more than an hour. If it drags on, I'll leave." She added napkins and silverware at each place. "I thought afterward we could get a bite to eat and then go over to Sawyers' Tree Farm. It should be early enough to put the tree up, and decorate, too."

"All right. That sounds like a good plan."

Jane walked over with the menus she'd picked out, and Emily smiled at her. "How does that sound, Jane? Do you want to put the tree up Friday night?"

"Sure. I might be totally zonked, but why not."

"We can do some baking next weekend, too. And some shopping for gifts. We have plenty of time to get ready for Christmas."

Dan gave her a helpless smile. "If you say so, Crash."

His favorite nickname—inspired by Emily's tendency to crash every deadline—made Jane laugh. Emily laughed, too, feeling relieved. Ruffled feathers seemed smoothed over. For now.

ON THURSDAY AFTERNOON, EMILY WAS DETERMINED TO BE THE FIRST car in the school parking lot so she could whisk Jane off to the mall before getting stuck in the usual bus-and-parent-pickup gridlock.

She had left the house at noon with a list of errands—the usual stop at Dillard's Drugstore for Lillian and Ezra, the post office and bank, and another visit to the Bramble, to pick up an antique tea set she had spotted there as a Christmas gift for her sister.

She was walking back to her car, the china carefully packed in a box, when she spotted Charlie Bates coming out of Krueger's Hardware. Emily stopped in her tracks. Had he seen her? She hoped not. He had been so nasty and bitter the last time they met; she didn't need another dose of that. She quickly crossed the street, though her car was parked on the same side as Krueger's. She would let him pass her and double back at the corner.

But Charlie crossed the street, too. He walked quickly and waved at her, clearly trying to catch up.

Emily slowly turned to face him. Her stomach fluttered with nerves, though she felt annoyed with herself for allowing him to intimidate her for even a second. She took a breath and raised her chin as he drew closer.

"Hello, Charlie," she greeted him calmly.

"Why, hello there, Napoleon. Enjoying life on Elba? Did you raise your army yet?"

Emily nearly laughed out loud at his greeting. "I had no idea you were a student of French history, Charlie. But you've lost me. I have no idea what you're talking about."

"So you say. Meanwhile, behind my back, you're marshaling your forces. Don't deny it. If there's anything I dislike more than a sneak, it's a liar."

Emily's back stiffened at the insult. She suddenly felt she might crush the box of china in her hands, her body grew so tense. "How dare you," she said quietly. "And how dare you blame me because your administration is just bumping along . . . and you obviously have no idea what you're doing."

She immediately felt annoyed with herself for sinking to his level. But he had gone out of his way to confront and insult her.

"Bumping along, huh? More like ambushed at every turn. You purposely stirred up that board meeting and made me a laughingstock. And now I hear you're meeting with the county executive this week. You and your anti-Bates group."

Emily didn't reply. She wasn't surprised that he knew about their appointment. He had to have some connections by now in the county seat. But she wasn't going to give him any information that he didn't have.

"I don't know what you're up to, Emily, not exactly. But I do know this—you're using this zoning debate to get back at me. Everyone knows it's just sour grapes and you're a sore loser. You're going to find out that the people want progress. That's why they picked me. You lost the election, and you're going to lose this battle, too."

Emily took a breath before she spoke. "Some people want more development in this village, and they voted for you. That's true. But once all the facts are clear and publicly known, I don't think your notion of progress will get very far." She stepped to the side and began to walk around him. "If you'll excuse me, I have to go."

"Fine words, as usual," she heard him call after her. "But you need some new hobbies, Emily, besides trying to undermine and embarrass me."

Emily tried to ignore him, but she could not resist turning once more to face him. "Good point, Charlie. You seem to have that covered all on your own."

She turned her back to him and crossed the street. If he tried to get in the final word, she didn't hear it. Dan had been right. Charlie—and probably others, as well—thought she was just taking part in this cause out of sour grapes. But the only opinion that mattered was the one she had of herself. As she gently set the box of china on the backseat, she didn't feel that good about losing her temper with Charlie. He did have a way of getting under her skin, no matter how hard she tried to keep her cool.

But after tomorrow, this entire situation will be out of your hands, she reminded herself. *Charlie might not change his idea of you. But others—people with a sense of fairness and decency—will see that you are not the ringleader or rabble-rouser he makes you out to be.*

And you are certainly not Napoleon in exile, scheming to take back your empire. The thought of that outrageous accusation finally made her smile.

"I'M DONE WITH THE UPSTAIRS, GRANDMA. I THOUGHT I'D START down here today—maybe that spare room at the back of the house? What color would you like in there?"

James was just finishing breakfast on Friday morning: his grandmother's usual hearty offering of eggs with all the trimmings, including the irresistible, freshly baked muffins. More of a Sunday breakfast, he thought, than one for a Friday morning. Still, he put another muffin on his plate, telling himself that all the farmwork he would be starting in a few weeks down in South America would get him lean and mean again.

"Plain old white is fine," Sophie answered, sitting down across from him. She looked tired and a bit distracted today. "As long as it looks clean."

"Easy enough. Does your wrist hurt, Grandma?"

"No, dear, not a bit. I think that's all healed now. Though your aunt Evelyn insists on taking me to Dr. Harding today. To follow up."

"It's a good idea," James agreed. "You don't seem yourself. Are you tired?"

She sipped her coffee, then sat back and sighed. "I didn't sleep well. Too much thinking . . . and praying. But when I woke up, I knew what I had to do."

"Do about what?"

She looked at him squarely. "About selling this place, moving out. The way your father and aunts have been after me to do. I'm going to do it. I want to stay, God knows. I'd like to pass away right upstairs in my bed, with Mac at my feet," she admitted boldly. "But I've come to see that's selfish of me. There will be no peace in the family until I agree to give up the orchard."

James felt the bottom of his stomach drop, as if he were in an elevator that had missed a floor. There had been so much talk, back and forth, in his family about this question that part of him never expected it to be resolved.

"I'm sorry, Grandma . . . This must be so hard for you. I wish you could stay here forever."

"Me, too, sweetheart." She glanced at him, her eyes glassy with tears. She forced a smile and reached over to pat his hand. "But my mind is made up, finally. That's a relief, too. It isn't what I want, but it's the right thing to do."

That was his grandmother—a woman of incredibly strong character and conscience. The quintessential mother, still making sacrifices for her children, still putting their happiness and comfort above her own. James knew if he could ever create a character on paper that was half the woman his grandmother was in real life, he'd really be doing something.

"When will you tell them?" he asked quietly.

"I'm going to tell Evelyn today. I'll take her up on her offer to have me live there. See how that works out." She glanced at him, a twinkle in her eye. James knew his grandmother and aunt did not get along all that well, and wondered what would come of that arrangement.

"Why don't you wait a few days, sit with it awhile? There's no rush, Grandma. You might change your mind," he said, knowing that was what he hoped would happen.

She laughed. "I will change my mind. That's the problem, honey. I've got to strike while the iron is hot. It's not just a whim. I know it in my heart—it's what I have to do. What the Lord has called me to do now, in my journey," she added. "That's what love is, dear. You need to see your loved ones happy and safe more than you care about yourself. Because their well-being is your happiness," she added. "When you feel that way about someone, you'll know you truly love them."

James nodded, but didn't reply. He had fallen head over heels with a few girls so far and had even thought he was in love once or twice. But he knew now that those relationships weren't real love. Certainly not the deep and lasting kind his grandmother was talking about.

"I promised your father and your aunts at Thanksgiving that I would think this question through. And I've kept my promise," she added. "So I expect, sprained wrist and all, they will let me have my last Christmas gathering here. That was the deal."

"I remember. I was sitting right there. If they argue, I'll stick up for you, Grandma."

She smiled. "I know you will. But I don't think I'll get much of a fuss once they get what they want. We don't get everything in life that we want, honey. But God knows what is best for us, and what is best for all involved, in our struggles. He has a way of working things out, if you get out of the way and let Him do His job. We usually see that later," she added. "I'm truly thankful for the years He gave me living under this roof, within these four walls. I've been truly blessed, James, since the day I arrived on this Earth, squalling my head off in that back room you're about to paint. So please, dear, don't feel sad for me." She patted his hand again. "I pray that when you reach my age and you look back, you'll feel the same peace and gratitude for your days."

His grandmother's certainty made him feel better. She did seem at peace with her decision, and he knew he had no right to talk her out of it, or even advise her to wait.

"I hope by then I have your way of understanding the world," he said. "It would sure help my writing."

Everything changes. Nothing stays the same. That was the only thing you could be certain of. His parents' divorce, growing up, and leaving home and trying to make his way in the world had taught him that already.

Still, his grandparents' house and orchard was a place that seemed eternal and unchanging, a safe haven. He had always assumed he could return to it and it would always be the same, no matter what. There were so many memories here for his entire family. So much family history, it seemed the Potter DNA had seeped into the wooden floors, and even into the apples that fell from the trees outside the kitchen window.

It would be so hard to think of this place and know it belonged to someone else. Or even worse, to know it had been knocked down and torn up, the land filled with new houses or something even more awful.

He gazed at his grandmother, feeding bits of muffin to Mac, who sat alertly at her feet. James didn't have the heart to ask questions that probed into the future.

What did his grandmother always say? "The answers are revealed in God's time, not our own." James wasn't a big churchgoer, but he decided he would leave all of his questions and the answers to Heaven for now.

EMILY SHOULD HAVE EXPECTED THE COUNTY SUPERVISOR WOULD make them wait. She shifted in her seat in the outer office and checked her watch again. Martin sat next to her, answering emails on his phone. Marion Ross and the group's attorney, Jack Rowland, had gotten restless and left the office in search of a drink machine.

"Does it always take this long to see him?" Martin asked.

"Yes and no. We're sort of small potatoes," she said honestly.

Twenty minutes later, an administrative assistant came out of the inner office. "Supervisor Thatcher will see you now."

William Thatcher rose from behind his desk and extended a hand. "Emily, good to see you. I read your group's letter. I understand your concern, but I don't know how the county can help. Cape Light is an incorporated village with its own laws and charter."

Pitch one, fastball, at least ninety-five miles per hour. Emily wasn't surprised. She had never met a politician willing to stick their neck out in a matter that didn't directly involve them. It was the first rule of staying electable. The group turned to her, obviously assuming she would plead their case.

"But you can, Bill. Once we explain how, I think you'll agree that the county is well within its rights to step in." She turned to introduce the others, hoping to pass the conversation to Martin and Marion. But Bill Thatcher seemed most interested and comfortable talking to her. The truth was, she was the only one able to field his questions with clear, succinct answers that pounded in the point that the county could and should step in and support their appeal.

Despite her expectation that Thatcher would not keep them long or be interested in the documents they prepared, he ended up calling in his expert on environmental impact and his zoning supervisor. Martin, Marion, and Jack looked pleased and very encouraged, but Emily watched the time pass with dread.

She closed the binder in her lap and picked up her purse. "I'm sorry, everyone. I have to go. My daughter is in a debate at the middle school. It's a big school assembly, and I have to get a good seat."

Bill Thatcher laughed. "I wonder where she gets that talent from."

Martin turned to her with an anxious look. "Can't you stay a few minutes more? I think it would be very helpful, Emily, especially if the zoning supervisor has questions."

Marion looked worried, too. "Can't you call and say you'll be a few minutes late?"

Emily knew she couldn't do that, and she had no intention of being late. But she could see that they were both worried about saying the wrong thing and obviously intimidated by the other officials coming in. Winning the environmental and zoning departments to their side today would be a huge boost.

She checked her watch again. "I guess I can stay a few more minutes. But I really need to go soon." Her group looked weak with relief.

Moments later, the environmental and zoning experts joined them. It took time to explain the situation again and more time to answer more questions. Emily stretched the five minutes she had to spare to seven and then rose from her seat.

"Sorry, I have to go. If you have any more questions for me, please get in touch. You have my phone and email, Bill." She said this quickly while backing up to the door. Her group stared back at her. *Like children left with a strange babysitter,* she thought. But she couldn't help that. *They'll be okay. You really don't have to take the world on your shoulders, Napoleon,* she told herself. *They can and will manage without you. Besides, this will be good experience for them. And a good lesson for you, too.*

She felt happy and relieved as she drove toward the middle school. She had done her part and, starting now, would concentrate on her family and the holidays. She was looking forward to picking out their Christmas tree after the debate. She had meant to take the boxes of ornaments down from the attic this morning, but that was no trouble. It was actually part of the fun, to make a human chain and hand them down and down again.

A light snow had begun to fall, and she thought how nice it would be at Sawyers' Tree Farm that night. Christmas carols would be playing, and colorful lights would be strung everywhere. The Sawyers served hot cocoa and even gave pony rides, which Jane was much too big for now, of course. But a trip to Sawyers' was a family tradition and would definitely get them all into a holiday mood.

The ride to the middle school from the Essex County offices was not long. Emily had timed it perfectly. Until she hit roadwork on the Beach Road.

"You've got to be kidding me!" she gasped, then followed the signs steering everyone around side streets in an endless detour. She checked the time on her watch. Now she was cutting it too close and was so annoyed with herself, she thought she might scream. Or cry.

Calm down. Take a breath. You're almost there. These school events never start on time. And Jane isn't the first to speak on her team. She's after Maddie and Lauren. Focus on the road and get there.

Repeating those words again and again, she soon pulled into the school lot and parked in one of the only spaces left, way at the back. She ran all the way to the building and then down the hallway. The school seemed quiet and empty. Not a good sign. She pulled open the auditorium door. The debate had already started.

Jane and her team sat on one side of the stage, behind a long table. Jane stared down at her notes. A boy from the other team stood at the podium, giving a statement. Emily was too distracted to hear what he said.

She spotted Dan in a middle row, right on the aisle. She was grateful for that and soon landed in the empty seat next to him.

"I got stuck at the meeting and hit construction on the Beach Road," she whispered. "I left myself plenty of time."

Dan didn't answer her; his gaze was fixed on the stage. Was he angry about something? She couldn't tell.

"Did I miss much?"

"You missed Jane. She just finished."

Emily sat back in shock. She wondered for a moment if she had heard him correctly. "How could that be? She was last on her team."

"They changed the order. I don't know why. You missed her. I thought she was going to cry when she didn't see you here."

Dan was definitely angry, and Emily didn't blame him. She sat back, feeling like she might start crying herself. She bit down on her lip, feeling two inches tall.

Emily forced herself to focus on the stage and the students speaking. But it was hard to settle her emotions and get her bearings again. Jane spoke several times in rebuttal, giving excellent answers that were unrehearsed and unscripted. Emily was very proud of her, though when she glanced at Dan to share her excitement, he still wouldn't meet her gaze.

When the debate ended, Jane's team was voted the winner. Emily was glad for them but could barely enjoy the victory, she felt so guilty. She and Dan filed out of the auditorium and waited in the crowded school lobby for Jane to appear.

Maddie's mother came up to them, beaming. "The girls were wonderful, weren't they?"

"They were terrific," Dan agreed. "They worked hard."

"Yes," Emily added, forcing a smile. She was relieved when Maddie's mother walked off. Dan hadn't said a word to her since telling her that she had missed Jane's argument. She could almost feel the cold waves of anger coming off him.

Finally, Jane made her way to them, through the crowded lobby.

"You were great up there, honey. We're so proud of you," Emily began. "And I'm so—"

"Good job, Janie." Dan cut her off, something he almost never did. But he was smiling at his daughter. "You spoke very well. Your whole team was very sharp."

"Thanks." Jane didn't seem that pleased. She looked angry. Actually, Emily realized, she was seething.

Of course, she's mad at me. She has every right to be. Emily felt awful and cast around for something positive to say. "You had some great rebuttals, honey. That's even harder than giving a statement."

Jane finally looked up at her. "Which you missed, Mom."

Emily winced, feeling like the worst mother ever. "Yes, I know, honey. I'm sorry. I left plenty of time to get here, but I . . ." She sighed, her voice trailing off. "I'm so sorry. Honestly."

Jane didn't answer. She wouldn't even meet Emily's eye. Emily felt as if she might cry, but didn't want to make it about herself. At that moment, she would have given anything to turn back the clock and make everyone at the meeting mad at her by leaving early instead of having Jane mad at her now.

"I know I messed up, but I really didn't mean to. And I did see most of it. You should be very proud," Emily added. "I bet you're hungry. Where should we eat? You pick the place. Then we'll get our tree."

Jane didn't answer. Emily could tell she was still upset and was not forgiving her so easily. At last Jane said, "Can we do the tree another night? Maddie is having the rest of the girls over to her house. Can I go there instead?"

"Sure, you can," Dan said before Emily even had a chance to respond. "We have the whole weekend to get the tree. You go have some fun."

"Great. Can you guys drop me off there on your way home?"

"Sure," Emily said weakly. She knew that Jane's eagerness to be with her friends instead of putting up the Christmas tree with them was her fault. And that Dan, who had been so set on the three of them getting ready for Christmas together, agreed to it that way felt like some kind of blow, though she suspected that he wanted Janie to have a good time with her friends instead of wading into her parents' deep-freeze zone.

AT HOME, WITHOUT A WORD, DAN STARTED COOKING DINNER—A mushroom and cheese omelet and a green salad. He put the news on while they ate, which he didn't usually do. Emily hated to eat with the TV on, but was grateful tonight for the distraction, especially since Dan barely spoke except to ask her to pass the pepper. After dinner, Emily offered to clean up.

"Fine with me," Dan said. "I have to work on my book. I have a chapter to finish."

Dan had another book coming out in the spring, this one about a town, not far from Cape Light, where colonial residents had disappeared quite mysteriously. People claimed the area was still haunted, and he had researched the question thoroughly.

"I can pick up Jane later. I'll text her and tell her to let me know when she's ready. I hope she has a good time with her friends," Emily added. "She needs to blow off a little steam."

Dan met her gaze. "Don't we all."

Before she could reply, he had turned and left the room.

It was about eleven when Emily drove over to Maddie's house to pick up Jane. She sent a text and waited in the driveway. Her daughter soon appeared at the door. She waved to her friends and ran down to the car, then jumped in the front seat and fastened her seat belt.

"How was the party? Did you have fun?"

Jane shrugged. "It was all right."

"What did you do? Just hang out?"

"We had this giant hero to eat, and we played a video game. Maddie's family has a humongous TV."

Jane often complained their family had the smallest TV in the universe. "I'm not sure about that, honey. But it's the smallest one we could find," Emily would always reply.

"Sounds like fun. Any boys there?" she asked in a teasing tone.

She had spotted a few on the opposing team and wondered if they had been invited.

"One or two." Jane shrugged. "The girls totally outnumbered them. I don't even know why they stayed."

Emily smiled again but didn't offer any theories. "I bet you were all worn out tonight. You did a great job. Dad and I were very proud of you," she said again.

Jane glanced at her and then looked out her window. "Thanks . . . even though you missed half of it."

Emily felt a pang. "It wasn't half, not nearly. But a very important part of your presentation. I know that, honey. And there's no excuse. I did get more caught up at the meeting than I expected, and then I hit construction on the Beach Road. The detour went on forever and—I ended up being late."

Her voice trailed off. Jane was still staring out her window. Emily wondered if she was even listening.

"The meeting I had today was important. It's a situation that will affect everyone in this town for years to come. It will affect you when you're an adult, if you ever decide to live here," she added. "But I know that doesn't make up for missing your big moment in the debate."

Jane sighed. "No, it doesn't, Mom. Remember how you kept telling me that if I was nervous to look for a friendly face, like you or Dad? I did feel nervous, and I looked for you. And you weren't there. I felt so bad . . . I lost my place for a minute and my brain totally went blank. I had no idea what I was supposed to be saying, even though I'd memorized that part backward and forward. And then I felt so awful, I just wanted to run off the stage."

Emily's heart ached. Dan hadn't told her about that. She reached over in the dark and squeezed Jane's shoulder. "Honey, I'm so sorry."

Jane took a breath. She seemed determined not to cry. "I got through it. And we won, so I guess it wasn't the worst thing."

Wasn't it? Or was hearing Jane describe how disappointed and abandoned she had felt the worst thing?

Emily felt awful, too upset and distracted to drive. She pulled over to the side of the road. Jane turned to her with a confused expression. "What's the matter? Is something wrong with the car?"

Emily shook her head and took a breath. "The car is fine. But I'm not. I need to tell you something. So please look at me while I'm talking." Jane turned, finally giving Emily her full attention, though Emily did notice a slight eye roll. "I need you to know that you are the most important person in the world to me. What you do and what you think and feel is more important than any issue or cause, or any job I've had or will ever have. Or any . . . anything. I couldn't love you more if I tried." Emily found her daughter's hand in the dark and took it in her own. "I'm sorry for what happened today. But please try to forgive me. And believe me?"

Jane stared straight ahead a moment, then looked down at their hands. "I know you love me, Mom, and I love you, too. But sometimes, I don't feel like all of that is true—that what I do and think and say is *that* important to you. You know what you always tell me . . . actions speak louder than words?"

"That's true," Emily admitted. She was aching to put her arms around her daughter, but she was sure that if she did, Jane would stiffen, and she wasn't sure she could bear that now. "Actions do speak louder. I just have to try harder, I guess. Someday, sweetheart, you will believe me. I promise."

CHAPTER ELEVEN

ᐧᐁ

*S*OPHIE SAT IN ONE OF THE FRONT ROWS AT CHURCH ON
Sunday morning. She preferred the back, but her daughter
Evelyn liked it up front better on the pulpit side. Sophie had to agree
that you could definitely hear Reverend Ben better; she wondered
what she had been missing all these years. She also had a good view
of the young family who came up to light the third candle of Advent.
It was almost Christmas—only one week left.

She remembered a time when she was a young mother, too, standing there with Gus and the girls, who were just in grade school. Lifting Bart up in her arms so he could have his turn, too. It seemed like
no time at all had passed since that Sunday. But, of course, decades
had gone by. That's the way she felt about a lot of things lately.

Since she had made the decision to leave the orchard, she had gotten so nostalgic. Anybody would be, she knew. But she didn't like to
wallow in sentiment and memories. She had always been a forward-

looking person, not one to moan and groan over situations she could not alter. And she didn't want to be any different now.

She shifted in her seat, reading the bulletin. She wore her best dress today, dark red with black velvet trim at the collar. She usually saved it for Christmas Day, but today was special, too. She thought of the announcement she had to make, and her stomach fluttered with nerves. Then she asked for God's help and forced herself to focus on the service.

Reverend Ben stood at the pulpit, spreading his arms in welcome.

"Let us come together for worship," he announced, and then began with the morning prayers.

To Sophie that always meant to cast aside the cares of the material world and set your sights on Heaven for a while. On the things that really matter and will never fade or crumble or pass away with time. Give your worldly concerns to the Lord for an hour and try to see them through His eyes. How small and insignificant they are. Don't you think the power that made the moon and stars, the sun that shines and the birds that fly, can fix these worries for you? Trust in Him and let your heart be light.

When it was time for the Scripture readings, she found her reading glasses at the bottom of her purse and read along with the words that Reverend Ben spoke aloud, from the Book of Luke, Chapter One.

"'My soul glorifies the Lord and my spirit rejoices in God my Savior,'" Reverend Ben read aloud, "'for He has been mindful of the humble state of His servant. From now on all generations will call me blessed, for the Mighty One has done great things for me—holy is His name' . . ."

My soul does glorify the Lord, Sophie reflected. *Even on this sad day, knowing what I have to say. Whatever He wants, I'll do,* she silently added to the verse.

When it came time for Joys and Concerns, Sophie raised her hand, and Reverend Ben called upon her first. She got to her feet.

"You can talk sitting down, Mom," Evelyn reminded her.

"That's all right. I want people to hear what I have to say." She held the edge of the pew to steady herself and lifted her chin. "I have one joy and one concern. I took a little fall last week. It was nothing at all, honestly. But I want to thank everyone for your phone calls and cards. That made me feel better a lot faster."

"We're glad to hear that, Sophie. And glad to see you back so quickly," Reverend Ben said.

"Thank you, Reverend. I have to add my concern now. Falling down did shake some sense into my old head. I've decided it's time to move in with my daughter Evelyn and her family and give up growing apples. Well, they'll still keep growing whether I'm there or not," she added with a grin. "But you all know what I mean. I won't say it was an easy decision for me," she admitted. "So I'm asking for prayers to help me through this big change in my life."

Her friends and neighbors looked back at her with surprise. Even Reverend Ben seemed surprised, though they had talked about it less than a week ago. "Of course we'll include you in our prayers, Sophie," he said. "And I'm sure many here would be happy to help you with the practical matters of moving. When the time comes."

"Thank you, Reverend. That's all I have to say, for now."

She sat down, her knees feeling suddenly watery—not the weakness of age, but her nerves giving out on her. It had taken more effort than she had expected to share the news and to show a bright face to the world.

"You did very well, Mom." Evelyn patted her shoulder.

Sophie nodded but didn't answer. Her announcement had very

likely been the hardest she'd ever had to make. Next to announcing her beloved Gus had passed on. It was one thing to tell her family about her decision—and even Zoey, though she had taken the news hard. But announcing it here made it so painfully real.

The choir had begun to sing one of her favorite Christmas songs, "O Come, All Ye Faithful." She tried to join in, but her mind wandered, wondering again if she was doing the right thing. *God, please, if I've spoken too soon or I'm making a mistake, please right it for me? I feel so confused today. This is much harder than I ever thought it would be.*

EMILY, DAN, AND JANE HAD GONE TO CHURCH TOGETHER AND planned to spend the rest of the day putting up their Christmas tree and baking cookies.

"Should we have lunch first?" Emily asked as they got into the car. "Or go straight to Sawyers'?"

"I vote for lunch," Dan replied. "It's hard to focus if your stomach is grumbling."

"Me, too," Jane said. "At Willoughby's."

"Willoughby's sounds great," Emily replied, grateful that Jane hadn't requested the Clam Box.

Dan nodded and turned on Main Street in that direction. "It's still early. There won't be too much of a crowd. I bet we have our tree up and decorated by dinnertime," he predicted cheerfully.

"And some cookies baked," Emily added, glancing back at Jane. She felt happy and relieved that they were back on track and getting on with their holidays. Jane seemed to have forgiven her after their heart-to-heart in the car. After huffing around the house Friday night,

Dan had let the topic go. He could see that she was mad enough at herself for both of them.

After a quick lunch at the bakery, they picked out a fine tree and went straight home. It took all three of them to get it standing straight and secure in the stand. Then Dan began to work on the lights, which were, as usual, tangled and missing a few bulbs.

Emily and Jane started their baking, promising Dan that they would only come out once in a while to advise on the Christmas tree lights.

"I like all white," Emily said as she measured out molasses for a gingerbread recipe. "Even though it's boring."

"All white can be pretty, but I think Dad's already strung the multi-colored. I don't want to be the one to tell him to take them all off again."

"Good point," Emily agreed. It felt good to be back in an easy, happy mood with her family, especially with Jane. She had thought about that in church this morning, saying a silent prayer of thanks.

"I can't believe Mrs. Potter is selling the orchard," Jane said. "That's so sad."

"It is sad," Emily agreed. "But I suppose it's just too hard for her to live there alone and run the place. I know her children help her, but I don't think any of them are interested in taking over the business. I guess that fall scared her. She's very lucky she didn't get hurt."

"I know. But I love going there to pick apples and peaches and berries in the summer. And she used to have that big barbecue on Memorial Day every year. Remember?"

Emily measured out the baking soda and added it to the bowl. "Yes, I do. The whole town would be there. She hasn't had that sort of party for a while," she added wistfully.

"I wonder who will buy it. I hope it's someone who wants to grow apples and won't just tear all the trees down."

Emily felt a pang in her heart hearing that possibility spoken aloud. If the new zoning laws went through, Potter's Orchard would be snatched up in a heartbeat by a developer. She was sure there was a flock of them circling the town like buzzards right now, waiting for valuable property to go up for sale. But she didn't want to get into all that today. She had sworn off any discussion of that issue until at least the first of January.

The open-space group had emailed her several times over the last few days, and had also sent some text messages. But she had answered with a quick note saying she was unavailable right now and would get in touch when she had some free time.

Jane was applying her impressive volleyball muscles to mixing the butter and sugar. "You know, Mom, I was thinking, maybe Potter's Orchard is a landmark. Like Grandma's old house, Lilac Hall? Maybe someone could say it shouldn't be torn down or changed, because it's a historic site—or someone could start a petition about it?"

Dan stood in the kitchen doorway holding an armful of tangled tree lights. "I'm going to pretend I didn't hear that." He glanced from Emily to Jane and back to his wife. "Is there a virus going around this house? Is it something in the water?"

"I don't know, dear." Emily shook her head, trying not to laugh but secretly gratified by her daughter's inspiration. "That's an excellent idea, Jane. I'm not sure if the orchard would qualify, but I like the way you're thinking. Very civic-minded."

She shared a smile with her daughter, then returned to the task at hand. "Let's finish mixing this dough and put it in the fridge. While it's chilling, we can decorate."

Jane seemed happy with that plan, and Dan shot her a look of sheer relief.

C.J. HAD COME HOME FROM COLLEGE SUNDAY NIGHT, AND CHARLIE had quickly put him to work at the Clam Box. C.J. didn't seem to mind, and even offered to close up on Tuesday night so Zoey could have the night off. Zoey had plenty left to do before Christmas, more shopping and baking with Lucy. But instead, she headed to the orchard. She had offered to help Sophie prepare for her Christmas Eve party, and there were only five days left. And the truth was, she wanted to hang out with James, too.

A few knocks on Sophie's side door caused Macintosh to sound the alarm. "Come on in," Sophie called. "The door is open."

Zoey walked into the kitchen, struck by the sight of James on a ladder, stringing Christmas lights around the room as Sophie directed from below. Christmas ornaments and an assortment of ceramic figures, tiny snow-covered houses, snow globes, and all sorts of holiday knickknacks covered every shelf and window ledge.

"That's it, honey, hang them sort of swoopy. I've got white candles for the windows and big snowflakes that hang on ribbons."

Zoey gazed around in awe. "It looks like a Christmas village in here."

"Thanks, dear. That's what I'm aiming for."

"Where did you get all this stuff? Did you buy out a Christmas store?"

"Of course not. Though I could probably open one." Sophie dropped into a kitchen chair, looking tired but pleased. "It's just piled up over the years. I've never put it all out at once, but this year, I decided to shoot the works. Most of this stuff will get passed on to whoever wants it or end up in a yard sale soon. You see anything you like, just let me know, okay?"

"Sure, Sophie. Thanks." Zoey shrugged off her khaki-green coat and forced a smile. *Anything you'd like as a remembrance or souvenir of the orchard,* Sophie meant.

Zoey felt as if her heart were on a roller coaster—her spirits boosted by the lavish, eye-popping display, then sliding down again, remembering the announcement Sophie had made at church on Sunday. Everyone had talked about it after the service, and at the diner, too. But Zoey had not seen Sophie since and could hardly believe it was true. "So, it's settled. You really are leaving here?"

"It is, dear. That fall I had was a warning, a message, I think. I'm going to heed it. I don't want to leave, heaven knows. But sometimes we have to step up and do things we don't want to do. For our own good—and for the people we love, too."

Zoey nodded. It was hard to hide her unhappiness, though she tried. "You sound as if you're okay with it. So I guess I will be, too."

"Thank you, Zoey. That's just what a dear friend should say. Isn't it, James?"

James was still on the ladder, draping the rest of the lights across the other side of the room. Zoey could see the big dining room through the doorway, decorated just as thoroughly.

"I feel the same, Grandma. As long as you're at peace, I won't try to change your mind."

"I know it's hard to fathom, but don't feel sad for me. I've had the most wonderful life in this house, on this land. A richer, happier life than most anyone I know. I'm truly grateful for that, and for all the memories. No one can ever take that away from me."

Zoey admired her attitude. She was sure that if she was ever in Sophie's position, she wouldn't be nearly so positive or grateful.

"I wonder who will buy the place," she mused. "I hope they don't change anything." The words had barely left her mouth before Zoey regretted them. *How insensitive can you get? Sophie must be worried about the same thing, and now you've made her feel worse.*

"That's my dearest prayer now," Sophie confessed. "And my biggest regret. Those trees . . . they're like my children. I do feel as if my life's blood runs in the branches, same as my own kin. I hate to abandon them. Makes me feel like a bad mother," she confessed.

"I know, Grandma. But maybe someone will come along who wants to run the orchard." James had come down from the ladder, and he patted his grandmother's shoulder. "There are a lot of young people interested in agriculture now—in organic farming and keeping farmland in a place like this open and undeveloped. I just saw a documentary on it a few weeks ago."

Sophie's laugh was incredulous. "It seems all the young people run off fast as they can to make a life in the city."

"It's true, Sophie," Zoey said. "I read about that, too. Look at James. He went to New York. And now he wants to work on a farm in South America."

"Good point. See, you have a young farmer right under your nose. I never thought of myself as a young agrarian type. But I guess I am," he agreed with a laugh.

James's impending departure felt like another loss, coming right on top of losing the orchard. But Zoey didn't want to dwell on that now.

"Maybe that's true. I didn't realize it was a tide among you young people."

"Do you mean a trend?" Zoey asked respectfully.

Sophie laughed. "Yes, that's what I meant, a trend. If you meet up with any of those young farmers, send them my way."

"We will, Grandma. Count on it," James promised. He glanced at Zoey. She could tell he, too, felt sad about his grandmother's decision.

"I don't know who will be celebrating Christmas here next year. Young farmers . . . old farmers. This house may even be knocked down by then," Sophie said honestly. "I want to be very careful who I sell to, but it's really in the Lord's hands. All I know is that we're going to have the best Christmas party ever, to celebrate and honor all the good times my family has known here. For three generations."

"What's going to be on the menu?" Zoey asked.

"Well . . . everything," Sophie replied with a grin. "We'll have a big punch and lots of starters. I'll make baked clams and get some raw clams, too. Your father likes that," she said to James. "The dinner will start with a corn and lobster chowder. And I'm cooking some sort of roast—beef or ham? Maybe both. Potatoes gratin and a roast goose with apple and chestnut stuffing. That's what my mother used to make every year on Christmas."

"I've never tasted roast goose. That sounds delicious," Zoey said, awed by Sophie's menu. If anyone could make all those dishes and more, it was Sophie.

"You'll have to try some. I still have her recipe. One year, she left the goose on the counter, waiting to be carved, and one of the dogs— a big hound and a real rascal—jumped up and stole it. He ran right under my brother's bed. The old wooden beds were high off the floor, and that dog crammed himself in a spot nobody could reach and gobbled up the goose in a minute flat. My mother was fit to be tied.

She chased the dog with a broom. But who wanted the goose anyway, after he'd had a few bites?"

Sophie laughed at the memory, and Zoey did, too, while Mac sat at her feet, looking like he wondered what all the merriment was about.

"Macintosh wouldn't do anything like that," James said. "Would you, Mac?"

"If he could move that ladder by himself, he would. He's not that well behaved." Sophie smiled, petting the dog's head. "I hope that wherever I end up, I can take him with me," she added in a quieter tone. "I would miss his company."

Zoey felt a tug in her heart. Of course Sophie would have to take her dog when she moved. The very idea of the two being separated was unthinkable. As unthinkable as Sophie leaving the orchard.

"If you can't take Mac with you . . . well, you just won't go," Zoey said.

Sophie met her gaze and smiled wistfully, then sat back and took a sip of tea. "We will surely cross that bridge when we come to it." She set down her cup. "Right now, we have some Christmas cooking to do. Find an apron and we'll get to work. We'll start on the chowder, and maybe bake some Joe Froggers."

"Good plan. I'm down with that," James said.

Zoey was familiar with Sophie's famous chowder, but not with the baking recipe. "What are Joe Froggers?"

Sophie laughed. "You never had my Froggers? Best in New England."

"And the biggest, I bet," James added.

"If I ever had them, I didn't know what they were called."

"They're giant cookies made with spices, rum, and molasses,"

Sophie explained. "Crisp on the edges and soft and chewy in the middle. James knows the history. He looked it up once when he was a little boy. Always curious. Do you remember, James?"

"Absolutely. About two hundred years ago, a couple in Marblehead, Aunt Crease and Old Joe Brown, ran a tavern next to a frog pond, and they got famous for baking giant spice cookies, as big as dinner plates. They named the cookies for the big frogs in their pond. People would come from all over to drink their spirits and eat their giant Froggers. Sailors liked them, too, because they stayed chewy a long time."

"I don't make them all that big. But we'll use a coffee can for a cookie cutter."

"That sounds large enough to me." Zoey happily put on her apron, clipped up her hair, and got to work. She had come to help Sophie prepare for her party, but she was also looking forward to spending time with James. Though their shifts often overlapped at the diner, it was different seeing him outside of work. But once he finished hanging the lights, he left the kitchen, taking the ladder. Zoey realized she would be alone in the kitchen tonight with Sophie while James was decorating elsewhere. Or maybe working on his writing.

That fine. I really came to see Sophie, she told herself.

But she did feel cheered a short time later when James returned. She was at the table peeling a huge pile of potatoes for the soup. He stood by, watching her. "Better pick up some speed there. Christmas is coming."

She tried not to smile at his teasing. The pile was huge, and she had hardly made a dent. "Guys can peel potatoes, too. It's not a gender-specific activity."

He laughed. "True enough. Let's see who can peel them faster."

Zoey rolled her eyes. "Why do men have to make a competition out of everything?"

"It's a mystery to me, too," Sophie agreed.

James picked up a paring knife and grabbed a spud, losing nearly half to the scrap heap as he struggled to cut off the skin. Meanwhile, Zoey peeled the skin off hers in a smooth ribbon.

"This is harder than it looks. How did you do that?"

"Just guide the skin between your thumb and the blade, and try to keep it thin. The goal is to get more than one French fry per potato."

"Thanks for the tip. This is definitely a marketable skill, worth learning."

"It is. Though I know you have loftier goals."

He met her gaze, his eyes dancing with amusement, but didn't reply.

They worked together awhile without talking. James improved with each try. Zoey focused on the task, all the time savoring the feeling of working with him. She felt so comfortable with James, not needing to say a word at all as they peeled their way through the pile and James forgot all about the contest.

Sophie hovered over a huge stock pot, tossing in ingredients for her chowder. She glanced over her shoulder. "It's a dull day that you don't learn something, James."

"Very true, Grandma. Zoey is always teaching me things. How to peel potatoes . . . how to stack glasses so they don't break . . . how to pack snowballs? She's a very interesting girl."

He smiled into Zoey's eyes, and she felt her breath catch—and nearly cut her thumb. *He's just being nice . . . and his usual flirtatious self. Better get a grip on the potatoes. And your imagination.*

Sophie's soup base was soon simmering, and the dough for the Froggers was mixed in big bowls. James helped for a while, then disappeared into another part of the house. After a few pans of the big cookies were baked, he poked his head into the kitchen again.

"How's it going in here?"

"We've been very productive. I can check two jobs off my list, thanks to Zoey," Sophie reported.

"Then it's time for a break. Come look. I have a surprise for you." James disappeared again. Mac jumped up from his bed and trotted after him, not needing to be asked twice.

"Wonder what he's up to. I guess we should go see."

Sophie took off her apron, and Zoey did the same, then took the clip out and fluffed her hair with her fingers. She had on jeans and boots and one of her favorite sweaters—a long sapphire-blue turtleneck that brought out the color of her eyes. She was glad to see she hadn't gotten any cookie batter or soup on it.

Not that I'm trying to look especially good or anything for anyone around here . . .

She followed Sophie into the front parlor, the sound of Christmas music greeting her on the way. Some old-fashioned singer—she couldn't remember his name—singing a cheerful song called "A Holly Jolly Christmas."

Sophie cried out in delight, clapping her hands as she stood in the doorway. "Mother of Pearl! James . . . what did you do?" Zoey pressed her hands to her face and could not contain a gasp as she surveyed the scene.

The room was dimly lit, glowing with a thousand lights—swooping strands of lights on the Christmas tree and twined in pine garlands on the mantel and around the big picture window. Votive candles in colored glass holders were spread around the room, giving off a spicy scent, and in the big hearth, flames danced in a freshly laid fire.

Every music box was turned on, and ballerinas twirled, wooden soldiers marched, and ice skaters swept around a plastic pond, arm in arm. The tree itself was an utter masterpiece, every bough covered with lights and ornaments—the type of ornaments you might find in an antiques shop, Zoey noticed, all too fragile-looking to even touch, along with nostalgic touches, like pictures of Sophie's children when they were in grade school, in faded paper frames with glued-on sparkles and bows. All in all, it was the most beautiful, magnificently decorated tree Zoey had ever seen, from the golden star on top to the crèche below, carefully arranged and sheltered by the lowest pine branches.

"Did we just get transported to the North Pole?" Zoey asked.

James was delighted with their reactions. "You wanted to use all your decorations this year, Grandma. So that's what I did."

"And then some, I think. I forgot I even owned half of this. Every one brings back some memory." Sophie picked up the tallest nutcracker from a row of three who stood at attention on a side table. "This was Gus's favorite. He brought home this set when he was in the army, stationed in Germany."

When she looked up at them again, Zoey could see the many lights reflected in her misty eyes. Zoey glanced at James and knew he also sensed his grandmother's distress. He quickly stepped over to a side table, where he had set up an old portable record player, the type Zoey had only seen in retro shops and in old movies.

"How about some music? Did you forget you owned all these great old records, too?"

Sophie smiled again. "Records? I forgot we even owned a record player."

"I found it in the attic. And a box of Christmas albums. Have we had enough of Burl Ives yet?"

"*That's* who it is. My dad always plays those songs in the diner during Christmas. I just couldn't remember the guy's name."

Sophie looked shocked. "Burl Ives is my favorite. He does do a nice version of 'Rudolph' on that album. And 'Silver Bells.'"

"How about this one?" James put another record on the turntable and carefully moved the needle to find the track he wanted. The song "Jingle Bell Rock" suddenly filled the room.

"That's a good one, too," Sophie agreed. "You need to be our DJ on Christmas, James."

"Happy to spin some tracks for you, Grandma." He walked over and took her hand, then led her to an empty space in the parlor and coaxed her to dance.

She was at first reluctant, letting him sway around her.

"Come on, Grandma. I know you can do better than that. I saw you cut the rug with Grandpa more than a few times."

Sophie laughed, looking shy and embarrassed. "Your Grandpa loved to dance, that is true. All right. In his honor, I can do a little better. Let me just remember how . . ."

Zoey stood back, smiling so widely her face nearly hurt as she watched James and Sophie dance around the parlor to "Jingle Bell Rock."

James led his grandmother with a firm but gentle touch, and she was soon dancing along smoothly and even let him spin her once, then laughed out loud.

"You dance like a professional, Grandma. You must have taken lessons. Or danced on the stage?"

"Don't be silly," she said, breathless when the song finally ended. "That was fun. We'll do some dancing on Christmas, too."

"Don't worry. I'll get the party moving," James promised. "You even have Alvin and the Chipmunks."

"I was wondering about Alvin, but I didn't want to say," Zoey joked.

The phone rang in the kitchen, and Sophie headed off to answer it as the caller spoke on the answering machine. "It's Evelyn, checking up on me. Wait till I tell her I was dancing in a Christmas wonderland. She won't believe it."

Zoey turned to James. "It was very sweet of you to do this for your grandmother. She's thrilled."

He shrugged, flipping through the stack of records again. "I had fun going through all this old stuff. I'm glad the record player works. The old music really makes it."

"No doubt." Zoey watched him put another album on. "What are you playing now?"

"You tell me." He set the arm down, and all Zoey could hear at first through the old speakers was a scratchy sound. Then she heard a voice that was unmistakable and the opening bars to "Blue Christmas."

"You're a little young, I guess," he teased her. "Maybe you don't know who this is."

"Everybody knows Elvis. And I'm only three years younger than you," she reminded him.

"And years past me in some ways, I must admit." He smiled and reached out his hand. "May I have this dance?"

Zoey felt speechless and suddenly glued to the spot. But he tugged her hand and pulled her forward, not waiting for an answer.

She fell into his arms and he smiled with quiet satisfaction, slipping one hand around her waist and tucking her other hand against his broad shoulder.

James had certainly been in good shape when he burst through the door that first snowy night. But a month of painting, carpentry, and chopping wood—not to mention carrying heavy trays of glasses and dishes around the diner—had added more muscles under his flannel shirt, Zoey noticed.

Zoey was not very adept at this type of dancing, but her feet seemed to follow his lead effortlessly as he guided her, gently and smoothly, around the small space. She smiled as he hummed along with the tune, then did a perfect Elvis imitation.

"... *Won't be the same, dear, if you're not here with me* ..."

"Pretty good. Maybe I should call you Elvis Potter instead of Harry Potter?"

He thought about it a moment. "It has a nice ring. I might use it for a pen name."

Zoey laughed. She looked up and met his gaze. He was laughing, too, but suddenly grew silent. The song had finished, and all she heard was the sound of the needle stuck on the last grooves. James didn't make any move to fix it.

"I'm glad I'm spending Christmas with you, Zoey. You're so pretty and clever and . . . just plain . . . wonderful," he whispered.

Zoey wasn't sure what to say. She felt her heart beating so fast, she was sure he could hear it, too. Before she could reply his head dipped down and he kissed her. A sweet, questioning kiss. His hold on her tightened and she leaned into his touch, surprised at first, then kissing him back. She wasn't sure how long it lasted. But they both heard Sophie's slippers scuffing down the hallway, and Mac's quick step trailing behind her. They jumped apart just in time.

James turned toward the record player, taking off the Elvis album and slipping it back in its cardboard cover. Zoey picked up a snow globe and pretended to be studying it, though she hardly saw it in her hand. If Sophie noticed anything out of the ordinary, she didn't let on. She walked into the room talking, as if they were all still in the middle of a conversation.

"Evelyn says there's a big storm on the way. An ice storm. Everyone is running around town buying up batteries and water and groceries. I guess we should have put on the news tonight."

"I heard there might be snow," Zoey said, "but not a storm."

James peered out the window. "It's started snowing. I hadn't even noticed. It already looks icy, too. I'll drive you home, Zoey."

"Not in that old truck," Sophie cut in. "You haven't even put the chains on. Zoey can stay over."

"Thanks, but I don't want to trouble you."

"It's no trouble. All the rooms are clean and freshly painted, thanks to James. Like a real hotel."

"Do you think it's that bad?" Zoey didn't mind spending more time with James and Sophie, but she didn't want to intrude.

"I haven't heard any plows yet. I'm not sure we will. No offense to your father," Sophie said, "but I don't think the problem with the trash and snow removal contract is completely settled yet. Evelyn doesn't seem to think so. It's another thing for her to worry about, the houses out here being snowed in. But we have a generator and plenty of food. I don't see any problem."

Zoey thought that for once the fretful Evelyn might be right. She knew that the village had made a handshake agreement and trash was being collected on a regular schedule again. But the contract was not signed, and her father still worried.

"I think you're right. If it was completely settled, we would have had a celebration at our house by now," she admitted.

It had actually been a relief to come to the orchard tonight. Lucy was trying hard to stir up Christmas spirit, but Charlie was tense and touchy and out at meetings till all hours of the night. Zoey felt bad for him, but there was no way she knew how to help.

"It's settled. You should stay." James turned to her and then back to the record player. "We have a lot more tunes to spin and Froggers to sample."

"And I was hoping for a Scrabble match," Sophie admitted.

"Perfect. But I have to warn you, I'm a master at that game," James said.

Zoey grinned. "So you say, Potter. Grab a dictionary and we'll see who's the master."

Sophie laughed. "Watch out, James. You may have met your match."

He looked surprised and intrigued. "You might be right, Grandma. I've been thinking the same thing myself."

It wasn't just his words but the way his blue gaze sought Zoey's that made her blush. She reminded herself not to take James too seriously. Even if she did believe him, where could this lead? He was off to South America in a week or two. Still, Zoey knew his disarming personality had just about melted her common sense and worn a steady path to her heart.

CHAPTER TWELVE

HARLIE TOSSED IN HIS SLEEP, TRYING TO CATCH A FEW MORE winks before the alarm went off. He had a crick in his neck and felt chilled to the bone. The mattress felt lumpy, and the quilt was barely past his knees. He punched up his pillow and quickly realized it was a wadded-up sweatshirt.

Then he remembered. He was not home in bed but stretched out on the nubby brown couch in his office, his down jacket tossed over his body as a makeshift blanket.

He sat up and rubbed his eyes, afraid to look outside, though he had been watching the storm through the night and into the early hours of the morning. He had also been talking on his phone to the fire chief, police chief, and all the town's support services until his throat was hoarse.

He walked to the window and pulled his jacket on. The heat in the building was off. He suspected the electricity was gone, too. Not a good sign, not a good sign at all.

He lifted the shade, and his heart fell. The world outside was a crystal palace—every tree, car, and building on Main Street coated with ice. Every phone and utility line hanging low with the glistening weight. He could not discern even a single tire track on the street. Or any sign that plows had passed.

Though he had called a backup list of every independent plow operator he could find, their light equipment hadn't made much of a dent. The snow was not very high, not by New England standards, but the icy coating over it had turned his village into a danger zone. He already knew from reports last night that the arctic blast had knocked down trees and tree limbs, crashing them into houses and cars. How would they even begin to clear that damage if the emergency trucks couldn't drive on the roads?

The phone rang and he answered quickly. "Village Hall, Mayor Bates."

"Charlie, it's me. Are you all right?"

The sound of Lucy's sleepy voice filled him with longing to be home, waking up with his family—and not feeling responsible for the entire village.

"I'm okay, honey. Just about to get things rolling again. I thought you were Rheinhardt," he said, mentioning the fire chief.

"I won't keep you. I know you have a lot to do. The power is off here, but at least we still have heat. Zoey stayed over at Sophie Potter's. They're all fine. Sophie even has a generator."

"Good, tell her to stay there. I'll pick her up later in the truck." Charlie felt relieved to hear Zoey was safe. The last thing he wanted was her driving on these roads. "I'm going to open the diner. At least I can set up a place for folks to get warm and get some food and coffee."

Charlie knew there was a lot more he needed to do. But that was just the way his mind worked—hot food and coffee seemed the obvious place to start.

"Good idea. How about the church? They have a generator, too. You should call Reverend Ben and see what he can do."

Charlie hadn't thought about the church, but it was a good suggestion. Maybe Reverend Ben could rally some church members and get them out shoveling?

"I'll bring the boys. We can help," Lucy added.

"Thanks, honey . . . but how will you get to town? I sent those independent plow guys out last night, but they didn't make a dent. I could have done a better job with my soup ladle."

"It's early. Maybe the sun will melt some of this down in a few hours. Just take it step-by-step. We'll get there—and take it step by step, too."

Charlie had heard the temperature would stay well below freezing today. But trust Lucy to come up with an optimistic possibility. Even walking seemed treacherous, but Charlie knew his wife would not be persuaded to stay home. The truth was, he did want his family near him today and needed their help and company.

"Sounds like I can't change your mind. Be careful, Lucy . . . And thank you," he added quietly.

"Don't be silly, Charlie. No need to thank me. See you later."

Lucy's call had been a short respite, tamping down some of his stress. He had barely hung up before he was feeling overwhelmed again. A binder with the town's emergency plan sat open on his desk, but he didn't bother to check it again. He had memorized every word last night. Not that it had helped him much.

The roads were the problem. If only the trash and snow removal company hadn't taken such a hard line last night. They had gone back to work the past few weeks on a handshake. But the contract was not signed and now, with the ice storm, the company owner had the upper hand: If Charlie didn't agree to the terms K&B wanted, the plows would not budge.

Charlie had tried all night to persuade him, reminding the man he couldn't act without the town council's consent. But he knew this was payback for the way he had strung out the situation, bickering about the yearly increases. Now the company owner claimed he couldn't get the drivers and snowplows out unless Charlie signed on the dotted line. An insurance liability, he said. He was sorry, but it couldn't be done.

No sense calling back this morning, Charlie thought. *Though I might call later, after conferring with the council.* Right now he had to check in with Police Chief Sandborn and Fire Chief Rheinhardt. He had to mobilize every village employee and volunteer, get them out on the streets digging, and even plowing where they could. He had to open the diner and set up the warming center, and check on seniors and folks living outside of the village who were completely snowed in. He had to call Reverend Ben, who could probably help by setting up the church as another center and calling around to some of the old people. And he had to do it all right now.

Not a prayerful man by nature, Charlie closed his eyes and took a breath. *God, please help me today,* he silently prayed. *Send a few helping hands my way? And please, remind me why I ever wanted this job.*

*   *   *

EMILY SLIPPED OUT OF BED, CAREFUL NOT TO WAKE DAN. SHE PULLED the bedroom curtain aside and blinked at the glistening shards of light. It was still very early in the morning, but the sky was clear and an icy coating reflected sharp, bright sunlight. The backyard looked beautiful—the trees and bushes, the birdbath and lawn, all coated in ice.

A beautiful disaster, Emily reflected. She could already tell the electricity was off, and she hoped that none of their pipes were frozen. Her first thought was to check in with the heads of the fire and police departments, then rush down to Village Hall.

That's not my job anymore, she realized wistfully. *This storm is Charlie's challenge to navigate.*

Down in the kitchen, the appliances were useless. She was about to go in search of the camp stove when her cell phone rang. She was surprised to see the caller was Reverend Ben.

"Emily? Did I wake you?"

"I'm just rattling around the kitchen. It's a mess out there, isn't it? Though very beautiful."

"God's handiwork is magnificent. Though magnificently inconvenient, too. I just spoke to Charlie Bates. The Clam Box has a generator, and he's opening it up as a warming center. He asked if I would open the church, too, but I'd already thought of that."

"That's a good idea." Emily had forgotten the diner had a generator.

"He's been working hard, Emily; slept in his office last night. But this storm was particularly nasty, and there's that problem with the snow-removal company. I hope the deacons and volunteers from the congregation can help clear the town, after they've finished digging out the church."

"I'm sure they will." She glanced at her own ice-covered driveway and thought of Dan, still in bed. "It will take a while for us to dig out. But I'm sure we can get down to the church later and help, Reverend. Is that why you're calling?"

"Not exactly, though I'm grateful for your offer." Reverend Ben paused. Emily was curious now, wondering what this call was really about. "I don't mean to meddle—or any disrespect to Charlie. But I think it's fair to say he can use some help, more than I can offer. And not just shoveling—some guidance and advice from someone who has faced this situation."

Emily didn't answer. She knew that Reverend Ben must have thought long and hard before making this appeal. She didn't want to seem stubborn or spiteful, but she needed to respect some boundaries here—Charlie's and those she had set for herself and her family.

"I know you mean well, Reverend. But Charlie is the mayor now. He calls the plays today. Even if I tried to help him, I doubt he would hear me out."

"I understand. And I know it's a long shot. But if ever there was a day that he *might* listen to and even welcome your advice, this would be the one," Reverend Ben mused. "'Blessed are the peacemakers,' Emily. And I don't need to remind you what the Scripture says about turning the other cheek?"

Emily smiled. "No, Reverend, you don't."

"The thing is, of all the people I know who love this village and everyone in it, you and Charlie are side by side at the top of the list. People need help today, Emily. It's an emergency. Charlie is smart but new at this job. You're an old hand. Maybe you two can put aside your differences and join forces? You would be a formidable team. And everyone in town would benefit."

Emily considered his words a moment. "That's good of you to say, but I'm not sure it's the right thing to do. Or even possible." She not only had Charlie's rebuff to consider but the reaction of her family. What would they say if she ran down to Village Hall today and declared herself Charlie's new deputy? She had just turned a corner with Dan and Jane. She didn't want to risk disappointing them again.

But she couldn't explain any of this to Reverend Ben, not this morning. "I appreciate your calling. I do, Reverend. But I have to think about this. It's not as simple for me as you might expect."

"I didn't think it would be. Stay safe. Please also remember, the church is open if you're looking for warmth and company."

If you don't go to the diner, he meant. Emily thanked him and ended the call.

Part of her knew she could help Charlie. But when she had tried to initiate a simple conversation with him on the street that day, he had answered with an angry, insulting rebuff. She certainly didn't need more of that.

You were giving out flyers for the open-space group, another voice reminded her. *Not the best way to win his trust.*

True. But why should I help him now? Let people see what they got when they voted for him instead of me.

It wasn't her nature to be spiteful, but Emily couldn't deny that's how she felt.

But Reverend Ben's words stuck in her head. Despite their differences, she and Charlie both loved the village and felt called to serve and protect the people who lived there.

Maybe I should go just for the sake of my friends and neighbors. Maybe there's some way I can offer some guidance without offending him?

Dan and Jane came into the kitchen together, both wearing sweatshirts over their pajamas. The heat was off, the house growing colder by the minute. Dan carried the big battery-operated radio they kept for emergencies.

"I just heard the forecast. It's an arctic blast. The ice is a real wild card. It's made a mess of everything. I just checked the street. I don't think a plow has come through yet."

Jane took a carton of milk from the fridge and sniffed. "I guess this is still good. But the fridge is off."

"There isn't much in there. I didn't get to the market yesterday. I knew we were getting snow, but I had no idea it would be this much," Emily added, realizing they were probably among the few who had not prepared.

"Maybe we could eat cereal?" Dan pulled open a cupboard and shook a box that sounded nearly empty.

"I hear the church is open as a warming center. And the Clam Box is, too. Maybe we should go there?"

"The Clam Box? You hate that place," Dan reminded her.

"I know, but . . ." Emily met her husband's knowing gaze. She could tell he already suspected something. "Reverend Ben just called. He spoke to Charlie this morning, and he got the feeling that our new mayor could use a little advice and support. From an old hand. He suggested I offer some help."

Dan looked incredulous. "I love Reverend Ben. But does he think for a moment that plan would actually work—short of some biblical-sized miracle?"

"He seems to think Charlie is worn out and willing to listen to anyone—including me. But I don't want to go if you two don't want me to. I promised to stop jumping into causes for every little village crisis. I'm fine with keeping that promise, honestly."

Dan peered down at her. "Do you really want to help Charlie? After everything he's said about you? I say let him sink or swim."

"That thought did cross my mind," she admitted, though not proudly. "But everyone needs advice once in a while. You gave me plenty my first term as mayor," she reminded him.

"True. But you weren't too stubborn to listen. Do you think he would even hear you out?"

"I said the same thing to Reverend Ben. But he made a good point. It's not about me and Charlie. It's about the people in this town, their well-being and safety. Families are trapped without power and are dealing with all sorts of problems. I'm willing to offer my knowledge and experience. But not if you think it's a bad idea. I guess I'm not sure what to do."

Dan gazed at her, his expression reflecting her own confusion.

"I think Mom should help Charlie," Jane said.

Emily turned to her. "You do?"

"People need you, Mom. Everyone is cold and stuck in their houses. It will be even worse tonight. You know what to do. Charlie wants to help, but I'm not sure he knows how."

Emily was touched by her daughter's understanding. "Okay, maybe I should try—if you come with me. If Dad wants to stay here, he can," she added, glancing at Dan.

"Don't be silly. Of course I'm coming. I agree with Jane. You know what to do. You should help today, if Charlie will let you. I know what I've been saying about you keeping your nose out of town business, but this is different." He sighed. "Besides, it's hard to refuse Reverend Ben. I think he knows that, too."

Emily smiled. "Yes, I think he does."

Dan's brow furrowed. "What do you think we did with those old snowshoes? A walk into the village will be like trekking over a glacier in Iceland."

Emily shrugged. "You're always dreaming about taking adventurous vacations, dear. This will be good practice."

Dan rolled his eyes, and Jane laughed. Emily just felt glad that her family was in her corner again.

"ZOEY? IT'S DAD. YOU'RE STILL AT THE ORCHARD, RIGHT?"

"Yep, we just finished breakfast." James was washing dishes, and Sophie was talking to Reverend Ben on her cell phone. Zoey walked into the mudroom to hear her father better. "Mom said you're opening the diner. I want to help."

"That's sweet of you, honey. I wish you were here, too. But I don't want you to drive. You wait there until the road is clear, and I'll pick you up."

"James said he'll drive me. He's going to put chains on Sophie's truck."

"That old heap? It's more dangerous than your car." Her father's voice was gruff and protective. "I know you always help me when you can, honey. I appreciate that. But you can help today by staying safe. Promise me, okay?"

"All right." Zoey felt frustrated. As much as she complained about working at the diner, this was one day she really wanted to be there with her family.

"Good girl. I'll talk to you later."

Her father ended the call, and Zoey walked back into the kitchen.

James had finished washing and was drying now. She picked up a towel and helped him. "Something wrong, Zoey?"

"That was my dad. He said you shouldn't drive Sophie's truck, even with chains on the tires. He says it's too dangerous."

James reached up to hook a frying pan on the rack that hung from the ceiling. "He might be right. We haven't been outside yet. You don't look very happy at the prospect of staying here today. Tired of my company already?"

Zoey finally smiled. "It's not that," she said, avoiding a direct answer to the question. "He set up the Clam Box as a warming center. I'm sure it's crazy busy, and my father has a lot of other things he needs to do today without being shorthanded at the diner. I bet everyone blames him for the mess the storm made. Working there is the one way I can help him."

"I'd like to help, too. I'm sorry he said we shouldn't take Bella. But maybe it's for the best. It would be hard to be stuck on the Beach Road in the cold if we didn't make it."

Or worse, Zoey thought, the light truck could slide right off the road and wind up in a ditch. Or go into a spin. Her father was right. It wasn't worth the risk. Still, she wished there was some way she could get there.

Sophie returned to the kitchen and hung up the phone. She looked as if she had just heard good news. "Guess what? I've arranged with Reverend Ben to set up here as a warming center, for people who live out this way and don't have generators. We have plenty of heat, food, and water—and the best decorations in town."

James did not look surprised. He knew his grandmother well. "That's good of you, Grandma. But how are they going to get here?"

"Sam Morgan is going to drive around and pick folks up. He has a big, heavy truck with a plow on the front. Reverend Ben said he's already been to town and back. His wife, Jessica, is coming to help me and some other ladies from the church, too. If you two could just put out some folding chairs in the living room and dining room and help me with the percolators, we'll be fine."

"I'll get the chairs," James said.

"Where are the percolators?" Zoey asked. Sophie was the only person she knew who owned two or even three giant coffeepots. Her house was as well-equipped for company as any catering hall. "I can set that up for you."

Sophie directed them, almost giddy with excitement. "They'll probably go through all the cookies we made, Zoey. But this is just as important as Christmas."

"It is," Zoey agreed. "And we can make more by then."

She set off on her job, glad to be busy.

The Clam Box was crowded, as Emily had expected. Luckily, three seats at the counter were free, and they claimed them quickly. She recognized faces from all over town—Grace and Digger Hegman, Frank Dillard, and Vera Plante. All the members of Charlie's town council were huddled in a booth in the back. Charlie was racing in and out of the kitchen, a cell phone pressed against his ear. He didn't seem to notice them.

The chalkboard that usually posted the day's special read: FREE FOOD AND HOT DRINKS—COFFEE, TEA, HOT COCOA. SANDWICHES, SOUP, AND DESSERTS. COMPLIMENTS OF MAYOR BATES AND HIS FAMILY.

He was on the right track there. Who could refuse a hot drink today? The mere scent of the coffee was wildly distracting.

Lucy swept past with a coffeepot, surprised to see them. "Emily,

Dan . . . coffee?" she asked. They both nodded quickly. She served them and set down a hot chocolate for Jane.

"It's very generous of you to open and do all this for the town," Emily said.

"It was Charlie's idea. We'll stay open as long as people need the shelter. I just hope the soup and sandwiches hold out."

"I'm sure people are grateful just to be in a warm place," Emily replied.

"Thanks, Emily. I'll tell Charlie you said that. Charlie, look who's here, Emily and Dan." Lucy announced their presence as if the two couples were all old friends, Emily noticed. Lucy did have wonderful social skills.

Charlie looked as if he didn't want to come over and talk, but Lucy kept waving her hand. Finally, he walked the short distance from the grill. "Hello, folks. How are you faring?"

"Our heat is off, but we don't have it too bad, compared to a lot of other families," Emily said.

"Any word on getting the roads clear, Charlie?" Dan asked bluntly.

"I've been working on it, believe me." Charlie was trying to sound upbeat and in control but tension shone through. "We've got town workers out shoveling Main Street and a crew of plow operators I hired coming through. There are a lot of roads. It's going to take time."

"Of course it will. That goes without saying," Emily agreed. "Have you called Tom Dempsey, up in Newburyport? He might be able to help."

Charlie stared at her. She held her breath and waited, expecting an explosion.

"Dempsey?" He squinted at her. "Sure . . . I spoke to his department, to his boss. Last night."

Emily suspected he was bluffing and didn't know who she was talking about. "That's good. I'm sure he can help you, since he supervises and schedules the routes of the plow trucks for that area. Once they get their roads clear, he might send one or two down here. He did that for the village one winter a few years ago. The village will need to cover the salaries and the supplies, of course. As I'm sure you know."

Charlie nodded. "Right. We talked about that . . . He's getting back to me."

Emily nodded, feeling satisfied this slim arrow had hit its mark. "Good coffee," she said sincerely. "I know it sounds trivial, but I really missed it this morning. I can't even think straight without coffee."

"Me, neither," Charlie agreed. He folded his arms over his chest. "So . . . anyone else who might not be listed in the emergency plan? Just wondering."

Emily considered the question, thinking of county and even state officials whom she might contact at a time like this. And some at the utility company, as well. "Let's see . . . now that you mention it, there are a few . . ." She paused. "It's so noisy in here. Maybe we should talk in the kitchen?"

"It is noisy. Come on back." Charlie headed for the swinging doors, and Emily got to her feet. She glanced back at Dan, who smiled at her with fingers crossed. Emily followed Charlie into the kitchen, feeling as if she were willingly walking into a lion's den, half expecting him to bite her head off.

Charlie's cook, Tim, ladled soup in a row of bowls on a large tray while Lucy waited to carry them into the dining room. If either of them thought there was anything odd about Emily and Charlie meeting in the kitchen, they didn't show it.

"Hot soup, coming through," Lucy said lightly as she sailed by.

Emily faced Charlie and took out her cell phone, then browsed her list of contacts. "There are a few more people you might reach out to—beyond the names in the plan," she said. "Let me see if I can find them for you."

"Why aren't they in the plan? That's what I want to know."

His tone wasn't accusatory, exactly. Just frustrated. Emily would have felt the same in his shoes.

"I guess it's because there's a network of people you get to know being in the job for a long time. People I developed relationships with, who knew me and were willing to help. Not because they had to, but because we were friends and colleagues. I hope they'll help you, too. It's worth a try."

Charlie seemed satisfied with that answer but still frowned at her. "That makes sense. But why in the world do *you* want to help me? I thought you'd be pleased as punch to see me fail."

That was even a harder question to answer. "I know we don't agree on a lot of things, Charlie. But one thing we do agree on is this town and the people in it. I know you would do anything to help everyone get through this mess safely. And I feel the same."

"True enough," Charlie admitted, a little reluctantly. "Though I never thought of it that way."

"I never did, either," she answered honestly. "But maybe we should. Even if it's just for today?"

He gazed at her a moment, then handed over an order pad and a pencil. "Okay. What would you do? Who would you call? I don't know if it's sleep deprivation or what, but I guess I'm willing to hear out anyone right now."

She knew that was as close as he would ever come to a thank-you, and she began to describe how she would deal with the situation, giving Charlie ample credit for the bases he had covered. He asked a lot of questions and seemed encouraged by her suggestions. When they were finally done, he had several pages torn from the order book with names to call from Essex to Rockport, all the way down to Peabody and up to Princeton, plus a list of jobs he could delegate to his staff.

"I'd better get back to the office. You've been a big help, Emily. I can't believe it . . . but I won't forget it."

"Happy to do what I can. Is there anything else? I can oversee one of those areas for you—the warming centers or checking on the elderly?" She wasn't sure he would want her any more involved than she'd been already.

"Let's see . . . the warming centers. That's a good spot. We have one at the church and one at Potter Orchard. Sam Morgan offered his house, too, for overflow. But they're a little farther out. We need to spread the word and find more transportation. Can you handle that?"

Emily tried hard not to smile. "I think so. Thanks for the assignment," she added. "I'll check in if I have questions."

"You do that." He suddenly stuck out his hand. "I know we're usually on opposite sides of every question. I can't promise it will ever be different. But I have to say, you surprised me today. You're all right, Emily Warwick. You sure know how to take the high road."

Emily shook his hand, pleased at his compliment. "Thanks, Charlie. You surprised me today, too."

A short time later, Emily met Dan back at the lunch counter. She saw Jane across the room, sitting at a table with a group of her friends.

"You were back there a long time," Dan said. "I thought Charlie might have pushed you in the freezer and thrown away the key."

"I didn't know what to expect either. But he did hear me out, and I gave him advice. I hope it helps." She took a sip of her coffee. It was cold but still tasted good. "We shook hands."

"That is big. You ought to tell Reverend Ben. He'll be pleased."

"Yes, he will," Emily agreed. "I hope you don't mind, but Charlie asked me to oversee the warming centers."

"I'm not surprised," Dan said with a smile. "What can I do to help?"

Emily was grateful for his offer and his understanding. "We need to make a ton of phone calls to start. Let's find a booth and a place to charge the phones." Luckily, she had remembered to bring the chargers.

This was not going to be easy. She didn't have any of the resources of her old office at Village Hall, but she didn't feel comfortable asking to do the job there. Even if she and Charlie had struck a truce, that was his command post and inner sanctum now.

I'm just a deputy today. Not the sheriff. And that's fine. More than fine. Just as it should be.

Charlie pulled on his down jacket and gloves and worked his way through the crowd to the door. He needed to get back to Village Hall, even though he was leaving poor Lucy and the boys shorthanded. C.J. didn't seem to mind so much, but Jamie kept sending him comically desperate looks, as if no one could survive bussing so many tables.

He saw Emily and Dan in a booth, talking on their cell phones and making lists on sheets of paper most likely borrowed from schoolkids doing homework at other tables. He could barely believe

Emily had come here. But the advice she had given him was golden, and he was eager to follow through.

He stepped out on to the street, wishing he could run to Village Hall, but forcing himself to tread carefully. At least there was some sand down. And his old friend Krueger was selling snow shovels and Ice Melt at half price. He stood in front of his store and waved. "Hang in there, Charlie. So far, so good," he shouted.

"Thanks, George. I'm doing my best."

A little farther down Main Street, Tucker and a few other police officers were helping shopkeepers clear the sidewalk.

"That's the way, folks. Everybody does their part. We'll get through this. Don't worry," Charlie coached them. "Help is on the way."

"That's the spirit, Dad."

It was Zoey, standing in front of the diner. The busboy, James Potter, was with her. Part of him felt relieved to see she was safe and sound, and the other part was upset that she had not kept her promise.

"I thought you were staying at the orchard. You promised me you wouldn't take that old truck out . . . Did you drive her here?" He turned from Zoey to James, already blaming him.

"No, sir. Sam Morgan gave us a ride. He's been shuttling people in and out of town all day. He brought some neighbors to my grandmother's and said we could ride back to town with him."

"I called you, Dad. You didn't answer," Zoey explained. "I thought it would be all right. Reverend Ben thought Sam's truck was safe enough for church members."

Charlie felt foolish for losing his temper. "I guess that was okay. Right now, the diner sounds like Fenway after a home run. I must have missed the phone."

"I just want to help, Dad."

"I'm sorry. That's sweet of you, Zoey. Don't mind me. I'm tired," he admitted. "Your mother and brothers will be thrilled to see you." He glanced at James. "You here to help, too?"

"Absolutely."

"Better get in there. It's a madhouse. I'll be in my office. And thank you, honey. You're a special girl. I always said that."

"Thanks, Dad. Good luck!"

Charlie waved and concentrated on his footing again. Tiny, careful steps, one behind the other, that was the only way he could get from A to B. It seemed a metaphor for his life lately. *But at least I'm moving forward,* he reminded himself. *One slippery step at a time.*

It was sometime after six that night when Emily called Charlie. She was at Sophie Potter's house, checking to see how many people were sheltered there and to see if Sophie needed any supplies. The house was filled, but it seemed under control, with Sophie at the stove, cooking up a storm of her own, a huge preholiday party.

"I think we've managed to get everyone who needs to be out of the cold tonight into one of the warming centers, Charlie. There's food and blankets for all, and most will have cots to sleep on, too."

"Good to know. And good job. I appreciate you stepping up." His words of gratitude were gruffly spoken. But he had thanked her, a surprising first in their relationship.

"I was glad to help. I can continue tomorrow, too," she added.

"All right, if you want to. No pressure. I'm going to stop by the church and see how they're doing. I'm letting folks stay over at the diner, too," he added. "There's no heat at our house. Looks like I'll be there with my family tonight."

"That makes sense," Emily said.

"Where will you be tonight, you and your family?"

Was he actually concerned about her—or just curious? Concerned, Emily decided. They disagreed about a lot of things, but she knew Charlie had a good heart underneath. Very far underneath, sometimes.

"I'm going to my sister's house. She and Sam have a generator, so they offered their place as a warming center, too. But it didn't seem as if we needed another in this area. And they live a bit farther out than Sophie, so it's harder to get to."

"Very true. Though we'll see how long these centers are needed. Sophie might need a break after a day or so. Let's see how it goes. Tomorrow is another busy day. Guess I'll check in with you in the morning, Emily."

"Good idea. Talk to you then. Stay warm," she added.

"Same to you and yours," Charlie said.

Emily said good-bye and ended the call.

"Who was that?" Dan asked. He had been walking around Sophie's house, socializing with all the storm guests, but now stood nearby.

"I had to check in with Charlie. I'm going to help him tomorrow, too."

"Reporting in to the mayor?" Dan teased. "Did you ever think you'd be working for him, Em?"

Emily smiled. "I'm not working for him, I'm just a volunteer. But no, not in a million years. Goes to show, you just never know what's going to happen when you wake up in the morning."

"Very true. This morning was a perfect example of that."

A few minutes later they called Sam, and he picked them up in his truck. They stopped at their own house for sleeping bags and over-night needs and then headed over to Sam's house.

Emily knew that her mother and Ezra had been the first to arrive, rescued by Sam early that morning. She wondered how her sister's nerves were holding up, stuck in the house with their mother all day. But there were many more people in the house, Emily realized, including Molly Willoughby, her husband, Dr. Matt Harding, and their youngest daughter, Betty, as well as Jessica's younger children, Tyler and Lily. Jessica had also invited her new neighbors, a young couple who had moved into an adorable little cottage on the pond that edged Sam and Jessica's property. Emily hadn't met them before, but she recalled their last name was Quinn. Jessica often mentioned the wife, Melissa. In the past few months, they had become good friends.

"Emily, Dan . . . give me your coats, you must be frozen." Jessica ran to the door to greet each of them with a hug. Their dog, a yellow lab mix named Sunny, followed at her heels.

"We're fine. We've been hanging around warming centers all day," Dan explained. "Grazing on coffee and donuts."

Sam had come in right behind them and laughed. "A crisis brings out the best in people. I've always said that."

"I haven't had a single donut," Emily protested. "I didn't want to spoil my appetite. I knew there would be something delicious cooking . . . Is that freshly baked bread?"

"Among other things. Molly's in the kitchen working her magic. Even I had to step aside for a while."

Jessica was a wonderful cook, but so was her sister-in-law, Molly. Emily was sure that between them, they had created a feast from whatever ingredients were at hand.

"Can I help?" Emily asked.

"Maybe later. You've been out all day working. Why don't you warm up and relax for a while? I'll make you some tea."

"I'd love that. Where's Mother?" she asked.

"She and Ezra exhausted themselves doing crossword puzzles. They worked their way through an entire book today. Now Ezra is reading, and I think she's taking a nap," Jessica reported in a quiet voice.

Emily smiled and walked into the big family room where a fire blazed in the huge stone hearth. Jessica had already started decorating for Christmas, and a row of wooden angels stood among pine boughs on the mantelpiece. Sam had carved the set for his wife during the early years of their marriage. A huge tree stood in the corner of the room, covered with lights but with no ornaments yet. At the other side of the room, in the dining area, a long table had been set for all the guests. But the room was empty now while most of the guests relaxed near the fire.

Emily spotted Ezra sitting in a chair, focused on a thick book. Matt was playing chess with Tyler, who was in middle school now and on a chess team, Emily had heard. Lily, who was six, had already pounced on Jane and persuaded her older cousin to play with her. They sat surrounded by a pile of dolls, and moments later Betty joined them.

Emily found her mother in an armchair by the fire, a book open on her lap, her head tilted back as she slept. She was about to tiptoe away when Lillian's eyes opened.

"Were you watching me while I slept? That's rather rude, Emily." She sat up straighter, smoothing her cashmere cardigan and pearls. Not her good pearls but the single strand she called her "everyday set." *But still, only my mother would wear pearls during an ice storm,*

Emily reflected wryly. She did have on a long wool skirt, thick stockings, and sturdy boots, which were some compromise with the situation.

"I wasn't staring. I was just checking to see if you were still asleep." Emily sat in the armchair on the other side of the hearth.

"I was. Until you stared me awake. Just as well. I don't know how I even fell asleep. I might as well be sitting in the middle of South Station with all the hubbub here today."

"I think it's very cozy. And calm," Emily added. "You should see the warming centers. Everyone's safe, but they're very crowded. I'm thankful we have a comfortable, private place to stay, instead."

Lillian sighed. "We could all be comfortable in our own homes if that fool mayor could do his job properly."

"Charlie has no control over the power company and how fast they can get the lines and transformers repaired, Mother. You know that."

Her mother's head tilted back with surprise. "So you're defending him now? Did you drink any free Kool-Aid at the Clam Box this morning?"

Emily had to laugh. Her mother was still very sharp for her age. Before she could answer, Molly called from the dining room, "Hey, guys, dinner is served. We have a lot of yummy food here. Please help yourselves."

"A buffet . . . I should have known." Lillian made a face as Emily helped her up from the chair and handed over her cane. Lillian had always disliked buffets; mixing all sorts of foods together on one plate was not her style. Neither was it her style not to sit and be served.

"Why don't you find a seat at the table and I'll make you a plate?" Emily offered.

Lillian nodded. "I'd appreciate that. You know what I like. None of Molly Willoughby's food, please." Her voice was very low, but she rolled her eyes. "It never agrees with me."

In the midst of this emergency, only her mother could complain about landing in one of the loveliest and most comfortable houses in the entire village and dining on food prepared by one of the most acclaimed cooks for miles around.

Emily smiled to herself as she took two plates and stepped up to the long table filled with an array of dishes—freshly baked bread, green salad, chili, a pasta dish smothered in melted cheese, and even a chicken curry.

She couldn't speak for anyone else, but she was very, very thankful to be here tonight with her family, and she said a quick, silent prayer for so many others in town tonight who were not nearly as cozy and comfortable.

She was also grateful that she'd had the chance today to help them as much as she had been able, and suddenly realized she also had Charlie to thank for that.

CHAPTER THIRTEEN

ON FRIDAY AFTERNOON, EMILY FOUND REVEREND BEN IN Fellowship Hall, chatting with Claire North and her husband, Nolan Porter. Though two days had passed since they all woke up to the ice storm, Fellowship Hall was still set up as a warming center, with long tables of hot drinks and a miscellaneous, ever-changing array of food. There were some tables for eating, others for socializing, and still others where people who were shut out of offices could work, with stations to charge cell phones and computers.

There were also some cots, folded up against a wall now, but used the first and second night after the storm. Emily did not expect anyone to stay over tonight. As she supervised the centers, she kept track of the attendance at each location, even interviewing people who came and went about their situations and needs.

Charlie had appreciated her efficient reports, in his way, she reflected with a wry smile. There were fewer people passing through this center than on Wednesday and Thursday, she noticed. But she still found the number concerning.

Sophie's house had been active on Wednesday and Thursday, but her visitors had thinned out. She was also at church today, balancing a big pot of soup on a hot plate. "I cooked this last night, but I don't think I'll have enough customers to use it up today. I thought you could use it here."

"Thank you, Sophie. We can." Emily was setting out another contribution of pastries and breads from Willoughby's Bakery as Sophie disappeared into the kitchen again.

She didn't mean to eavesdrop but couldn't help overhearing the minister's conversation with Claire and Nolan.

The couple managed the Inn at Angel Island for Liza and Daniel Merritt, who lived half the year in Arizona now. Claire had lived on the island most of her life, and Nolan was a fairly new arrival. The island, a tiny jewel set in Cape Light harbor, had been hit hard by the storm. The slim land bridge connecting the island to the mainland had been washed out, and Emily had heard that at first, the only help for the island's residents had been Coast Guard boats that had arrived on Wednesday and evacuated a few elderly and sick residents.

"There were no guests staying over Tuesday night when the storm hit, luckily. Nolan and I had all we needed and then some," Claire reported.

"Except electricity," her husband added. "Still without power, but we're managing. We lost a shutter or two, but there was no major damage to the inn."

"We did feel isolated," Claire admitted. "Weeks go by when I don't set foot off the island. But it's different when you know you can't."

"I'm glad you could get back to town. It's good to see you both.

Will you be back tomorrow for the Christmas Eve service?" Reverend Ben asked. "We're starting earlier than usual. We know there are still concerns about traveling, especially at night."

The older couple looked relieved. "We were going to stay over at Vera Plante's house, even though she's still without power, too," Claire said. "But that's good to know, Reverend. Thank you."

Claire and Nolan left, and Reverend Ben came over to chat with Emily. Or maybe he was just drawn by the scent of the soup? He lifted the lid and inhaled a savory aroma—a combination of rich broth, vegetables, beans, and maybe even some chicken.

"This smells delicious. What kind of soup is it?"

Emily smiled. "You'll have to ask Sophie. She just delivered it."

Sophie appeared in the pass-through window between the kitchen and the hall. "Storm soup. I toss in all the perishables I can find in the fridge. And some herbs and such. A chicken or two doesn't hurt, but you can make it fine without."

"Sounds like a once-in-a-lifetime opportunity," Reverend Ben observed. "I may have a cup for lunch. It was generous of you to bring this here, Sophie, in the midst of running your own center."

"I was just telling Emily it's slowed down out there, Reverend. I think folks are getting back to normal."

"The town has stepped up to get the roads clear and clean up the fallen trees and other debris," Emily said. "But there are still a lot of pockets in the village without power. There's nothing the town can do about that. That part is up to the utility company."

Reverend Ben nodded. "Yes, I know. I'm concerned about Christmas Eve. Even though we're holding the service at four o'clock, I'm worried about what will happen afterward. Will people go back to their cold, dark houses? That doesn't seem much like Christmas to me. I'm afraid the church can't really accommodate them here, either. Willoughby's has been very generous, and so have many church members who can cook, but I don't think we can hold a Christmas party, not on such short notice."

"I've been wondering about that, too. I thought that maybe the Clam Box would be open," Emily said. "But Lucy told me just about all their supplies are gone, and they haven't gotten any deliveries this week. Charlie is sending his cook, Tim, to Boston today to buy what he can, but he's not sure what he'll find."

"I still have plenty in my deep freeze. And my pantry." Sophie had come out of the kitchen and set a pan of corn bread on the table, next to the soup. "I stocked up for my family Christmas party, and I tend to keep an ample supply of food on hand anyway. You'd think I still had a houseful to feed."

"You mean you'd give it to the diner or serve it here at church?" Emily asked.

Sophie looked confused. "The diner? Why would I do that?" She leaned over and nearly whispered, "I'm pretty sure that whatever I do with that food, it will be tastier than what's served at the Clam Box. No offense to Charlie Bates."

Emily knew that was true. But she still didn't understand. She could tell from Reverend Ben's expression that he was puzzled, too.

"So you want to cook it at home? And bring it here?"

Sophie shook her head again, strands of her white hair flying loose from her bun. "I want to have a Christmas party at my house and serve it all there. Clean that deep freeze right out, and the pantry. It does occur to me that I'm probably leaving there very soon, and I certainly can't take it with me, as the saying goes."

"That's most generous of you, Sophie. Honestly." Reverend Ben hesitated, seeming overwhelmed by the offer. "But we are talking about a huge group coming into your house—more than arrived for the warming center."

"I understand, Reverend. That's the best part. I persuaded my children to let me hold our family Christmas gathering this year, and I've been thinking it would be a celebration of all the beautiful years I've spent in that house—and my entire family, before me. What better way to celebrate, and honor those years, than to open the doors and invite everyone in town to join in the party?" Her face was beaming, Emily thought, with the light of her inspiration, generosity, and loving heart. "I know I've got to leave soon, but I'd rather go out with a bang, as they say."

Reverend Ben began to look intrigued. "It's an ambitious idea, but it would give so many people the gift of Christmas who would otherwise be cold and isolated. I can't find fault with it," he admitted. "In fact, I think it might work, coming from such heartfelt, generous intentions."

"We'll all help you," Emily promised. "There are a lot of people at church who have volunteered at the warming centers and asked if there was any sort of celebration for Christmas Eve. I'm sure they'll help you and contribute dishes to your dinner, too."

"God will send plenty of helping hands. I'm not worried about that. He always does when you set out on the right path. Remember the story about the loaves and fishes?" Sophie reminded them, the note of faith in her voice pure and clear as a bell. "We just need to spread the word—to the congregation and out in the village."

"We do. There's not much time. But I'll work on that and announce it at the service, as well. Mrs. Honeyfield can make some flyers for the bulletin about the party, and directions to the orchard, too."

"I'll post flyers in town," Emily offered, thinking a Loaves and

Fishes Potluck Open House Christmas Party would be the most apt description, but also wondering how many would get the joke.

"How about your children, Sophie? Maybe you should speak to them first before we get started on these plans?" Reverend Ben's tone was gentle and respectful. Emily wondered about that, too. Would Sophie's children even allow her to offer her house like this? If they did object, she definitely couldn't blame them.

Sophie sighed. "I'm not saying I plan to deceive them. But it's still my house, my deep freeze, and my doors to open to whomever I please. It won't be that way for always, but it is for now. So, I don't see any reason to ask their permission. Though I do hope they come," she added sweetly.

Reverend Ben glanced at Emily. "Fair enough. Though we insist that you accept as many helpers as we can rally. Emily will help you figure out what you need."

"Absolutely. I'm free to talk right now if you can, Sophie."

"I am, too," Reverend Ben said. "Right after I get a bowl of that delicious soup and some corn bread."

"Help yourself, Reverend. There's more where that came from. Plenty more," Sophie promised.

EMILY COULD HARDLY REMEMBER SEEING SO MANY PEOPLE IN THE sanctuary for the Christmas Eve service—or any occasion. She was very glad she had pushed herself, for once, to arrive on time with her family. Jessica and Sam had picked up her mother and Ezra and saved them seats up front. Her mother's doing, Emily guessed.

Her nephew Darrell, Jessica's oldest son, was back from Texas, where he was finishing a degree in computer science. He had always been a bright boy, interested in how things worked. He sat beside Sam, just as tall as his father now. Tyler and Lily sat between their parents, with Ezra and Lillian close to the aisle. Emily and her family sat on the other end of the pew, arriving with a few minutes to chat and catch up, though the main topic of conversation seemed to be how many people had come tonight for the service.

"I can't remember ever seeing this many—including every Christmas Eve and Easter holiday since I was a girl," Jessica said.

"Me, neither," Sam agreed. "What a turnout. I think it's great."

Lillian glanced at them, a sour expression on her face. "Who are all these people? Not members of our congregation, I can tell you. Just riffraff. They descend for Christmas Eve, the big party night, but will disappear once the hard work starts again."

Emily shared a glance with her sister, but neither replied. There was a grain of truth to her mother's words. Some people only attended church on Christmas and maybe Easter. But did that mean they shouldn't be welcomed for these most important days? That wouldn't honor the spirit of compassion that Reverend Ben worked so hard to share with his flock. Besides, there might be potential new members here tonight. There were many who seemed familiar to her, families that had passed through the warming center in Fellowship Hall over the last few days and now were interested in what went on in the sanctuary. The thought made her smile. It seemed to her the way Christmas should be, strangers coming together, warmed and welcomed, given material comforts and nourishment, and spiritual comfort and nourishment, too.

Bright, trumpeting organ notes sounded the start of the service. Everyone turned to watch the choir march up the center aisle, with Reverend Ben walking at the very end. They were singing the processional

"Joy to the World," and Emily felt a little catch in her chest. Everyone here had shared a momentous experience this week and had, by the grace of God, come through it relatively unscathed.

As her gaze followed the choir moving toward the risers, she caught sight of Charlie Bates and his family. She almost didn't recognize Charlie, who was dressed in a navy blue suit, white shirt, and bright red tie. He looked quite dignified, and Lucy looked lovely in dark blue velvet. Their boys and Zoey were also dressed in their best for the holiday. She couldn't say for sure, but she had a feeling that Charlie shared her feelings here tonight, of relief and gratitude that he had been able to help and protect people.

"Merry Christmas, everyone." Reverend Ben stood at the front of the sanctuary and greeted the congregation. "It's wonderful to see so many coming together for worship here tonight. I want to welcome everyone, most especially all our visitors. I hope you'll enjoy this service and visit us again in the new year."

He gazed out at the crowd a moment, then began the announcements. After the usual mention of monthly meetings, he looked up with a huge smile. "And I have a very special announcement to add. More of an invitation, I'd say. But I will hand this part over to another member of our congregation . . . Sophie?"

Sophie Potter sat in the middle section, among her many relatives, who took up several rows of seats. Her grandson James, who sat next to her, gently helped her to her feet.

"After tonight's service," Sophie began, "you are all invited back to my house. Every last one of you," she added, her gaze sweeping the sanctuary. "Whether I've known you for years or we never, ever met, you are all very welcome to my house for the biggest and most wonderful Christmas party anybody in this town has ever seen. We've got plenty of food, more than enough to feed everyone in this sanctuary. But if you'd like to bring a dish, that would be fine, too. And please, don't be shy," she urged in her warm, motherly tone. "I know how many families are still stuck in cold, dark houses. That's no way to celebrate Christmas Eve, and it pains me to think of you all alone like that tonight. Come to my house and stay as long as you like. Or just drop by to say hello and grab a bite. All are welcome. I mean that sincerely. The directions are in the bulletin. But I expect you can follow a line of cars that will be leaving here tonight. The more the merrier, as they say. And you'll be doing a good deed by making an old woman very happy."

Many were softly laughing and talking quietly about the invitation, Emily guessed. Many families had a warm house to go home to tonight and had their own plans. Her family would be going back to Jessica and Sam's, though they had all agreed to stop at Sophie's house first for a little while. Emily also wanted to make sure the town hostess with the mostest really did have all she needed for such an ambitious gathering.

"Yes, please come to Sophie's tonight," Reverend Ben repeated. "It will be wonderful to celebrate the holiday with our church family, after all we've been through."

The choir sang the introit, and Reverend Ben came down from the pulpit to call the congregation to worship and recite the opening prayers.

When it came time for Reverend Ben's sermon, the large audience sat very still and quiet. He stared down at the pages on the pulpit and shuffled them around a bit, uncommonly slow to begin. Then he looked up, blinking behind his gold-rimmed glasses, a small, gentle smile forming.

"I prepared a sermon for tonight, of course. I've been working on it for weeks, actually, based on our Advent theme of spiritual gifts. But, for some reason, I feel inspired to put these fine thoughts aside for tonight." He closed the folder that held the typed sermon and looked back up again. "I will speak from the heart—or perhaps, my soul?—part of the divine spirit that we all share.

"I have been very distracted the last few days by images of the nativity," he explained. He glanced over his shoulder, his gaze falling on the crèche that was set up on the altar. "Such a familiar scene, we don't even see it anymore. Do you know how that is? How we become blind and desensitized to sights that are so familiar? But this week, for some reason that perhaps only God knows, I looked at the scene and was struck by a new insight, a new way of seeing it. Yes, it is a symbol of the humble birth of our Lord and how he entered the world in such a modest, low way to share our humanity.

"But it is also a scene of community, cooperation, a coming together of so many diverse players in this joyful drama. Characters of high birth and low. A tradesman and his young wife, seeking a new home. A shepherd and a king. A wise man and even an angel. All from different backgrounds, with different perspectives on the world and different opinions, I'm sure. But their differences seemed suddenly trivial, eclipsed by their common experience, the awe-inspiring experience that connected them, that brought them to common ground, both literally and spiritually. The recognition and adoration of the baby Jesus.

"Can you imagine the situation that night? Certainly, it was a crisis. Mary, forced to give birth outdoors, on a bed of straw, in a flimsy shelter alongside farm animals. Uncommonly rough, even for those days. But out of that crisis, opportunity arises. A chance for some to show their best nature, to share the experience of this young couple, not cast them aside. To aid and support this homeless family. To bring gifts and to simply respect and value them. All these very different people, brought together by the wonder of Jesus's birth. All experiencing the same revelation, the same joy in their hearts.

"I wasn't studying tonight's Scriptures when this insight came to me. I wasn't even sitting at my desk, staring into space, wondering what to say, as is often the case." His admission made many laugh.

"I was in Fellowship Hall, working in our warming center, filling the coffee percolators for the umpteenth time. Making sure everyone had enough blankets, pillows, and cell phone chargers. Surprised and grateful when the donations of food continued to come in. There were no barn animals wandering about. I don't think so, anyway," he added in a bemused tone that brought more laughter. "Only a diverse group of people, mostly strangers, brought together by an unexpected challenge, and showing their best side, their highest selves. Forgetting their differences and focusing on their common experience and the similarities deep inside.

"Finally, I thought of the beautiful, innocent baby in this scene. A baby who responds the same to the admiration of the shepherd or the king. A baby who doesn't know the difference between any of the different faces surrounding him. He reaches toward all of them with equal love. Because that is the way God has created and loves us. We are all equal in His eyes and all worthy of love, respect, and care.

"Maybe the message of the manger scene that I have overlooked for so long is simply this: In the eyes of God, our differences are infinitesimal. We are each unique, but equally wonderful, equally loved and valued. It is our challenge here, in this world, in this 'manger scene' of our own making, to see each other and treat each other just that way. To ignore the differences, the external experience, and look deeper. Down to the essential level of spirit. The way the infant looks up at each one of us, with so much love and trust.

"Sometimes we need a crisis, like a huge, destructive storm, to remind us. But the opportunities are then abundant to show care and love to each other. To express the qualities in our nature that are truly a gift from God. And we are continually reminded to look for the light that shines in each and every one of us. To feel the connection of our love for Him, and our love for each other."

The sanctuary was silent as Reverend Ben bowed his head and stepped away from the pulpit. The choir stood and began singing "It Came Upon the Midnight Clear."

Reverend Ben's sermon had put into words so many feelings Emily had experienced the past few days—but couldn't quite put her finger on at the time. He had a gift that way. She knew she would be mulling over these thoughts for a long time, well past Christmas.

WHEN THE SERVICE ENDED, ZOEY FELT AS IF HER FAMILY WERE THE only people in the whole world who were not going to Sophie's house. Lucy seemed willing to go, but Charlie insisted that they have Christmas Eve on their own, just the family. He was closing the diner as a warming center and they would have their dinner there, since they still didn't have heat at home. Zoey guessed that Charlie needed a break from being in the midst of the entire village. He had barely had a minute off all week long. She could understand that, but it was hard for her to miss the party, since she had helped Sophie prepare and knew how much good food and fun Sophie was anticipating. It was going to be the party of the year, maybe even of the decade.

Across the sanctuary, she watched the Potter clan empty out of their pew. Evelyn herded everyone to the side door, eager to beat the guests back to Sophie's house.

Zoey searched the group for James but didn't see him. Her parents and brothers were on line to wish Reverend Ben a merry Christmas, a mission that could take until New Year's Day, Zoey thought. She worked her way to a side door and stepped outside, greeted by the crisp night air and sharp, bright stars that covered the sky above the village green.

She felt alone and dispirited, not at all in a Christmas mood. She wondered how she would get through the night. She had a secret and it felt like a weight pressing on her chest. It was a secret from her parents, but she believed she was doing the right thing, keeping this from them. The mature thing. Her parents would be proud of her, if they knew. But the whole point was for them *not* to know.

She had been watching the mail the last few days—trying to be the first to the delivery before her mother or father. Which wasn't hard, since they were both out working so much. She'd received a letter yesterday, offering her the internship at the center. She had to read it a few times to make sure she understood the message. Then she felt so happy, she wanted to dance and scream. Then she remembered she couldn't take the job.

End of story. You've faced much tougher situations and disappointments, she reminded herself. *This is nothing. Besides, you knew better. It was dumb to go to the interview, knowing you could never take the job.*

She wasn't going to tell her folks and start another fight—or make them feel super guilty. And she didn't want to ruin everyone's Christmas with a big drama. Charlie was right. He had this one chance to be mayor, but she would have a lot of opportunities. She had to give him this. A special Christmas present. Even if he didn't realize it.

Someone tugged on her sleeve and she turned to see James, his face inches from her own. "Hey. I've been looking all over for you. I thought you left."

"Just slipped out to wait for my folks. It was so crowded in there. I thought you left with your family."

"I escaped the iron grip of Aunt Evelyn. It's all hands on deck, but I think they can manage without me for a little while. Are you coming to the orchard tonight? I hope so," he added. His blue eyes sparkled, as bright as any of the stars.

Zoey shook her head. "I'm sorry . . . I don't think I can. We're having Christmas Eve at the diner. There's still no power in our house. I don't think I'll be able to make it out there."

James looked surprised and disappointed. "Maybe later? I think the party will go on awhile. I can pick you up," he offered. "Maybe your whole family will come. They know they're invited, right?"

"Yes. And I'll remind them, but I think my dad wants to just lay low tonight. He's burned out from dealing with the storm and talking to everyone in town all week."

"I get it." James nodded, sounding sympathetic. He took her hand and caught her gaze. "It won't be the same without you. I was hoping we could dance to another Elvis song," he added. "Maybe you'll be able to slip away. I'll hope for the best, as my grandmother always says."

"I will, too," she promised, though she wasn't sure she could muster much hopeful energy tonight.

James leaned over and kissed her cheek. She felt happy again and wished she could go with him to Sophie's at that very moment.

They both heard his father calling from the parking lot, "James, where are you? We're leaving."

He gave her hand a quick squeeze, then vanished into the darkness. When she turned, Lucy was standing on the church steps, waving to her. "Zoey? We're going to the diner now. Dad is bringing the car around."

Zoey shook her head. "It's okay, I'll walk." Her hands dug in her pockets as she headed across the green toward Main Street.

It was going to be the longest Christmas Eve of her life.

IT HAD SEEMED AN ODD IDEA TO HER TO SPEND CHRISTMAS EVE AT the diner, but once the rest of her family got there, it didn't seem odd at all. Her mother had set up a small Christmas tree on one of the tables and their presents were stashed underneath. Her father disappeared into the kitchen and returned wearing a Santa cap. He set out some tasty snacks on the counter and carried around a tray of glasses filled with his famous Christmas punch. He had turned on Christmas music and sang along as he passed out the cranberry potion.

"I bet you don't know who this is singing," Charlie said.

Zoey took a sip of punch—mainly cranberry juice and ginger ale, but it was tasty. "Bet I do. Burl Ives."

Charlie looked surprised. "Very good. Best Christmas album ever."

"It's Sophie's favorite, too," she said, though she wasn't sure he heard her.

"Is this box for me? Is this the video game I asked for?" Jamie stood near the tree, shaking the gifts.

Lucy took the box from his hands. "We'll see. We're not opening gifts yet. We have to eat dinner."

"What's for dinner? I'm starving." C.J. had worn a tie and jacket and his good wool pants to church, but now he yanked off the neckwear and draped his jacket over a chair. "Can I turn on the TV?"

"No, sir," Charlie replied. "No TV on Christmas."

"Thank heaven," Lucy said with a sigh. A big table in the center of the room was covered with a red tablecloth and set for five. She added a centerpiece of pine and holly and two diner candles. "See, it's just as nice as home."

It really wasn't, but Zoey appreciated her mother's effort to make it so. And her father's. It was certainly better than their cold, dark house. Even candles and a fire in the hearth couldn't dispel the shadows these last few nights.

"I think it's fun," Zoey said, determined to at least act cheerful. "The table looks very pretty. Can I help you with the food?"

Lucy had folded green napkins into little hat shapes and paused at the table to prop one up. "Thanks, dear. It's all ready. I made a roast and mashed potatoes."

Jamie took a seat and tucked the cloth napkin into his collar. He also wore his best clothes: a navy blue blazer, a white dress shirt, and a red tie. Zoey thought he looked like a miniature banker or lawyer. He enjoyed dressing up and didn't rip his tie off nearly as fast as C.J. always did.

"Church was so long," Jamie said. "All the singing made me hungry."

"Singing can't make you hungry, dummy." C.J. sat down and shook his head.

"Don't call your brother names, please?" her father said.

Her mother carried in the roast, and Zoey carried the side dishes. "I loved the singing," Lucy said. "That was the best part. I hope we can sing some carols later, before we open the presents."

Her brothers groaned together, making Zoey laugh. When they finally settled down, her mother asked everyone to bow their heads and said grace.

"Well said, Lucy. Thank you for that prayer. And for this delicious dinner. What a feast."

"Thank you, Charlie. Enjoy, everyone."

Zoey passed the serving plates around and filled her own dish. The meal did look good, but she couldn't help but wonder what they were eating at Sophie's house right now.

"Did you see how many people were headed for the orchard?" Lucy was obviously thinking in the same direction. "It looked like a car parade heading out of the church parking lot. I'll bet half the town will be there."

"At least they have someplace to go. I can do without a big crowd tonight, everyone asking me when the roads will be clear and the power back on. I just want to relax and enjoy Christmas."

"I understand," Lucy said. "It's been a long week, and a very hard one."

So much for hoping, Zoey thought.

"I bet they're having fun." Jamie pushed a string bean around his plate. "All the kids in my class are there."

"Another reason to steer clear," her father said. "The noise must be deafening."

"It's a big house. People will spread out," Zoey said.

Lucy tilted her head to one side. "A big party can be fun. It's very good of Sophie to open her home for people who still don't have power or any way to cook a dinner. But we have everything we need. It's much cozier here."

"I agree. This is the perfect place for us to celebrate Christmas." Charlie smiled and gazed around the table. "Merry Christmas, everyone. Now, let's eat up so we can get to those presents."

A short time later, they were sitting by the tree and Charlie was passing out the gifts. Zoey was surprised when she opened a big box and found a pair of high boots that she had really wanted. "How did you know I wanted these, Mom?"

"I saw you eyeing them in the store when you thought I wasn't looking. I have my ways, you know."

Zoey felt touched by her thoughtfulness. She got some other great gifts, too—clothes that she had wanted and some books and art supplies. And it felt good watching her parents and brothers open the gifts she had chosen for them. She had bought Lucy a pair of comfort clogs for the hospital; she was on her feet so much at work. And Zoey had found a fancier, less practical gift for her, too.

"Oh, Zoey . . . this is beautiful." Lucy unfolded the flowered scarf Zoey had chosen and wrapped it around her shoulders. "Don't I look elegant?"

"You always look just right to me," Charlie answered. "But those flowers do look nice with your eyes and your dress."

Her mother seemed pleased and kept the scarf on. It did go well with her blue dress. She put her arm around Zoey's shoulders and gave her a hug. "I love it, honey."

When it was Charlie's turn to open his present, he tore off the wrapping, then carefully lifted the box cover. "Well . . . I'll be. I thought I was getting a pair of earmuffs."

"It's a desk set, Dad, for your office in Village Hall. I thought the mayor should have something special."

"This is special, all right." Charlie seemed impressed, even a bit awed, as he examined each piece of the fancy leather set—a desk blotter, a pencil holder, a note holder, and even a pricey pen and pencil set. "This looks expensive, Zoey. I think you overdid it."

"Do you like it?"

"I'll say. It belongs on a judge's desk. No, the president of the United States," he corrected himself. "You were way too extravagant—"

"You need that, Dad. Besides, you gave me a big raise. I could afford it," she added with a grin. "There's something else for your office. On the bottom of the box. Do you see it?"

He dug through the box again and came up with the last tissue-wrapped packet. He tore off the paper and smiled at the family portrait Zoey had framed for him.

"That's perfect, honey. Just what I need to give me a boost when things get rough down there."

"Things are going better now," Lucy assured him. "You did a lot the last few days to get us back to normal. People are grateful."

"After a shaky start," Charlie agreed.

Zoey was about to agree. She, too, had heard some good reviews of her father's performance as mayor the last few days. But before she could comment, her cell phone buzzed. She pulled it out from her pocket and found a text message from James:

Haven't given up on you. I can pick you up. My dad's car, not the truck. I know your father hates Bella.

When she looked up, she found her parents watching her. "Everything okay?" Lucy asked.

"It's James. He wants me to come to the orchard. Can I go? He said he can pick me up with his father's car."

Her parents exchanged looks. Charlie sighed. "I don't know. Christmas Eve is a time to be with your family."

"That's true," Lucy agreed. "But Zoey helped a lot with the party preparations, and she is close to Sophie. It's probably the last time Sophie will have a big get-together in that house."

Zoey's phone buzzed again with a text:

Everyone in town is here. They're all asking about your dad. They want him to come. I'm not just saying that to get you here . . .

Charlie leaned close, as if sensing his name had been mentioned. "What's he saying now?"

"He said everyone in town is there, and everyone is wondering if we're coming. They're asking for you, Dad. They want you to come."

"Me? Why would they want to see me?" he scoffed, but Zoey could tell he felt good about that report.

"Because you're the mayor, dear, and we've all just muddled our way through a big ordeal, and now folks are relieved and celebrating," Lucy replied.

"Can we go, Dad?" C.J. asked. "My friend Mike just texted me, too. He says it's awesome."

"I guess I've been outvoted," Charlie said, but he seemed pleased. "Let's clean up a bit and get our coats on."

CARS LINED THE NARROW LANE THAT LED TO SOPHIE'S HOUSE. Luckily, a car parked close to the house was pulling away, and Charlie quickly claimed the spot. "You'd think it was the county fair in there," he mumbled.

"At least we don't have far to walk," Lucy said, balancing the large bowl of Christmas pudding she had made for their family's dessert.

"I'll carry that. You take my arm, Lucy," her father said gallantly.

Her mother had packed up the desserts she had prepared—a big Christmas trifle and an orange spice Bundt cake. Zoey carried the cake and followed them. The front door was open, and guests streamed in and out, many also carrying trays of food and gifts.

They stepped into a scene of light, music, and laughter. Zoey had never seen Sophie's house so active or filled with so many people—children and their young parents, old people, and everyone in between. The most well-to-do people in town were there, like Lillian and Ezra Elliot, and the most humble, like Grace Hegman and her father, Digger. She saw Reverend Ben and his family, including his daughter, Rachel, her husband, and his grandchildren. She even saw Santa—a guest in a full Santa suit—with a flock of kids buzzing around him as he gave out small toys and candy.

Sam and Jessica Morgan, along with their family, were there. Even though they had power in their house, Sophie had insisted that they come. Zoey even saw Tim, and Trudy with her husband, though Zoey hardly recognized her coworker out of her waitressing uniform.

She carried the cake back to the kitchen and found Sophie in the center of a flock of women busily keeping the party running—washing at the sink, putting food in the oven, and taking other dishes out to the many tables set up around the house.

Sophie suddenly noticed she was there and called out to her. "Zoey, I'm so glad you could come. Merry Christmas, sweetheart." She pulled Zoey close, and Zoey hugged her back.

"My mom made this cake, orange spice."

"Looks delicious."

"Can I help you with anything?"

Sophie shook her head. "Absolutely not. You did more than your share already, young lady. You go enjoy yourself. I'll be out in a minute."

Zoey slipped out of the kitchen and looked around for James. There were candles everywhere and fireplaces glowed, shedding a warm, flickering light throughout the house. The amazing decorations that James had arranged had not gone to waste, Zoey realized. It was almost as if James had guessed there would be a spectacular party here, deserving such a grand display.

Long tables, covered with bright tablecloths, seemed to bend under the weight of all the many platters, with Sophie's roast goose front and center. There were spicy scented baked hams and roast turkeys, with all possible side dishes, along with an array of casseroles and tempting entrées the many guests had contributed. Even though Zoey had already eaten with her family, she felt her mouth water at the sight. *This is the closest thing I'll ever see to a medieval feast,* she thought.

In one corner of the front parlor, Grace Hegman played Christmas songs on the piano. Other guests, including Emily Warwick and her husband, Dan Forbes, had gathered around to sing along.

Among the familiar faces of church members and townspeople, Zoey spotted the Potter clan—James's father, his aunts, and all his cousins. She had never met his older sister, Miranda, but Zoey recognized her from photos. She had come up from North Carolina with her family and stood near the Christmas tree, balancing a baby on her hip.

Every time Zoey turned around, she saw Santa Claus again. A tall, lean Santa, she noticed, despite the padding under his suit. She caught his eye and realized it was James. The beard and suit had fooled her, but he could never disguise those eyes.

"Excuse me, Santa, but your reindeer are blocking the driveway," she said.

"Thank you, miss. I'd better be going, anyway. But I do have one more present to give out . . ." He searched inside the bag and came up with two small packets. "Do you know anyone named . . . Zoey?"

Zoey felt herself blush. "I think I do . . . and I think she has a gift for you, too."

"For me? How thoughtful. Why don't you find this Zoey and tell her to meet me outside on the porch?"

"That's a good idea. I'll give her the message right away."

Zoey grabbed her coat from the pile on a bench in the foyer and found the gift she brought for James, which she had left under the tree. When she stepped out on the porch, it was suddenly quiet. She could still hear the voices and music from inside, but the sounds seemed muffled and distant.

She watched the party through a window for a moment, as if watching a movie with the sound turned very low. Sophie had emerged from the kitchen, though she still wore her apron. She moved around the parlor, talking a few minutes with each of her guests. She no sooner started one conversation than some other guest walked over and hugged her hello, or thanked her for opening her doors—and heart—in such a grand way. Little children ran up to her, asking permission to attack the cookies and cakes or wondering when the gifts would be opened. Piles of presents sat under the tree. Zoey had left one there for Sophie, a present she had asked for, in a way.

Even Lillian Warwick, sitting in a high-backed chair by the fire, looked remarkably content, one hand clasping Ezra's as he stood by her side. Sophie looked happiest of all, absolutely glowing with an inner light of love and contentment. This night was surely all she had hoped for.

Zoey felt someone standing nearby, and James stepped out of the shadows. The only thing left of his costume was the red gift sack. He had exchanged the red suit and white beard for a fisherman knit sweater and jeans, along with his handsome, beardless face and heart-stopping smile.

"Santa sent me. He had to go," he greeted her.

"It's getting late. He has a lot of ground to cover," Zoey replied, remembering James would be leaving for distant points on the globe himself soon. Another thing she didn't want to think about now.

"You looked lost in some deep thoughts out here. I bet you missed seeing his sleigh fly off the roof."

"I did," she admitted. "I was looking in at the party. There are so many people here. And your grandmother has some connection to each of them, either family or friends, neighbors or members of our church. She's like an apple tree," Zoey decided. "Her roots to this place go so deep. It's hard to believe she'll ever leave here."

James laughed and brushed her hair from her cheek with his warm hand. "You sound like the writer now. But I know what you mean. I can't quite get my head around the idea that our family is giving up this place. I'm not sure it's really hit her, either. I'm just happy she got her wish—to hold this big party for her last Christmas here."

"Me, too. But I bet Sophie isn't surprised by how amazing it is. She'll just say something like, 'That's God's way. You hand Him your troubles, and He figures things out better than you ever can.'"

"You nailed it. That's *exactly* what she said, just this afternoon, when we were setting up the tables and chairs."

Zoey laughed with him but also felt a twinge of envy. Sophie's faith was so strong. Zoey did pray from time to time, and did have faith, but not nearly as much.

James pulled a paper gift bag out from Santa's red sack. "Getting back to Santa, I promised him I would give you these." He handed her the two tissue-covered packets, and Zoey felt suddenly shy, handing over his box.

"What is this?" He shook it and listened, reminding Zoey of Jamie. "You open yours first," he said.

"All right." Zoey took a breath and opened the smaller packet first. Inside, she found a slim silver bracelet. It had some writing on it and she brought it closer to the window in order to read the inscription. *She believed she could, so she did.* The words touched her heart. She looked back at him, feeling tongue-tied.

"I saw it in a shop in town. It reminded me of you. Even if you don't get that internship this winter, I know you're going to do great things in your life, Zoey. You're just that kind of person."

"Thank you . . . that means a lot to me. That you would say that," she said quietly.

"Open the other one," he coaxed her.

Zoey had forgotten there even was another gift. This packet was about the same size but a bit lighter. She pulled off the paper and found what looked like a leather wallet. Not a wallet exactly, more of a small black leather book cover, stamped with gold writing. She opened it, but didn't see anything inside.

"It's a cover." He seemed amused at her confusion. "For your passport."

"Thanks," she said politely. "I don't have a passport, but I guess I should get one someday."

"I think you should get one right away. You'll need it to visit me. Maybe over spring break?"

The reassurance that he wanted to continue their relationship after he left should have made her happy. But Zoey's heart fell with the sudden reminder of his departure. Soon, James would be thousands of miles away. "Spring break? Maybe . . ."

If I quit school and manage the diner full-time. And if my parents both get head injuries. Even if I had the airfare, does James really think my dad will let me go to South America to see him?

But she knew he meant well and didn't want to sound snide. Especially not tonight. She forced a smile. "I should have a passport. You're right. I'll get one right after Christmas," she promised. "Want to open your present now?"

"I thought you'd never ask." His package was a bit bigger and heavier. He tore off the paper and uncovered two books. One was a novel, the other a blank book with a black leather cover for his writing.

He picked up the blank book first and smoothed his hand over the cover. "This is beautiful. It's almost too good to write in. I'm used to the shabby notebooks I pick up in the market."

"I thought you could use something special for your trip."

"This is special, all right. Thank you." He picked up the novel next and read the title with reverence, "*On the Road*. This is great. I love this book. How did you know I love Jack Kerouac?"

Zoey shrugged. "Maybe because you carry the paperback around with you constantly and study it the way Sophie reads her Bible? The guy in the bookstore said this is a new edition. It's got a copy of his original manuscript. He typed it on long strips of paper and taped it together?"

She didn't totally understand, but when the book had caught her eye, the bookseller explained that Kerouac had typed the novel on eight strips of tracing paper and taped it together to make a scroll. This new edition reproduced the first, unedited manuscript.

"Wow . . . I really wanted this. I heard about it, but I didn't realize it was out yet." James eagerly flipped through the pages, then stopped to read her inscription.

Zoey knew it by heart.

To James—

I know this is a writer you admire. I'm sure that one day, I'll be seeing your books in a big display just like this one. I hope you find a lot of interesting stories to tell in your travels. Good luck and happy landings!

—Zoey

He looked up at her, his eyes glowing with emotion. "Thank you, Zoey. These are the best Christmas gifts I've gotten in a long time. Since . . . I can't remember when."

Zoey smiled. She was so pleased that he liked the presents she had chosen. Before she could say a word, he pulled her close and gave her a long, tight hug. "Merry Christmas," he whispered in her hair.

"Merry Christmas, James," she whispered back.

He pulled back a bit and kissed her. A long, sweet kiss that made her rise on tiptoe and hold him close again. Their embrace felt as though they were moving to a new place in their relationship, even closer and more trusting. But at the same time, Zoey sensed a note in their kiss that was bittersweet, the beginning of a farewell that was certain to come.

James stepped back but still held her hands. "I really hope you come and visit me. I'm definitely going to Peru. I got an email back from the organization and the farm owner there yesterday. He offered me a job and I accepted."

Zoey felt stunned, even though she had expected this news almost from the first day they met. "Great. Congrats." She tried to sound cheerful and wondered if she was pulling it off. "When do you leave?"

"That's the bad part. Very soon. The day after New Year's."

"Monday, January second," she said. She felt as if someone had knocked the wind out of her—hollow and aching inside.

"That's right." He nodded, looking as if he wondered how she knew the calendar so well.

Zoey knew the date because that was the same day her internship was supposed to start. "That's soon," she said. Nine days away.

"Yes, it is." He sighed. "But I don't want to turn it down or ask for a delay. It's a good spot and I might lose it."

"Sure. You need to take it. That was your plan. It's all worked out." He looked grateful for her understanding. Zoey did understand, and yet she suddenly felt distant from him. She knew that he cared for her—but apparently not that much if he could leave here so easily.

Lucy had been right, after all. Zoey had been foolish to get so involved with him. To think it was fine to fall for him, knowing this was only a brief stopover in his travels.

"I had some news this week, too," she said suddenly. "I got the internship."

She hadn't told anyone and hadn't even planned to tell James. But it had suddenly spurted out. Maybe she wanted him to know interesting things were happening in her life, too?

"Wow, that's great. I knew they would pick you." He hugged her close a moment and stepped back. "When do you start?"

Zoey slid her glance away from his. "I don't start, actually. I still can't take it."

"Did your parents say that?" His tone was protective, as if he wanted to argue with her parents on her behalf.

"You're the only one who knows. I don't want to put them in that spot right now. My father just had the worst week of his life." Somewhat of an exaggeration, but not much. "I know he still needs me to manage the diner, and I don't mind so much now. It's only a few weeks. I can stick it out."

James sighed. "You're very noble, on top of all your other wonderful qualities. I don't think I'd be nearly as selfless."

Zoey didn't bother to debate. She didn't think so, either.

"I think it's wonderful that you love your family so much. I really do," James continued. "But what about your own life—your own goals? You're not a child anymore. You don't have to do what they say. The sooner you realize that, the better for you. Honestly, I'm just telling you from experience."

His well-meaning advice made her angry. She didn't need James Potter to tell her that she had her own life. What did he know about her life, anyway?

"I'm not doing this because my parents say I have to. Or even because I'm afraid they'll be angry and we'll argue. I'm doing it because I love them, James. I want to help my father. He worked very hard to be mayor. That's all he's ever wanted. You don't live here, so you don't get that part. He has this one chance to do it right. I want to give that to him, if I can. I certainly don't want to make it harder for him."

James stepped back, his expression serious. "You're right. I don't live here. I probably shouldn't butt in. But maybe I see things clearer because I don't have all that baggage in the way. It's a waste that you got this opportunity and you can't take it. What would your father do if you broke your leg or something? He would have to figure it out. I think you should go for it, Zoey, and not worry about what your parents say."

Zoey sighed and stared back at him. "Easy for you to say. You do whatever you like. You say you want to travel and write, but I think you just want to get away from your father. Run off to Peru. Good idea. Good for you," she nearly shouted. "I really don't need your advice. You don't understand my life at all."

James looked upset, and Zoey knew she had probably gone too far. But she couldn't help it. James suddenly seemed different to her. Not the caring, sensitive guy she had thought he was.

"I'm sorry," he said quickly. "I don't know how we got into this." He reached for her hand, but she pulled away and headed for the door, suddenly chilled.

She turned and met his glance one last time, her heart feeling as if it had just cracked open. "I'm sorry, James. I . . . can't do this. I don't do good-bye very well. I guess that's something else you don't really know about me."

She felt bad for unloading on him. And sorry now that she let herself get so involved with him in the first place. What she said was true. She didn't do good-bye very well, though she'd had more practice than most people.

She walked into the house through the side door, leaving James out on the porch with his thoughts. The party was thinning, but everyone was still so distracted, no one noticed her slip back in. She left her coat in the mudroom and took a moment to compose herself. Was she crying? She hoped not. She ran a tissue under her eyes and dabbed her nose.

She pulled off the bracelet James had given her and tucked it in her pocket. She would stick it in the back of a drawer when she got home. Maybe take it out someday, when thinking about James didn't hurt anymore.

Maybe when I'm old as Sophie, she decided.

CHAPTER FOURTEEN

⟊

*Y*OU'RE UP EARLY, GRANDMA. I THOUGHT YOU'D BE TIRED
    from the party."

"I'm fine. Never felt better." Sophie turned from the sink to find
James in the kitchen doorway, with bedhead and a day's growth of
beard shadowing his lean cheeks. He sure looked tired—and not in a
very good mood for Christmas Day.

"Merry Christmas, James."

"Merry Christmas, Grandma. I'm glad you got your Christmas
wish," he added. "Was the party all you'd hoped for?"

"Was it ever. And then some." She shook her head in disbelief.
"There's not even much cleaning up to do. Everyone pitched in before
they left. But I do want to get a few things in order. A few more folks
from church are coming by soon to help and take away all those folding chairs and tables we borrowed from Fellowship Hall."

"I can help with that." James sipped his coffee, staring into space again.

Sophie had rarely seen anyone so glum on Christmas and wondered what was going on. "There are still a few gifts to open. Why don't we do that later?" she suggested.

"Sure. Whenever you like."

"I already opened the gift Zoey left for me. A large-print Bible. Just what I wanted. Remember when I fell on the steps and was going on about it?"

James nodded, barely smiling. "I do. That was thoughtful of her."

"It was. As usual. I got her a little something, too. Maybe she can stop by this afternoon and open it."

"I think she's busy with her family."

Something in his tone piqued Sophie's radar—a hint of friction between them? But she didn't feel comfortable asking questions. Young people had to work things out for themselves. *What was meant to be, will be,* she reminded herself.

"Well, I'm sure to see her before the New Year. Before you go," she added, thinking of the plans James had made for his departure. "Did you tell her about Peru?"

"I told her last night. She was happy for me," he said in the same flat tone.

Sophie wondered now if that was it. It only made sense. Of course, Zoey was disappointed to see him go. And he felt bad, too. Anyone with eyes in their head could see how the two got on. It was a shame, but they were headed in different directions right now.

The good Lord did have a way of bringing people back together who belonged together, she knew that as well. Best to just let this settle, like a bottle of cream, and see what rises to the top.

"I'm going to put the extra dishes away in the china closet. You get a bite to eat for yourself," she told him.

"I'm not that hungry right now. Guess I overdid it at the party. I'll take Mac for a walk if you don't need me right now."

Macintosh loved to be outside, in any kind of weather, though Sophie could not recall the last time anyone had taken the dog for an official walk. He was an independent old hound who walked himself. But she could see that James was restless and a bit dispirited. She thought fresh air would do him good.

"Good idea. He'll follow you. But take some treats in your pocket in case he goes chasing a rabbit or some other critter."

The dog knew he was being talked about and jumped up from his bed. He ran to James and put both paws on the young man's knees, staring up with an imploring look.

"Okay, buddy. You're on. Let me get my coat and gloves."

Sophie was already in the dining room, working on her dishes, when she heard them leave. She returned to the kitchen a short time later and stood drying another stack of dishes that needed to be stored.

A knock sounded on the side door and she checked the time. Church volunteers already? It seemed too early for that. She opened the door to find her new neighbors, Melissa and Tom Quinn, a young couple who had moved into the area a few months ago. She had seen them last night at the party.

"Merry Christmas, Sophie. I hope we're not disturbing you?"

"Not at all, come on in. I was just cleaning up a bit."

"I heard people talking about that last night, and we came to help. Tom brought you some firewood," Melissa said, turning to her husband.

"You must have used at least a cord last night," Tom said. "We have plenty. I'll stack it on your porch later."

"Thank you so much. That's very generous of you. I was wondering what my son would say when he saw how low that pile is," she added with a laugh. "Take off your coats. Would you like some coffee or tea? I was just about to sit down a minute."

Melissa took off her coat and reached into her big leather bag. She handed Sophie a parcel wrapped in a cloth. "The wood is sort of a Christmas present. This is, too."

Sophie unwrapped the cloth and found a beautiful handmade bowl with a dark blue glaze.

"Isn't this beautiful? I love the color. It's perfect for my kitchen," she added, feeling a tight spot in her heart, wondering how long she would even have her own kitchen. But the girl could not have known that. She meant only good.

"Melissa made it. She's a potter," Tom said proudly.

"Are you? My granddaughter Miranda is an artist, a jewelry maker. She used to have a studio right out there in the barn."

Melissa glanced at Tom. "Yes, we know. We were talking to her last night."

"She told us that you're planning on selling your property, the house and the orchard?"

Sophie nodded. "Yes, I am. I have to. It's gotten too much for me, and my children have been after me awhile to go. The orchard especially is hard to manage at my age . . . though it never felt like work," she added. "I grew up here. I was born right in this house, and I've lived here ever since."

Melissa smiled sympathetically. "That must make it even harder."

"It does," Sophie said. "Or it will, once I sell and go. My children are going to put the place up right after the New Year. I don't know how long I'll stay after that. My grandson James has been here the last few weeks, but he's leaving in a few days, too."

"You can't live alone here, is that it?" Tom asked.

"I'd stay until I died in my bed," Sophie said honestly. "But I have to see common sense, too. I can't stay all alone anymore. The winters are too long and hard. I suppose I could find a companion of some kind. But my kids say, just let it go. So . . . here we are."

She looked up at the young couple, realizing she had been lost in her own worries and probably rambling. "I'm sorry, I didn't mean to bore you with my troubles. So, tell me about yourselves. Your aunt left you a little cottage down the road, Melissa?" she recalled. "On the pond near the Morgan property?"

"That's the one. We need to make some improvements, but it's very comfortable, for now," Melissa said. "Tom grew up in Vermont, and I grew up in the Berkshires. We met in college and lived in Portland awhile. But we both wanted to move back to a more rural place."

"Cape Light is perfect for you, then," Sophie said.

"Almost," Tom agreed. "Right now, we're looking for a piece of land to cultivate. I studied agriculture. I've been working on organic farms, and I'm ready to start my own."

"Good for you. You know, my grandson was just telling me there are a lot of young people interested in farming again. I didn't really believe him . . . but here you are."

"Yes, here we are." Melissa smiled at her.

Sophie suddenly understood the reason for their visit. Aside from the lovely Christmas gifts.

"Do you think you'd be interested in selling just your property, Sophie—the orchard and outbuildings?" Tom asked.

"We don't really need the house. We're not sure we can afford the property with the house, too," Melissa said honestly.

"Or maybe you would consider leasing the land to us, and we would cultivate it? I would keep the orchard," he said quickly. "Though I'd turn it green."

Sophie's head was spinning. Were these young folks sitting at her kitchen table—who suddenly looked like angels to her, complete with halos and wings—really offering to buy the orchard, to keep her trees and take good care of them? To even let her keep living in the house if she liked? She pressed her hand to her chest. She could barely breathe.

Melissa looked at her with alarm. "Sophie, are you all right?" Melissa jumped up from her chair, looking ready to administer first aid or call 911.

Sophie caught her breath and laughed. "I'm perfectly fine, dear. I'm just so happy, I don't know whether to laugh or cry. You can't know what this means to me, to hear you say you'd like to buy the orchard and keep growing apples. And I can stay in this house, too." She shook her head. She was crying now and took a tissue from her pocket to dry her tears. "You can't know. It's an absolute . . . miracle," she said finally.

Melissa reached over and touched Sophie's hand. "You'd be helping us, too," she said. "We've been looking for months for the right place. We know you probably have to talk this over with your family. We don't want to create any problems for you, or any trouble. But this place is just perfect for us. It would mean the world to us if we could work this out."

"It's our dream come true," Tom said.

Sophie lifted her head and smiled at him. "I know . . . that's what makes it perfect. Now that you two have found your way here, I feel certain in my heart that it *will* work out."

Sophie heard the side door open and then Mac's paws clicking on the wooden floor. He raced into the kitchen, straight to his water bowl, where he lapped furiously. James soon followed, his cheeks red from the cold and his hair wind tossed. Or maybe he hadn't combed it yet. He had taken a shower but he had not shaved, Sophie noticed. Was he growing a beard for Peru?

"This is my grandson James," Sophie said. "Maybe you've already met?"

"Yes, last night when he bore a strange resemblance to Santa." Tom stood up and offered James his hand. "Nice to see you, James. Merry Christmas."

"Merry Christmas," James said to both of them. He turned to Sophie. "Your dog took me for quite a hike, Grandma. I checked the trees. It doesn't look like the storm did any damage. But some of the wire supports on the new row of Granny Smith saplings were loose. I can fix that for you before I go."

"You sound like you know your way around an orchard," Tom said.

"A little. I used to stay here for a few weeks every summer. My grandpa would always have us in the orchard, helping him. We used to call it Apple Camp."

Melissa laughed. "What a good idea! I'm sure a lot of eco-minded parents would sign their children up for that camp."

Sophie laughed, too. "You'll have to jot that down. It's always nice to figure out a few ways to bring in some extra money. I kept bees and had a cutting garden, too. We had a little shed on the road that sold fresh flowers, honey, fruit, and my pies and preserves."

James looked confused. He turned to Tom. "Are you thinking of opening up an orchard around here?"

"Yes, they are," Sophie answered. "You remember those young farmers you were telling me about? Well, here they are. Melissa and Tom want to buy my property and keep the trees and grow vegetables on the land, too. Isn't that amazing news?"

James looked stunned. He slowly smiled. "That is amazing. I know what I said, but—"

"You didn't really believe it," she finished for him. "Well, I did. All things are possible with God, James."

"I guess so, Grandma. This is certainly proof."

Someone knocked on the door, then pushed it open. "It's just me, Sophie," Sam Morgan called out. "We're here to pick up the tables and chairs. We'll start with the stack on the porch."

James rose and pulled his jacket on. "I'll help them."

"We will, too," Melissa said as she and Tom got up to follow. She turned to Sophie for a moment. "We'll talk more about the details. Can we call you tomorrow? Or maybe you'd like us to deal with a realtor?"

"You can deal with me," Sophie said quickly. "I'm still the owner here." She was reminding herself as well, she realized. She didn't need Bart and some real estate broker raising all sorts of objections and hurdles for these young people. *We'll get our ducks in order first,* she decided. *Then I'll tell them.*

I trust you to iron out the practical details of all this, Lord, she added, offering a silent prayer. *You've taken me this far; I know you won't let me down now.*

SOPHIE WAS THANKFUL THAT IN THE DAYS AFTER CHRISTMAS, NONE of her children mentioned putting her house up for sale, or any of the heavy issues that had hovered over their holidays. Maybe they had agreed among themselves to give her a few days' grace—to simply savor the success of her Christmas party and recuperate from that event.

Or maybe they were all too busy with their own lives.

Whatever the reason, she was thankful. The days between Christmas and New Year's Eve provided just enough time for her to talk over the sale and terms with Melissa and Tom. And enough time for them to get their finances in order and even get a preapproval from the bank for a mortgage.

She still hadn't quite figured out how to share the news with her family when Bart called on Thursday night. "I was thinking of coming up tomorrow," Bart said. "I want to say good-bye to James before he leaves for Peru."

James was leaving Monday. It was getting close. But Sophie had a feeling Bart had other business on his mind as well.

"That would be fine, Bart. I'll tell him you're coming. I'll make a nice lunch," she added.

Once they had hung up, Sophie wished her son would come that very night. She felt suddenly on edge and wanted to get the conversation over with, though she felt it would be best to tell all three of the children at once.

God, give me strength. I'm leaving this in your hands. I'll do whatever pleases you, she promised.

She felt even more nervous the next day as she prepared for her son's visit. Her hands trembled, and she dropped a cup as she carried it to the table. Luckily, it was empty and didn't break.

James jumped up from his chair and picked it up for her. "Are you all right, Grandma?" He had been lost in his thoughts, writing in his book, but now carefully helped her into a chair.

I might ask you the same, she nearly replied. He had been moping around the house the last few days, ever since Christmas Eve.

Maybe having second thoughts about his trip? Or maybe it was something going on with Zoey? Zoey had stopped by for a few minutes the day after Christmas, but James had been out and she hadn't asked after him.

"I'm fine, dear. Just some nerves about seeing your father. He and your aunts have been quiet as mice lately about selling the house. But I have a feeling that's why he's really coming."

"You haven't told them about Melissa and Tom?"

"Not yet. I want to tell them all at once. And I needed a few days to work things out with the Quinns. We haven't put anything in writing yet, but we agreed on a price. I think it's a fair one, and I hope your father agrees."

"It sounds serious."

"It is. I gave them my word. They have the means to buy this place and a letter from the bank to prove it. But I expect a landslide of objections from your father and your aunts."

"I do, too," James said. "But I'm in your corner, Grandma. I think this is a great solution for you. I hope they can see that."

"I do, too, dear." She patted his arm.

The doorbell rang. Sophie looked at James. Only strangers rang her doorbell. "I'll get it," James offered.

"No, let me." Sophie took off her apron and smoothed her dark red dress. Mac trotted after her, barking along the way. She pulled the door open and was surprised to see Fran Tulley.

The Tulleys had not come to her party. Power had been restored to their street, and Sophie had heard in church that Fran and Tucker had a houseful, with their married children home for Christmas.

Sophie was not sure why Fran would be all the way out here today, but thought it might be some church business. Along with her purse, Fran had a pile of folders tucked under one arm.

"Nice to see you, Fran. Did you have a good holiday?"

"It was wonderful. My son and daughter-in-law are still here. I wasn't going to work at all this week, but I told Bart I could spare some time today."

Sophie was confused now. "Bart asked you to come here?"

"Yes, he said to come around noon. He told me you're ready to list the property, and he wants me to work up an asking price." Fran looked surprised and embarrassed. "Are you sure he didn't tell you? We've all been so busy with the storm and the holiday, it's easy to forget things."

Sophie paused and counted to three before answering. It was so easy to tell old people they had forgotten something. *Did I do that, too, when I was younger?*

"Maybe that's what happened. *Bart* must have forgotten to tell me he asked you here," she said mildly. She noticed another car turn onto the property and recognized her son's blue sedan. "Here he comes now. No harm done. We'll work this out." She ushered Fran inside and shut the door. "Bart will be a while. He drives up that lane very slowly."

"It is bumpy. You really need to pave it," Fran said as she followed Sophie into the kitchen.

Sophie caught her grandson's eye and smiled. "People say that. I guess we'll see."

Fran took off her coat and quickly set up shop at the kitchen table, with a notebook computer, folders that said BOWMAN REAL ESTATE, and a long yellow pad.

Bart soon came through the side door without knocking. He stamped some snow off his feet and called out from the mudroom, "I'm here, Mother. Is Fran here yet? I'm sorry, I forgot to tell you she was coming."

Sophie glanced at Fran. "That's all right. I guessed something like that must have happened."

Bart walked in and kissed her cheek, then greeted Fran and James. Her grandson had begun setting out the lunch she had made, fixings for sandwiches and salads.

But Bart didn't seem interested in eating. "I thought it would be a good idea to let Fran look over the property while I'm here. We need to get started with the listing."

"Yes, dear, I understand. Let's all have a bite first. No need to rush, is there?"

Fran glanced at Bart, then back at Sophie. "I've already had some lunch, but I wouldn't mind coffee."

"Coming up." James was at the stove and served coffee all around.

Sophie sat down at the head of the table and waited for James to return. "Let's say a little blessing over the meal." Her guests bowed their heads and joined hands. "Dear Lord, thank you for a wonderful Christmas. As you can see, we're still enjoying your bounty and the leftovers. Please watch over all of us in the new year and keep James safe in his travels. Most of all, please keep us mindful of your word. Help us trust in you with all our hearts and lean not on our own understanding. In all our ways help us submit to you, and know that you will make our paths straight."

Sophie lifted her head and smiled. She glanced at her son. She knew he had faith, but her open way of expressing her own made him uneasy at times. He cleared his throat and looked down at the table. "Very nice blessing, Mother."

"Thanks, son. The words just came to me. That's the way it is sometimes. Try some of that Virginia ham, it's very tasty. And there's turkey, too."

She passed her son a platter and then passed a bowl of potato salad to Fran, who had decided she was hungry after all. "What a pretty bowl," Fran said.

"A Christmas gift from a new friend, Melissa Quinn. She and her husband, Tom, just moved in down the road. That old cottage on the pond, near the Morgan property?"

"I know the one. It was passed on in a family trust," Fran replied.

"That's right," Sophie said. Mac started barking and ran to the side door before they heard a knock. Bart was about to bite into the sandwich he'd built for himself, but paused. "Must be Evelyn. I told her I'd be here."

Sophie was not surprised. Her son had planned an ambush, but she was well prepared.

"I'll get it, Grandma," James said.

"You sit. I'll see who's there." She glanced out the kitchen window as she headed to the mudroom, happy to see the Quinns' green truck parked behind Bart's car.

Lord, if I'm doing the wrong thing, I'm sure you'll let me know pretty quickly, she silently prayed. Then she pulled open the door and welcomed the young couple in.

"I hope we're not here too early," Tom said.

"You said noon, but we thought you might want to visit with your son awhile," Melissa added.

Sophie helped them off with their coats and herded them toward the kitchen. "Right on time. We were just sitting down for lunch."

The curious stares of Fran and Bart greeted Sophie and her guests as they walked in. "This is my son, Bart Potter, and Fran Tulley, a friend from church," she explained, not wanting to scare them.

Fran looked surprised at that introduction, but didn't contradict her. "This is Melissa and Tom Quinn, my new neighbors. We were just talking about you. Fran was admiring that bowl you gave me," Sophie explained.

The Quinns stood beside her, looking a bit uneasy. Bart jumped up and offered his hand. Sophie had taught her children good manners, and he had not forgotten.

"Have a seat, you two. Have a bite to eat. Get them some coffee or tea, James," Sophie told her grandson as she sat. She would have done it herself, but she didn't dare leave the couple alone with Bart and Fran.

Bart glanced at his mother curiously, as if to say, "We have family business to discuss. Why in the world did you invite them here?"

Sophie ignored his dark looks. Fran looked confused, too. "So . . . how do you like Cape Light? Have you been in the cottage very long?" Fran asked politely.

"We came in September," Melissa said. "We like it very much."

"The cottage suits them fine," Sophie jumped in. "But they've been looking for some property to cultivate. Tom's studied organic farming, and he likes the idea of apples," she added. "So we talked about them buying this place, and we've come to an agreement."

Fran sat back in her seat, looking the most surprised. She turned to Bart. Bart looked surprised as well, but Sophie could tell from the grim set of his mouth he had been expecting her to toss up some obstacle to his reasonable, well-meaning plan.

"A deal to buy the orchard? Well . . . I guess we can consider all offers," he said in a smooth tone. "Once Fran works up the figures. But we were hoping for a buyer who would take the house and land. It will be harder to sell the pieces separately."

Tom seemed about to speak, but Sophie held up her hand. "That's just it—why it works so well for me and why I've given my word to them." She caught her son's eye with a look he knew well. "If the orchard is taken care of, I see no reason why I can't stay on in the house. I plan to find a nice companion who will live here and help around the house, as needed."

Bart shook his head. "Mother, we've been through all this. You promised us," he reminded her.

"I did," Sophie agreed. "But that was when I thought I couldn't burden you and your sisters with worrying about me living here all alone and taking care of the property, too. It seemed selfish to put that responsibility on you, along with worrying about my well-being. But now these young people have appeared out of the blue. They love the trees and will take good care of them. That was part of my prayers, too."

"It would be easy to divide the house and property," Fran said. "I've already looked into that question." She searched through her folders and flipped one open.

Bart glanced in her direction and back at his mother. "That still doesn't solve the question of you staying here."

"It does for me, son. Don't you see? With these lovely people taking over the orchard, it's a sign that I am meant to stay. My dearest prayer is to spend the rest of my days—be it one or one thousand— right under this roof. There's nothing wrong with me but old age, thank the Lord. With a companion, I'll be fine. I'm going to try. No matter what you or your sisters say."

Bart looked about to object again and just shook his head.

He turned to Tom Quinn. "I don't know what sort of agreement you have with my mother. But, as you can see, the issue is more complicated than she's told you."

"I think we've struck a fair price, sir, if that's what you're worried about." Tom also had a folder of papers with him and handed it across the table to Bart.

"Here's a list of recent sales of comparable properties," Tom said.

"And we have a letter from our banker there, too. There shouldn't be any problem with a mortgage," Melissa added.

James had been so quiet that Sophie had almost forgotten he was there. He suddenly jumped up in his chair. "Dad, I think we should go outside with Tom and Melissa and walk the property. They have a lot of great ideas for the orchard and the land. We can show them the equipment in the apple shed and talk about the sale of that as well."

Bart looked up at his son, seeming surprised at the idea. "All right. I could use a breath of fresh air." He got up from his chair and looked back at his plate. "Save my lunch, Mother. I barely got to eat a bite."

Sophie nodded. "Take your time. It will be right here."

"I think I'll be going, too," Fran said. "It doesn't look like you need my help after all."

"I'm sorry to take you out of your way today, Fran. As you can see, this is all new to me," Bart apologized.

Fran shrugged. "All's well that ends well." She smiled at Sophie as she pulled on her coat. "I couldn't quite imagine you leaving this place, either," she confessed. "You're like a village landmark or something by now. I mean that in the nicest way."

"That's a very nice compliment, Fran." Sophie laughed. "Maybe I should get a bronze plaque and wear it around my neck. Then my children would stop pestering me."

Fran laughed and hugged her good-bye. "Thanks for the lunch. I can find my way to the door. Happy New Year, everyone!" she called back.

"Happy New Year, Fran," Sophie answered, feeling that her own prospects for the new year were ever so much brighter.

As Fran left from the front door, Bart, James, and the Quinns left from the side of the house. Sophie ran to the kitchen window to watch them begin a tour of the property.

James was such a clever boy. That inspiration had come from Heaven above, actually, she corrected herself. Either way, she was sure that some time with Tom and Melissa would convince her son they were the perfect people to take over the Potter land. Bart acted as if he didn't care who bought the place, but she knew, deep down, he felt an attachment to the orchard and his family home—when he was able to silence the very practical, businesslike voice inside him.

Just as the group emerged from the barn, she saw Evelyn's car pull up. Sophie was relieved to see Bart summon her over and introduce her to the Quinns. She had not been looking forward to explaining it all to Evelyn while the others were out.

"Thanks again, Lord. It's going along beautifully," Sophie said as she watched from the window, washing up a few dishes.

A while later, the group came back inside. Sophie had fresh hot tea and coffee and a platter of cake and cookies ready. Sweets did tend to help people act and speak sweeter to each other, she had found.

"Did you have a good walk?" she asked as they came in.

"We did," Bart replied. "We had a good talk, too. There are some more details to work out, of course. But I'm tending to agree with you, Mother. I think the Quinns are good buyers for the property." He glanced at his sister. "What do you say, Evelyn?"

Evelyn shrugged. "I trust the business details to you, Bart. But I'm happy to see the orchard go to a family who will keep it running. I know that means the world to Mother."

Sophie didn't reply. Her heart felt too full of gratitude, and her eyes felt watery, too. "Thank you both. I knew that once you got to know Melissa and Tom, you would understand that I was doing the right thing."

"In that respect," Bart agreed, not yet letting her off the hook for the living-alone idea. "The conversation is not entirely over, Mother."

"No, it isn't," Evelyn agreed.

"We can see you have more to talk about, and we don't want to intrude," Tom said. He offered his hand to Bart and then to Evelyn. "Please call me soon to iron out the rest of the agreement."

"I will, Tom. Good to meet you," Bart said. Good-byes were exchanged all around, and the Quinns showed themselves to the door. James went outside with them. "I'm going to close up the barn and find Mac. He's been out long enough, too."

"Good idea. Thanks, honey." Sophie faced her children and took a steadying breath. Neither of them had sat at the table yet, and she didn't want to, either. Best to have this out on her two feet, she decided.

"Bart told me you plan to stay in the house," Evelyn said.

"With a live-in companion," Sophie cut in. "I can find one easily—"

Evelyn held up her hand, like a crossing guard directing traffic, and Sophie's heart fell. "That may not solve our problem. You had James here with you, and yet you managed to fall."

"That could happen at your house as well," Sophie pointed out reasonably. "Even if you put me in a wheelchair, there's no guarantee I'll never take a spill. But I aim to hire a professional, someone who's been trained to care for an old woman like me."

Evelyn and Bart exchanged a glance. "Bart and I talked it over outside," Evelyn said at last. "If you hire a professional caregiver, and if you agree to follow some basic safety guidelines, we're willing to try it . . . for six months," she added.

"We'll be keeping a close eye on you. No driving or cleaning out gutters, and no climbing ladders of any kind," Bart reminded her. "If there's the least reason for concern, we'll have to revisit this question."

"And we get to meet and approve of the person you hire to live here. Before you give your solemn word again, Mother," Evelyn added.

Sophie felt her cheeks grow warm. She had acted behind their backs with the Quinns, it was true. But she believed the Lord forgave her for that. As Fran had said, all's well that ends well.

"Of course you'll help interview my companion. I had no intention of doing it without you," she promised. She suddenly felt light, almost giddy with happiness. "So it's all settled? I can stay in my house—me and Mac?"

"Yes, it's settled," Bart said gruffly. "Amen to that."

"Amen," Evelyn echoed. "I'll call Una. She's been burning up my cell phone line."

"Yes, call your sister. Give her the good news. You're very good children, and I love you all dearly. I don't tell you enough," she added.

Evelyn and Bart glanced at each other and laughed.

"I would never say that," Bart replied, patting his mother's shoulder. "But we do deserve a little special credit today."

She agreed with that. And she was sure the good Lord did, too.

Thank you for bringing them both around to my point of view, she said silently. *Thank you for this happy day and all its blessings.*

CHAPTER FIFTEEN

On New Year's Eve, the diner closed at three o'clock. It wouldn't open again until Monday. Christmas and New Year's Day were practically the only days of the year Charlie closed entirely.

Zoey watched the clock. It had been a very slow and boring day, even though Saturdays were usually busy. She had spent most of the time at a table in the back, figuring out her schedule for the next semester. She was working with just her mother and father, but there had been hardly any customers all day. She had harbored some crazy fantasy James would stop in to say good-bye, though part of her knew it was best if she didn't see him at all.

They hadn't been in touch since Christmas Eve. She had managed to avoid his work shifts; it wasn't that hard, since she made up the schedules. He was leaving on Monday, so she really ought to stop thinking about him now.

Still, she wondered what he was doing tonight to bring in the New Year. Packing, probably? That wouldn't take too long. Everything he owned fit in a backpack. Her friend Laurel was having some people from school over, and Zoey had promised to go there. Better than staying all alone in her room while her parents had company downstairs. She would only sit around moping about James—and might even give in to the ever-present urge to text or call him.

And the point of that would be? It's not like he's going to come back from Peru and see me on weekends, she reminded herself. *Maybe someday I'll write him a letter.* Though she doubted she would ever work up the nerve to do that, either.

"Three o'clock, on the nose," Lucy announced. She had the broom and dustpan out to sweep up. "Flip the sign and see what your father's up to, will you, honey? I need to get home and get ready for my company."

As eager to leave as her mom, Zoey ran back into the kitchen. Charlie had it well under control. "You go help your mother. Remind her to shut off the ice maker."

"All clear in the kitchen. Dad said to shut off the ice maker. I can do it," Zoey announced as she walked out again.

Lucy didn't answer. Zoey looked around for her and found her at the back of the diner, standing next to the table where Zoey's laptop and books were spread out. Lucy looked up from a sheet of paper she was reading and stared at her.

"Zoey, what is this?"

Zoey walked closer and glanced at the paper her mother held out to her.

"How did you find that? Did you go through my things?" Zoey said, feeling suddenly and totally upset.

"I found it on the floor, under your chair. You got that internship and you didn't even tell us?"

Zoey stepped back. She nodded, a lump in her throat. "I went on the interview a few weeks ago. For the experience," she added. "I never thought I'd get it."

Her mother shook her head. "I'm not mad at you for that part. But why didn't you tell us you were chosen? This is a big honor, honey. Why did you keep it a secret?"

"I knew I couldn't take it. I already promised Dad I'd work here over winter break. He was going through so much with the storm, I didn't want to make more problems for everybody. So I thanked them and said it wasn't going to work out."

Lucy stared at her, her eyes wide and glassy. She let out a long breath. "You just sit here. Don't move until I say," she warned.

Zoey sat down. She knew her mother was going to tell her father. But there was nothing she could do.

Lucy marched to the kitchen and pushed open the door. "Charlie? Come out here."

"I'm almost done, Lucy. I'll be right out."

"Come out here now. We need you," her mother insisted.

She heard her father grumble and the squeak of his kitchen shoes as he hurried out to the dining room. "What is it—that ice maker leaking again?"

Lucy held out the letter. "Remember that internship Zoey wanted? Look at this. They chose her, out of everyone who applied."

Her father took the letter and read it quickly, then looked back at her mother. "When did this happen?"

"I don't know. Ask Zoey. She says she already turned it down, because she promised you she would work here."

Charlie stared at her. "Zoey . . . you didn't, did you?"

Zoey nodded. "I sent an email yesterday. I said I was very honored and grateful, but I had to help with a family situation. I didn't want to bother you, Dad," she explained. "You were dealing with so much in town with the storm. I promised I'd help you. I didn't want to go back on my word."

"You did that for me?"

Zoey just nodded. "I want to help you, Dad."

He shook his head and cleared his throat. "Honey, that's just about the nicest thing I ever heard. I feel awful about this—"

"See? That's just what I mean," Zoey interrupted. "I didn't want you to feel bad. That's why I didn't tell you."

"Well, now we know," Lucy said gently. "I don't think it's any accident I found that letter, either."

"Your mother's right. You take this job. It's important, and a lot better use of your time than working here. I see that now. I'll figure it out," Charlie promised.

"Besides, I changed my schedule at the hospital for January. I'm working more nights and can help here during the daytime," Lucy added.

"And I'll find someone else to fill in," Charlie promised. "For goodness' sake, if I can dig this town out after the storm, practically singled-handed, I can figure this out, too."

"*But I already turned it down.*" Zoey couldn't hide her frustration. "They probably gave the spot to someone else by now."

Charlie pulled out his cell phone, pushed his glasses on, and started dialing the center, reading the phone number off the very fine print on the letter. "I'll call them right now and tell them your plans changed."

Lucy checked her watch. "Do you think the place is still open?"

Zoey knew it was. There were plenty of parents who had to work a full day on Saturday, even if it was New Year's Eve.

"If it's closed, we can leave a message. Maybe they didn't fill the spot. And if they did, maybe they'll take you, too," her father said. "Never hurts to ask."

Zoey heard the line ring and felt mortified. She couldn't let her father speak for her, as if she were an immature high school kid. She snatched the phone away, then walked as far as possible from her parents.

Beth Foster, the woman who had interviewed her, answered. Zoey quickly explained why she was calling.

Ms. Foster heard her out and took a moment before she replied. "We did offer the placement to another candidate, Zoey. But I was very sorry that you couldn't accept. I think, under the circumstances, we can take two interns this winter. Why don't you come in on Monday and we'll figure it out? There's an orientation from nine to three."

"Thank you so much. I'll be there. Thank you, Beth." She turned to her parents, who both looked very nervous, waiting to hear the answer.

"Ms. Foster told me to come in on Monday. They might be able to use two interns."

Charlie walked over and hugged her. "What did I tell you? Persistence wins the day."

Of course her father would have a corny motto to mark the occasion. Not quite her story, but Zoey didn't argue. She was too happy.

Lucy hugged her, too. "I'm glad I grabbed the broom today. Please don't keep things from us, honey. Even if you think it's for our own good?" She stood back and caught Zoey's eye. "We're certainly not perfect parents, but we always want the best for you. Please trust in that. We love you so much."

"I know," Zoey said, hugging her back. "It's totally mutual."

* * *

"I'm glad we got here early. Not a seat left in the house." Emily's mother had to shout to be heard above the din in Village Hall. She gazed around at the standing-room-only crowd with an astonished expression. "Quite a turnout for the day after New Year's. I hope Bates can keep things under control. Though I doubt he's learned his lesson."

"Never mind Bates. I hope the crowd bodes well for our side," Ezra said.

"I do, too. But it's hard to say," Emily answered honestly.

She had expected high attendance at this meeting, the first of the new year. The open-space group had been working hard to encourage their members to make their voices heard tonight. Their opponents had apparently done the same.

Charlie and the council entered through a side door and took seats at the long table in the front of the room. Emily noticed that Charlie had his gavel handy again.

"Welcome, everyone," he began. "Thanks for coming out tonight. It's another cold one out there, but at least we all have our heat on, and we can put that ski underwear away for a while. That storm does make you grateful for the little things." A few people laughed, including Ezra, earning a sharp look from Lillian.

"First up on the agenda tonight, the proposal for new zoning. Town residents will have the opportunity to vote this law onto the books at a special election . . ."

He paused to put on his reading glasses and glanced down at a binder that was open on the table in front of him. Emily recognized it—the town bylaws. At least the bylaws would be handy when the open-space group made their move. She spotted Martin Becker sitting on the edge of his chair, a sheaf of papers in his lap, looking like a tiger about to spring on his prey.

"The bylaws state that a special election can be called by a majority of the council within forty-five days of the motion passing." Charlie looked up at the audience. "I open the floor to comments. But I'm warning all of you, if it gets disorderly in here, the council will vote. Whether you all had your say or not."

"He's a megalomaniac," Lillian muttered. "He's going to force this through, no matter how many people object."

"Calm down, Mother. Let's just listen." Lillian knew the open-space group had come with a plan to derail their opposition, but Emily had not divulged the details to her—or to anyone, except for Dan. It was vital that their plan did not get out and give the zoning group a chance to counter it.

George Krueger was the first at the microphone. "The residents of Cape Light want closure on this question. We need to put it to a vote, the sooner the better. I say the council votes on the motion and we set a date for the village to vote."

Fran Tulley was the next in line. "I agree with George. Most of us voted you in on this question, Charlie. We'd like to see you move along with your promises and vision for the village."

Her mother made a huffing sound. "Of course she would say that. She's just seeing dollar signs, all those big properties on the Beach Road broken up and sold to builders."

Ezra shook his head. "Doesn't look good for our side. Oh dear, what a night."

Emily felt bad, seeing him so distressed, but Martin Becker was next at the microphone. She touched Ezra's arm. "Look, it's Martin. Don't worry. He's got something up his sleeve."

"Well, it better be good," Lillian whispered back.

"Mayor Bates, town council members, I'm speaking for the residents who oppose new zoning laws, those who joined the open-space group and signed the petitions we've presented to you."

"We know who you are, Marty," Charlie said. "Just get on with it. We don't have all night."

"All right. Here's a letter from the county, signed by the county executive, the county zoning supervisor, and the county's supervisor of environmental impact." Martin held the letter up, displaying the bold stamp of the county on the letterhead. "I won't bother to read it aloud, but it's an order to the town council to freeze this question for twenty-four months so that a full review by an independent group can be conducted."

"What do they think they're going to review?" George Krueger interrupted.

"They'll be looking at the effects of the new zoning proposal on the area's infrastructure and environment, and particularly the impact on wildlife and the local ecosystem."

Charlie looked dumbfounded. Then his eyes narrowed. "That's a lot of official signatures, Marty. Congratulations. But what does the county have to do with our business? We're an incorporated village. We run our own show here."

"I understand," Martin said. "However, there is a bylaw in our village constitution that supports this action. I have a copy of that as well. In fact, an attorney at the county supervisor's office has also written a letter explaining that this is fully within their powers."

Emily watched Charlie's confident expression melt. He stood up and held out his hand. "Can I see that, please?"

"Of course. I have copies for each of you." Martin walked up to the table and handed out the letter. He turned to the audience.

"We also have copies for residents. If anyone would like one, please raise your hand."

Every hand in the room went up, and the noise level suddenly rose. "Ho, ho! Way to go, Marty!" Ezra laughed and slapped his knee. "What a brilliant maneuver!"

Lillian gave Emily a squinty stare. "A well-intentioned man. But I see the handiwork of a master here. This is your doing, Emily, isn't it?"

"I knew about it, but I couldn't tell anyone, Mother. Sorry."

"From the sound of it, you not only knew, you were the one who cooked this up. What does Martin Becker know of village bylaws?"

Emily smiled but didn't reply. "Look, the mayor is ready to speak. Let's be quiet."

Charlie had been in a huddle with the council members, their hands covering their microphones as they frantically whispered to each other. Carl Nelson, the village attorney, began searching the bylaws.

While Martin handed out information packets to the audience, Art Hecht walked up to the microphone. He waved his copy of the letter from the county.

"This is a load of baloney. It's our town, and we can do what we want without a bunch of county bureaucrats butting into our business." He looked up at Charlie and the town council. "Are you really going to give in to this without a fight?"

Charlie had returned to his seat, his back ramrod straight, his expression grim. He banged his gavel for the first time that evening.

"I understand you're upset, Art. But let's tone it down a notch.

Carl Nelson has just looked over the letter and checked the bylaws up here. It appears that this action is within the rights of the county, and our village must abide by this directive."

"You're kidding, right?" someone else shouted out.

Carl, the town attorney, leaned forward to speak. "This is not a request we can argue or fight. Not without the village taking the county to court, where we would probably lose and spend a great deal of money and also tie up this question for much longer than twenty-four months. The bylaws are very clear. I advise the town to comply."

"I agree with Carl," Charlie said. "And so does the rest of the council. We accept these documents into the minutes. The proposal for new zoning is tabled for twenty-four months, for a period of review, as so directed in this letter."

Charlie tapped his gavel. It wasn't exactly a bang, Emily noticed. She watched him shake his head, then scan the audience, his eyes finally finding her. She stared back at him and shrugged.

To her surprise, he smiled. It was the smile one would grant a worthy opponent across a battlefield. Emily smiled back.

"Twenty-four months? That's just enough time for a new mayor to come in," someone shouted out.

"You never know what's going to happen, fellas. This is politics," Charlie said. He cleared his throat and checked the agenda. "On to the next item. The town has finally signed a contract with K&B Carting . . ."

"That is enough time for a new mayor to come in. Or an oldie but goodie," Lillian murmured.

"Not a chance, Mother," Emily replied, though she did feel very happy and relieved to see the plan had worked.

"You say that now. But you've saved the village from certain disaster. From complete extinction, actually. Word will get out. They'll want you back, mark my words."

Word would get out if her mother had anything to do with it. But Emily had no time to get into this conversation again.

"I've got to go, Mother. Jessica and Sam will take you home. They're sitting across the room. We've already arranged it."

"Yes, I noticed them there. All right, you run along. Your work is done here."

"Good show, Emily. You should be very proud," Ezra added in a hushed tone. Emily touched his arm and thanked him as she slipped out of her seat and headed for an exit at the back of the room.

Once outside, she walked quickly down Main Street and met Dan and Jane at the Beanery.

"Did we win, Mom?" Jane greeted her.

"Yes, honey. *This* time, I think we did. I think the entire village won, for years to come."

"Someday, even Charlie will agree with that," Dan said.

"You never know. Stranger things have happened," Emily replied.

"Well, we're very proud of you, Jane and I," Dan said, glancing at his daughter. "I know I put up a fuss when you started to help that group, but I can see now it was very important and your help made all the difference."

"Thank you, honey. That's nice of you to say. But I know why you felt upset, both of you. I promise not to get carried away on any more causes. Honestly."

Dan took her hand. "But that's just the point, Emily. That's who you are. I was wrong to ask you to change totally. I know you're still trying to figure things out, to find your way after being mayor for so long. But we wouldn't want you any different."

"He's right, Mom," Jane agreed. "You wouldn't be you."

Emily suddenly felt as if she might cry. "I don't want to be mayor again, so you don't have to worry about that. But I probably will be drawn to causes and issues from time to time. I guess I can't help that," she admitted.

"As long as it's occasional, I won't object. And as long as it doesn't interfere with any vacation plans." Dan checked his watch. "Which reminds me, we'd better get moving, or we'll miss the talk."

Emily linked her arm in his as they left the café. Jane trailed alongside, toting a knapsack of schoolbooks and her laptop. They were headed for the library, where Emily and Dan were going to attend a presentation on ecotourism, to help plan their trip, and Jane was going to work on a research project.

Emily felt lighthearted, as if a load had been lifted. She was not only happy about the outcome of the zoning question but also relieved to put aside politics and focus on her family. They needed her love and attention as much as the village of Cape Light did. Even more.

No matter what her mother said, or how much she goaded or stroked Emily's ego, Emily was sure she would never want to be mayor again. But she could see now that she still wanted to serve and help. She always would. It was part of her DNA. These sideline efforts would never be the same as "running the show," as Charlie liked to say. But Emily thought now they might even be better.

ON THE TUESDAY AFTER NEW YEAR'S, ZOEY WOKE UP AND REALIZED that James was gone. He had taken off for his new life in South America.

Well, at least she, too, had a sort-of-new life, working at the center. It was a relief to be out of the diner, which just reminded her of him. She felt an aching emptiness deep inside—and regretted that she had not gotten in touch after their argument.

But he never made a move to get in touch with you, she reminded herself as she finally got out of bed. *Which probably means he didn't want any big farewell scene, either. Maybe this is the best way for both of us. Sophie must be wondering what happened, but she probably understands.*

Zoey didn't need to be at the center until noon, and Sophie had left a message on her cell phone Sunday, saying she had big news to share and asking Zoey to stop by sometime.

Zoey decided to stop at the orchard on her way to Beverly. She had been avoiding James since Christmas Eve, and the result was that she had also avoided her dear friend. Sophie needed her support now more than ever, with her move coming up. And Zoey planned to be there for her—now that the coast was finally clear to visit.

Zoey hadn't even told Sophie yet about the internship. She could hardly wait to see her friend's reaction.

She pulled up the bumpy private road and parked at the side of the house, behind Bella. She had just gotten out of her car when Mac raced out of the barn, barking and wagging his tail. Zoey expected to see Sophie follow. And saw James instead.

She felt shock and something else—something that was a lot like happiness. But she quickly covered over both reactions with what she hoped was a neutral expression.

"Hey, Zoey. Are you all right? You look a little pale. Like you just saw a ghost."

She lifted her chin, determined to keep her composure and not look as if she cared so much. *It's just as well to run into him,* she decided. *It's probably better to say good-bye and take this chance to talk things out, if we can.*

"I'm just surprised to see you. Weren't you supposed to leave yesterday?"

"Well, my plans changed. I got an offer to work on a different farm." He came closer and stood with his hands in the pockets of his jacket, his blue gaze fixed on her in a way she found unnerving.

"Is this another farm in Peru? Or that one in Chile you were talking about?"

"Actually, it's right here, in New England. It's not exactly a farm yet. It's an orchard, but new people are taking over, and they want to grow vegetables and herbs, and increase the honey production, too."

Zoey didn't understand at first. Then she thought he had to be teasing her. She squinted up at him. "You mean, *this* orchard?"

"I do." He looked as if he wanted to laugh but was trying hard not to.

"How can that be? Did Sophie find a buyer already? I didn't even know she put it up for sale. But she left me a message that she had some big news."

"It's big news, all right. You know my grandma. She has her own way of doing things. She found this young couple, the Quinns. They live down the road, and they just happened to be shopping around for an orchard." James laughed and shook his head. "But she's keeping the house, and she's going to stay here. With a live-in companion. And I'm going to stay here, too."

"You are?" Zoey's eyes grew wide. She blinked, not knowing if she wanted to laugh or cry.

"The Quinns offered me a job. And I decided to take it."

Zoey was so amazed by that news, she could hardly breathe. She looked out at the trees, then back at James. "I don't understand. Are you sure this is what you really want? Traveling around and having new experiences . . . that was your dream. I didn't mean to belittle it, either, when we had that fight. I said a lot of mean things on Christmas Eve. Things I wish I could take back now. I'm so sorry—"

"I'm sorry, too, Zoey." He met her gaze with a solemn look. "I should have gotten in touch with you and apologized. But I had some real thinking to do."

"Me, too." She had to summon her courage for what came next. "I'd be lying if I said I wasn't glad to hear that you're staying, James. But you had your heart set on traveling. I don't understand what's made you change your mind. I'd hate to think it was anything I said."

"No, not at all. But getting to know you has made me see a lot of things differently. There's plenty to write about right here, right under my nose. And I still want to visit all those places someday. But I know now it wouldn't be any fun without you, Zoey. My heart was set on traveling. But now it's set on you—stuck on you, I'd have to say. What do you think?"

Zoey felt her heart melt. He actually looked nervous, waiting for her answer. She reached up and looped her arms around his neck. "I think that traveling together to Peru, or anywhere with you, is an excellent plan. And I'm thinking it's going to be a really great new year. Which I didn't think at all a few days ago."

He smiled and pulled her close. "I feel the same about that, too. Happy New Year, Zoey."

"Happy New Year," she whispered back, knowing that she had never meant it more.

Their lips met in a deep, warm kiss. Zoey was swept away on a wave of joy and a feeling of connection and belonging to someone that she had never quite known before. When they finally parted, she noticed that James's eyes looked glossy and bright. Was he about to cry, too? She was sure a few tears of happiness had slipped from her eyes. They stared at each other and laughed.

"Let's walk a little. I'll show you some of the changes the Quinns want to make."

James put his arm around her shoulders, and she wound her arm around his waist. They headed toward the rows of apple trees, their steps timed perfectly together. Zoey knew she would remember this day for the rest of her life. She had never been quite so blissfully happy.

SOPHIE WATCHED THEM WALK INTO THE ORCHARD AND SIGHED. It was a relief to see James and Zoey make up. James had been a basket case ever since Christmas Eve. She'd had to bite her tongue a few times to avoid saying, "Just call her up. Talk it out."

But she didn't want to meddle. Though she did leave that message to get Zoey over here and get it over with. That wasn't meddling, exactly. Just stirring the pot.

They're both strong willed. But meant to be, she decided. *I wasn't worried, not really.*

She gazed out the window again and saw them in the distance now. Just a young couple, holding hands as they walked through the orchard. She saw herself and Gus. *We must have looked just like that, walking that same path, way back when. Everything comes full circle, doesn't it?* She closed her eyes, her gratitude for all that had come to pass these past few days welling up inside.

Thanks again, Lord, for all your help. For making everything that seemed so wrong turn out right. Much better than I could ever expect, or imagine.

I'll be right here when you need me. Until then, I'll enjoy the peace and joy in my heart. And the miracles you send every day in my world.

JEWISH SPIRITUALITY
From the Sixteenth-Century Revival
to the Present

World Spirituality

An Encyclopedic History of the Religious Quest

1. Asian Archaic Spirituality
2. European Archaic Spirituality
3. African and Oceanic Spirituality
4. South and Meso-American Native Spirituality
5. North American Indian Spirituality
6. Hindu Spirituality: Vedas through Vedanta
7. Hindu Spirituality: Postclassical and Modern
8. Buddhist Spirituality: Indian, Sri Lankan, Southeast Asian
9. Buddhist Spirituality: Chinese, Tibetan, Japanese, Korean
10. Taoist Spirituality
11. Confucian Spirituality
12. Ancient Near Eastern Spirituality: Zoroastrian, Sumerian, Assyro-Babylonian, Hittite
13. Jewish Spirituality: From the Bible to the Middle Ages
14. Jewish Spirituality: From the Sixteenth-Century Revival to the Present
15. Classical Mediterranean Spirituality: Egyptian, Greek, Roman
16. Christian Spirituality: Origins to the Twelfth Century
17. Christian Spirituality: High Middle Ages and Reformation
18. Christian Spirituality: Post-Reformation and Modern
19. Islamic Spirituality: Foundations
20. Islamic Spirituality: Manifestations
21. Modern Esoteric Movements
22. Spirituality and the Secular Quest
23. Encounter of Spiritualities: Past to Present
24. Encounter of Spiritualities: Present to Future
25. Dictionary of World Spirituality

Board of Editors and Advisors

Volume 14 of
World Spirituality:
An Encyclopedic History
of the Religious Quest

JEWISH SPIRITUALITY

FROM THE
SIXTEENTH-CENTURY REVIVAL
TO THE PRESENT

Edited by
Arthur Green

CROSSROAD • NEW YORK

1987
The Crossroad Publishing Company
370 Lexington Avenue, New York, NY 10017

World Spirituality, Volume 14
Diane Apostolos-Cappadona, Art Editor

Printed in the United States of America

Library of Congress Cataloging in Publication Data
(Revised for vol. 2)

Jewish spirituality.

(World spirituality ; v. 13–14)
Includes bibliographies and indexes.
Contents: v. 1. From the Bible through the Middle
Ages – [v.] 2. From the sixteenth-century revival to
the present.
1. Spiritual life–Judaism. 2. Spiritual life–
Biblical teaching. 3. Rabbinical literature–History
and criticism. 4. Judaism–History. 5. Judaism–
20th century I. Green, Arthur, 1941–
II. Series.
BM23.J487 1986   296.7   85-11287
ISBN 0-8245-0762-2 (v. 1)
ISBN: 0-8245-0763-0 (v. 2)

Contents

PREFACE TO THE SERIES   ix

INTRODUCTION   xi

ACKNOWLEDGMENTS   xvii

Part One: Renewal
The Post-Medieval Age

1   The Safed Revival and Its Aftermath
    R. J. Zwi Werblowsky   7

2   Halakhah and Kabbalah as Competing Disciplines of Study
    Jacob Katz   34

3   The Contemplative Practice of Yiḥudim
    in Lurianic Kabbalah
    Lawrence Fine   64

4   The Uplifting of Sparks in Later Jewish Mysticism
    Louis Jacobs   99

5   Typologies of Leadership and the Hasidic Ẓaddiq
    Arthur Green   127

6   ḤaBaD: The Contemplative Ascent to God
    Rachel Elior   157

7   Rabbi Israel Salanter and His Psychology of *Mussar*
     Immanuel Etkes   206

8   The Traditional Piety of Ashkenazic Women
     Chava Weissler   245

                    Part Two: Challenge
                     The Modern Age

9   Secularization, "Spirit," and the Strategies of
     Modern Jewish Faith
     Arnold M. Eisen   283

10 Law and Sacrament: Ritual Observance in
     Twentieth-Century Jewish Thought
     Paul Mendes-Flohr   317

11 Revelation and the Bible according to
     Twentieth-Century Jewish Philosophy
     Rivka Horwitz   346

12 Spiritual and Anti-Spiritual Trends in Zionism
     Ehud Luz   371

13 The Renewal of Jewish Spirituality: Two Views
     Laurence J. Silberstein   402

CONTRIBUTORS   433

PHOTOGRAPHIC CREDITS   435

INDEXES   437

Preface to the Series

THE PRESENT VOLUME is part of a series entitled World Spirituality: An Encyclopedic History of the Religious Quest, which seeks to present the spiritual wisdom of the human race in its historical unfolding. Although each of the volumes can be read on its own terms, taken together they provide a comprehensive picture of the spiritual strivings of the human community as a whole—from prehistoric times, through the great religions, to the meeting of traditions at the present.

Drawing upon the highest level of scholarship around the world, the series gathers together and presents in a single collection the richness of the spiritual heritage of the human race. It is designed to reflect the autonomy of each tradition in its historical development, but at the same time to present the entire story of the human spiritual quest. The first five volumes deal with the spiritualities of archaic peoples in Asia, Europe, Africa, Oceania, and North and South America. Most of these have ceased to exist as living traditions, although some perdure among tribal peoples throughout the world. However, the archaic level of spirituality survives within the later traditions as a foundational stratum, preserved in ritual and myth. Individual volumes or combinations of volumes are devoted to the major traditions: Hindu, Buddhist, Taoist, Confucian, Jewish, Christian, and Islamic. Included within the series are the Jain, Sikh, and Zoroastrian traditions. In order to complete the story, the series includes traditions that have not survived but have exercised important influence on living traditions—such as Egyptian, Sumerian, classical Greek and Roman. A volume is devoted to modern esoteric movements and another to modern secular movements.

Having presented the history of the various traditions, the series devotes two volumes to the meeting of spiritualities. The first surveys the meeting of spiritualities from the past to the present, exploring common themes that

A longer version of this preface may be found in Christian Spirituality: Origins to the Twelfth Century, *the first published volume in the series.*

can provide the basis for a positive encounter, for example, symbols, rituals, techniques. Finally, the series closes with a dictionary of world spirituality.

Each volume is edited by a specialist or a team of specialists who have gathered a number of contributors to write articles in their fields of specialization. As in this volume, the articles are not brief entries but substantial studies of an area of spirituality within a given tradition. An effort has been made to choose editors and contributors who have a cultural and religious grounding within the tradition studied and at the same time possess the scholarly objectivity to present the material to a larger forum of readers. For several years some five hundred scholars around the world have been working on the project.

In the planning of the project, no attempt was made to arrive at a common definition of spirituality that would be accepted by all in precisely the same way. The term "spirituality," or an equivalent, is not found in a number of the traditions. Yet from the outset, there was a consensus among the editors about what was in general intended by the term. It was left to each tradition to clarify its own understanding of this meaning and to the editors to express this in the introduction to their volumes. As a working hypothesis, the following description was used to launch the project:

> The series focuses on that inner dimension of the person called by certain traditions "the spirit." This spiritual core is the deepest center of the person. It is here that the person is open to the transcendent dimension; it is here that the person experiences ultimate reality. The series explores the discovery of this core, the dynamics of its development, and its journey to the ultimate goal. It deals with prayer, spiritual direction, the various maps of the spiritual journey, and the methods of advancement in the spiritual ascent.

By presenting the ancient spiritual wisdom in an academic perspective, the series can fulfill a number of needs. It can provide readers with a spiritual inventory of the richness of their own traditions, informing them at the same time of the richness of other traditions. It can give structure and order, meaning and direction to the vast amount of information with which we are often overwhelmed in the computer age. By drawing the material into the focus of world spirituality, it can provide a perspective for understanding one's place in the larger process. For it may well be that the meeting of spiritual paths—the assimilation not only of one's own spiritual heritage but of that of the human community as a whole—is the distinctive spiritual journey of our time.

EWERT COUSINS

Introduction

THIS SECOND VOLUME OF *Jewish Spirituality* takes us into two periods different from any that had preceded them and radically different from each other. The rapidity of change in the geographical locus of Jewish life, the political situation of Jewry, and the degree of loyalty of Jews to their ancient traditions have been tremendous. Indeed, it is hard to believe, in the long sweep of Jewish history, that the great revival of spiritual lore that took place among the Safed Kabbalists happened a mere four hundred years ago.

The period of the sixteenth century through the eighteenth in Jewish history was at one time set aside by scholars as an age of little creativity or originality. The period, in fact, hardly has a name; it is later than medieval but surely not yet modern. Since most of Jewry lived in areas relatively little affected by the Renaissance or the Reformation, it is hardly appropriate to characterize the age in Jewish history by those names. "Enlightenment," a rather loaded term, to be sure, belongs to the closing decades of the eighteenth century in Germany, as the emerging modern West began to break through its medieval repression and stereotyping of Jews and as a Jewish literature emerged that participated in the Enlightenment culture of Europe.

In choosing "Renewal" as an epithet for this period, I mean to suggest that in fact Jewry did go through a Renaissance of its own in the sixteenth century, one mostly unrelated to the European phenomenon of a century earlier. In the century that followed the Expulsion from Spain, two new Jewries began to take their place as the primary centers of Jewish creative life: the Sephardic center in the Ottoman Empire and the Ashkenazic center in the Polish-Lithuanian kingdom. In both communities, each in its own way, a revival took place in the areas of talmudic studies, Kabbalah, popular devotional literature, and liturgical/poetic creativity.

The closing century of Jewish life in Spain was a period of relative decline in Jewish literature. A few isolated thinkers continued to write, but only on the eve of the Expulsion is there to be seen a true flurry of creative activity.

But the century following the tragedy of 1492 was indeed a time of awakening. From the self-critical historical writings of Judah ibn Verga and the biblical commentaries of Isaac Abravanel to the great "Summa Kabbalistica" of Meir ibn Gabbai's *Avodat ha-Qodesh* to the messianic longings of Eliezer Berukhim Halevi, the sixteenth century reveals itself as a time of reflection and profundity. The dislocations of the new exile clearly have set their mark upon the age.

It was in the last quarter of this century that a most unusual and intense gathering of Jewish savants and mystics took place in the Galilean town of Safed, a community composed of the children of Spanish exiles, Jews from other parts of the Ottoman Empire and the Near East, and a few stray Ashkenazim from Europe. There Joseph Caro completed the great halakhic oeuvre that still serves as guidepost to daily praxis in the life of the observant Jew. Poets such as Shlomo Alkabez and Eliezer Azikri composed hymns that are still among the devotional highlights of Jewish worship. Most significant, kabbalists including Moses Cordovero, Alkabez, Isaac Luria, Hayyim Vital and others brought about a renewal of Jewish occult teachings on an unparalleled scale.

The Kabbalah of Safed represents neither a continuation of the old Zoharic teachings nor an entirely new departure. In its various schools it is rather an amalgam of the entire corpus of earlier Jewish esotericism, one Kabbalist emphasizing one stream while his neighbor might choose another. Ancient *merkavah* speculations, magical and numerological lore, the devotional teachings of Ashkenazic Hasidism, the theosophy of the Zohar and the mind-expanding mystical exercises of the Abulafian "Jewish Sufi" school all found their place in the Safed corpus. Each of the two new schools that emerged from the Safed crucible, that of Cordovero and that of Luria, represents a new blending of all these ancient sources, along with the creative vocabulary of a new generation of thinkers.

The intense devotional atmosphere of the Safed study-houses found avid followers among Jews as widespread as those of Italy, Poland, and Yemen. Tightly knit brotherhoods of mystics, such as those around Shalom Shar'abi in eighteenth-century Jerusalem, Moses Hayyim Luzzatto in Padua, and Israel Ba'al Shem Tov in Miedzybozh all reflect attempts to preserve or re-create the seemingly magical aura of Safed. A new genre of popular Jewish hagiography was born around the legendary lives of Luria and Vital, providing the inspiration for the tales of the righteous that were to become so central to eastern European Hasidism.

An anonymous Hasidic preacher near the turn of the twentieth century perhaps said it best. Quoting the mishnaic dictum "The world stands on three things: Torah, Worship, and Deeds of Lovingkindness," he divided

Jewish history into a naïve periodization. From the time of Moses to that of Isaac Luria, he claimed the "world," meaning Jewish existence, was based on Torah study. From Safed onward, he said, devotion became the central pillar on which that "world" was founded. More than any specific teaching or terminological innovation, the legacy of the Safed Revival and its two-hundred-year aftermath, including both the mystical heresy of Sabbatianism and the popular piety of Beshtian Hasidism, is the possibility of a Jewish life based on the intensity of inward devotion.

Our essays in this section discuss numerous aspects of Jewish spiritual life in this formative period of renewal. An overview of the Safed Revival is provided by R. J. Z. Werblowsky, well-known for his study of Joseph Caro as a figure who embodied the mystical as well as the legal spirit of his age. Louis Jacobs and Lawrence Fine go forward to explore specific aspects of mystical teachings in the late sixteenth century. These three essays will for the first time provide the English reader with a full outline of Lurianic teaching in its major dimensions. The distinguished historical sociologist Jacob Katz discusses the inevitable tensions between Kabbalah and halakhah that emerged in the wake of this revival.

Turning from Safed to eastern Europe, the editor's own contribution to this collection deals with the crucial theme of leadership in early Hasidism. Rachel Elior gives an important summation of HaBaD theology, again offering a much-needed first opportunity for the English reader to explore in detail an important school of Jewish religious thought. Chava Weissler discusses the usually neglected area of women's religious lives in a pioneering attempt to read collections of simple supplications written by or for women as a map to the religious consciousness of Jewish women in eastern Europe. The non-Hasidic area of east European pietism is treated in Immanuel Etkes's study of the Lithuanian Mussar movement in the mid-nineteenth century.

* * * * * * *

The fate of Jewish spirituality in modern times requires an entirely different sort of treatment. From the late eighteenth century on, first in Germany, then in eastern Europe, and most recently in the Near East as well, large numbers of Jews have chosen to live their lives outside the patterns of traditional Judaism. This disaffection was made possible in the first instance from without, by the acceptance of Jewry into polite "post-Christian" or "nondenominational" society in the Western world. For a century and more Jews were drawn away from the seeming narrowness and confinement of the ghetto or shtetl and its intensity, attracted by the greater personal freedom and higher standards of cultural achievement to be seen in the outside world.

In response to this mass desertion of Jewish tradition, new Judaisms arose that hoped to retain the faithfulness of Jewry to at least some semblance of its heritage. Reform and liberal Judaism in the West as well as early cultural Zionism in eastern Europe are to be seen as strategies for Jewish survival, attempts to "hold the fort" when it seemed that all might indeed be lost to the tremendous pressures of assimilation. Our lead essay in this section, that by Arnold Eisen, deals most provocatively with the uses of "spirit" as a way of making Judaism somehow more palatable to Jews living in an essentially skeptical age.

The rapid pace of progress in the nineteenth and early twentieth centuries, in both the technological and social realms, left most Jews feeling that their religion was a relic, even if a beloved one, of an earlier age. When the Hasidic *rebbe* moved from his small town to Warsaw, Vienna, or New York, he tellingly took the name of his shtetl as well as its lifestyle, along with him, as though proclaiming his irrelevance to urban Jews along with his faithfulness to his ancestors. Jews coming of age after the First World War, whether in Europe or America, were increasingly ignorant of and distanced from the old way of life. There emerged in the early twentieth century a self-proclaimed "secular" Jewish culture, using the vehicles of both Yiddish and Hebrew, which sought to reshape Jewry in line with a modern, irreligious, and generally socialist view of life.

Already at the turn of the century, however, small circles of serious thinking Jews emerged who tried to reappropriate or reformulate the Jewish tradition without sacrifice of their own participation in the modern world. Dissatisfied by the perceived shallowness of liberal Judaism yet unable to proclaim themselves Orthodox, these thinkers struggled to articulate a Judaism that made sense to them. With the notable exception of Hermann Cohen and Franz Rosenzweig in Germany, most of these thinkers were associated in one way or another with the Zionist reassertion of Jewish national identity. Such diverse figures as Ahad Ha'Am (Asher Ginzburg) in eastern Europe, Martin Buber in Germany, Mordecai M. Kaplan in America, and Gershom Scholem in Jerusalem each sought to develop a spiritual counterpart to the political and cultural revival that was fast becoming the new Jewish reality. Among these, Buber and Scholem joined with such other figures as Hillel Zeitlin and Abraham Joshua Heschel in seeing in Jewish mysticism or Hasidism the prototype for a new vision of Judaism—or at least, in Scholem's case, the seed out of which such a new Judaism might germinate.

These thinkers are treated, singly and collectively, in the ensuing essays of this volume. Rivka Horwitz studies the theory of revelation, a touchstone of conflict for all Jewish moderns, in the writings of Franz Rosenzweig. Laurence Silberstein deals with Buber and Heschel as modern and universalist thinkers nevertheless rooted in the very particularistic soil of Judaism. Paul Mendes-Flohr uses an important new document from the legacy of Gershom Scholem as a way back to consideration of the all-important conflict between Buber and Rosenzweig on the issue of law and commandment. Ehud Luz reviews the issues of Judaism, Jewish identity, and modernity as they were treated by the formative generations of the Zionist community in the Land of Israel.

* * * * * *

The period of Jewish history that began in late-eighteenth-century Germany has ended. We whose identities were formed after 1933, 1945, 1948, and 1967 are no longer modern Jews. After 1933 we no longer believe in the possibility—or attractiveness—of assimilation. In the face of 1945 and the realization of what had happened in the death camps, we surely no longer worship at the temple of human progress. The year 1948 heralded the fact that the central project to which world Jewry would commit itself in the latter half of the twentieth century was to be the building of a free and secure Jewish state in the Land of Israel. All else, including both the ongoing demise of the much larger Jewish community in North America and the various attempts to slow or prevent that demise, took a back seat to the riveting drama of events as they unfolded in the Holy Land, both for good and for ill.

But it was in 1967 that the emerging new age of Jewish history was truly born. Forced to confront the bleakest of its nightmares, world Jewry discovered within itself a deep and abiding loyalty to Jewish existence. Assimilation, intermarriage, and indifference notwithstanding, the tremendous number of American Jews who have participated in "missions" or other sorts of trips to Israel bear witness, as do their vast monetary contributions, to an ongoing sense of connection. Among their children a not insignificant number have begun to return to Judaism on a more seriously religious plane, including a large number of "returnees" to Orthodoxy, even of the would-be pre-modern variety. The intensely spiritualized nationalism of Gush Emunim in Israel and the surprising vitality and attractiveness of Lubavitch and other ultra-Orthodoxies are among the signs of this new age; the Judaism emerging from them could hardly be seen as belonging to the age called "modern."

This same emerging era sees growth and development outside of Ortho-doxy as well. Those influenced by Buber and Heschel join with émigrés from the Hasidic community in an attempt to find a serious Jewish spirituality for those who cannot, for whatever reason, find their place wholly within the law. The vitality shown by the Havurah movement, the Jewish feminist movement, and the Reconstructionist movement are all hopeful signs on the North American scene. The tremendous growth of Judaic studies in American universities will, it is hoped, produce a better-informed Jewish public and will lead some, at least, to a deeper examination of self as well as sources. The great number of Jewish classics now available in English translations, along with the many English-language monographs written on them, should have some effect on the highly literate Jewish com-munity. While there is little question that a significant number of American Jews will continue to disaffiliate or simply lose all interest in Jewish life, the creative survival of a smaller but more seriously committed community seems assured. The varieties of spiritual creativity that are beginning to emerge from that community have not yet reached maturity.

The current scene in Israel is somewhat less promising, at least at the moment of this writing. Israeli society learned from eastern Europe that one had to choose either an Orthodox or a "secularist" way of life as a con-temporary Jew. Most Israelis, especially those of Sephardic or Near Eastern background, are really neither of these, but a new pattern of self-definition has not yet emerged. Religion as defined by the Orthodox rabbinate is held in derision by most outside their camp. A highly significant battle for the soul of modern Orthodoxy is taking place, the protagonists being extreme religious nationalists on one side and the small but highly articulate religious peace camp on the other. But this struggle too leaves most Israelis unmoved. It seems that more basic issues such as land, security, survival, and relations with neighbors will have to be solved before Israel can take the place it surely should have as the cradle of a new Judaism for the emerging new age in our history.

Arthur Green

Acknowledgments

As preparation of *Jewish Spirituality* draws to a close, I wish to acknowledge the assistance of several people without whose help the editing of these volumes would have been impossible. Rabbi Jonathan Chipman of Jerusalem translated several essays in this volume from the Hebrew. The essay by Jacob Katz was translated by Elliot Horowitz. Caryn Broitman served as editorial assistant and Muriel Weiss typed the bulk of the manuscript. My thanks go out to all of them.

This volume is dedicated to the memory of Professor Alexander Altmann, whose passing was announced just as the volume was going to press. Most of the essays here are by his friends, his students, and his protégés. I know he would have been proud to see it.

For reprint permissions, we express our gratitude to the Jewish Publication Society of America for permission to quote from their translation of the Holy Scriptures; to Stephen Mitchell for a selection from his *Into the Whirlwind* (Garden City, NY: Doubleday, 1979); to Dr. David Goldstein for the use of two poems from his *Hebrew Poems from Spain* (London: Routledge, 1965); to Daniel Matt for a selection from his *Zohar: The Book of Enlightenment* (New York: Paulist, 1983); to Dvir and Co. for the translation of C. N. Bialik, *Selected Poems* (1981); to October House for the selection from Jacob Glatstein's *My Brother Refugee,* in the translation of Ruth Whitman (*The Selected Poems of Jacob Glatstein,* 1972); to the University of California for the use of S. Shalom's *Guard Me, O God,* from Ruth Finer Mintz's *Modern Hebrew Poetry* (1966).

Part One
RENEWAL
The Post-Medieval Age

Soul's beloved, compassionate Father,
Draw Your servant to Your will.
Let him run, swift as a deer,
To kneel before Your majesty.
Sweeter is Your love to him
Than honey from the comb,
Than any taste of pleasure.

Glorious, radiant, cosmic light,
My soul is faint for love of You.
Heal her, I pray, O God,
Show to her Your splendrous glow.
Then will she be strengthened, cured,
Your maidservant forever.

O Faithful, may Your tender mercies
Reach Your son who loves You greatly.
In deepest longings has he sought
To gaze upon Your mighty splendor.
My God, my heart's delight,
Come quickly; be not hidden.

Reveal Yourself, my Dearest; spread over me
The shelter of Your peace.
Your presence lighting up the world,
We shall rejoice, exult in You.
Hurry, Lover, time has come,
Grant me Your grace
As You did of old.

Eleazar Azikri

Rock of my heart, my Holy One,
Creator of All, knower of all secrets

You know my heart.
You know how fiercely the holy fire burns within me,
     For we are part of God above, His Presence dwelling in
     our hearts.

Like a harp my heart wails for You,
Flesh and heart as one long but for God,
Our portion forever.
My soul longs to be in Your courts,
     O Lord,
My whole being cries out for the living God
A fiery flame in my heart burns in longing;
Mighty waters will not quench this love,
Nor floods drown it.

My heart is drawn to your endless light
So that its light too glows endlessly.
Beyond all limit is my love for You;
My one desire,
To cleave to you forever.

Yet you have told us that such is not Your will,
That flesh and blood cannot be so attached to you.
You rather seek out our service, our deeds,
For those above we were sent into this lowly world.
And so You tell us not to burn for You too much,
To reduce that fire in the heart,
To make an empty space instead.

So I come before you, Lord, to ask You:
"Teach me how to do this thing,
To temper the fire, to lower the light,
That it not run too fast to You, as it desires,
And keep me from Your service.

Nathan of Nemirovin
Liqqutey Tefilot 49
(adapted)

A father and his son, travelling together in a wagon,
   came to the edge of a forest.
Some bushes, thick with berries,
   caught the child's eye.
"Father," he asked, "may we stop awhile
   so that I can pick some berries?"
The father was anxious to complete his journey,
   but he did not have it in his heart
   to refuse the boy's request.
The wagon was called to a halt,
   and the son alighted to pick the berries.

After a while,
   the father wanted to continue on his way.
But his son had become so engrossed in
   berry-picking
   that he could not bring himself
   to leave the forest.
"Son!" cried the father, "we cannot stay here all
   day!
   We must continue our journey!"

Even his father's pleas were not enough
   to lure the boy away.
What could the father do?
Surely he loved his son no less
   for acting so childishly.
He would not think of leaving him behind—
   but he really did have to get going
   on his journey.

Finally he called out:
   "You may pick your berries for a while longer,
   but be sure that you are still able to find me,
   For I shall start moving slowly along the road.
As you work, call out 'Father! Father!'
   every few minutes, and I shall answer you.
As long as you can hear my voice,
   know that I am still nearby.
But as soon as you can no longer hear my answer,
   know that you are lost,
   and run with all your strength to find me!"

Shmelka of Nikolsburg Sholom
Divrey Shemuʿel 124

1. "Ketubah," 1648, Rotterdam.

ספר

תְּהִלָּה

לְיוֹם הָרִאשׁוֹן

אַשְׁרֵי

הָאִישׁ אֲשֶׁר לֹא הָלַךְ בַּעֲצַת רְשָׁעִים וּבְדֶרֶךְ חַטָּאִים לֹא
עָמָד וּבְמוֹשַׁב לֵצִים לֹא יָשָׁב ׃ כִּי אִם בְּתוֹרַת יְיָ חֶפְצוֹ
וּבְתוֹרָתוֹ יֶהְגֶּה יוֹמָם וָלָיְלָה ׃ וְהָיָה כְּעֵץ שָׁתוּל עַל פַּלְגֵי
מָיִם אֲשֶׁר פִּרְיוֹ יִתֵּן בְּעִתּוֹ וְעָלֵהוּ לֹא יִבּוֹל וְכֹל אֲשֶׁר
יַעֲשֶׂה יַצְלִיחַ ׃ לֹא כֵן הָרְשָׁעִים כִּי אִם כַּמֹּץ אֲשֶׁר הַ
דְּפֶנּוּ רוּחַ ׃ עַל כֵּן לֹא יָקֻמוּ רְשָׁעִים בַּמִּשְׁפָּט וְחַטָּאִים
בַּעֲדַת צַדִּיקִים ׃ כִּי יוֹדֵעַ יְיָ דֶּרֶךְ צַדִּיקִים וְדֶרֶךְ רְשָׁעִים
תֹּאבֵד ׃

לָמָּה רָגְשׁוּ גוֹיִם וּלְאֻמִּים יֶהְגּוּ רִיק ׃ יִתְיַצְּבוּ
מַלְכֵי אֶרֶץ וְרוֹזְנִים נוֹסְדוּ יָחַד עַל יְיָ
וְעַל מְשִׁיחוֹ ׃ נְנַתְּקָה אֶת מוֹסְרוֹתֵימוֹ וְנַשְׁלִיכָה מִמֶּנּוּ

2. Aryeh Judah Loeb ben Elhanan Katz, "Prayer Book," 1716/7, Vienna.

3. Title Page, *Shomer Emunim* by Joseph Ergas, 1736, Amsterdam.

4. Israel David Luzzatto, "Sukkah Decoration," ca. 1775, Trieste.

5. Jacques-Emile-Edouard Brandon, *Silent Prayer, Synagogue of Amsterdam, "The Amida" ("La Gmauida")*, 1897.

6. Isidor Kaufmann, *Friday Evening*, 1920.

1

The Safed Revival
and Its Aftermath

R. J. Zwi Werblowsky

General Considerations

THE PRECEDING PART of this collection (*Jewish Spirituality: From the Bible through the Middle Ages*, World Spirituality, vol. 13; part 3, "Reflections: The Medieval Age") dealt with the Middle Ages, and the following part will describe the modern age. In a work the overall organization of which is chronological (from the biblical to the modern period), one would naturally expect the chapter entitled "The Safed Revival and Its Aftermath" to cover the otherwise nameless intermediary period between medieval and modern. Putting it that way is, of course, to let the cat out of the bag and to pose the problem of what, in more technical jargon, is known as the "periodization of history." The reader need hardly be reminded that neither Saadiah, Bahya, Maimonides and the author of the *Zohar* nor Thomas Aquinas, for that matter, was aware of being "medieval." The term "Middle Ages" was invented by Renaissance admirers of classical culture: that which was in between the original (i.e., Greco-Roman) and the renewed (i.e., Renaissance) "classical" culture, was "middle." Having said that much, we have also said that the usual periodization is an extremely dubious matter, and of doubly dubious applicability to Jewish history. In one sense the Jewish Middle Ages came to an end in the second half of the eighteenth century only (in some areas even later); in another sense even the seventeenth- and eighteenth-century ghetto was affected by the osmotic pressures of changing and ultimately "modern" Europe. Chronologically, the epoch under consideration in this section begins with the expulsion of the Jews from the Iberian peninsula. In Italy the Jewish communities came into contact with Renaissance culture. Kabbalah and messianism saw an unprecedented, even feverish, revival. Gershom Scholem has argued that the

Sabbatian movement, and especially its aftermath, played a significant role in preparing the way for the modern types of Jewish experience. Martin Buber interpreted the Ba'al Shem Tov as the Jewish spiritual "reply" to Spinoza. Hasidism, with its mystical highs and popular superstitious lows, developed in the East at the same time that in the West the Enlightenment prepared the way for emancipation and eventual modernization. The period under review thus exhibits its own inherent and authentic values, as well as the characteristics of an age of transition. There is little point in fighting terminological windmills. Let us accept, therefore, the given framework while keeping in mind its inadequacy and its limitations.

The aforementioned problems of periodization as well as of description are compounded by the difficulty of isolating specific characteristics and styles. How do we perceive the relationship of continuity and change? Judaism, like many other religions, is a culture of quotations. And under the cover of quotation and commentary both continuity and change find shelter. A sixteenth- or seventeenth-century author would quote the Talmud, Midrash, Maimonides and the *Zohar* "synchronically" and without worrying about compatibility or incompatibility. In fact, what to us appear to be incompatibilities are to believers both theoretical and practical compatibilities, and they rarely ask themselves whether in the act of quoting they did not go far beyond the quotation.

A further difficulty is introduced by the necessity of dividing, or rather chopping up, an integral subject (*in casu* Jewish spirituality) into more detailed topics. It is almost impossible to separate a discussion of the contemplative ideal from that of the "love of God" or to detach a consideration of the techniques of spiritual attainment from a consideration of psychological issues. Every religious system has its "anthropology," that is, its doctrines concerning the nature of humanity—for example, the origin and essence of the soul (or multiple souls), its relation to "reason," namely, the "rational faculty" or "intellectual soul" on the one hand, and to the body on the other, the location of the "lower" passions and of the tendency to sin and evil etc. Many ethical and especially mystical systems, in keeping with their meditative and at times introspective character, tend to elaborate the psychological aspects of their anthropology. Similarly, psychological and cosmological doctrines are closely interrelated, since traditional imagery often uses a spatial idiom, speaking, for example, of the "descent" or even "fall" of the soul (from where and through which cosmic spheres?) as well as of its subsequent ecstatic or meditative, "ascent." This holds true of Jewish, both kabbalistic and nonkabbalistic, as well as many non-Jewish systems in the East and in the West. (Needless to add that Western systems are greatly indebted to gnostic as well as Neoplatonic traditions.) Jewish sixteenth- and seventeenth-century psychological doctrines are a continuation of, at times even simply identical with, earlier medieval conceptions of philosophical and/or kabbalistic provenance.

A word should also be said about that protean term "spirituality." For the purposes of the present work it is taken to mean the inward side of religious life. This definition is adequate as far as it goes, but it has its limitations and even dangers, since it may unintentionally foster the impression that a religious phenomenon that focuses on contemplation, meditational practices, or the more emotional aspects of religion is more "spiritual" than the so-called external forms of observance. But in its intentionality every religious act includes inner dispositions and states of mind, such as belief in god(s), the desire and quest for salvation, the wish to obey God's voice and to do his will, faith, etc. There is no a priori reason to assume that an anti-Sufi Sunnite Muslim, bent on punctiliously obeying Allah's law as delivered through his Prophet, is less "spiritual" than a Sufi mystic.

The Eve and Aftermath of the Safed Revival

As the previous remarks concerning periodization have indicated, or at least implied, the overall title of this chapter should be taken with a grain of salt. We are dealing, in fact, with the period stretching from the Expulsion (end of the fifteenth century) to the beginning of the modern age. But since the present work is not a textbook of social, cultural, or even religious history, we shall focus on what seem to us, perhaps arbitrarily, the most salient and significant phenomena in terms of "spiritual life." To repeat what has already been said: The period under review is partly a continuation, indeed in many ways still part, of the Middle Ages, yet also an age of transition, characterized by upheavals and convulsions, to something not only chronologically but also qualitatively different—the modern age. The Jewish Middle Ages ended with both a bang and a whimper.

Although the Safed Revival should, technically speaking, be dated in the second quarter of the sixteenth century, our account must begin, for reasons noted before, at the end of the fifteenth century, that is, with the completion of the Christian *reconquista* and unification of Spain, and the Expulsion— after a century of increasingly virulent anti-Semitism—of the Jews from the Iberian peninsula. Few events between the destruction of the temple and the Chmielnicki massacres in the Ukraine (1648) have had such traumatizing character. Even the horrors of the First Crusade with its destruction of whole Jewish communities did not produce such major cultural shifts and spiritual movements. Needless to say, the Expulsion also caused major demographic shifts and movements. Iberian refugee Jewry spread over the Mediterranean world, that is, North Africa, Italy, and especially Turkey, where they were welcomed by the Ottoman rulers for economic-political reasons. Palestine being part of the Ottoman Empire, which so hospitably welcomed Sephardic Jewry, the Holy Land could now play a role that has no parallel in preceding centuries. The Cossack massacres of 1648 caused a reversal in the migratory trends of Ashkenazic Jewry. Whereas in the late Middle Ages the flow had been from the west, where kings and rulers expelled their Jews, to eastern Europe (where the Polish kings received them for economic reasons), the human tide now swept back to the west. Soon after the Sephardic ex-marranos had begun to settle in Amsterdam, an Ashkenazic "refugee" community established itself there also. For a better understanding of Sephardic history, a reminder may be useful here to the effect that whereas the Mediterranean (and subsequently Oriental) Sephardim are the descendants of Jews who left Spain as Jewish expellees in quest of new homes, the western Sephardim (in the Netherlands, London, and subsequently the new world) were marranos who had lived for generations as pseudo-Christians, and in terror of the Inquisition, until they could escape. As we shall see, the kabbalistic revival associated with the small town in Galilee, Safed, actually had its origins in the new centers of Jewish life in the Turkish Balkans.

One of the results of the Expulsion was the decline of philosophy, a decline that had set in already in the preceding century. No doubt there were philosophers continuing the medieval tradition whose high-water mark had been Maimonides, and there were those who absorbed contemporaneous Renaissance influences; but as a major and powerful cultural and spiritual force, philosophy lost its preeminence. The kabbalists held philosophy responsible for the weakening of Judaism in Spain; its interpretation of the mizwot—more allegorical than genuinely spiritual in their view—had contributed to the erosion of observance and to a weakening of commitment and fervor. Confirmation of this view was found in the fact that, unlike the communities in the Rhineland during the First Crusade, which preferred without exception martyrdom to apostasy, Spanish Jewry produced many thousands of "new Christians" and marranos already in the century preceding the Expulsion. The Kabbalah, until then a secret and esoteric doctrine taught to choice initiates only, became popularized and influenced—indeed, finally, as a result of the impact of Safed, even dominated—Jewish piety and spirituality.

Mysticism is not necessarily messianic. On the contrary, it can be argued that mysticism, because of its contemplative immersion in the absolute, the eternal and unchanging, the "everlasting now," operates in a climate very different from that of messianism. It is sufficient, in that connection, to study the lack of messianic tension in Maimonides' doctrine of *devequt*, in Bahya's doctrine of abandonment to and love of God, or in the teachings of the early kabbalists. Messianism presupposes a certain relationship to the time process, that is, history as a goal-directed sequence of changes ending in a social, political, moral, or even cosmic, fulfillment. The amazing achievement of the Safed Revival was its explosive (as subsequent developments showed) combination of kabbalistic mysticism and messianism—and a short-term messianism to boot, that is, messianism not on the horizon of a distant future but as an immediate expectation. The combination is well expressed in the subtitle that G. Scholem chose to give to his massive and magisterial study of Sabbatai Sevi: "the Mystical Messiah." The dismal and shameful end of this "Great Awakening" left in its wake a trail of confusion and disarray. The Kabbalah too had been compromised as a whole and, as a result, declined, especially in its public and social role. In due course it even came to be viewed by the spokesmen of the new Enlightenment as the very incarnation of superstitious obscurantism, worse than even rabbinic talmudism.

The social and economic conditions of European Jewry continued to go from bad to worse. The combination of this social-cultural decline with the post-Sabbatian spiritual disarray prepared the way for two diametrically opposed developments. In the West, the movement known as the European Enlightenment, though itself not devoid of anti-Jewish elements, merged with ideals of toleration and even tolerance, the demand for a "civil betterment" of the Jews and their status, and from there it moved to emancipation and ultimately modernization. It produced the type of Jew that will be the subject of part 2 of this volume. In eastern Europe the economically and spiritually pauperized masses, bereft of their messianic enthusiasm and dream as a result of the Sabbatian debacle and pushed into the role of religious pariahs by the talmudic scholasticism of the rabbinic elite, eagerly responded to the new message of mystical revival on a popular level— Hasidism. When the Enlightenment reached the ghettos of eastern Europe, Hasidism in its turn appeared to be the very incarnation of medieval obscurantism and popular superstition, and thus it made its dialectical contribution to the emergence of rationalism and modernity among Polish and Russian Jewry. It is only in our generation that disillusionment with Enlightenment rationalism, combined with a postromantic penchant for mystical spirituality plus a melancholic nostalgia for the *shtetl* that had disappeared in the flames of the Holocaust, have led to a renewed interest in Hasidic spirituality.

One more type of spirituality should be mentioned before we take a closer look at the kabbalistic revival associated with Safed. This is the type of piety that is concerned with the strict observance of God's commandments as spelled out in halakhic tradition, with the study of Torah, and with the cultivation of the religious and moral virtues—it being understood that the latter too (e.g., humility, loving-kindness, charity, self-control), being prescribed by the Torah, were essentially religious virtues. The consciousness of sin and the consequent preoccupation with repentance and atonement give this type of piety a markedly penitential and ascetic character. But this asceticism is not so much a matter of mortification for its own sake as a penitential discipline for atoning for past failures and transgressions and a moral discipline of self-control for the purpose of avoiding future sin and suppressing the inclination to evil. Asceticism can easily combine with philosophical and mystical piety (i.e., suppressing the lower appetites and passions in order to enable the soul to rise to higher levels and to cleave to God) on the one hand, and with messianic fervor (since the Messiah will appear only after Israel has atoned for all its sins) on the other.

At this point another methodological problem raises its head. We can reconstruct the spiritual life of past ages by means of literary documents only. We cannot study it by means of a living encounter with the living representatives of that spirituality. But texts have to be cross-examined for what they say no less than for what they leave unsaid. Thus, many ascetic and theological writers may well have been kabbalists or may have been influenced by kabbalistic ideas, without giving the slightest hint of it in their writings. As a result, scholars often debate whether these authors were kabbalists or not. R. Jonah of Gerona and his *Epistle on Repentance* represent one such case. The voluminous and influential writings of the great Rabbi Loew of Prague (1525–1609), whom later legend credited with creating a *golem*, are another example. Probably very few of the many thousands of pious people edified by one of the most beautiful manuals of the spiritual life, the *Path of the Upright* by Moses Hayyim Luzzatto (1707–1747) guiding the aspirant from the basic virtues of prudence, fervor, humility, etc. to the ultimate aim, the gift of the Holy Spirit, ever realized that its author was a charismatic kabbalist who in states of trancelike inspiration even composed a second *Zohar* and, moreover, was at the center of a feverishly messianic circle.

Safed: Mystical Messianism

There can be no doubt of the messianic character of sixteenth- and seventeenth-century spirituality, especially in its kabbalistic form. Yet there seems to be a difference between theological systems whose structure is essentially messianic (e.g., Lurianism) and those which, as philosophic-mystical systems, are outwardly and even structurally nonmessianic (e.g., Moses Cordovero and his school)—though from biographical and other sources, including our knowledge of their liturgical practices, we can deduce that the motivation and emotional driving force were thoroughly messianic. We can illustrate this state of affairs with testimonies that incidentally also bear out our earlier statement to the effect that the Safed Revival did not begin in Safed but in the new centers of Sephardic Jewry in the Balkan provinces of the Ottoman Empire. The pre-Lurianic circle of kabbalists in Safed included such luminaries as Moses Cordovero (perhaps one of the most learned and profoundest thinkers in the history of the Kabbalah), Joseph Karo (known to posterity mainly as the great Talmudist and codifier of rabbinic law), and Solomon Alkabez (best known as the author of the hymn *Lekhah Dodi,* which quickly became one of the main features of the Sabbath Eve service). Karo and Alkabez went to Safed from Greece, where they had been members of kabbalistic brotherhoods that cultivated charismatic phenomena such as instruction by celestial mentors and other manifestations of the Holy Spirit. The theoretical and systematic writings of Cordovero and Alkabez betray little messianic tension. Yet the life of these brotherhoods was centered not only on the reception of heavenly graces but also on "raising the *Shekhinah* from the dust," that is, contributing to the redemptive union of the *sefirot* and thereby to hastening the advent of the Messiah. The famous epistle of Alkabez, describing the Shavu'ot Night Vigil in R. Joseph Karo's house is particularly instructive in this respect. The celestial voice urges the sufferings of the *Shekhinah* and praises the brethren for "raising her up" through their devotions, thus clearly emphasizing the messianic character of these exercises. In the second place we also learn that kabbalistic-liturgical innovations were made not only in Lurianic Safed but also in pre-Lurianic circles long before Safed became the recognized spiritual center. Alkabez's account is given in an epistle addressed to the brethren in Salonica, who are upbraided for having held the vigil during the first night of Shavu'ot only but not during the second night. Evidently the pious kabbalists congregating in Karo's house were fully aware of being in spiritual communion with brethren in Salonica engaged in the same liturgical and mystical devotions. The evidence agrees with allusions contained in Joseph Karo's mystical diary, *Maggid Mesharim*, which seem to imply that such kabbalistic brotherhoods existed in several centers (Salonica, Adrianople, Nicopolis). These kabbalistic groups clearly felt themselves bound together in some kind of mystical communion. On one occasion the celestial voice announced to Karo that the arrival of Solomon Alkabez in Adrianople—armed with recommendations from Karo—had triggered a religious revival there and that "the holy brethren [there now] illuminate you, and you illuminate them, and [both of] you [together] illuminate the holy brethren in the metropolis of Israel [i.e., Salonica] and they [of Salonica in turn] illuminate both of you."

We also know the names of some of the central charismatic figures of the time, for example, the great talmudic and kabbalistic scholar R. Joseph Taytazak of Salonica, who was vouchsafed heavenly instruction. The short and meteoric career of the strange ex-marrano and visionary Solomon Molkho need not be recounted here in detail. The brilliant young marrano courtier from Lisbon met the messianic adventurer David ha-Re'ubeni in 1525, performed upon himself the operation of circumcision, and was henceforth visited by dreams and visions. Some of his predictions actually came to pass exactly at the predicted time (e.g., the overflow of the Tiber in 1530, and the earthquake in Lisbon in 1531). After escaping from Lisbon (ca. 1526) he spent some time in Turkey in the circle around Taytazak in Salonica, before proceeding on his ill-fated "mission to the Pope." Imprisoned by order of Charles V and sentenced by the Inquisition, he was burned in Mantua in 1532, eight years before the date he had predicted for the advent of the Messiah. His career and martyrdom made a profound impression—so much so that for a long time the many references in Karo's mystical diary to the "beloved Solomon" were held to refer to Molkho. Only subsequent research showed that they refer to Karo's disciple and associate Solomon Alkabez.

The growing messianic fervor was undoubtedly one of the main factors in the movement to the Holy Land, which resulted in Safed's (rather than Jerusalem, for reasons that are irrelevant to our present purpose) becoming the center and fulcrum of the great mystical revival.

Mention has already been made of the messianic motivations underlying the spirituality of even those kabbalists whose theological systems are not overtly and patently messianic. In other words, devotional, spiritual, and ascetic life had a markedly messianic slant. This characteristic became increasingly prominent in Safed, not only in legend (e.g., the story about Luria's disciple Abraham Halevi Berukhim, who in 1571 saw a woman dressed in black—none other than the incarnate *Shekhinah*—weeping at the

Wailing Wall in Jerusalem) but also in new devotional practices. A popular but still eminently readable account of the mystical and pious ideals, values, and practices that were cherished and cultivated in this remarkable community of saints was given by Solomon Schechter in his beautiful essay "Safed in the 16th century."[1] Some of the liturgical innovations have been described and analyzed by G. Scholem. One of the most interesting was the habit of *gerushin* ("exile wanderings," lit., "banishments") for the double purpose of sharing the exile of the *Shekhinah* and obtaining heavenly inspirations and illuminations. Moses Cordovero has left us an account of these mystical peregrinations in the Galilean countryside around Safed and at the tombs of the talmudic masters in the area. These wanderings had nothing in common with romantic notions of communing with nature. They incidentally also illustrate one of the main characteristics of kabbalistic spirituality: not simply emotional experiences of ecstatic closeness to God (as, e.g., in later Hasidism in eastern Europe), but the desire of inspired insight into kabbalistic mysteries and the revelation of mystical interpretations of Scripture. One or two illustrations must suffice here. "On Friday, 10 Shevat in the year 5308 [= 1548 C.E.] we went into the exile of the King and Queen [i.e., the two *sefirot* symbolized by these names] as far as the ruins of the Beth ha-Midrash in Nabartin [in Galilee], and there I hit upon the novel kabbalistic interpretation. . . ." Or again, "We went as far as Kefar Biryah, where we entered the Synagogue and devoted ourselves to matters appropriate to *gerushin;* and my master [Alkabez] decided upon the innovation that in the summer months especially we should on occasion walk barefoot, in the mystery of the *Shekhinah* 'withhold thy foot from being unshod' [Jer 2:25]." This practice of *gerushin* also illustrates the parallelism of individual ascetic-mystical life, on the one hand, and the fate of the Godhead-in-exile, especially in its aspect of *Shekhinah,* on the other. Mystical communion and the ascent on the *scala mentis ad Deum* are thus not "egoistical" experiences, but are meant to contribute to the work of redemption. As one of Cordovero's disciples, Elijah de Vidas, put it in his well-known manual *Reshit Hokhmah (The Beginning of Wisdom), devequt* or communion with God is the "cleaving with one's soul, and having as one's sole aim the union of the *Shekhinah* and the separation from her of all *qelippot* ["shells," namely, evil, demonic powers], and similarly the separation from one's own mind of all alien [i.e., sinful or worldly] thoughts." The parallelization of the two spheres is an important step toward their complete identification in the mystical doctrine of later Hasidism. The rationalistic character of these mystical illuminations imitating—albeit on an inspirational level—the discussions in the talmudic schools, is well illustrated by Cordovero's account:

Again we wandered on the 15th day of Shevat, my master and myself alone, and the words of Torah were shining in us and the words were spoken of themselves. We went as far as the tomb of Rabbi Joseph of Yokrat and on our return we discussed the verse [Micah 7:15] "According to the days of thy coming out of the land of Egypt will I show him." For my master asked . . . and replied. . . . Thereupon I commented . . . and my master added to this by saying . . . enlarging very much on the subject because the words were shining forth of themselves.

So far the proceedings of that day. Thanks be to God that we were vouch-safed all this, for these things are all supernal, infused without reflection whatsoever they are sweeter than honey, the gift of the Queen to them that wander with her in exile.

We were still in the study of Rabbi Simon bar Yohai in Meron when I con-cluded my exposition of this subject. Then we fell down [in prayer] in the sepulchre of Rabbi Simon and Rabbi Eleazar, and with my lips still moving I said a short prayer from the depths of my heart. Then my master arose and expounded Deuteronomy 25:17–19 in a manner different from his previous explanations, and so did some other participants.

Elsewhere, Cordovero speaks of

What I and others have experienced in connection with *gerushin*, when we wandered in the fields with the kabbalist Rabbi Solomon Alkabez, discussing verses from the Bible suddenly, without previous reflection. On these occa-sions new ideas would come to us in a manner that cannot be believed unless one has seen or experienced it many times. The gifts which I received and which fell to my part during these *gerushin* by God's mercy upon me I shall set down in a special tract.

The messianic temper of the Safed kabbalists is also evident in their feeling of living at a crucial, in fact eschatological, moment in history. This awareness was already present, although in a very low key, among the early kabbalists. But it was greatly intensified in the sixteenth century. They were living at a turning point of history, marked by the revelation of the ultimate mysteries of divine wisdom and more especially the Lurianic teachings. In fact, the revelation and spread of kabbalistic doctrines were regarded as an essential sign of, and factor in, the process of historic growth toward the messianic era. The mystical experience of the kabbalists thus was not merely one of individual fulfillment or salvation through *gnosis*, but very definitely that of a *kairos*. R. Isaac Delattes of Mantua clearly expresses this conviction and mood in his approbation permitting, or rather justifying, the printing of the *Zohar* (1558). Printing the *Zohar* was tantamount to the hitherto esoteric Kabbalah "going public."

Contemplation, Communion with God, and Mystical Illumination

We shall revert later to the messianic aspects and results of the Safed Revival. At present we must note that it was primarily a major upsurge of genuinely mystical life. The kabbalists earnestly and devotedly sought the immediate presence of God—*devequt*. For them, as for M. H. Luzzatto in the eighteenth century, the mystical ladder led via the moral and ascetic virtues to the gift of the Holy Spirit. For that reason, the so-called "Baraitha of Rabbi Pinhas ben Yair" was a favorite text with all moralists and contemplatives.

Penitence, strict observance of the law, and moral and spiritual perfection, though undoubtedly efficacious in hastening the advent of redemption, were mere preliminaries which "man should do and live by them"; but the life intended here was the *vita contemplativa* of communion with God (*devequt*), which in sixteenth-century Safed acquired an almost erotic quality reminiscent in many ways of Sufi piety. On the love of God Maimonides states:

> And what is the proper love? That one love God with a great, excessive, and mighty love until one's soul becomes permanently bound in the love of God like one who is sick of love and cannot distract his mind from the beloved woman but always thinks of her—when lying down or rising up, when eating or drinking. Even greater than that should be the love of God in the hearts of His lovers, meditating constantly upon Him as He commanded us [Deut 6:5 "And thou shalt love the Lord thy God] with all thine heart and with all thy soul." This is what Solomon meant when he said allegorically (Cant 2:5) "for I am sick of love," and the whole *Song of Songs* is an allegory on this subject.

Or the injunctions of Bahya ibn Paquda, "He [the lover of God] will not sleep but on the couch of His love, and will not wake up but with the sweetness of His remembrance," were taken up and lived out with an emotional intensity that was enhanced by the corporate life of the kabbalistic brotherhoods. Eliezar Azikri in his ascetic manual accepts all the consequences of violent love: sleeplessness ("and one should be strong as a lion and arise after midnight and give praise to Him, practise solitude and enjoy His love"), calling God fond names, and singing to the Beloved: "It is the custom of passionate lovers to sing, and since the love of our Creator is wonderful, passing the love of women [cf. 2 Sam 1:26], therefore he who loves Him with all his heart should sing before Him." It is true that the love lyrics of the Safed mystics fall short of the literary perfection of Yehudah Halevi and Moses ibn Ezra, whom they tried to emulate, but they prove at least that the urge to sing was too powerful to be contained: "One of the most important expressions of the flame of passion is that the lover should sing songs of love before Him. Therefore I shall place before you some of the love songs that we sang with great joy in the brotherhood of Hearkening Companions [cf. Cant 8:13]." The best known and, in Schechter's phrase, most "vividly erotic" of these mystic bards was Israel Nagara, whose hymns have found their way into many a prayer book.

As has been remarked earlier, the two supreme aims of these mystics were the exaltation and redemption of the exiled *Shekhinah* and the immediate adhesion to or communion with God—"without any partition whatsoever." *Devequt* was possible because of the profound awareness that the mystic's heart was God's true dwelling. This idea is, of course, more at home among Sufis than among theosophical kabbalists, and it is quite obvious that those among the Safed authors who use this kind of language draw heavily upon such writings of earlier kabbalists as have, in fact, absorbed Sufi influence. But the deceptively simple idea of the heart as God's dwelling is enormously complicated once it is integrated in the context of kabbalistic theories on the relation of the divine *sefirot*-macrocosm to the human microcosm. At times it is difficult not to get confused by the bewildering detail in which kabbalists describe the analogous structures in the descending chain of emanations, all identically "sealed" with the Holy Name YHWH. Nonetheless, the basic idea is frequently expressed in movingly simple words. Azikri repeatedly impresses upon his readers:

> And thou, man, know that thy soul is the seat of God . . . the principal dwelling place of the *Shekhinah* is in the heart of the Jew . . . and so also has Rabbi Simon bar Yohai explained the verse [Deut 23:15] "For the Lord thy God walketh in the midst of thy camp"—the "midst," that is the heart which is in the midst of thy "camp," i.e., the body, . . . How much, therefore, should man sanctify himself in body, heart and soul, since he is a temple of the Holy King. . . . "Prepare to meet thy God, O Israel" [Amos 4:12], for thy soul is His throne and thine heart is His footstool [cf. Isa 66:1] . . . "and where is the place of His rest?"—it is in the heart, as the sages have said: God exists in the hearts of His lovers. . . . He who receives a king in his house, would he not sweep it and clean it? Since the hearts of Jews are His house we should sweep from them all the rubble and dust of sinful thoughts.

The royal road to *devequt* was solitary contemplation and the reduction of all talk, business, and social intercourse to the barest minimum. Even if one is in the world, one should not be of it: "The light of the face of the Living King rests on thine head; keep silent in His fear. And if thou speakest, speak to Him alone and the listener [i.e., your partner in worldly intercourse] may hear. In this way thou wilt practise constant *devequt*." The relation to the world and its duties is therefore an indirect, oblique, and external one. The two types of mystical solitude—the seclusion of the hermit and the seclusion "in" the world—are exemplified by Noah in the ark, and Azikri's interpretation of Gen 6:9 on two mystical levels corresponds exactly to the two stages of *Abgeschiedenheit* distinguished by all mystics and so beautifully expressed in one of Tersteegen's stanzas:

> Ich wählte vormals Ort und Zeit
> Zum Beten und zur Einsamkeit;
> Nun bet' ich stets im stillen Sinn,
> Nun bin ich einsam wo ich bin.

Azikri says:

> It is written [Gen 6:9] "and Noah walked with God." This signifies that he secluded himself with his Creator and avoided human company. Or else it may signify that he was so advanced in the practice of solitude that even when he was among men these did not distract him, for they were as non-existent in his eyes. . . . A man in the company of others is like unto one who has fallen into the sea—unless he swims well he will be drowned; but if he flees society and secludes himself with his Creator, then he is like one in a boat, saved and in communion with God.

The use made here of the image of the sea is extremely significant and suggestive. For whereas in mystical literature generally this commonplace metaphor signifies the Divine Infinite in which the individual soul (the "drop") loses itself, it here means the world which threatens to swallow the contemplative. He must therefore isolate himself "in a boat" and fall back on his own, solitary personality, which can then enter into communion with God. The maintenance of the personality as implied by the image of the boat on the infinite sea is an apt illustration of the meaning of *devequt* as compared with the radical "annihilation-in-unification" type of Sufi *unio mystica*.

But solitude is more than withdrawal from the world or society; it is also withdrawal from one's body, that is, something very near to ecstasy. Prayer is therefore an act of double withdrawal. A man's home should be the house of the Lord, where he can be alone, particularly at night:

> Even as one should make an effort and settle in the Holy Land, so the next step on the spiritual ladder should be the effort to spend the greater part of one's day and night in the Synagogue and the House of Study. There one should find rest and peace and joy, as the sages have said: Synagogues and Houses of Study are Paradise for the righteous and a prison for the wicked.

A son should offer savoury meat to his father and mother...and God delighteth in His creature arising at midnight to practise *devequt* with Him in solitude. Life is nothing but the reality of God's light shining on man; how could man remain unaware of it? "The light of God illumines thy face and thus thou livest; when He hides it, immediately man perishes. How then canst thou hide thy face and not contemplate Him always?" This realization is particularly important during prayer, which involves *devequt* of double withdrawal. The Rabbis have taught that at prayer there should be no interception between the worshipper and the wall. This signifies [immediate communion with] the *Shekhinah*, for which one has to remove all evil thoughts *or even thoughts that are not evil* from one's heart.... Another explanation is that the body should not intercept [between the soul and God] but should be as nonexistent so that the soul can cleave to the divine soul as a magnet to an iron.... You should make an effort to concentrate your mind with *devequt* whenever you utter the name of God, and this is the meaning of the phrase [1 Sam 1:15] "I have poured out my soul before the Lord," removing all partitions. It behooves us to abstract the body from the soul during prayer, as Rabbi Jonah of Gerona has already written.

It is interesting to note how the extreme demands of *devequt* turned solitude into a major virtue in spite of the strong social motives operating in the community. There were not only the devout brotherhoods, banding together in pursuit of redemption and perfection, the corporate visits to the tomb of Rabbi Simon ben Yohai and the study of the *Zohar* there, and the habit of mutual confessions of sin. There was also the more general and all-pervading stress on the value of performing all religious ceremonies and divine commandments "in company." On the other hand, the opposite tendency was no less strongly at work, extolling solitude as a *sine qua non* of the truly perfect state. The stress on solitude had appeared in earlier periods too, but had never combined in such extraordinary fashion with powerful social values and motives. The problem is a well-known one in the sociology of religion: the hermit's cave becomes a monastery, and ascetic contemplatives combine in religious orders to form model social organizations. It seems that the social habits and values of the Safed kabbalists helped to integrate the individual mystic in an ideal, normative community which gave him spiritual security and support, and which provided him with a fund of energy and discipline on which he could constantly draw. But he was never allowed to forget that in seeking God he was always a *monos pros monon:*

How can you fail to practise solitude with God? Behold, most of your time you are alone: alone in your mother's womb, alone when you sleep, the body is lonely and the soul is lonely; the body is solitary in the grave and the soul is solitary in Paradise, for "every righteous soul has a [separate] dwelling place according to its dignity".... Therefore hearken unto my voice, always walk with Him and do not separate yourself [from Him] for a moment, but seek Him and ye shall find Him, He will not part from thee. O how good and how pleasant is His company.

Characteristically enough, this exhortation knows of no expectation of life eternal in the happy company of saints (whose counterpart in traditional Jewish eschatology is eternal study in the celestial academies in the company of all the prophets, teachers, and rabbis), but the utter solitude of the soul, transfigured by the bliss of solitude fulfilled in the presence of the divine Beloved. The community is something to be left behind and forgotten:

"I and He, save, I beseech thee" — this means when I and He are alone at the proper times of solitude, as expounded in [Bahya ibn Paquda's] *Book of the Duties of the Heart*. Alternatively it can mean that "even when I am among people . . . no created thing will come between me and you [i.e., God] for compared to Him they are all as nothing, and I and He are quite alone."

Azikri avers that solitude was the traditional practice of Jewish mystics:

We find in the ascetic writings of the ancients that the pious used to practice ascetic solitude and *devequt*, which means that when they were alone they withdrew their minds from all worldly things and concentrated [lit., bound] their thoughts on the Lord of all. . . . This is the meaning of the report in the *Mishnah* [*Ber.* 5:1] "the early *hasidim* used to wait [i.e., prepare themselves] one hour before praying [and one hour afterwards] in order to concentrate their mind on God." The commentators explained this to mean that they cleared their minds from all worldly things, concentrating on the Lord of all with fear and love. They thus took off nine hours from the study of Torah and devoted this time to solitary contemplation and *devequt*. Then they would imagine the light of the *Shekhinah* above their heads as though it were flowing all around them and they were sitting in the midst of the light. So also have I found it [described] in an old manuscript of the ancient ascetics. And while in that [state of meditation] they are all trembling as a natural effect, but [spiritually] rejoicing in trembling as it is written [Ps 2:11], "Serve the Lord with fear and rejoice with trembling."

The theme is resumed again by Azikri toward the end of his book:

The fifth condition [for the attainment of the state of *devequt*] is the practice of solitary contemplation as described above. . . . At the appropriate times one should withdraw to a secluded place where one cannot be seen by others, lift up one's eyes on high to the one King, the Cause of all causes, like a mark for the arrow [of the contemplative ascent]; "as in water face answereth to face, so the heart of man to man;" [Prov 27:19], and similarly as man turns his face to his God so also will He turn to him and they will cleave together [in mystical communion]. This I have heard from my master and teacher, the holy and pious Rabbi Joseph Sagis, and this was also his practice. Similarly I have found in the writings of Rabbi Isaac of Acre that this was the practice of some pious men in his time and you will find the same in the writings of Maimonides, Naḥmanides, Baḥya ibn Paquda, and Rabbi Jonah of Gerona.

Here the extreme practice of *devequt* almost reaches the point where it ceases to be compatible with the traditional Jewish virtues of *talmud torah* and of the "performance of the divine commandments in community." Azikri's manual recommends a spiritual practice that would lead to the experience of *devequt,* but does not make it clear to what extent and in what sense this experience is ecstatic or not. We cannot even be sure that Azikri really gives us the whole story. But taking his manual as it is, we should note that it teaches no mystical techniques or formulas beyond the purely spiritual practice of contemplation, prayer, solitude, and the intense yearning of love. There are no indications that the mystic aspires to illumination in the sense of revealed knowledge and celestial indoctrination. All that he seems to seek is the immediate, mystical awareness of the presence of God. For other kabbalists *devequt* was definitely a more active and, at the same time, more "revealing" state. At the very outset of their mystical quest they asked for more—and apparently received more. Thus, Vital's *Gates of Holiness* was composed because, as the author says:

> I saw exalted souls, though but few, desiring to ascend, but ignorant of the [mystical] ladder. They study ancient books to seek and to find the paths of life, the way wherein they must walk and *the work that they must do* in order to raise their soul to its supernal root and make it cleave to Him who is eternal perfection, according to the manner of the ancient prophets who were in a state of communion with their Creator throughout their lives.

Here the cat is very quietly let out of the bag in the apparently harmless association of the practice of *devequt* with prophecy. The notion that the "prophet" is the ideal type of the perfect man implies that the prophetic *charisma* is the fruit and hence also the necessary concomitant or result of proper *devequt:*

> By means of their *devequt* the Holy Spirit rested on them, teaching them "the way where light dwelleth" and enlightening their eyes with the mysteries of the Torah . . . to cleave unto Him . . . for the prophet cleaveth to God by drawing down the influx of prophecy and divine blessing on the nether beings.

The cognitive, intellectual element in contemplation reasserts itself here, since *devequt* is the means for obtaining the Holy Spirit, namely, the prophetic influx, which is identical, to all intents and purposes, with the revelation of kabbalistic mysteries and doctrines.

According to Vital, the original prophetic tradition was continued thus:

> [By] ancient *hasidim* known as "ascetics" [lit., "Pharisees"] . . . who retired into
> the caves of rocks and into the desert, withdrawing from all social inter-
> course. Some of them were *hermits in their own houses,* living [at home] as
> in a desert and praising their Creator without interruption, day and night,
> with the study of Torah and the Psalms of David . . . until their mind cleaved
> with a mighty force and passion to the supernal lights.

But the mystic tradition was lost, and in its stead came dubious attempts to
secure illumination by methods that made it difficult to distinguish celestial
from demonic inspiration:

> In the end despair of ever discovering this wonderful wisdom seized the hearts
> of men . . . [and as a result] some began to adjure the angels by the power of
> the Holy Names, expecting light, but behold there was darkness because the
> angels [that appeared] were very inferior ones, appointed over worldly affairs
> [and not over spiritual matters] and composed of good and evil elements so
> that their revelations too were a composite of good and evil, truth and
> falsehood and all manner of vanities such as [magical] healing, alchemy, and
> the techniques of amulets and magical formulae. . . . Would God that their
> hearts were set only on [the study of] Torah and [the performance of] the
> commandments:

The "Four Travelers" to the garden of mystical knowledge are held up as
warning examples.

> It is true that the four heroes of the talmudic legend risked too much by
> attempting to attain the highest mystical reaches, whereas "we should be
> happy to attain the lower manifestations of the Holy Spirit such as the appa-
> rition of the Prophet Elijah, which, as is well known, was vouchsafed to
> many, or such as the apparition of the souls of departed saints . . . and *even
> in our time I have seen holy men who have attained this.*" Another form [of
> charismatic illumination] is that man's own soul, if it is much purified,
> appears to him and guides him on all his ways. All these methods are within
> the reach of worthy adepts even in our own time.
> In fact, we have heard and seen ourselves how choice spirits have in our
> time attained the degree of [direct inspiration by] the Holy Spirit whereby
> they could foretell the future. Some of them possessed wisdom that had not
> been revealed to previous generations. Nevertheless, the danger of involve-
> ment with the demonic world is very real whenever "prophetic" experience
> is actively solicited: "But it requires great discrimination and much experience
> to find out the truth [about these matters], for perhaps it was an alien, impure
> spirit that was with him."

Vital's ladder of ascent begins with counsels of moral and ascetic perfection and ends with almost magical formulas which so alarmed the publisher

of the little book that he left them in manuscript. His pious reticence is an eloquent tribute to the magical character of Vital's mystical instruction, for our printed text ends with this announcement: "Thus speaketh the printer: this fourth part will not be printed for it is all Holy Names and Secret Mysteries which it would be unseemly to publish." We may ignore, for the present, the extremely complicated and confusing ontology and anthropology that Vital outlines as the background of his theory of prophecy and inspiration. According to this system of combined anthropology and cosmology, ideal human nature is such that contact with the highest, divine sphere is possible and even necessary if human beings are to fulfill their proper function and purpose in the cosmic household. In spite of the proliferation of intermediate, emanated "worlds" in Lurianic Kabbalah, there is an essential unity to this great chain of being. The "lower" is always also the "outer" cover, garment, or shell, surrounding the preceding "higher" — namely, more "interior" — level of existence to which it is related as body to soul. This unity or repeated mystical analogy of infinite cosmic levels is emphatically brought out by another formulation according to which all "worlds," that is, stages of emanation, share the same anthropomorphic structure in spite of the vast hierarchical differences between them. From the celestial *anthrōpos* down to earthly humanity the same structure infinitely repeats itself. Already the exalted world of divine *sefirot* mirrors the even higher sphere of the *'Adam Qadmon*. It is thus easy to see how the human being is in principle fit to attain the state of prophecy. One merely has to establish immediate contact with the highest—that is, deepest and most hidden—divine sphere. One can do this by making use of the structure of the cosmos, the chain of being, and the essential identity of one's own structure with that of all the higher worlds. The requirements for this ascent are that one purge oneself of matter and the passions, sanctify one's soul by strict observance of the divine commandments, acquire perfect humility and constant joy, and practice contemplative *devequt*.

The specifically magical element of Vital's theory of contemplation and prophecy inheres in his refusal to admit that inspiration automatically follows *devequt*. Between the attainment of *devequt* and the influx of the Holy Spirit there must intervene a specific magical-meditative activity whose effect is to "trigger off," as it were, the downward movement of the divine influx. A rough outline of Vital's *scala contemplationis* would be somewhat like this:

1. Ascetic purification and sanctification, preparatory to *devequt* proper.

2. Meditation, preceded by complete withdrawal of the mind from all bodily and material things and sensations and by absolute mental vacuity owing to the absence of sense impressions. In this connection it is important

to note that in Vital's terminology the word *hitpashtut* does not mean ecstasy. The term is used only in the description of this second stage of contemplation, and its connotation is purely negative: withdrawal from material sensations. Actually, Vital, like many earlier kabbalists, knows no ecstasy *sensu stricto* because the soul does not leave the body behind except in the lowest form of inspiration—dreams. There is no real ascent or *Himmelsfahrt* of the soul such as was cultivated in some other systems. *Hitpashtut* means the abstraction of the mind from worldly mental contents so that the imaginative faculty, which continues to function, can exercise itself on other, higher realities. The same imaginative faculty that usually works on material supplied by the senses is now free to imagine and contemplate more spiritual things.

3. A purely imaginative ascent of the soul to its individual "root" or source in the higher world:

> Then the imaginative faculty will turn a man's thoughts to imagine and picture [mental contents] *as if* it ascended in the higher worlds up to the roots of his soul . . . until the imagined image reaches its highest source and there the images of the [supernal] lights are imprinted on his mind *as if* he imagined and saw them in the same way in which his imaginative faculty normally pictures in his mind mental contents deriving from the world. . . .

The decisive role attributed here to the imaginative faculty is clearly dependent on Maimonides' theory of prophecy. According to Vital's adaptation of it, the essence of mystical meditation is "contemplation *as if*." What makes this contemplative but purely imaginative ascent as seriously real as the less sophisticated and more ecstatic *Himmelsfahrt* of earlier adepts is the underlying doctrine of the "magical" power of all acts of meditation and concentration, particularly when supported by the right formulas. The meditative ascent, though taking place in the imagination only, thus makes the same real impact on the higher worlds and has the same effects on the soul as would a real ascent through the heavens in which the soul ecstatically left the body.

> This influx and substantial light [which as a result of the contemplative exercise is infused into the mystic's soul] is what is called "Thought" (*mahashavah*). Understand this well, for it is no vain thing. If this were not so [that imaginative meditation produces these results], then the whole kabbalistic doctrine concerning the right "intentions" and devotions at prayer (*kawwanot*) and concerning [the mystical significance of] man's good and evil thoughts were as good as nothing. You will now understand why prophecy is not only possible *but necessary;* it is as if a man held fast to the end of the bent down branch of a tree: when he shakes it [his bit of branch] with sufficient strength, then *of necessity* the whole tree is shaken with it.

4. In his imaginative ascent the mystic contemplates the ten *sefirot*. Opening himself to their irradiation he exalts and raises them to the highest sphere of *Eyn Sof*. From this highest point the light is then "reflected" and flows back ('*or hozer*). The contemplative who draws the light in the reverse direction, down on his own "soul root," thereby also irradiates the *sefirot* themselves, which are now illumined by the reflex light flowing down from *Eyn Sof*. The mystic then proceeds to conduct and direct the light farther downward through the innumerable worlds and stages of the kabbalistic cosmos, down to his rational soul and from there down to his animal soul, which is the seat of the imaginative faculty and therefore the *locus* where the prophetic, that is, spiritual-imaginative, experience takes place: "and there [in his animal soul] these [heavenly, spiritual] things will be pictured in material images by the imaginative faculty, and then he will apprehend them *as if* he saw them with his bodily eyes." Occasionally the imaginative faculty may even externalize or project the effects of this "light," so that the experience becomes one of external sense impressions such as of the apparition of angelic messengers, the hearing of voices, etc. Vital sums up the whole process in these words:

> The thought of the prophet expands and rises from one level to another . . . until he arrives at the point where the root of his soul is sunk [in the divine world]. Next he concentrates on raising the light of the *sefirah* to *Eyn Sof* and from there he draws the light down, from on high down to his rational soul and from there, by means of the imaginative faculty, down to his animal soul and there all things are pictured either by the inner senses of the imaginative faculty or by the outer senses.

So far our brief summary of Vital's *itinerarium mentis* follows the account in *Sha'arey Qedushah*. Practically all its main elements have a respectable ancestry in kabbalistic literature and practice, and regarded in isolation they hardly appear very original. The "magical" effect of concentration and meditation (*kawwanot*) is an axiom of kabbalistic tradition, and so is the anthropological-cosmological microcosm-macrocosm doctrine, which turns the whole universe into a huge chain of being that can be operated by a human being, small and insignificant as that being may appear to be. That the contemplative ascent was not an actual journey—as, for example, among primitive shamans—was also known among kabbalists, though even as a purely imaginative adventure it required the knowledge and use of holy names, formulas, and the like. Obviously, every single step during the ascent as well as during the no less dangerous descent had its appropriate and specific formulas and names. One need only read Abraham Abulafia or the fourteenth-century Spanish work *Berit Menuhah* to form an idea of the breadth and weight of the tradition on which Vital could draw.

Yet all these elements taken together do not add up to Vital's thoroughly original formulation. His important and decisive innovation resides in the definitely and *necessarily* magical character which he imparts to the contemplative exercise and which depends on his unprecedented and original distinction between "magic formulas" (*hashba'ot*) and "mystical formulas" (*yihudim*). The crucial point, as far as the magical character of Vital's system of meditation is concerned, is the transition from the contemplative ascent to the reverse movement of drawing the light, that is, the divine influx, down (*hamshakhat ha-mahashavah*). This all-important reversal can be effected only by special intense meditations and formulas (*yihudim, hazkarat shemot*). The use of "holy names" is indispensable in the Lurianic system of meditation. This fact is indisputable. Its inconsistency with Vital's repeated and grave warnings against the use of *hashba'ot* (magic formulas, lit., *Beschwörungen*) is more apparent than real. It is true that Vital never tires of stressing the dangers inherent in the use of such formulas. Their use can be risked with impunity only by saints in a state of perfect purity; otherwise the adept lets himself in with the demonic powers and is lost. Vital instances the well-known cases of Joseph della Reyna and Solomon Molkho (!) as warning examples. This "practical Kabbalah" is to be eschewed, particularly by the present generation so gravely deficient in purity and saintliness, and living in an age in which only the lowest "world of *'Asiyyah*" is accessible to *hashba'ot* and can be magically manipulated. The saints of ancient times, whose spiritual lives moved on higher planes than the "world of *'Asiyyah*" could and did use holy names during their mystic ascent in order to unlock the various celestial gates and to gain access to particular celestial "worlds," "stages," or "mansions." These formulas were effective because each was appropriately applied to the individual angel or guardian in charge of a particular *sefirah*, region, or celestial "gate." Vital thus completely absorbs the venerable *Merkavah* tradition of pacifying, exorcizing, and coercing the celestial powers and keepers of the gates. But by prohibiting or at least discouraging its practice, he to all intents and purposes also eliminates it. However, what Vital discards is the use of formulas to aid the mystical ascent (*hashba'ot*); what he insists on and actually develops as a major feature of his system are special formulas for reversing the flow of the divine light (*yihudim*). Without *yihudim*, the influx from the highest point in *Eyn Sof* to the lowest *terminus* in the animal soul cannot be brought down.

It is important to realize clearly the nature of the difference between illegitimate *hashba'ot* and indispensable *yihudim*. The former, according to Vital, were never meant as an alternative to *yihudim*; the practice of the latter is therefore untouched by the condemnation of *hashba'ot*. The one is concerned with effecting the ascent, the other with bringing about the reverse flow of the divine light and its infusion into the soul. The difference between legitimate and illegitimate use of holy names is therefore not one of pure (spiritual) versus selfish (magical) intentions. No doubt this is how the difference was understood by earlier schools of magical contemplation. Thus, according to Abraham Abulafia the same formulas might be used legitimately—if the aim was communion with God and the state of prophetic perfection—or sinfully—if the purpose was the acquisition of magical power. This latter possibility is not even discussed by Vital in the present context; it is too obviously damnable to merit consideration. The distinction, for Vital, is not between unselfish and holy versus selfish and worldly use of the magical power of the divine names, but between formulas of ascent and formulas of descent. Originally both were used and taught. The disciple of the prophets of old were taught the following, in addition to the *kawwanot* and *yiḥudim* that are indispensable even today:

> Certain prayer-formulas and divine names to be used against the guardians of the celestial gates . . . and in this way they ascended higher and higher. . . . And concerning the gate-keepers and the holy names it is thus: they adjured [the gate-keepers] with the power of the appropriate Holy Name. In fact, the whole *Merkabah*-vision of the prophet Ezekiel is nothing but an account of such an ascent by means of *hashba'ot*. But today it behooves the adept to sanctify himself to such a degree that he can pass the gates without special incantations.

However, once "inside," namely, "high up"—whether aided by formulas or not—the mystic still has to meditate, to raise the lights to *Eyn Sof*, and finally to reverse their flow and direct it downward.

The possibilities of pneumatic life are clearly stated by Vital:

> Concerning the manner of attaining the Holy Spirit I have already explained . . . that there are five manners: the Holy Spirit [in the narrow sense], the souls of departed saints, angels of the type called *maggidim*, Elijah, and dreams. Every one of these can be mediated through Elijah and without resorting to any [magical] act, purely as a result of a man's saintliness and his devotion to the law. It is also possible to attain all these by means of specific actions, but one must be worthy for this and well-prepared for illumination.

The rejection of *hashba'ot* consequently only means that formulas employing power over angels and ministering spirits should be excluded from the mystical exercise and that the initial ascent should be effected solely by means of ascetic discipline, piety, and contemplative *devequt*. In a way, the halfheartedness of Vital in this matter comes out in the fact that, in spite of his grave warnings, he did write down the practical method of *hazkarat shemot;* if the technique remained largely unknown, this was due to the printer's discretion and not to Vital's. But in any case we must fall back on the method of *yihudim,* for without it there is no attainment of prophecy:

> For this drawing down of the influx (*hamshakhat hamahashavah*) certainly never comes about by itself but [is effected] solely by the *kawwanot* and *yihudim* transmitted to the disciple by the prophet who taught him the art of prophecy. . . . By these *yihudim* he was then enabled to draw down the light and the influx according to his wish, and this is the ultimate purpose of the whole subject of prophecy.

Gnostic Mythology and Messianic Outburst

It is not our purpose here to expound in detail the kabbalistic theories and doctrines underlying much of this spirituality. But a short summary is indispensable if we are to understand the explosive messianic charge inherent in the system. [See also the more detailed discussions by Fine and Jacobs in the essays to follow.—ED.] According to Isaac Luria (1534–1572), a primordial cosmic catastrophe occurred at the very heart of God's creation. The channels or "pipes" through which the creative light-essence of God poured into creation-in-the-making could not contain this powerful light. They broke and collapsed, and the divine light "sparks" fell into chaos. Since then these sparks are in the grip of demonic powers, much as Israel (the earthly counterpart of the *Shekhinah*) is in the grip of the Gentile powers. Both are in exile, and both yearn to return to their source. The history of the world, with its progress and setbacks, is really the history of the struggle for this restoration. The two major setbacks had been the fall of Adam and the destruction of the Temple, but in fact it was not only Israel that was in need of salvation but the whole cosmos, even God Himself. The Lurianic system contained a world view in which God and humanity were bound together by much closer ties than in orthodox theology. This is not the traditional picture of a God completely independent of the world and bringing to it a kind of condescending paternal benevolence. God and human beings need each other, and hence every human act acquires a new and powerful significance. Human persons are not just sinners passively waiting for divine grace; they are not merely free agents working out their own salvation; they are decisive factors in the universe, beings whose activities are vitally related to the inner life of the Godhead. The human was created after the primeval catastrophe ("the breaking of the vessels") as God's helper in the struggle for the restoration of the perfect order and the conquest of the demonic powers. Israel's task consists in living a life of sanctity, mystical concentration, and fulfillment of the divine commandments, and, by so doing, bringing about the salvation of the world. God Himself is incomplete as long as the divine sparks are scattered and imprisoned in fallen matter and in fallen souls. God and humanity are united in the great work of salvation (*tiqqun*), which will redeem the world, the soul, Israel, and God himself. This mystical framework—one could almost call it a gnostic-type mythology—was able to absorb the whole traditional system of Jewish life and observance. Far from exhibiting antinomian tendencies, the Lurianic system viewed the halakhic tradition with its commandments and ritual as nothing less than the method by which the cosmos would be restored and reordered. "Doing the will of God," which had formerly meant carrying out his commandments and observing his law—and thereby acquiring blessing and a long life (or eternal felicity)—was now transformed by contemplative concentration into a process of mystical redemption. It represented a "sacramentalization" of the life of even the humblest Jew.

Luria's career in Safed was short, since he died very young. But undoubtedly he was the most charismatic as well as the most original of the Safed kabbalists, and his influence on the small band of chosen disciples was almost hypnotic. For a short time after his death his teaching was jealously guarded by his disciples as a highly esoteric lore that could be imparted only to the elect few. But inevitably the teaching spread, as more manuscripts (often surreptitiously copied) began to circulate and as missionaries of the new kabbalistic gospel reached all parts of the Jewish Diaspora. Understandably enough, it was not so much the esoteric doctrine as its messianic high voltage that galvanized the public and crystallized its apocalyptic mood. The terrible Cossack massacres of 1648 may well have intensified this mood at least among Ashkenazi Jewry. The messianic event took place in May 1665. A young kabbalist rabbi of unstable temperament—in fact, so unstable and exhibiting such bizarre behavior that he was forced to leave his hometown of Smyrna and his family and to go to a place where he was a stranger—took up temporary residence in Jerusalem, but also there attracted attention. Finally he proclaimed himself—or rather was proclaimed by a prophet—as the Messiah, the anointed of the God of Israel. According to G. Scholem in his magisterial account of this astounding movement, Sabbatai Sevi was not merely unstable but a clear case of manic-depressive psychosis, whereas his prophet, Nathan of Gaza, was a charismatic visionary and by far the stronger personality.[2] Messianic pretenders and messianic movements have been a constant feature of Jewish history, but they were usually local and very short-lived phenomena. Never before had a messianic movement spread like a bushfire and engulfed Jewry from England to Persia, from Germany to Poland and Russia, from Italy to North Africa, from Holland to the Yemen. Turkey and the Turkish Balkans, and of course

Palestine, were at the epicenter of this cataclysm. The messianic fever was not restrained by the sad fact that nothing had changed. Kabbalistic doctrine had an answer for that. It had taught the believers that change would begin in the invisible spheres of the mystical cosmos and gradually spread outward. Only in the end, when the Messiah had accomplished and consummated his mission, would the fullness of redemption become manifest also on the outer levels of our social and political reality. When the agitation among the Jews became too much for the Ottoman authorities, Sabbatai was arrested (February 1666), imprisoned, and subsequently exiled. But the movement continued to flourish and was not even squelched by Sabbatai's converting to Islam in order to save his skin. An apostate messiah! Many believers lost their faith—much as 1600 years earlier many believers had lost theirs after the crucifixion. But there are messianic theologies that thrive on paradox—and the more stunning the paradox the profounder it is claimed to be—and in this case the answer was given by developing Lurianic kabbalism to its utmost limits: the Messiah must descend into the abyss of sin and evil in order to conquer sin and evil. A small band of believers followed the Messiah into apostasy and survived as a crypto-Muslim sect in Turkey until early in the twentieth century. Others held fast to the faith, living as orthodox Jews but believing that the Messiah, a unique manifestation of a uniquely divine soul, had to fulfill his unique mission of bringing about salvation in his own unique and mysterious way. Sabbatai died in 1676 in the small Albanian town whither the Turkish authorities had exiled him. The movement petered out, leaving behind it a trail of shame, disarray, a discredited Kabbalah, and a deep suspicion regarding messianic enthusiasm. Scholem has argued that the messianic outburst played a significant role in the conditioning of Jewry for the transition into modernity. The great awakening and the vision of a new world had irremediably shattered the old world. But although the new world of the Messiah failed to dawn, the old world remained shattered nonetheless, and many were ready for an alternative type of new world.

The Aftermath and Other Developments

For the Jewry of eastern Europe, the new world of the Enlightenment and emancipation, civil rights and modernity, was still generations away. The messianic dream was shattered—or rather ceased to be an immediate expectation within reach—and once more became a long-term hope. But the misery and the material as well as spiritual pauperization of the present were very much in evidence. Hasidism was one answer. The talmudic-rabbinic elite looked down upon this revival type of mysticism with a great deal of contempt and at first also accused it of being an offshoot of the Sabbatian "heresy." In a sense it was, but that is the least important part of it. It is also true that the founder, R. Israel Ba'al Shem Tov (or, abbreviated, BeSHT), and his immediate disciples did not come from the ranks of the rabbinic scholars. But they taught the simple folk the rejoicing in the communion with God and the practice of the presence of God in everyday life. If such communion was difficult to achieve, there was the hasidic master, the saintly man and guide (i.e., the rabbi as mediator rather than scholar) to help. Hasidism saw itself as standing in the line of kabbalistic tradition. In actual fact, however, and in spite of the use of kabbalistic terminology, the new mystical revival had shifted away from the traditional Kabbalah in general and from the high-pitched messianic fervor of Lurianism in particular. It was a demessianized mystical spirituality. Not that Hasidism relinquished the traditional messianic faith—that essential element of historic Judaism—but, in terms of their actual and immediate spiritual aspirations (and barely recovering from the Sabbatian debacle), the early hasidic masters, so G. Scholem argued, somehow "neutralized" the explosive dynamite of imminent messianism and taught a way to the practice of the presence of God that would be accessible even to the simplest and lowliest. It should not come as a surprise that students of Hasidism have found analogies, at least in certain details, with other, also non-Jewish, manifestations of spirituality, from St. Francis to Zen. The Hasidic way was not devoid of elements of enthusiasm, ecstasy, and emotional excess. Nevertheless, though first held in contempt (and this contempt persisted as part of the attitude toward Hasidism among many sections of orthodox Jewry), Hasidism conquered a large part of eastern European Jewry and established itself as a valid and legitimate form of Judaism. Decline was inevitable, but the history of this decline (including the foolish superstitions that seem to become a necessary part of every mystical mass movement, the hereditary "dynasties" of hasidic masters combined with a degenerate and presumptuous doctrine of "mediation," the fact that the movement spread at a time when the Enlightenment and the new rationalism caused other segments of Jewry to cross over into the modern age etc.) is not our present concern.

Mention has already been made of another type of spirituality which is often neglected—perhaps because less spectacular, less exotic, and more rational than the Kabbalah. Very often this type of piety was propagated by men who, as we know, were themselves kabbalists but who felt that this part of their teaching should be reserved to the chosen few only. It is a spirituality usually called *mussar*. The term may cause confusion since it is nowadays mainly associated with the nineteenth-century movement that developed as a non-Hasidic orthodox reaction to the spirit of the Enlightenment, which, coming from Germany, penetrated eastern Europe. (The term Hasidism too, having a long history in the vocabulary of Jewish piety, is subject to similar confusions.) *Mussar* found expression in writings usually described as "ethical literature," sometimes in the form of homiletical compositions, sometimes in more systematic, semiphilosophical form, often also in the form of "ethical wills." Each author dealt with the cardinal virtues and disciplines (love of God, fear of God, humility, avoidance of sin) against a larger theological background, and each author did so in his own way and with his peculiar borrowings from philosophical and kabbalistic terminology. Perhaps the most outstanding work in this genre is the *Path of the Upright* (already mentioned earlier in this essay) by R. Moses Hayyim Luzzatto (1707–1747). No matter what the author's (hidden kabbalistic?) motives were in writing this tract, it served as a nonkabbalist manual of piety and as a guide to moral and religious self-discipline and training, aiming at the attainment of spiritual perfection. The ascent on the ladder of virtues follows the sequence of an old talmudic saying: "The knowledge of Torah leads to watchfulness, watchfulness to zeal, zeal to cleanness, cleanness to abstinence, abstinence to purity, purity to saintliness, saintliness to humility, humility to fear of sin, fear of sin to holiness, and holiness leads to the gift of the Holy Spirit." An eighteenth-century kabbalist and mystic writes an exoteric spiritual manual by way of expounding a talmudic dictum. As is the case also in other religious traditions, Jewish spirituality makes it history, often a revolutionary one, by hiding the facts of change under a cloak—which, in fact, is far more than a cloak—of continuity.

Notes

[1] In *Studies in Judaism*, 203–306.
[2] Scholem, *Sabbatai Sevi: The Mystical Messiah.*

Bibliography

Most histories of Judaism deal with the Safed Revival, its spirituality, and the messianic outburst that followed it. In addition to the general histories, special mention should be made of the following works.

Schechter, Solomon. "Safed in the 16th Century." In *Studies in Judaism*, 203–306. 2nd series. Philadelphia: Jewish Publication Society, 1908.

Scholem, G. *Kabbalah.* Jerusalem: Keter, 1974. Pp. 67ff. and the relevant entries in parts 2 ("Topics") and 3 ("Personalities").

———. *Major Trends in Jewish Mysticism.* New York: Schocken Books, 1946. Chaps. 7 and 8.

———. *The Messianic Idea in Judaism.* New York: Schocken Books, 1971.

———. *On the Kabbalah and Its Symbolism.* New York: Schocken Books, 1965. Chaps. 3 and 4.

———. *Sabbatai Sevi: The Mystical Messiah.* Princeton, NJ: Princeton University Press, 1973.

Werblowsky, R. J. Zwi. *Joseph Karo: Lawyer and Mystic.* 2nd ed. Philadelphia: Jewish Publication Society, 1977.

2

Halakhah and Kabbalah as Competing Disciplines of Study

Jacob Katz

Halakhah and Aggadah

POSTBIBLICAL JUDAISM is distinguished by the central position its scale of values assigns to the study of Sacred Scripture, both in its "written" and "oral" varieties. The study of Torah is obligatory for each and every individual and is considered a religious commandment of the first rank, raising the performer's esteem both in his own eyes and in the eyes of others.[1] It differs in one respect from other obligations of the Jewish religion: its observance can be limitlessly extended or, in the language of the Mishnah, "no definite quantity is prescribed" (*Peah* 1:1). Therefore, the student of Torah can attain many possible levels until the upper limit of "one whose study is his craft" (*h. Ber.* 16b, *h. Shab.* 11a), that is, one who devotes himself to the performance of this commandment and also makes it the main concern of his life.

The phenomenon of granting central importance to an intellectual activity permeated by an aura of holiness manifests itself clearly throughout the life of the Jewish people. In theory, the aura of holiness applied only to foundation layers of Scripture and oral tradition, the latter regarded as having been revealed at Sinai. In fact, however, all that had become interwoven, through the centuries, with those fundamental layers by means of exegesis or amplification enjoyed a similar aura. There were, to be sure, differences of opinion from time to time with regard to some of the literary products of these processes—popular legend, rationalistic philosophical views, and bold kabbalistic conceptions, which some embraced and others rejected.[2] Those, however, which gained acceptance were accorded the status of sacred literature whose study was considered the fulfillment of a commandment.

Nonetheless, not everything recognized as worthy of study was awarded equal status, and the question of priority with regard to certain segments of what was broadly considered *divrey Torah* was never satisfactorily resolved. During the rabbinic era, Scripture, Mishnah, Midrash, Talmud, laws, and legends vied for position in the scale of priorities.[3] In the post-talmudic era, philosophy and Kabbalah entered the fray. It appears that the dividing line between the two major areas of study throughout the generations falls between what was called, in a general sense, *halakhah* and what was known as *aggadah* (including philosophy and Kabbalah). By the first is meant all that applies to determining the definitions, details, and directives of the practical commandments. The second category applies to subjects dealing with matters of "belief and opinion," among whose roles is the giving of meaning to the practical commandments, both their general principles and their specific details.

Ostensibly, the two elements of this tradition of learning complement each other, for the practical directives of the halakhah without explanations from the realm of "beliefs and opinions" would be simply pointless decrees and, on the other hand, Judaism's system of beliefs and opinions includes, by definition, the notion of binding commandments revealed at Sinai. In fact, the obligation of engaging in both spheres of study was unanimously accepted. But the division of time between them and the question of emphasis upon one sphere or another always remained open. Certainly there were always to be found students who distinguished themselves primarily in halakhah or who specialized in aggadah,[4] philosophy, or Kabbalah. The choice between them could well have been determined by individual talents and proclivities, for it is clear that a creative command of halakhah demands different kinds of abilities than does a similar mastery of aggadah, philosophy, or Kabbalah.[5] However, the decision could also be a matter of absolute preferences, for despite the mutual dependence between halakhah and its sister disciplines, the competition between them for esteem never ceased, neither in the public domain nor in the hearts and minds of individuals.

The primacy of halakhah was ostensibly assured both on account of its inherent characteristics and because of the manner in which a knowledge of it was acquired. The halakhot are the very basis of the Torah: only through them can one come to know one's religious obligations. A broad knowledge of the halakhah establishes one as an authoritative guide in religious practice for the public and serves as the prerequisite for appointment to such positions as religious judge or head of a *yeshiva*. A mastery of halakhah cannot be attained without a degree of intellectual effort of which not all are capable, thus contributing to the prestige bound up with it. A knowledge of aggadah, by contrast, is more easily attained, and its mastery neither provides formal religious authority nor does it pave the way for the attainment of prestigious positions.

Nevertheless, it is conceivable that the aggadist will feel that he, more than the halakhist, penetrates the mysteries of the religion, for it is he who points the way to others in studying the divinity and seeking its proximity in the conquest of the evil instinct and the purifying of one's mind. Not for naught did the sages say, "If you desire to know The One Who created the world, study aggadah" (*Sifre ' Eqev* 49:11, 12). Furthermore, they themselves accepted the existence of an unmediated path to the study and knowledge of God—that which was known as *ma'aseh merkavah*. Whatever its precise nature, it was considered a means of initiating the elite into the revelation of divine commandments that were hidden from the masses. In the wider sense of the term, *ma'aseh merkavah* was also included in the notion of aggadah, and it was explicitly assigned a superior status to that of halakhic debate in the famous statement concerning R. Yohanan b. Zakkai, of whom it is said "that he did not leave [unstudied] Scripture, Mishnah, Gemara, halakhah, aggadah . . . great matter or small matters. "Great matters" mean the *ma'aseh merkavah*; "small matters" mean the discussions of Abbaye and Rava (*Sukkah* 28a).[6]

Aggadah as Philosophy and Kabbalah

Post-talmudic halakhah enjoyed immense and variegated expansion, but in its essence—in its characteristic manner of thought and its dogmatic directives—it remained basically unchanged. This was not true of the aggadah, whose exegetical role was gradually entrusted during the Middle Ages to the two disciplines of philosophy and Kabbalah, both of which were relative upstarts.[7] Moreover, the conceptual system of the aggadah itself was, to a considerable degree, wrenched from its original meaning and understood in terms of these new disciplines. And just as these disciplines raided the terrain of the aggadah, so too they inherited its problematic relationship with the halakhah. The questions of priority and primacy in relation to the halakhah attached themselves now to philosophy and Kabbalah, though in a somewhat different form.

Philosophy came to medieval Jewish society as a result of the latter's contacts with the non-Jewish worlds of Islam and Christendom. Once it arrived, however, it was absorbed—at least so far as those who espoused it were concerned—in Jewish intellectual tradition. In the eyes of such men as Abraham ibn Ezra and Maimonides, philosophy was not an alien growth in the midst of Judaism but rather was considered the only path toward verifying and properly understanding the principles of faith. In fact, they interpreted the religion's own sources—scriptural verses and talmudic statements—as commanding philosophical study toward that end.[8] They were able to find explicit support for their position in the words of the sages concerning *ma'aseh merkavah*, which they identified with metaphysics. Thus they were able to infer not only that philosophical study of this sort was permissible (as long as one took the necessary precautions) but also that it was, in fact, considered a *mizwah*—as it had been for R. Akiba and his colleagues in their day.[9]

Modern scholarship has come to the conclusion that the Kabbalah too, at least in the early stages of its development, was both stimulated and influenced by non-Jewish sources.[10] These sources, however, remained beneath the surface; thus, unlike philosophy, Kabbalah succeeded in presenting itself—from the time that it first appeared in the public realm in twelfth-century Provence—as a purely Jewish phenomenon. Furthermore, it was accepted as the deepest layer of revelation, whether from Sinai or through such accepted channels of divine inspiration as prophecy or "the revelation of Elijah."[11] For this reason its alleged link with the talmudic tradition of *ma'aseh merkavah* seemed reasonable and was, in fact, accepted by many. For the same reason, however, it could not avoid the problem implicit in the distinction between "great matters" and "small matters." Its adherents were liable to demand for Kabbalah primacy over the study of halakhah—and not necessarily on the basis of the above-mentioned talmudic distinction. The Kabbalists suffered the same fate as the philosophers: once they immersed themselves in attempting to understand the divine essence and that of the Torah, this activity became more attractive to them than conventional Torah study. The parallel in consciousness between the proponents of philosophy and those who favored Kabbalah is clearly evident and was actually expressed by R. Elijah Mizrahi, who wrote: "The study of *ma'aseh merkavah* relates to the Creator, both in the view of the Kabbalists and of the scholars of philosophy, and Talmudic wisdom deals with the commandments."[12] Why involve oneself only in expressions of will when the path has been broken for coming into contact with the Creator Himself?

Zohar—The Turning Point

Kabbalah's demand for primacy over the halakhah did not arise immediately with the appearance of the former upon the Jewish scene. In its early stages of development—in the Provençal *Sefer ha-Bahir* and in the writings of the Gerona kabbalists through (and including) Nahmanides—the Kabbalah entirely preserved its esoteric character. The question regarding its study was whether it was permitted at all, and for whom. In the homilies of *Sefer ha-Bahir* the commandment of Torah study is included among those to which kabbalistic meaning is attached.[13] Although it was given metaphysical significance—providing assistance to the divine forces so that they might carry out their activities—Torah study's content was not altered thereby but retained rather its plain meaning—the study of the exoteric (*nigleh*), to use a concept which crystallized only later.[14]

R. Ezra of Gerona, in his commentary on the Song of Songs, provides a list of the 613 commandments which, following Maimonides, includes also that of Torah study.[15] Although his primary intention in the work is to glorify esoteric wisdom, he does not claim greater metaphysical value for its study than for the study of halakhah.[16] A similar view is espoused by his friend R. Azriel in the latter's *Commentary on the Aggadot.*[17] R. Ezra saw in the esoteric interpretation of the Torah a necessary complement to its straightforward interpretation, and he did not seek therefore to limit knowledge of this method to a specific circle. This tendency, however, encountered opposition. R. Isaac the Blind's warning to the Gerona kabbalists not to disseminate their esoteric teaching publicly[18] and the effort of Nahmanides to express his (kabbalistic) views in such a way that they would be comprehensible only to initiates[19] both indicate that the hedge of secrecy surrounding the Kabbalah had not been burst. Kabbalah remained within the ken of a select few and did not, therefore, cause halakhah any loss of ground in the public domain.

This situation continued without significant change until the critical turning point in the history of the Kabbalah, which came about with the publication (in the late thirteenth century) of the *Zohar.* In the triangle composed of halakhah, philosophy, and Kabbalah, there now occurred a revolutionary shift. R. Moses de Leon adapted to his own needs the criticism voiced by Maimonides against the scholar who limited himself to exoteric study only.[20] His major composition, the *Zohar,* was nothing less than a new light cast on the foundations of the Jewish religion, including its biblical traditions and its institutions, commandments, and daily practices. This kabbalistic midrash (which covered most of the pericopes of the Pentateuch) by its very existence constituted a form of protest against the rationalistic exegesis of the Torah and was, in fact, understood and presented as such by its author.[21]

In the *Zohar,* as opposed to its immediate successors the *Ra'aya Meheimna* and the *Tiqquney Zohar,* the opposition between esoteric and exoteric study is neither stressed nor even sensed. In the *Zohar's* narratives, which are presented as the actual background against which the homilies of its protagonists were delivered, Torah study plays an important role. Many of them open with the words "Rabbi so-and-so was studying Torah," without even the slightest hint that mystical study is intended. Similarly, all that is said in the *Zohar* in praise of Torah study and in disparagement of its neglect refers, without doubt, also to exoteric study.[22] If the *Zohar* exaggerated in either direction, it was merely overemphasizing the talmudic tradition, which elevated Torah study to the highest position in the scale of the commandments. It was seen not only as a key to observing the Torah's commandments but also as a means of achieving direct contact with the divine sphere. The *Zohar*, in its characteristic manner, was able to portray the process of making contact with one of the divine *sefirot* and fortifying it through the act of Torah study. A distinction was evidently made between the study of Scripture and the study of oral tradition with regard to the specific operation of the act upon the *sefirot*.[23] No special kabbalistic significance, however, was attributed to the study of esoteric lore.

Assertion of the Primacy of Kabbalah

The *Zohar*'s influence upon the decision in favor of esoteric study came as a result of its very "appearance" (in the late thirteenth century). Students of Kabbalah now had at their disposal a wide-ranging corpus that inspired awe on account of its antiquity and also enchanted readers by means of the aura of mystery that pervaded its pages. Whether or not this atmosphere was created as a conscious response to philosophical rationalism, the result was the supplantation of any study demanding sharp and vigorous thought—including straightforward halakhic study.

This dialectical development is manifestly clear in the pages of the *Ra'aya Meheimna* and the *Tiqquney Zohar*. They continue in the *Zohar*'s path, but the illumination they gain through esoteric understanding of the Torah causes a heavy shadow to fall upon the study of its plain meaning. It sometimes appears, in fact, that these ardent kabbalists have been so completely alienated from halakhic discourse that they regard it as a painful burden whose sole purpose is to torment them.[24] How far, precisely, did they go in their negation of halakhah? Modern scholars of Kabbalah have offered various points of view on the question. The correct one seems to be that of Gershom Scholem, who asserts that they did not question its validity for their own time though they did envision a future messianic era, in which the Torah with its laws and commandments intended for our earthly existence (*torah de-beri'ah*) would be replaced by a sublime and purely spiritual one (*torah de-'azilut*).[25] The practical implications of this theory for the present applied to the study of Torah—granting highest priority to kabbalistic study, through which one gained access to the realm of the higher emanations even while maintaining an everyday existence. And, in fact, later authors who fought to provide a basis for the Kabbalah's claim to primacy vis-à-vis the halakhah made use of the relevant passages in the *Ra'aya Meheimna* and *Tiqquney Zohar,* as we shall see.

Although there had now erupted a more or less open battle between exoteric and esoteric study, the major front passed, in the above-mentioned triangle, between halakhah and kabbalah, on the one side, and philosophy, on the other. Talmudists distanced themselves from philosophy even if they had not developed an affinity for Kabbalah. Two Spanish representatives of this position were R. Solomon ibn Adret (d. 1310) and, two generations later, R. Nissim Gerondi. This talmudic autarchy is reflected also in Profiat Duran's description of one of the three competing schools of thought among Spanish Jewry of his day—the late fourteenth and early fifteenth centuries.[26] The three groups offer differing opinions concerning "the wisdom of the Torah through which may be attained . . . ultimate felicity."[27]

Duran describes the three positions in order to argue for a fourth (his own): granting primacy to the study of the Bible, which had been suffering from neglect.[28] His description reflects a situation in which talmudic study had risen in esteem, especially that of the "pilpulistic" variety—seeking intellectual satisfaction rather than practical implications—which had come to enjoy ideological support on religious grounds.[29]

The kabbalists, according to Duran, criticize the insularity of studying only halakhah, preferring to complement the latter with their own teachings—with no intention, however, of weakening it or causing it harm. A deliberate attack of this sort, surpassing even the *Ra'aya Meheimna* and *Tiqquney Zohar* in its criticism, did come from the author of the two books known as *Qanah* and *Peli'ah.* Thus unique and rather isolated author (who seems, as Israel Ta-Shema has suggested, to have lived in Byzantium rather than Spain[30]) expressed the view that exoteric study was worthwhile and necessary only insofar as the material studied contained hidden secrets. Therefore, he claimed, the discerning student could extract kabbalistic meanings from between the lines of the halakhic debate. One who did not, could not, according to *Sefer ha-Peli'ah,* be considered a "sage," even if he had studied *Sifra, Sifre, Tosefta,* and the entire Talmud; "for what use has he from all these if he does not seek to know their source and foundation—for all their words are hidden secrets."[31] This unique manner of argumentation is evident in the *Sefer ha-Qanah* as well. Its author opens many of his discussions with critical questions concerning Talmudic statements which are intended, evidently, to make them appear baseless. The questions are formulated according to the conventions of halakhic debate, whereas the answers he provides seek to read kabbalistic meaning into the talmudic texts. The implication is that, without resorting to Kabbalah, the words of the Talmud would remain logically undermined.[32]

Profiat Duran's casual testimony concerning the increasing esteem enjoyed by talmudic studies among Spanish Jewry of his day is corroborated by R. Joseph Yavetz's observations on the situation at the time of the Expulsion. The latter asserts that never before had Spain been as full of *yeshivot* and their students as it had been at that moment, "with the students divided into several groups—some would spend six or seven years with the great rabbis, sharpening their minds like a razor." This phenomenon, however, was seen by Yavetz in essentially negative terms, for he felt that such intensive study had failed to achieve its desired end of "practice and piety."[33] His judgment of his generation, colored by the experience of decrees and expulsion it had suffered, is framed in categories of innocent and guilty. The former, in his opinion, consisted of naïve believers who sacrificed their lives for their faith, in contrast to the latter, the intellectuals (*maskilim*), whose learning may have been talmudic or philosophical. Although his ire was directed primarily at those "addicted" to philosophy (which he regarded as responsible for weakening the faith of his generation), the talmudists were not free from blame. Their excessive involvement in *pilpul*, he claimed, prevented them from attaining "the Torah's ultimate end." Furthermore, most of them were not religiously motivated in their study; "therefore they were not able to defend their generation," by which he meant that they did not serve as a model of self-sacrifice to the masses when they were put to the test.[34]

The question that arises from such a description is: Where were the kabbalists, masters of that which he saw as "the highest wisdom . . . through which we might adhere to this great name"?[35] Yet elsewhere he indicates that he did not regard Kabbalah as necessary knowledge, seeing the revelation of its secrets, rather, as a reward awaiting the pious in the next world.[36] In fact, it is unclear whether Yavetz himself was well versed in its teachings. Hardly a trace of them is evident in his sermons or commentaries. Nonetheless, R. Joseph seems to have shown an interest in spreading the Kabbalah publicly.[37] Be that as it may, in his description of pre-Expulsion Spain, he mentions those intellectuals "entirely lacking in this wisdom (the Kabbalah) who scoff at it . . . and at its scholars."[38] In his critique of the generation's leadership, however, the kabbalists are not presented as a group elevated above the rest, whose behavior could have served as a model to the masses.

R. Judah Hayyat, in contrast, was hardly equivocal concerning the need to acquire the secrets of the *Merkavah* while humanity still resided in this world. Knowledge of the "secret reasons" is, according to him, readily accessible, "and those who taste of it taste of the delicacies preserved for the righteous in the next world." Only few, however, actually attain this level, since the majority, he asserts, have distanced themselves from kabbalistic wisdom, whether out of low esteem for its worth, denial of its validity, or the fear of misunderstanding it.[39] Hayyat launches an all-out attack against those who deny themselves, to his mind, both the fulfillment of the Torah (especially in the matter of prayers) and the sense of elevation and clinging to the divine which accompanies its fulfillment. In fact, he goes so far as to assert that the masters of the Kabbalah are ten times superior to the masters of Bible and Mishnah.[40] This rather daring opinion found support in the words of the *Zohar* and *Tiqquney Zohar*, in which Hayyat was well versed. He was also one of the first to make use of *Sefer ha-Qanah* for elevating the esoteric Torah above the exoteric. If, in the case of R. Joseph Yavetz, the experience of the Expulsion and the harsh decrees that preceded it intensified his opposition to philosophy, in the case of R. Judah Hayyat, this same experience strengthened his belief in the almost magical power of the Kabbalah. He attributed his own salvation at the end of a long road of suffering in Portugal, North Africa, and Italy to his devotion to the study of Kabbalah and to his assiduous collection of *Zohar* manuscripts, "so that most of its existing sections came into [his] hands."[41]

The Relation between Halakhah and Kabbalah

The tension between the competing attractions of exoteric and esoteric teachings did not always burst outward (sometimes it was intentionally kept quiet), but it played an important role, nonetheless, in determining the relation between the two. In the thought of R. Meir ibn Gabbai, a young contemporary of the Spanish exiles who developed his ideas in their new colony in Turkey, Kabbalah clashed head on only with philosophy.[42] Already in the introduction to his youthful work *Tola'at Ya'aqov* (written in 1507 when he was 26), R. Meir joined the ranks of those who criticized the Maimonidean effort to explain the commandments on the basis of human reason. He even hinted at his opposition, in principle, to Maimonides' effort to incorporate philosophy into the hallowed Jewish tradition by means of identifying its subjects with *ma'aseh bereshit* and *ma'aseh merkavah*. In his systematic work of kabbalistic thought, *'Avodat ha-Qodesh*, written during the years 1523–1531,[43] he expressed this opposition more forcefully, quoting from such predecessors as ibn Adret and R. Yom Tov Ashvili, while adding to their own criticisms. In his view, external forms of wisdom were excluded from any possible comparison with the Torah in all its parts, exoteric and esoteric. It was possible, however, to compare the *ma'aseh merkavah*, that is, the teachings of the Kabbalah, with "the debates of Abbaye and Rava"—the halakhah in its widest sense. These "could be included within one category . . . but would be distinguished by their relative stature" ('*Avodat ha-Qodesh,* part 4, chap. 1 [1b]).

In R. Meir's view, then, complete harmony reigned between the two parts of the Torah, the esoteric and exoteric, with the obligation of study falling upon both. The study of halakhah is perceived as necessary, first of all, so that one may know how the divine directives are to be carried out. Halakhic knowledge, however, hardly suffices as a means of achieving spiritual perfection. The latter can be achieved only by also gaining a knowledge of the reasons for and the secrets of the commandments—and these are hidden in the "esoteric lore." The "exoteric" is no more than a body or a container, "and one who studies only the body and the vestments of the Torah, denying that there is anything besides them, removes the Torah's soul and denies its essence . . . and it would be better had he never been created" ('*Avodat ha-Qodesh,* part 4, chap. 1 [52a–b]). Such statements are only, of course, echoes of the judgments of the *Ra'aya Meheimna* and *Tiqquney Zohar,* from which ibn Gabbai frequently quotes to support his views. In greatly stressing the value of the esoteric over that of the exoteric, R. Meir was able to find support also in the talmudic distinction between the "great thing" and the "small thing," which, according to his interpretation, applied to these two sections of the Torah respectively.[44]

To be sure, it is not merely a theoretical position that is being discussed here, for R. Meir clearly identifies personally with this evaluation. He himself studies both varieties of Torah but finds inspiration and satisfaction only while dealing with the esoteric teachings, in which he demonstrates independence and originality of thought. This attitude is expressed biographically in the concluding words of his youthful work. There he apologizes to the reader for any errors that might be found in the book, which he attributes to three possible factors: first, the difficulty of the work (and profundity of the subject) in relation to his young age; second, the heavy burden of supporting himself and his family, "and the third, that I did not cease studying, even in the middle of the night, the debates of Abbaye and Rava" (*Tola'at Ya'aqov,* 47b). He therefore implies that the obligation of talmudic study stood in the way of his dealing in sufficient depth with the esoteric subject matter of his book.

The attitude toward halakhic study expressed in this casual confession at the end of *Tola'at Ya'aqov* is reflected also in the body of the work. The stated purpose is to guide the reader in performing the daily prayers and their auxiliary commandments (*zizit, lulav,* etc.) in the best manner possible. In order to do so one must first know the laws connected with these commandments, but, more important according to R. Meir, one must be familiar with their symbolic meaning according to the Kabbalah.[45] The preparation of the work required the author to involve himself in the relevant halakhic and kabbalistic material. Significantly, with regard to the former, he chose to rely upon readily available reference works (primarily the *Tur Oraḥ Ḥayyim*[46] without delving into the original talmudic sources. His primary energies are devoted, rather, to giving kabbalistic meaning to the laws—a task at which he is both original and politic, although in this also he relies, of course, on preexisting tradition rooted especially in the *Zohar*.[47]

The reluctance to enter into halakhic debate is especially noticeable in those places where R. Meir encountered differences between the various codifiers on small points of ritual, or where the *Tur* cites multiple opinions without deciding between them. In such cases, he could not, as guide to the Jew desirous of serving God properly, simply leave the matter hanging. He chooses instead to bypass the halakhic thought processes of the codifiers, allowing his decisions to be determined either by the authority of the *Zohar* or in favor of the practice which best lent itself to kabbalistic explanation. The preference for Zoharic authority over that of the codifiers is made explicit by R. Meir (*Tolaʿat Yaʿaqov*, 17b, 20a), and in doing so he merely continues and perhaps expands a tradition that was accepted among kabbalistically inclined scholars in Spain, as I shall explain elsewhere.[48]

In some instances, however, R. Meir prefers not to rely formally on Zoharic authority, providing only the kabbalistic reason on the basis of which he arrives at his halakhic decision.[49] In allowing the kabbalistic explanation to serve as the basis for determining actual practice, R. Meir takes a radical step which such bona fide halakhists as R. Joseph Karo and R. David ibn Zimra (though both were devotees of Kabbalah) were unwilling to take.

In fact, ibn Gabbai appears before us as one who is knowledgeable in the fundamentals of halakhah and who continues in its study for the sake of the commandment to do so, like other Jews loyal to tradition. In describing the order of the Jew's day, following the *Tur* (*Oraḥ Ḥayyim* #155), he states the obligation, following the morning prayers in the synagogue, "to enter the *bet ha-midrash* to study Torah or to hear [its study]" (*Tolaʿat Yaʿaqov*, 22a). Torah study, in his view, is necessary in order to provide guidance for actual practice, but it also functions, on the kabbalistic level, "to create harmony and perfection in the divine world."[50] This double purpose can be achieved at any level of study—whether intensive or merely passive—thus R. Meir's phrase "to study or to hear" (which is absent from the *Tur*).

No reference is here made to in-depth study of the halakhah or novel interpretations of its statements, and there is no indication that R. Meir himself actually achieved such a level or even aspired to it. He demonstrated independence and originality of mind, as we have seen, only in kabbalistic study. Whether we regard this as a matter of character (for the psychological traits suitable for creativity in halakhah are not the same as those appropriate for original kabbalistic thought), or whether we relate these tendencies to his devotion to Kabbalah (the available biographical data do not furnish a satisfactory answer), ibn Gabbai's mastery of Kabbalah and its mastery of him are both characteristic of his personality.

Safed

In contrast to the individual biographical dimension, a causal relationship between attachment to the mystical aura of Kabbalah and a weakening involvement in halakhic study can be shown when speaking of an entire group in which such a dual tendency is shown. We find a group of this type among the Jewish population of Safed during the period of its efflorescence, from the third decade of the sixteenth century until just before the century's end. Signs of such blossoming in the spiritual sphere (in contrast to the economic and organizational sphere) are to be found in the considerable talents demonstrated in the traditional areas of Jewish cultural creativity—halakhah, homiletic and ethical literature, poetry, and especially Kabbalah.[51] Activity in these areas was not sharply divided between individuals and, on occasion, the same person might be active and even prolific in several different fields.[52]

Halakhah was less susceptible than any other field to becoming the province of a few. Acquiring the method of talmudic study was part of the education of every Jew; daily devotion to study was considered an obligation; and fulfilling it more or less satisfactorily was considered a prerequisite for membership in the creative elite. Furthermore, those exceptional individuals who were productive on the literary level, even in such non-halakhic subjects as ethics, homiletics, and Kabbalah, required nevertheless a wide knowledge of halakhah. These subjects centered on the practical commandments, whose details could not be known without recourse to the halakhic sources. Literary productivity in nonhalakhic subjects, then, is certainly no indication of having abandoned halakhic study. Under the special conditions that obtained in Safed during the period under discussion, there were additional reasons for the learned elite to persevere in halakhic study even if their hearts were drawn rather to Kabbalah. For, in Safed, talmudic scholars were entitled to economic benefits—exemption from taxes, and welfare payments for the needy among them from funds donated by benefactors, coming from both near and far.[53] Entitlement to such benefits required proof, and it seems that this was furnished through association with one of the leading *yeshivot* in town or through joining one of the groups that studied together regularly in one of the local synagogues or halls of study. It is well known that the public institutions of learning intended for advanced scholars limited themselves almost exclusively to halakhic study. Every other sort of study—whether homiletic, ethical, or kabbalistic—was carried on outside the walls of these public halls of learning. This was done either individually, in temporary groupings, or in regular associations which were especially characteristic of the Safed kabbalistic "scene."[54] There is no evidence that members of these associations were entitled to the benefits reserved for talmudic scholars or even that they demanded for themselves such special considerations. Their official status continued to be determined on the basis of their relationship to public institutions of learning. It is a fact that even the most outstanding kabbalists filled positions in the "houses of study"—whether as heads of academies or simply as regular members of study groups.

In the competition between halakhah and Kabbalah for the attention of students, the latter was initially at a disadvantage. The study of Talmud, which at the beginning of the century was quite undeveloped in Erez Israel,[55] received a powerful push forward with the arrival of R. Jacob Berab in Safed during the 1520s.[56] Berab brought with him the analytic method of 'iyyun, which had been developed in the academies of Spain during the final generations before the Expulsion. This method guided the student in detailed analysis of the discussions of the Talmud and its commentaries on the basis of clearly defined and articulated principles. It gave students a methodological tool for active study, permitting them to develop novel interpretations while engaged in dialectical debate—something that was done, as Dimitrovsky's researches have shown, through the regular group study of students in the advanced academies.[57]

The halakhah was then in the midst of one of its periods of greatest expansion and prosperity—a sign of such periods being that scholars found their full intellectual satisfaction in halakhah, sensing almost no need to complement it with other studies. And, in fact, it seems that this type of scholar, whose intellectual interests did not extend beyond the realm of halakhah, was not absent from Safed in this period.[58] Side by side with these, however, appeared individuals with a marked tendency toward mystical experience, metaphysical thought, "poetic" thinking, and the cultivation of emotionally intense religious sentiment. The activity of the latter group charged the atmosphere of the city and marked the historical image of the period, as it emerged from the literary sources, with a distinctive stamp. Many of this generation were caught between these two opposing forces—the immense intellectual challenge of talmudic *pilpul,* on the one hand, and the magical appeal of the world of mystery and fervent religious experience, on the other.

This situation is reflected in the cultural history of Safed during the period under discussion, but it also finds literary expression, matter-of-factly, in the programmatic treatise *Or Ne'erav* of the greatest of its first generation of kabbalists—R. Moses Cordovero.[59] "Ramak" sets out in this work to attack those who set themselves apart from kabbalistic study, and, as part of his effort, he presents a schematic portrait of his opponents. From his comments, it may be inferred that there were indeed those in Safed of his time "who distanced themselves from this wisdom" for the reasons he cites—fear of delving into the unknown, fear of error, or hesitation to embrace its study "since one's belly is not yet full of the bread and meat of the Talmud" (*Or Ne'erav,* part 1, chaps. 1–5; Brandwein, p. 8). His comments on the kabbalists themselves, on their attitudes toward esoteric and exoteric teachings—the problem that here occupies us—are those of a firsthand witness and product of close observation, both of himself and his colleagues. Cordovero divides those who study Kabbalah into three types. The first comes to esoteric study without sufficient preparation in exoteric teachings. The second is the talmudic scholar who engages in kabbalistic study not out of any inherent interest but only because some familiarity with the subject was considered necessary for a well-rounded Torah education. The third type, the only one deemed desirable, consists of those "who follow the straight path—who study part Scripture, part Gemara, and its teachings, which are for us like Mishnah and part this wisdom (Kabbalah) for its own sake in order to penetrate its secrets . . ." (*Or Ne'erav;* Brandwein, pp. 15–16).

It seems that this deliberate division of study refers to the talmudic advice (*Kiddushim* 30a) to devote one's time one-third to Scripture, one-third to Mishnah, and one-third to Talmud. Since, however, the Talmud came to be used as a source for halakhic decision, its study was considered akin to Mishnah, leaving the final third, the true end and final completion of the first two, for Kabbalah.[60] We do not know if anyone actually sought to encourage practical implementation of this scheme, for it is merely a theoretical proposal of an ideal program, leaving open the possibility of compromise.

Ramak advises those of the first type to get themselves in the habit of studying some *pilpul,* as far as they can understand it, as well as some Mishnah, Talmud, and the rudiments of halakhah, "so that they should not be akin to one who gazes at the stars and pays no heed to the ditch that lies beneath his legs." The order of study is presented here in inverse order. *Pilpul,* that is, the give and take of halakhic debate, is actually the final rather than the initial stage. It is necessary, however, for introducing

students to the habit of thinking abstractly—a precondition for studying
Kabbalah, "so that they might not come to attribute corporeal properties
to things celestial" (*Or Ne'erav;* Brandwein, p. 15). In practice, therefore,
Ramak is willing to be satisfied with little. The student of Kabbalah must
acquire the basic rudiments of exoteric knowledge so that the gates of the
esoteric may be opened before him.

The qualitative advantage of kabbalistic study over other kinds of Torah
study is made explicit and experienced in Cordovero's words. All Torah
study leads one to cling to the divine, since "the Torah is all-divine and is
composed of the name of God"; but there are different gradations, "and one
who engages in divine matters undoubtedly clings more closely" (*Or
Ne'erav;* Brandwein, p. 32). This seems to be less a theoretical position than
a testimony to the author's more uplifting experience while studying
Kabbalah than while studying other portions of the Torah. Esoteric study
exercised greater attraction than did the study of exoteric literature, and the
kabbalist struggled with himself not to be drawn excessively after his
inclination, for it conflicted with the obligation to persist in exoteric study.
Cordovero attributes such spiritual struggle to the arch-kabbalist R. Simon
b. Yohai, who, he claims, almost abandoned talmudic study on account of
his infatuation with Kabbalah (*Or Ne'erav;* Brandwein, p. 33), and it seems,
rather, than Ramak is actually speaking of himself. Unlike many kabbalists
who had limited exoteric credentials, Ramak was known as a reputable
Torah scholar and was deemed capable of serving as religious judge (*dayyan*)
in a city as full of scholars as Safed.[61] The struggle between esoteric and
exoteric which occurred inside him was therefore a competition between
equals, and the decision between the two was a conscious one. Although
Ramak does provide a kabbalistic explanation as to why one who studies
"this wisdom" will attain a higher level of spirituality than one who studies
more superficial matters (such as the laws), it is clear that, at base, his view
is rooted in subjective experience (*Or Ne'erav;* Brandwein, pp. 33–35).[62]

Ramak buttressed his demand for setting a degree of knowledgeability in
exoteric literature as a prerequisite for esoteric study, as we have seen, with
the claim that the two systems did not require very different modes of
thought. The study of Talmud and Codes serves, therefore, as a means for
preparing one to understand kabbalistic teachings and for confirming them,
and thus it must precede chronologically. However, once the possibility
arises of gaining knowledge of Kabbalah through the method of *gerushin,*[63]
the inherent difference between it and halakhah emerges more clearly,
especially with regard to the emotional and intellectual challenges involved
in their study. An atmosphere of irrational tension pervaded kabbalistic
study—the opposite of the mentality that obtained among those engaged in

the analysis of talmudic passages or the classification of points in halakhah. To move back and forth periodically between the two worlds obviously demanded considerable effort, and we have already noted the difficulties encountered by Ramak in preserving his ties with both. Such tensions would presumably result if not in a declining involvement in halakhah then in a weakening desire to increase and improve one's knowledge of it.

In Cordovero's apology for continued exoteric study, notably absent is the recommendation to strive for novel interpretations—the higher achievement of those who distinguish themselves in the halakhah. His creative abilities and those of others like him were now channeled toward the world of mystery. Justification for this tendency was provided by placing Kabbalah uppermost in the scale of Torah studies.

I believe that signs of this shift are evident in the religious culture of Safed during its entire "golden period." It excels in the realm of halakhah in the great codifying enterprise of R. Joseph Karo (the *Bet Yosef* and *Shulḥan 'Arukh*) and in the rich responsa literature. These constitute a kind of cross-examination of the sources in order to determine on their basis the norms of individual and communal conduct. If, as a consequence of the codifying effort, halakhic novellas emerged, these were simply a by-product of the process. Actual talmudic novellas constitute only a small fraction of Safed's literary-cultural productivity.[64] Codification is, at base, static in character. The dynamic element in the religious culture of Safed during its "golden period" is represented by Kabbalah and the ethical-homiletic literature and poetry that were influenced by it. It is hardly surprising that they placed their distinctive stamp on the image of the period as it was portrayed both within Jewish tradition and in modern historiography.

R. Isaac Luria

The general characteristics of Safed's culture during this period apply also to the individual considered by later generations to be its leading representative, R. Isaac Luria. As a student of R. David ibn Zimra and a kind of disciple-colleague of R. Bezalel Ashkenazi (the author of *Shiṭṭah Mequbeẓet*, in the compilation of which Luria took a small part), he was capable, upon moving from Egypt to Safed at the age of thirty-six, of assuming immediately the position of head of a *yeshiva*.[65] Of his standing in Safed, and also of his accomplishments in the realm of halakhah, we may learn from a query and responsum which passed between him and R. Joseph Karo. The question turned on a business matter (the amount due one who had invested money with another so as to receive half the profits, when the latter [active] partner died while transporting the goods overseas) in which Luria himself was evidently involved. R. Joseph Karo addresses him in terms of great respect but finds serious fault with his interpretation of the words of Maimonides. He furthermore accuses Luria's general argument of lacking internal logic, which led Karo to exclaim, "I wonder about the soundness of your reason."[66] And, in fact, a close analysis of Luria's comments on the subject reveals that he is generally well versed in halakhic concept but, nevertheless, not quite up to precise halakhic thinking.

This degree of familiarity with the sources was sufficient for gaining recognition as a *talmid ḥakham*. It certainly would be inaccurate to describe every person who taught Torah publicly as a profoundly learned scholar. Those who actually attained a sovereign mastery of the concepts of halakhah and its winding paths of thought were few in number, and there is no sign that Luria ever joined their ranks or even aspired to do so. It appears that his exoteric study was carried out essentially as the fulfillment of an obligation. His mind was preoccupied with the pressing problems of kabbalistic thought, and it is likely that he did not cease to long for the world of the esoteric even while he was involved in exoteric study.

Illuminating from this perspective is the testimony of Luria's student R. Hayyim Vital, concerning his master's conduct while he taught Talmud publicly, "when he read the *Halakhot* among the 'associates,' he would ask a question with such strenuousness that he would become very tired and sweaty. When I asked him why he did so he answered that halakhic activity is intended to destroy the 'husks' (*qelipot*) which are represented by the questions, and this requires very considerable effort. . . ."[67]

Luria's answer alludes, of course, to the words of the *Ra'aya Meheimna* discussed above, according to which the entire enterprise of halakhic study, with its method of questions and *pilpul*, is built upon a foundation of negation and castigation, to which the external forces ("husks") are attracted. The novel aspect of his formulation, however, is the translation of this notion into ritual, and this innovation seems to have escaped the attention of scholars. Involvement in *pilpul*, raising questions and seeking to resolve them, became an act of purification—destroying the evil foundation, the *qelipah*, which was hidden inside them.[68]

What effect did this new ritual baggage have upon the actual intellectual process of study? According to one tradition, each day Luria would explain a law six ways on the level of *peshat*, parallel to the six "profane" weekdays, and then would explain the same law in a seventh, "secret" manner in honor of the Sabbath.[69] It is difficult to imagine that a study method of this sort was consistently maintained. Whatever the case, efforts to subordinate study to any superimposed schema or to require the student to cultivate special "intentions" not related to the subject could have had only a detrimental effect upon concentration in straightforward study.

It is certain, in any case, that the study of halakhah itself was allotted only limited space in Luria's spiritual world—and not in its highest echelons. His involvement in such practices as solitude, yiḥudim, and visiting the graves of the holy, constituted a deviation from the way of life of the professional scholars who limited themselves to the "four ells" of the halakhah. The inspiration he strived for through these activities was more important to him than the study of Torah, as we know from the testimony of two of his disciples, R. Eliezar Azikri and R. Hayyim Vital. The former reported hearing from his master that contemplation in solitude "is seven times more useful to the soul than study."[70] R. Hayyim Vital, Luria's disciple, reports that when he himself became lax in performing yiḥudim, partially because he preferred to devote more time to Torah study, his master urged him nonetheless to perform them daily "for they are greater than Torah study."[71] R. Hayyim Vital himself, of course, also valued such spiritual exercises, but on account of his characteristic mood shifts, he sometimes found them ineffective and preferred to return to his studies. The desire to concentrate on study served as an excuse before his master for discontinuing the yiḥudim, but the latter decreed unequivocally that study is the less important of the two. Study certainly did not lose its value, but it was simply relegated to a lower rung by force of values considered more sublime.

R. Hayyim Vital's Offensive—
The Superiority of Kabbalah

The story concerning R. Hayyim Vital and his master points to the consistently problematical nature of the relationship between exoteric and esoteric in the former's life. In fact, Vital's problem was more acute than his master's, for he possessed demonstrated ability to distinguish himself in the realm of halakhah. This is evident both from his literary estate and from the positions which he filled in Safed, Jerusalem, and Damascus.[72] There is no reason to doubt his testimony that at the age of fourteen he attracted the attention of R. Joseph Karo, who asked R. Moses Alsheikh to keep an eye on the talented boy and to teach him as "much as he could."[73]

The ambience of Safed, however, suffused as it was with the mysteries of the Kabbalah, penetrated the heart of the young scholar, who became caught up in it especially after he met Luria and became his disciple. As is well known, Vital became the standard-bearer of the Lurianic system in Kabbalah, and his devotion to esoteric study came to overshadow his involvement in exoteric matters. The tradition he received from his master regarding the inferiority of halakhah vis-à-vis Kabbalah was enough to bring about such a shift in the direction of his life. He, for his part, moreover, lent additional theoretical support to the preferential status accorded esoteric study. It seems that, in the aftermath of Luria's death, the voices of those who harbored doubts concerning the study of Kabbalah were more frequently heard. In fact, there were some who linked his untimely death with the punishment awaiting those who delve too much into matters beyond their understanding.[74] Vital saw such accusations as bordering on the blasphemous, and it is not surprising that he felt it necessary to launch an offensive against all those who belittled the value of Kabbalah or refused to study it.

For his ammunition in this struggle, R. Hayyim drew primarily on the *Zohar, Ra'aya Meheimna,* and *Tiqquney Zohar,* whose criticism of those who limit themselves to exoteric study he brings to bear on the reality of his own day (*'Ez Hayyim,* 1a–b). He advances the notion that the study of halakhah, by its nature, is study *not* for its own sake but for the sake of reward. The reward is the knowledge of how to conduct oneself properly in this world. Those, however, involved in Kabbalah, he claims, study Torah for its own sake (*'Ez Hayyim,* esp. 3a). Vital develops this bold thesis at considerable length and does not shy away from its logical consequences.

The basic curriculum, however, remains fundamentally untouched even according to R. Hayyim's proposal. Before beginning Kabbalah, one must first study Mishnah and Talmud, following the view of the sages: "let one not enter the *pardes* until he has filled his belly with meat and wine." In two matters, however, he departs from the accepted program. The beginning student must pursue biblical and talmudic studies to the extent his mind can absorb them, after which he should strive to know his Creator through the "true wisdom," as David commanded Solomon (1 Chr 28:9): "Know the God of your father and love him." But if one finds the study of Talmud too difficult and demanding, Vital asserts, it is better for him to abandon it after trying his hand at it, and to turn rather to the "true wisdom" of Kabbalah.[75]

No less radical was Vital's conclusion with regard to one who did enjoy success in the study of halakhah. Such a person, he says, "must devote an hour or two each day to halakhic study . . . intending thereby to remove the evil husk which causes questions to arise which no man can understand . . . and afterwards he should intend to adorn the lady herself, who is the Kabbalah" (*'Ez Hayyim,* 2a). In recommending that most of one's time be spent in Kabbalah and only a small fraction in halakhah, he saw no reason why pursuing such a program would prevent people like himself from serving as public instructors and religious judges. On the contrary, he claims that those who limit themselves to the halakhah "because they abandon the tree of life, are not helped by God . . . and they therefore declare the pure impure and prohibit that which is permissible and declare unsuitable for use that which is suitable, and other obstacles result from their actions on account of their many sins" ('*Ez Hayyim*, 2b). One may infer from these words that one who devotes his primary energies to esoteric study will merit divine aid even when he renders decisions in exoteric matters. And this is not for naught, for only in their superficial appearance do halakhic decisions actually arise from debate rooted in exoteric sources. In truth they are linked to the "inner character of the Torah, as is known to the initiated" ('*Ez Hayyim*, 2b). The exoteric and the esoteric realms are intertwined, and if the study of the former constitutes preparation for the latter, in the end a mastery of exoteric sources depends upon one's ability to penetrate the world of "the hidden."

The Effect of the Spread of Kabbalah

The palpable impact of the Kabbalah of Safed upon the course of Jewish history expressed itself, as is well accepted, in the bursting forth of the esoteric teachings from their previously enforced isolation. These teachings, which had until then been in the domain of a privileged few—or, at the most, elite groups—now entered the public domain. This shift occurred as a consequence of the dissemination of abridged versions of books, halakhic decisions, as well as homiletic and moralizing treatises which had begun, as a matter of course, to absorb the principles of kabbalistic teaching.[76]

This process, as is known, was of such considerable consequence that it changed the face of Jewish culture and brought about a shift in the religious consciousness of the great bulk of world Jewry. It goes without saying that this shift also affected the problem that occupies us here—the relationship between exoteric and esoteric study. How did the spread of Kabbalah affect the study of halakhah? A comprehensive and thorough answer to this question would demand attention to developments in communities as far afield as the Ottoman Empire, Italy, as well as central and eastern Europe. We shall deal here only with the last, where the spread of Kabbalah occurred during one of the halakhah's great spurts of creativity.

One of the signs of this creative flowering is the distinctive method of study employed in the large *yeshivot* of central and eastern Europe, such as those of Cracow, Lvov, Prague, and Vilna.[77] This method had two dimensions. On the one hand, it was customary to extract exhaustively all possible meaning from the texts under study (Talmud, codes, and their commentaries), and this type of study, carried out with precision, gave birth to the rich exegetical and codificatory literature of the sixteenth and seventeenth centuries. On the other hand, the heads of these academies and their students were drawn to the cultivation of the method of *ḥilluqim* ("distinctions"), which consisted of debate arising from questions and answers conceived on the basis of various formalized schemes. Generally, those engaged in the *ḥilluqim* were themselves fully aware of the sophistic character of their novel interpretations.[78] In the realm of theological thought, however, these same generations were lacking in originality. They relied exclusively on ancestral tradition—talmudic aggadah and medieval philosophy—whose ideas were reformulated by preachers and homilists in accordance with the needs of the hour and the tasks of their contemporaries.[79]

It was this cultural situation which the Kabbalah of Safed encountered upon its arrival in the Ashkenazic communities, and its influence there can be gauged by its impact on a typical representative of the period—R. Isaiah Horowitz, the "Shelah."[80] R. Isaiah was educated in the *yeshivot* of the great scholars of Poland and was trained in their method of halakhic study. With regard to "beliefs and opinions" he came under the influence of the Safed Kabbalah and saw in it the only legitimate interpretation of Judaism. In his work *Sheney Luḥot ha-Berit*, he seeks to lend kabbalistic meaning to accepted religious practice (including many new ritual details that he added on his own for the sake of enrichment).[81] Yet in his newly introduced laws or in those regarding which there were differences of opinion between the codifiers or regional differences in practice, he generally devoted his attention first to clarifying the matter from the point of view of halakhah without resorting to kabbalistic notions.[82] His attachment to Kabbalah did not sever his links with halakhah but did influence his style of studying the latter and the degree of his devotion to it. In his youth, R. Isaiah was accustomed to producing novellas in the fashionable pilpulistic manner, but when he matured he became alienated from it and graphically expressed his regret at having done so. The method of *ḥilluqim* had been criticized by other scholars for various reasons. But R. Isaiah was the only one to have seen it as a "criminal offense" worthy of confession (*Sheney Luḥot ha-Berit*, "Massekhet Shavuot," 30b), and this seems to be linked to his mystical conception of both parts of the Torah, esoteric and exoteric.

In the beginning of his book, R. Isaiah establishes the principle that the "exoteric" is not a separate entity from the "esoteric," as the masses believe, but rather a later stage in a single progressive revelation (*Sheney Luḥot ha-Berit*, "Toledot Adam," 3b, 12a). The conflict between "the great thing" (*ma'aseh merkavah*) and "the small thing" (the discussions of Abbaye and Rava), which occupied the minds of generations, was here peacefully resolved by declaring them one and the same. This identification had already been hinted at by R. Hayyim Vital, as we have seen, but Horowitz made the claim more explicitly and, furthermore, utilized it as a guiding principle with far-reaching implications. In fact, the very effort to combine within a single work the clarification of laws from the point of view of halakhah and their explanation from a kabbalistic perspective hinged upon this principle.

An integral characteristic of the *hilluqim* style of *pilpul* was the willingness of its practitioners to admit openly that they felt no obligation for their novellas to be actually "the Torah's own truth." Various justifications were provided for this concession. R. Isaiah cites three of these and decisively rejects them all, asserting that the study of Torah cannot be utilized simply as a means to an end. It must be all truth without the slightest admixture of falsehood—which disqualifies the whole (*Sheney Luḥot ha-Berit*, "Massekhet Shavuot," 30b). The method of study which many had embraced and which he, too, had pursued regularly in his youth, was now, in R. Isaiah's opinion, virtually a criminal offense. This shift was doubtless rooted in the kabbalistic conception of the Torah which he had since absorbed into his thought.[83]

The identification of esoteric and exoteric teachings remained a theoretical construct for Horowitz and did not lead to the blurring, in practice, of the lines between the two disciplines. Even when halakhic and kabbalistic discussions deal with the same subject, they receive separate treatment in the *Sheney Luḥot ha-Berit*. The obligation of study, however, remained in force with regard to both, and the question of how to divide one's time between halakhah and Kabbalah presented itself before R. Isaiah. His decision was more conservative than that of R. Hayyim Vital. He advised his sons that the majority of their day be spent in exoteric study, although the highest transcendence was to be attained through esoteric study. Although the study of halakhah is enveloped in a shroud of mystery, only the study of the mysteries themselves brings one to a true knowledge of God "and one who has not encountered this wisdom has not truly seen light 'and the fool walks in darkness' (Eccl 2:14)."

As one who had stood at the head of esteemed *yeshivot* throughout central Europe, R. Isaiah was bound by their accepted curricula of study, which accorded primary importance to Talmud and which regarded every other type of study, even that of kabbalistic works, as merely subordinate. Upon arriving in the Holy Land in 1621, however, he was free to determine his own daily schedule, and it seems that he then permitted himself to grant pride of place to the Kabbalah. This transition is evidently reflected in his commentary on the words of the Talmud (*Ketubot* 75a) concerning the relative merits of the scholars in Babylonia and Palestine. Abbaye stated there that the scholars of Palestine were worth twice as much as those of Babylonia, and Rava had replied that when a Babylonian comes to Palestine, he becomes worth twice as much as a Palestinian scholar. R. Isaiah relates these observations to the question of esoteric versus exoteric study. The scholars of the Holy Land "engage much more in the study of the secrets of the *ma'aseh merkavah,* which is the 'great thing' and those in Babylonia study, on the contrary, almost exclusively the 'small thing'—the discussions of Abbaye and Rava—and the 'great thing' almost not at all" (*Sheney Luḥot ha-Berit,* "Bet Ḥokhmah," 12b). In exoteric study, the scholars of Babylonia excel over those of the Holy Land, as Abbaye noted. However, as Rava noted, the Babylonian scholar who "ascends" to the Holy Land, is even greater, for he can apply his skill in talmudic *pilpul* to the study of Kabbalah, while devoting to it his greatest energies in the manner of the scholars of the Holy Land. It is hard to avoid seeing in this commentary a reflection of the path R. Isaiah himself had traveled and an attempt to justify his own change in practice upon ascending from "Babylonia" to the Land of Israel.

Ḥasidim and Mitnagdim

R. Isaiah's method was able to forestall the displacement of exoteric by esoteric study. Although the Kabbalah was recognized as a necessary source for understanding the essence of the Torah and the commandments, the place of halakhic study, according to the principles of the method, remained secure. Nevertheless, it is a fact that the absorption of kabbalistic ideas on a broad scale, from the second half of the seventeenth century on, is paralleled by a relaxation of the previously intense cultivation of talmudic study. The flowering of the halakhah in Poland-Lithuania and even Bohemia-Moravia reached its peak during these generations. There are clear explanations for this phenomenon—the decrees of 1648–1649 and the disasters that followed in their wake, the withering of the Councils of the Lands, and the decline in the economic and organizational power of the communities—this at a time when the *yeshivot* were institutionally supported and supervised.[84] It is distinctly possible, however, that unseen forces played a role in this process as well. Recurring demands that students not limit themselves only to halakhah on account of its being insufficient if not complemented by Kabbalah, undoubtedly lowered the stature of the talmudists.[85] At the same time, preachers devoted considerable efforts to encouraging scrupulous self-examination for sins, arousing as well a powerful yearning for purification through acts of repentance, according to the teachings of the kabbalists. The study of Torah ceased to be regarded as a sufficient means for gaining favor in the eyes of God.[86]

This process of putting aside talmudic study as a consequence of finding greater satisfaction in more emotionally charged religious activity received wide public expression in the Hasidic movement. Torah study was deposed from its preeminent position in the scale of religious values. This shift, moreover, was not inadvertent, but became rather a declared tendency in most segments of Hasidism.[87] Unlike the circles of kabbalists, where esoteric study interfered with exoteric study, in Hasidism the study of halakhah was abandoned in favor of the religious experience, arising from participation in the life of the comm004ity at whose center was the Zaddiq.

To be sure, the ḥasid was commanded to teach his sons the fundamentals of the written and oral Torah, and the commandment of Torah study did not expire when one reached adulthood. However, one was able to fulfill these obligations in the ḥeder and house of study. In the former, one received a rudimentary knowledge of Torah, and in the latter this knowledge could be both broadened and deepened through individual or group study. The institution that was conspicuously absent in the Hasidic sphere was the yeshiva. According to the tradition that one of its leading figures, R. Hayyim of Sanz, received from his father-in-law, R. Baruch Teomim Frankel, this was the fruit of conscious deliberation.[88] Not that Hasidism needed to undermine the yeshivot, for their disappearance, as we have seen, preceded the emergence of Hasidism. However, the Hasidic leadership made no attempt to revive these institutions. This indifference was rooted in the nature of the Hasidic leadership, for even though it included talmudic scholars of the first rank, their authority did not stem from their knowledge. The Rebbes who did not excel in talmudic study and who arrived at their elevated positions as a result of their religious inspiration or on account of charisma inherited from their fathers could not have been interested in the creation of competing sources of religious authority in the form of yeshivot and their heads. The role of providing halakhic knowledge was fulfilled by the local House of Study, and the secondary objective of the yeshiva—serving as a consolidating social-religious framework—was fulfilled by the Hasidic assembly around the Zaddiq.

The situation was otherwise in the "Mitnagdic" domain. Here the disappearance of the yeshivot left a vacuum, and the ensuing sense of enduring loss encouraged R. Hayyim of Volozhin, as is well known, to work toward improving the situation.[89] The foundation of a yeshiva on his part was not simply an act of restoration, for the new institution he created was different from those of previous generations in its standing within the community, its organization, and its program of study. Furthermore, the yeshiva came as a response to the challenge emerging from the Hasidic camp, with which its founder was engaged in ideological confrontation. The yeshiva could not satisfy itself with the cultivation of halakhic study alone; it had to supply those who so desired a spiritual experience, similar to the one which Hasidism provided, on a grand scale, to its adherents.

In fact, R. Hayyim followed in the steps of Hasidism by having recourse to the wellsprings of Kabbalah. He did so, however, not in the manner of the latter, but rather by skipping, as it were, the Kabbalah's stages of development since the days of R. Isaiah Horowitz. If R. Isaiah identified exoteric and esoteric—while allowing each to remain a separate discipline of study—R. Hayyim followed the identification to its logical end, granting exoteric study in full the metaphysical qualities that had previously been associated solely with esoteric study. His work in Jewish thought, *Nefesh ha-Hayyim*, which has been much studied even by modern scholars, is intended primarily to prove the identification, using both esoteric and exoteric sources.[90] So it was on the level of reason and intellect. On the level of emotion and inspiration, however, the work seeks to remove the barrier between esoteric and exoteric study, to provide a sense of involvement in metaphysical processes to one engaged in the interpretation of talmudic texts—as if one were involved in uncovering the secrets of the divine. With the latter he has in reality nothing to do, for R. Hayyim had no intention of having Kabbalah studied in his *yeshiva*, reserving its study for exceptional individuals like himself, if for anyone. The question of the relation between esoteric and exoteric study here arrived finally at its paradoxical resolution—the former was set aside and its former function and weight were assigned to the latter.

Notes

1. See G. F. Moore, *Judaism in the First Centuries of the Christian Era* (Cambridge, MA: Harvard University Press, 1959) 2:239–47. The fact that such a prominent characteristic of the Jewish religion has not yet been historically researched in a comprehensive manner testifies to the state of Judaic scholarship with regard to all matters pertaining to the early foundations of normative Judaism.

2. In *San.* 99a reference is made to *aggadot shel dofi*. R. Nachman Krochmal in chap. 14 of his *Moreh Nevukhey ha-Zeman* pointed to the distinctions between more and less acceptable types of aggadot. See *The Writings of Nachman Krochmal*, ed. Simon Rawidowicz (London: Ararat, 1961) 238–56.

3. See, e.g., *Hag.* 10a, *Bab. Mez.* 33–ab and the effort at compromise (one-third Scripture, one-third Mishnah, and one-third Gemara) in *Qid.* 30a. See also L. Zunz, *Ha-Derashot be-Yisrael* (Jerusalem: Bialik, 1947) 25 nn. 15–18.

4. The special status of aggadists was described in particular by I. H. Weiss (*Dor Dov we-Dorshaw* [Vilna, 1893] vol. 3, chap. 11) according to his characteristic mode of historical explanation.

5. See Zunz, *Derashot*, 33.

6. On the matter of *ma'aseh merkavah*, see G. Scholem's study *Jewish Gnosticism, Merkabah*

Mysticism, and Talmudic Tradition (2nd ed.; New York: Jewish Theological Seminary, 1965). For the various interpretations given to the statement concerning R. Yohanan, see below.

7. I have discussed the point at length in my article "Post-Zoharic Relations between Halakhah and Aggadah," in *Jewish Thought in the Sixteenth Century*, ed. Bernard D. Cooperman (Cambridge, MA: Harvard University Center for Jewish Studies, 1983 [distributed by Harvard University Press]).

8. This issue has been given the serious treatment it deserves by Herbert A. Davidson, "The Study of Philosophy as a Religious Obligation," in *Religion in a Religious Age*, ed. S. D. Goitein (Cambridge, MA: Association for Jewish Studies, 1974) 53–68.

9. See Alexander Altmann, "Das Verhältnis Maimunis zur jüdischen Mystik," *Monatsschrift für Geschichte und Wissenschaft des Judentums* 80 (1936) 308–28; and Davidson, "Study of Philosophy," 63–64.

10. See G. Scholem, *Reshit ha-Qabbalah* (Jerusalem: Schocken, 1948) 12–16; idem, *Ursprung und Anfänge der Kabbala* (Berlin: de Gruyter, 1962) 9–15.

11. See Scholem, *Major Trends in Jewish Mysticism* (New York: Schocken, 1941) 17–18; see also idem, "Religious Authority and Mysticism," in *On the Kabbalah and Its Symbolism*, trans. Ralph Manheim (New York: Schocken, 1965).

12. Cited in *Kesef Mishneh* to Maimonides' *Hilkot Talmud Torah* 4:13. I have not seen this sharp formulation noticed in scholarship.

13. *Sefer ha-Bahir*, ed. Reuven Margaliot (Jerusalem: Mossad Ha Rav Kook, 1951) #185.

14. The concepts "exoteric" and "esoteric" (*nigleh* and *nistar*) used in the sense of two dimensions of the same entity appear, as is well known, throughout the history of philosophy and Kabbalah. In later usage, however, they signify two segments of Jewish tradition, halakhah and Kabbalah respectively. The standard dictionaries have not taken this change of meaning into account, and I have not succeeded in identifying its first appearance. The usage appears frequently in the writings of R. Isaiah Horowitz, and it could well be that it spread from there to others. G. Scholem (*Encyclopaedia Judaica* 10:494–95) provides a list of the various terms for Kabbalah but omits the term *nistar* ("esoteric"). In my work I have found it convenient to resort to this dichotomy.

15. On R. Ezra's dependence on Maimonides, see my article "Halakhah and Kabbalah—First Contacts" (Hebrew), in *The Yizhak Baer Memorial Volume* (Jerusalem, 1980) 160.

16. The text of the commentary is included in *Kitvey Ramban*, ed. H. D. Chavel (Jerusalem: Mossad Ha Rav Kook, 1964) vol. 2; see esp. pp. 428–29, 525. See also Georges Vajda, trans., *Le commentaire d'Ezra de Gérone sur le cantique des cantiques* (Paris: Aubier Montaigne, 1969).

17. See *Commentary on Talmudic Aggadoth by R. Azriel of Gerona*, ed. Isaiah Tishby (2nd ed.; Jerusalem: Magnes Press, 1982) 97.

18. See Scholem, *Reshit*, 156; idem, *Ursprung*, 349–51.

19. Scholem, *Reshit*, 148–50; Efraim Gottlieb, *Studies in the Kabbalah Literature* (Hebrew) (Tel Aviv: Tel Aviv University, 1976) 88–95.

20. See the introductory remarks to his work *Or Zaru'a* in Alexander Altmann's edition *Qovez 'al Yad* n.s. vol. 9 (19) (Jerusalem: Mekizzey Nirdamim, 1980) 248. Altmann, in his own introduction (*Qovez* 235–43), explores at greater length the relationship between the two authors.

21. Scholem, *Major Trends*, 201–2 and nn. 151–54.

22. Isaiah Tishby, *Mishnat ha-Zohar* (2 vols.; Jerusalem: Bialik, 1961) 2:374–75.

23. G. Scholem, "The Meaning of the Torah in Jewish Mysticism," in *On the Kabbalah* (cited in n. 11 above).

24. See the famous passage in *Zohar* 3:153a. The parallel passages are cited and analyzed by Tishby (Mishnat ha-Zohar, 2:375–98, esp. 383).

25. See Scholem, "Meaning of the Torah," in *On the Kabbalah*, 66ff. Tishby (*Mishnat ha-Zohar*, 2:375–98) questioned Scholem's view in a lengthy and substantive discussion but admitted in

conclusion that the *Ra'aya Meheimna* and *Tiqquney Zohar* both contain contradictory statements on the matter which cannot be reconciled (p. 395). It would seem that, in contrast to Tishby's method of analyzing each relevant passage in detail, a more synoptic approach to the material would yield a better understanding of the author's views.

26. See Isaac Profiat Duran, *Ma'aseh Efod*, ed. Friedlander (Vienna, 1865 [reprint Jerusalem, 1970]) 4–10. On Duran, see Isadore Twersky, "Religion and Law," in *Religion in a Religious Age*, ed. S. D. Goitein, 74–77, 80–82.

27. Duran, *Ma'aseh Efod*, 4.

28. Ibid., 9.

29. Ibid., 14, 18.

30. Israel Ta-Shema, "Where were the Books *Ha-Qanah* and *Ha-Peli'ah* composed?" in *Studies in the History of Jewish Society in the Middle Ages and in the Modern Period Presented to Prof. Jacob Katz* (Jerusalem: Magnes Press, 1980) 56–63. Ta-Shema there cites the various authors who have dealt with the complicated question of the authorship of these two books.

31. *Sefer ha-Peli'ah* (Koretz, 1784) 4a.

32. See, e.g., *Sefer ha-Qanah* (Cracow, 1794) 7b–8a. The halakhic statements of this book have not yet been analyzed by the scholars working on it. The method of halakhic thinking utilized in the work would provide important indications with regard to the time and place of its composition. Research in this direction would, in my opinion, probably confirm Ta-Shema's view concerning the work's non-Spanish provenance.

33. Joseph Yavetz, *Or ha-Hayyim* (Warsaw, 1871) 1b.

34. Ibid., 1b, 4a, 8a.

35. Joseph Yavetz, *Commentary on Avot* (Warsaw, 1880) 3:9, p. 30b.

36. Yavetz, *Or ha-Hayyim*, 6b.

37. R. Judah Hayyat testifies that it was R. Joseph who encouraged him, while both were residing in Mantua after the Expulsion, to compose his famous commentary *Minhat Yehudah* on the *Ma'arekhet Elohut*. See the latter work (Mantua, 1558) 3a.

38. *Or ha-Hayyim*, 6a.

39. *Ma'arekhet*, 1a.

40. Ibid., 1a–2a.

41. Ibid., 2b–3a.

42. Of his life only little is known. See Israel Zinberg, *A History of Jewish Literature*, trans. and ed. Bernard Martin (Cleveland, OH: Press of Case Western Reserve University, 1974) 5:40–49. His kabbalistic views have been treated at length by Efraim Gottlieb. See the latter's *Studies in the Kabbalah Literature*, index, s.v. "Meir ibn Gabbai." On ibn Gabbai's thoughts, see also G. Scholem, "Traditions and Commentary as Religious Categories in Judaism," in *The Messianic Idea in Judaism* (New York: Schocken, 1971) 298–300.

43. Cited according to the Lvov 1849 edition.

44. See *'Avodat ha-Qodesh*, part 4, chap. 1 (1b).

45. See the introduction, esp. pp. 55–56a.

46. He cites the *Tur* on p. 17b but utilizes it much more than he indicates. Other works mentioned are *Abudarham* (21a) and *Sefer ha-Manhig* (24b).

47. Other kabbalistic works he draws on are *Sefer ha-Qanah* and *Sefer ha-Bahir*.

48. See the expanded version of my article "Post-Zoharic Relations between Halakhah and Kabbalah" (Hebrew version in *Da'at* 4 [1980] 57–74; English version cited in n. 7 above), which will be included in a collected volume of my articles.

49. See, e.g., *Tola'at Ya'aqov*, 12a, 29a, and my article cited in the preceding note.

50. This is the formulation of Efraim Gottlieb in his description of Meir ibn Gabbai's thought (*Studies*, 54).

51. The history of Safed during this period has attracted considerable scholarly attention. See

Naphtali Ben-Menahem, "A Bibliography of Publications on Safed" (Hebrew), *Sefunot* 6 (1962) 475–503. The classic study of the subject is still Solomon Schechter's 1908 essay "Safed in the Sixteenth Century: A City of Legists and Mystics" (available now in *The Jewish Expression*, ed. J. Goldin [New Haven, CT: Yale University Press, 1976] 258–321). Despite the numerous studies, we are still in the dark with regard to such fundamental issues as the structure of social life, relations between various groups, etc.

52. E.g., R. Solomon Alkabez in poetry and Kabbalah, R. Moses Galante in halakhah and Kabbalah, and others in a similar fashion.

53. See Meir Benayahu, "The Tax Concession Enjoyed by the Scholars of Safed" (Hebrew), *Sefunot* 7 (1964) 103–4. The support given, from public or private sources, to professional Torah scholars is mentioned in many sources. See, e.g., *Responsa of R. Moses Trani*, part 3, nos. 48, 66, 96.

54. On associations of kabbalists, see Schechter, "Safed in the Sixteenth Century"; and, more recently, David Tama, *Studies in the History of the Jewish People in Eretz Israel and Italy* (Hebrew) (Jerusalem: Reuben Mas, 1970) 95–100.

55. See the letter published by Abraham Ya'ari, *Igrot Erez Yisra'el* (Tel Aviv: Masada, 1943) 171.

56. See the excellent article of H. Z. Dimitrovsky, "Rabbi Ya'aqov Berab's Academy" (Hebrew), *Sefunot* 7 (1963) 41–102.

57. Ibid.; also Meir Benayahu, "R. Ḥiyya Rofe and his book *Ma'aseh Ḥiyya*" (Hebrew), *Areshet* 2 (1960) 109–29.

58. This type is perhaps best represented, among the leading scholars of the generation, by R. Moses Trani. His work *Bet Elohim* (Warsaw, 1872) sums up the principles of rabbinic Judaism from a classic, rationalistic point of view. For criticism of the views of the kabbalists, see *Bet Elohim*, 28a, 47b.

59. The work was first published in Venice in 1587 and will here be cited according to Y. Z. Brandwein's edition (Jerusalem, 1966). For details concerning Cordovero's life, see Joseph Ben-Shlomo, *The Mystical Theology of Moses Cordovero* (Hebrew) (Jerusalem: Bialik, 1965) 7–33.

60. This attempt to fit the talmudic scheme to later conditions is comparable to that of Maimonides (*Hilkhot Talmud Torah* 1:11–12) with Kabbalah, however, replacing philosophy. See I. Twersky, *Introduction to the Code of Maimonides* (New Haven: CT: Yale University Press, 1980) 189–92.

61. See Ben-Shlomo, *Mystical Theology*, 8–9.

62. A decidedly subjective aspect of kabbalistic activity may be found in the technique of *gerushin*, which Cordovero, by his own testimony, was in the habit of practicing, on the outskirts of Safed, with his fellow kabbalist R. Solomon Alkabez. Through the random recitation of verses they expected to receive divinely revealed (kabbalistic) secrets. See *Sefer Gerushin* (Venice, 1600); R. J. Z. Werblowsky, *Joseph Karo: Lawyer and Mystic* (2nd ed.; Philadelphia: Jewish Publication Society, 1977) 51–55. See also the chapter by Lawrence Fine in this volume.

63. See the preceding note.

64. On R. Joseph Karo's novellas on three talmudic tractates, see Dimitrovsky, "Berab's Academy," 94–95.

65. The biographical information concerning R. Isaac Luria can be found in G. Scholem's article in *Encyclopaedia Judaica*, 2:572–78, available also in his *Kabbalah* (New York: New York Times Book Co., 1974) 420–28. On his method in public halakhic study see below.

66. See *Responsa Avkat Rokhel* (Leipzig, 1859) #136. On Luria's economic activities see Scholem, *Encyclopaedia Judaica*, 2:572–78, n. 140.

67. Isaac Luria, *Ha-Kawwanot* (Lemberg, 1863) 6a.

68. For another Lurianic tradition concerning the spiritualization of halakhic study, see Jacob Zemah, *Naggid v. Mezawweh* (Lublin, 1929) 15a.

69. Ibid., in the name of *lequtim*.

70. Eliezar Azikri, *Sefer Haredim* (Zolkiew, 1778) 76b.

71. *Sefer ha-Hezyonot*, ed. Z. Aescoly (Jerusalem, 1954) 149.

72. Some of his responsa are included in the collection of his son, Samuel. See *Be' er Mayyim Hayyim* (MS Oxford 832). For the positions filled by Vital, see Scholem, *Encyclopaedia Judaica*, 2:171–76; also Meir Benayahu, "R. Hayyim Vital in Jerusalem" (Hebrew), *Sinai* 30 (1952) 65–75.

73. *Sefer ha-Hezyonot*, p. 2. Eventually R. Moses Alsheikh granted ordination to Vital as part of the revival of that institution by the scholars of Safed. The latter, however, was then forty-seven. See Meir Benayahu, "The Revival of Ordination in Safed" (Hebrew), in *Yizhak F. Baer Jubilee Volume*, ed. S. W. Baron et al. (Jerusalem: Historical Society of Israel, 1960) 256–66.

74. See R. Hayyim Vital's introduction to his *'Ez Hayyim* (Warsaw, 1891) 2a, where he mentions "the view of those few mistaken Torah scholars in our time who give a bad name to Kabbalah, asserting that anyone who studies it will die an early death." This was written when Vital was thirty—that is, a year after Luria's death.

75. Vital here evidently has in mind the talmudic saying "If a student does not see progress in his studies after five years, he never will." There, however, the meaning is that there is no future for that student in further study, whereas Vital, in contrast, sees it as a suggestion to move on to the next stage of study.

76. Scholem, *Major Trends*, 250–51.

77. See M. A. Shulvass, "Torah and its study in Poland and Lithuania" (Hebrew), in *Bet Yisra' el be-Polin*, ed. Israel Halperin (Jerusalem, 1954) 2:13–35; and H. H. Ben-Sasson, *Hagut we-Hanhagah* (Jerusalem: Bialik, 1959) 18–33.

78. On this method, see H. Z. Dimitrovsky's comprehensive article "On the Pilpulistic Method" (Hebrew), in *Salo W. Baron Jubilee Volume* (Jerusalem: American Academy for Jewish Research, 1974) 3:111–81.

79. See Ben-Sasson, *Hagut*, 11–17, 34–54.

80. The most recent biographical study is Eugene Newman, *The Life and Teachings of Isaiah Horowitz* (London, 1972).

81. The work was originally published in Amsterdam in 1648; it is cited here according to the Warsaw 1862 edition. R. Isaiah's son testifies in the introduction to the work that it contains four hundred new laws and customs which his father introduced.

82. On Horowitz's method in applying Kabbalah to halakhic matters, see Ben-Sasson, *Hagut*, 19–22.

83. This is made explicit in his use of Psalm 101:7, the verse used by R. Akiba as a warning to his colleagues entering the *Pardes* (*Hag.* 145) in criticism of students of the exoteric (ibid.).

84. See my study *Tradition and Crisis: Jewish Society at the End of the Middle Ages* (New York: Free Press of Glencoe, 1961) 217ff.

85. Ibid., 220ff.

86. On the activity of preachers during the period preceding the rise of Hasidism, see B. Z. Dinur, *Historical Writings* (Hebrew) (Jerusalem: Bialik, 1955) 1:83; Joseph Weiss, "The Beginnings of Hasidism" (Hebrew), *Zion* 16 (1951) 46–105; and, most recently, Mendel Piekarz, *The Beginning of Hasidism* (Hebrew) (Jerusalem: Bialik, 1978).

87. See Joseph Weiss, "Torah Study According to R. Israel Ba'al Shem Tov," in *Essays Presented to Chief Rabbi Israel Brodie . . .* (London: Soncino Press) 151–69.

88. *Responsa Divrey Hayyim* of R. Hayyim of Sanz, Y. D. #47, cited by Assaf, *Meqorot* 4 (Tel Aviv, 1948) 4:210–11.

89. See M. S. Schmuckler's biography, *Toledot R. Hayyim me-Volozhin* (Vilna, 1920); and now Shaul Stampfer's dissertation, "Three Lithuanian Yeshivot in the Nineteenth Century" (Hebrew) (Hebrew University, 1981) esp. chap. 2.

90. See Emmanuel Etkes, "Shitato . . . shel R. Ḥayyim me-Volozhin . . ." (Hebrew), *Proceedings of the American Academy for Jewish Research* 38–39 (1972) 1–45 (Hebrew section); and Norman Lamm, *Torah Li-shmah* [*Torah for its own sake*] (Hebrew) (Jerusalem: Mossad Ha Rav Kook, 1972).

Bibliography

Davidson, Herbert G. "The Study of Philosophy as a Religious Obligation." In *Religion in a Religious Age*, 58–68. Edited by S. D. Goitein. Cambridge, MA: Association for Jewish Studies, 1984.

Schechter, Solomon. "Safed in the Sixteenth Century: A City of Legists and Mystics." In *Studies in Judaism*, 202–85. Second series. Philadelphia: Jewish Publication Society, 1908.

——. "Saints and Saintliness." In *Studies in Judaism*, 148–81. Philadelphia: Jewish Publication Society, 1908.

Scholem, Gershom. "Devekut, or Communion with God." In *The Messianic Idea in Judaism*, 203–27. New York: Schocken Books, 1971.

Twersky, Isadore. "Religion and Law." In *Religion in a Religious Age*, 69–82. Edited by S. D. Goitein. Cambridge, MA: Association for Jewish Studies, 1984.

3

The Contemplative Practice of Yiḥudim in Lurianic Kabbalah

LAWRENCE FINE

ISAAC LURIA (1534–1572) is one of the several greatest figures in the history of the Jewish mystical tradition and the preeminent personality among the kabbalists of Safed in the sixteenth century. Despite the fact that Luria lived in Safed for a period of only two years, from 1570 until his death in 1572, and that a range of teachers including Moses Cordovero and Solomon Alkabez had already established Safed as a mystical community of very considerable importance, it is Luria's name that is traditionally identified with the renaissance that occurred in this city. The reasons for this are twofold. First, Isaac Luria's charismatic personality not only produced a significant discipleship in Safed itself but also generated a powerful legendary and hagiographical tradition, which developed over the course of the succeeding generations. Second, Lurianic teachings and practices were greeted with considerable enthusiasm in diverse parts of the Jewish world from the late sixteenth century on.[1]

Although Isaac Luria's fascinating and intricate mythological teachings have been studied extensively by modern scholars, most especially in the work of Gershom Scholem and Isaiah Tishby,[2] much less attention has been given to what might be called the devotional side of Luria's teachings. Scholem and Tishby have described and analyzed the Lurianic *idea*, the complex gnostic myth according to which a crisis within the life of the Godhead resulted in the scattering of divine sparks in material reality. But the religious practices by which the process of "mending" or "restoration" (*tiqqun*) was to be accomplished have been treated in mostly general terms. A fuller understanding of Lurianic Kabbalah calls for thorough analysis of the variety of spiritual *disciplines* which this teacher imparted to his students. For Lurianism was no mere theoretical system, a set of intellectual abstractions. *It was a lived and living phenomenon, the actual "world" of a historically observable community.* The ultimate goal of this community was a *pragmatic* one requiring mystical action—nothing less than the return of all existence to its original spiritual condition, a state synonymous with the manifestation of the messianic age.

In pursuit of this goal Isaac Luria guided his circle of followers, approximately thirty-five of whose names we know, toward the cultivation of a rigorous form of piety, at the center of which was a set of contemplative techniques.[3] One of the most important of these, and one that is illustrative of the entire Lurianic enterprise, was the practice of meditative exercises known as *yihudim* ("unifications"). The present study seeks to explore the meaning of Lurianism in general by reference to this rather unusual religious practice. At the same time, our study of this particular Lurianic discipline will shed light on the critical role that devotional practices played in sixteenth-century Safed as a whole. This is the case inasmuch as Luria's teachings—their highly distinctive character notwithstanding—are ultimately a complicated variation on a basic theme shared by all the kabbalists of this community: the return of all things from the state of exile to one of redemption.

The Mythological Teachings of Isaac Luria

Any attempt to understand the discipline of contemplation in Lurianic Kabbalah requires at least a general familiarity with the theological and mythological themes that stand at the root of Luria's system. Indeed, the mystical workings of the Godhead and its highly complex nature constitute the focus of contemplation for Isaac Luria and his disciples. Lurianic myth describes in intricate detail three events in the life of God: the *zimzum*, or "self-limitation" of God; *shevirat ha-kelim*, or "breaking of the vessels"; and *tiqqun*, or "reconstruction" and "mending" of the flaw which occurred by virtue of the *shevirah*.

The idea of *zimzum* appears to have no place at all in the Kabbalah of the *Zohar*. Whereas the latter conceives of the initial action of the Godhead as an *outward* one—the self-disclosure of the deepest hidden Self, known as the *Eyn Sof*, by means of the *sefirot*—Luria describes the first movement as a step *inward*, as a withdrawal of God into Himself. *Zimzum* is the process by which He contracts His essence, retreating "from Himself into Himself," abandoning a space within Himself thereby creating an "empty" region. This step inward seeks to solve this problem: how is the existence of the world possible if the Infinite, that is, the *Eyn Sof*, fills all reality? Luria's answer is that by withdrawing into His own depths the *Eyn Sof* establishes room for creation, for actuality that is not *Eyn Sof.* *Zimzum* does not suggest the concentration of God's power *in* a place, but its withdrawal *away* from a place. The space created is a mere infinitesimal point in contrast with God's infinity. Nevertheless, from the human perspective it is the space in which all dimensions of existence are formed, both on the spiritual and on the corporeal level.

Prior to *zimzum,* the various powers of God, the *sefirot,* were harmoniously balanced without any discernible differentiation. In particular, the opposing forces of Mercy (*Hesed*) and Stern Judgment (*Din*) existed in perfect unity within the essence of the divine. In the process of *zimzum,* however, *Eyn Sof* gathered in one place all the "roots" of Stern Judgment, leaving them behind in the region now abandoned. This resulted in a separation between *Din* and *Hesed* and the establishment of a measure of independence for the forces of Judgment. Thus, the *zimzum,* from one point of view, may be regarded as an act of self-limitation or self-imposed "exile" within God for the purpose of separating out and eliminating the forces of Judgment. More radically formulated, the purification of the divine organism of all elements of potential evil took place in this process, the "dross" within God was purged from His innermost being.

This empty space, into which all the forces of Judgment were concentrated and in which all processes of emanation and creation take place, is called *tehiru* ("vacuum"). Besides the roots of Judgment, an additional positive residue of divine light, known as *reshimu* ("traces"), remained in the empty space. A third element, a ray from God's hidden essence, entered the *tehiru* and acted upon the existing mixture of *reshimu* and *Din.* This illuminating ray or *qav ha-middah* ("cosmic measure") serves as a permanent link between the *Eyn Sof* and the *tehiru.* It seeks to organize the *reshimu* and *Din* that have filled the empty space, and which are inherently opposed to one another.

The form of the divine produced by this first ray of light which penetrates the *tehiru* is termed the "Primordial Man" ('*Adam Qadmon*). Entering the *tehiru* like a beam of light, it is the first and highest shape in which the divinity proceeds to manifest itself following the *zimzum.* In the Lurianic schema it indicates a realm of divinity above the four "worlds" of '*Azilut, Beri'ah, Yezirah,* and '*Asiyah.*[4] Luria employs two different images to describe the emanative process from '*Adam Qadmon*—"circle" and "line," (*'iggul we-yosher*). The ten *sefirot* originally took shape in '*Adam Qadmon* in the form of concentric circles, the most external circle remaining in close contact with *Eyn Sof.* Following this, the *sefirot* reorganized themselves in a line—more specifically, in the shape of a human body.

The lights shining from 'Adam Qadmon's "ears," "nose," and "mouth" constituted a collective or perfectly unified structure. In this state the sefirot were as yet undifferentiated and needed no vessels to contain them in the course of their emanation. However, the light issuing forth from the "eyes" of 'Adam Qadmon emanated in a different manner. They were atomized or separated into different sefirot so as to require their containment in special vessels (kelim). These vessels, composed of a "thicker" light, were to serve as "shells" for the purer light.

The vessels designed to contain the upper three sefirot emanating from the "eyes" of 'Adam Qadmon, namely, Keter, Hokhmah, and Binah, performed their task properly. The light flowing into them was held within the vessels and their emanation was orderly. At this juncture, however, the vessels that were supposed to shelter the lower sefirot from Hesed through Yesod proved to be insufficiently strong for the task. Under the impact of the simultaneous flow of light into these six lower vessels, the latter shattered and were dispersed into the tehiru. This event is known as shevirat ha-kelim, the "breaking of the vessels." While the vessel containing the final sefirah, Malkhut, also cracked, it did not completely shatter as did the others.

Most of the light that had been contained in the vessels returned to its divine source, while the remainder fell below into the tehiru and attached themselves to the now broken shards of vessels. From these shards of broken vessels the powers of the qelipot, that is, "husks" or "shells" were produced. These husks are the evil forces of the "other side," the sitra 'ahra. In addition to constituting the source of evil, the broken shards are also the basis for the material world. The sparks of light that failed to return to their source above remained trapped, as it were, among the qelipot. The qelipot, in turn, are constantly nourished and strengthened by the holy sparks attached to them. Indeed, were it not for the sparks attached to the qelipot, the latter would be altogether lifeless and powerless.

In a way, then, that is strikingly similar to the mythic systems of the gnostics of late antiquity, Lurianic mythology depicts the descent of divine or transcendent light into the world of gross materiality. Imprisoned, these sparks yearn to extricate themselves from their exiled condition. Gershom Scholem summarized the effect that this catastrophic event exerted on the otherwise orderly process of divine emanation in these words:

> Its repercussions are manifest in every single detail of Lurianic cosmology. But for the breaking of the vessels, everything would have occupied its rightful and appointed place. Now everything is out of joint.... Henceforth everything is imperfect and deficient, in a way "broken" or "fallen." That which should have occupied its appointed and appropriate place has moved somewhere else. However, this situation of not being where one ought to be,

namely, of being removed from one's rightful place, is what is meant by the term "exile." In fact, since the breaking of the vessels, exile is the fundamental and exclusive—albeit hidden—mode of all existence. In Lurianism the historical notion of exile had become a cosmic symbol.[5]

According to some explanations in the Lurianic literature, the catastrophe occurred by virtue of the weak structure or differentiated character of the lights emanating from the eyes of 'Adam Qadmon. That is, their disorganization created an instability that led to the breaking of the vessels in which they were contained. From another point of view, the shevirah took place as a result of the further desire to separate the dross from the holy, a cathartic process that served to expunge all elements of evil from within God. Whatever the cause, the kabbalists all agreed that the shevirah constituted the decisive event in the cosmological process.

The challenge that Lurianic teaching now faced was to determine how to mend the injury suffered by the Godhead. Tiqqun refers to the processes by which restoration and repair were to be accomplished. They constitute the greatest part of Lurianic theory and are complex in the extreme. The primary medium for tiqqun was the sefirotic light that continued to issue from 'Adam Qadmon following the "breaking of the vessels." This sefirotic light was now reorganized under five new structural principles known as parzufim ("faces"). These parzufim, or configurations of divine light, were intended to restore order to the confusion produced by the shevirah. The sefirah Keter was reconstituted as the parzuf of 'Arikh 'Anpin (lit., "the Long-Faced One," i.e., "the Indulgent One" or "Forbearing One") or 'Attiqa Qaddisha ("the Holy Ancient One"). The sefirot Hokhmah and Binah were reformed as the parzufim of 'Abba ("Father") and 'Imma ("Mother") respectively. The fourth parzuf is that of Ze'ir 'Anpin ("the Short-Faced One" or the "Impatient One"), which contains the six lower sefirot, from Din through Yesod. The final parzuf is Nuqva de-Ze'ir, the "female of Ze'ir," representing the sefirah Malkhut, or Shekhinah. This parzuf contains two aspects: Raḥel and Leah.

The process by which these parzufim manifest themselves is described in language of human development: conception, pregnancy, birth, suckling, and maturity. The "parents," 'Abba and 'Imma, engage in union known as ziwwug, which results in the creation of Ze'ir 'Anpin. Yeniqah (suckling) is the process by which Ze'ir 'Anpin is nourished after its departure from the womb of 'Imma. By the power of this suckling Ze'ir is able to grow and comprise the six lower sefirot.

In its original state, union between 'Abba and 'Imma was constant. The two lower parzufim, Ze'ir 'Anpin and Nuqva de-Ze'ir, were likewise in a state of unity with one another. These two pairs of male and female were each looking "face to face" in a perpetual condition of marriage.

According to Lurianic teaching, the soul of the first man, Adam, was made up of all the various "worlds" and was intended to extricate and reintegrate the divine sparks that still remained within the qelipot. When Adam was created, the cosmic process of tiqqun had virtually been completed. It was his task to finalize the restorative process through contemplative exercises. He was capable of doing so as his body was a perfect microcosm of 'Adam Qadmon. Through his mystical activities Adam could have separated the holy sparks from their demonic shells, thus reestablishing the primordial unity of all things. Having purged the realm of holiness of the final vestiges of dross, the qelipot would have sunk beneath the lowest spiritual world of 'Asiyah and lost all their power. The cosmos would have achieved its original state of perpetual communion with the divine light, and the historical process would have come to a close.

None of this came about, however, because of Adam's failure. Instead of accomplishing his great task, Adam sinned, interrupting his own communion with the upper spheres and attaching himself to the lower worlds. As Gershom Scholem aptly formulated it, Adam's sin parallels on an anthropological level what occurred on the ontological plane through the "breaking of the vessels." Among the many injurious consequences, Adam's sin transformed the relationship of Ze'ir 'Anpin and Nuqva de-Ze'ir to one of "looking back to back," (aḥor-be-aḥor). Likewise, the "female waters" (mayyim nuqvin), the power that ascended from Nuqva de-Ze'ir to arouse the energy of Ze'ir, was cut off. In turn, the "male waters" (mayyim dukhrin), the power that flowed from Ze'ir to Nuqba de-Ze'ir during ziwwug, ceased to flow. The harmonious existence of the "worlds" dependent on the union of these two parzufim was thrown into disorder and confusion. The "worlds" which had begun to rise and to return to their proper position when Adam entered the Garden of Eden, once again fell below. The entire "world" of 'Asiyah descended into the realm of the qelipot, and good and evil were again thoroughly mixed in with each other. Humanity and all reality in the world of 'Asiyah became materialized. Finally, the sin of Adam caused the sparks of all human souls that had been contained within his own to fall and become imprisoned as well within the qelipot; there they help to nourish the evil powers of the lower world.

Tiqqun, therefore, involves two fundamental aspects. First, it means the gathering of the divine lights that had fallen into the realm of the qelipot by virtue of the "breaking of the vessels." It necessitates the complete separation of the holy from the "shells" which entrap it. In addition, it means the gathering of all the holy souls likewise imprisoned in the qelipot. The

Lurianic expression "raising of the sparks" (ha'alat ha-nizozot) includes both of these responsibilities.

But precisely how is tiqqun to be achieved? If it is each individual's obligation to help bring about tiqqun, what is one to do to accomplish this? The human task, according to Isaac Luria, is essentially a contemplative one. Every religious action, regardless of the kind, requires contemplative concentration on the parzufim and various combinations of the divine name in order to "raise up the fallen sparks." The primary focus of attention is the reunification of the parzufim Ze'ir 'Anpin and Nuqva de-Ze'ir. Every action done in the world below—the material world—accompanied by concentration on the dynamics being initiated through such action, causes the "female waters" within Nuqva de-Ze'ir to become aroused and ascend with the 288 sparks that were believed to be attached to the broken vessels. The "female waters" act as spiritual "chemicals" which bring about—even if only temporarily—ziwwug or harmony between male and female within the Godhead. The crucial point here is that such reunification depends entirely on the efforts of human beings. This is a process that can only be set in motion through the contemplative exercises of kabbalists whose souls are thoroughly cleansed and purified. Thus, the focus of contemplation is the inner dynamics of reorganization and restructuring that occurs in the course of acts of devotional piety.

The kinds of activities by which the kabbalist seeks to accomplish these goals can be divided into three basic categories: liturgical prayer, the performance of all other mizwot, and the practice of yihudim.[6] The same general contemplative idea characterizes each of these types of activity, and Hayyim Vital's versions of Luria's teachings spell out the proper mystical intentions (kawwanot) in great detail. But the practice of yihudim stands out as a rather extraordinary meditative discipline for reasons that will become clear as we turn our attention to a description of these exercises.

Qualifying for the Practice of Yihudim

Intrinsic to virtually every traditional system of meditation is a stage in which the future adept must become prepared so as to be fit and worthy for successfully mystical practice. According to Luria, the attainment of prophetic inspiration or the Holy Spirit is not possible without having first passed through such a stage. The yihudim are not to be practiced by just anyone; nor are they to be performed casually. Rather, intense and methodical effort must be exerted by an aspiring adept in order to train himself to become worthy of even beginning the practice. The qualifying activities that Vital describes are of three types, which we may broadly label ethical, ritual, and penitential.

The Cultivation of Moral and Spiritual Qualities

In the first place we find rules prescribing the kinds of spiritual and moral qualities that an individual who wishes to achieve mystical inspiration must cultivate. One such quality, for example, which Luria considered essential for anyone seeking to perform the *yiḥudim*, is joyfulness (*SRH*, 33).[7] Whenever one performs a religious act, be it study of Torah, prayer, or the like, great heartfelt joy is indispensable. The joy of performing God's will ought to be regarded as greater than all material wealth. Correspondingly, no quality of spirit prevents the possibility of divine inspiration as much as sadness. Vital reports that sadness prevents the soul from receiving supernal light, although the feeling of sadness while confessing one's sins is appropriate. In one of his own treatises, Vital suggests that happiness strengthens a person, enabling one to love God and cleave to Him, whereas sadness derives from *Sama'el,* the power of evil.[8] Moreover, the *Shekhinah,* the female presence of divinity, cannot reside in a place where sadness exists.[9]

A closely related spiritual trait with which Isaac Luria appears to have been particularly concerned was the avoidance of anger, inasmuch as it inhibits the prospects of prophetic inspiration. Citing a talmudic passage from *Pesaḥim* 66b which states that a prophet's inspiration will depart when he is angered, Vital writes that Luria was more stringent with regard to this matter than all other transgressions. Whereas all other sins cause damage to one of the soul's "limbs," the sin of anger injures the soul as a whole, altering it completely. When one is angered, one's highest level of soul (*neshamah*) leaves and is replaced by a lower stratum of soul (*nefesh*) from the side of the *qelipot.* Citing Job 18:4, "Thou that tearest thyself in thine anger," Luria teaches that anger "tears" the soul making it *trefa* (lit., "torn"). Following earlier rabbinic and Zoharic traditions, Luria goes so far as to identify anger with idolatry.[10] When one is angered, one is filled with a "strange god" whose removal can be brought about only through great acts of repentance. The danger of anger is such that it draws one to sin and makes divine inspiration impossible. Because it damages the soul in its entirety, atonement requires personal *tiqqun* of every aspect of one's being. As with sadness, anger makes one vulnerable to the powers of evil, which are prepared to occupy the void created by the departure of holiness.

Qualities of modesty, which are stressed in both classical rabbinic and medieval Hebrew literature, are also considered of great importance in order to qualify oneself for divine inspiration. One must conduct oneself in meekness, humility, and fear of sin (*SRH*, 34).[11] Correspondingly, one should avoid pride, jesting, gossip, and pedantry. An individual ought not be too strict or severe even if there should be significant cause. Nor should one indulge in "idle" conversation, that is, in talk unrelated to Torah or spiritual matters (*SRH*, 34).[12] All of these standards were typical of rabbinic and medieval piety and ethics. Moreover, they were of concern generally to the kabbalists of sixteenth-century Safed who wrote treatises on kabbalistic ethics and repentance. The particularly Lurianic feature, though, is the stress on the notion that failure to meet these standards results in severe injury to the soul, diminishing or even rendering impossible the attainment of divine inspiration.

Special Acts of Ritual Piety

The second category of qualifying activities involves a variety of ritual observances and special acts of piety designed to qualify one to perform the *yihudim*. The basic purpose of these customs was to destroy the power of the demonic and to purify the soul. Such purification necessitated an ongoing war with the powers of evil, whose persistence prolonged the work of *tiqqun*.

As Hayyim Vital reports, Luria informed him that attainment of the Holy Spirit depends, among other things, upon the care and contemplative concentration with which blessings of enjoyment (*birkhot ha-nehenin*) are carried out. This is especially true in the case of enjoying food:

> Since through him [blessings over food recited with proper mystical intention] the strength of these *qelipot* which cling to physical foods, and cleave through them to man who eats them, is abrogated. And by virtue of the blessings over them [i.e., the food] recited with mystical intention, he removes these *qelipot* from them, purifies his physical self, and becomes pure, ready to receive holiness. And he [Luria] warned me carefully in this regard. (*SRH*, 34)

Luria also enjoined his disciples to practice the custom of rising at midnight for the purpose of praying and studying through the night, an activity especially efficacious in qualifying one for the performance of *yihudim*. In *Sha'ar Ruaḥ ha-Qodesh* (34–35), Vital records that the midnight vigil will be effective only for one who has performed certain deeds during the day, including causing others to repent, giving charity anonymously, and reading the literature of the *Poseqim* (rabbinic legal decisions). As we shall see, the most favorable time to perform the *yihudim* is also at midnight.

Other important acts of piety included strict observance of the Sabbath in all its details, entering the synagogue with great awe and trembling, and wearing *tefillin* (phylacteries) the entire day. Furthermore, the attainment of the Holy Spirit requires the regular study of Scripture, Mishnah, Talmud (i.e., Gemara) and Kabbalah (*SRH*, 35).[13] In this connection, one particular activity that Luria regarded as essential to achieving divine inspiration was intensive study of the law (halakhah) (*SRH*, 35).[14] According to Luria, the *qushia*, the difficult problem in a legal argument requiring resolution by intellectual acumen, represents the evil "shell" which covers the "brain," the holy element. In resolving the halakhic difficulty, a person must concentrate on breaking the *qelipah*, which will result in disclosure of the halakhah, the holy inner core. The latter consists of secrets of the Torah and kabbalistic knowledge. The person to whom such intensive study comes easily is required to spend an hour or two each day engaged in it. One who finds it difficult should study only halakhic rules or conclusions (*dinim*) rather than neglect the study of Torah by dwelling on complex arguments.

Hayyim Vital also records those practices which other students of Isaac Luria told him they received from the mouth of the master. In the name of Jonathan Sagis, Vital reports that Luria regarded ritual immersion as essential to attainment of the Holy Spirit (*SRH*, 36).[15] Immersion was deemed a purifying exercise of such significance that it was to be practiced with the utmost regularity. Vital adds, however, that Luria himself could not practice ritual immersion for six months during one winter because of illness, though he suffered no loss of divine inspiration.

Abraham ben Eliezer ha-Levi Berukhim told Vital that Luria related to him that the following activities were conducive to mystical inspiration: avoidance of "idle" talk, rising at midnight and weeping on account of our lack of mystical knowledge, and study of forty or fifty pages of *Zohar* each day without intensive reflection (*SRH*, 36). Samuel Uzeda reported that he was informed by Luria that anyone who passes forty successive days without speaking anything but words of Torah will become prepared to achieve mystical inspiration and knowledge.

The basic purpose of these customs and rituals is clear. They are intended to cleanse the soul and thereby render it receptive to divine inspiration. This can be done only by destroying the power of the *qelipot* and by preventing the infiltration of evil into the purified soul. The task of *tiqqun*, the removal of the demonic forces from the lower world and the lifting up of the sparks of holiness, entails a never-ending battle. Laxity or passivity on the part of an individual fortifies the evil powers and entrenches their position, whereas the continuous cultivation of particular spiritual qualities and the performance of special acts of piety destroy their potency.

Acts of Penitence

The third category of qualifying exercises is acts of penitence known as *tiqquney ʿawonot*. The Lurianic kabbalists, as was the case with all of the sixteenth-century Safed mystics, possessed a profound sense of their own sinfulness. The feelings of guilt harbored by these individuals derived from several sources. In the first place, collective sin was, of course, among the traditional explanations for historical calamity and suffering in Jewish theology. The consciousness of exile weighed particularly heavy on the Safed kabbalists precisely because they were convinced that the sins of the generation of the Spanish Expulsion were responsible in some way for the tragic events that had befallen Iberian Jewry at the end of the fifteenth century. This sense of shared guilt and failure was continually reinforced by the belief that the exile was prolonged by virtue of every *new* transgression, a kabbalistic notion based on the conviction that every sin reiterates Adam's primordial transgression. Just as Adam's sin resulted in the disunification of the *Shekhinah*, the female quality of the Godhead, from Her spouse, *Tifʾeret*, *every* sin deepens the *Shekhinah*'s exile. Elijah de Vidas, the author of the popular sixteenth-century kabbalistic treatise *Reshit Ḥokhmah* (*The Beginning of Wisdom*), puts it in these straightforward terms: "It is appropriate for a person to arouse himself in repentance when he considers that the *Shekhinah* is exiled on his account, as it is written: 'And for your transgressions was your mother put away' (Isa 50:1)." It is this belief that the fate of the Godhead itself was bound up with the kabbalist's action which served as the most powerful source of guilt. Israel is responsible not merely for its own exiled historical situation, but for the rupture within the life of deity as well.

Isaac Luria prescribed specific penitential acts whose purpose, in the words of Hayyim Vital's son Shmuel, was to "mend his [i.e., the kabbalist's] soul" and "cleanse him from the filth of the disease of his sins." Afterward, writes Shmuel Vital, he would be prepared to perform the various kinds of *yiḥudim*. Hayyim Vital himself introduces the *tiqquney ʿawonot* with a discussion of the relationship between one's soul and sin. The following passage provides a lucid account of the Lurianic theory of sin and the effectiveness of genuine repentance:

> Man is created from matter, and from form which consists of soul (*nefesh*), spirit (*ruaḥ*) and super-soul (*neshamah*), the divine portion from above, as it is

said: "and [God] breathed into his nostrils the breath (*neshamah*) of life" (Gen 2:7). And his body is dark matter from the side of the "shell," luring and preventing man from [achieving] perfection of his soul [in order] to cut it [i.e., his soul] off from the Tree of Life . . . and so "there is not a righteous man upon earth that doeth good and sinneth not" (Eccl 7:20). And it is known that sin is a blemish, stain and rust in the soul, and this is the sickness of the pure soul. When it [is immersed] in filth and stain, it is unable to perceive and achieve the true perfection, which is [attainment of] the mysteries of the Torah. . . . And the transgression becomes a barrier separating the soul from her Creator, preventing her from perceiving and comprehending holy and pure supernal matters, as it is said: "The law of the Lord is perfect, restoring the soul" (Ps 19:8). . . . When the soul is pure and unblemished, then the supernal holy matters take shape in her, and when she dwells in rust and stain everything becomes bittersweet [i.e., evil appears as good]. [This is] similar to the sick person who, when he is ill, abhors the good things and loves things which aggravate his illness. The doctor, in order to restore his health, gives him spices including gall, by which his nature will return to what it originally was, and his health as before.

So, too, the sick soul, to remove the sickness from her, must receive the bitterness of medicine and "return" in [the form of] mortifications and fasts, sackcloth and ashes and stripes, ritual immersions, and purifications from filth and the stains of sins. [This is] in order to be able to attain and comprehend supernal matters, which are the mysteries of the world. . . . (*SRH*, 39)[16]

Only the weapons of ascetic piety are potent enough to cleanse the soul entirely of the filth that clings to it. Luria himself, proclaims Hayyim Vital, is the diagnostician and healer of diseased souls! (*SRH*, 39–40).[17] Luria's powers stem from the spirit of prophecy which he possessed, meriting him divine light and esoteric knowledge with which to teach his followers. But Luria only revealed his knowledge to those disciples who were completely pure and worthy. To this end he prescribed for each of his students personalized penitential activities to meet their specific needs:

He [Luria] would not reveal any of the mysteries of this holy knowledge to one in whose soul he perceived, with the [aid of the] Holy Spirit, a blemish—until he gave him penitential acts to straighten out all he did crookedly. And like the expert doctor who prescribes for each sick person the proper medicine to cure this illness, so too [Isaac Luria] may he rest in peace, used to recognize the sin, tell him where he incurred a blemish, and prescribe for him the penitential act needed for this transgression in order to cleanse his soul, so that he could receive the divine light, as it is written: "O Jerusalem, wash thy heart from wickedness, that thou mayest be saved" (Jer 4:14). (*SRH*, 40)

Luria did what any good physician would do: he carefully diagnosed the specific maladies which his "patient" had and prescribed the appropriate cure. Among the diagnostic techniques that Luria had at his disposal, according to Hayyim Vital, was the capacity to discover the character of a person's sinfulness by feeling his pulse and by reading the letters and signs engraved upon his forehead, an esoteric science known as metoposcopy. These and other techniques are discussed in considerable detail in the writings of Hayyim Vital.

Along with diagnoses Luria specified the penitence necessary for particular transgressions. Vital informs us that he recorded all of the *tiqquney 'awonot* which he heard from his teacher's mouth for the sake of those who needed to purify their souls. The character of these exercises can be illustrated by reference to several typical instructions.

One *tiqqun*, for example, prescribes the penitence for the sin of merely thinking about a transgression. A fast of eighty-seven days is required to atone for this sin. A person must concentrate on the name of God, *YHWH*, as it is written out *plene* (*bi-millui*) so as to spell the name of each letter. The numerical equivalent (*gematria*) of this name equals 45 (*SRH*, 41).[18] By adding up the number of letters utilized in this spelling, that is, 10, plus the number of letters involved in spelling out the *millui* of the *millui*, that is, 28, and the 4 letters of the simple *YHWH*, we arrive at 42. Adding 45 and 42 the figure of 87 is achieved, accounting for the fast of 87 days. This is a relatively simple, though representative, example of the way in which the technique of *gematria* is used to derive practical results. It is based on the conviction that the numerical equivalents of names and words are not arbitrary, but suggestive of the "meaning" or "power" of the name or word.

Another *tiqqun* is prescribed as atonement for the transgression of the *miẓwah* of honoring one's father and mother (*SRH*, 48). According to Luria, the *parẓufim* of 'Abba (Father) and 'Imma (Mother) are associated with the divine name *YaH*. The *millui* of *YaH* equals 26, which is the number of fasts required to atone for this sin. In addition, 26 lashings are prescribed. Performance of the penance atones for the sin, not merely by raising the sinner's consciousness with regard to his act but also by "mending" the damage done to the relevant parts of the divine structure through such transgression. Thus, the number 26 is of the utmost significance for the penitent. By concentrating on the proper number of fasts and lashings, their relationship to *YaH* and the *parẓufim* of 'Abba and 'Imma, the individual repairs the injury suffered by the Godhead.

Another *tiqqun* is that required for one who has publicly humiliated another person. He must roll upon thorns called *ortigas* (*SRH*, 49).[19] Luria derived this practice from Proverbs 24:31, "The face thereof was covered with nettles." The word "face" is taken to mean the face of one who has been put to shame in public. Just as the humiliated person is covered with "nettles," the guilty part must suffer affliction with thorns.

Still other mortification practices were enjoined as acts of repentance. Transgressions involving sexual matters called for particularly severe affliction.[20] For example, a person who has had intercourse with the wife of another man must submit to a fast of 325 days, which corresponds to five times the *gematria* of the name *'ADoNaY.* For every one of the fasts he must don sackcloth and rub dust on his forehead, traditional signs of mourning. Moreover, the final portion of each meal that breaks a day of fasting must be dipped in dust before eating. In this case Luria equates the number 325 with 320 "judgments" (*dinim*) whose severity is "sweetened" by adding five times the letter *'alef* from the five times *'ADoNaY.* In other words, it is concentration on the name *'ADoNaY,* whose source is in the *parzuf Nuqva de-Ze'ir,* that atones for this transgression. The wearing of sackcloth and the application of dust signify the reunification of the *parzufim Ze'ir 'Anpin* and *Nuqva de-Ze'ir.* This is possible because these two *parzufim* are symbolized by heaven (*shamayim*) and earth (*'arez*), the *gematria* of which equals that of the Hebrew words for sackcloth and dust, 681.

One who is guilty of having had intercourse with a menstruating woman must fast for a total of 59 days, which corresponds to the *gematria* of the word *niddah* (menstruant). Moreover, he must be lashed and ritually immerse himself in water each day. He is not permitted to sleep on his bed during the days of fast.

While the kabbalists of the sixteenth century regarded properly carried out sexuality within the context of marriage a mystical rite of vital significance, the abuse and misuse of one's sexual powers were viewed with the most severe anxiety. Misuse of generative powers, illegitimate lust, and passion strengthen the realm of the "other side" (*sitra 'ahra*), the forces of evil. Strict penance, though, is able to disentangle the improperly mixed elements of holiness and impurity.

Virtually every one of the *tiqqunim* involves a certain length of fasting. Hayyim Vital indicates a number of reasons for engaging in such fasts. A person is to regard himself as a *sacrifice* in which the blood and fat are given up to God through abstention from eating. Such a spiritualized interpretation of fasting is related to the conception that a person's sins initiate a breach within the letters of the divine name *YHWH.* Sacrifice, through fasting, draws the separated letters near to one another again, reuniting the totality of God's being.

We also find that fasting constitutes atonement for that which one has already eaten. Luria taught that the soul of a deceased sinner will undergo a process of transmigration (*gilgul*) and may come to reside in an animal or vegetable. When a person consumes meat, it is possible that the soul of such an Israelite dwells within the food. During a period of fasting a penitent should concentrate on the *tiqqun* or "repair" of what he has eaten with the intention of raising up the soul of the departed sinner.

It is clear that the ritual exercises prescribed by Luria for expiation of sin and purification of the soul were not intended to be mere physical afflictions or punishment for its own sake. Rather, they were to cleanse the soul by calling to mind the blemish within it and the damage done to the corresponding elements within the Godhead. The emphasis rests with the proper attitude of repentance and the mending which such repentance accomplishes. The immediate goal of these penitential exercises, and of the qualifying activities as a whole, was personal preparedness for the sake of indulging in a higher order of contemplative ritual, a subject to which we now turn.

The Time and Place for the Practice of *Yiḥudim*

The practice of the *yiḥudim* is an independent exercise, detached entirely from the format of traditional prayer and the performance of other *miẓwot*. The total setting suggests an experience quite different from these other vehicles for Lurianic contemplation. According to our sources, there are two places in which the *yiḥudim* can be performed: at the grave of a *ẓaddiq* (a righteous individual) or in one's own home (*SRH*, 108). The reason for performance at the grave has to do with the fact that one of the essential goals of the *yiḥudim*, as we shall see, is to commune with the soul of a departed *ẓaddiq*. They *can* be carried out in one's home, but far greater purity on the part of the adept is necessary in order to bring about the communion of souls (*SY*, 4).

Certain days were considered more propitious than others for the practice of *yiḥudim* (*SRH*, 108). Practice at the grave could be done on all days except for the Sabbath, new moon (*rosh ḥodesh*) and festivals. On these days the souls of the righteous (*nefashot*), which normally hover above the grave, ascend to the "terrestrial paradise" and are thus unavailable for communion. Although all other days are acceptable, the most preferable are the eve of the new moon and the eve of the fifteenth day of the month. On these days an individual is considered likely to be more spiritually prepared. In the case of *yiḥudim* performed at home, all days are acceptable—including the Sabbath, new moon, and festivals. Although both types of *yiḥudim* can be adequately practiced at any hour of the day, the "favored time" is after midnight. If one performs the devotions at home, it is particularly important to wait until the midnight hour.

This separation of the *yiḥudim* from the context of conventional prayer is not without significance. The history of mysticism suggests that, in general, the devotion of mystics tends toward private experience. Mystical prayer is characterized by an unusual degree of concentration and intensity, as well as by a concern for the highly personal apprehension of God or the sacred. Jewish mystics, however, have always had to deal with the entrenched tradition of communal prayer, according to which a quorum of ten is required for public worship. As a consequence, the earliest kabbalists gravitated toward the use of traditional liturgy for their meditative activities.

In Isaac Luria's case, the practice of contemplation in private, as with the *yihudim,* is understandable from several points of view. Although the *kawwanot* (mystical intentions) of prayer remained tied to communal worship in Lurianic devotion, the nature of the contemplation involved tended to shift the emphasis from collective dynamics to individual experience. The *kawwanot* of prayer are of an extremely complex character, requiring intense and lengthy concentration. Moreover, the *primary* focus of contemplative attention is no longer directed toward the text of the prayers themselves as much as toward the sefirotic system to which the words of prayer correspond. These factors must have necessarily led to an increased withdrawal into oneself in the course of prayer.

From this privatizing tendency it was an easy transition to meditation divorced altogether from regular communal worship. Such a move allowed for the development of freer techniques for raising up one's soul and contemplating the intricacies of the divine world. Moreover, the added dimension of communion with the soul of a *zaddiq* called for a technique and a setting other than that of communal devotion. It is thus not surprising that alongside of the elaborate system of *kawwanot* of prayer, Isaac Luria fashioned a meditative ritual detached from public worship.

Communion of Souls with the Departed

One of the essential goals of the practice of *yihudim* is mystical communion between the soul of the adept and that of a departed *zaddiq,* as noted earlier. Hayyim Vital's account of the process of communion is contained in a series of short "introductions":

> Be aware that in the case of all possible *Yihudim,* if you perform the *Yihud* by actually stretching yourself out on the *zaddiq*'s grave [i.e., in a prone position], you should contemplatively "intend" that by virtue of your stretching out on top of him you also cause the *zaddiq* to stretch out his soul (*nefesh*), which will then spread out in his bones that are in the grave: [whereupon] he comes "alive" and his bones become like a "body" to the soul that is stretched and spread out within them. This [particular] soul is the one that remains over the grave, as is known, which is the secret meaning of: "And his soul mourneth over him" (Job 14:22). And it is as if this *zaddiq* lives in body and soul at this moment.

> And if you perform the *Yihudim* in your house, without prostration, there is no need to practice the contemplative intention indicated above. However, you must *always* concentrate upon raising up your soul (*nefesh*) and that of the *zaddiq* while they are bound to one another, your soul included with his, regardless of whether you perform the *Yihudim* while prostrated at the grave or while at home. You must also concentrate your attention upon that root within Adam from which both your soul and that of the *zaddiq* derive. And concentrate upon arousing that root, for it is the "limb" within Adam from which the soul of this *zaddiq* originates. By doing so you can raise up his soul through the mystery of the "female waters." (*SRH*, 75)[21]

We have here what is surely a most unusual and extraordinary ritual. When performed at the grave of the *zaddiq*, the adept's prostration arouses the *zaddiq*'s soul. This, in turn, "activates" his bones so as to revive him temporarily, as if he were actually alive. The quasi-magical nature of this practice is evident. What distinguishes it, in part, from actual magic, however, is that the physical act by itself does not suffice to accomplish the intended goal; rather, a *contemplative* effort is required. In fact, we see that the physical act can be dispensed with altogether if necessary. What is more significant, the ultimate goal of this activity is a *spiritual* one, the ascent of the soul along with that of the *zaddiq* to the upper realms. Nevertheless, the theurgic tendency so essential to most forms of kabbalism may be said to be taken in this case to something of an extreme.

The "soul" referred to in this passage is the *nefesh*, the lowest of the various parts of soul described in kabbalistic literature. In earlier Kabbalah the soul is generally considered to have three aspects. In an ascending hierarchy they are the *nefesh* (soul), the *ruah* (spirit), and the *neshamah* (super-soul). The *nefesh* is immediately present and active in every individual; the two more elevated levels, however, are *latent* and become manifest only in the case of one who is spiritually aroused, having striven to develop oneself through religious activity. Such activity assists in the development of the higher powers of cognition and represents the fullest maturation of the soul. Later kabbalists—including the Lurianists—added two additional levels of soul. Known as *hayyah* and *yehidah*, these are considered to represent still higher stages of spiritual attainment, present in only the most select figures. According to the teachings of Lurianic Kabbalah, these five parts of the soul correspond to the five *parzufim* of 'Adam Qadmon. Further, every one of them is associated with each of the "worlds" of '*Azilut, Beri' ah, Yezirah,* and '*Asiyah,* producing an elaborate hierarchy of soul-ranks. The most exalted level of soul, for example, has its origin in the *yehidah* of the *sefirah Keter* in the highest divine world of '*Azilut.*

According to Lurianic teaching, the various parts of the soul return to their respective places of origin following death. However, the *nefesh*—or, more precisely, the *lowest* grade of *nefesh*, "*nefesh* of the lower world of 'Asiyah"—hovers over an individual's grave. It is this grade of *nefesh* to which our passage refers. If, however, the contemplative kabbalist has himself attained higher levels of soul, such as *ruah*, or *neshamah*, he can attempt meditatively to bind these to the *ruah* and *neshamah* of the *zaddiq* with whom he is seeking to commune. In order to understand the nature of this contemplative goal it is necessary to delineate in somewhat greater detail the notion that certain souls have affinity for one another.

As we indicated earlier, Luria taught that the soul of Adam was originally made up of all the future souls of humankind. The structure of this soul was complex: it possessed 613 "limbs" or "parts," each one corresponding to one of the 613 *mizwot* in the Torah. (Each of these "limbs" of Adam's spiritual body reflected the corresponding "limbs" of 'Adam Qadmon, making Adam a lower configuration of the supernal *anthrōpos*, itself the paradigm for all reality.) Every one of the 613 "limbs" of Adam's soul was itself a fully developed configuration, subdivided into 613 additional parts or "roots." In turn, each of these major "roots" (*shoresh gadol*) comprised a number of minor "roots" or sparks; every such spark is an individual soul. There exist, as a consequence of this intricate subdivision, "families" or groups of souls which derive from common "roots" within Adam's original soul. The critical point is that these "families" have a special attraction and affinity for one another, sharing, as they do, the same source. Because of this they are uniquely qualified to assist one another in the task of raising up souls from the now materialized realm of the world of 'Asiyah. The knowledge of one's soul-ancestry—knowledge that Isaac Luria was able to give his disciples—was thus of crucial importance to the contemplative kabbalist.

It is this affinity of souls that constitutes the basis for the communion of souls to which our passage refers. Because of their natural kinship, the soul of the adept can "arouse" the corresponding aspect of soul of the *zaddiq*. In turn, the soul of the *zaddiq* can assist in their simultaneous ascent to the upper realms. The desire to raise up one's soul is thus much more than a private matter; it forms part of the continuous struggle to restore all the elements of holiness that have descended into the material sphere to their proper place above. What appears to be primarily a personal act of *tiqqun* partakes in the far larger task of messianic restitution. The redemption of the individual soul is a small but absolutely vital part of the infinitely complex effort to redeem divinity as a whole.

Luria's notion of soul-communion also drew on themes developed in the *Zohar*. In speaking of the fate of the soul after death, the *Zohar* teaches that the lower souls (*nefashot*) remain in this world, hovering over the grave, in order to protect the living. When the living come to them and beg for mercy, the souls of the departed inform their spirits (ruḥot), setting off a chain reaction of celestial communication:

> We have learned that when the world requires mercy and the intervention of those righteous ones, that which is in the world (i.e., the *nefesh*) to shield mankind, ascends, goes and flits about the world to tell the spirit, and the spirit ascends, removes itself and tells the super-soul, which informs the Holy One, blessed be He. Then God has pity on the world and the reverse process takes place, the super-soul telling the spirit and the spirit, the soul. (*Zohar* 3:70b)

Our Lurianic sources utilize this motif for their own purposes. Vital's text (*SRH*, 109), as well as that of Joseph ibn Tabul (folio 175a), cites the continuation of the above *Zohar* passage, according to which the living inform the souls of the departed righteous when the world is in distress so that they might cleave "soul to soul" with the righteous. Although no ritual of prostration upon the grave is suggested here, the *Zohar* is describing a simplified prototype of the Lurianic notion of soul-communion. Of particular interest is Moses Cordovero's comment on the Zoharic passage under consideration.

> This is the meaning of "soul bound up with soul"—this is when he "pours" his soul upon the grave of the *zaddiq*, cleaving soul to soul, and speaks with the soul of the *zaddiq*. He informs him of the world's distress, and the soul of the *zaddiq* arouses other souls.... (Cordovero's *Zohar* commentary in Abraham Azulai's 'Or ha-Ḥammah, 3:56a)

Cordovero also reports that such a practice was performed by "men who worked wondrous things in Spain." It is not clear exactly what Cordovero means by the term "pour" in this comment, but it does appear that he has in mind something akin to Luria's practice. It is possible that the peregrinations (*gerushin*) carried out by Cordovero and Solomon Alkabez, in which they wandered from grave to grave in the environs of Safed and had experiences of automatic speech in which they uttered kabbalistic interpretations of scriptural verses, were inspired by the Zoharic tradition.

We know of the practice of visiting the gravesites of important rabbis and teachers in the Safed area from a variety of sources. There are reports as early as the thirteenth century of visits to the cave of Hillel and Shammai in Meron—a small village near Safed—in order to pray for rain. Even before the Spanish Expulsion, visits were made to the grave, in Meron, of Shimon bar Yohai, whose mystical teachings the *Zohar* purports to contain. Testimony by various Safed kabbalists, Joseph Karo, Moses Cordovero, Abraham Galante, and Eliezar Azikri indicate the widespread custom of visits to Shimon bar Yohai's grave for study, prayer, and meditation.[22] Karo's *maggid*, or angelic mentor, for example, informs him that Shimon bar Yohai and his son Eliezer reveal heavenly mysteries to those who study *Zohar* at their graves.[23] It is clear, then, that by the time Isaac Luria arrived in Safed, the custom of visiting the graves of sages for various devotional purposes was already quite common. Such a practice, along with the conceptions found in the *Zohar* described above, is likely to have served as the framework for his own technique of soul-communion at the graves of *zaddiqim*. Nevertheless, Luria's ritual represents a far more complex and elaborate meditative exercise.

Contemplation upon Divine Names

While maintaining a state of cleaving to the soul of a *zaddiq,* the adept moves on to a second stage of practice. The focus of meditation is now on an intricate array of divine "names." These "names" correspond to the *parzufim* and their multiple subconfigurations, whose unification is effected through formalized and sustained concentration. Like the *parzufim,* the "names" of God constitute a vast and complex "map" of the divine structure.

Although the most characteristic symbolism employed in kabbalistic literature to describe the inner workings of God is that of the *sefirot,* the kabbalists also conceive of the emanation of deity in terms of the revealing of divine *language*. In this symbolism the Torah comprises a network of "names," each of which signifies a particular concentration of divine power or energy. As such, these "names" possess a fullness of meaning not exhausted by human language. It is not surprising that the Lurianic "names" are only to a limited extent conventional words at all. In a way that is highly reminiscent of the seemingly arbitrary combining of Hebrew letters characteristic of Abulafian mysticism, Luria's divine "names" are, to a considerable degree, beyond rational understanding altogether. For the contemplative, however, to exercise one's concentration successfully upon the "names" of God is to reorganize theurgically and restructure the life of the divine.

Unification of Male and Female within Divinity

As an example of this contemplation we turn to one of the *yihudim* that exhibits some of the essential elements of these meditations (*SRH,* 110–11). It is concerned with the unification of *Hokhmah* and *Binah* (the *parzufim* 'Abba and 'Imma), as well as that of *Tif'eret* and *Malkhut* (the *parzufim* Ze'ir 'Anpin and *Nuqva de-Ze'ir*), the totality of which represents the complete tetragrammaton, YHWH.

Analysis of this meditation requires an understanding of the relationship between the tetragrammaton and the structure of 'Adam Qadmon.

According to Luria, the figure of 'Adam Qadmon, as indicated earlier, possesses four structural dimensions: eyes, ears, nose, and mouth. Each of these is the source of different parzufim, which, in turn, correspond to various forms of the tetragrammaton. The "organs" of 'Adam Qadmon can thus be conceived of as divine lights which combine to form names, the expression of which represents different aspects of the divine structure. According to this conception, the tetragrammaton can assume four basic forms; these are known as the names 72, 63, 45, and 52 and are based on different spellings (milluim) of YHWH:

1. Name 72 is expressed by millui de-yudin[24] and is written out as follows: YW"D H"Y WY"W H"Y. The gematria of this name is 72.

2. Name 63 is expressed by millui de-yudin with an 'alef in the waw and is written as follows: YW"D H"Y WA"W H"Y. The gematria of this name is 63.

3. Name 45 is expressed by millui de-'alfin,[25] which is written as follows: YW"D H"A WA"W H"A. The gematria of this name is 45.

4. Name 52 is expressed by millui de-hein,[26] which is written as follows: YW"D H"H W"W H"H. The gematria of this name is 52.

In addition to representing one of the parzufim that make up the entire divine structure, each of these names corresponds to one of the four letters of the simple tetragrammaton. This set of associations can be summarized as follows:

"Organ" of 'Adam Qadmon	Parzuf	Name	Letter
eye	'Abba	72	Yud
ear	'Imma	63	Heh
nose	Ze'ir 'Anpin	45	Waw
mouth	Nuqva de-Ze'ir	52	Heh

This meditation begins with the attempt to unite the upper "parents," Hokhmah and Binah ('Abba and 'Imma). The adept concentrates on the name YHWH within Hokhmah and on the name 'EHYH within Binah. He mentally joins these two names by interspersing their letters—thus forming the single divine appellation: YAHHWYH"H. After concentrating on this name, the adept is instructed to turn his attention to the name 72, itself corresponding to Hokhmah/'Abba. Contemplation of the name 72 serves to stimulate the initial unification of Hokhmah/'Abba and Binah/'Imma. The name 72 also corresponds to the quality of divine compassion, HeSeD, the gematria of which is 72. This Hesed helps to facilitate the love between the upper two *parzufim*. The meditative action represents the first letter of the simple *YHWH*.

In the next stage the adept concerns himself with the completion of this unification by attempting to bring about the ascent of the "female waters." He does this by concentrating on the name 63, whose source is *Binah/ 'Imma*. The ascent of the "female waters" aroused by an individual's contemplation of the name 63 acts as the catalyst that finalizes the unification of *Ḥokhmah/'Abba* and *Binah/'Imma*. This action represents the second letter of the simple *YHWH*.

Following this the adept is instructed to turn his attention to the uniting of the lower two *parzufim, Tif'eret* and *Malkhut* (*Ze'ir 'Anpin* and *Nuqva de-Ze'ir*). He contemplates the name *YHWH* within *Tif'eret* and the name *'ADNY* within *Malkhut*. In his imagination he combines the two names by interspersing their letters, thus forming: YAHDWNH"Y. He then turns his attention to the name 45, which itself corresponds to *Ze'ir 'Anpin*, the contemplation of which serves to stimulate the initial unification of the lower two *parzufim*. This action represents the third letter of the tetragrammaton, *Waw*. In the second stage, an individual finalizes the uniting of *Ze'ir 'Anpin* and *Nuqva de-Ze'ir* by raising up the "female waters" from *Malkhut*. This is achieved by contemplation on the name 52, itself rooted in *Nuqva de-Ze'ir*. This corresponds to the fourth letter of the tetragrammaton, *heh*.

Through this meditation, then, both sets of male and female within *'Adam Qadmon* are united with one another, *'Abba* and *'Imma, Ze'ir* and *Nuqva de-Ze'ir*. The net result on the theosophical plane is the total reunification of *YHWH*. Inasmuch as each *parzuf* corresponds to one of the four letters of the simple *YHWH*, when the *parzufim* are brought into proper relationship to one another through contemplation, the tetragrammaton itself is restored to its primordial state of unity. The following chart outlines this meditative exercise.

Ia. Unification of *Ḥokhmah* and *Binah:* YAHHWYH"H
YUD HY WAW HY (72)

Ib. Arousal of "female waters" to complete unification:
YUD HY WAW HY (63)

IIa. Unification of *Tif'eret* and *Malkhut:* YAHDWNH"Y
YUD HA WAW HA (45)

IIb. Arousal of "female waters" to complete unification:
YUD HH WAW HH (52)

Achieving Prophetic Inspiration

We are now in a position to ask about the nature of the *experience* itself that the adept underwent in the course of practicing the *yihudim*. What were the effects upon the psyche and the body of the contemplative kabbalist, and what were the ultimate consequences of his practice? What partial answers we are able to provide to these questions derive from two kinds of sources. First, we rely upon fragmentary and incidental statements in the theoretical accounts describing the *yihudim* in Hayyim Vital's *Sha'ar Ruah ha-Qodesh* and *Sha'ar ha-Yihudim*. Second, Vital has recorded his own experiences during the performance of *yihudim*. These valuable reports are preserved in *Sha'ar ha-Gilgulim* and Vital's mystical diary, *Sefer ha-Hezyonot*.

According to our sources, the flow of divine power set off by the uniting of male and female, *Ze'ir 'Anpin* and *Nuqva de-Ze'ir*, in the course of meditation, constitutes the source of divine inspiration which the successful adept attains—either in the form of prophecy or the Holy Spirit.[27]

> All of the prophecy of prophets derives only from [the *sefirot* of] *Nezah, Hod* and *Yesod* within *Ze'ir 'Anpin*—because from there an illumination shines upon *Malkhut*, the feminine [aspect of *Ze'ir 'Anpin*]. From this illumination prophets draw their prophecy.... There is no comprehension for any prophet or seer except by means of *Nuqva de-Ze'ir*. (*SY*, 1)

That prophetic inspiration derives from *Nuqva de-Ze'ir* is in complete accord with the traditional kabbalistic notion of prophecy through *Malkhut*. Uniting the *parzufim* of *Ze'ir* and *Nuqva de-Ze'ir* provides an individual with divine inspiration and enables him to speak words of "prophecy." The Holy Spirit or the spirit of prophecy begins to rest upon him and manifests itself through spontaneous unreflected speech, a form of motor automatism. Prophetic utterance such as this requires great power of concentration and is not easily achieved:

> There is one who begins to achieve some inspiration (*hasagah*) and the Spirit (*ha-Ruah*) rests upon him. But it [i.e., the Spirit] does not possess perfection with which to cause the voice of prophecy and the Holy Spirit to dwell upon his lips and tongue. Without speaking, he only feels at the moment of *yihud* that his hair stands up, his body and limbs shake, his lips tremble—but the power of speaking is not in his mouth. (*SY*, 5)

This condition may afflict an adept only after he has already achieved a certain degree of inspiration. The spirit speaks within him but does not manifest itself vocally. Luria thus prescribes several particular *yihudim* whose specific function is to invest the adept in need of special assistance with the power to bring forth prophetic speech:

If the person who performs *Yihudim* has already obtained some arousal on the part of his super-soul, which speaks to him by means of some *Yihud* which he has performed, but he does not yet have the strength to bring forth the speech upon his lips from the potential to the actual—he should perform this *Yihud* before he does the other one. (*SRH,* 115–16)

Although Vital writes in one place that "God will reveal to him wondrous things from His Torah," the speech itself, which the contemplative either hears from without or utters from his own mouth, derives from the *zaddiq* with whom he is communing: "On account of these *Yihudim,* they [i.e., the *zaddiqim*] reveal to them secrets of the Torah and matters of the future" (*SY,* 3). In *Shivhei ha-'Ari,* we read the following about this process:

And how is this mystery of communion (*devequt*) performed? Let a righteous person stretch out on the grave of one of the *Tanna'im* (early rabbis) or one of the prophets, and cleave with his soul (*nafsho*) to that of the *zaddiq,* and with his spirit (*ruho*) to his spirit. Then the *Tanna* begins to speak with him as a man talks to his friend—and answers all that he asks, revealing to him all the mysteries of Torah.[28]

Isaac Luria's Performance of Yihudim

Before turning to Vital's autobiographical accounts, we take notice of an interesting passage in *Shivhei ha-'Ari,* which describes Isaac Luria's own performance of *yihudim.* Though there appears to be little other testimony concerning Luria's performance of these exercises, it is reasonable to assume that he engaged in the same contemplative exercises that he prescribed for his disciples.[29]

Once the Rabbi went to prostrate himself upon the grave of Shemayah and Avtalyon in *Gush Halav,* at a distance of one *parsa,* for the purpose of inquiring of them the true secrets of the Torah. For such was his custom. Whenever he desired to speak with a prophet or a certain *Tanna,* he would go to his grave and lay himself down upon it, with outstretched arms and feet, "putting his mouth upon his mouth . . ." [2 Kgs 4:34], as did Elisha with Habakkuk. He would contemplate a *Yihud,* and elevate the soul, spirit and super-soul of this *zaddiq* through the mystery of the "female waters." . . . He would bind his soul, spirit and super-soul to those of the *zaddiq,* and bring about supernal unification. By means of the *Yihud* the soul of this *zaddiq* would be invested with a new light, greater than that which he had previously. In this way the dry bones which lie in the grave revived; the soul, spirit and super-soul of that *zaddiq* descended to his bones, bringing him to actual life, speaking with him (i.e., Luria) as a man speaks to his neighbor, revealing to him all the secrets of the Torah concerning which he asks of him. All these *Yihudim* are in my possession, written down, praised be God. For the Rabbi transmitted them to his disciples, all ten of whom successfully practiced them. As a consequence, the *zaddiqim* [with whom they commune] spoke to them, answering all their questions. However, they possessed the strength to do this only during the Rabbi's lifetime. After his death their efforts were without success, with the exception of our teacher, Rabbi Hayyim Calabrese, may God protect and preserve him, who successfully practices them to this day. (*Shivḥei ha-ʾAri*, 5)[30]

The Experiences of Hayyim Vital

Turning to Vital's account of his own experiences, we learn that Luria prescribed particular *tiqquney ʾawonot* for sins which Vital had committed.[31] Among other things, Vital had indulged in alchemical studies during the years 1566–1568, just prior to his taking up with Luria—a practice that he later regretted. He also needed to purify himself for having become angry with his wife, for having drunk forbidden wine with an apostate, having cursed his parents, and having committed a minor sexual transgression on his wedding night. Luria told him that he would have to undergo a two-and-one-half-year period of absolution in order fully to qualify himself for contemplative experience. Vital also reports that Luria reproached him for failing to practice *yihudim* regularly. In the following text we learn the importance that Luria attached to the performance of these meditations:

> One day I visited him [i.e., Luria], a whole month having passed during which I had performed none of the *Yihudim* he had prescribed for me. Recognizing this by looking at my face, he said to me: "'If you leave me for a day I shall leave you for two' (Jerusalem Talmud, *Berakhot* 9:5; 14d). You cause great harm by failing to perform the unifications for it causes the souls who wish to become attached to you to become separated from you." I excused myself in that I desired only to study the Torah at that time, especially since those souls did not come to me as openly as they should have done. He replied that in spite of this I must not fail to perform these unifications daily. It is more important than the study of the Torah since it unifies the upper worlds and so serves the dual purpose of Torah study and unification. He warned me that when I perform the unifications my intention should not be only for the purpose of attracting the soul but in order to put things right on high.
>
> He also said to me, when I went with him to the sepulcher of Rabbi Akiva, that Rabbi Akiva had told him I was to mention Rabbi Akiva's name ten times consecutively before each of the three daily prayers, evening, morning and noon. As a result he will become impregnated in[32] me and will greatly assist me. He told me that there was no need for me to say "Rabbi Akiva," only "Akiva."
>
> He also said to me that until the festival of Tabernacles in the year 5334 (1573) I shall require real assistance, that he should assist me whenever I perform unifications. But from then onwards I shall require no assistance

whatever, for then compensation will have been made for the two and a half years I had sinned by failing to study the Torah. Furthermore, until that time, even if he did assist me, it was only on occasion for it could not then have been permanent, but that from that time onwards it would be permanent, God willing.[33]

What is truly remarkable in this passage is what it reveals about the status assigned to the practice of *yihudim*. Contemplative devotion is more important than the study of Torah! Insofar as the real and *ultimate* goal of the study of Torah is the unification of the upper worlds, a ritual that accomplishes this more directly has priority. This serves to illustrate perfectly the fundamental transformation of values to which Lurianic piety testifies. Every dimension of religious life is now directed toward clearly defined mystical goals: it is the *contemplative* act, the attainment of divine inspiration, the restoration of the cosmos, which demand one's every waking moment.

Although Hayyim Vital refers in quite a number of places to this practice of *yihudim*,[34] we possess only a single *detailed* description of the actual physical experience he underwent in the course of engaging in one particular meditation. In the absence of other such accounts by Vital, or by any of the other students to whom personalized instructions were given by Isaac Luria, we are dependent on this passage for any sense of what the performance of *yihudim* was like from the adept's point of view.

On the eve of the New Moon of the month of 'Elul in the year 5331 (1571) my master of blessed memory sent me to the sepulcher of Abbaye and Rava.[35] There I prostrated myself at the grave of Abbaye of blessed memory and first performed the unification of the Mouth and Nose of the Holy Ancient One ('Attiqa Qadisha or 'Arikh 'Anpin). Sleep fell upon me and then I awoke but I saw nothing. Then I again prostrated myself on Abbaye's actual grave and I performed the unification recorded in my master's own handwriting, but as I was engaged in combining, as is well known, the letters of the Tetragrammaton with those of 'Adonai, my thoughts became confused and I was unable to combine them, so I ceased from reflecting on that combination of letters. It then seemed to me in my thought as if a voice was saying to me: "Retract! Retract!" many times and I thought to myself that these were the words Aqavyah ben Mahalalel addressed to his son, as is well known. (Mishnah 'Eduyot 5:7) So I tried again to combine the letters and this time I was successful. It then seemed to me in my thoughts that they were saying to me: "God will provide Himself the lamb for a burnt-offering, my son" (Gen 22:8) ('elohim yir'eh lo ha-seh le-'olah beni) and it seemed as if they were explaining the meaning of the verse to me, namely, I was apprehensive that I had not performed the first unification adequately but it was not so. It had, in fact, been effective before God, hence: "God will provide Himself the lamb." And it seemed in my thoughts as if they were explaining to me that the whole of the first unification I had performed was hinted at in the verse. For the initial letters of 'elohim yir'eh lo ha-seh have the numerical value of forty-six, the same as that of the Tetragrammaton and 'Eheyeh. And the initial letters of ha-seh le'olah beni form the word hevel ("breath") of the Supernal Mouth which I had in mind while performing that unification. And it seemed to me as if they were saying that Hillel the Elder is hinted at in the initial letters of lo ha-seh le-'olah but I failed to grasp the meaning of this. Behold, all this passed through my mind.

Then a great dread and trembling seized hold of all my limbs and my hands trembled. My lips, too, were trembling in a highly exaggerated manner, moving quickly and concurrently and with great speed as if a voice was perched on my tongue between my lips. It said with great speed more than a hundred times: "What can I say? What can I say." I tried to steady myself and prevent my lips from moving but was unable to still them at all. Then I had in mind to ask for wisdom upon which the voice broke out in my mouth and on my tongue, saying, more than twenty times, "Wisdom, Wisdom." Then it repeated many times: "Wisdom and knowledge." Then it repeated: "Wisdom and knowledge will be given to you from heaven like the knowledge attained by Rabbi Akiva." Then it repeated: "And more than that of Rabbi Akiva." Then it repeated: "Like that attained by Rabbi Yeiva Sava." And then it repeated: "And more than that of Rabbi Yeiva Sava." And then it said: "Greeting to you." And then it said: "They send you greetings from heaven." All this was said at a great speed, repeatedly many times, utterly wondrous, while I was in a waking state and while prostrated in the sepulcher of Abbaye.

Then I went to my master of blessed memory who said to me that I was most effective in performing these two unifications one after the other and this was, indeed, the right way to perform them. The reason I had received no response after performing the first unification was because they were waiting until I had performed both. And my master of blessed memory said to me that when I returned from that place and entered my house he saw the soul of Benaiah ben Yehoiada going along with me. He told me that Benaiah did not belong to my soul root, but the reason he accompanied me was that he is always revealed together with anyone who performs the supernal unification. For this was his habit during his lifetime on earth as we have stated elsewhere.

My teacher of blessed memory said to me at the time of the afternoon prayer that if I shall be worthy on the coming Sabbath, the soul of Rabbi Yeiva Sava will remain with me for ever, never to depart, as do the other reincarnations. Through him I shall be worthy of receiving powerful illuminations, especially during the 'Amidah prayer while reciting the benedictions "the years," "the shoot" and "hearkening to prayer." The reason for it is that Rabbi Yeiva Sava also reveals himself to the saints just as Benaiah does, as we have explained. Furthermore, he belongs to my soul root. Therefore, if I shall be worthy of having him reveal himself to me he will disclose to me, God willing, marvellous things.[36]

Hayyim Vital's experience, as described in this text, consisted of two distinct stages. The first stage involved the contemplation of the *yiḥudim* themselves. His initial efforts at unification appeared to him to be unsuccessful. His mind became confused after attempting a second *yiḥud*, following which he heard a voice uttering the request of the dying Aqavyah ben Mahalalel to his son.[37] We learn from Vital's diary that this sage was one of the various *zaddiqim* who comprised his *gilgul* ancestry. Having heard this voice he returned to contemplation of the second *yiḥud*, which he successfully completed. Again he heard a voice which this time uttered a scriptural passage (Gen 22:8), the *notariqon* and *gematria* of which elucidated the meaning of the *initial yiḥud*. The initial letters of several words in this passage, forming as they do the word *hevel* ("breath"), indicated to Vital the mystery of the supernal Mouth intended by the first meditation. This demonstrated to him that it had been successful after all.

Having achieved a level of inspiration in which he heard the external voices of others speaking *to* him, Vital entered a more intense stage of experience. He was overcome with physical trembling and began to utter short phrases repeatedly and quickly in the manner of automatic speech. He was apparently "possessed" by the voice that was speaking through his mouth, unable to control himself at all. The substance of the disclosure elicited after his having asked "for wisdom" consisted in a confirmation of the exalted status of his soul. He is promised the attainment of knowledge exceeding that of Akiba, a famous rabbinic teacher of the first century, and that of Yeiva Sava, a figure in the *Zohar*. According to Vital's diary, both of these men were part of his *gilgul* ancestry. The exceptionally elevated status of his soul, the transmigrations through which it had gone, and the unlimited possibilities for mystical illumination of which he was capable were themes with which Vital was continually preoccupied.

One of the initial and essential goals of many forms of contemplation is that of separating oneself completely for a period of time from the realm of normal sensation. The purpose or effect of doing so is to provide the conditions under which one can achieve an altered state of awareness of one variety or another. In Vital's account several elements appear to contribute to such an effort. In the first place, arising at night to engage in the *yiḥudim* clearly served to establish a quiet, nondistracting environment. Besides the various mythic associations with which the Safed kabbalists viewed the hour of midnight, the *effect* of practicing devotional activities at such a time would be to create an opportunity for undisturbed concentration. Elsewhere, Vital adds that the adept is to seclude himself and close his eyes while concentrating (*SRH*, 117, 130). The very deprivation of sleep might

reasonably contribute to inducing an altered state of consciousness. Suscep-
tibility for this would be enhanced if one was fasting as well.

While these physical conditions may help explain what happened to Vital
as reported in this text, there can be no doubt that the primary means by
which he entered into the kind of state described here was the concentration on the letter combinations themselves. Intense contemplative concentration for sustained periods of time upon the various names of God must
have served the purpose of enabling an individual to exclude from the
mind's consciousness all external sensation and bring about the unusual
experience suggested by Vital. Vital himself explicitly states elsewhere that
the contemplative "must exert intense powers of concentration, turn his
heart from all external thoughts, and divest his soul of its bodily aspect"
(SRH, 111).

The central feature of Vital's experience was that of hearing voices com-
municating to him and through his own voice. In his diary, Sefer ha-
Hezyonot, he reports having asked his teacher, Luria, whether the voice of
the zaddiq which he hears is *actually* that of the zaddiq himself or merely
his own voice. Luria assures Vital that the voice which he has experienced
is indeed that of the zaddiq, inasmuch as the soul of the zaddiq invests itself
in Vital's heart through proper concentration. As Vital reports it: "From
there [i.e., from Vital's heart] the sound of the zaddiq's speech ascends to my
mouth (ma'aleh dibburo be-fi) and speaks with my mouth, whereupon I hear
his voice."[38] Elsewhere in his diary Vital indicates that sometimes the voice
of the zaddiq speaks *to* him rather than through his own voice. When he
is restricted to this lesser experience, it is apparently on account of laxness
in fulfilling his religious responsibilities.[39]

Unreflected automatic speech such as this was quite well known among
the Safed kabbalists of the sixteenth century. The gerushin or mystical peregrinations of Moses Cordovero and Solomon Alkabez, Joseph Karo's
experiences of a mentor angel or maggid, Luria's own technique of inducing
a maggid, and Vital's technique of communing with the soul of a departed
zaddiq through the contemplative recitation of passages from the Mishnah,
are all examples of experiences resulting in the revelation of mysteries of the
Torah and esoteric knowledge in the form of unreflected automatic speech.[40]

The Status of Heavenly Revelations in Safed

It remains for us to consider briefly two related matters that may help to
clarify the broader significance of the contemplative ritual we have studied.
The attempt to acquire kabbalistic knowledge through personal and direct
revelatory means stands in distinct contrast to traditional rabbinic methods

of developing teachings on the basis of various types of textual inquiry. Different hermeneutical styles may be brought to bear upon such inquiry— logic, for example, in the case of rabbinic law or medieval rationalism; moral or narrative concerns in the case of midrash aggadah or moralistic literature. The common factor, however, is the essentially *intellectual* process of study- ing an existing text or texts for the purpose of clarifying, interpreting, or furthering meaning. For meaning is believed to reside within the texts themselves; one need only apply the appropriate techniques of inquiry to ferret out the meaning of the text. This was the case not only for the rabbis of late antiquity; it was true also for the medieval philosophers, biblical exegetes of various types, as well as most of the early kabbalists.

In the case of the *yiḥudim* (as well as the other techniques mentioned earlier involving the revelation of mystical knowledge) appeal is not made to the inherent meaning of existing texts, but to a "heavenly" source. The successful adept is said to acquire the inspiration of the Holy Spirit, or to achieve the level of prophecy, even if it is only a minor degree of prophecy. Knowledge is regarded as deriving *directly* from "on high" rather than from an individual's own intellectual powers. Whereas the talmudic sages went out of their way to deny the possibility of further prophecy, claiming instead that the privilege of understanding the meaning of Torah is now a more "earthly" one, the kabbalists of Safed in general, and Isaac Luria in particular, reassert the contention that more direct channels of communica- tion are entirely appropriate, even preferable.

Isaac Luria himself was believed by his disciples to be exemplary in this regard. It was not his intellectual acumen that served as the basis for his authority as a teacher, but his *intuitive* and *contemplative* acumen. It was his knowledge of esoteric sciences and arts, his having merited the revela- tions of Elijah, his having been invested with the Holy Spirit, his ability to "read" the lines on a face, his capacity to recognize the identity of the souls hovering above graves, which accounted for his authoritative position. Moreover, according to Lurianic teachings, other persons could potentially acquire similar kinds of abilities. With Lurianism, then, we witness the emergence of a new point of view with respect to the acquisition of divine truth. The phenomenon of charismatic experience, in which individuals had direct access to the "heavens," was elevated to a status that it had not enjoyed for centuries.

Revelatory Knowledge as Messianic Gnosis

Finally, how are we to understand the immense preoccupation with the revelation of new mystical knowledge on the part of the Safed kabbalists?

The answer to this question has to do, in large part, with the messianic aspirations of the community as a whole, and Lurianic mysticism in particular. For it was believed that the revelation of esoteric knowledge was both a signal of the coming redemption and a means by which to facilitate the messianic era. In the literature of the *Zohar*, particularly the *Ra'aya Meheimna* and *Tiqquney Zohar*, the eschatological aspect of kabbalistic knowledge forms a significant theme. The Torah of the "Tree of Life" is a *concealed* Torah, and contains the mystical meanings that will be completely revealed in the messianic future.[41] This messianic Torah is, however, partially revealed through the *Zohar* itself. Not only will the esoteric layer of meaning prevail in the redeemed future, but the very study of the *Zohar* will *facilitate* the redemption.

With the popularization and democratization of kabbalistic life that took place in the sixteenth century, this idea assumed great importance. Kabbalistic knowledge was, ideally, no longer to be restricted to small circles of initiates, but was to become the property of the people at large. It was precisely such an argument that prevailed in the debate in Italy over the question of printing the *Zohar*. Writing in the middle of the sixteenth century, Isaac Delattes argued that "the merit of studying the book *Zohar* is sufficient to deliver us and to overturn our exile."

The importance of kabbalistic knowledge as a feature of the messianic age is no less important to Lurianism. Sin and exile caused the exile of the inner secrets of the Torah; in the "end of days," however, they will be revealed once again. The redemption of holiness, which lies at the heart of Lurianic mysticism, extends even to the redemption of the Torah itself! Whereas now only fragments of the deepest mysteries of the Torah are within reach, in the messianic future every Israelite will achieve knowledge of the entire Torah. But the revelations merited in the unredeemed state are not merely foreshadowings of redemption; they are actually *instrumental* in hastening the messianic age. The communications that some merited as a consequence of contemplative exercises were conceived of as salvational in and of themselves, *gnosis* in the truest sense.

Notes

1. This legendary tradition was preserved in two influential works, *Shivḥei ha-'Ari*, written by Solomon Shlomiel of Dresnitz during the first decade of the seventeenth century, and *Toldot ha-'Ari*, compiled sometime in the middle of the same century. *Shivḥei ha-'Ari* comprises stories about Luria which, for the most part, are compatible with the personality about whom we learn from the information scattered throughout the works of his actual disciples, especially those of Hayyim Vital. In contrast, *Toldot ha-'Ari* is much further removed from what we know about Luria, containing as it does many folkloristic tales such as those, for example, which emphasize

Luria's supposed miracle working. These traditions have been studied by M. Benayahu in his *Sefer Toldot ha-ʾAri*. Concerning this literature, see also J. Dan. *Ha-Sippur ha-ʿIvri Beyemei ha-Beynayim*, chap. 11. With regard to the dissemination and influence of Lurianic Kabbalah, see G. Scholem, *Sabbatai Sevi*, part 1.

2. See G. Scholem, *Major Trends in Jewish Mysticism*, lecture seven; I. Tishby, *Torat ha-Ra weha-Qelipah be Qabbalat ha-ʾAri;* idem, "Gnostic Doctrines in Sixteenth Century Jewish Mysticism," *Journal of Jewish Studies* 6 (1955).

3. Hayyim Vital (1542–1620), Luria's chief disciple and the person responsible for the most elaborate versions of Lurianic teachings, lists Luria's students in *Shaʿar ha-Gilgulim* of the *Shemonah Sheʿarim* (pp. 171–72), and in Vital's mystical diary, *Sefer ha-Hezyonot* (Jerusalem: Mossad ha Rav Kook, 1954) 217–20. (All references to the books that make up Vital's version of Lurianic teachings, the *Shemonah Sheʿarim* [*Eight Gates*], are to the Yehudah Ashlag edition [Tel Aviv, 1962].)

4. The conception of a series of four "worlds" or divine realms above the terrestrial world goes back to thirteenth-century Kabbalah. These include: *ʿOlam ha-ʾAzilut*, the "World of Emanation," that is, the realm of the ten *sefirot; ʿOlam ha-Beriʾah*, the "World of Creation," that is, the divine throne and chariot; *ʿOlam ha-Yezirah*, the "World of Formation," that of the angels and of *Metatron;* and *ʿOlam ha-ʿAsiyah*, the "World of Making," that world closest to the terrestrial realm and sometimes identified with the terrestrial world itself. The doctrine underwent considerable development in sixteenth-century Safed, especially at the hands of Moses Cordovero and Isaac Luria. From the point of view of Lurianic Kabbalah, all of the worlds, including that of *ʿAsiyah*, were originally of a purely spiritual character. With the "breaking of the vessels," however, *ʿAsiyah* descended and became mixed in with the realms of impurity and materiality brought about as a result of the shattering of the divine vessels.

5. G. Scholem, *Sabbatai Sevi*, 34.

6. The contemplative intentions (*kawwanot*) to accompany prayer are described in *Shaʿar ha-Kawwanot*, the *kawwanot* of *mizwot* in *Shaʿar ha-Mizwot*, both of Vital's *Shemonah Sheʿarim*. The *yihudim* are discussed in detail in *Shaʿar Ruah ha-Qodesh* (hereafter *SRH*) and *Shaʿar ha-Yihudim* (hereafter *SY*). References to *Shaʿar ha-Yihudim*, which is not part of the *Shemonah Sheʿarim*, are to a reprint published in Jerusalem: Mekor Hayyim, 1970.

7. Cf. *Shaʿar ha-Mizwot*, 1–2; *Shaʿar ha-Kawwanot*, 1:2. Another Safed author, Elijah de Vidas, writes that joyfulness in the performance of the commandments enables one to destroy the evil (*qelipot*) which imprisons the *Shekhinah* (*Reshit Hokhmah* [Venice, 1593], *Shaʿar ha-ʾAhavah*, chap. 10). An extreme formulation of the importance of joy is reported by Moses Galante in the name of his brother Abraham. He states that the joy with which a *mizwah* is performed is more important than the *mizwah* itself! See *Kohelet Yaʿaqov* (Safed, 1578) 36a.

8. *Shaʿarei Qedushah* (Constantinople, 1734) part 2, gate 4.

9. This notion goes back to *Berakhot* 31a, *Hagigah* 5b, *Shabbat* 30b.

10. See, e.g., *Shabbat* 105b, *Nedarim* 22b; *Zohar* 1:27b; 2:182a–b; 3:179a. Concerning the value of avoiding anger, see Moses Cordovero's rules of piety, no. 2, printed as part of an appendix to S. Schechter, "Safed in the Sixteenth Century: A City of Legists and Mystics," in *Studies in Judaism* (Philadelphia: Jewish Publication Society, 1908) 292; idem, *Tomer Devorah*, chap. 1, part 5; *Shaʿarei Qedushah*, part 2, gate 4; *Shaʿar ha-Gilgulim*, 24; Eliezar Azikri, *Sefer Haredim* (Jerusalem, 1958), *Mizwot ha-Teshuvah*, chap 4.

11. Cf. *Shaʿarei Qedushah*, part 2, gate 4. Elijah de Vidas devotes an entire "gate" to discussing humility in *Reshit Hokhmah*, *Shaʿar ha-ʿAnawah*. See also his *Tozaʾot Hayyim* (Jerusalem, 1971) 5–7.

12. Cf. *Shaʿarei Qedushah*, part 2, gate 5; Cordovero's rules of piety, nos. 6, 9, and 10 in Schechter, *Studies*, 292.

13. Vital discusses the significance of the various levels of study in *Sha'ar ha-Mizwot, Parashat We'ethanan;* cf. also Vital, *Ta'amei Mizwot* (Jerusalem, 1972), *Parashat We'ethanan.*

14. Cf. *Sha'ar ha-Mizwot,* 79; M. Benayahu, *Sefer Toldot ha-'Ari,* 336; Vital's introduction to *'Ez Hayyim* (Warsaw, 1891).

15. For *kawwanot* to accompany ritual immersion see *Sha'ar ha-Kawwanot,* 24–26; cf. *Sha'ar ha-Mizwot,* where immersion is said to cleanse one who has had a nocturnal pollution. The same reason is given by Abraham ben Eliezer ha-Levi Berukhim in his rules of piety (Schechter, *Studies,* 297, no. 6).

16. The basis for the analogy of the sick body to the sick soul appears to be drawn from Maimonides, *Mishneh Torah, Hilkhot, De'ot,* chap. 2; *Shemonah Peraqim,* chap. 3.

17. Concerning the theme of Luria as healing doctor and diagnostician of the soul's injuries, see *SRH,* 14; and Benayahu, *Toldot ha-'Ari,* 156–57. In this connection, see L. Fine, "The Art of Metoposcopy: A Study in Isaac Luria's Charismatic Knowledge," *AJS Review* 11 (1986) 1.

18. The apparent severity of the amount of fasting is mitigated in two ways. Vital explains that a day of fasting does not include the night and that two successive days of fasting which do include the night are equivalent to twenty-seven days, whereas three consecutive days and nights are equivalent to forty days of fasting (*SRH,* 25–26). *Millui* consists of spelling out the full name of each letter and adding up the numerical value of the combined letters. *Gematria* is the technique of determining the combined numerical value of the letters of a word or phrase and relating it to other words or phrases of numerical equivalence. Through *millui* (and other manipulative techniques) the *gematria* of a word can be greatly increased. The technique of *millui* can be extended so as to calculate the *millui* of the *millui,* and so on.

19. The term *ortigas* is Spanish for "nettles." Among the various extreme self-afflictive acts Abraham ben Eliezer ha-Levi Berukhim was reported to have practiced was that of rolling upon a bed of thorns which felt like fire to his flesh (*Sefer Toldot ha-'Ari,* 226).

20. Sexual transgressions for which Luria prescribed *tiqquney 'awonot* included relations with a menstruating woman, adultery, relations with an animal, necrophilia, homosexuality, and nocturnal pollution.

21. This text is paralleled in Joseph ibn Tabul's discussion of the *yihudim* preserved in MS Jewish Theological Seminary 931 (Deinrod 430), folios 175a–180a.

22. See the references in M. Benayahu, "Devotion Practices of the Kabbalists of Safed in Meron" (Hebrew), *Sefunot* (Jerusalem: Ben Zvi Institute, 1962) 9–40.

23. Joseph Karo, *Maggid Mesharim* (Venice, 1649), *Parashat 'Emor.*

24. *Millui de-yudin* refers to spelling the letter *heh* in *YHWH* with the letters *heh* and *yud.*

25. *Millui de-'alfin* refers to spelling the letter *heh* in *YHWH* with the letters *heh* and *'alef.*

26. *Millui de-hein* refers to spelling the letter *heh* in *YHWH* as *heh-heh.*

27. Our sources do not distinguish between the term prophecy (*nevuah*) and Holy Spirit (*Ruah ha-Qodesh*). They appear to be used interchangeably, each being a form of "inspiration" (*hasagah*). From other Lurianic contexts, however, it would seem that when care is taken to differentiate between the two, prophecy is clearly deemed a more exalted state of inspiration. This is the case, for example, in Hayyim Vital's discussion about Luria's concept of maggidic revelations, where we learn that prophecy has its origin in the *sefirah Tif'eret,* whereas the Holy Spirit derives from the *sefirah Malkhut.* See L. Fine, "Maggidic Revelation in the Teachings of Isaac Luria," in *Mystics, Philosophers, and Politicians,* ed. J. Reinharz and D. Swetschinski, esp. 147–49.

28. Benayahu, *Toldot ha-'Ari,* 157 n. 6.

29. See Benayahu, *Toldot ha-'Ari,* 157, 199, n. 2. See also *Shivhei ha-'Ari* (Bardejov, 1929) 17, where a tradition is reported concerning Luria's performance of *yihudim* at the grave of Rabbi Shimon bar Yohai in Meron.

30. The text refers here to the incident in 2 Kings 4 in which the prophet Elisha revives the dead child of a Shunammite woman: "Then he went up and lay upon the child, putting his mouth

upon his mouth, his eyes upon his eyes, and his hands upon his hands; and as he stretched himself upon him, the flesh of the child became warm." According to a legendary motif in the *Zohar* (1:7b; 2:44a–45a)—upon which the text under discussion apparently draws—the revived child was the prophet Habakkuk.

31. *Sha'ar ha-Gilgulim*, 127–28, 132–37; *Sefer ha-Hezyonot*, 146–47, 152–54, 157.

32. *'Ibbur* ("impregnation"), in contrast to the doctrine of *gilgul* (transmigration of souls), refers to the entry of an additional soul into an individual sometime during a person's lifetime rather than at birth. This extra soul generally inhabits a person's body for a limited period of time. This doctrine, which goes back to thirteenth-century Kabbalah, became especially prominent in Lurianic doctrine. Impregnation was believed to constitute an opportunity for a soul which belonged to a now deceased individual to fulfill some *mizwah* which it had not fulfilled during the lifetime of the deceased.

33. Vital, *Sefer ha-Hezyonot*, 149–50; cf. *Sha'ar ha-Gilgulim*, 136. We have drawn on the translation of this passage from *Sefer ha-Hezyonot* by L. Jacobs, *Jewish Mystical Testimonies*, 130–31.

34. See, e.g., *Sefer ha-Hezyonot*, 5, 16–17, 25–26, 28–29, 36, 149–51, 172–73; *SRH*, 131–32, 141–42.

35. Vital describes the cave of Abbaye and Rava, famous rabbinic sages of fourth-century Babylonia in *Sha'ar ha-Gilgulim*, 185.

36. Vital, *Sefer ha-Hezyonot*, 170–72. This translation is drawn from Jacobs, *Jewish Mystical Testimonies*, 131–33. A slightly different version is found in *Sha'ar ha-Gilgulim*, 140–41.

37. Aqavyah ben Mahalalel was a first-century sage who was offered the position of president of the Sanhedrin if he would renounce four of his decisions in which he disagreed with the majority opinion. He refused to do so until, in the hour that he was about to die, he told his son to retract these four opinions on his behalf (Mishnah *'Eduyot* 5:6–7).

38. *Sefer ha-Hezyonot*, 16.

39. *Sefer ha-Hezyonot*, 25. Vital draws precisely such a distinction in his account of a technique of soul-communion using the recitation of passages from the Mishnah. Here too, the experience of hearing a voice speaking to you rather than through your own voice is attributed to an individual being unfit for the higher level of inspiration. See L. Fine, "Recitation of Mishnah as a Vehicle for Mystical Inspiration: A Contemplative Technique Taught by Hayyim Vital," *Revue des études juives* 141 (1982).

40. Concerning Cordovero's *gerushin* and Karo's maggidic experiences, see R. J. Z. Werblowsky (Oxford, 1962) esp. 51–54, 257–86. Luria's maggidic theory and Vital's technique of Mishnah recitation are studied in this writer's articles indicated in notes 27 and 39. An analysis by Moshe Idel of manuscripts comprising the anonymously authored *Sefer ha-Meshiv*, a fifteenth-century kabbalistic work written in Spain prior to the Expulsion, suggests this book's critical influence in the development of the kind of revelatory techniques mentioned here. *Sefer ha-Meshiv*, which contains heavenly revelations deriving from God and from various angels, especially the angel Azriel, influenced Safed kabbalists Moses Cordovero and Ovadiah Hamon. Moreover, there is evidence that Luria's student, Hayyim Vital, was familiar with *Kaf ha-Qetoret*, a work that stands in intimate relationship to *Sefer ha-Meshiv*. In the light of these facts, Idel suggests the influence, even if indirectly, of *Sefer ha-Meshiv* on Isaac Luria's exaltation of personal and direct revelatory experience. See M. Idel, "'Iyyunim be-Shitat Ba'al Sefer ha-Meshiv," *Sefunot* n.s. 2 (17) (Jerusalem: Ben Zvi Institute, 1983) 185–266; also G. Scholem, "Ha-Maggid shel R. Yosef Taitazak weha-Giluyim ha-Meyuhasim Lo," *Sefunot* 11 (Jerusalem: Ben Zvi Institute, 1971–77) 69–112.

41. Concerning these themes, see G. Scholem, *Sabbatai Sevi*, 11–12, 17–22.

Bibliography

For general background to Safed piety, the classic essay by Schechter is still valuable reading. A more recent introduction to the religious life of Safed, studied through translated primary texts, is Fine, *Safed Spirituality. On the Kabbalah* by Scholem contains important essays on specific themes related to the Safed experience. *Sefer Safed* (ed. Benayahu and Yizhaq), two volumes on the history of sixteenth-century Safed, includes a wide range of valuable essays in Hebrew by leading scholars. The second of these volumes contains a lengthy bibliography.

Lurianic Kabbalah, particularly its mythological issues, is the subject of lecture seven of Scholem's classic *Major Trends*, which also contains a list of the important older scholarship on Lurianism. Scholem also discusses Lurianic ideas—especially their messianic orientation—in his *Sabbatai Sevi*, part 1. The most sustained treatment of Lurianic mythology, however, is the work of Tishby.

The literature of sacred biography, or hagiography, which developed in the decades following Isaac Luria's death, was studied by Benayahu. In this connection see the critique of Benayahu by Tamar, "'Al ha-Sefer," in which Tamar disputes Benayahu's controversial contention that *Sefer Toldot ha-'Ari* served as the source for *Shivhei ha-'Ari*, not the reverse, as is widely considered to be the case. These narratives about Luria are also analyzed by Dan in his study of the Hebrew story in the Middle Ages. Concerning the question of the perception of Luria by his discples, see the article by Pachter, as well as the rejoinder by Tamar. The problem of Luria's relationship to his followers and their collective self-understanding is taken up by Fine in "Metoposcopy."

Other techniques for the achievement of mystical experience developed by Isaac Luria or his disciple Hayyim Vital have been studied in the following articles by Fine: "Maggidic Revelation"; "Recitation of Mishnah"; "The Study of Torah." A closely related phenomenon, Joseph Karo's maggidic experiences, was the subject of a full-length study by Werblowsky. Translations into English of some of Karo's and Vital's mystical experiences are found in Jacobs.

Benayahu, Meir. *Sefer Toldot ha-'Ari.* Jerusalem: Ben Zvi Institute, 1967.

——, and Ben Zvi Yizhaq, eds. *Sefer Safed.* 2 vols. Jerusalem: Ben Zvi Institute, 1962–63.

Dan, Joseph. *Ha-Sippur ha-'Ivri Beyemei ha-Benayim.* Jerusalem: Keter, 1974.

Fine, Lawrence. *Safed Spirituality.* New York: Paulist Press, 1984.

——. "The Art of Metoposcopy: A Study in Isaac Luria's Charismatic Knowledge." *AJS Review* 11 (1986) 79–101.

——. "Maggidic Revelation in the Teachings of Isaac Luria." In *Mystics, Philosophers, and Politicians: Essays in Jewish Intellectual History in Honor of Alexander Altmann,.* 141–57. Edited by J. Reinharz and D. Swetschinski. Durham, NC: Duke University Press, 1982.

——. "Recitation of Mishnah as a Vehicle for Mystical Inspiration: A Contemplative Technique Taught by Hayyim Vital." *Revue des études juives* 141 (1982) 183–99.

——. "The Study of Torah as a Rite of Theurgical Contemplation in Lurianic Kabbalah." In *Approaches to Judaism in Medieval Times,* volume 3. Edited by D. Blumenthal. Chico, CA: Scholars Press, in press.

Jacobs, Louis, *Jewish Mystical Testimonies.* New York: Schocken, 1977.

Pachter, Mordecai. "Demuto shel ha-'Ari be-Hespedo R. Shmuel Uzeda." *Zion* 37 (1972) 22–40.

Schechter, Solomon. "Safed in the Sixteenth Century: A City of Legists and Mystics." In *Studies in Judaism,* 202–85. Second series. Philadelphia: Jewish Publication Society, 1908.

Scholem, Gershom. *On the Kabbalah and Its Symbolism.* Translated by Ralph Manheim. New York: Schocken, 1965.

——. *Major Trends in Jewish Mysticism.* 3rd ed. New York: Schocken, 1954.

——. *Sabbatai Sevi: The Mystical Messiah.* Princeton, NJ: Princeton University Press, 1973.

Tamar, David. "'Al ha-Sefer Toldot ha-'Ari." In *Mehkarim be-Toldot ha-Yehudim be-Erez Yisrael U-be-Italyah,* 166–93. Jerusalem: Rubin Mass, 1973.

——. "Al Aggadat ha-Ari ve-al Hespedo shel R. Shmuel Di-Uzeda." In *Mehkarim be-Toldot ha-Yehudim be-Erez Yisrael U-be-Arzot ha-Mizrah,* 107–18. Jerusalem: Mosad ha-Rav Kook, 1981.

Tishby, Isaiah. *Torat ha-Ra' we-ha-qelipah be-qabbalat ha-'Ari.* Jerusalem: Akademon, 1971.

4

The Uplifting of Sparks in Later Jewish Mysticism

Louis Jacobs

LTHOUGH FOR CONVENIENCE' SAKE we shall refer, in this essay, to light as a kabbalistic symbol for the divine, it should be noted that, for the kabbalists themselves, light and the other symbols they use are really more than symbols. They are not mere pointers to the reality; in a sense they are the reality itself. For the kabbalists, light, for example, really exists on high as a spiritual object. It is that entity which is the true source of physical light. Again, for them, the Hebrew language is not simply a convention. The Hebrew letters are the material form assumed by the sacred alphabet on high. God really did say: "Let there be light" (Gen 1:3) by combining those spiritual forces represented by the letters *'alef, waw,* and *resh* to form the spiritual word for "light," *'or.* Echoes of the Platonic "idea" are heard in all this.

Edwyn Bevan has shown how ubiquitous is the light symbol in the religions of humanity: how, from the earliest times, light has impressed humans as most closely associated with our thoughts of the divine.[1] Among the reasons for the emergence and persistence of the light symbol to represent the divine are that light dispels darkness and so is a symbol for knowledge, for admission into the mysteries, for the sudden realization of the truth, as in the expression "a flash of illumination." In the darkness something hostile may be lurking. There is danger to life there, making us welcome the safety and security afforded by light. The enemy uses the darkness to pursue his nefarious ends so that light becomes synonymous with the good, darkness with evil. Again, the brilliance of light, its shining quality, is extremely attractive, exercising a powerful fascination in itself, quite apart from its usefulness. Still another property of light, which has made it serve as a symbol in Neoplatonic thought (especially relevant to the

Kabbalah), is the way in which a luminous body apparently sends forth emanations of its substance without any force coming into play or any loss being suffered. To whatever distance these emanations reach, they remain always one with the luminous body.

The kabbalists have the Hebrew Bible and rabbinic literature as the background to all their thinking. In these works light symbolism for the good and for the divine occurs frequently. The passages are innumerable, but for our purpose we need refer only to the Psalms: "light is sown for the righteous" (97:11); "the Lord is my light and my salvation" (27:1); "at the brightness before Him" (18:23); "the commandment of the Lord is pure, enlightening the eyes" (19:9); "thy word is a lamp unto my feet, and a light unto my path" (119:105). In the vision of the divine chariot seen by the prophet Ezekiel (chapter 1), a passage that formed the basis for mystical speculation in Judaism, the divine is described in terms of flashing lights and the colors of the rainbow.

It is not, therefore, surprising that for the kabbalists, in Bevan's felicitous phrase, "the numinous is essentially the luminous." The classical work of the Kabbalah, the *Zohar*, has a title meaning "Illumination," even though the title is not original with the work. In the *Zohar*, the entities on high and their relationship with one another are described in terms of lights flashing, being reflected, producing sparks, and the like. It is necessary to repeat, however, that the kabbalists are thinking of the spiritual sources of light. In his defense of the Kabbalah, the Italian kabbalist Joseph Ergas (1685–1730), for instance, writes:

> There are many who think of God as a great, pure, refined light, and the like, because they think that this is not to describe Him in corporeal terms. But this is the most extreme error and confusion. For although light is the most ethereal of all tangible things, it is still a matter. And there is nothing which can be imagined which is not an image of a material thing. . . . For whatever is grasped by the intellect is incorporeal but whatever is grasped by the imagination is corporeal, since the intellect is incorporeal whereas the imagination belongs to a man's physical nature. Even when he imagines entities that are incorporeal he does so as if they were corporeal. . . . When you find, in the works of the Kabbalists, that they refer to the activities of *Eyn Sof* and the *sefirot* in terms of light, it is not that these are lights in themselves.
>
> Because it does not lie within the capacity of our intellect, while clothed in the material body, to apprehend the being and essence of the spiritual entities . . . the Kabbalists attributed to these entities the name "light" since of all things perceived by the senses light is the most precious. Furthermore, light has certain properties similar to those of the entities that are emanated. . . . From all that we have said, you will appreciate that since light has qualities resembling those of the spiritual entities it is proper, as do the Kabbalists, to describe the *sefirot* and their functions in terms of lights. It was

never their intention, Heaven forbid, to suggest that the *sefirot* are really lights. The *sefirot* are not corporeal substances, Heaven forbid.[2]

Ergas, developing his argument, suggests the following reasons for the suitability of light symbolism for the spiritual entities on high: (1) Light proceeds from its source and yet is not detached from it. Where the source is removed, no light remains—unlike wind, for example. It is possible to fill a balloon with wind and preserve it there detached from its source. In similar fashion, the *sefirot* are emanations of *Eyn Sof* and yet always remain attached to their source. (2) Light traverses objects and fills them without suffering any change. The colors of the objects into which the light penetrates are in them, not in the light. In similar fashion the *sefirot* penetrate all created things, endowing them with vitality, and yet the *sefirot* themselves suffer no change. (3) The effect of the light depends on the nature of the substance it illumines. The coarser a substance the less receptive it is to the illumination; the more refined a substance the more effective will be the power of the illumination. In similar fashion all change is not in the *sefirot* but in the capacity of creatures to receive their power.

It must be noted that Ergas is an apologist for the Kabbalah and is, therefore, more rationalistic than other kabbalists. For all that, his associates would agree that the light of which the Kabbalah speaks is in no way physical.

We must now turn to the kabbalistic doctrine of the *sefirot* and the wide-ranging elaborations of the Lurianic Kabbalah in order to appreciate the significance of the idea of holy sparks. Although the Kabbalah is sometimes spoken of as if it were a single, though complex, system, it is more correct historically to see it as a number of systems developed in different ages. The later kabbalists acknowledge, in the main, two great systems. The first of these arose in the twelfth century in Spain and the Provence to find its fullest expression, at the end of the thirteenth century, in the *Zohar*. The second is that of Isaac Luria (1534–1572), taught by him in Safed to a few chosen disciples. The Lurianic Kabbalah is based on the earlier Kabbalah; Luria's ideas appear to have resulted from his profound and sustained reflection on the *Zohar*, but there are several new features that make it, essentially, a completely new system. The Lurianic kabbalists admit to its originality, attributing the new revelations to Elijah, who appeared to their saintly master. To these new features belong the doctrine of the holy sparks.

Although an outline of the Lurianic Kabbalah has been offered in the preceding essay in this volume, it seems best to restate that outline here in the particular detail required by our subject, the motif of the holy sparks. The question this version of the Kabbalah seeks to answer is how a finite world, containing evil, falsehood, multiplicity, and imperfection, can have emerged from the perfect and infinite Godhead. The Lurianic Kabbalah is concerned not only with the sefirotic processes but also with that which preceded them—at least, at the stage when the *sefirot* begin their emergence as differentiated entities from out of the recesses of *Eyn Sof.* The first step in the process is one of contraction or withdrawal—*zimzum.* In order to make room, as it were, for the *sefirot*, *Eyn Sof* "withdrew from Himself to Himself" to leave an "empty space," the primordial space into which, eventually, space and time as we know them emerged. The *zimzum* was bound to be incomplete; otherwise its purpose would have been defeated. Nothing can come into being in the absence of God's power. The "empty space" is thought of as a circle with *Eyn Sof* surrounding it on all sides in equal measure. So as to prevent a "space" empty of *Eyn Sof* entirely, a "thin line" of *Eyn Sof*'s light permeates the "circle" but does not traverse it completely. Moreover, a "residue" of the light of *Eyn Sof* remains even after the withdrawal. This aspect of *Eyn Sof*, remaining in the "empty space," forms the "body" of *'Adam Qadmon,* "Primordial Man," now no longer understood, as in the Zoharic scheme, as a synonym for the sefirotic realm but as a stage prior to the emergence of the *sefirot*, though embracing them in its fullness as unrealized and undifferentiated entities.

After the emergence of *'Adam Qadmon,* the *sefirot* had to be constituted as separate and distinct entities, each with its own function, though infused with the light from *Eyn Sof.* For this to take place two aspects of each *sefirah* had to be emanated. First, there was required the emanation of the "vessel" of each *sefirah*, and, second, this had to be filled with "light"; the combination of "vessel" and "light" constituted a complete *sefirah* with its own separate identity. The process is envisioned in terms of lights flashing from *'Adam Qadmon* and then recoiling. The light first beams downward and then returns, leaving behind a residue from which the "vessel" is formed. After the formation of the "vessel" in this way, a second light is beamed from *'Adam Qadmon* and returns, leaving behind a second residue to form the light which fills the "vessel," thus completing the formation of the *sefirah.* These lights stream from the ears, nostrils, mouth, and eyes of *'Adam Qadmon.* Lights streamed from the ears, nose, and mouth of *'Adam Qadmon* and then returned, but this was no more than a preparatory stage at which "vessels" and "lights" are united, the ground being made ready for the constitution of "vessels" and "lights" of separate *sefirot.* When, after this, lights stream from the eyes of *'Adam Qadmon,* they strike the residue of the earlier lights that have emerged, the impact removing some of the light so as to form a "vessel." The "vessels" are now ready to receive further streams of light from the eyes of *'Adam Qadmon* so that the lights filling the "vessels" will produce the *sefirot* as separate and distinct entities. Now the nearer the *sefirot* are to *'Adam Qadmon* the more powerful are their "vessels," since the lights forming these do not have to travel over such a vast "distance" as the lights that form the "vessels" of the lower *sefirot;* light becomes fainter as it is distanced from its source. Thus, since the *sefirot* emerge in a descending order from higher to lower, the "vessels" of the three higher *sefirot* are stronger than those of the lower *sefirot,* great strength being required if the "vessels" are not to be overcome by the impact of the tremendous power of the lights which stream from the eyes. The basic idea behind all this is that there is tension in the whole creative process. Too much of the divine love and power is as ineffective in producing that which is other than God, as it were, as too little. The lights streaming downward cannot achieve the total effect all at once. First there has to be the flash and the recoil to allow the "vessels" to be fortified in a gradual process. The divine Other can only emerge from concealment in a kind of trial and error, "reaching and yet not reaching" in the language of the Kabbalah.

When the lights from the eyes of *'Adam Qadmon* streamed forth toward the "vessels," only the "vessels" of the three higher *sefirot* were sufficiently strong to endure the impact. The "vessels" of the seven lower *sefirot,* weaker than the others, could not endure the light streaming into them and they were shattered. This is the stage known as the "breaking of the vessels" (*shevirat ha-kelim*). Again we have the theme of the control of the divine love in the creative process. Genesis 16:31–39, which tells of the death of the Edomite kings before there reigned a king over the children of Israel, is given a mystical interpretation. The "kings" who died are the seven lower *sefirot,* compelled to pass away before sovereignty could emerge. Rabbinic ideas about God creating worlds and destroying them before he finally created this world are similarly laid under tribute to the kabbalistic doctrine. The "worlds" are those of the *sefirot,* which had to be destroyed before there could emerge the proper balance.

When the "vessels" were shattered—or, in the other metaphor, when the kings died—the lights returned to their source; but not all the lights returned. "Sparks" of the lights remained, adhering to the broken shards in order to keep them in being. Furthermore, even the higher *sefirot,* though they suffered no breakage, fell from their higher place to a lower one. Thus, at this stage everything was in disarray. The higher *sefirot* were in the wrong place, as it were; and, as for the lower *sefirot,* all that remained of them were their broken "vessels" with the "sparks" attached to them. The whole sefirotic realm needed to be reconstituted. This process of reconstitution is called *tiqqun,* brought by means of lights streaming from the forehead of *'Adam Qadmon.* For the *sefirot* to be prevented from suffering the fate that had previously befallen them, it was necessary for them to be ordered as *parzufim*, meaning "configurations." A *parzuf* is a particular combination of all ten *sefirot*. The point here is that while single *sefirot* on their own are incapable of endurance because the "vessels" become too weak to contain their lights, when the *sefirot* come together in a *parzuf*, they fortify one another. The lights from the forehead of *'Adam Qadmon* meet the broken "vessels" and the "sparks" which vivify them and also meet the fallen higher *sefirot*. Under the impact of these lights the *parzufim* are constituted. But after the reconstitution, things are not exactly as they were before. There is no complete restoration; the *parzufim* require further assistance before there can again be complete harmony on high. This task of providing the *tiqqun* for the *parzufim* is the responsibility of Israel.

There are five *parzufim*: (1) *'Arikh 'Anpin* ("Long Face," i.e., Longsuffering); (2) *'Abba* ("Father"); (3) *'Imma* ("Mother"); (4) *Ze'ir 'Anpin* ("Small Face," i.e., Impatient); (5) *Nuqva* ("Female"). Each one of these contains all ten *sefirot* but represents in particular one of the *sefirot*, around which the other nine are configured. For instance, *'Arikh 'Anpin* represents the *Keter* aspect of the *sefirot*, in which, as yet, there is no separation of Mercy and Judgment but all is love, whereas *Ze'ir 'Anpin* represents the *Tif'eret* aspect, where Mercy and Judgment are separate but harmonized. This is the meaning of *'Arikh 'Anpin* as "Longsuffering" and *Ze'ir 'Anpin* as "Impatient" or less whole and complete. It must further be noted that the six *sefirot* from *Hesed* to *Yesod* are grouped around *Tif'eret* so that the *parzuf Ze'ir 'Anpin*, while containing all ten *sefirot* (as do all the *parzufim*), stresses the aspect of *Tif'eret* and the other five. In the total correspondence with the *sefirot*, *'Arikh 'Anpin* corresponds to *Keter*; *'Abba* to *Hokhmah*; *'Imma* to *Binah*; *Ze'ir 'Anpin* to *Tif'eret* (and the other five); and *Nuqva* to *Malkhut*.

There are worlds without number, but, in the main, the Lurianic Kabbalah, relying on stray references in the later *Zohar* literature, speaks of four worlds, one beneath the other, each of which comes into being by means of the sefirotic processes and each of which contains all five *parzufim* since it is through the *parzufim* that the divine, sustaining energy is conveyed to all. In descending order, the four worlds are (1) *'Azilut* ("World of Emanation"), the realm of the *sefirot* proper; (2) *Beri'ah* ("World of Creation"), the realm of the heavenly throne; (3) *Yezirah* ("World of Creation"), the realm of the angelic hosts; (4) *'Asiyah* ("World of Action"), the realm from which the finite universe emerges and the finite universe itself. *'Adam Qadmon* is also called a realm or a world, so that there are five worlds, each corresponding to one of the *parzufim*. Although the five *parzufim* are in all the worlds, each corresponds to one of the worlds.

All creative activity is by means of the special divine name, the tetragrammaton, the four letters of which are *yud, heh, waw, heh*. These letters correspond to the *sefirot* thus: *yud* represents *Hokhmah;* the first *heh, Binah; waw, Tif'eret* and the other five (the numerical value of *waw* is six); and the last *heh, Malkhut. Keter* is too elevated to be represented by a letter but is denoted by the tittle of the *yud*.

There is a further elaboration of the tetragrammaton as the creative power in the universe. The four letters of this name can be spelled out in full in four different ways, as has been outlined in the preceding essay (see above, pp. 83–86), resulting in the 72, 63, 45, and 52 letter names of God.

These four combinations are given the following names: (1) 'aV ('*yyin*=70; *bet*=2; =72; (2) SaG (*samekh*=60; *gimmel*=3; =63); (3) MaH (*mem*=40; *heh*=5; =45); (4) BeN (*bet*=2; *nun*=50; +52). All four are found in all worlds but they are especially apportioned each to the four worlds in descending order. Moreover, each of them is itself divided into the four so that it is possible to speak of the SaG of 'aV; the MaH of 'av; the BeN of 'aV, and so forth. Similarly, each of the *sefirot* can be divided into ten so that there is the *Hesed* of *Gevurah;* the *Hesed* of *Hesed;* the *Gevurah* of *Hesed,* and so forth. Again, since each *parzuf* contains all ten *sefirot* and all five *parzufim*, it is possible to speak of the Ze'ir 'Anpin of 'Abba; the 'Abba of Nuqva; the *Keter* of *Binah;* the *Binah* of *Hokhmah,* and so forth. All is relevant to the human task since these complex associations correspond to this or that human act by means of which one can "put right," perform the *tiqqun,* for this or the other category on high.

Before we proceed to consider the doctrine of the holy sparks it will be helpful to set it all out in diagrammatic form.

	Sefirot	Parzufim	Worlds	Letters	Names
1.	Keter	'Arikh 'Anpin	'Adam Qadmon	Tittle of *yud*	–
2.	Hokhmah	'Abba	'Azilut	yud	'aV
3.	Binah	'Imma	Beri'ah	heh 1	SaG
4.	Tif'eret plus five	Ze'ir 'Anpin	Yezirah	waw	MaH
5.	Malkhut	Nuqva	'Asiyah	heh 2	BeN

The further extremely complex relationships, such as the division into the letters of the Torah, the vowel points, the crowns of the letters, and the musical notes, are part of the whole system, but to examine these in detail would demand a whole volume and would take us beyond the scope of this inquiry. For our purpose it is sufficient to sketch the main outlines only.

The Holy Sparks

As we have seen, the sparks adhering to the broken vessels helped in the reconstitution of the *sefirot* into *parzufim* and the formation of the world of '*Azilut,* the sefirotic realm. But there was an overspill of these sparks from the world of '*Azilut;* thus was the world of *Beri'ah* constituted. The overspill from this world resulted in the emergence of the world of *Yezirah,* and, in turn, from this world there was an overspill that brought about the world of '*Asiyah.* The idea here is that fewer sparks are required for the formation of the worlds as they descend; less energy is needed to keep lower worlds in existence, so that as the sparks flash out those which are redundant insofar as that world is concerned spill over to create the next lower world. There is a further overspill from the world of '*Asiyah* and it is this which nourishes the *qelipot* or demonic forces. In this way the effect of the breaking of the vessels results in holy sparks being imprisoned among the *qelipot.* It is the human task to reclaim these sparks for the holy and by so doing perform the necessary *tiqqun,* assisting the fallen worlds to be restored to their former harmonious state. The reclaiming of the sparks from the *qelipot* is achieved by rejecting evil, that is, by obeying the negative precepts of the Torah. So far as the highest *qelipah* realm, the ambiguously holy/ unholy world of *nogah* is concerned, the sparks therein are reclaimed by directing aright the natural drives of the body and so bringing this *qelipah* into the realm of the holy. Furthermore, in a very elaborate scheme, every detail of the precepts of the Torah is directed toward this or that aspect of the *parzufim.* Every evil deed not only keeps the holy sparks imprisoned among the *qelipot* but also sends baneful impulses on high to disturb further the harmony among the *sefirot.* Conversely, every good deed sends beneficent impulses on high to promote harmony among the *sefirot* and reclaim the holy sparks.

In kabbalistic exegesis, the creation narrative in the first chapter of Genesis does not refer to the emergence of this world but to the emanation of the *sefirot* and, in the Lurianic school, to the whole process as described. The verse (Gen 1:2) states that the spirit of God (*Elohim*) hovered over the face of the waters. In the rabbinic midrash, the name *Elohim* denotes judgment, sternness, severity. The reference is said by the Lurianic Kabbalah to be the breaking of the vessels, the restriction of the divine light, and hence the emergence of severity and judgment, albeit for the sake of God's love, so that creatures might come into being to benefit from his goodness and share it forever. The spirit of judgment, then, hovered over the waters, that is, the lights were too powerful and the vessels too weak for the process to be completed. The word for "hover" is *merahefet*. If the first and last letters are detached from this word and placed together they form the word *met*, "death," referring to the death of the "kings." When these two letters have been removed from the word, we are left with the letters *resh, peh, het* (*resh*=200; *peh*=80; *het*=8) with the numerical value of 288. The number of holy sparks to be rescued is consequently said to be 288. The significance of this number becomes clearer when it is recalled that the highest of the four divine names, the name 'aV, has the numerical value of 72. Four times 72 (four because there are four divine names— 'aV and the other three—and four letters in the tetragrammaton) is 288.

In the extremely bold sexual symbolism that the kabbalists favor, the unification or harmonization among the *sefirot* is described as *ziwwug* ("copulation"). First there takes place the *ziwwug* of *'Abba* and *'Imma* and then of *Ze'ir* and *Nuqva* (*Tif'eret*, the male principle; and *Malkhut*, the female principle, personified as the *Shekhinah*). The male principle, *Tif'eret*, is given the rabbinic name for God: "The Holy One, blessed be He" (*qudsha berikh hu* in Aramaic). For *ziwwug* to take place, both male and female orgasm are required; the male orgasm is described as "male waters"; the female orgasm as "female waters." The "male waters" are attained through the flow of grace and power from above, from the higher *sefirot*, but (here is the most startling aspect of the whole doctrine) the "female waters" are provided by humans who send on high the reclaimed holy sparks. The holy sparks provide the "female waters," so that the sacred marriage can take place. (Again and again the kabbalists issue the sternest warnings against taking this in any physical or corporeal way, but solely as descriptions of complex relationships between spiritual entities in the sefirotic realm).

At first it was intended for the *tiqqun* and the reclaiming of the holy sparks to be performed by Adam, whose great soul embraced all the souls of humanity. If Adam had obeyed God the *tiqqun* would have been completed and harmony restored throughout all creation. But, as a result of Adam's disobedience, there was a second cosmic fall, repeating, as it were, the original breaking of the vessels. Adam's soul became fragmented, each of his descendants having a mere spark of Adam's mighty soul. Thus the Lurianic school thinks of two kinds of sparks. The first are those which fell when the vessels were shattered. The second are the sparks of Adam's soul. It is not only the sparks in creation that require reclamation, but, in addition, every soul has to assist in its own *tiqqun*, that is, in the perfection of that particular spark of Adam's soul. A vast cosmic drama is being played out with the human being in the central role. Each individual has to engage in the dual task of restoring his or her own holy spark, an inheritance from the first father of the human race, and one has to reclaim the holy sparks in creation, both of which are achieved by keeping the precepts of the Torah. (Occasionally it is hinted that the process applies to all the descendants of Adam—not only to Jews—but this is infrequent. The kabbalistic doctrines are addressed primarily to Jews, to whom the Torah has been given, every detail of which corresponds to some aspect on high.)

The bare performance of the precepts is not sufficient, however, for the rescuing of the sparks and the achievement of the *tiqqun*. The mystical adept must be thoroughly familiar with all the details of the sefirotic map, so that when he carries out the precepts he has the required *kawwanot* ("intentions"), by which his mind is directed to the particular detail his act puts right. For instance, each festival in the Jewish calendar has its own particular *tiqqun*, its special promotion of harmony among the *parzufim*. As an observant Jew, the mystic will naturally keep the festivals in the way the law demands. But of him much more is required. He must be fully conscious at every stage of his observances of that which his efforts put right on high. The spiritual exercises of the kabbalists are, consequently, in the nature of prolonged meditations on the complex relationships among the *sefirot* and the *parzufim*. Some opponents of the Kabbalah based part of their objection on this very point, arguing that the kabbalist becomes so absorbed in the *kawwanot* that he has no time to think of God!

There is a mystical formula, incorporated into the prayer books in the seventeenth century, whereby the kabbalist directs his heart to the *tiqqun* before he carries out any of the precepts. In its fuller form this declaration reads: "I perform this for the sake of the unification of the Holy One, blessed be He, and His *Shekhinah*, to unite the name *yud, heh* with *waw, heh*, by means of that Hidden and Concealed One, in the name of all Israel." The letters *yud, heh*, the first two letters of the tetragrammaton, represent, respectively, *Hokhmah* and *Binah* (with *Keter*, represented by the tittle of the *yud*). The performance of the precepts brings about the unification of *Tif'eret* and *Malkhut* (corresponding to the *parzufim Ze'ir 'Anpin* and *Nuqva*), represented by the letters *waw, heh*, the third and fourth letters of the tetragrammaton. This produces the further unification of the higher and lower *sefirot* and thus the unification of *yud, heh*, with *waw, heh*. It is all brought about by the power of *Eyn Sof* ("Hidden and Concealed"). And it is performed in the name of all Israel, each individual being only a spark of Adam's soul. In many versions of the formula there is the addition: "And I perform it in love and fear," representing the love of God, corresponding to *Hesed*, and the fear of God, corresponding to *Gevurah*. One who approaches God in love and fear brings into play on high the divine *Hesed* and *Gevurah*, united and harmonized in *Tif'eret*.

The Lurianic Kabbalah also has a strong messianic thrust. The doctrine runs that although Adam had sinned and by so doing prevented the restoration of the sparks, his descendants were given a second chance when the Torah was given to Israel. By their willing acceptance of the demands of the Torah, the Israelites were set to put right the whole realm of the *sefirot*, restoring the harmony Adam had failed to achieve. The sentence of death, decreed on Adam, was annulled and they were destined to become immortal. But these privileges were forfeited at the time of the worship of the golden calf. The catastrophic breach was repeated and all was in disarray again. The process of reclaiming the sparks now had to be a gradual one; only to be completed in the far-off messianic age. The risk of a third catastrophic failure could only have been avoided by a step-by-step restoration rather than an immediate storming of the heavens. But, so soon after the Expulsion from Spain, the Lurianic kabbalists seemed to have felt that redemption could no longer be allowed to tarry. Their aim was to hasten the process. They developed the theory that in the age in which they flourished the store of souls from Adam had almost been exhausted. The great ones of the past possessed souls from the head of Adam, with a progressive degeneration then setting in, and the souls of the sixteenth century were seen as deriving from the heels of Adam. Moreover, most of the sparks in creation had already been reclaimed. All that was needed for the Messiah to come was for the few remaining souls with sparks from Adam to rescue the correspondingly few sparks in creation. A final effort of great power was seen to be required in order to rescue the few remaining sparks from the *qelipot*. The members of the Lurianic school were ascetics, seeking, by holy living, self-denial, prayer, and the practice of the *kawwanot*, to complete the task of *birur* ("selection"), the total rescue of all the holy sparks and their complete separation from the domain of the *qelipot*.

The whole process, from beginning to end, is seen by the Lurianic school as one of exile and redemption. The first act of *zimzum*, the "withdrawal," betokened a kind of exile, with the filling of the "empty space" a partial restoration. This process was repeated when the vessels were shattered and then reconstituted in the form of *parzufim*, in Adam's sin and the giving of the Torah, in the worship of the golden calf and the task of restoring the fallen sparks. It is small wonder, then, that the exile of the *Shekhinah* and her redemption occupy such a prominent place in the Lurianic scheme.

New rituals were introduced by the Lurianists with the express purpose of hastening the redemption, of restoring the *Shekhinah* to her spouse. There are two aspects of the *Shekhinah* in Lurianic thought, two *parzufim* (each of the five *parzufim* is further divided into two, making a total of ten) known as *Raḥel* and *Leah* (the biblical stories represent, chiefly, for the kabbalists, the relationships on high, though, of course, the historicity of the matriarchs and the other biblical personages is not denied). The mystic rises at midnight to recite various scriptural verses and prayers intended to restore the *Shekhinah* from her exile. The passages are arranged in two parts: somber *tiqqun Leah* and the *tiqqun Raḥel*, in which the note of consolation is sounded more emphatically. The custom of rising at midnight to mourn for the exile of the *Shekhinah*, like other Lurianic rituals, was later adopted by many devout Jews who made no claim to being mystics or kabbalists.

On the even of the new moon, the ritual of the Minor Day of Atonement (*Yom Kippur Qatan*) was introduced for the same reason. In the Kabbalah, *Tif'eret* is symbolized by the sun and *Malkhut*, the *Shekhinah*, by the moon; the waxing and waning of the moon represents the exile of the *Shekhinah* and her eventual return from exile. Since the reunification of the *Shekhinah* with her spouse depends on the reclaiming of the holy sparks, the eve of the new moon festival is made into a day of repentance and confession of sin in preparation for the new effort required in order to bring on the hoped-for event. This practice, too, was later adopted in many Jewish communities.

Another liturgical innovation by the kabbalists is the prayer recited before the performance of the precept of counting the Omer (Lev 23:15–16). There are seven weeks from the second day of Passover to the festival of Pentecost, the traditional anniversary of the giving of the Torah. The *tiqqun* of which the kabbalists speak involves chiefly the restoration of the seven lower *sefirot*. Only these were shattered; the three higher *sefirot* only fell from their place. Each *sefirah* contains all the others, so that, as we have noted, one can speak of *Ḥesed* of *Ḥesed*, *Gevurah* of *Ḥesed*, and so forth. To each day of the Omer period one of the forty-nine combinations is allotted, beginning with *Ḥesed* of *Ḥesed* on the first day and ending with *Malkhut* of *Malkhut* on the last day. Every sin brings in its wake a *pegam* ("flaw") in one of these combinations, but through carrying out the precept the flaw is removed and the *tiqqun* process assisted. When all forty-nine days have been counted and all seven *sefirot* in their forty-nine combinations have been restored, the Torah can be received in purity. The mystical prayer recited each day before the counting reads:

> Sovereign of the Universe! Thou didst command us through Moses Thy servant to count the Omer in order to purify us from our *qelipot* and our contaminations. As Thou hast written in Thy Torah: "And from the day on which you bring the sheaf (*'omer*) of wave offering—the day after the sabbath—you shall count off seven weeks. They must be complete: you must count until the day after the seventh week—fifty days" (Lev 23:15–16), so that

the souls of Thy people Israel will be cleansed from their filth. Therefore, may it be Thy will, O Lord our God and God of our fathers, that, in the merit of the counting of the Omer which I have this day counted, there should be a restoration of that which I have flawed in the *sefirah* (adding whichever of the forty-nine combinations is appropriate for that day). And may I be purified and sanctified in the holiness which comes from on high. Amen, Selah.

The idea of the purification as extending even to the sefirotic realm in this connection is based on the Zoharic notion that the counting of seven times seven here represents the counting by the *Shekhinah* of her days of impurity just as a menstruant must count seven days before she can be with her husband (Lev 15:28). Ritual purity has been raised to the level of profound mystery.

Especially through prayer, with the mind on the special *kawwanot*, each soul can rescue the holy sparks and assist in the *tiqqun* process. This is not understood as the same *tiqqun* performed repeatedly. Each day has its own *tiqqun*. Each prayer is a new *tiqqun*. No two prayers, even if they have the identical words, achieve the same result. For example, the disciples of Hayyim Vital describe the *tiqqun* performed through the early morning prayer and ablutions (*Peri 'Ez Hayyim, Sha'ar ha-Tefillah*, chap. 4). We must first note that, strictly speaking, the world of *'Azilut* is unaffected by the *qelipot* and requires no *tiqqun*. The lowest of the four worlds, *'Asiyah*, is given over entirely to the *qelipot*, and it is here that the rescue operation is required. But, through the rescue of the holy sparks in *'Asiyah*, the other two worlds, *Beri'ah* and *Yezirah*, are also put right. It is, in fact, in these that the actual *tiqqun* is achieved. However, as we have seen, each of the worlds contains all four, so that there is the aspect *'Asiyah* of *'Azilut*, where the *tiqqun* is required. The kabbalist writes:

> This is the meaning of prayer and its mystery. Man must rise up early in the morning, relieve himself, and wash his hands. He must put right the four worlds by means of his deeds and his words. He performs the *tiqqun* by deed when he relieves himself. The act corresponds to the World of Action (*'Asiyah*) so when he evacuates his bowels he should have the intention (*kawwanah*) of cleansing the World of Action from the *qelipot*, namely, the *'Asiyah* of *'Asiyah*. After this he should have the intention of putting right *'Asiyah* of *Yezirah*. This is achieved when he puts on the small garment with the fringes attached. . . . After this, when he puts on the *tefillin*, he should have the intention of putting right the *'Asiyah* of *'Azilut*. . . . And then, when he dons the large *tallit* and wraps himself around with it, there is the overall and surrounding *tiqqun*. Thus far the *tiqqun* performed by deed. And now the *tiqqun* performed by word of mouth. When he recites the order of the sacrifices there is achieved the *tiqqun* of *Yezirah* of *'Asiyah*. When he recites

the songs of praise there is achieved the *tiqqun* of *Yezirah* of *Yezirah.* This is followed by *Kaddish, Barekhu,* and the *Shema'.* These correspond to the *Beri'ah* of *Beri'ah,* and when the *Shema'* is recited there should be the intention of performing the complete unification.

The above is a very small example of how the process operates. The purpose of the *Peri 'Ez Ḥayyim* is to put all the kabbalistic doctrines to work by showing the particular intentions required when the rituals are carried out, demonstrating how each detail has its special correspondence in the supernal realms. By means of the whole range of Jewish observances the various *tiqqunim* are achieved; each observance, each individual, and each hour and day make its own contribution to the complete *tiqqun* through the rescue of the holy sparks from the *qelipot* until the great cosmic drama reaches its finale.

The Lurianic Kabbalah won adherents in many parts of the Jewish world, especially in Italy, Turkey, Germany, and Poland. The Lurianic *kawwanot* were practiced by individual kabbalists in isolation, but small groups of *mekhawwenim* (those who practiced the *kawwanot*) were also to be found, such as the group in the famed Klaus in the Galician town of Brody. A circle of *mekhawwenim* was formed by Gedaliah Hayyon, in Jerusalem in the year 1737. In Bet El, as the conventicle was known, prayer with the Lurianic *kawwanot* was engaged in until the present century. Hayyon was succeeded in the leadership of the circle by his son-in-law, Shalom Shar'abi (1720–1777), a renowned Yemenite kabbalist. Shar'abi produced a prayer book, *Nehar Shalom* (Salonika, 1806), containing all the *kawwanot.* The elitist nature of Bet El has been described by Ariel Bension, the son of one of its members:

> The center consisted of a small group of the intellectual elite, whose mystic joy lay in the heart of the silence which enveloped them in its seven veils for centuries. Living in a retirement that screened it off from the vulgar gaze of the public the group pursued its upward course, striking the synthesis between conviction and action. It was a community agreed to live in unity and sanctity. Of those who sought to enter its portals it demanded the attainments of the scholar and the self-abnegation of the ascetic. Thus it missed the masses. . . . In Beth-El joy was attained by no artificial means, but by silent meditation, by introspection in an atmosphere in which music, blending with men's thoughts, induced a forgetfulness of externals. Each man's eyes were turned inwards. Seeking to mine the wealth of his own soul he found there the wealth of the universe. Amazed at his own discovery of the hidden treasure the mystic pursues his course upwards until he attains the ecstasy that brings him to the mystery of creation, where sits Joy enthroned. In a silence in which alone the soul may meet its God, destroyed worlds are reconstructed and restored to their pristine perfection. And this is the aim

of the *Kavanoth*—the meditations on the mystic meaning of certain prayers with intention bring restoration. In a song which follows the meaningful word, continuing and deepening its meaning—even as a pause in the rendition of a symphony is but the continuation of the music—this worldless song attains that which cannot be reached through the medium of words. And the word of prayer, arising at a given moment from the throats of all Israel, attains its highest form in the silence of Beth-El, imaged in song by the Master seated on his divan and surrounded by silent, thought-inspired mystics.[3]

The following brief statement of the *berurim* (the "selections") in prayer by Shalom Shar'abi, the second and most famous leader at Bet El, is typical of the practice of the *kawwanot* at this center.

All this applies to the weekdays. But, afterwards, on the Sabbath, as a result of the prayers, those *berurim* that have been refined and put right on the weekday now emerge once again in order to be refined and put right though the supernal *parzufim* more than could have been achieved during the weekday, each prayer proportionally, until the Afternoon Prayer (of the Sabbath). Then *Ze'ir 'Anpin* ascends to the place of *'Arikh 'Anpin* and then all the *berurim* ascend to become combined and put right by means of the 'aV of the 'aV and the 'aV of the SaG of *'Adam Qadmon.*

Prior to this statement, Shar'abi had observed that the weekday prayers have the effect of refining (performing the *berurim*) the various stages in the divine process but only as a beginning. On the Sabbath these find their more complete refinements as they ascend even higher. We have seen that the four names, 'aV, SaG, MaH, and BeN, are present in all four worlds and they are present, too, in the world of *'Adam Qadmon.* Thus, on Sabbath afternoon the prayers complete the refinement process begun on the weekday and continued on the Sabbath, until toward the end of the Sabbath the *berurim* extend even to the highest of the high, to the 'aV of the 'aV of *'Adam Qadmon.* All this the mystic is required to have in mind before he begins to recite the prayer. During the prayer itself, various other complex associations in the realm of the *parzufim* are required to be in the mind, and these are provided by Shar'abi.

The Sabbatian Heresy

The movement founded by the false Messiah Sabbatai Sevi (1626–1676) and his prophet Nathan of Gaza, despite its antinomian departure from Jewish tradition, managed to win over to its redemptive fervor a large proportion of Jews of diverse social classes in many lands. Historians have been puzzled by the astonishing successes of Sabbatianism; but, however the special factors that led up to the new messianic enthusiasm are to be understood, there is no doubt that the movement's theology is based on the Lurianic Kabbalah, with the doctrine of the holy sparks occupying a prominent place—though the doctrine was completely recast in order to justify the messianic revolution.

Nathan of Gaza encouraged Sabbatai Sevi to believe that he was the long-awaited Messiah, maintaining that with the advent of Sabbatai, the *tiqqun* had received its fulfillment, all the holy sparks having been successfully reclaimed. A new era had been inaugurated. Even the practices of the Torah were no longer required in their traditional form. Their purpose had been the rescue of the holy sparks, and that task had been accomplished, rendering them superfluous. What had hitherto been sinful was now permitted, even mandatory, as a joyous celebration hailing the completion of Israel's mission. Sabbatai carried out certain acts, sternly forbidden in the Jewish sources, such as the eating of tallow, a food unpalatable in itself but precisely for that reason an instance of sin not for self-gratification but for its own sake. Sabbatai recited over the tallow the benediction: "Blessed art Thou, who hath permitted that which has hitherto been forbidden." In the new theology, the soul of the Messiah now occupied a prominent place in the whole cosmic scheme; that soul had been present in a mysterious way even at the time when the vessels were shattered. In the traditional Lurianic system, all the emphasis is on the *age* of the Messiah, when the *tiqqun* will have reached its fulfillment, not on the *person* of the Messiah (though, as Orthodox Jews, the Lurianic kabbalists obviously did believe in a personal Messiah).

When the stormy career of Sabbatai Sevi ended in his conversion to Islam, the hopes of all but his most faithful devotees were dashed. These were obliged to develop an even more radical theology in order to justify his apostasy. With the coming of the Messiah in the person of Sabbatai Sevi, it was argued, all the holy sparks dispersed for the children of Israel to reclaim had already been rescued. In this sense it was indeed true that the mission had been successfully completed. But there still remained holy sparks among the Gentiles, and these awaited their rescue. In order to achieve this final restoration it was necessary for the Messiah to descend into the domain of the *qelipot*, here represented by Islam, to elevate the holy sparks still imprisoned there. Long after Sabbatai's death, his still-faithful followers became enamored of this intoxicating idea of the holy sin, adopting it as a rule for all believers, not only as a task to be undertaken by the Messiah alone. These later Sabbatians outwardly kept all the observances of the Torah but secretly endeavored to rescue by the performance of illegal acts the holy sparks imprisoned among the *qelipot*. This involved a complete reversal of the Lurianic Kabbalah. In the Lurianic scheme it is never permitted to attempt to rescue the holy sparks through sinful acts. On the contrary, refraining from sin was one of the ways in which the sparks were to be rescued and the restoration completed.

Hasidism

Hasidism, the movement inaugurated in eastern Europe by Israel Ba'al-Shem-Tov (ca. 1700–1760) and his disciples, claimed to be "a new way of serving God." The Hasidic writings are in the conventional Hebrew and Aramaic of traditional Judaism, so that the novelty of the teaching can only be discerned by reading between the lines and by observing how the older vocabulary has been adapted to express ideas that had never been intended. In these texts there is to be found a subtle blending of the old and the new, resulting if not in a completely original doctrine at least in marked new emphases. Hasidism utilizes the concept of the holy sparks to a far greater degree than the Lurianic kabbalists themselves. But although on the surface nothing has changed, in effect the whole concept has undergone a radical transformation. Close examination of how the doctrine fares in Hasidism reveals several significant points of departure. The extent of the Sabbatian influence is still debated by scholars but it cannot be denied that Hasidism, like Sabbatianism, used the teachings regarding the holy sparks in order to advance its own theological position. The *mitnaggedim*, the rabbis, and communal leaders who opposed Hasidism, recognized this; although they believed that Luria's idea came to him by divine inspiration, they still declared Hasidism to be heretical and its adherents sectarians.

First, it has to be appreciated that while some Hasidic masters did engage in severe denial and mortification of the flesh, their ascetic mode of life belonged to their background as Lurianic kabbalists or to individual temperament. It was only incidental to the Hasidic way of life, which stressed the idea of *'avodah be-gashmiyyut,* "divine worship through the use of material things." This involved a positive embrace of things of this world as means toward the greater service of God. The Hasidic ideal and the asceticism of a few of the masters were in flat contradiction. Students of religious psychology are able to quote many examples of such contradictions existing side by side in the religious mind. In the essential Hasidic doctrine, God is to be worshiped not only by the study of the Torah, prayer, and the observance of the precepts but also, and particularly, by engaging in worldly pursuits with God in mind. Little is made in the Lurianic Kabbalah of the holy sparks residing in food and drink and in other worldly things except when the discussion has to do with their rescue through the performance of the precepts—eating and drinking as sacred acts on the festivals, for example, or eating unleavened bread on Passover. Otherwise, abstinence and holy living are the way in which the sparks are rescued. In Hasidism, on the other hand, the holy sparks clamor to be rescued by the *hasid* fully engaged in the world. When attending to his material needs for the sake of God, the *hasid* is carrying out acts of divine worship. For him to lead an ascetic life is to shirk his duty of rescuing the holy sparks. Traditional Judaism also knows of eating for the sake of heaven, that bodily appetites should be satisfied not out of hedonistic motives but in order to keep the body strong and healthy for the service of God. In Hasidism, worldly pursuit in the spirit of holiness is not simply a means to the noblest of ends; it is an end in itself. "For the sake of heaven" means, in Hasidism, that the true motivation must be to carry out the heavenly task laid upon humanity, that of rescuing the holy sparks.

Various theories have been advanced to account for the Hasidic transformation. It is likely that the Sabbatian notion of the holy sin, though never adopted in its stark form by Hasidism, paved the way, at least, for the spiritually adventuresome idea of finding the holy in the depths of the material. It is also highly likely that the early Hasidic masters, witnessing a lack in the spiritual life of the masses, for whom asceticism could have no appeal, wished to encourage a far greater participation in the religious life on the part of the ordinary Jews. Another factor, no doubt, was the harsh economic reality for the Jews in eastern Europe. Of what use was it to preach that the world was to be lost for the soul to be gained to people who had so little of the world to lose in any event? The lesson needed was that God is very near to all and near to these people in their travail, that the world is shot through with divinity. Downtrodden simple Jews needed to hear that they, too, could draw near to God, even if removed from the niceties of rabbinic learning, by perceiving the divine vitality in all things. The description of Hasidism as "mysticism for the masses" certainly contains some truth.

Second, the Lurianic kabbalists were elitists; they alone knew the secret method of reclaiming the holy sparks. Yet anyone with the necessary qualifications was allowed to join the mystic circle in order to participate in the tremendous cosmic engagement. Hasidism was, on the contrary, egalitarian. It was open to every Jew to become a *hasid*, no matter how humble his origin and attainments. (The very word *hasid*, meaning in the rabbinic and medieval literature "saint," now denoted a follower of a spiritual guide and mentor who numbered quite ordinary Jews as well as the learned and saintly among his followers.) But what Hasidism gave with one hand it took away with the other. All the *hasidim* were treated as equals but their lives now revolved around the *zaddiq*, the holy man, the guru-like figure, the righteous leader whose commands must be obeyed even by the Almighty himself. In some versions of Hasidism it is the *zaddiq* alone who can attempt the perilous task of reclaiming the holy sparks residing in the material. But more generally the *ḥasid*, too, is encouraged to embark on the great adventure, yet he can only hope to succeed because he is aided by the *zaddiq*, to whom he owes allegiance and whose mystical aura embraces his followers to elevate their souls.[5]

Third, as Gershom Scholem has shown, in Hasidism each individual, or at least each *zaddiq*, has his own unique sparks to reclaim.[6] There is nothing of this in Luria. True, in the Lurianic scheme each individual is called upon to elevate his own spark of Adam's soul. In this respect, each individual has his own task to perform even according to Luria. But the sparks found in creation as a result of the breaking of the vessels are in no way peculiar to each individual. All must engage in the task, each in accordance with his soul-root. In Hasidism the two sets of sparks—those belonging to Adam's soul and those residing in the material universe—are intimately connected. The task of the individual is to rescue those sparks in creation that belong to him, having an affinity with his soul-root. There are sparks in creation waiting for him to rescue them because they are his and he alone can perform that particular task. The development of the doctrine in this way is perhaps due to the renewed Hasidic emphasis on the individual as unique. It is because of this that we find many a Hasidic tale of a master being propelled by a force beyond his control to journey to distant places for no other purpose than to carry out there some task, otherwise neutral or insignificant, that would have the effect of rescuing the holy sparks held there captive by the *qelipot*—these sparks awaiting the coming of the one rescuer whose soul-root is close to them in the divine scheme. The princess enslaved in the ogre's castle will consent to be rescued by the knight in shining armor to whom she had plighted her troth.

A few examples must now be given of how the doctrine of the holy sparks is treated by the Hasidic masters. The doctrine appears frequently in the first Hasidic work to be published, *Toledot Ya'aqov Yosef* by Jacob Joseph of Polonnoye (d. ca. 1784). In one passage Jacob Joseph speaks of two kinds of intentions when eating.[7] The simple intention is to gain strength for God's service. The higher and more difficult intention is for the purpose of elevating the holy sparks in the food. God has given us the desire for food and drink as an inducement to elevate the holy sparks. This is the spiritual aspect of eating and drinking, concealed by the physical pleasure, just as an honest woman whose face is veiled may be mistaken for a harlot. The zaddiq sees through to the reality. His thoughts are not on the pleasure he obtains, only on the holy sparks to be rescued.

The grandson of the Ba'al-Shem-Tov, Baruch of Medzhibozh (1757–1810) is said to have gone even further in his enthusiasm for the idea of reclaiming the holy sparks through engagement in the world. In the work containing Baruch's teachings, *Bozina di-Nehora*, there is a remarkable homily on the following text:[8] "If a man has two wives, the one beloved, the other hated, and they have borne him children, both the beloved and the hated . . . he may not make the son of the beloved the firstborn before the son of the hated, who is the firstborn; but he shall acknowledge the firstborn, the son of the hated, by giving him a double portion" (Deut 21:15–17). The beloved wife represents the service of the one who worships God by studying the Torah and prayer. This is "beloved" to those who observe it since that is, indeed, how the majority understand worship. Not so the worship engaged in by the zaddiq when he engages in worldly things for the purpose of reclaiming the holy sparks. People find it very strange that such an activity should be termed divine worship, failing to see that while the zaddiq eats, drinks, and engages in commerce no differently from other men, his intentions are quite different. This aspect is represented by the "hated wife." It is the child of the hated wife, however, who is to receive the double portion that is the right of the firstborn. The result of this type of worship, its "child," is twice as valuable in God's eyes and must have priority, though repellent to men. Baruch himself conducted a splendid "court" with magnificent furniture, tapestries, and even a court jester. His many opponents were not slow to criticize him for departing from the simple life of his grandfather. Evidently he sought to justify his opulent life-style on the grounds that it was all for the purpose of reclaiming the holy sparks. Perhaps in overcompensation, Baruch roundly declares that the Torah holds this way to be greatly superior to that of study and prayer. Such an extreme view does not appear to have been shared by the majority of the masters, and it is certainly a far cry from the original idea of reclaiming the sparks as found in Luria. The novelty of his approach is acknowledged by Baruch himself when he describes this way of worship as "hated." It should be noted that Baruch speaks of the zaddiq, evidently holding that the ordinary hasid is incapable of having God in mind when following worldly pursuits.

According to legend, another Hasidic master, Abraham Joshua Heschel of Apt (d. 1825) was almost obsessed with the idea of reclaiming the holy sparks inherent in food. He is said to have eaten colossal meals whenever he could, with his mind on God as he ate, in order to rescue more and more sparks. In his work *Ohev Yisra'el*, the Apter examines the tradition that "inverted nuns" (i.e., the Hebrew letter *nun*) are to be inserted in the Torah scroll before and after the small section: "And it came to pass, when the Ark set forward . . ." (Num 10:35–36).[9] The traditional explanation of this phenomenon is that the *nuns* are like our inverted commas and are intended to show that this passage is out of place, that it does not belong here. The Apter, very anachronistically to be sure, but obviously with an eye on the Hasidic practices of his day, remarks that the section refers to the stages of the Israelites' journeys through diverse places in the wilderness. These journeys were necessary in order to rescue, by means of the holy Ark which went with the people and the holiness of Moses and their own holiness, all the holy sparks residing in those unclean places. The letter *nun* has the numerical value of 50, pointing to the 50 gates of Understanding (*Binah*). The rabbis (*Nedarim* 38a) speak of 50 gates of understanding (*binah*), 49 of which were open to Moses. Even the great leader was unable to pass through the fiftieth gate. In the Kabbalah, this is made to refer to the *sefirah* of *Binah,* the mother of the seven lower *sefirot,* which has 49 gates (seven times seven). On their holy journeys, aided by the holiness of the Ark and Moses, the people were able to draw down from on high even the illuminations from the fiftieth gate so as to rescue the holy sparks imprisoned in those places among the corresponding 50 gates of impurity. When the sparks, who had imagined that their cause was lost and that they were doomed forever to remain in captivity, saw the great illumination reaching down to them from all 50 gates on high, they sprang out to meet them and so could be elevated to their source by the holy people. This is the mystery of the inverted *nuns* and, indeed, this small section is "out of place" since the true home of the holy sparks was not among the *qelipot.* It is interesting to compare the Apter's homily with the Sabbatian idea of the descent of the Messiah into the realm of impurity in order to reclaim the sparks residing there. Possibly in conscious reaction to the Sabbatian doctrine, in the Apter's homily it is the *nun,* representing the sacred realm on high, that descends (is "inverted"). Moses and his people, on the contrary, do not descend and only elevate the sparks after their release from imprisonment through the descent of the celestial powers.

The Hasidic emphasis on the need to rescue the holy sparks through engagement in the world naturally presented its own temptations. It became all too easy for worldly men to indulge their appetites and ambitions under the guise of sanctity. The apparently worldly *zaddiq* may not have been worldly at all, because his intention is solely for the rescue of the sparks, but who was to know whether, in fact, his motives were pure? Even among the Hasidic masters themselves there is a realization of how open to abuse the doctrine is. Ze'ev Wolf of Zhitomer (d. 1800), in his book *Or ha-Me'ir,* for example, is extremely critical of the *zaddiqim* of his day who journey periodically to elicit contributions from their followers for their own upkeep.[10] Ze'ev Wolf is opposed to the practice, refusing to believe that these much-traveled *zaddiqim* only journey from place to place for the purpose of reclaiming the holy sparks. After all, he says, beggars too are decreed by fate to go from house to house to solicit donations. Only the holiest of men can be sure that their need for travel is induced by God so that they might rescue the holy sparks. Such journeys may, in reality, be nothing more subtle than the desire to be supported by others without having to work for a living. It may be only the decreed fate of the abject beggar. According to Ze'ev Wolf, discernment is imperative. Not every urge is to be seen as the call of the holy sparks to be delivered. Before responding to the urge, the *zaddiq* must be sufficiently confident in his spiritual power to elevate the sparks. He must know with certainty that when he sets out to rescue the sparks he will succeed in his task because he really is a holy man. Lacking such confidence, he can easily fall prey to self-delusion. Instead of rescuing the sparks, he himself will become enslaved by the *qelipot*.

In a number of passages in Hasidic writings it is suggested that the taste of food and drink is the spiritual aspect of that food and drink, the holy spark that sustains it. At the end of the work *No'am Elimelekh* by the early Hasidic master Elimelech of Lizensk (1717–1787) there occurs this passage:

> Before washing the hands preceding a meal, recite the penitential prayer of the *Ari* (Luria) of blessed memory. After eating the piece of bread over which grace before meals has been recited, say: "For the sake of the unification of the Holy One, blessed be He, and His *Shekhinah*. I do not eat, God forbid, to give enjoyment to my body but only that it be strong to worship God. Let not any sin, transgression, evil thought, or bodily pleasure prevent the unification by means of the holy sparks in this food and drink." Whenever one eats and drinks, he should have in mind that the taste he experiences when he swallows the food and imbibes the drink is the inward part of the holy sparks which reside in that food and drink; and that, through chewing with the teeth and digesting with the stomach, the inward part of the food becomes refined so that it does not become a surplus wherewith the outside ones are fed. His soul will then benefit from the inward part of the food, the residue becoming waste matter to be expelled for the outside ones. He should also have in mind that as soon as he will feel a need to evacuate his bowels he will not, God forbid, keep the waste inside his body to contaminate his mind and render his soul abominable by keeping the excrement and urine inside his body for a single moment. And, as he eats, he should depict to himself the letters of the word *ma'akhol* ("food") in their "Assyrian" (square Hebrew) form, and should have in mind that numerically they total 91, the numerical value of the Tetragrammaton and *Adonay*.[11]

The meaning of this last statement is that the tetragrammaton represents *Tif'eret* while the name 'Adonay represents *Malkhut.* The word *ma'akhol,* equal in its numerical value to that of *Tif'eret* and *Malkhut,* suggests the idea that by eating in a spirit of consecration the unification is brought about of these two *sefirot* through the rescue of the holy sparks.

From the earliest period, the *hasidim* were very fond of tobacco. The complaint that the *hasidim* waste their time in smoking is reiterated in the polemics of the *mitnaggedim,* collected by Mordecai Wilensky in his *Hasidim u-Mitnaggedim.*[12] The main reason for this addiction to the weed, claim the *hasidim,* is also because of the need to elevate the holy sparks. The argument runs that tobacco was unknown in Luria's day because the time had not yet come for the very subtle sparks in tobacco to be released by smoking. But now that almost all the coarser sparks had received their restoration, tobacco was sent by God so that the Hasidic masters should elevate these "new" and subtle sparks! A similar defense of tobacco is found in the work *Ozar ha-Hayyim* by Yitzhak Eisik of Komarno (1806–1874).[13] This author informs us, in the name of his father-in-law, that one of the Ba'al-Shem-Tov's disciples thought ill of a colleague who stooped to retrieve his pipe, which had fallen to the ground during his prayers. On reflection, however, he came to appreciate that there are subtle souls which can only find their *tiqqun* through the most ethereal of substances. This is the "sweet savor unto the Lord" mentioned in Scripture in connection with the sacrificial system. Also found in Hasidic sources is the idea that smoking corresponds to the incense in Temple times, having the same effect of elevating the holy sparks.

Another aspect of the sparks from Adam's soul was seized on by the Hasidic writers. This was the idea that the souls of his descendants were present in Adam's soul in families or groups, each with its own soul-root. Since Adam's sin, when the souls were scattered, Adam's descendants each receive their souls in this pattern of roots. Furthermore, a soul not yet perfected while in one body has to return to another body in order to perform the *tiqqun* it requires. The doctrine of *gilgul* ("transmigration of souls") features prominently in the Lurianic Kabbalah. The return to earth may be in the form of an animal or a bird, but more often it is in the form of another human being. There are many descriptions among the kabbalists of this or that scholar or saint having the soul of an earlier, perhaps biblical, spiritual hero. Sometimes it is not necessary for the soul of a saint to return to inhabit another body entirely. He may find his *tiqqun* by only partial residence in a body that already has its soul. This is known as *'ibbur,* impregnation. This means that the soul of the departed is impregnated into another soul, the latter still in the body, for mutual assistance in performing the *tiqqun* each of them needs. All these ideas were accepted implicitly by the Hasidic masters. Hasidic legend tells of certain masters having the souls of saints who lived long ago and with whom they share the same soul-root. It was also believed that there are sparks of souls waiting to be restored in various kinds of food, especially in fish, which is why the *zaddiqim* made a point of eating fish on the Sabbath. This notion is probably behind the tale referred to above of the disciple of the Ba'al-Shem-Tov and his pipe. It is as if the souls of the greatest of saints can only bear to return to earth if they are allowed to reside in tobacco, that is, in the refined form of rising smoke, so that when the *zaddiq* smokes his pipe he elevates the soul of the departed and it finds its *tiqqun*. This is the reason, too, for the many tales of disciples going from master to master without finding spiritual rest until they discover a master with the same soul-root as themselves. It is also the reason why a *zaddiq* is able to assist his followers. The *zaddiq* knows of his follower's previous existences on earth and so is able to advise him on the special *tiqqun* he requires in his present existence.

In one other important respect the development of the holy sparks doctrine in Hasidism differs from the Lurianic Kabbalah. In Lurianic thought the mystical adept must not only have in mind the rescue of the sparks but also—indeed, primarily—the precise *tiqqun* he achieves by that rescue. When, for example, he carries out a particular precept, his mind must be on the details of the complex relationships he intends to achieve among the *sefirot* and the *parzufim*. These are the Lurianic *kawwanot*, referred to earlier. For a reason to be noted shortly, Hasidism urges the mystic to leave the *kawwanot* aside, dwelling only on the intention to rescue the holy sparks. This is certainly the attitude adopted by the majority of the Hasidic masters, though some of the masters, as expert kabbalists, still practiced the *kawwanot*. They did so, however, as kabbalists, not as *hasidim*. The *HaBaD* movement in Hasidism also had a way of its own in the matter of contemplation.[14] In a sense, *HaBaD* is a separate system rather than a movement within Hasidism.

Why did the Hasidic masters virtually abandon the Lurianic *kawwanot*, even though they believed implicitly that Luria was the recipient of divine inspiration? The answer is to be found in the Hasidic idea of *devequt*, attachment to God. *Devequt* means that the mind of the *hasid* must always be on God, even though such an ideal is extremely difficult to attain. The *mitnaggedim* rejected the *devequt* ideal, considering it to be undesirable, since, if the mind is to be on God when studying the Torah, for instance, the texts will never be mastered, requiring as they do sustained and undivided attention. If the *hasid* has his mind on God when studying, say, the intricate talmudic discussions about property rights, he is, to be sure, engaging in a devotional exercise, but he is not really studying at all. There is much tension here even among the *ḥasidim,* many of whom were talmudists of distinction, and who evidently limited the *devequt* ideal to the period before and after study. During their studies, they admitted, the mind must be concentrated not on God but on the subject studied.

For the same reason that *devequt* found a rival in Torah study, it found a hindrance in the practice of the *kawwanot.* How could the mind of the mystic be on God alone when it had to be absorbed in the details of the sefirotic scheme? Of course these details were themselves part of the divine processes, and thought of them was really thought of God. Yet the very fact that there is a system worked out in rich detail with a host of complex symbols tended to create a dichotomy between simply having God in mind and concentrating on the arcane symbolism. Thus, the Hasidic emphasis on *devequt* tended to make the doctrine of the *kawwanot* something of an embarrassment. It was impossible to deny the truth of the sefirotic picture, and yet to dwell on it was to frustrate the *devequt* imperative. The usual way out adopted by the *ḥasidim* was to postulate that in the later generations, unlike in the time of the great Lurianists, it was no longer possible to reconcile the *kawwanot* with the *devequt* ideal. Men of these inferior generations have their work cut out in achieving *devequt* without having to cope with the distraction of the *kawwanot.* To concentrate on reclaiming the holy sparks for the sake of God was enough, it was argued, and the various *tiqqunim* were achieved automatically as a result of such concentration. There was no longer any need, nor was it desirable, to have the *kawwanot* in mind. Among those spiritually weaker generations God allows, as it were, the processes to continue and the perfections to be achieved without conscious devotion to the actual details. Some of the Hasidic masters even discouraged the study of the Kabbalah precisely because *devequt* is an exercise of pure devotion, not a matter of studying difficult texts. This is why there are so few references in the Hasidic texts to such topics as the combinations of the divine names and the associations among the *sefirot* and *parzufim.*

The Lurianic *kawwanot* are explicitly rejected by the chief disciple of Elimelech of Lizensk, Kalonymos Kalman Epstein of Cracow (d. 1823) in his work *Ma'or wa-Shemesh,* a work studied extensively by the *ḥasidim* and hence as authoritative as can be in a literature that is more impressionistic than systematic, more personal than official. Kalonymos Kalman's statement reads:

> In our generation it is improper to have in mind the *kawwanot* of prayer handed down to us in the Prayer Book of the Ari, of blessed memory, whether from the written text or by heart. So did I hear it from my master

and teacher, the holy rabbi, the godly man, head of all the Exile, our teacher Elimelech, may the memory of the righteous and holy be for a blessing. He said that one should not think or reflect on the *kawwanot* of the divine names. Instead he should bind both his external and internal self, that is, his vital force, his spirit, and his soul, to *Eyn Sof*, blessed be He. As a result he will bind all the revealed worlds and all the inner aspects of the worlds to Him, blessed be He. His thoughts should be so attached to the pleasantness of the Lord that he has no time, not even for a moment, to have the *kawwanot* in mind. When a person's prayers are of this order, the *kawwanot* and unifications are offered automatically.

What has happened, in effect, in Hasidism, is the continued use of the Lurianic vocabulary and a belief in its efficacy in controlling the upper worlds without any suggestion that the Lurianic intentions are still relevant. The Hasidic ideal, to which all else is made subordinate, is that of *devequt*, where the total concentration of the mind is on God. While all the Hasidic masters refer repeatedly to the reclaiming of the holy sparks, this terminology has now become virtually synonymous with the acknowledgment of the sacred in material things, the recognition that there is a vital force that keeps them in being. Humanity's rescue of the holy sparks has now come to mean the constant awareness of the divine energy suffusing all creation. The elevation of the sparks really amounts to the elevation of the finite universe to its source in God. Indeed, in a nonsystematic way, there is a definite panentheistic thrust in most varieties of Hasidism. Everything is in God; he is both transcendent and immanent. The rescue of the holy sparks thus comes very close to meaning that all the veils concealing God from humanity must be stripped away and only the divine glory seen in such power that the material world dissolves into nothingness.

The doctrine of the holy sparks, it can be said in summary, had its origin in the earlier Kabbalah but was only developed in the Lurianic school, where it is connected with the whole process by which God emerges from concealment to become manifest in his creation. The Lurianic mystic reclaims the holy sparks from the domain of the *qelipot* by an ascetic mode of life and the performance of the precepts. All the details of the manifold rituals are directed toward these processes in the worlds on high. The mystical adept, thoroughly at home with the higher realms and their correspondences, has all this in mind when he engages in the task of elevation. There are the sparks from Adam's soul, which he is also required to elevate in the same process. When the task of elevation is complete, when all the holy sparks have been restored to their proper place, the Messiah will come and the world will be perfected. Among orthodox kabbalists the doctrine has continued unchanged to the present day. It found its expression, particularly, among the mystics at Bet El. Sabbatianism gave a heretical turn to the doctrine. The role of the Messiah there becomes far more central and the world of *tiqqun* has been established, Sabbatai Sevi being the promised Messiah. Even before Sabbatai's apostasy, the idea that the holy sparks may be redeemed from among the *qelipot* through a descent into their impure domain is found in Sabbatai's sinful acts, legitimized in accordance with the new theology. After Sabbatai's conversion to Islam, the idea of the "holy sin" is given further prominence by the crypto-Sabbatians. With the rise of Hasidism the doctrine again took a new turn. In this movement, much emphasis is still placed on the need to reclaim the holy sparks, but the doctrine is now pressed into the service of the *devequt* ideal with its concomitant of serving God through engagement in the world. The rescue of the holy sparks is now much more a personal and individualistic affair, and the role of the *zaddiq* in the process has become highly significant. The belief that the *tiqqunim* on high really take place is not abandoned, but there is no longer any need to dwell on the details. The *tiqqunim* take place automatically when the *hasid* is faithful to his own ideal of *devequt*. In most versions of Hasidism there is less interest in the mystical life as theosophical reflection than in direct awareness and personal experience of the divine. The holy sparks have become almost synonymous with the recognition that all is in God. The Hasidic master Moses Teitelbaum of Ujhely (1759–1841) can say that Moses at the burning bush did not see a special bush created for the purpose. He rather saw the divine vitality which burns in every bush to keep it in being.[15] This comes very close to Elizabeth Barrett Browning's words:

> Earth's crammed with heaven,
> And every common bush afire with God;
> But only he who sees, takes off his shoes,
> The rest sit round it and pick blackberries,
> And daub their natural faces unaware
> More and more from the first similitude.

Notes

1. Edwyn Bevan, *Symbolism and Belief* (London: Collins, 1962) 110–33.

2. Joseph Ergas, *Shomer Emunim* (Jerusalem, 1968) 2:11, pp. 59–61.

3. Ariel Bension, *The Zohar in Muslim and Christian Spain* (London: G. Routledge, 1932) 242–46.

4. The passage is translated from the Hebrew text in *Siddur ha-Ge' onim we-ha-Mequbbalim*, ed. M. Y. Weinstock (Jerusalem, 1970–73) 7:37.

5. On the authority of the *zaddiq*, see the treatment by A. Green in chap. 5 of this volume.

6. G. Scholem, *The Messianic Idea in Judaism*, 176–202.

7. Jacob Joseph of Polonnoye, *Toledot Ya'aqov Yosef* (Warsaw, 1881) *'emor*, p. 225.

8. Baruch of Medzhibozh, *Bozina di-Nehora*, ed. R. Margaliot (Lemberg, 1930) *ki teze*, p. 59.

9. Abraham Joshua Heschel of Apt, *Oher Yisra'el* (Jerusalem, 1962) *be-ha'alotekha*, p. 177.

10. Ze'ev Wolf, *Or ha-Me'ir* (Jerusalem, 1968) *zaw*, pp. 95d–96d.

11. Elimelech of Lizensk, *No'am Elimelekh*, ed. G. Nigal (Jerusalem, 1978) *Zettel Qatan*, vol. 2, no. 15, p. 617.

12. Mordecai Wilensky, *Hasidim u-Mitnaggedin* (Jerusalem: Bialik, 1970) p. 39 n. 20, p. 54, and elsewhere in the book.

13. Yitzhak Eisik of Komarno, *Ozar ha-Hayyim* (Lemberg, 1869) vol. 3, *qedoshim*, p. 171 b.

14. On this, see the discussion by Rachel Elior in chap. 6 of this volume.

15. Moses Teitelbaum of Ujhely, *Yismah Moshe* (Jerusalem, 1976) *noah*, vol. 1, pp. 286–29a.

Bibliography

Somewhat surprisingly there is no work devoted solely to the doctrine of the holy sparks. The doctrine is treated as part of the Lurianic scheme in Scholem, *Major Trends*, in the chapter on Isaac Luria and his school, and in Tishby. For the doctrine in Sabbatianism, see Scholem, *Sabbatai Sevi*. A number of the essays in Scholem, *Messianic Idea*, are relevant. On the doctrine in Hasidism, the chapter in Scholem, *Major Trends*, is still one of the best treatments. Jacobs, *Hasidic Thought*, contains a number of extracts, some of which are referred to in this essay, from the classical Hasidic works. The doctrine of the holy sparks in connection with the enjoyment of food is treated in Jacobs, "Eating."

Jacobs, Louis. "Eating as an Act of Worship in Hasidic Thought." In *Studies in Jewish Religious and Intellectual History: Festschrift A. Altmann*, 157–66. Edited by Siegfried Stein and Raphael Loewe. University, AL: University of Alabama Press, 1979.

——. *Hasidic Thought*. New York: Behrman House, 1976.

Scholem, Gershom. *Major Trends in Jewish Mysticism*. 3rd ed. New York: Schocken, 1954.

——. *The Messianic Idea in Judaism and Other Essays on Jewish Spirituality*. New York: Schocken, 1971.

——. *Sabbatai Sevi: The Mystical Messiah*. Princeton, NJ: Princeton University Press, 1973.

Tishby, I. *Torat ha-Ra' ve-he-qelipah be-qabbalat ha-'Ari*. Jerusalem: Akademon, 1968.

5

Typologies of Leadership and the Hasidic Ẓaddiq

Arthur Green

The Question of Leadership

No issue was more central to the emerging Hasidic communities of the late eighteenth century than that of leadership.[1] Conceived in the midst of both a Jewish community and a larger Polish society beset by crises of public office, the phenomenon that was to be called Hasidism bore at its very heart an image of master and disciples, bound together by bonds at once esoteric and personal, an image that stood out in relief against those corruptions of leadership that many had come to revile. It was in fact participation in such a relationship that defined one's sense of belonging to the Hasidic movement, at least in its heyday. For that movement the term *hasid* (unlike all of its many previous usages) implies the question: "*Hasid* of whom?" The term here functionally means "disciple" in addition to the usual and literal "pious one" or "lover of God." The disciple stood in relation to the *rebbe*, or master, a relationship that is the subject of much discussion in both the early theoretical literature of Hasidism and the later tales.[2]

The complex of ideas, distinctive religious practices, and patterns of lifestyle that were to make up the nascent movement was first taught by a generation of rabbis and preachers in the Ukraine, a group much influenced by earlier mystical (including messianic) teachings and marked by a strong sense of alienation from the contemporary leadership of the Jewish communities. That leadership is frequently caricatured in the preaching of the age, Hasidic and non-Hasidic alike. Both rabbis and lay leaders were held up to derision, the former for the twin sins of pride and self-distancing from the community, the latter for their high-handedness in the conduct of community affairs. These same homilists, especially those outside the

Hasidic camp, also viewed the common folk of their times as extraordinar-
ily sinful, a generation appropriate to, if not responsible for, its woeful
leadership. Accurate or not, it was the perception of many thinking Jews in
mid-eighteenth century Poland that they lived in the most awfully sin-
ridden of times, a time when extremes of purgation were required to return
Israel to the pious norms of old.[3]

The first published work of Hasidism, the *Toledot Ya'aqov Yosef*, is much
concerned with these questions.[4] Alternatively blaming flock and shepherds
for leading one another down the path toward sin, it is Jacob Joseph of
Polonnoye who first crystallizes the question of leadership as a central
preoccupation of Hasidic thought. Though himself a rabbi serving in
various distinguished communities,[5] he viewed himself as a disciple of one
who had no rabbinic title or ordination, a rather unusual situation in so
authority-centered a tradition as premodern Judaism. His "teacher," as he
generally calls him, Israel Ba'al Shem Tov, was a sage of a rather different
sort from the normative rabbinic figure.[6] Though sharing most of the values
of the latter, including dedication to both Torah study and life within the
tradition, the Ba'al Shem saw himself generally as a teacher of "the fear of
heaven" and spiritual wakefulness rather than of the tradition itself. The
numerous quips and epigrams that the *Toledot* quotes from him uniformly
point in this direction; he is the teacher who can *use* the language of tradition to point to a religious consciousness of a depth beyond that which the
ordinary talmudist is called upon to see.[7] Accompanying this, he has the
power to look into human souls and call forth their healing in a way that
goes beyond the stock-in-trade of the usual Ba'al Shem, purveyor of both
amulets and herbs, folk doctor, and expert on the names of God and angels.
The BeSHT as depicted in the sources is a charismatic holy man; it was this
figure (rather than the *Toledot* himself, a rather retiring scholarly type) who
was to provide the model for leadership in the new movement. While
operating wholly within the context of tradition, Hasidism was to call for
a major transformation of values: simple devotion was to be placed over
abstruse learning, the joy of service over penitential brooding, and the
rediscovery of God's all-pervasive presence over the sense of longing and
exile. The transformation was to be effected by a new sort of leader, himself
the personal embodiment of the movement's teachings. The image of this
leader is already found in the descriptions of the Ba'al Shem Tov himself
as recorded in the popular hagiographic work *Shivhey ha-BeSHT*.[8]

Hasidism must be viewed as both a religious and a social movement.[9]
Innovations in spiritual teaching or devotional practice offered by its teachers
functioned also as guideposts toward the establishment of a new community, an alternative form of social organization that stood over against the

much-troubled traditional *kahal*. Rather than owing primary loyalty to the geographically defined corporate body of Jewry, Hasidism in practice suggested that truly pious Jews might constitute themselves in disciple-groups around a particular master, these translocal loyalties to be represented in each town by a conventicle of *hasidism* who espoused a particular path.[10] These *kloizlekh* or *minyanim*, first of *hasidim* in general and later of particular Hasidic groups, would, by the very nature of things, be more closely related to one another than they would to the community at large, an institution that early Hasidism did not deem much worthy of support. Unlike earlier pietistic conventicles, these Hasidic groups saw the expansion of their own circles as an essential part of their mission. The Hasidic *minyan* in a town could not simply be left alone to worship God and glory in its master. It strove—and in the long run often successfully—to dominate the entire Jewish community, at least in matters of the spirit.

Whence the authority for such innovation? Here was, in the circles around both the BeSHT and his successor the Maggid of Miedzyrzec, a group of ready leaders with a message that was soon to show itself of tremendous power to attract a following. But in what terms might the role claimed by such figures, termed by their opponents "newcomers from nearby"[11] be legitimated? Authority to lead the community has, by all the canons of Jewish tradition, only one legitimate source: the word of God. That source, in turn, might be invoked in either of two ways, either through a claim of direct revelation of God's will or by means of the normative chain of tradition, the legitimacy of rabbinic interpretation. Neither of these, however, could the early leaders of Hasidism invoke with full force.

The Ba'al Shem Tov and others in the early circles were surely motivated, in fact, by some sense of divine call. The religion of spiritual revival that they taught is by its very nature one in which the devotee is likely to have a deep sense of personally appointed mission. The BeSHT spoke rather openly about experiences of transcendence and messages from heavenly sources: we need only refer to his well-known letter to R. Gershon of Kuty to see that this is the case. But to claim legitimacy on the basis of heavenly journeys alone was a highly dubious business. Formally speaking, prophecy had ended with the destruction of the Temple; prophetic voice had been "taken from the prophets and given" either to the sages or to "fools and children"—depending on which version of the ancient saying one chooses. Since then, again in a formal sense, we "pay no attention to heavenly voices."[12] Of course, we know that such pronouncements were often observed in the breach and that especially in the sorts of popular mystical circles from which Hasidism sprang there was always much attention paid to dreams, "ascents of the soul," and various other personal illuminations.

The real reason why authority could not be based on such claims lay much closer to home. Such dreams and "prophecies" were the stuff of which the recent and well-remembered Sabbatian claims had been made; they had a dangerous association with the very sort of mystical heresy from which Hasidism was at pains to dissociate itself.[13] While the early leadership of Hasidism fully believed in the reality of heavenly voices and angelic messengers (as did its most trenchant opponent!), it saw good reason not to locate the source of its authority in these. There were those who claimed, as we shall see later, a degree of prophetic mantle for the new movement, but this was done in a cautious and somewhat secondary way.

The normative claim to authority already belonged to the rabbinate, the very sort of rabbinate against whom Hasidism was set in opposition. No one could claim, on purely talmudic/halakhic grounds, that the rabbis loyal to Hasidism in the early days were the leading luminaries of their time. Though Hasidism was far from being the movement of the unlettered masses that later romantics made it out to be, its leadership surely was not prepared to battle the rabbinate on the latter's own turf. Those with the finest pedigrees of learning—and family—from Elijah Gaon in Vilna to Rabbi Ezekiel Landau in Prague, were known to be unsympathetic to the new movement and its leaders.

The Zaddiq

Hasidism found its way out of this dilemma by proposing another sort of claim for its leaders, one that was highly innovative in its usage here though having the needed venerable associations in the earlier history of Judaism. It was not as bearer of either revelation or tradition, but rather as zaddiq, that the Hasidic leader was to claim his mantle. His authority was of a different order, one that bypassed the controversial matter of the *word* of God and went directly to another cosmological line, one that had ever existed in Judaism side by side with the centrality of Torah, though previously always in a somewhat secondary way. The zaddiq, "righteous one" or holy man, was known to the talmudic sources as one who stood at the very center of the cosmos[14] and could, by virtue of his meritorious deeds, intervene to reverse the decrees of heaven. For such figures (often called both hasid and zaddiq in the early sources) it had always been the virtue of meritorious action rather than learning or traditional authority that had lain at the core of their powers to attract a following. The zaddiq's merit sustains the universe: what greater claim than this need be made for the leadership of a religious community? The authority of the zaddiq was not opposed to that of Torah either in earlier or in Hasidic times, but rather stood side by side with it, exemplifying another aspect of Jewish religious ideology. While not in conflict with the values of Torah, the *zaddiq*'s authority was of a different order and of different historic lineage as well. Since the Middle Ages, this ancient figure of piety and power (for the *zaddiq*'s power was said to be able to annul a divine decree) was associated with the aspect of divinity called *yesod* by the adherents of Kabbalah. *Yesod* (lit.: "foundation") is the ninth of the ten *sefirot* or aspects of the divine self, the one that gathers together all the forces from above and causes them to flow into the feminine *Shekhinah* or "Community of Israel." As such, *yesod* is identified with the male procreative organ, with the "covenant" of sexual purity, and with Joseph, the original *zaddiq* who became such by resisting Madame Potiphar's wiles. The deeds of the earthly *zaddiqim*, or kabbalists, are essential in aiding the *zaddiq* above to continue that flow of life that sustains the universe. This kabbalistic association tended to highlight the term *zaddiq* among the various appellations of the pious and probably indirectly affected the use of this term to designate the Hasidic master.

Well known and almost archetypically Hasidic is the interpretation offered in several of the movement's early sources of a talmudic passage in praise of Rabbi Hanina ben Dosa, a famous wonder-worker and *hasid* of the first century:

> The Talmud says that "a heavenly voice came forth and said: The whole earth is sustained for the sake of (*bi-shevil*) Hanina My son, but Hanina My son has to do with only a ration of carob from one Sabbath eve to the next." See the second chapter of Berakhot. A famous question is asked on this text: Why is the latter part of it needed? [Why bother to mention what Hanina ate?] I have seen an answer in the book *Yad Yosef* which says that this latter phrase offers a reason for the former: the whole world is sustained for the sake of Hanina *because* he makes do with but a ration of carob. It is because of this that his merit suffices to sustain the entire world.
>
> But in the name of my teacher: Hanina My son forged a path (*shevil*) or a pipeline to draw divine bounty into the world. This is the meaning of "the world is sustained by the *shevil* of Hanina My son." The words of the wise are gracious. To me it appears that he not only made such a pathway or pipeline, but that he himself was called *shevil* or channel, since the bounty flowed through him. This would be an esoteric reading for "Blessings to the head of the *zaddiq*" (Prov 10:6). (*Ben Porat Yosef* 80b; ed. Warsaw 1883; based on Berakhot 17b)[15]

The *Toledot* first quotes a non-Hasidic reading of the talmudic passage, one that suggests the ascetic feat as the reason for Hanina's world-sustaining merit.[16] He then offers the BeSHT's reading of the passage as a contrast, one that emphasizes the charismatic side of Hanina's deed. The question as to the latter phrase has not really been answered by the new interpretation, but the focus has been shifted: Hanina *is* the path by which the cosmos is sustained. It turns out that the BeSHT's reading too is not original; recent scholarship has shown that it is already to be found in the *Two Tablets of the Covenant*, an early seventeenth century work by Isaiah Horowitz that enjoyed immense popularity in later pietistic circles.[17] But no matter: our interest is in the *use* made of such a reading in Hasidism, not in its originality. In the Hasidic context the reading is no longer abstract: its frequent repetition serves to underscore a claim made by a known and specific group of people to be the successors of Hanina, the ẓaddiqim who will sustain the world in this time. In the following text R. Menahem Nahum of Chernobyl makes a similar claim, here referring to a talmudic parallel in which Hanina is not mentioned:

> The fact is that "ẓaddiq is the foundation of the world" (Prov 10:25). He is the foundation and the channel through which divine bounty and life flow down into the world and to all creatures. It is all by his *shevil*, for he sets out the pathway and road which this life-flow will follow. By means of his constant attachment to the Creator he becomes a dwelling for the letter Aleph, the cosmic Aleph that lives within him. Thus Scripture says: "I shall dwell in their midst" (Exod 25:8). Thus he is truly a part of God, and has a place, as it were, with Him. This is the portion of his soul, a part of the Aleph. He also has a place among created beings, however, since he shares with them the letters *Dalet Mem* (=*DaM*, blood); the animal soul is contained in his blood just as it is in all creatures. How right and proper, then, that he be the intermediary between the blessed Creator and the full world, binding all to Him so that bounty flow to His creatures along the path that he, the ẓaddiq, has set out by his devotion and attachment. Thus did the rabbis say of the verse "for this is the whole of man ('aDaM – Eccl 12:13) – the entire world is created by the *shevil* of this one." They said it in the present tense . . . for Creation is constant. "He renews each day the work of Creation." By the constant flow of His life into His creatures the act of Creation is ever taking place. This is the meaning of "this is the whole of 'aDaM – it refers to the ẓaddiq, who unites in himself Aleph with *DaM*. Constant Creation happens only through his path. . . . Thus Onkelos translated "He holds fast to heaven and earth" he binds the whole world to its Creator. . . . (*Me'or 'Eynayim, yitro;* ed. Jerusalem 1966; p. 109; quoting *Yoma* 38b)

The figure described in these texts is one familiar to the students of "holy man" traditions in the most diverse religious contexts. He is a figure at once human and mythic, a spiritualized Hercules, if you will, holding the world aloft by his own inner strength and ever renewing creation's bond to its source. Such a being, in some traditions identified with God more fully as Avatar or Incarnation, elsewhere as the prophet reborn or the first man *redivivus,* is indeed hinted at from the very earliest sources of Jewish esotericism. Elements of it are found in aggadic discussions of Abraham, Jacob,

David, Elijah, and especially Moses. He is given prominence in the medieval Kabbalah, particularly through the protomessianic figure of Rabbi Simeon ben Yohai as described in the *Zohar*.[18] In the popular religious culture of the later Middle Ages, these ancient holy-man traditions developed in two directions at once. One of these emphasizes the hidden and therefore potentially ubiquitous presence of such figures. A folk tradition reaching back to talmudic times speaks of a certain number of *hidden ẓaddiqim* (usually thirty-six) for whose sake the world is sustained. But here their anonymity is essential to the legend: not only does it protect the virtue of humility, but its very point seems to be that you never know if the stranger before you might not be such a one, and you are to treat him accordingly. The *ẓaddiq* tradition in this sense is parallel to that of Elijah, the mysterious and virtuous stranger ever in your midst.[19] Another offshoot of this tradition points to well-known individuals of the present or the recent past as possessors of the holy spirit or of some special "influence" in the upper realms. Such tales were told of many great rabbis; the veneration of holy men's graves, widely attested in Jewish popular religion at least from the later Middle Ages, is an outgrowth of belief in the dead *ẓaddiq*'s power to intervene on high for the faithful he has left behind. The *Zohar*, which is to be seen in its narrative portions as an artful usage of these popular traditions, spurs their development further. Here the two lines meet, as such well-known figures as Rabbi Simeon and his friends encounter anonymous elders, children, and donkey-drivers who turn out to be hidden saints and revealers of secrets. In the later Kabbalah as well, especially after the Safed revival, legends about the *ẓaddiqim* and their powers were widespread, some of these entering that genre of hagiography (*shevahim*) that so influenced Hasidism.[20] In the esoteric literature of the Sabbatian movement, the term is used as a cipher for the Messiah, but again in veiled ways. Other Sabbatian charismatics are referred to rather openly and daringly as prophets (*navi'*) and are frequently designated by the term *hasid*, but it appears that there *ẓaddiq* was generally reserved for the Messiah himself.[21]

The figure of the Hasidic *ẓaddiq* emerged most specifically out of the homiletical and moralistic literature of the seventeenth and eighteenth centuries, a body of writings often influenced by Sabbatianism but not wholly dependent on it. Much scholarly attention has been focused on this literature in recent times, and there is no need here to repeat, other than in brief summary, what has been said elsewhere. The homiletic literature of the age, obsessed as it was with sin and its corrosive effect on both soul and cosmos, was concerned largely with the question of penitence. The moralizing preacher, himself a penitent, to be sure, saw himself as extending a helping, even saving, hand to those who heard his sermons or read his books. The very nature of this position made him an intermediary between the sin-ridden public and the will of heaven contained in the message that he bore. This image of self held great fascination for the preachers of the age, especially insofar as they saw themselves as not living utterly beyond the temptation toward sin in their own lives. (Think of the fascination with self-image in the psychotherapeutic community of our own day and of the problematic of the therapist's own healing and its relationship to his or her abilities as a professional.) In the course of such discussions, older images were evoked of the *zaddiq* descending into hell to redeem the souls of those who suffered there: thus were the preachers depicted as rescuing their hearers from the pit of damnation that was sure to await them upon their deaths. Such a preacher was frequently a tormented figure, seeing himself as his community's last or best hope for reconciliation with God and yet at the same time ever aware of his own inadequacy to the task.[22] Though such preachers were not called *zaddiqim* and no miracles were ascribed to them, they saw themselves as linking heaven and earth, moral intermediaries between God and his people.

Speaking out of this tradition, the early teachers of Hasidism forged some essential final links. Charged with a new sense of religious optimism, they spoke against excessive brooding over one's sins and largely set aside the penitential/ascetic rigors of the earlier preachers' world view. This lessened the sense of inadequacy inherent in the leader's self-identification as *zaddiq*, or in his claim to provide the link between his people and the God whom they sought to serve. The preacher linking the sinner to God, identified already earlier with the *zaddiq* saving the souls of the wicked, could now be identified as well with another aspect of the *zaddiq*, the pillar on whom the earth is set or the forger of that *shevil* by which God's grace comes down to save the world.

The term *zaddiq*, as found in Hasidic writings of the movement's first three generations (until about 1800), by no means uniformly designates the leader of a Hasidic community. On the contrary, the term is generally used in its earlier sense—one that combines a normative notion of moral righteousness (*zaddiq* as opposed to *rasha'*) with an overtone of that mythic/mystic figure to whom we have alluded. As such, "*zaddiq*" may remain that hidden one of the folk tradition and also be a normal model toward which all should aspire. The *Toledot* belongs essentially to the earlier homiletic tradition in the ways it speaks of *zaddiq*. *Rebbe* as well as rabbi is generally designated by R. Jacob Joseph by the normative *talmid ḥakham*. In the writings of the Maggid's school, even in the very *zaddiq*-centered *No'am Elimelekh,* the term still usually has a general, or at least ambiguous, sense; the reader frequently is given the impression that he too, with the proper awareness and behavior, might reach that state. It is in that school, however, that a new dimension is added to the term *zaddiq*. In a sense, it is the preacher who now comes back to haunt the Hasidic *zaddiq*. It is somehow wrong, or at least inadequate, for the righteous one to live alone in his righteousness, even if that righteousness bears the merit that sustains the world. A new typology is developed in these writings (though it too has earlier precedents),[23] one that pits the *zaddiq* "who is only for himself" against the one who serves as "*zaddiq* for himself and for others."

"The *zaddiq* blossoms like a palm tree, tall as a cedar in Lebanon" (Ps 92:1). There are two types of *zaddiqim*, both of them completely righteous. The difference between them is as follows: One is ever attached to God, blessed be He, doing the task that has been placed upon him. He is the *zaddiq* only for himself, but for no other. He does not cause his righteousness to flow forth to others. Thus he is compared to the cedar which, as our sages noted, does not bear fruit. He is a *zaddiq* only within himself, not bearing the fruit of bringing others back to the good, so that *zaddiqim* might multiply in the world. This one does only for himself, reaching high and adding to his reward. The second *zaddiq* is rather likened to the palm tree, one that bears fruit or "blossoms." He brings forth the precious from the cheap, causing good to blossom and increase in the world. Of this our sages spoke when they said: "In the place where penitents (*ba'aley teshuvah*, lit., 'masters of penitence') stand, absolute *zaddiqim* cannot stand." They meant to speak of the second *zaddiq*, the one who is called 'master of penitence,' for he is master and lord over repentance as he brings others back to the good. "He brings many back from sin" (Mal 2:6) as he makes for penitence in the world. Surely his reward is greatly redoubled over that of the first *zaddiq*, even though he too is completely righteous. (Dov Baer, *Or Torah*, Psalms; ed. Jerusalem 1968, p. 119)[24]

"But My servant Caleb, because he was of another spirit, and he followed Me wholly" (Num 14:24). There are two kinds of *zaddiqim*. There are some who need to be set aside and separated from people, for when they are among people [or: in public situations] they might fall from their proper rung. Then there are *zaddiqim* who mingle pleasantly among people and converse with them, not falling from their own rung and in fact bringing others back to the good. Thus have I heard from my master and teacher ... Dov Baer ... "Holy flesh has never turned rotten" (Avot 5:5)—he interpreted as "whoever is holy flesh" —a complete *zaddiq*— "never rots, even when he is among people and speaks with them." This is "My servant Caleb, because he was of another spirit" —even when speaking with them, but did not fall from his rung, "he followed Me wholly." (*No'am Elimelech, shelah*; ed. Nig'al, pp. 403f.)[25]

Many elements of the tradition have converged in the making of these statements. The ancient belief that the *zaddiq* sustains the "world" is now given a social context; it is the very particular "*oilem*," in the Yiddish usage, of his community that he sustains and justifies before God, as well as the cosmos as a whole. As heir to the *mokhiaḥ* of the immediately preceding generations he is teacher and spiritual healer, binding himself to God and humanity and holding them together. But as heir to the talmudic *ẓaddiq* he is also supernatural intercessor: his merit bears within it the power to negate the divine decree. The responsibility of bearing such power calls forth in him a quality antithetical to that usually found in the psyche of moralizing preachers: like the prophets of old, he becomes *defender* of Israel as they are judged by God. The intense devotion of the *ḥasid* to his master stems in part from the confidence that this master, who has high standing in the heavenly realms because of his own righteousness or that of his ancestors, stands ready to sacrifice all for the sake of his disciples. In psychological terms it may be said that the *rebbe* is thus a true father figure, both in embodying the values of tradition and in his willingness without limit to defend his "children" either from divine judgment or demonic threat.

So much for the hidden *ẓaddiq*. If he is to help others along the path, it becomes fully legitimate for him to reveal himself to them. True, it is theoretically possible to combine both virtues: to keep one's own constant attachment to God a secret and, posing as a poor sinner among others, to preach the word of God to them. But if the preacher/*ẓaddiq*'s work is to be done effectively, better that he discard his mask and set himself to the social and religious task in earnest. For *ẓaddiq* to serve a social function, as leader and rallying point for a spiritual community, he must also be identified. There thus emerges in Hasidism a remarkable group of religious teachers and charismatic figures who are identified by their followers and (though only obliquely) by themselves as *ẓaddiqim*. The meaning attributed to this term here and in later common speech—*ẓaddiq* as leader of a community of *ḥasidim*—is entirely original to Hasidism.

The Search for Paradigms

The preoccupation with leadership brought about in Hasidism a new reading of the earlier tradition, one in which diverse sources were combed for the light they could shed on the question of *ẓaddiq* and his relationship to community. Precisely because the term did not have a tradition of public leadership associated with it, models of leadership that would serve as paradigms for his proper role were to be sought elsewhere. It is not surprising that, for a community in which preaching took so central a role, it was to Scripture that Hasidic authors most frequently turned for guidance in the ways of proper leadership. In fact, the writings of more immediately past generations had rather little to offer on this question that had now become so crucial. It is hard to find postbiblical, or at least post-talmudic, sources in which the nature of proper leadership is a central topic of Jewish intellectual concern. In the medieval and later communities, proper leaders for the Jewish community were judged by standards essentially extrinsic to the question of leadership itself. The most defined leader role was that of rabbi. The rabbi, however, was trained and evaluated primarily in relationship to Torah; his "pastoral" skills were quite secondary to his learning and mastery of talmudic law. The *hasid* of medieval Germany and later Safed was such by virtue of his extraordinary acts of piety. While these frequently had to do with the realm of the interpersonal, they did not necessarily show the skills and responsibilities appropriate to leadership. On the contrary, the humility appropriate to such an ideal type might well keep him from seeking out such a role. Communal lay leaders were judged for honesty, in accord with the rigorous standards of the talmudic civil code. It was taken for granted, apparently, that such virtues as learning, piety, and integrity would make for fitting leadership. These were, after all, the values that the community was to hold in high regard, and they could best be supported if exemplified in its leaders. Such barely self-conscious notions of leadership seem to have generally sufficed, despite periodic complaints and reports of abuses.

If later Jewish history was lacking in treatments of this leader theme, however, the pages of Scripture itself were a virtual textbook on the question. From Moses and Aaron in the wilderness to David in battle and the prophets of calamity and consolation in Jerusalem and in exile, the Bible is filled with concern over the issue of proper and responsible leadership and the relationship between God's people and those He has appointed to minister to them. The three figures of prophet, priest, and king immediately come to mind; the proper role of each of these three and the not infrequent clashes between them bespeak the very essence of ancient Israel's unique religious situation.

The same is true, though to a lesser extent, of late Second Temple and early rabbinic times. There too were new religious leader-ideals in the making, not least because all three of the biblical models had run their course. Once prophecy was deemed at an end, it was only the interpretive authority of scribe or sage that could claim access to the divine word. Kingship and priesthood were identified wholly with the houses of David and Aaron, respectively, the one consigned to the messianic future and the other, much discredited after Hasmonean times, about to become vestigial with the Temple's destruction. The new types that emerged in their stead, the scholar/sage and the wonderworking *hasid*, were both reflections of types to be found elsewhere in the Hellenistic world. The unceasing attempts of the Midrash to convert Moses into rabbi and David into leader of the Sanhedrin reflect a pseudohistory that seeks to legitimate the rabbi by proclaiming him a biblical type.[26] The *ḥasid* had a greater chance of identifying with such a model of Elijah or Elisha, but he too was essentially a creation of the new era, searching the tradition for ancestors of his spirit.

A similar process now took place in Hasidism, an age of renewed creativity in leadership types, again born of the collapse of previously available models. And again the earlier tradition is combed in search of precedent or archetype with whom the present leader might identify. All of the biblical models—priest, king, prophet, as well as the rabbinic *ḥasid* and sage—are to be found in early BeSHTian Hasidism's descriptions of its *zaddiq*. The wide range of earlier models accessible to Hasidic preachers gives to their discussions of *zaddiq* a rich and varied texture. The interplay between the literary figures of these texts and the actual social institution is a complex one: the theoretical literature of Hasidism (almost all of it, we must remember, originally delivered as oral sermons)[27] both reflected and created the *zaddiq* as a living figure. Here as in other areas we see a dialectical relationship between Hasidic theory and social form. In examining the various models to which the literature appeals, we seek to cast our net wide and examine such paradigms of leadership as they are found throughout the writings of early Hasidism, not limited to any single author or school. We should at the same time note, however, that here as in most things it is the *Toledot* and the Maggid who appear as "original" sources, upon whom most other Hasidic preachers draw.

The *Zaddiq* as Priest

The figure of priest is very widespread in Hasidic discussions of the *zaddiq*. It is hard to find a collection of Hasidic homilies arranged according to the weekly Torah-reading cycle that does not, somewhere in Exodus or Leviticus, apply biblical mention of the *kohen* to the leader of its own day. In one place the *zaddiq*/priest may be offering the inward sacrifice on the altar of the heart; elsewhere he may be robed in the spiritual equivalent of the priestly garments, purifying the defiled of soul, or calling forth the divine bounty by the power of his blessing. All of these are priestly functions which go to the very heart of the *zaddiq*'s function in the Hasidic community. The following source, an unusually extended treatment of this subject, takes the form of a running comment on the opening Mishnah of *Berakhot* and a portion of the Gemara's discussion of it. We shall be well advised (unlike the original) to begin by quoting those talmudic texts in full:

> Mishnah: From what time does one recite the *Shemaʿ* in the evening? From the hour the priests come in to eat of their heave-offering, until the end of

the first watch. These are the words of Rabbi Eliezer. But the sages say: until midnight.

Gemara: From when do the priests eat of the heave-offering? From the time when the stars come out. Then teach [that *Shema'* be recited] from when the stars come out! We are being taught something by the way [in the present formulation, namely] that the priests eat of the heave-offering from the time the stars come out.

Comment: This is the meaning of "From when does one recite the *Shema'* in the evening": When will we be able to call out to God so that He will hear all our prayers, "in the evening," in this bitter exile which is the dark of night? "From the hour when the priests come in to eat of their *TeRuMaH* (heave-offering)." The priests are the *zaddiqim;* they draw forth holiness and *devequt.* "Their *TeRuMaH* refers to the raising up of the shekhinah, *TaRuM He*" [Uplift the letter *He,* = shekhina]. This is their "eating," as is said of Abraham "He stood over them beneath the tree and they ate" (Gen 18:8). Torah was not given to the angels: when they came to Abraham they heard words of Torah, the Tree of Life, from his mouth. The holiness they drew forth in this manner was their "eating." The Gemara asks on this: "From what time do the priests eat of the heave-offering? From the time when the stars come out." When will this level be attained, that from which such holiness and *devequt* can be drawn forth? "When the stars come out" —when our righteous messiah arrives, as in "a star courses forth from Jacob" (Num 24:17). . . . "Then teach: From when the stars come out," for the "priests" will "eat" at the same time that the "stars" appear! The Gemara answers that the text "taught us something by the way": the Tanna teaches us that in walking "by the way" of God's path and His holy Torah, by following in the paths of the *zaddiqim,* one can attain to great holiness, even to the holy spirit, now too, in the exile. (*No'am Elimelech, wa-yiggash;* ed. Nig'al, pp. 139f.)

The *zaddiqim* are today's priests, "eating" of holiness as the Temple priests ate of the heave offering. It is interesting that the spiritualization of the sacrifice suggested in this comment brings together *zaddiqim* and angels, both of them (though for different reasons) unable to partake of the offering in its corporeal form. At the same time, here even the supposedly most *zaddiq*-centered *No'am Elimelech* insists that such a path is open to anyone who follows it and that its rewards may even include attainment of the holy spirit, a degree of prophetic revelation. This is typical of the early literature of Hasidism, where the identification of *zaddiq* with a specified elite has not yet become clear. In the following passage, his identity as leader is clearer, though it has to be reinforced by joining the "new" term to a more conventional one (*ha-zaddiqim ha-hakhamim*).

"The Lord spoke to Moses saying: 'Command Aaron and his sons thus. This is the teaching concerning the burnt offering ('*olah*): it is that which ascends on its firewood all the night until morning . .' (Lev 6:1–2)."

RaSHI comments that "command" implies urgency, both immediate and for later generations. . . . Now surely the Torah is eternal and applies in each generation. These holy Scriptures (in my humble opinion) show the way of God to the wise righteous ones (*ha-zaddiqim ha-hakhamim*), the way to draw the souls of oppressed Israel (God save us!) to the blessed and exalted God. This was the deed of Aaron and his sons as well, as they offered the sacrifices of Israel, sin and guilt offerings or wholly burnt sacrifices, each as appropriate to him and in accord with his own needs. In doing so they would uplift and draw near the souls of Israel, each according to his needs and character. In this way is the passage one of "urgency, both immediate and for later generations" — even though there are no sacrifices in these times, the *zaddiqim* of each generation draw near [to God] the souls of Israel by means of their pure worship and the teachings (*torah*) they offer in truth and wholeness, with inner direction of the heart and in fear and love [of God]. Thus Scripture afterwards says: *zot torat ha-'olah* (lit., this is the teaching concerning the burnt offering) *hi ha-'olah* [i.e., it is the teaching that ascends as an offering]. (*Degel Mahaneh Ephraim, zaw*; ed. Jerusalem 1963, p. 152a)[28]

Such passages from the homiletic sources are reminiscent of the tale later told of Abraham Joshua Heschel of Apt, who so clearly "recalled" his prior incarnation as high priest in the Temple that he was drawn to reciting the Yom Kippur account of that service in the first person: "Thus did I count . . ." and so forth.

The image of prayer or inward devotion as a spiritual sacrifice is an ancient one, originating in the earliest Jewish sources[29] and a favorite of Jewish moralists throughout the ages. But the notion that there is an *officiant* at such sacrifice, be he called *zaddiq, hakham,* or any other name, is new in Hasidism. He is the one through whom, in some readings, such devotion must be directed to reach its source; for others he is the instructor in this cult of the inner temple or the model of its ideal fulfillment. All these have to do with the essential model we have already seen, that of *zaddiq* as source of blessing or as channel for the flow of divine life into the world. He draws Israel near to God as he draws divine blessing down to his people. Although such descriptions do not accompany the delineations of priestly function in the biblical text itself, which are deliberately this-worldly, there is, in a broader sense, something priestly about them — a sense that the Hasidic authors (greatly aided by the *Zohar's* freely mythic depictions of the cult)[30] have no difficulty in perceiving.

Another area in which priesthood is important in the *zaddiq's* image has to do with healing, again relating to his position as the arouser of God's mercies and the bearer of His life-flow into the world. In functional terms, a major part of the *zaddiq's* role in Hasidic society was that of healer; it was particularly in times of illness or medically dangerous situations such as childbirth that disciples—and other ordinary folk—came to seek out the *zaddiq's* blessing. Here he was acting as a priestly holy man, in a way that probably would have been quite familiar to the Orthodox clergy just across the town square. Quite naturally, it is in homilies on the Torah portions *tazriy'a* and *mezora'*, ever the bane of Jewish preachers' lives, that one is likely to find comments on the *zaddiq* in the role of priestly healer.

> "The priest will go outside the camp and see that the leprous sore has healed from the leper" (Lev 14:3). "From the leper" appears to be redundant. It seems, however, that the *zaddiq* has to come to the lower rungs in order to raise up souls from there. Those souls who desire to cleave to him he will be able to raise up with him, but not so with those that do not want to attach themselves to him. . . . "The priest will go outside the camp" — coming to the lower rungs, to raise up the "leper." The priest "sees" — he draws forth wisdom, which is identical to "sight" and allows for transformation. "And the leprous sore has healed" — but Scripture adds "from the leper" for the will to cleave to the priest must come from the leper himself. Only then can the priest raise him up to wisdom, effecting that transformation which cures his sore. (*Orah le-Hayyim, mezora'*; ed. Jerusalem 1960, p. 238)

> "When a man has in his skin . . . a leprous sore, he shall be brought to Aaron the priest or to one of his sons the priests, and the priest shall look at the sore . . . and if the hair in the sore be turned white or the sore appears to be deeper than the skin, it is leprosy. The priest shall look at it and proclaim him unclean" (Lev 13:2–3). The letters of *NeGa'* ("sore") are the same as those of *'oNeG* ("joy"); if one does not take care, however, this sore becomes "leprous." Scripture then speaks of what one should do to set one's deeds aright. *He shall be brought to the priest*—the perfect *zaddiq* is called a *priest;* he should attach himself to the *zaddiqim. The priest shall look . . . and if the hair in the sore be turned white*—the *zaddiq* must see the condition of the sore. He must determine whether the white divine fluid [of compassion] has been turned "by a hair," by one of those minor sins which are like "mountains hanging by a hair" or whether the *sore appears to be deeper than the skin,* the affliction, heaven forfend, be more than skin-deep. In either case, it is a *leprous sore; the priest shall look at it and proclaim him unclean;* he must show him to understand the great damage he has wrought in all this, teaching him the ways of return and true penitence so that he make good all those bad and shameful qualities that he bears. (*No'am Elimelech, tazri'a;* ed. Nig'al, p. 309)[31]

The powers of priesthood, including the ability to bless, to heal by the conferral of divine blessing, and to discern—intuitively or by secret sign—the "clean" from the "unclean" in the moral domain, have now all been "naturally" assumed by the *zaddiq.* The use of exegesis as an instrument of social change is particularly striking in these passages. This identification with the ancient priest allows the *rebbe* to assert the sort of claim that had been defined as outside the purview of the "normative" rabbinate for many centuries. The charismatic leader has now found a locus of authority more venerable, certainly more mysterious, than that of the rabbi himself. Priest-hood (a religious institution in full vigor among the surrounding Eastern Orthodox population), with all its mysterious power to bless and transform, was a notion that called forth memories of ancient grandeur but was now represented, in the persons of *kohanim*, by only a pitiable vestige. The *zaddiq* as priest—even a priest who could arouse a degree of awe among non-Jews—was for the *hasid* a living religious symbol that combined grandeur, the warmth of pastoral care, and true magic.

The *Zaddiq* as King

Although the priesthood continued to exist in Israel, if only in vestigial form, the figure of king was one that had long been relegated to historical memory. Royal imagery continued to exist in postexilic Judaism only with regard to the kingship of God, expressed mostly in a liturgical context. The figure of king remained alive, however, partly through this sacred usage and partly because of the influence of the surrounding culture: Hasidism was created in a period when the doings of kings and their courts were very much present in the public mind, from the failure and dissolution of the Polish kingdom to the awesome pomp of the Romanovs and, if one includes the opening decades of the nineteenth century, through the period of Napoleonic adventure and the restoration of royal legitimacy. No wonder that a tradition in search of authority would seek to partake of the symbols of royalty, indicating power and legitimacy at once.

There were various aids in the sources of tradition that made this usage, audacious on the face of things, somewhat more accessible. While the widely quoted "*Man malkhey? Rabbanan*" ("Who are kings? The rabbis") does not seem to be an authentic quotation from the Talmud, the gist of the idea that rabbis have quasi-royal authority is to be found.[32] In recounting the power of true *zaddiqim* to affect the will of heaven, God himself is quoted by one well-known rabbinic source as saying: "Who rules over Me? The *zaddiq*, for I issue a decree and he nullifies it" (*Mo'ed Qatan* 16b). It was also considered perfectly proper, in the formal Hebrew of the Middle Ages and later, to speak of a rabbi in terms echoing those of royalty. Thus, a chronicler telling of a rabbi's tenure in a particular town might readily say, "His reign began in year so-and-so, and he occupied the rabbinic throne, judging the people in equity. . . ."

The Hasidic sources use this metaphor in their own way, again rather casually allowing the homiletic mode to carry over "naturally" the earlier image into their own circumstances.

"Set a king over yourself, as the Lord your God chooses. From among your brethren take a king. . . . As he sits upon his throne he shall write out this second Torah in a book, before the Levitical priests" (Deut 17:15, 18). RaSHI comments on "this second Torah" that the king is to write two Torah scrolls, one to remain in his treasury and the other to be carried with him to and fro. This comment, the original source of which is in the Talmud (*Sanhedrin* 21b), makes no sense. Of what value to him is the scroll that just lies in his treasury?

We know, however, the statement "Who are kings? The rabbis." The sages are truly kings, as Scripture says: "Through me [wisdom or Torah] do kings rule" (Prov 8:15). But the fact is that even if a person learn the whole Torah and all the holy volumes and teachings of the sages, this still will not bring him to repentance or remove the curtain that separates him from God, not until he cleaves to God's holy ones, the *zaddiqim* of the generation. Thus have I heard from my master and teacher, the man of God Elimelech, of blessed and sainted memory; a person must choose one *zaddiq* in his generation to be his master. And who is the one he should choose as master, teacher, and intimate? When he sees a *zaddiq* all of whose comings and goings are conducted in accord with the holy Torah, who is lax neither in the Torah's own commands nor in matters ordained by the rabbis, while in his heart there burns a pillar of fire as he performs the unifications, this thought being visible in his deeds—such a one should he choose as master.

This is the meaning of "set a king over yourself"; "king" here refers to rabbis. "As the Lord your God chooses"—whom should you choose? Scripture goes on to answer this by the words "he shall write this second Torah," according to RaSHI's interpretation. He should have two scrolls, the one that is "carried with him to and fro" refers to the justice of his deeds and the way he conducts himself. The "treasury" in which the other scroll remains refers to his heart, burning with the fire of Torah, proclaiming God's unity in love and fear. Such a "king" whose thought is to be seen also in his deeds, is the one whom you should choose. All this belongs to that *zaddiq* as tradition received from those sublime holy men who were his own masters; these are the "levitical priests" of whom the verse speaks. (*Ma' or wa-Shemesh, shofetim*; ed. Tel. Aviv 1964, pp. 219d–220a)[33]

To this rather typical set of criteria for choosing a *rebbe*, we may add a Hasidic insistence on the *need* for a relationship that bears this kingship within it; the *hasid* cannot exist in purely egalitarian circumstances.

"From among your brethren take a king" (Deut 17:15). The sages add that his fear should be upon you. Now it sometimes happens that you meet a man who treats you as his friend and equal, acting as though you were two brothers, with no difference of rank. In fact, however, this person stands on a higher rung [of spiritual attainment] than you, and it would be fitting for him to hold the ruler's sceptre over you. It is because he is so humble that he sees himself as being just like you, relating to you as brother and equal. Of this situation I warn you: "From among your *brothers* take a king." Even if he acts as though he were just your brother, you must make him king, until his fear is upon you like the fear of the kingdom. Now this can be a terrific struggle, that of taking one who is acting as brother and making him into awesome king. That is why Scripture chose the word *mi-qerev* ("from among") for use in this verse; Q-R-V also refers to battle. Enough said. (*Ahavat Shalom, shofetim;* ed. Lvov 1850, p. 76a)[34]

There are other places in the literature where the specific language of royalty is avoided but where something of the king–subject relationship is bespoken nonetheless. In HaBaD circles the term *nasi'*, or prince, was chosen to refer to the *rebbe,* and these sources will speak of a particular event as having taken place during the *nesi'ut* of one occupant or another of that dynastic throne. Approbations and introductions to books, hotbeds of hyperbole in any case, will commonly contain some element of regal language. Appropriation of a degree of royal style happened rather early in the history of Hasidism and was quite widespread. It was Baruch of Miedzhybozh (ca. 1750–1812), the BeSHT's grandson, and Mordecai of Chernobyl (1770–1837), who first established "courts" in which it was expected that the *rebbe* live in grand manner. Already in 1798 the bitter anti-Hasidic polemicist David of Makarov described the Hasidic masters as "seated each upon his throne, with royal crowns on their heads."[35] This and other anti-Hasidic descriptions, including those of Abraham Baer Gottlober, while poisoned with a hatred of their subject, surely have some basis on which to build their mockeries, or else their claims would have been of little power. The very notion of inherited dynasty, the right to authority in the Hasidic community by virtue of birth, smacked of royalism. This claim, loudly proferred by Baruch of Miedzhybozh in justifying his prerogative over against those of all his rivals, became normative early on in Hasidism's history. By the second decade of the nineteenth century most Hasidic communities were led by sons or grandsons of the original group around the BeSHT and the Maggid.

Chief heir to the royal lifestyle of the earlier Ukrainian courts was Israel of Ruzhyn (1796–1850), great-grandson of the Maggid. The luxury in which he and his household lived was legendary and aroused opposition both within and without the Hasidic community. Accompanying the life of pomp and great wealth in the Ruzhyner's "court" was a trumpeting of the claim of Davidic descent that had been a tradition in the Maggid's family. Here the style and traditional symbols of kingship came together, and the evocation of royal language in description of the Hasidic master would forever afterward call forth the image of this most controversial figure. Of course Ruzhyn and its defenders had a series of responses to all the charges laid against them, including the assertion that the *rebbe* derived no pleasure from the great wealth and power that were amassed in his hands, or that his grand manner of living was but a ruse to keep the accuser from discovering his true humility.

"He is the trustee over all My household" (Num 12:7). The *zaddiq* is a channel of flow. A pipeline, through which water is to be carried, must be kept clean, no mud or refuse from within the water being allowed to stick to it. If mud does accumulate within the pipe, the water will cease its flow. So it is with the *zaddiq:* he has to keep himself from enjoying any benefit from that which flows through his pipeline. He concerns himself with all these worldly matters but profits from them not at all. Thus he becomes "the trustee over all My household." All of the rich man's fortune passes through the hands of the trustee, but he takes not a cent of his master's hoard. That is why he is so trusted. The *zaddiq* is like Moses [of whom Scripture here speaks] in his own generation: all matters of this world pass through his hands, but he derives no benefit from them.[36]

Such a defense is, to say the least, difficult to document, and Rabbi Hayyim of Sanz spoke for many, both *hasidim* and *maskilim,* when he declared "war" on the Ruzhyn-Sadegora dynasty and its way of life.

But the utility and positive value of the royal claim should not be dismissed too quickly. One still can sense even in those groups that stood far from Ruzhyn and its abuses a measure of royalty in the way *rebbes* of contemporary Hasidic courts conduct themselves and in the manner of the *hasidim* when in their presence. If description in royal terms had served to strengthen the claims made for Hasidic leadership, it also supplied to that leadership the texture of pastoral concern and deeply personal *noblesse oblige* that it sought. Jewish images of sacred kingship, we should recall, had long been colored with the sort of compassionate and warm hues that typify the aggadic descriptions of God's loving relationship with His children, the house of Israel. The sense of Israel as "children of the King" was underscored in Hasidism, where the disciple could also feel himself belonging to the "palace" of a beloved earthly father figure who was revered in the royal manner. "The greatest evil," according to an old Hasidic saying attributed to R. Aaron of Karlin, "is when the King's son forgets who he is." The sharp contrasts between the loving descriptions of God's kingship that filled Jewish literature and the harsh and frightening earthly kingship of the nations as it related to its Jewish subjects were mitigated for the *hasid* by the presence of holy royalty, or at least a representative of God's kingship on earth—a psychological factor that should by no means be dismissed. The *rebbe's tisch* or Sabbath meal table, usually the setting where Hasidic teachings were offered, typifies a peculiar combination of priestly and royal elements. That table was, for the *hasid,* a true altar; *shulhan domeh la-mizbeah* ("the table is like an altar") in Hasidism came to bear particular reference to this holy table. Here was the earthly priest performing the mysterious sacraments of which all would take part. This table is at the same time that of a great Polish lord, one at which he and his men joined in feasting and singing. In that "palace," as it is frequently described by visitors and later writers, the *hasid* could forget for a while his Jewish disenfranchisement from the world of royalty and pomp. He was indeed seated at the earthly embodiment of the *shulḥan shel ma'alah*, at once the heavenly table, at which the divine king partook of spiritual repast with the souls of the righteous, and the sacred altar of the ideal temple.

The Ẓaddiq as Prophet

We have already indicated that the third type of biblical leader, the prophet, could be invoked by Hasidism only with some difficulty. It would seem at first glance that this should be the most accessible of the models for post-biblical Jews: one need claim neither Davidic nor Aaronic lineage to be a prophet. But the discrediting of prophecy in the age of apocalypse, the association of further claims to revelation with faiths that established themselves as being other than Judaism, and the defined and closed canon of scriptural authority all led Judaism, at least formally, to declare that it was done with prophecy. "Better sage than prophet" counsels one rabbinic saying (*Baba Batra* 12a)[37], and another, in a legal context: "We pay no attention to heavenly voices." This rather rigid and monolithic view of the Jewish tradition, although important in establishing the rule of law in the post-biblical Jewish community, has been shown to be lacking as a complete description of Jewish spiritual activity for almost every period of Jewish history. Something like the religion of apocalypse continued to thrive among the early rabbis despite their formal rejection of "prophecy" in their time. A historical line may be traced from near-prophetic apocalypse into the heavenly "voyaging" that took the form preserved in the sources of *merkavah* literature.[38] These later journeys lack prophetic message, to be sure, but they contain elements that clearly link them to prophetic vision on the one hand and rabbinic aggadah and liturgy on the other. Medieval Jewry, even before the emergence of Kabbalah, was dotted occasionally with various figures who claimed one degree or another of direct access to heavenly truth. The term "prophet" was mostly (though not universally) taboo, but there were "lesser" and more legitimate sources of revelation that could be claimed: the "holy spirit," the "revelation of Elijah," prophetic dreams, and so forth.[39] From the thirteenth century, these were very much in vogue among writers of the kabbalistic tradition, including some who provided actual instructions for the attainment of the holy spirit. This is especially true of that school within medieval and later Jewish mysticism known as "prophetic kabbalah." Recent historical research has shown that this strand of mystical praxis, long intentionally hidden by the self-censorship of the mystics and the reluctance of printers, played a major role in the new growth of Kabbalah in the sixteenth century and had not a little influence on certain aspects of Hasidism. In these sources, most of which are preserved only in manuscript, the prophetic claim is made quite openly.[40]

The revival of prophecy that both heralded and characterized the Sabbatian movement, highly reminiscent of that which accompanied the early church, was both culmination and negation of all the above. Here the would-be prophets violated the tradition's univocal definition of prophetic legitimacy: they spoke against the law, favoring abrogation of the commandments, at first selectively and later *en masse*. The radical wing of the Sabbatian movement, that which represented conversion to Islam in the Ottoman lands and gave birth to the well-remembered and much-hated Frankist sect in Poland, had made ample use of the charismatic vehicle, a use that could not but bring such phenomena into disrepute for the much more conservative Hasidic circles. For all their brashness in tone, even the most outspoken of the Hasidic leaders sought to maintain a position within the general Jewish community, and to answer their critics and persecutors within the theological language that both held in common.

Nevertheless, there is talk of prophetic revelation in some Hasidic circles; certainly the possibility of attaining prophetic states in our day is not denied. Well known is the claim of the Maggid that prophecy might in fact be *more* easily attainable to us than it was in the days of the Temple, a claim that stands in direct, if gentle, contradiction to the rabbinic sources quoted earlier. When the king is on the road, says the Maggid, he is more easily approachable for a commoner than when he is protected by all the royal claptrap of his life in the capital. So is it easier to attain to the "holy spirit" in our own day than it was in the times of the prophets, who required "oaths and periods of aloneness" before the spirit would come upon them (*No'am Elimelech, wa-yeshev;* ed. Nig'al, pp. 109f.)[41] Such a distinction makes it clear that the Maggid lives in a world where possession by the holy spirit is a not-uncommon occurrence and one that does not require a great deal of rigorous preparation.

Of the Maggid's circle, it was particularly the well-known preacher Wolf of Zhitomir who nurtured this openness to prophetic experience. In his *Or ha-Me'ir,* one of the longer and more profound collections of Hasidic homilies, the distinction between mystical religion and prophecy seems to break down altogether. The true *ḥasid* in the intensity of his prayers as well as the *zaddiq* while preaching can reach a state in which "the *shekhinah* speaks from within his mouth."[42] In these discussions, it is the act of prophetic inspiration that interests the Hasidic authors rather than the figure of the prophet himself. There are passages, however, in which it is precisely on prophetic authority that the Hasidic leader draws, despite all the difficulties inherent in such a usage. In the homilies this claim will typically take the form of identification with Moses, sometimes also making for the association of those who oppose the *zaddiq* with the classic enemies of prophetic authority. In the following passage R. Benjamin of Zalozhtsy proceeds from a discussion of Korah's rebellion against the seemingly arbitrary character of purification through the ritual of the red heifer:

> In our generation as well we may see one who serves God in great love, pure of body and whole of mind, worshipping by means of some form that no one else can understand. . . . The *zaddiq* is like Moses; he is "mind" [*da'at*] as Moses was the mind of all Israel. Whoever opposes him is like Korah. This is why the rabbis asked "What did Korah see . . ." meaning "What does the one who is like Korah see in the *zaddiq* who is like Moses [that leads him to rebel]?" They answered: "He saw the red heifer," meaning that he saw some practice he could not comprehend. But just as in the case of the red heifer, the one who is "mind" understands its meaning, and only to others is it [an incomprehensible] statute. (*Torey Zahav, qorah* 83d–84a)

This identification of the *zaddiq* with Moses as the collective mind of Israel also places him in a kabbalistic realm significantly beyond that which is ordinarily claimed. Here the *zaddiq* has "risen" from association with *yesod*, the ninth in the sefirotic decade, to *da'at*, third by the usual Hasidic count. The authority of such a figure is indeed absolute, for he "knows" by a connection to the inward roots of knowledge that which others may never hope to comprehend. No wonder then that the enemies of such a figure can be identified with the classic rebel of the Mosaic tale, long seen by rabbinic tradition as one who had refused to accept Moses' divinely authorized interpretation of the law.

There was yet another aspect of the prophetic role, specifically that of Moses, that was assigned to the *zaddiq:* the role of intercessor or defender of Israel before the divine throne. Although the term "prophet" is not used in the Hasidic sources that discuss this function, the model is clearly that of Moses standing before God following the incident of the golden calf, pleading with, cajoling, and demanding of God that He not destroy His people. This ability to argue with God and to demand of Him a standard of justice or loyalty to His covenant higher than that which appears to rule in His world is a central part of the prophetic legacy. Abraham at Sodom and Moses on Sinai serve as models for a rule assumed both by biblical prophet and by later *zaddiq* or *hasid*. This sense of the ability to speak frankly and harshly to God (*le-hatiah devarim kelapey ma'alah*)[43] and to achieve the desired end of course again depends on the righteousness, courage, and utter unselfishness of the one who does so. In this it is not entirely separable in the mind of the tradition from the power of *zaddiqim* to nullify the divine decree, though here the distance from magic is even greater.

We shall not deal further here with the influence of the rabbinic/medieval figures of *hasid* and *zaddiq* on the *zaddiq* of BeSHTian Hasidism. These, along with their development through the twin channels of Safed and ongoing Ashkenazic folk pietism, formed the basis for the newly emerging leader, to which all the biblical imagery of which we have spoken was added. The collections of Hasidic tales frequently contain accounts of miracles wrought by such early *zaddiq* types, bearing testimony to the fact that their intended readers saw a continuity between the *zaddiqim* or *hasidim* of prior ages and those who followed the path of the Ba'al Shem Tov.

The *Zaddiq* as Rabbi

Perhaps the strangest employment of an earlier leadership model among the *hasidim* was that of conventional rabbi: *zaddiq* in the garb of *talmid hakham*. Here the very form that had been seen as abused and debased in the times of Hasidism's origin, and the office of those who in so many cases led the opposition to the new movement, is itself claimed as the mantle of the Hasidic leaders. We must be particularly cautious here, because of the misleading possibilities of terminological confusion. In the writings of the *Toledot* and some others, as we have noted, the emerging Hasidic leader is in fact regularly referred to as *talmid hakham,* the *true* scholar/sage as distinct from those who had let this mantle become soiled. Such passages cannot really be used to claim the use of rabbinic justification for the *zaddiq*. But there are others where the matter goes beyond that of terms.

> It is known that the written Torah and the oral Torah are all one, not to be separated from one another at all. Neither can in fact exist without the other; the secrets of the written Torah are revealed only through the oral, without which it would be but half a book. In interpreting the Torah and revealing its secrets, the sages at times even uprooted something from the text, as in the case of the prescribed forty lashes for punishment, of which they permitted only thirty-nine. All this they did by the power of the Holy Spirit that appeared in their midst, so that the very wholeness of the written Torah depends upon the oral tradition. That is why "he who says that a certain inference [as derived by the rabbis] is not from the Torah" or that "a single statement of the rabbis" is not Torah, is as one who denied the Torah of Moses our Teacher. Everything depends upon the interpretation of the rabbis. . . .

Until they had interpreted it, the Torah was not considered complete, but only half-finished; it was the rabbis, through their interpretations, who made the Torah whole. *Such is the case for each generation and its leaders; they complete the Torah. The Torah is interpreted in each generation according to that generation's needs, and according to the soul-root of those who live at that time. God thus enlightens the sages of the generation in [the interpretation of] His holy Torah. He who denies this is as one who denies the Torah itself, God forbid.* (*Degel Maḥaneh Ephraim,* bereshit; ed. Jerusalem 1963, 6a)

Here the Hasidic reading has done precisely that which it would seem is most difficult for it: the new leadership has usurped the rabbinic role precisely in the place where it originated and where its power most critically lies—in the interpretive function. The lineage of rabbinic authority has been wordlessly transferred to the Hasidic master; it is entirely clear to the reader of this passage that R. Ephraim, the grandson of the Baʿal Shem Tov, refers to the Hasidic master/leader rather than to the duly appointed local rabbi (*mara de-atra*, in the traditional parlance) when he speaks of "the sages of the generation." Of course we should recall that R. Ephraim, like a number of other Hasidic leaders, served as both *rav* and *rebbe* in Sudilkov, so that for him the distinction may not have been a live issue. The same may be said of Levi Yizhak, author of this very striking parallel to the passage we have just read.

A basic principle in the service of God: We Israelites are obliged to believe in two Torahs, one written and the other oral, both given by a single shepherd. The meaning is as follows: the written Torah was given us by Moses, God's faithful servant, in writing etched on the tablets, black fire on white fire. The oral Torah given to Moses is its interpretation, including "everything a faithful student was ever to discover." This means that the oral Torah as it was given to us essentially follows the interpretation offered by the *zaddiqim* of the generation. *As they interpret the Torah, so it is.* This great power has been given us by the Creator out of love for Israel, His chosen people. All the worlds follow their will [as manifest] in Torah. Thus did the sages say: "The blessed Holy One issues a decree, but the *zaddiq* may nullify it." (*Qedushat Levi,* yitro; ed. Jerusalem 1958, p. 134 [emphasis added])

Here *rav* and *zaddiq* are a single figure, the interpretive function and the righteous power to negate a heavenly decree fully identified with each other! The interpretation *becomes* that which the sage says because of his power to effect change in the uppermost realms, which is where the true Torah dwells. The hermeneutical function reveals itself to be a magical one, as the text changes itself to conform with the interpretation offered by the true *zaddiq.* Here we have something that goes beyond the ongoing presence of the heavenly voice in the deliberations of the rabbis, as documented in the teachings of kabbalists in an earlier age.[44] It is neither the learning of the rabbi nor his role as an authorized interpreter in the chain of tradition that makes him a spokesman for the word of God. It is rather his power, the power of his righteousness, if you will, as *zaddiq*, that makes him the vehicle for revelation in his day. Here the secondary tradition within Judaism, as we have described it above, has indeed become dominant, as the *zaddiq* becomes master over Torah itself.

Thus far the claims for *zaddiq* as the true interpreter of Torah remain within the aggadic realm. There, it may be argued, the claim is a relatively safe one. Medieval kabbalists had already called for complete freedom of interpretation so long as no matter of law is to be affected. This claim is found echoed in Hasidism, explicitly so in the literature of Bratslav.[45] We see in Hasidism a sort of compromise: homiletic license has indeed been given to the *rebbe*, while legal authority is to remain in the hands of the *rav*. In fact, this is the way Hasidism has functioned through much of its history, careful traditionalism in legal matters providing a safe context for theological radicalism and spiritual boldness. The final text we record here is not intended to show the breakdown of traditional legal authority among the *hasidim*—not even in the unique sect called Bratslav. It does, however, demonstrate in theory the final handing over of authority, *halakhic* authority, to the *zaddiq*, and for that reason it is worthy of note. The speaker is R. Nathan of Nemirov, the famous disciple of R. Nahman. His *Liqqutey Halakhot* is an extension of R. Nahman's teachings to cover the institutions of Jewish life, through the form of a series of homilies following the order of the *Shulhan 'Arukh*. Here he deals with the laws of clean and unclean birds, which, it will be recalled, are listed in the Torah but not given any defining characteristics:

> "The signs of permitted fowl are not made explicit in the Torah, and the sages say that permitted fowl is eaten only by tradition. . . ."
>
> The "fowl" or "bird" here is Metatron, who is of the tree of knowledge of good and evil, which is also the permitted and the forbidden, the pure and the defiled. Scripture says: "Of the tree of knowledge of good and evil you shall not eat" (Gen 2:17). It is forbidden to us to partake of anything in which good and evil are combined, as in the tree. Our eating is uplifted essentially through the oral Torah, the six orders of the Mishnah. These are given over to the *zaddiqim*, those who separate the good from the evil, the permitted from the forbidden. That is why we are told to follow all that the true *zaddiqim* and sages of each generation teach us, as Scripture says: "You shall not turn aside from them, right or left" (Deut 17:8.2), and the sages add "even if they tell you that right is left or that left is right." Purifications are required in each generation, to uplift good from that evil with which it was comingled through Adam's sin of eating of that tree. Not everyone can perform such purifications, however, but only the true *zaddiq* of each generation. Ordinary

people, those who have not fully and wholly repented, are not yet at rest. They themselves are like the tree of knowledge of good and evil, sometimes doing what is proper, and sometimes otherwise. Surely then they do not have the power to separate the evil from the good. The true *zaddiq* of each generation is one who has already pushed evil aside altogether; he is like a Sabbath, and he has the strength to effect those purifications, uplifting the sparks that dwell within each thing. He can distinguish good from evil, permitted from forbidden.

The oral Torah was given only to the *zaddiqim,* who are the sages of the generation; since they have set evil aside so fully, the power of purification lies in their hands alone. The rabbis chose this commandment of the pure fowl to indicate this fact: permitted fowl is eaten only by tradition. The fowl is Metatron, the one who represents the tree. Since good and evil are combined in him, it cannot be eaten. Were it not for the *zaddiqim* and sages of the generation, to whom the oral Torah has been given, we would not be able to eat of it at all; it is "eaten only by tradition." The same is true of other eating; it too is possible only through the generation's sages. It is only that the rabbis revealed this more clearly here, since the bird itself is a symbol of that tree. We have only the wise men of our time on whom we can rely; the Torah chose not to offer signs for the pure fowl in order to teach us that we must depend on them, for they alone have the power to transform that tree of knowledge. (*Liqqutey Halakhot, yoreh de'ah, simmaney 'of tahor* 1; ed. Jerusalem 1950, p. 68)

The *zaddiq* has come full circle: the new leader who stands in the place of the normative rabbinic figure has now become the voice of tradition itself. In this final claim we see Hasidism at its boldest and most audacious stage. That most essentially halakhic area, the realm of *issur we-hetter* (the forbidden and the permitted), has now been transformed and removed from the hands of the *rav* to those of the *rebbe.* No wonder that the rabbinic establishment fought so hard to squelch such a movement! At the same time, however, we see here the conservative streak in Hasidism that was to determine its later character. For as tradition is given over into the hands of the *zaddiq,* he himself takes on the mantle of spokesman for that tradition and becomes its greatest defender. The history of Hasidism bears witness to the fact that in this wedding of normative authority to the charismatic spokesman, it is chiefly the charismatic who is transformed as he feels the mantle of tradition and the responsibility for its maintenance bear down weightily upon him.

Notes

1. There has not yet been a full treatment of the leadership motif in the literature on Hasidism. The matter has been touched on, however, in the writings of many scholars. See especially B. Z.

Dinur, *Be-Mifneh ha-Dorot* (Jerusalem: Bialik, 1955) 83–227; J. Weiss, *"Reshit Zemihatah shel ha-Derekh ha-Hasidit,"* Zion 16 (1951) passim; idem, *Studies in Eastern European Jewish Mysticism* (Oxford: Oxford University Press, 1985) 183–93; M. Buber, *The Origin and Meaning of Hasidism* (New York: Harper & Row, 1960) 128–49; S. Dresner, *The Zaddik* (London: Abelard-Schuman, 1960) 75–141; M. Piekarz, *Bi-Yemey Zemihat ha-Hasidut* (Jerusalem: Bialik, 1978) 280–302; S. Ettinger, "The Hasidic Movement: Reality and Ideals," in *Social Life and Social Values of the Jewish People* (=*Journal of World History* 11/1–2 [1968]) 251–66.

2. The ancient term *hasidim* was used to describe the BeSHT and his followers from the very beginning of the movement. In this usage they were seen as part of a broader phenomenon of pietists who had been on the increase since the end of the sixteenth century, when the term was given new life by the Safed Revival. In the early anti-Hasidic polemics (1772) the term is widely used and is the object of wordplays (*hasidim/hashudim*, "suspect ones") in such a way as to make it clear that this is the regular designation of the group. See M. Wilensky, *Hasidim u-Mitnaggedim* (Jerusalem: Bialik, 1970) 1:59 (*kat hashudim*, the suspect sect); 62 (*u-mekhanim shemam hasidim*, self-proclaimed pietists), and frequently. It seems that the Polish documents from 1740 on Miedzybosz recently found by M. Rosman (the publication of which is at this writing still awaited) also use a term that translates *hasid*. None of this, however, implies the specific meaning of *hasid* as "disciple," coming in place of the expected *talmid*, as in the phrase *hasid shel mi*. This usage is documented only much later and seems to originate in common speech rather than in the literary sources. *Shivhey ha-BeSHT* (published 1815; ed. Jerusalem: B. Mintz, 1969) does not yet know this usage, referring to the BeSHT's disciples as *anashav* (p. 143), *anshey segulah de-BeSHT* (p. 75), *anshey havurta qadishta* (p. 144), *ha-sarim le-mishma'ato* (p. 147), or simply *talmidim* (p. 53), but not *hasidim*. The same is true in the Yiddish version of this text, first published in 1816: *zayne layt* (p. 12b), *zayne hekhste layt* (p. 23a), *mekurovim* (p. 25a), etc. The usage is found only in the later (post-1864) tale literature.

The master of this *hasid* is referred to by a number of terms in the literature, a matter that sometimes leads to misunderstandings or imprecision. His main title in the homiletical literature is *zaddiq* (lit., "righteous one") but most usages of this term in the early Hasidic sources do not refer exclusively to the leader of a Hasidic disciple group. He is also called *rav* (rabbi), *talmid hakham* (scholar), *mokhiah* (preacher), etc., but none of these is a specific term restricted only to this usage. The Hasidic master was a new institution, for which a precise term did not exist in the vocabularies of those who wrought it. The term *rebbe* in the specifically Hasidic sense does seem to occur in the Yiddish version of *Shivhey ha-BeSHT*: ". . . un zol im on nemen far eyn rebbe" (21c).

3. The homiletical literature of the period has been extensively studied, especially for questions of class attitude, social protest, and in an attempt to distinguish both Sabbatian and Hasidic preaching from that of others. See especially the works by Dinur, Weiss, and Piekarz cited in n. 1.

4. See Dresner, *The Zaddik;* and G. Nig'al, *Torot Ba'al ha-Toledot* (Jerusalem: Mossad ha-Rav Kook, 1974).

5. Jacob Joseph was rabbi in Shargorod, Rashkov, Nemirov, and Polonnoye. See Dresner, *The Zaddik*, 256 n. 4, based on S. Dubnov, *Toledot ha-Hasidut* (Tel Aviv: Dvir, 1930–31) 94.

6. See G. Scholem, "Demuto ha-Historit shel Rabbi Yisra'el Ba'al Shem Tov," *Molad* 18 (1961) 335–56.

7. Determining the teachings of the BeSHT is one of the great difficulties in research on Hasidism, since R. Israel left no book of his own and all the later Hasidic masters, despite their highly divergent views, sought to claim the original master as their own. Of first rank in any attempt to characterize the BeSHT's teachings are those few writings which he did leave. To date there are only two short texts that are regarded by most scholars as unimpeachably his: the letter he sent to his brother-in-law Gershon of Kuty, first published by Jacob Joseph of Polonnoye in 1781 (translation in L. Jacobs, *Jewish Mystical Testimonies* [New York: Schocken, 1977] 148–55),

and a commentary on Psalm 107, printed in several Hasidic prayer books and edited critically by R. Schatz in *Tarbiz* 42 (1973) 154–84. Second in importance are the many quotations in the name of "my teacher" in the works of Rabbi Jacob Joseph himself. These were later combined with some other materials to form the *Keter Shem Tov* (Zolkeiv, 1794–95); they are yet to be the subject of thorough scholarly examination in their own right. Attention should also be paid, though with greater caution, to the direct heirs of the BeSHT in the Ukraine, and especially to his two grand-sons, Moses Hayyim Ephraim of Sudilkov (*Degel Mahaneh Ephraim* [n.p., 1808?]) and Baruch of Miedzybozh (*Buzina di-Nehora* [Lvov, 1880]). Still further caution is needed with regard to quota-tions from the BeSHT in the writings of Dov Baer of Miedzyrzec and his disciples, who clearly used the authority of the BeSHT for teachings that took a somewhat different direction. An uncritical but most important collection of materials attributed to the BeSHT is *Sefer Baʿal Shem Tov*, ed. Simeon Mendel of Gavartchov (Lodz, 1938). That work is somewhat marred by excessive dependency on writings from the Zydachov/Komarna dynasty.

It is clear from all the above that the BeSHT was not a "kabbalist" as the term was generally used in the eighteenth century (this despite the reported designation as such in the Polish docu-ment mentioned in n. 2); he refers only seldom to the symbolic language of contemporary kabbalists. He does, however, frequently quote and comment on passages from the *Zohar*. It is also hard to characterize him as a "preacher"; his teachings as reported are short and aphoristic rather than homiletical in the typical lengthy style of the day. He seems to have been especially fond of the pungent play on words, as frequently reported by Jacob Joseph.

8. There is an extensive scholarly literature on *Shivhey ha-BeSHT* and its various recensions. See especially the treatments by C. Shmeruk in *Zion* 28 (1963) 86–105; A. Ya'ari in *Kirjath Sefer* 39 (1964) 249–72, 394–407, 552–61; A. Rubenstein in *Tarbiz* 35 (1966) 174–91, in *'Aley Sefer* 6/7 (1979) 157–86, and in *Sinai* 86 (1980) 62–71, 89 (1981) 59–68, 90 (1982) 269–79. Y. Mondschein has published a full introduction to his facsimile edition of a *Shivhey ha-BeSHT* manuscript (Jerusalem, 1982) containing important material of a textual nature. Mondschein has also replied to one of Rubenstein's articles in *Tarbiz* 51 (1982) 673–80. A literary-structuralist approach to the *Shivhey ha-BeSHT* has been developed by Y. Elstein in his article in *Jerusalem Studies in Jewish Folklore* 2 (1982) 66–79 and in his book *Paʿamey Bet Melekh* (Ramat Gan: Bar Ilan University, 1984).

Shivhey ha-BeSHT unquestionably contains materials that faithfully reflect the period of the BeSHT's lifetime and information about him and his circle. The historian who makes use of this work has to learn to distinguish the purely legendary material that has been included within it from those portions that contain a grain of historical fact. These distinctions are not made easily and do not depend on the question of the various separate strands from which the work was woven and their editing, to which so much scholarly attention has been devoted. The specific content of each individual tale must be weighed carefully, compared to what is known from non-legendary sources, held up against historical realia, etc.

9. See the sources cited in n. 1 and add to them the work of Jacob Katz in *Tradition and Crisis* (New York: Schocken, 1971) 231–44.

10. On the separatist self-perception of medieval German-Jewish *hasidim*, see I. Marcus, *Piety and Society* (Leiden: Brill, 1981) passim.

11. The phrase is found in the epistle sent by the Vilna community to that of Brest-Litovsk, based on Deut 32:17. The document was part of *Zemir 'Arizim we-Harvot Zurim* (Aleksnits, 1772). It was republished in Wilensky, *Hasidim*, 1:59. The accusation that the *hasidim* are spiritual "new-comers" or innovators is widespread in the bans.

12. *Baba Batra* 12a; *'Eruvin* 7a. See N. N. Glatzer, "A Study of the Talmudic-Midrashic Inter-pretation of Prophecy" (1946), reprinted in his *Essays in Jewish Thought* (University, AL: University of Alabama Press, 1978) 16–35, as well as E. Urbach, "When did Prophecy Cease?" *Tarbiz* 17 (1946) 1–11; idem, "Halachah and Prophecy," *Tarbiz* 18 (1947) 1–27.

13. References, mostly in the form of veiled hints, that the accusation of Sabbatianism was made

against the early *hasidim,* are widely found in the anti-Hasidic polemical literature. See Wilensky, *Hasidim,* index s.v. "Shabbatai Zevi," "*Shabta' ut,*" "*Shabta' im.*"

14. See *Hagigah* 12b: "*Zaddiq* is the foundation of the world," quoting Prov 10:25. I have discussed this matter in "The *Zaddiq* as Axis Mundi in Later Judaism," *Journal of the American Academy of Religion* 45 (1977) 327–47. See also the various treatments of the *zaddiq* by G. Scholem: the chapter "Zaddik" in his *Von der mystischen Gestalt der Gottheit* (Zurich: Rhein-Verlag, 1962) [Hebrew version in *Pirkey Yesod be-Havanat ha-Qabbalah u-Semaleha* (Jerusalem: Bialik, 1976)]; "Three Types of Jewish Piety," *Eranos Jahrbuch* 38 (1969) 323–40; "The thirty-six Hidden Tsadikim in Jewish Legends" in *The Messianic Idea in Judaism and Other Essays on Jewish Spirituality* (New York: Schocken, 1971). On *zaddiq* in the rabbinic sources, see R. Mach, *Der Zaddik in Talmud und Midrasch* (Leiden: Brill, 1957).

15. For other references to Hanina in the writings of Rabbi Jacob Joseph, see Dresner, *The Zaddik,* 277 n. 33. This teaching of the BeSHT is also quoted at the beginning of *Keter Shem Tov,* #3. See also *No'am Elimelech,* ed. G. Nig'al (Jerusalem: Mossad Harav Kook, 1978) 11a (56).

16. *Yad Yosef* by Joseph Zarfati, printed in Venice in 1616, and in Amsterdam in 1700. The passage quoted is found at the beginning of *lekh lekha* (ed. Amsterdam 12b): "They mean that because he made do with the bare necessities, a high moral rung, the whole world was sustained 'for the sake of Hanina my son'; the reason for this was that 'Hanina was satisfied with a measure of carobs from one Sabbath to the next.'"

17. M. Piekarz, *Bi-Yemey Zemihat ha-Hasidut,* 16ff. It is noteworthy that this statement is one of the very few rabbinic-type *divrey Torah* that the *Shivhey ha-BeSHT* (ed. Jerusalem 1969, p. 149) also attributes to the Ba'al Shem Tov.

18. See Y. Liebes, "The Messiah of the Zohar," in *Ha-Ra'ayon ha-Meshihi be-Yisra'el* (Jerusalem: Israel Academy of Sciences, 1982) 87–236.

19. On Elijah the prophet, see the psychological study by Aharon Wiener, *The Prophet Elijah in the Development of Judaism* (London: Routledge and Kegan Paul, 1978) and the works quoted in Wiener's bibliography (pp. 225ff.).

20. See J. Dan, "On the History of the Hagiographic Literature," *Jerusalem Studies in Jewish Folklore* 1 (1981) 82–100.

21. *Zaddiq* as a designation for Sabbatai Sevi is found in a source included in A. Freimann's *'Inyeney Shabbatai Zevi* (Berlin: Mekizzey Nirdamim, 1912) 54. This passage is discussed by Y. Liebes in the important treatment of the *zaddiq* theme in his "*Zaddiq* the Foundation of the World: A Sabbatian Mythos," *Da'at* 1 (1978) 37ff.; see esp. nn. 29–31; cf. Liebes's comments also in "The Messiah of the Zohar," 114 n. 118.

22. See J. Weiss, "Reshit Zemihatah." Despite a certain tendency on Weiss's part to exaggerate in the psychological analysis of these materials, I agree with his claim that evidence can be found in the sources of guilt over the (perhaps inevitable) failure of the preachers' mission.

23. Cf. Piekarz, *Bi-Yemey Zemihat ha-Hasidut,* 107ff.

24. Parallels to this text, connecting the distinction made here to that between Noah and Abraham as leaders of their respective generations are found in the writings of Rabbi Jacob Joseph. See Dresner, *The Zaddik,* 152ff., 284 n. 23.

25. In the previous passage, the Maggid had referred to both types as "complete *zaddiqim,*" though this is promptly undercut by the ensuing discussion. The sharp language in which the dichotomy is expressed by Elimelech leaves no doubt that only one of the two is worthy of respect.

26. This is the essential insight of I. Heinemann's *Darkhey ha-Aggadah* (Jerusalem: Hebrew University, 1954). On the Hellenistic background of the rabbi as wisdom teacher, see H. Fischel, *Rabbinic Literature and Greco-Roman Philosophy* (Leiden: Brill, 1973). On the rabbi in the broader religious context of late antiquity, especially Babylonia, see J. Neusner, "The Phenomenon of the Rabbi in Late Antiquity," *Numen* 16 (1969) 1–20, 11 (1970) 1–18. See also Neusner's "Rabbis and Community in Third Century Babylonia," in *Religions in Antiquity,* ed. J. Neusner (Leiden: Brill, 1970).

27. See my "On Translating Hasidic Homilies," *Prooftexts* 3 (1983) 63–72.

28. In the continuation of the same passage, however, it turns out that the individual worshiper is to see himself as *kohen*. This shift is a good example of the ambivalent relationship between the democratization of Jewish spiritual life and the promulgation of a new charismatic elite, both of which are typical of early Hasidism. The passage quoted here contains plays on both the words *qorban* (QRV, "draw near") and *'olah* ('LH, "raise up").

29. The idea of prayer as spiritual sacrifice is quite ancient. It may be traced to Scripture itself (Hos 14:3) and is found in the Qumran literature (1QS 9:4; 10:6). A more radical expression of this idea, in which the worshiper places himself on the metaphoric altar, is found in Romans 12:1. See M. Newton, *The Concept of Purity at Qumran and in the Letters of Paul* (Cambridge: University Press, 1985). Compare with Philo *On the Special Laws* 1.270 and *Who Is the Heir* 184. Rabbinic sources also see prayer as spiritual sacrifice, *'avodah sheba-lev* (*Ta'anit* 2a). *Numbers Rabbah* 18:21 attributes to Rabbi Simon the view that the worshiper at prayer sacrifices his own fat, blood, and soul. This motif becomes a favorite of later Jewish moralists; see I. Tishby, *Mishnat ha-Zohar* (Jerusalem: Bialik, 1982) 2:183–246.

30. For the *Zohar*'s treatment of the Temple cult, see Tishby's *Mishnat ha-Zohar*, 2:183–246. The *Zohar*'s views on this topic are the subject of a doctoral dissertation currently in progress by Rabbi Seth Brody at the University of Pennsylvania.

31. Cf. the discussion of *zaddiqim* and preachers as healers in Piekarz, *Bi-Yemey Zemihat ha-Hasidut*, 120ff.

32. *Gittin* 62a, *rabbanan iqeru melakhim* ("rabbis are called kings"), apparently often confused in later quotation with *Nedarim* 20b, *man mal' akhey ha-sharet, rabbanan* ("Who are the angels? Rabbis.").

33. Kalonymos Kalman Epstein of Cracow (d. 1823), author of this work, was a leading disciple of Elimelech of Lezajsk.

34. *Ahavat Shalom* contains the sermons of Menahem Mendel of Kossov (1768–1826), progenitor of the Kossov/Vyznitsa dynasty.

35. Wilensky, *Hasidim*, 2:210.

36. Quoted in *Orot Yisra'el* (Jerusalem: n.p., n.d.), a collection of Ruzhyn teachings, p. 152.

37. See n. 12 above.

38. See M. Himmelfarb, "From Prophecy to Apocalypse: The *Book of the Watchers* and Tours of Heaven," in *Jewish Spirituality: From the Bible through the Middle Ages*, ed. A. Green (World Spirituality 13; New York: Crossroad, 1986) 145–65. On the prophetic links of the early Enoch literature, see G. W. E. Nickelsburg, "Enoch, Levi, and Peter: Recipients of Revelation in Upper Galilee," *Journal of Biblical Literature* 100 (1981) 575–600. M. E. Stone has a very interesting note on prophetic models for Enoch in his "Lists of Revealed Things," in *Magnalia Dei: The Mighty Acts of God: Essays on the Bible and Archaeology in Memory of G. Ernest Wright*, ed. F. M. Cross et al. (Garden City, NY: Doubleday, 1976). [My thanks to M. Himmelfarb for her help with this note.]

39. See A. J. Heschel, "Inspiration in the Middle Ages," in *Alexander Marx Jubilee Volume*, Hebrew Section (New York: Jewish Theological Seminary, 1950).

40. See the discussion by M. Idel in his forthcoming *Religious Experience in the Thought of Abraham Abulafia* (Albany: State University of New York Press, 1988).

41. Cf. the parallel sources quoted by R. Schatz-Uffenheimer in *Quietistic Elements in Eighteenth Century Hasidic Thought* (Jerusalem: Magnes Press, 1968) 175ff.

42. See the discussion in the forthcoming work by M. Idel (*Religious Experience*), which serves to update the treatment in Schatz-Uffenheimer, *Quietistic Elements*.

43. M. W. Levinsohn-Loewy, *Sefer Hashanah: The American Hebrew Yearbook* (1938) 113–27.

44. See Scholem, *Messianic Idea in Judaism*, 300ff., quoting the kabbalists R. Meir Ibn Gabbai and R. Isaiah Horowitz.

45. See the sources quoted in my *Tormented Master* (University, AL: University of Alabama Press, 1978) 330 n. 5.

6

ḤaBaD: The Contemplative Ascent to God

RACHEL ELIOR

THE HASIDIC MOVEMENT, which originated in the eighteenth century, was one of the most exciting spiritual phenomena in Jewish history, in its vitality, continuity, variety, and scope. This multifaceted movement, the successor to the mystical tradition of the Kabbalah, attempted to embody its mystical teachings within new social frameworks. It contained a number of different trends, which developed and changed during the course of its two-hundred-year history by adopting distinctive and varied shapes.

Among the major streams with a distinctive character and influence was the ḤaBaD movement. ḤaBaD—from the initials of the Hebrew terms *ḥokhmah* ("wisdom"), *binah* ("understanding"), *da'at* ("knowledge")—was the name of the movement established by Rabbi Shneur Zalman of Lyady (1745–1813), who was among the principal disciples of R. Dov Baer (the "Maggid") of Miedzyrzec (d. 1772). R. Shneur Zalman's doctrine developed in dialectical relationship with that of the Maggid, while he established a unique Hasidic community in Belorussia and the Ukraine in the 1780s. His book *Liqqutey Amarim,* generally known by its popular title, *Tanya,* was first published in 1797. This work, considered the ideological manifesto of this school of Hasidim, was a kind of spiritual handbook—alongside Joseph Karo's halakhic code, *Shulḥan 'Arukh.* It intended to expound the mystical ideas underlying the quest for God, while clarifying the implications of Lurianic Kabbalah for Hasidic worship.

Ḥabad literature had two main concerns: (1) the formulation of a systematic mystical theosophy, based on kabbalistic thought and its Hasidic interpretation; (2) the propagation of Hasidism and detailed guidance in the Hasidic path of *'Avodat Ha-Shem* (a central Hasidic term, usually translated as "divine service" or "divine worship," but understood as including not only prayer or other strictly "religious" activities, but all aspects of the individual's life in both the activist and spiritualist version, according to Ḥabad).

Because of this attempt to bridge the gap between theoretical mystical truths and their practical implementation, the entire system of Ḥabad reflects the dialectic between spiritualism and activism, and the interplay between mystical interests and social-ethical concerns. This is because its teaching is concerned not only with speculative theology but also with the role of spiritual values and the pneumatic orientation in the daily life of the individual member of the community. It also addresses the implications of a mystical way of thought for a comprehensive religious world view, entailing commitment to the observance of Torah and *miẓwot* and strict loyalty to the commandments of the halakhah.

In Ḥabad, as in other Hasidic movements, one may find simultaneously the two contradictory tendencies of quietistic spiritualism and aspiritual activism. Along with abundant expressions of quietistic, spiritual concerns, seeking self-abnegation in the act of passive contemplation, withdrawal from worldly involvements, and communion with God, there is an activist element, demanding involvement in the material world in terms of practical *miẓwot* and Torah study, on the one hand, and relationship to the concrete world on a social level, on the other. The uniqueness of Ḥabad literature, which is an outstanding attempt to bridge mystical truths and their practical implications, lies in the formulation of a complex dialectical theosophic framework, which grants an important place to both aspects of religious experience.

Its essential innovation lay in the formulation of a religious outlook concentrating upon divinity: its essence, its nature, the stages of its manifestations, its characteristics, its perfection, its differing wills, its processes, the significance of its revelation and the possibilities of its perception—that is to say, a theocentric approach whose assumptions are formulated beyond the bounds of kabbalistic esoterism. These new spiritual truths were very carefully examined against the traditional commandments and accepted halakhic approaches. Great care was taken to present the new ideas as an attempt to formulate a new religious consciousness, rather than a new religious praxis, and as shedding light on the hallowed, traditional praxis from a new theocentric viewpoint.

In the light of the new relationship between God and the world, between finitude and the Infinite, the religious life was given a new spiritualist perspective and theocentric orientation. All was to be directed toward the realization of the divine will and the deciphering of it in the various levels of existence, far beyond the limits of the halakhic command and the ethos that follows from it. Contemplation of both the hidden and the revealed divine essence, of the nature of its connection with the world, the significance of its wills and of the immanent law governing its activity in the cosmos, are understood by Ḥabad as the essence of the divine worship demanded of humanity, encapsulated in the term *yiḥud* ("unification").

Ḥabad stresses the dual character of this unification—the upper *yiḥud* and the lower *yiḥud*. The upper unification *(yiḥud ha-ʿelyon)*, is identified with the spiritualistic worship of God, involving negation of the world and its inclusion within the Godhead by a deliberate effort to transcend the boundaries of existence, time, and space. *Yiḥud ha-taḥton*, the lower unification, signifies the drawing of divinity into the lower realms, making it dwell in the world through Torah and *mizwot* and divine worship in concrete reality. As a result of the essentially dialectic structure of Ḥabad theosophy, which is concerned with both spiritual transcendence of the world and divine immanence in the world, and which is directed in principle toward the two goals of the double divine will and the dual-focused worship on the part of human beings, one may easily misinterpret its world views, drawing far-reaching conclusions on the basis of one book or one chapter, when in fact these relate to only one aspect. Indeed, the spiritualist, quietistic dimension and the concrete, aspiritual activist dimension are organically interwoven with each other.

Ḥabad teaching, found in scores of books and tractates, is extremely multifaceted. The fundamental dialectic lying at the basis of this teaching cannot be adequately expressed by one or another narrow perspective on the broad scope of interrelationships among the various dimensions. Its uniqueness must be fathomed by examining its teachings and writings against the broad perspective of its spiritual context, including the kabbalistic tradition, on the one hand, and its social and historical background, on the other. In examining the Ḥabad tradition, one must bear in mind that the books, sermons, documents, and letters were all written in a sociocultural context in which the halakhic and kabbalistic associations were taken for granted, so that a passing allusion was sufficient to make its meaning clear.

In terms of the historical context, one must take into account that the views of Ḥabad were formulated at the end of the 1780s and in the 1790s, following the death of R. Dov Baer of Miedzyrzec, during a period of severe attacks from both within and without. On the one hand, other Hasidic groups were severely critical of the Ḥabad interpretation of the Maggid's teachings and of the Hasidic and kabbalistic heritage;[1] on the other hand, this was the period of the sharpest attacks by the opponents of Hasidism, the Mitnaggedim, against Hasidism in general and Ḥabad teaching in particular.[2] These two factors decisively influenced the presentation and formulation of spiritualist teachings, as the consideration of avoiding exacerbation of the antagonisms among the rival camps was always a primary one for Habad leadership.

The picture presented by Habad literature reveals a living spiritual entity in process of becoming and in its self-questioning. These are not anthologies of kabbalistic teachings or polished volumes of Hasidic theory, but works expressing the vivid religious experience of those seeking closeness to God, struggling with established paths as well as breaking through to new ones within the framework of kabbalistic thought and its Hasidic interpretation.

Habad literature is concerned with four primary subjects: (1) the doctrine of Godhead (*Torat ha-Elohut*)—the formulation of a mystical theology; (2) the doctrine of the soul (*Torat ha-Nefesh*)—descriptions of the psychology of religious service; (3) divine service (*'Avodat Ha-Shem*)—guidelines for the mystical spiritualist worship of God and the shaping of states of mind expressing religious obligations over and above the time-hallowed halakhic practices, which were seen as self-evident; (4) the suprarational (*'Avodah sheme'ever le-ta'am we-da'at*)—confrontation with the religious problematics which follow from the contradictions among mystical axioms, their Hasidic interpretation, the demands of the halakhah, and personal experience.

Each of these areas was subject to extensive discussion based on the kabbalistic heritage, and exciting attempts were made to find the ethical, rational, and intellectual equivalents to the mystical tradition, testing the limits of rational thought and attempting to break through to the transrational. In contrast to these daring attempts in the areas of thought and speculation, we find in Habad, as in Hasidism generally, absolute and strict loyalty to the demands of the halakhah, combined with extreme conservatism in everything pertaining to religious praxis and the traditional ethos, which revolved around the study of Torah and the observance of the *mizwot*. However, despite its conservative appearance, there is no doubt that religious life underwent a far-reaching spiritualistic transformation. Such subjects as the relationship between spirituality and materiality, self-resignation, ecstasy, communion with God, contemplation, and faith, were all subject to detailed discussion, sharp polemics, precise examination, and daring definitions.[3]

Mystical Theology

The Habad theory of divinity is rooted in an acosmic understanding of the world, in which there is only one true reality, the divine, every other reality being seen, in the final analysis, as illusory. The doctrine of acosmism denies the substantial reality of the world's existence and claims the exclusive existence of the divine entity. In this acosmic approach, the world has no independent existence, and the entire cosmos is dependent on one being which negates the independent reality of its parts, and even their totality, the world, so that there is only one true reality—the divine reality.

> For there exists in the world no entity other than Him . . . for there is no true substance other than Him. For if, because of the vessels and the conceal-ment, other entities appear to be substantial, in reality they are not sub-stantial at all. For He, may He be blessed, is the substance of all substances, and there exists in reality no other substance but Him. (R. Aaron Ha-Levi, *Sha'arey ha-Yihud weha-Emunah*, I:2)[4]

The doctrine of the absolute nature of God's existence, which denies the true substance of every other being—expressed in the formula, "there is nothing apart from Him"—lies at the center of Habad theology. It provides the basis for a profound encounter with the meaning of the existence of the world—which seems to contradict the axiom of the exclusivity of divine existence—and an analysis of its revealed and concealed, or true and appar-ent, essence. Its acosmic doctrine is rooted in a challenge against the limits of human perception, or against the empirical view and rational criteria for judging reality—assuming that there is only one reality, the divine reality that fills the entire cosmos, and that any other apparent reality is an illusion. "From the standpoint of the Infinite, blessed be He, all the worlds are as if literally nothing and nihility" (R. Shneur Zalman, *Tanya*, 320). Acosmism is based on the divine viewpoint according to which all other existence is lacking in substance. This understanding is based on the distinction between existence (*qiyyum*) and substance (*yeshut*): things apart from divinity exist but are insubstantial, there being only one true substance—the divine Being. Any perception of reality as possessing substance in itself is merely short-sightedness, illusion, or falsehood, as in the following sharp words of R. Shneur Zalman: "Even though it appears to us that the worlds exist, this is a total lie" (*Torah Or* [1899], Tisa, p. 86b).

Existence is itself perceived merely as an image, a kind of radiance which emanates from the divine source, which is nullified relative to its source, and has only an illusory existence, being entirely dependent on the divine substance that sustains it (cf. R. Shneur Zalman, *Tanya*, 155, 174). Existence, in which God as a tangible entity is absent to human perception, is thus transformed into an insubstantial illusion, while divinity becomes the only substantial reality, even if it is not within the immediate field of human perception. In the light of the postulate of the exclusive existence of God, Habad worship centers on the understanding of apparent, visible reality and the uncovering of the underlying divine essence, while apprehending the former's illusoriness. In other words, humanity is called upon to uncover the divine unity of reality, beyond the seemingly real cosmos.

The Ḥabad theological position that "there is nothing but Him" (R. Shneur Zalman, *Tanya*, 155, quoting Deut 4:35) relates to the claim that there is no separate, independent existence apart from the one all-encompassing existence—that of the Infinite—thereby adding an important dimension to the idea of divine immanence. This is a major theological concept that was discussed and developed in all branches of Hasidic literature and occupied a central place in the doctrines of all Hasidic teachers. A fundamental axiom of Hasidism generally is that God is immanent in all things and that the world only exists by virtue of the immanent divine reality that it embodies. Habad adds to this the argument that the Infinite incorporated within itself the entire cosmos, in its substance, being itself the only truly existing substance, and all other existing things being mere manifestations thereof. Reality exists within divinity, while divinity penetrates all of existence, which is unified through it and exists by virtue of the divine substance ('*azmut*). Therefore, God and visible reality are in fact one. Reality has no independent existence and does not bring about multiplicity within God. Divinity contains everything, and there is nothing that exists in a substantial way outside of it.

> All created things in the world are hidden within His essence, be He blessed, in one potentia, in coincidentia oppositorum (*hashwa'ah*), for He is the Creator of all, and there is nothing outside of Him, and nothing is concealed from Him, and He, may He be blessed, is equally present throughout the entire creation, that is, that all of reality must exist by virtue of His essence in all its details, for He brings them about into existence, and by His potency they came to be revealed. (R. Aaron Ha-Levi, *Sha'arey ha-'Avodah*, III:29)

The independent existence of separate things (i.e., seemingly nondivine reality) is related to God's perception of these separated things. If, from the divine viewpoint, the realm outside of divinity itself is without separate or independent existence, then the understanding of reality as separate from God is itself illusory: "In the Holy One, blessed be He, the created things and the world are not a distinct entity from Him, heaven forfend, for there is nought but Him, be He blessed, and all things exist only by the truth of His existence" (R. Aaron Ha-Levi, *Sha'arey ha-'Avodah*, III:7).

This radical pantheistic position served as a platform on the basis of which one could distinguish between true and illusory existence, grounded in the apprehension of existence as rooted in one essence, whose different dimensions are all aspects, phenomena, or projections thereof. This substance is

God, and the world is nothing but a revelation or manifestation of His essence. The conclusion to be derived from this view is the belief in the unity of God throughout the entire cosmos, and the awareness of the nullification of the substantive existence of the world.

Habad Hasidism taught seven basic axioms concerning the relationship between God and the world:

1. *Pantheism.* God is the exclusive substance, and the world is nothing but a mode, projection, or expression of this infinite being. The existence of the visible world depends on the existence of that element which sustains it—God.

2. *Acosmism.* From the divine viewpoint, the world is lacking any distinct or discrete existence. Creation does not constitute a change within God (see R. Shneur Zalman, *Tanya,* 219), since "everything is like vanity and nihility compared to His essence and substance (*Mahut we-'azmut*)."

3. *Creation.* The divine being is the creator, originator, and sustainer of the world at all times, and the world is dependent on Him, as it is constantly being created (see *Tanya,* 144, 231).

4. *Immanence.* Divinity is present everywhere in absolutely equal substantiality. The distinction from the human point of view between "finite" and "infinite" is epistemological and not substantive. "For the being and substance of the Infinite, blessed be He, is equal in the upper and lower realms" (see *Tanya,* 143). From the divine point of view, there is total equivalence of all the various manifestations of existence, both physical and spiritual, the only distinction being on the level of human perception thereof.

5. *Panentheism.* All that exists is within God; however, "the worlds do not take in Him any essence at all, in terms of His truth, for there is nothing but Him" (R. Aaron Ha-Levi, *Sha'arey ha-'Avodah,* III:22). Divinity is present in reality, which is united with it, since the realm outside of God has no independent, substantive existence.

6. *The world as manifestation of God.* The world is an essential and necessary manifestation of God. One cannot speak of God's existence without God. God incorporates the world within Himself.

> It is known that the Infinite, blessed be He, is called "Infinite Perfection," that is, that His glory, be He blessed, encompasses the entire process of emanation, from the very highest to the very lowest level. . . . And He, may He be blessed, is present in every detail, from the head of all levels to the smallest worm in the sea . . . and He brings them into existence, divides them and creates everything with His power, be He blessed." (R. Aaron Ha-Levi, *Sha'arey ha-Yihud weha-Emunah,* I:6)

7. *Dialectical reciprocity.* To the central assumption of Ḥabad theology—
"the life and existence of the worlds which live and exist come from His
potency, in His own substance, may He be blessed, and there is nothing else
but Him, for there is nought without Him" (*Sha'arey ha-Yiḥud weha-
Emunah,* 4)—one must add the dialectical principle that God has no separate
existence without the world, because the world—which is nothing but a
manifestation of the substance of God—is understood as an expression of
God's infinite perfection and of His desire for self-perfection, both in its
substance, which is united with God and in its real manifestations, which
are separate from it.

Underlying these assumptions is the question of the nature of divine
presence in the world and its causes, which constitute the background to
a panentheistic-acosmic world view which claims that everything which
exists is in God, while simultaneously denying real existence to the world.

The panentheistic-acosmic viewpoint is expressed in the Ḥabad concept
of coincidentia oppositorum (*hashwa'ah*), which defines the absolute divine
unity in all existence, or the understanding of the substantial equality of
divine existence in all worlds. According to Ḥabad acosmic doctrine, the
character of divine existence in the world implies the absolute unity of the
divine in all aspects of being or the substantive equality of divine existence
in all the worlds, despite the apparent difference. The unity of the divine
is not a simple one, but is rooted in the equivalence of those opposing,
different natures which constitute reality. This substantive equivalence of
divine reality in all of existence, both in principle and in action, is expressed
in the concept of coincidentia oppositorum (*hashwa'ah*). *Hashwa'ah,* which
is the dynamic aspect of the concept of unity or its practical translation,
expresses the essential interdependence between the created and the divine
reality. It implies that all attributes, including their opposites and contradictions, share a common root equalizing them with the Infinite, in such
a way that differences are nullified. This point of contact between the finite
and the infinite, between God and creation, in which reality shakes off its
multiplicity and reaches toward nihility and abnegation, and in which all
existing things are equalized in their root, is the subject of the acosmic
orientation and mystical consciousness of Ḥabad. *Hashwa'ah* is the development within Ḥabad of the kabbalistic and Hasidic concepts of "the attribute
of nothingness" (*midat ha-ayin*),[5] the element within the divine which
allows for contradictions, in which the specific attributes of various elements are negated and equalized in their being, and within which all
changes from one state of being to another occur. *Hashwa'ah* is the
equivalent of coincidentia oppositorum—the dialectical characteristic of
"the existence of two opposites in one subject," which is the true meaning

of unity. The dialectical law of the union of opposites and their merging in infinity becomes a basic law, applicable to all the worlds from the divine point of view, expressed in the term "the power of equalization" (*koah ha-hashwa'ah*), which "includes all the diverse things of the world in one potency."

Equalization is a dialectical concept which, on the one hand, defines the nature of the existence of the world within divinity and, on the other hand, describes the nature of the presence of the divine substance in the different aspects of existence. "All the worlds in all their details are included in the power of His equalization" (R. Aaron Ha-Levi, *Sha'arey ha-'Avodah*, IV:22). "And He, blessed be He, is their power, in the aspect of His equalization and His perfection, blessed be He, which encompasses all the parts of the world in one potential and in equalization" (R. Aaron Ha-Levi, *Sha'arey ha-Yihud weha-Emunah*, I:14). "But this is generally called His attribute of flowing into all the details of all levels in the aspect of equalization" (*Sha'arey ha-Yihud weha-Emunah*, II:30).

The concept of the power of *hashwa'ah* is used to described the divine substance as encompassing all aspects of existence—a view known in the study of religions as panentheism—and is also identified with the process of transition from unity to differentiation, or the drawing down of the divine substance into various aspects of existence. However, the uniqueness of the Habad approach lies in its presentation of the "power of equalization" as the dialectical axis on which the two principal processes of divine existence take place—the transition from infinity to finitude, and the transcending of finitude in infinity:

> For the entire intention is that His equalization, blessed be He, be revealed in actuality, that is, that all of reality, in all of its levels and all of its details, should be revealed, and that nevertheless they be unified and connected in their value, that is, that they be revealed in their differentiated essences and that nevertheless they be united." (*Sha'arey ha-Yihud weha-Emunah*, IV:5).

The divine intention is that, simultaneously, the coincidentia oppositorum be revealed in its details and be united at its source. The manifestation in detail of *hashwa'ah* signifies the transition from infinite to finite, from nihility to existence, while its unification in the divine source means the transcendence of the finite in the infinite. The dialectical relationships between the finite and the infinite, the revealed and the concealed, the existent and the divine, are manifested in the process of coincidentia oppositorum, which expressed the union of opposites and the dynamic relationship between them. The Lurianic conceptions explaining the inner law governing divine life—abundance and contraction, withdrawal and self-expression—took on a new meaning in their Habad interpretation, which anchored them in the two-directional process of coincidentia oppositorum.[6] This process—parallel to the active dimension of divinity and its being, uniting opposites in which finite and infinite are made equivalent—became a governing principle in Habad dialectics in general.

Acosmism, which denies the reality of the world and argues that the "apparently-separate-from-God" appearance is, in fact, identical with the manifestation of the divine substance in the cosmos, leaves unanswered the question of the transition from the infinite to the finite, or of the active motivation of the process of creation and the reason for the world's existence. Habad theology's answer to this question is rooted in the concept of manifestation of the divine wholeness. The aim of creation is the fulfillment of God's will to create a separate, nondivine reality, which is in fact illusory. The purpose of this step is the manifestation of divine perfection within the aspect most opposed to its spiritual being—the depths of material reality, the world of separation and limitation, or in kabbalistic terminology, the world of opposition and of qelipot ("shells"). The transition from abstract being to that which exists in actuality takes place because of the divine will to manifest His perfection, as the divine perfection implies "inclusion of all the opposites": "for He is called the perfection of all, and we call perfection only that which is made through encompassment of all opposites, as is known" ('Avodat ha-Lewi, Wa-yehi, 77). Divine perfection requires the existence of its opposite for the sake of its own encompassing quality: this opposite was made through creation. Creation is understood as a means of attaining divine perfection, because it manifests the formation of "the inclusion of opposites":

> The entire principle of the creation and emanation of the worlds is that He, may He be blessed, is of the quintessence of simplicity, and one may not attribute to Him anything belonging to the realms of existence and limitation, and we see the coming into existence of the worlds, which emanated in the aspect of limitation and being, which is the attribute of descent. And this is in order to reveal His perfection, precisely through the opposite. . . . But all these aspects only pertain from the point of view of the worlds, but not from that of His substance, for He is absolutely simple, and there is none but Him at all. . . . For in terms of His own substance, may He be blessed, He is infinitely, immeasurably distant from these aspects, so that His intention, may He be blessed, was that His unity and His uniqueness, blessed be He, be manifested, even in terms of these aspects, through the existent and the limited, and then His perfection will be revealed, for He is the perfection of all, for the essence of perfection is that even those opposites which are opposed to one another be made one, as is known. ('Avodat ha-Lewi, Wa-yehi, 74; cf. R. Shneur Zalman, Tanya, 317)

The creation of the world is understood as the bringing into being of the divine opposite, which was required for that realization of perfection conditional upon the inclusion of opposites. Divine perfection can be revealed only through the manifestation of the divine unity in its opposition and the inclusion of the opposites in oneness. The assumption that "the revelation of every thing is through its opposite" (see R. Aaron Ha-Levi, *Sha'arey ha-'Avodah*, II:10) became a universal principle pertaining to the realms of spirit and matter. The second, related principle was that divine perfection depends on the existence of the opposites and their transformation into their divine antithesis. The assumption that "the essence of (divine) perfection is revealed precisely through distance and the opposite" conveys the quintessence of the dialectic of relationships between God and the world, as the existence of the world becomes a condition of the revelation of Godhead and its full realization, just as divinity is the absolute condition for the existence of the world. This view of the relationship between the reason for creation and the manifestation of divine perfection is very close to the pantheistic idea, which sees the cosmic process as the actual coming-into-being of God or the manifestation of aspects of the divine being which are only expressed in creation.

In the Habad conception, creation and reality are understood as stages in the process of becoming of God, as the manifestation of the divine perfection demands the cosmic process which makes it possible for divinity to be revealed in all its dimensions and aspects. However, this is not a one-time or unidirectional process, but a dialectical one, as God's perfection and His manifestation are conditional on the transformations from the infinite into the finite and back again into the infinite: "For this is the purpose of the creation of the worlds from infinity into finitude, that they be transformed back from the finite into the infinite" (Rabbi Shneur Zalman, *Torah Or*, wa-yeze, 44).

One must distinguish between two kinds of transformation. The first transformation, from divine infinite substance into finite essence, is the process defined as the manifestation of *hashwa'ah*. The latter transformation, from finite being back to infinite being, is defined as *yihud* ("unification") or as the restoration of the coincidentia oppositorum to its source. This double dialectic is the aim of the divine will and the way to the manifestation of His perfection within the finite and negation of the finite at one and the same time: "For the essence of His intention is that His coincidentia be manifested in concrete reality, that is, that all realities and their levels be revealed in actuality, each detail in itself, and that they nevertheless be unified and joined in their value, that is, that they be revealed as separated essences, and that they nevertheless be unified and joined in their value"

(R. Aaron Ha-Levi, *Sha'arey ha-Yihud weha-Emunah*, IV:5). Divine perfection is expressed through this paradox of unity and multiplicity at once; divinity achieves its perfection by the double and contradictory law of manifestation through opposition and discrimination, on the one hand, and restoration of unity and incorporation, on the other—processes known in kabbalistic terminology as "contraction" (*zimzum*), "breaking" (*shevirah*), and "restoration" (*tiqqun*).[7] However, whereas in the Lurianic Kabbalah both "breaking" and "contraction" take place in the theogonic realm, with which humanity is uninvolved, and only *tiqqun* belongs in the human realm, in the Habad system humanity takes part in both processes, since neither is ever completed and both are understood as continuous processes: "But His essential intention, may He be blessed, was not manifested at the time of the Creation, for His essential intention was that there be further revelation . . . for the essence of the manifestation of this aspect is through the service of man" (R. Aaron Ha-Levi, *Sha'arey ha-Yihud weha-Emunah*, V:15; cf. IV:24).

The worship demanded of human beings for the realization of this divine perfection as the unification of opposites is anchored in the response to the double divine will—of the becoming of the finite as an expression of the divine will for manifestation and actualization, and the return of existence to its source and its negation as an expression of the divine will to be concealed and annihilated. Humans are called to draw divine existence into the very depths of the material world through their service of Torah and *mizwot* (and "service through transformation," for the select few), on the one hand, and, on the other, to return the finite to its divine source by the worship of negation (*bittul*), elevation of sparks, communion with God and ecstasy. These two tendencies—the drawing of divinity into the finite and the annihilation of the finite within God—are indiscriminately intertwined, and the divine intention is realized only by the fulfillment of the two contradictory wills, which express the paradoxical lawfulness of the union of opposites. This form of worship, which draws its inspiration from both divine wills, is focused on the "finite" (*ha-yesh*)—its true essence as against its revealed appearance; its lofty source as against its mundane manifestation; and its acosmic truth as against its cosmic appearance. Reflection upon these different relationships of "finite" and "infinite," both from the divine and the human point of view, is at the focus of Habad thought.

The theological relation between *ayin* and *yesh*—the "mystical nihil" and the "finite," or between God and the world, parallels the dialectical relationship between substance and manifestation, which is also the dominant relationship among all these opposites.

Godhead—that substance which gives life to the cosmos in all its manifestations—cannot in itself be revealed. Its only possible appearance is by means of "clothing," "instruments," or "concealment"—that is to say, through finitude and the world. The relationship between the two dimensions is one of total mutual dependence: the expression of substance depends on the existence of tools for its manifestation, whereas the very existence of this manifestation is dependent on the substance that brings it into existence. The fact that substance and manifestation are two separate categories, while at the same time interconnected, is emphasized. There is no manifestation without substance, and substance cannot be understood without manifestation. This is so even if manifestation does not necessarily express the substance, while the independent existence of substance does not depend on its manifestation.

Divinity, which according to the acosmic axiom is the only true essence, requires the creation of vessels for its expression. The process of creation of vessels is that of the formation of the finite, the finite being tested against these two categories of substance and manifestation. The substance of the cosmos is the divine essence itself, while its appearances seem to be its total opposite, because they embody differentiation and separation rather than the unification of the divine. The revealed cosmos exemplifies finitude, limitation, and discrimination, as opposed to the infinite, unlimited nature and unity of the divine being. The relationship between these two categories in the becoming of the cosmos—substance and manifestation—is a changing dialectic relationship, dependent on human acts and consciousness. The revealed cosmos expresses the divine purpose of revelation through contradiction, and apprehension of the substance of true being, despite its contradictory external appearance, is the fulfillment of the divine intention. Humanity is called upon to recognize these two categories, while annihilating manifestation within substance.

The main requirement of Habad divine service is to recognize these two approaches in terms of which reality is to be perceived. In order to define clearly the distinction between these two dimensions, Habad coined the two expressions *koah ha-yesh* (the potence of the finite) and *gilluy ha-yesh* (the manifestation of the finite). The former relates to the essence of the true connection between God and reality, to the divine will to bring about the reality, to the divine life within reality which sustains it at every moment, the causality of the coming into existence of the finite, etc. The latter relates to the manifestation of this potentiality and the embodiment of the revealed finite, as they are understood from the human point of view of concrete reality. Humanity is called upon to bridge the gap between the divine point of view, "which even in its aspect of absolute finitude is the aspect of His substance, may He be blessed" (R. Aaron Ha-Levi, *Sha'arey ha-Yihud weha-Emunah*, IV:26)—that is, the identification of material reality with the divine substance—and human empirical experience, which teaches us that material reality has a distinct, separate essence. The "potential of the finite," which is identified with the divine substance, was transformed into "absolute existence" after many concealments—that is, was transformed from divine potential to "hiddenness" and "opposite"—because of the divine will to self-manifestation.[8] Added to the basic assumption concerning the divine essence of materiality is a distinction between this essence being *in potentia* or being realized. Its being carried out in action—the becoming of the cosmos—takes place by contractions. However, the separate and distinct essence the cosmos formed by this process of *zimzum* exists only in terms of human perception and not from the divine point of view.

> He, may He be praised, is equal in heaven and on earth, for finitude does not conceal for Him, in spite of the fact that He is the creator of all and through Him they act, and He exists in all details of the levels. Nevertheless He, may He be blessed, is alone, without distinction, in terms of His potency of paradox, which is drawn from the potency of his equalization, which may do anything, to bring into existence and to give life, without any concealment or distinction at all. All this is from His point-of-view, may He be praised, but from our point-of-view existence appears as a separate and distinct substance. (R. Aaron Ha-Levi, *Sha'arey ha-'Avodah*, III:10)

A double paradox lies at the basis of this mystical theology. The first paradox relates to the understanding of Godhead as both united and divided. Indeed, it is defined by the arational duality of its being: "two contradictory opposites which cannot be comprehended by the human mind." This paradoxical duality uniting opposites underlies the unity of the divine: "As He is infinite, may He be blessed, and He is completely one and all division comes from Him, may He be blessed, nevertheless He is absolutely simple ... and understand this well, and remember this rule, for this is the root and basis of the unification" (R. Aaron Ha-Levi, *Sha'arey ha-Yihud weha-Emunah*, I:11).

The second paradox involves the understanding of emanated reality as bereft of divine essence, on the one hand, and divinity as united in reality, on the other hand: "Therefore they are called emanated, for they are a new existence unconnected to His essence, for He, may He be blessed, is without all these, and is nevertheless immanent in them" (*Sha'arey ha-Yihud weha-Emunah*, I:13).

The paradox of simultaneous unity and multiplicity and of existence and nihility is an expression of the more general problem of immanence and transcendence, with which kabbalistic thought had been concerned for generations, and which acquired a new dimension in Ḥabad thought. The acosmic outlook transcends the ranking of existence within the divine reality, because of the principle that divinity is the one and exclusive essence and that nothing exists apart from it. Duality, change, differentiated reality, and limitation are all nullified within the Infinite; they are merely imaginary, existing only from the point of view of created beings, while from the divine point of view all existence is totally equalized within the divine essence.

At the same time, because of the obvious difficulty in a simple identification of visible being with the totality of the divine essence, there must be a quantitative, if not a qualitative, ranking of this substance. This is accomplished by postulating the existence of a realm of His essence unapprehended by human beings: "For He, blessed be He, is absolutely equal even from the point of view of the worlds [i.e., immanence], but the potential of His equalization is neither known nor perceived, and is remote from apprehension [i.e., transcendence]" (R. Aaron Ha-Levi, *Sha'arey ha-Yiḥud weha-Emunah*, V:19). The conclusion to be drawn from this acosmic-immanentist argument concerning the equivalence of the forms of existence of God throughout the cosmos is thus qualified by the insistence on the inability of the human understanding to apprehend the "power of equalization" or by the contention of divine immanence.

Here we are not referring to transcendence in terms of substance, which distinguishes between various aspects of the divine essence (i.e., a concealed God and a revealed God), but transcendence of consciousness. This is because in acosmism, which recognizes one divine essence, the distinction between divinity and its appearances or emanations has no reality, since from the divine point of view all is one, and any differentiation exists only from the human point of view. Thus, any such differentiation exists only in perception and not in substance—the former being associated with the mistaken, illusory human point of view, the latter being connected with the absolute, unitary divine point of view. As we have said, the main emphasis is on the idea that the human's limited perception, which cannot apprehend the unity of the divine, may not lead one to an approach that suggests a change in the divine substance on its various levels. In other words, the understanding of divinity as transcendent is simply the outcome of the human's limited perception; divine transcendence then becomes an object of perception rather than a substantive reality. In Ḥabad terminology, "He who surrounds all worlds" (*sovev kol 'almin*—R. Shneur Zalman, *Tanya*, 134–36) is a concept relating to the transcendent aspect of divinity in the sense of his nonmanifestation to human perception or awareness (see

R. Aaron Ha-Levi, *Sha'arey ha-yihud weha-Emunah*, IV:9, 21), whereas in the kabbalistic perspective this concept refers to the divine light which breaks out of the boundaries of limited existence (vessels) and contact with the material and the world, because it is unable to tolerate its limitations.

"He who fills all worlds" (*memale' kol 'almin*; R. Shneur Zalman, *Tanya*, 111, 142) refers to the immanent aspect of the divinity or, in kabbalistic language, to the divine being which is condensed within the "vessels," within finite existence. However, because of the claim that this limitation has no ontic status from the divine viewpoint and that the "vessels" exist only within human thoughts, there is no substantial distinction between the two.

The uniqueness of the Habad conception, which yearned to decipher the divine unity within reality in terms of its acosmic assumptions, lies in its expression of full awareness of the cognitive transcendence in which the divinity is enshrouded, a transcendence that is expressed in the perception of reality as seemingly without divinity, despite the fact that the opposite is the case. The reason for this polarity in the perception of God, which may be defined as a tension between immanence (in actuality) and transcendence (stemming from the limitations of human comprehension), is rooted in its dialectical theology, which subjects the relationships of humanity and God to the realms of contradiction and paradox.

This perception of reality is based on two contradictory assumptions. In terms of God's true existence, or "from the divine point of view," the divine is everywhere immanent. There is absolute equivalence among all the different manifestations of reality. The only distinction stems from the level of human perception, which is able to stand the divine manifestation in its contracted form but not in its fullness. The confrontation with the paradox between immanence (the theoretical, the substantial, the unfelt, the longed-for in the formula "'The whole world is filled with His glory' [Isa 6:31], and no place is empty of Him") and transcendence (which one experiences and at the same time denies) or that between truth from the divine point of view ("for the worlds are not perceived by Him as substance at all, for in His truth, may He be praised, there is naught but Him at all," that is, the acosmic truth) and the limitations of the sense perceptions (which perceive in the world a separate being, separating between humanity and God) is solved the moment that the concealed is transformed into the object of faith, and the revealed, the concrete, and the empirical are transformed into illusion. The refusal to submit to the limitations of sense perception and the creation of different methods for the transformation of concrete reality into something insubstantial, meaningless, and illusory, lie at the very foundation of the spiritual service of God. The fundamental Hasidic outlook, which argues that the sense of distance between humanity and God is nothing but an illusion, lies at the basis of Habad doctrine, which confronts it from an ontological and epistemological viewpoint and wishes to understand both the nature of the divine closeness and the essential meaninglessness of his distance, by means of a dialectical mysticism. *This mysticism transforms transcendent existence, absent in God as a tangible substance, into a meaningless illusion, while the immanent God, who is outside the range of immediate fixed human apprehension, is transformed into the exclusive substantial reality.*

The Duality of Perception

Despite the fact that, from an ontological point of view, reality is one—namely, the divine substance in the unity of its many manifestations, which themselves have no substantial existence—there are a number of ways of perceiving this true reality: the human viewpoint, which cannot avoid deducing the truth of existence from visible reality and is thus necessarily mistaken, and that of the true reality, as it is perceived from the divine viewpoint. In Habad thought, the distinction between the divine and the human point of view and the nature of the relationship between finitude and infinity are of central importance. The attempt to reconcile these two points of view or to transcend the limits of human perception, which perceives reality as a distinct entity, and to enter into the realm of divine perception, in which infinite and finite are united, is one of the central goals of the spiritualist tendency within the Habad system of divine worship. The attempt to reconcile visible reality and its divine source, which is the true reality, undergoes various stages of examination and reflection, beginning in the rational-logical sphere and ending in the irrational-mystic. Confrontation with the contradiction between true existence from the divine point of view and humanly visible reality implies an understanding of the nature of the divine unity within limited reality (see R. Shneur Zalman, *Tanya*, 246, 258) that requires one to assume that the criterion of substance lies within one's point of perception.

> The coming about of substantiality ex nihile (*yesh me-ayin*) is in Hebrew called *Beri'ah* (creation). Such created substance, in fact, is also esteemed as naught before Him; that is, it is essentially non-existent in relation to the force and light that effulges in it from the kelim of the ten sefirot . . . just as the ray of the sun. . . . However, this is so only "before Him," relating to His blessed knowledge, from netherwards. But in relation to the knowledge from below upwards, created substance is [in such a knowledge and apprehension from below] an altogether separate thing. For the force that effuses it is not apprehended at all. (R. Shneur Zalman, *Tanya*, 258).[9]

The conflict between these two approaches is crystallized in a theory expressing the transition from an ontological perception of being (beyond human understanding) and an epistemological approach. That is, the understanding of reality as divine is replaced by its being understood as an epistemological criterion for its concealment and manifestation in the different aspects of human perception:

> What follows from all we have said above is that we must consider two aspects of Infinitude, may He be blessed—namely, one aspect from the point-of-view of Himself, and the other aspect, from the point-of-view of the worlds. That is, from the point of view of His Essence, one may not depict him with any attributes or differences of levels, or any activities, because of His simplicity; but from the view-point of the world, we must consider the aspects of the contraction of light, and emanation of potentialities from Him, may He be blessed, who exists in every detail. And there is nothing in the existent world which is not done in accordance with His intent, may He be blessed, and His flow into them, literally, in an active sense, except that He is united in them and is not changed in them, and this is the perception from the view-point of the revealed worlds, which are divided. But nevertheless, we must depict His unity in all its divisions without change or distinction. But in terms of His own point-of-view, even though he is drawn down in them and contracted within them, and they are all united in an overwhelming unification . . . one cannot describe, with regard to His essence, may He be blessed, any division or separation at all, for one may say that, even though they are divided into different levels, nevertheless He is one of them: for He is equalized in them, in the very model of His potencies, may He be blessed, which cannot be perceived within the realm of apprehension or understanding at all. . . . And the second consideration, which is that of the view-point of the worlds, contains two aspects, namely, as they are towards Him, may He be blessed, and as they are towards us, and we must assume and imagine that, towards us, what seems as limited and separate existence, towards Him, may He be blessed, are unified in a perfect unity, without any change or distinction at all (R. Aaron Ha-Levi, *Sha'arey ha-Yihud weha-emunah*, II:32)

The distinction suggested here between the two points of view is a perceptual one and not an essential one: the divine point of view, known in Habad literature by the term *le-gabaw* or *legabei didey* (regarding Him), which understands the true nature of reality, is contrasted with human understanding, *le-gabey didan* (regarding us), which perceives reality in an illusory, mistaken manner. Existence is not separate from divinity but is completely unified with it, because the concept of concealment and hiddenness does not refer to divinity, but is only valid from the human point of view. The unity of divine substance in all of its visible manifestations, which seems to contravene this unity, is in fact beyond the distorting nature of sensory, perceptually based consciousness. Therefore, the fact that reality seems to contradict the nature of the divine unity from the human viewpoint is not an ontological but an epistemological question.

What is then proposed here is a dual, bilateral perception of reality. From the divine point of view, reality embodies the manifestation of the divine essence of being, but from a human point of view, which by its nature lacks this all-encompassing view of things, being is understood in terms of hiddenness, concealment, and the absence of divinity.[10] The manifestation of the divine to human comprehension is dependent on concealment, but the uncovering of this concealment, which is theoretically within human capacity, is the precondition for apprehension of the true revelation.

In the acosmic outlook, the substantial distinction between finite and infinite is negated and transferred to the epistemological plane. The claim of absolute equivalence of the divine substance in all manifestations of reality is tested against the epistemological criterion of revelation and concealment and is transformed from a question of substance into one of apprehension. As a result of this conception, a substantial effort is devoted to uncovering the nature of the finite, and a double, spiritual interest is crystallized: on the one hand, an attempt to break through the boundaries of the finite and the borders of comprehension in order to perceive the reality of the divine, while the locus of confrontation is in the human soul (i.e., the spiritualist interest); on the other hand, a conscious renunciation of the possibility of human apprehension of the divine unity beyond its revelation to human consciousness through Torah and *mizwot* (i.e., the a-spiritual interest).

The Theory of the Soul

In addition to the three dialectical tendencies discussed above—corporealization and annihilation, the human and divine viewpoints, the extension of the real and the negation of the real—there is an additional dialectical structure found in the Habad doctrine of the soul,[11] built upon the assumption that the ontological duality of the divine essence is reflected in the structure of the human soul. The basic assumption of Habad psychology, borrowed from the Lurianic doctrine of the soul, is that the human being possesses two souls—a divine soul and an animal soul—reflecting two parallel structures expressing concealed and revealed relationships, unity and diversity in the cosmos as a whole.

The divine soul is "a portion of God above"—the divine element present in the human, originating in the *sefirot* and representing recognition of the true, integrated reality, the longing of the spirit to return and cling to its source, and the restoration of the finite to the infinite (see R. Shneur Zalman, *Tanya*, chap. 2). The animal soul is rooted in the "bright shell" (*qelipat nogah*), which unites within itself good and evil and represents the appearance of differentiated reality, the worlds—that reality which does not perceive itself as a part of the divine unity—as well as the longing after the illusory reality with which one ought not to be satisfied (see *Tanya*, chap. 1).

These two souls are interdependent: the divine soul is the source of vitality and a condition for the existence of the animal soul, while the animal soul is the garment allowing the manifestation of the divine soul and its individual existence. The relationship between these two souls (which includes parallel frameworks of intellectual potences and ethical characteristics which correspond to the system of *sefirot* and the system of *qelipot*) is not a static one. The divine soul wishes to transform the animal soul, to incorporate it within the Godhead, and to change its very essence, while the animal soul wishes to alter the nature of the divine soul and bring it down into physical reality. The purpose of the descent of the divine soul and its embodiment in the animal soul is the same as that of the creation of the world as a whole—namely, "to reveal His glory, may He be blessed, in the lower realms." As in the former case, this takes place through its opposite. The uniqueness of the Ḥabad doctrine of the soul does not lie in its components, which are by and large borrowed from earlier kabbalistic doctrines, but in its theocentric orientation, which states that the relationship between the divine soul and the animal soul correspond to relationships between the physical and the spiritual which exist in the cosmos as a whole. As we have said above, the dominant factor in this relationship is interdependence: the physical cannot exist without the spiritual, which sustains it, and the spiritual cannot be manifested without the material in which it is embodied. The spiritual is revealed by means of the physical, but wishes to negate and incorporate the physical within its own essence.

The innovation of the Ḥabad approach consists in its understanding of the different parts of the soul as different levels of awareness of the divine being as separated or as united, while drawing a parallel between the unification of the divine within the worlds and that of the divine soul within the animal soul.

Ḥabad doctrine contains a parallel, dual structure of positive and negative spiritual forces, which share a common source despite their separate manifestations. These structures are known by different names, dependent upon the context within which they are discussed. At one pole is the Infinite, the holiness, unity, revelation, the Good Urge, all represented in the divine soul; at the other pole are the finite, the "Other Side" (*sitra 'aḥra*), separation, contraction (*zimzum*), hiddenness, and the Evil Impulse, all of which are represented in the animal soul. The dialectic between finite and infinite is simultaneously one between the animal soul and the divine soul, between evil and good, between the "Other Side" and holiness. Thus, a meta-morphosis in any one of them bears consequences for the rest as well. The central role of the doctrine of the soul in Habad derives from this—that the locus of theogonic events passes to the human soul, in which the two dialectic elements of manifestation and concealment are represented within the guise of the divine soul and the animal soul. The relationships between the different parts of the soul are not circumscribed within the confines of human psychology, but are first and foremost the reflection of different situations within the divine reality and different levels of awareness of the divine being as separate or as united.

Both souls reflect the dialectic of annihilation and realization in the divine reality. The divine soul, whose descent into the world is in order "to reveal His glory, may He be blessed, below," longs to return to its divine, supernal source, while the animal soul, whose purpose is to enable the divine soul to be revealed, wishes to descend to the depths of corporeality.

The animal soul is the focus of religious life, as it constantly confronts the challenge of change of essence, spiritual metamorphosis and struggle between its natural inclinations (toward fragmentation and corporealization) and that which is expected of it (annihilation and incorporation). The animal soul represents empirical-sensory cognition, the posture or con-sciousness of reality which must be changed and the illusory consciousness against which battle must be done, separation and division, the being which ascribes to itself separate existence in place of the unitary consciousness which is the goal of religious worship. The divine soul, on the other hand, represents the mystical consciousness of the divine nature of the cosmos, absolute unity, and the divine point of view. The process of transformation of the animal soul into the divine soul is one in which separation is transformed into unity, and an ever-changing, transient consciousness based on sensory experience is transformed into one based on mystical perception. This is, in fact, the essence of the transformation of evil into good, since in Habad thought evil is first of all a reality lacking any substance, which is nothing more than an expression of mistaken differentiative perception (see R. Shneur Zalman, *Tanya*, 20, 74), while good expresses a unified percep-tion and cognition of the trust of existence.[12]

There was a dialectical assumption in Habad that the maximal realization of the spiritual element is possible through its revelation by its own opposite and that the cognitive confrontation with this situation of opposi-tion, its abstraction and restoration to its source, brings about expression of the truth of its existence. The implication of this idea of the relationship between the divine soul and the animal soul, or of the relationship between God and manifest reality, is that of a dialectical manifestation of divinity through its opposite. Confrontation with reality, while recognizing its function as a manifestation of the divine reality, set as its goal the restoration of the contradiction to its source, the revelation to divinity. This approach granted principal importance to reality and to finitude and to their function in the totality of the divine wills and demanded that they be understood as part of the totality of processes and tendencies, and not in isolation.

The struggle with existence, its cognitive confrontation, and the metamorphosis within it all occur in the realm of the soul and the apprehension or anticipated consciousness. The animal soul represents seemingly separate reality, the self-being that sees itself as being separated from God, while the divine soul represents the true reality, conscious of its divine origin and of the negation of its external reality or being to its true essence, which longs to be included in a comprehensive unity within God.

The Habad doctrine of the soul emphasizes the dynamic, transformative element in religious life; there are no static, uni-meaning values, but everything is expressed or realized in processes of embodiment and expansion, confrontation and change between the poles of the physical and the spiritual, the animal soul and the divine soul. It was not created through an interest in psychology, but from a theological point of view relating to what occurs within the human being and the soul as such. The human being is rather understood as a vehicle for serving the divine goals of revelation by means of transformation and as a stage for the occurrence of the metamorphosis of the hidden divine being into revealed reality, on the one hand, and for the restoration of revealed being to its substantial source, on the other.

The Worship of God ('Avodat ha-Shem)

The Habad approach to divine worship is based on its dialectical theology, which ascribes to God two tendencies or contradictory wills pertaining to the process of creation:

> As the purpose of the descent and drawing down of the light of His Divinity, may it be blessed, was that it be embodied in the created beings and grant them life through the process of contraction (zimzum) . . . until they come to exist in the manner of finite or separated being, this is so that afterwards the finite be abnegated in the infinite . . . and this gives pleasure to Him, may He be praised, that there is a finite that is abnegated, and it is precisely this that He wills." (R. Shneur Zalman, Torah Or, Bereshit, 9)

The aim of creation was rooted in the divine will to create a finitude, separated from Himself, a seeming nondivine cosmic reality which, in terms of its true existence, is only illusory. The purpose of the service of God is to negate or annihilate this distinct being, to strip its corporeality, and to cause it to ascend through the levels of spirituality until the previous divine unity is restored. However, this is not the single divine will that guides humanity in its relationship to the world, since this relationship must be based on the awareness of the permanent dialectical relationship between God and existence. The process of creation is interpreted as an expression of the divine will to reveal His perfection, a perfection expressed in the dual will of simultaneous concretization and annihilation of the nondivine cosmos. As divinity did not fully express its will in the act of creation, this perfection depends upon human worship.

All Ḥabad divine worship, in both its "spiritualistic" and "nonspiritualistic" aspects, is inspired by this tension between creation and God.[13] Corresponding to these two dimensions of the becoming of the finite as an expression of the divine will to be revealed and the annihilation of the finite as an expression of the divine will to be concealed, there are two commandments relating to the service of God. One is the drawing down of divinity into the finite (A), and the second is annihilation or self-abnegation of the finite to God (B). The drawing down of the divine will into the finite, or its unification in the cosmos, is expressed in the service of Torah and *mizwot,* and the annihilation of the finite and its restoration to its divine source are expressed in the service of *biṭṭul* (self-abnegation), contemplation, communion, ecstasy, and other means of incorporation of the physical in the spiritual through spiritualization. (A) "The essential worship is to draw down the light of the Infinite, blessed be He, into the realm of the Finite, that the glory of God be revealed specifically in the sense of manifestation of the Finite, and in this worship . . . the essential intention is revealed in its inwardness" (R. Aaron Ha-Levi, *Shaʿarey ha-ʿAvodah,* I:33). (B) "Just as they [i.e., the worlds] are united by His power, may He be blessed, in the aspect of upper unification (*yiḥuda ʿilaʾa*), so must they be united in the aspect of the lower unification (*yiḥuda tataʾa*), that they be annihilated towards Him, may He be blessed, that they not be made manifest as existing and separate in terms of their own essence" (R. Aaron Ha-Levi, *Shaʿarey ha-Yiḥud weha-Emunah,* V:19).

As a counterpart to the duality of the divine will, a dual submission of the human will is demanded: on the one hand, self-abnegation of the human will to the divine will in the sense of annihilation and utter lack of individual will; on the other hand, the realization of the divine will as defined through one's obligation to fulfill or perform Torah and *mizwot,* through which divine will is revealed in the cosmos.

The teachers of Ḥabad stressed the uncompromising necessity of both dimensions of divine service—pertaining as they do to the two different divine wills and the two aspects of human submission—by several pairs of mutually dependent concepts, such as inwardness and externalness, breathing and blowing, going and returning:

> But the phrase "all that has breath" [Ps 150:6] is specifically used, because the term *neshamah* (soul) comes from the word *neshimah* (breath), for man has the characteristic of going and returning (or "running back and forth" [*razo' wa-shov;* Ezek 1:14]), and also because it is said of breath itself, "I will pant and I will gasp" [Isa 42:14]. . . . And the aspect of *razo'* (ascending) of the soul is that of self-sacrifice at the time that one recites *Shema'*—that is, the surrendering of one's will, because the soul is the will . . . that is, that he uproot his will, which is implanted in the vanities of this world, to have only one will, directed toward his Father in heaven, as is said, "Whom have I in heaven but thee" [Ps 73:24], that he has no other desire or will whatsoever, that is, when he reflects in his heart that there is nothing but Him, and everything is annihilated in Him, may He be praised. . . . And whoever delves deeply into this matter, and more, will understand in his heart that he should not turn to aught but to God himself and his will will be only towards Him, may He be blessed, to cling to Him with yearning of the soul. And as it is in *razo'* [i.e., the movement towards God], so shall it be in *shov* [i.e., the return to the material world] as well, that "these things which I command you this day [shall be on your heart; Deut 6:6]. . . . For the holy One, blessed be He, has naught in this world but the "four ells" of the *halakhah,* by means of which His dwelling is made specifically in the lower realms, for this is His wisdom and His will, etc., and it is incumbent upon every man that your heart run out and return to the One. (R. Shneur Zalman, *Torah Or,* Miqeẓ, 72)

These two aspects of the worship of God, which relate to the two aspects of the divine will, are parallel to the two Lurianic symbols of *shevirah* (breaking) and *tiqqun* (restoration). However, whereas in the Lurianic myth *shevirah* relates to the theogonic realm and *tiqqun* is partially connected to the human realm, here the two realms are understood as corresponding to the two tendencies of the divine will—differentiation and integration, manifestation and concealment—as well as being subject to human worship and to human consciousness of them, as an expression of the duality of the divine will.

The two aspects of the relationship of material reality to the sustaining spiritual element—on the one hand, drawing it into the world and, on the other, abnegation toward it—are understood within the broad categories of realism and spiritualism, which dictate a bifurcated approach to the service of God: that which draws Godhead down from above, relating to the God residing in reality, the immanent divinity, seeking to worship God within the givens of time and place; and that which seeks to annihilate the limits of the body and of finitude and to break beyond it, to negate the cosmos and to incorporate it within the divine Nothingness, out of its longing for the transcendent Godhead (see R. Shneur Zalman, *Tanya*, 85). The fact that these two tendencies are mutually contradictory is no obstacle to this teaching, in which paradox and the dialectic of contradiction, "two opposites in one subject," is a fundamental element.

> There are two aspects in the worship of God: one, the intense love, with burning fire, to leave the body. . . . This is the aspect of "great love," which the vessels of the heart cannot contain, for the heart cannot contain such tremendous ecstasy. Thus, it cannot stand in the vessels of its body and wishes to leave the material vessel of the body. The second is that of ecstasy which dwells in the heart, and whose concern is to draw down divinity from above to below, in the various kinds of vessels, through Torah and *miẓwot*. (R. Shneur Zalman, *Torah Or*, wa-yishlaḥ, 49)

The mystical theology of Ḥabad is based on the dialectic between the physical and the spiritual, the real and the divine, the concrete and the abstract, the immanent and the transcendent, the finite and the infinite, the limitations of human perception and the truth of divine reality, the animal soul and the divine soul. The religious effort demanded of the human being entails the discovering of the abstract essence of visible, concrete appearance or the exposure of the divine substance of the physical realm in every dimension of existence and being. From another point of view, the implication of this demand is the liberation of human consciousness from the bonds of the illusion of the concrete and its orientation toward the truth of reality from the divine point of view or, in Ḥabad terminology, *bittul ha-yesh we-hasagat ha-ayin* (abnegation of the finite and apprehension of the infinite)—that is, the revelation of the truth of reality as united within a seemingly differentiated reality.

Worship through Self-Abnegation (*bittul*)

The acosmic view, asserting the nihility of creation, demanded that the consciousness of this nihility become the basis for a spiritualist worship which sought the restoration of the finite to the infinite, a form of worship known in Ḥabad terminology as *'avodah be-bittul* ("worship through negation").[14] The concept of *bittul* expresses the awareness that the human being is nullified or seen as nothing in relation to the divine element, and the human's relationship to reality is seen as negated in contrast to the divine element that enlivens it.

The fundamental relationship between God and that which He created is expressed by *bittul*, the value that most expresses the uniqueness of God demanded by the acosmic approach. *Bittul* is the ideal archetype of the mystical life, or the basic orientation of finite and infinite. It is not to be understood as an everyday practice (even though it is meant to be attained at the time of prayer), but as a fundamental attitude which serves as the basis for the relationship toward all divine worship. The centrality of the concept of *bittul* within Habad is parallel to that of *devequt* ("communion") in Hasidism generally. In pre-Habad Hasidism, *bittul* was not a value in itself, but a means toward attaining the desired communion, whether as a stage toward its attainment or as a means of acquiring the passivity that is conducive to the ecstatic state of being moved by the divine Spirit. In this Hasidic approach, *bittul* is understood as a stage in the acquisition of the highest human perfection, which involves the destruction of natural forces in order to allow the divine to act within humans.

In Habad, *bittul* is understood as the spiritual practice derived from the acosmic assumption and as humanity's portion in the dialectical process of divine concretization and annihilation. Thus, the dominant interest in the process of *bittul* is the theocentric one, understood as aiding in the realization of a dimension of the divine not realized at the time of creation. Hence, the negation of the finite is not understood simply as an expression for the human being's mystical longings, but as an obligation incumbent upon the human being, who serves as a tool of the divine dialectic of concretization and annihilation.

The significance of the service of negation is based on the assumption that the spirit is able to negate physical reality: according to Habad psychology, the divine soul's yearning toward its source and its desire to cling to its root are the source of the very possibility of *bittul* (see R. Dov Baer, *Ner Mizwah we-Torah Or: Sha'ar ha-Emunah*, 66a–b).

The service of *bittul* begins with *hitbonenut* ("contemplation"),[15]—rational, intellectual speculation on the finite and the infinite, of being and nothingness. In the Habad lexicon, contemplation (*hitbonenut*) is derived from *tevunah* ("understanding") (see R. Shneur Zalman, *Iggeret ha-Qodesh* [*Tanya*, 246–47]). Its aim is to grant the human a perspective beyond the artificial constraints of ordinary consciousness. The goal of contemplation is for one to understand, within human limitations and in the realm of the ratio and the intellect, the greatness of God who "fills all worlds" and "surrounds all worlds"; to comprehend His apparent distance from humanity, and His actual closeness to humanity, to apprehend the truth of existence—a perception of the world as if it is not and of reality as illusory—and to recognize Godhead as the exclusive reality and source of the life of the cosmos. *Hitbonenut* is defined as a means of perceiving the divine unity and is explicated within a detailed, systematic framework of the processes of understanding and of apprehension.

R. Dov Baer, the son of R. Shneur Zalman of Lyady, wrote a detailed treatise on this subject entitled *Quntres ha-Hitbonenut* (*Tract on Contemplation*).[16] In the introduction, the subject is defined as follows:

> The nature of this tract is that it speaks about the divine unity, in every detail of the structure of manifestations of the ten *sefirot* of Emanation, Creation, Formation and Action—in short, everything that man is able to bring close to his understanding in apprehension embodied and grasped in the mind and the heart, in all details of the structure or order of the emanation, from the first stage of contraction [i.e., of the divine substance—*zimzum*] down to the end of the World of Action, and this is called, the tract on Contemplation. (R. Dov Baer, *Ner Miẓwah we-Torah Or, Shaʿar ha-Yiḥud,* Introduction)

The teachers of Ḥabad interpreted the kabbalistic doctrine of emanation as a way of perceiving the unity of the divine substance, despite its different manifestations. *Hitbonenut,* or contemplation of the doctrine of emanation, became a tool for perceiving the divine unity, while contemplating the spiritual structure of reality in relation to the infinite and the significance of immanence and transcendence (see R. Dov Baer, *Liqqutey Bi'urim,* 57a).

Contemplation of the greatness of God, in the sense of directing one's thoughts and understanding toward Him, constitutes a fundamental imperative. The continual consciousness that the world is filled with and surrounded by divinity is the essential subject of contemplation, whose purpose is to bridge between the transcendental experience of a world without divinity and the immanent longings for a world united with divinity. The underlying assumption is that intellectual reflection will bring about a mystical-ecstatic arousal which will transcend the limits of sensory cognition.

> For when the intellect in the rational soul contemplates and immerses itself exceedingly in the greatness of God, the way in which He fills all worlds and encompasses all worlds, and in the presence of Whom everything is considered as nothing—there will be born and aroused in his mind and thought the emotion of awe for the Divine Majesty, to fear and be humble before His blessed greatness, which is without end or limit, and to have the dread of God in his heart. Next, his heart will glow with an intense love, like burning coals, with a passion, desire and longing, and a yearning soul, towards the greatness of the blessed *Eyn Sof.* This constitutes the culminating passion of the soul (*kelot ha-nefesh*) of which Scripture speaks. (R. Shneur Zalman, *Tanya,* chap. 3, p. 14; Eng., I:32)

The purpose of *hitbonenut* is the understanding of God's paradoxical presence in the cosmos, which simultaneously unites his existence and his nonexistence, known as "the knowledge of his unity." In order to attain this knowledge, one must comprehend the theosophic-kabbalistic meaning of the concepts of *zimzum*, emanation, the theory of the *sefirot*, and other subjects known as "knowledge of the Kabbalah." The purpose of this contemplation is to serve as a means for the excitation of the soul to mystical arousal, for breaking out of the boundaries of finite and empirical consciousness, and to achieve unio-mystica.[17] The path of rational contemplation is open to all, including those who lack the pneumatic capability, although the ultimate goal is the transition from intellectual understanding and rational contemplation to pneumatic unity, self-abnegation, and expiration of the soul (*kelot ha-nefesh*).

Habad was attacked from several quarters for its teaching of contemplation, which facilitated the rational study of kabbalistic esotericism, by its daring attempt to create rational intellectual parallels to kabbalistic-mystical concepts and to remove the esoteric aura surrounding the study of these subjects in the mainstream kabbalistic tradition.[18]

Habad historiography suggests that its opponents within the Hasidic camp thought that "worship should only be via the moral traits (*middot*) and through simple faith, and that augmentation of contemplation of divinity is unnecessary, and that, to the contrary, enhanced knowledge of divinity, if not coupled with the actualization of the attributes of the heart, will make it less than worthwhile. But "our teacher" [i.e., R. Shneur Zalman] argued the knowledge of Divinity as being the principal matter."[19]

Those theological and mystical principles which were known in Habad as "the words of the living God" (*divrey Elohim hayyim*) were the main subject of contemplation and were articulated and explained in the most rational and logical way possible, including detailed instructions concerning the attainment of the goals of *hitbonenut*. The teachers of Habad argued whether rational contemplation was an end in itself or a prior condition and instrument for the attainment of ecstasy (*hitpaʿalut*), or whether the fact that an individual can grasp the inclusion of the entire cosmos within divinity by means of rational contemplation means that he is exempt from the mystical-spiritualistic enthusiasm which seeks the unchanging God beyond the world. In the eyes of both its supporters and its critics, Habad was characterized by the centrality it gave to the rationalistic posture which sought the point of contact among human intellect, physical reality, and the divine essence, and saw the knowledge of divinity as the essential thing. In fact, the Habad outlook was unique in its confidence that rational contemplation does lead to suprarational apprehension and that this apprehension is not dependent on pneumatic being but on an intellectual method (which is described) of study of theological principles and contemplation of their meaning for the service of God.

The acquisition of these theological-mystical suppositions and their detailed knowledge were a precondition of pneumatic-spiritual and transrational experience. The transition from the rational-intellectual to the suprarational stage required, in addition to profound study of the Kabbalah, of Hasidism, and of prayer (see R. Dov Baer, *Liqqutey Bi'urim,* 61a), an ability compounded of the annihilation of individual awareness, the obliteration of consciousness, and the negation of the will, which are believed to prepare the human soul for the mystical experience of incorporation within the divine. Habad Hasidism confronted the question of the relationship between intellectual contemplation—that *hitbonenut* which entails "intellectual ecstasy" (*hitpa'alut ha-sekhel;* R. Menahem Mendel, *Derekh Mizwotekha,* 39)—and emotional ecstasy—"excitation of the heart" (*hitpa'alut ha-lev*). Its teachers wrote detailed tractates clarifying the correct and incorrect relationship between intellectual and emotional effort within the worship of God. The criterion was the mystical attainment of communion and abnegation, against which both "contemplation of the mind" and "excitement of the heart" are measured.

The introduction to R. Dov Baer b. Shneur Zalman's *Quntres ha-Hitpa'alut* (*Tract on Ecstasy*) contains evidence of the great tension surrounding this question:

> The time has now come when it is my clear duty to explain thoroughly for all our fraternity the fundamental principles of Hasidism. For many—indeed, practically all, great and small—delude themselves, are mistaken and walk in a crooked path. . . . For instance, there is the matter of that type of confusion, of which all our fraternity is guilty, regarding contemplation in prayer. When a man dwells in understanding on the subject and is successful in his mind's efforts, he forbids himself the category of heart-ecstasy, which seems to him to be forbidden for a number of reasons. For rumor has it that ecstasy interferes with comprehension. He forbids mind-ecstasy too.[20]

R. Shneur Zalman's disciple, R. Aaron Ha-Levi, devoted many pages to refuting the claim that *hitbonenut* without "arousal of the heart" is the principal matter, arguing that the entire validity of *hitbonenut* depends entirely on the ecstatic or transrational arousal that it brings about.[21]

According to his view, *hitbonenut* represents the way of rational worship, which is limited to the finite realm, and is itself nothing more than a means serving the realm of transrational experience, but lacking in significance as a goal in itself, despite its great importance. According to another view, that of R. Dov Baer b. Shneur Zalman, by means of intellectual contemplation one attains the highest possible levels of self-abnegation and unity with God

(*Sha'arey Teshuvah*, I:87, II:27). The goal of *hitbonenut* is to apprehend the truth of reality—the perception of the world as nonexistent and of divinity as possessing the only true existence, or the denial of visible reality and the apprehension of the exclusive reality, that of God, while distinguishing between apprehension of the extension of the divine substance within the world (immanence) and contemplation of that non-emanated divine substance which is not coterminous with the cosmos (transcendence). The former apprehension must precede the latter and is the subject of contemplation.

The concept of *bittul* (negation) is the central concept in Habad spiritual-istic teaching, which expresses the ethos demanded by the acosmic thesis—the incorporation of the finite and its nullification within the infinite.

The service of *bittul* requires one to acknowledge the finite realm and to understand its place within the divine scheme from various points of view, expressing the level of unity of spirit within matter—"for to that which is not finite the term *bittul* does not apply at all" (R. Aaron Ha-Levi, *Sha'arey ha-'Avodah*, II:21).

The principal possibility of negation of finitude is based on the under-standing of reality and the infinite. The finite is formed for the sake of the divine will to reveal his wholeness in the lower realms. It was formed through many contractions (*zimzumim*), which conceal and hide the power of divine *hashwa'ah* ("equalization"). These contractions are meaningless from the divine point of view, for which the finite and the infinite, the revealed and the hidden, are equal, but they are meaningful from the human point of view, which cannot withstand a divinity that is not concealed. This axiom relating to the existence of the finite and its contraction from the human point of view alone opens the way for the negation of the finite, which does not in fact actually exist, in order to apprehend the divinity embodied in reality.

> From God's point of view, above and below are equal in Him, may He be blessed, As is light, so is darkness, and the emanation is only according to our perception and from the aspect [viewpoint] of the created worlds, from infinite to finitude, that they not be negated in existence . . . that is, the truth of His unity, may He be blessed, is equal in the upper and lower worlds. . . . And in order to bring about finitude from absolute infinity, there must be the aspect of contraction. (R. Shneur Zalman, *Torah Or*, Miqez, 80, 71)

The finite, in its potential, is identified with the divine substance, while its actualization, realized through the process of *zimzum*, brings about the separate essence of the finite. But this essence or being only exists from the human point of view, but lacks any existence from the divine point of view.

Worship in *bittul* embodies the realization of the divine will since, by it, the manifestation of the divine, which is not revealed under any other circumstances, occurs: "Therefore, when the lower beings are united in the worlds and devote their souls to God by negation of the finite as revealed unto us, thereby performing His will, then His will, may He be blessed, is awakened in the cosmos through His own substance, which is not in the capacity of drawing down; and this apsect is called 'surrounding all worlds'" (R. Aaron Ha-Levi, *Sha'arey ha-Yihud weha-Emunah*, V:24).

One finds within Habad literature many different kinds of service of negation, accompanied by complex discussions relating the service of *bittul* to the doctrine of the soul and the understanding of the finite. The three main kinds of negation are "negation in relation to the transrational substance," "negation of understanding and knowledge," and "negation of feeling and ecstasy." This threefold division is based on the theoretical axiom which interprets the relationship of the spiritual and the physical in terms of three categories: potential essence, the manifestations of this essence, and its reflections (or: potential, actual, and reflective). This scheme refers to the relations of spirit and matter on all levels, toward which human worship is directed. The service of *bittul* thus reflects simultaneously different levels of human self-consciousness and awareness as well as the relationship between human will and the divine will within which the human being longs to be annihilated.

The theoretical basis for this threefold categorization of the service of negation is rooted in the understanding of the role of the finite and its relation to the divine manifestation, by its division into potential, actual, and reflective stages of the divine unification within the worlds. In kabbalistic terminology, this parallels "complete holiness" (*qedushah gemurah*), "brightness" (*nogah*), and "dross of kings" (*sigey melakhim*) (see R. Aaron Ha-Levi, *Sha'arey ha-'Avodah*, II:21).

The guiding principle is that "outside of the realm of the finite, *bittul* does not at all apply" (*Sha'arey ha-'Avodah*, II:21), that is, the service of negation requires acknowledgment of the finite and an understanding of its position within the divine creation from various points of view, which expresses the unification of spirit within matter.

On the highest level, symbolized by the "world of emanation" and of worship known as *bittul mi-zad ha-'ezem* ("negation of the substance"), the finite is expressed from the divine point of view. This is an acknowledgment of the acosmic position, which sees the finite as without substance in terms of its own true existence—from the divine point of view—and its understanding as a means of concealment of divinity from created beings. From the human point of view, on the highest levels of negation, that of negation from substance, there is no feeling at all, so that the question of self-consciousness is inapplicable. The human being ascends beyond that view which distinguishes between contradictory elements and awareness of them and achieves realization of the aspect of equalization (unification of opposites) by understanding, on the one hand, that reality is denied of the divine essence, and yet he perceives divinity as united with reality, on the other hand—and includes them all in one potentiality. The emphasis upon the lack of self-awareness stresses incorporation within the divine unity, while losing the awareness of distinct consciousness.

The second level of negation expresses the recognition of the unification of divinity with the world, which is still understood as a separate being from God, *bittul* expressing "the understanding of His expansion, may He be blessed, throughout the worlds, and that there is nothing apart from Him, and that He, may He be blessed, is unified in all actions" (R. Aaron Ha-Levi, *Sha'arey ha-'Avodah*, II:21). This paradoxical approach says that "the unification is because all the worlds and all of the aspects within the world are manifested on the level of division, yet He, may He be blessed, is nevertheless unified within them" (*Sha'arey ha-'Avodah*, II:21). In this negation, one is still aware of the finite as a separate existent being, deriving the truth of existence—the fact that existence is a projection of the divine being and lacks substance of its own—from manifest reality. Here finitude understands its source, or the manifest understands its potential, while remaining separate in its being and its awareness of it. This negation is known as *bittul be-haskalah we-da'at*—negation through understanding and knowledge.

The third level of negation is defined as an emotion, which is an application of the sensory reflection that distinguishes among essences and understands their unity, despite the distinctions felt by human consciousness. On this level, the relationship between divinity and existence as two distinct elements is emphasized, because as the distance between them becomes smaller, so does the love become smaller, according to the Habad outlook, as "feeling and ecstasy are towards that which is remote in its essence, but as we draw closer to it the ecstasy becomes less, until at the point of the love that one feels for oneself, one is completely without ecstasy" (*Sha'arey ha-'Avodah*, II:21). In principle, the discussion of *bittul* focuses upon *bittul be-da'at* and upon negation of substance—that is, *bittul shele-ma'lah min ha-da'at* (transrational negation). The distinction between the two levels of *bittul* appears on the level of the unity of the worshiper with God. On the lower level there is a distinction drawn between two essences, the worshiper and the object of worship: the worshiper approaches God but is yet separated from Him, in the sense that the worshiper is still conscious of himself as an independent entity and distinct from God. On the higher level, the consciousness of the uniqueness of the divine negates the existence of anything apart from God, including the being of the worshiper himself, who is united with God. The act of approach can only take place between two distinct essences, but the awareness that only one essence exists brings about the negation of the other in respect to it.

Bittul be-da'at, negation from the aspect of revelation, depends on *hitbonenut* and causes communion from below to above, while *bittul mi-zad ha-'ezem* (negation in terms of substance) is "uninterrupted, even at the time that he does not meditate," while the communion which it brings about comes from above to below. The ultimate object of *bittul be-'ezem* is the transcendent divine substance, while the other levels of *bittul* make do with the aspects of divinity embodied in the various "vessels", that is, the immanent aspect of divinity, or some other limitation accessible to humanity.

Both forms of *bittul* are necessary and are interdependent, *bittul be-da'at* being a stage in human apprehension which distinguishes between opposites, while *bittul* which is above reason unites and annihilates opposites within the all-inclusive unity. Nevertheless, the achievement of this trans-rational *bittul* is dependent on the realization of *bittul be-da'at* (see R. Aaron Ha-Levi, *Sha'arey ha-Yihud weha-Emunah,* II:40). The ultimate goal—awareness of the absolute unity of the divine being, or of the unity of being and the mystic nihil as "literally one essence," and of the misleading nature of sensory-based human perceptions—must confront the double reality visible to the eye, with the finite and the infinite, with all their contradictions. At the time of this confrontation, human consciousness comes to encompass more and more of reality, until and at the highest stage it enables one to transcend the limitations of this reality.

Bittul is understood as one of the general foundations of the cosmos, its significance being that each and every creature and reality contains the potential for annihilation within its source. *Bittul* is not only an act on the part of created beings but also a divine principle present in the entire cosmos. The basis of the transition from the concrete to the abstract exists in potential throughout creation, but the active potential within the creation, with its transformative possibilities, is present only in one's thought and consciousness, and only by its means is the transition from the corporeal to the spiritual at all possible. The goal of the worship of abnegation is to realize and actualize this given potential—that of negation to the source.

This negation is contingent upon a certain consciousness of the nature of the divine reality of the cosmos and an understanding of the divine unity, in which the divine essence exists in the world, while its essence is unchanged. This consciousness likewise asserts that there is no reality apart from the divine one, so that everything which seems to refute this position must be seen as if it is nonexistent. There is no argument in Habad over the fact that reality appears to be separate from divinity, but rather over its perception as such. The demand is to perceive reality as divine, despite the fact that it appears to be the opposite—indeed, precisely because this is so. Habad masters admit that, as material reality seems lacking in divinity, the recognition of its divine nature becomes that much more difficult: "Without understanding His unity, may He be blessed, in the worlds, even if one believes that 'the whole world is full of His glory' [Isa 6:3] all the worlds appear to be purely material, and the Holy One, blessed be He, is infinitely denied within the material realm" (R. Aaron Ha-Levi, *Sha'arey ha-Yihud weha-Emunah*, introduction). Spiritual worship is based on an understanding of the nature of the divine union within the worlds, which cannot be judged on the basis of appearances, but through cognition, faith, and reflection. Thus, *bittul* expresses the preference for the spiritual value of reality above its manifest, apparent material value.

According to the acosmic view, reality, which is seemingly distinct from divinity, is united with divinity "in a tremendous unification," and the aim of *bittul* is to understand its true stature as the realization of the divine will, despite its apparently being the opposite. The bridge between the understanding of reality as it is and as it appears to our eyes is performed by means of *bittul*. In other words, *bittul* is an expression of the effort contained in the unique vision of reality from the divine viewpoint to abandon the human perception, which sees existence as separate from divinity and as an expression of the recognition of the truth of reality, and not of its illusionary, visible appearance. "The negation of the worlds and their unification is such that the worlds are not understood as an essence in themselves, but as united with Him, may He be blessed, until nothing is revealed but the light of His substance that is united with them" (R. Aaron Ha-Levi, *Sha'arey ha-Yihud weha-Emunah*, IV:32).

One might see the worship in *bittul* as "practical acosmism," as that form of praxis which seems to be demanded by the acosmic assumption and as the best expression of this consciousness. The performance of *bittul* demands total abnegation of the individual self and the total elimination of the element of personal interest within divine worship. This demand entails, as well, the annihilation of human will, a lack of personal interest, and a state of unawareness. The hour of prayer was the period set aside for the performance of negation in practice, but such statements as "and that they should also be as a permanent remembrance all day that the world and his body and his soul are not an essence at all, in this knowledge he attached himself to Him, may He be blessed" (R. Aaron Ha-Levi, *Sha'arey ha-'Avodah*, IV:39) take the service of negation above and beyond a certain time period, to become the general spiritual orientation of divine service.

The teachers of Ḥabad differed in their opinions concerning the possibility of achieving perfect *biṭṭul* and the role of the various imperfect forms of *biṭṭul* in relation to complete *biṭṭul*.²² The uniqueness of the Habad view lay in this: that, despite the aiming for absolute *biṭṭul*, for the annihilation of human will and the denial of all desires and interests, there was room for longings and achievements which were of a lower but more realistic order and which opened the way for those who are prevented from attaining *biṭṭul* in the fullest sense but whose consciousness and feeling nevertheless lead them on this path (see R. Aaron Ha-Levi, *Sha'arey ha-'Avodah*, Sha'ar ha-Tefillah, chaps. 40, 41).

Transrational Perception – Faith

The highest level, that of *biṭṭul mi-zad ha-'ezem*, or "abnegation beyond reason and comprehension" (*biṭṭul me-'ever le-ta'am we-da'at*), cannot be attained by means of rational categories, as its basic assumptions conflict with that reality which is understood by the intellect. Only by means of the "transrational" dimension may one grasp that divine reality in which "two contradictory things," or the transcendent and immanent viewpoints, "may be held at once": "For in truth, He is above knowledge and intellect and understanding, for the Infinite, blessed be He, is not within the realm of knowledge and understanding at all, but is above the intellect, for in the transrational realm two opposites may be contained in one subject" (R. Aaron Ha-Levi, *Sha'arey ha-'Avodah*, III:19). The aspect of *biṭṭul* that transcends reason is also defined through the concept of faith: "Abnegation is that aspect of faith which is above understanding and apprehension" (R. Aaron Ha-Levi, *Sha'arey ha-Yiḥud weha-Emunah*, III:26). Faith is seen not as the opposite of knowledge but as a stage that goes beyond it, to be reached only after one has realized the limits of knowledge and consciousness to their fullest extent. To understand that "the worlds are not related to Him at all" one makes use of the abnegation of the intellect, because the religious fulfillment of this position must precede its understanding. But knowledge cannot aid in perceiving the unity that flows from it, for "negation in one's substance," because this transrational level cannot be comprehended by the human understanding. The effort to abnegate existence "above reason" expresses the supreme human endeavor to arrive at the divine point of view of true reality and to overcome the limitations of material experience, in order to transcend the limits of the finite and the restricted.

As we have mentioned, the point of departure of the Habad system is the duality of perception, which distinguishes between the divine point of view, which perceives the true reality, and the human point of view, which is imprisoned in the illusory empirical perception and which is derived from an apprehension of reality as it appears. The service of *biṭṭul* beyond reason is defined as within the realm of the impossible, because it expresses the apprehension of the divine point of view and the complete abandonment of the human viewpoint. However, this impossibility is occasionally achieved when one breaks out of the limits of the finite and comprehends the nature of the divine unity in existence. After the limits of knowledge have been exhausted, the intellect is no longer the vehicle for this mystical awareness, but other tools are needed, expressing transrational modes of consciousness. Faith plays a crucial role here, as a transrational form of consciousness; this type of religious worship is defined in the concept "to adhere on the level of not-knowing" (R. Aaron Ha-Levi, *Sha'arey ha-Yihud weha-Emunah*, II:32) or "to believe with a faith which is above intellect and apprehension" (R. Shneur Zalman, *Tanya*, 165). Faith entails a relationship to a realm which is not understood or subject to perception, along with the willingness to exclude certain areas from rational categories, to define them in the realm of the paradox and to leave them without an answer. Various events occurring within the divinity—the transition from the infinite to the finite, the simultaneous unity of the *sefirot* within the Emanator and their separation from him, the unity of opposites within the Emanator, and the creation of finitude from infinity—all these areas are beyond human comprehension, and must remain so. This position, which acknowledges the presence of realms of divinity which are beyond the limits of rational apprehension, and which accepts the a-rational unity as a definition of divinity, is faith.[23]

Faith is based on a dialectic contradiction, which recognizes the impossibility of its resolution and the dissatisfaction with the limits of consciousness, which cannot answer the paradox at the root of all existence—the presence and the nihility of God within the cosmos. This supreme paradox is embodied in the question of divine "being" and "non-being" with regard to the world, and in the relationship between unity and nihility of God within reality, from the divine and human points of view.

Reality is governed by a paradox, consisting of two contradictory religious positions, which determines reality's existence: one that demands God's immanence in the world, and one that denies it from him; or put in other terms, the immanentist position taught by Hasidism, against the transcendent position, inherited from Lurianic Kabbalah, which had made creation dependent on God's self-contraction and subsequent abandonment of the world. The two approaches both contradict and simultaneously affirm each other. Immanence and transcendence are interdependent, because the logical possibility of creation depends on the contradiction between the two. Were immanence to attain its full and logical conclusion of identity between the cosmos and divinity, there could be no cosmos; and were transcendence not to extend itself into immanence, there could be no cosmos, for God would remain hidden within himself. The problem of divine finitude and infinity lies at the focus of Habad's paradoxical understanding of the relationships between God and the world, and they become the subject of faith, which is defined as "two opposites in one subject."

One must stress the Habad axiom that those contradictions originating within the limitations of human thought have no ontological existence within the divine being and possess no objective existence, because the distinctions between the contradictions at the root of existence—that is, the unity and nihility of God within the cosmos—or between true reality and illusory reality are distinctions existing only within human consciousness. The fact that it is beyond human capability to overcome these is itself the meaning of that divine transcendence which is beyond the limits of awareness. The profound gap between the apprehension of the paradoxical divine essence and the capacities of human perception can only be bridged through faith, by submission to paradox.

It must be emphasized that "transrational faith" is not at all naïve, and is not to be confused with simple faith. It is sustained by the realization of the limits of knowledge and the acknowledgment of the limitation of intellectual consciousness which is unable to confront the dialectical contradiction lying at the basis of existence, and the assumption of the existence of a transrational realm, the relation to which is premised on relinquishing any hope of its apprehension. The recognition of the existence of this realm does not exempt one from a profound confrontation with the limits of human cognition, with discursive thought, with rational clarification and the exhaustion of those questions to which it is possible to give an answer. Only confrontation with the dialectic region of existence through "reason and understanding" can bring one to the "transrational"—to that realm of passive annihilation of realization of the divine unity within reality.

The performance of faith, and of transrational *bittul,* demands that one break through the bounds of cognitive transcendence in which divinity resides. There is no doubt that this religious approach, underlying the conceptions of negation and faith, which refuses to suffice with the cosmos known to the limitations of human cognition, is a transcendental one, insofar as it negates the possibility of encountering God within the realms of existence and insists on the obliteration of this reality on the way toward the meeting with that which is beyond it. The worship of negation is not intended to exhaust the multiplicity of relationships between God and the world, but is only one side of them—that which strives to restore finitude to infinity, while the perception of the relationships between God and the world as a whole are essentially dialectical, expressing simultaneously the contradiction between the two and the world as manifestation of divinity. The former is expressed by the service of *biṭṭul,* whereas the latter, in which the world is understood as the place in which the divine will is made manifest, is embodied in the service of Torah and *miẓwot.* The highest expressions of the worship of *biṭṭul* are dependent on an existential-religious situation in which the elements of human personality and self-interest are entirely obliterated. This worship is totally dedicated to the divine substance and expresses a willingness to entirely depart from the limitations of the finite, that is, to die (see R. Aaron Ha-Levi, *Sha'arey ha-'Avodah,* Petah ha-Teshuvah, chap. 12).

This radical departure from the world and commitment to an extreme anti-existentialist position characterized the transition from intellectual speculation upon the nature of the finite and the infinite to the ecstatic effect involving that *biṭṭul* which transcends mind and reason, known as *mesirat nefesh* ("self-sacrifice"), which is the transrational stage following the abnegation of reality through contemplation:

> Thus, he must first negate the finite by means of contemplation during *Shema'* and Prayer, and unite it in the aspect of Man, which is the divine soul, to arouse the unification through the attribute of intellection and understanding; and then, by means of intellect and understanding, he will turn over his soul to the level which is above knowledge, known as *mesirat nefesh* above knowledge and understanding. (R. Aaron Ha-Levi, *Sha'arey ha-'Avodah,* III: 20 [22]).

The gap between the intellectual negation of existence, which is addressed to every individual, and *mesirat nefesh* and that abnegation which is beyond reason, is very great, involving the complete negation of human nature, a radical anti-existential stance, conscious abolition of the reflective consciousness, and longings for the extinction of the soul within divine union. The obliteration of the reflective consciousness, in order to free oneself of the finite, combined with active readiness to die, to reject life and to surrender one's individual will, for apprehension and knowledge, is true *mesirat nefesh.*[24]

> But to feel disgust for his life, literally, to be on the level of "my soul expires," with extinction of the soul . . . that he literally sacrifices (his soul) with his

will and his substance and with all ten of his powers. And the focus of his life is to be absorbed in the source and to be drawn into the body of the kind, and to be disgusted with his life, even with that life necessary for Torah and worship and survival of the species—he does not desire that life at all, but only to cling to the source. (*'Avodat ha-Lewi,* Shemot, Wa-'era, 17)

And the true connection is by means of the blue thread, because blue (*tekhlelet*) is called *esha tekhela* (lit., "blue fire," read as a wordplay on *kilayon,* destruction), which consumes and burns all things, that is, the complete extinction and destruction of the finite, in the aspect of *nefilat apayim* ("prostration," i.e., the *Tahanun* prayer) in which he gives over his soul to death, that is, that he does not in truth wish to be alive in a finite existence, but "to you, O Lord, do I elevate my soul" [Ps 25:1], in the sense of extinction and absence of the finite, and this aspect is that of connection, that of *sovev* and *memale* (i.e., transcendent and immanent), as mentioned above. (*'Avodat ha-Lewi,* Tezaweh, 47b).

The derivation of the term *tekhlelet* from *kilayon* (extinction) transforms the blue thread of the *zizit* into a symbol of the vehicle connecting finite and infinite existence. By means of the obliteration of visible, finite being and its negation within true being, divinity, he attains his mystical ideal— the annihilation of separate existence and its absorption within God.

Surrender to the paradox of the simultaneous existence and nonexistence of God within the cosmos and conscious submission to nonknowledge, express one's willingness to sacrifice everything and to sacrifice one's being. Within a religious teaching, all of whose efforts are directed toward penetration to the depths of divine unity, the renunciation of this knowledge on behalf of the divine substance is a very great sacrifice, and the level of "to be negated and to adhere to that aspect which is not known" is the very summit of the religious effort. Fulfillment of the goal of worship—perceiving the divine essence of the finite in its true existence—is dependent on consciously relinquishing its apprehension through the intellect, the imagination, or the consciousness.

At the same time, as all of creation is an illusion from the divine point of view, it follows that human perception and the imagination of the contemplator embody infinite capability and force, since existence is not concealment of God at all. From the divine viewpoint, created beings are always close to Him, and partitions only exist from the human point of view.

This perception of the finite as an illusion, which lies at the very basis of the acosmic teaching, transforms the removal and abnegation of the finite into an effort strictly within the context of human consciousness, since from the divine point of view it does not really exist. From a mystical viewpoint, the abnegation of reality is understood as a precondition of the unification with God, expressing the consciousness of nihility and nothing-ness necessary to attain the desired state of literal unity of the soul with God. One abandons all those elements which separate the human realm from its divine essence—human will as a separate will; human consciousness as entailing reflective thought, which distinguishes between the thinker and the object of thought; the human perception of opposites, which is replaced by the understanding of reality as unified; and the personal, specific interest in individual existence. This was replaced by various stages of ecstasy, on the various levels of *bittul*, and by the annihilation of the individual as possess-ing self-consciousness, will, reflection, and every other dimension that separates him from the truth of his existence. The extinction of conscious-ness and the emptying of being prepared the way for unity with God, in the course of the ascent from the concrete realm to the abstract: at the peak of this unity, the human no longer exists as a separate being, and the human being's essence is entirely united with divinity. One finds in Habad literature descriptions of this experience of mystical annihilation:

> Then all men's wills, attached to separate matters from His very substance, are all considered as naught, for they are included in this essential will which pertains to all his substance. . . . That is to say, his whole being is so absorbed that nothing remains, and he has no self-consciousness whatsoever. . . . And from the attribute of this pleasure is made manifest the aspect of simple will, for this will causes the ascent of the soul to be absorbed in the substance of the Infinite, blessed be He, in the very essence of absorption, that is, that all the substance of his soul is included and connected within it. . . . And this is "my soul shall glory in the Lord" [Ps 34:3] that all of his soul is totally absorbed within God. (R. Dov Baer and R. Hillel of Paritsh, *Liqqutey Bi'urim*, 55a–b)

Despite the mystical longings expressed in Habad literature, it must be emphasized that the relationship between the aspect of rational-intellectual reflection and the mystical-ecstatic orientation—or, in Habad terminology, "ecstasy of the mind" (*hitpa'alut ha-moah*) and "ecstasy of the heart" (*hit-pa'alut ha-lev*)—was by no means a simple or unequivocal one, but rather one that raised many difficulties, as may be seen from the documents and writings of this period.

Although *hitbonenut*—that is, contemplation and ecstasy of the mind—was clearly interpreted as a religious imperative, subject to detailed instruc-tions and guidelines, the mystical, ecstatic, and emotional implications derived from this effort remained problematic. As the greatest part of Habad literature deals with explicating and defining the various means of spiritual worship of God and the formation of guidelines of a mystical and contemplative character, a difficulty arose concerning the setting of objective criteria for spiritual worship. Communicable external expressions for its testing—over which there were differences of opinion—needed to be found. Another aspect of the problem was the great fear of vulgarization, both of the acosmic teachings in general and of the doctrine of divine immanence in the cosmos in particular, so that an entire literature appeared that dealt with fixing and defining limits against the cheapening of religious worship and false interpretations of the spiritual teachings and mystical enthusiasm.[25] There is no doubt that the strong emphasis on "anti-spiritualism" is the outcome of the awareness of the balance needed in the light of the spiritual teachings and their dangers.

From R. Dov Baer's *Quntres ha-Hitpa'alut* (*Tract on Ecstasy*), from the introductions to R. Aaron Ha-Levi's works, and from other writings of the disciples of R. Shneur Zalman and of his son, one can see that there was both a theoretical and a practical confrontation with spiritual values and their implications for daily life. Some circles opposed and even prohibited the practice of "ecstasy of the heart"; on the other hand, others forbade "ecstasy of the mind."

The distinction between the authentic and the false in all of the various kinds of worship, particularly concerning the question of *hitpa'alut ha-lev*, is based on the object of the worship: "he does not call out to God, but only to make his own voice heard"—that is, true divine worship requires that it be dedicated entirely to God and based on forgetting of self. On the contrary, unfit service is that which pretends to be directed toward God but in fact is directed toward the individual himself. The critical test for the desired state is "lack of feeling for his own self entirely, with the divine ecstasy felt in the heart of flesh" (R. Dov Baer, *Quntres ha-Hitpa'alut*, 11), while the dangers of misleading and falsification in spiritual-emotional worship are spelled out in detail:

> The exact opposite of this is the external ecstasy of the fleshly heart, with an inflammatory enthusiasm of strange fire, which stems only from the heating of the blood, and possesses nothing whatever of the fire of the Lord. It is no more than a laying bare of heart and flesh with sparks of fire, by which a man warms himself in order to sense the aspect of ecstasy—and it is a most excessive error. (R. Dov Baer, *Quntres ha-Hitpa'alut*, 9)

The distinction between physical ecstasy and spiritual ecstasy is very sharply drawn. Not only are these two different states, but there are also many intermediate stages, which indicate failure, whether in the physical or the spiritual pole, as opposed to the optimum, defined as "total removal of the finite." The criterion for the attainment of the various degrees of *hitpa'alut* is the degree of consciousness of self and external reality. The various teachers of Ḥabad differed with regard to the relationship between self-consciousness and the degree of authenticity of the ecstasy, its motivations, its implications for different kinds of worship, and the essential underlying interest.

The Service of Torah and *Miẓwot*

Within the teaching of Ḥabad, a conscious distinction is drawn between the mystical ideal, which sees the "knowledge" of God and his unity as the goal of spiritual worship, and which longs to depart from corporeality and that form of service which expresses the performance of God's will in the realm of practical action, of Torah and *miẓwot*. The former strives to abstract the borders of space, time, being, and consciousness, whereas the latter is interested in manifestations of the divine within the limits of given reality, in which it sees an accessible embodiment of the divine will. This distinction between spiritual worship and material service is simultaneously one between passive and active service. The category of passive spiritualist service includes love and fear, contemplation and knowledge of the divine unity, communion and ecstasy, abnegation (*biṭṭul*), self-sacrifice, and faith. The active sacramental service entails knowledge of the revealed Torah, the study of its laws, and the performance of the *miẓwot*.[26]

Ḥabad teaching clearly stated that no practical conclusions regarding religious practice are to be drawn from the acosmic approach, which sees creation as a mere illusion and imaginary thing and seeks to transcend corporeality. Rather, one must fulfill Torah and *miẓwot* in practice and cling to the sacramental ethos of practical action at the same time that one subscribes to the ultimate truth of the acosmic view in theory and sees in it a binding religious consciousness: "It is forbidden to believe that creation is merely an illusion, for all of Torah and *miẓwot* are performed within corporeal, material reality as it is, yet we are also obliged to believe that the cosmos is literally void and nothingness!" (*'Avodat ha-Lewi,* Be-haʿalotkha, 21b).

Precisely because the main emphasis of Ḥabad teachers was on pneumatic worship, which stresses spiritualist and contemplative values, extra emphasis is placed upon the practical performance of *miẓwot*.

A man should not think that his main concern should be the study of this knowledge . . . [that is], knowledge of His unity, may He be blessed, in order through this understanding to be excited in his soul, to serve Him, may He be blessed, with love and fear and self-sacrifice and abnegation . . . but the main practice should be the study of that Torah which is revealed to us, namely the Talmud and *posqim* . . . in order to know the laws, which involve the performance of His blessed will." (R. Aaron Ha-Levi, *Sha'arey ha-Yiḥud weha-Emunah*, Petaḥ u-Mavo She'arim)

Because of the dialectical approach, which in principle sees both material and spiritual worship as valid expressions of the respective divine wills for concretization and annihilation, one does not find any open indication in Ḥabad of a confrontation between mystical and halakhic values. If tension does exist between the demand for complete transcendence of corporeality and the finite world, on the grounds that one who adheres to physical existence cannot cleave to God since the *mizwot* themselves require a material consciousness and physical actions, Ḥabad teaching dealt with this by means of the dialectic of essence and revelation, or the duality of perception.

At the basis of the relationship to Torah and *mizwot* is the paradox which places alongside one another the understanding of material existence as utterly lacking in substance from the divine viewpoint, and that which interprets it as the domain within which the divine is manifested. Thus, at the very basis of the desired service lies an understanding of the double relationship between divinity and reality. The statement of the essential divine intention — "the revelation within the aspect of the finite, specifically, which is called 'the acceptance of the yoke of the Kingdom of heaven'; that is, that the act of negation take place through the aspect of the yoke and negation of self-will towards Him, may He be blessed, without any understanding or *middot*" (R. Aaron Ha-Levi, *Sha'arey he-Yiḥud weha-Emunah*, IV:26) — generates a new definition of the relation between the human and divine wills. The act which most expresses the submission of the human will to the divine will is that of the fulfillment of Torah and *mizwot*, which embodies the divine will within the finite world of limitation and being. However, the effort to comprehend this will beyond the limitations of material borders and being places the service of negation in the center. The fulfillment of the divine will through Torah is clarified out of the need to find a communicable religious basis embodying the infinite will within finite reality.

Torah and *mizwot* are considered from two differing viewpoints, the divine and the human. In the former, Torah and *mizwot* symbolize the divine will to be revealed within reality, whereas in the latter (human) viewpoint, they express the possibility of encountering God within the finite realm.

The basic assumption that the essence of the Torah, which embodies the divine will, is extremely elevated, while its concrete manifestation perceived by humanity is extremely inferior, is examined from several dimensions. From the divine viewpoint, the revelation of the divine will within the

Torah is the same in the upper and lower spheres, as is true of every other aspect of being, even though the divine unity within creation is not clear to humans, despite its truth. As we have said above, from the divine point of view the divine will is equal in its limited and its limitless existence, insofar as the infinite and the finite are equal in that perception which negates substantial existence to every limited being. Therefore, the discussion concerning the relationship between the transcendent divine will and its manifestation in Torah corresponds to the discussion of the principal transition between infinite and finite reality.

The contrast between the elevated source and essence of the Torah and *mizwot* as divine will and their inferior manifestations, which are compared with darkness, sackcloth, and concealment, parallels the essential contrast between infinity and the finite. From this view of the contradiction between essence and revelation, the demand arose to uncover the truth of the Torah through its manifestations, which express the opposite of this truth.

The divine essence embodied in Torah may only be encountered by removing the apparent barriers created by the finite or by the abnegation of revealed being and by recognition of the lack of differentiation in the substance which was emanated; however, the manifestation of the light of the infinite in terms of the world and its adherence to the divine substance as limited or contained in the vessels, demands the service of Torah and *mizwot*.

The double nature of the Torah—"for the Torah speaks entirely on the level of finitude and limitation and practical commandments, yet nevertheless there is hidden within it His inner will, and of His true wisdom, which are seemingly two opposite things" (*'Avodat ha-Lewi*, Wa-'era, 14)—expresses well the manifestation of the divine will in the sense of limit and finitude. The finite, as has been mentioned, is the expression of the divine will that is manifested by means of its opposite, while the corporeal Torah and *mizwot* express that finitude and opposite which conceal the divine unity and the supernal divine essence contained therein. Habad teaching is not satisfied with the service of Torah and *mizwot* in the simple sense as a means toward encountering the divine will, but it contains a radical insistence upon the need to comprehend the spiritual essence embodied in Torah, which must be discovered and revealed within the bonds of the finitude of its physical manifestation.

The dual divine intention, of "revelation through the vessels" (*hitgalut mizad ha-kelim*) and "transcendence of the limitations of the vessels" (*yezi'ah mi-gidrey ha-kelim*), which parallels the manifestation through the finite and abnegation of the finite, dictates the relationship to the service of Torah and *mizwot,* on the one hand, and to the service of *biṭṭul,* on the other. The Torah in its corporeal manifestations symbolizes separate finite existence, or the divine will embodied within the finite, while *biṭṭul* symbolizes the disembodied divine substance beyond finitude. The Torah expresses the divine emanation in the finite, its drawing down and realization, while *biṭṭul* expresses the negation of finitude and its annihilation. The Torah is defined within the limitations of the vessels, while the principle of *biṭṭul* transcends the limitations of the vessels. In other words, divine perfection is manifested by drawing divinity down into the world by means of Torah and *mizwot* (see R. Dov Baer, *Sha'arey ha-Emunah* 68a), while simultaneously finitude is negated and restored to its divine essence through the service of negation-of-the-finite and contemplation. The dialectic within the dual divine intention of manifestation within the finite, on the one hand, and negation of the finite to the divine nihil, on the other—which demands of humans that they "draw Divinity down into the vessels" and together with that "transcend the limits of the vessels"—lies at the very basis of the entire Ḥabad conception of divine worship. The relationship between *biṭṭul* and the service of Torah and *mizwot* is one of "running and returning" (*razo' wa-shov*): *biṭṭul* is the running—the leap into the spiritual spheres—while the performance of Torah and *mizwot* is the "return"—to corporeal reality. The attainment of *razo'* ("running") is intended to illuminate, upon its return to reality, the darkness of the *shov* ("return").

The relationship between the two aspects of divine service is not a permanent one, but is presented differently by different authors, so that one sees a certain difficulty pertaining to the relationship between spiritual service and material service and a defense of the role of Torah and *mizwot* in the light of their dual significance. The two contradictory dimensions of the Torah—that which represents concealment, *zimzum,* and hiddenness, and that which embodies the divine substance—gain a new status from the point at which it is determined that the preferable service in the present world relates to reality as it seems to exist, devoid of divinity, and to God in His unattainable transcendence. Reality may be approached through the divine commandments of Torah and *mizwot.* In the future, divine service will relate to a reality in which God's presence is immanent, "for in the future His substance, may He be blessed, will be made manifest in all creatures, that is, that His glory, may He be blessed, will be clearly revealed in all of reality, for then the Torah will be revealed in its root" (R. Aaron Ha-Levi, *Sha'arey ha-'Avodah,* IV:9). The use of the dimension of time to bridge the dual face of the Torah, in its spiritual essence and corporeal manifestation, sharpens the assumption that the understanding of the Torah as the embodiment of the divine will is not concerned with the present but with the future, and that the relationship between the two dimensions is the clarification or full realization of the present, corporeal Torah, in order to apprehend the spiritual Torah and to be revealed in the future. The service of Torah and *mizwot* is thus understood as a consequence of the historical, cosmic situation in which reality finds itself—the Exile (*galut*). The significance of this *galut* lies in the absence of manifestation of the divine unity within reality, as a result of which existence is in a situation of hiddenness and separation, in which the service that must follow from this reality is in concealment, that is, within the Torah and *mizwot* embodied in physical acts.

This situation of *galut*, requiring hiddenness and corporealization, applies to all the aspects of existence, to the human soul and to the Torah. From this, one arrives at the conclusion that the adherence to the divine substance within the realm of being ought to be by means of the vessels and the corporeal being—which exist only from the human point of view but are not immanent within the divine substance itself, on the one hand, and do not represent the divine existence revealed to us through its contractions, which are capable of apprehension, on the other hand.

The separate, corporeal nature of the earthly manifestations of Torah and *mizwot* transform them into a means of struggle, which embodies the efforts to elevate the evil to good within the finite realm of existence separated from divinity. The forum for this struggle is the human soul, in which one also finds the two elements of divine essence *in potentia* (the divine soul) and its active manifestation (the animal soul), which are parallel to the divine essence embodied in Torah and its lower manifestations within limited being given over to us. This duality, embodying the divine intention—the manifestation of divinity within the finite, on the one hand, and the incorporation of the animal soul within the divine soul, as an expression of the incorporation of the finite in the infinite, on the other hand—is accomplished by means of Torah and *mizwot*. In brief—the service of Torah and *mizwot* is intended to grant expression for the religious attempt to encounter the divine life concentrated within the vessels in a manner subject to human apprehension. It also helps one recognize the transcendent limits of the mind and the cognitive distance of human beings from holiness, despite its influx upon them and their existence within it. The religious demands and spiritual struggle characterizing the world of Habad Hasidism are based on a decisive change in inner religious consciousness, not one in external ritual or ethos. The deepening of human awareness, the broadening of consciousness, and the breakthrough in the limits of comprehension, together with the reexamination and reinterpretation of the entire accepted religious tradition in the light of the new perspective, stand at the center of Habad's interests.

Notes

1. See D. Z. Hillman, *Iggerot Ba'al Ha-Tanya;* A. I. Brawer, "On the Dispute Between Rabbi S. Z. of Lyady and R. Abraham Kalisker" (Hebrew), *Kiryat Sefer* 1 (1924) 140–52, 226–38.

2. On the role of Habad in the polemics between Hasidism and Mitnaggedism, see M. Wilensky, *Hasidim u-Mitnaggedim* (Jerusalem: Bialik, 1970); R. Elior, "The Minsk Debate" (Hebrew), *Mehqerey Yerushalayim be-Mahshevet Yisra'el* 4 (1982) 179–235; and the Habad sources cited in the bibliography of this article.

3. See L. Jacobs, ed., *Tract on Ecstasy* (London: Vallentine, Mitchell, 1963); R. Elior, "The Controversy over the Leadership of the Habad Movement" (Hebrew), *Tarbiz* 49 (1980) 166–86.

4. All references in this paper to the writings of R. Aaron are to section (lit., "gate") and chapter. Thus, I:2 refers to "gate" I, chap. 2.

5. See G. Scholem, *Reshit ha-Qabbalah* (Jerusalem: Schocken, 1948) 139–40; R. Schatz-Uffenheimer, *Ha-Hassidut ke-Mistiqah,* index, s.v. *ayin* (nothingness); J. G. Weiss, "The Great Maggid's Theory of Contemplative Magic," *HUCA* 31 (1960) 139–40.

6. On the fundamental concepts of Lurianic Kabbalah, see the discussions in this volume by L. Fine (chap. 3) and L. Jacobs (chap. 4).

7. In Lurianic Kabbalah, *shevirah* ("breaking") and *zimzum* ("contraction") are stages in the transition from unified divine being to discrete, differentiated reality. For an explanation of the role and significance of these concepts, see the works cited above in n. 5; see also G. Scholem, *Sabbatai Sevi: The Mystical Messiah (1626–1676)* (Princeton, NJ: Princeton University Press, 1973) 22–43.

8. "Likewise, the entire attribute of separation-out of holiness comes from *hipukh* (opposite)—for the manifestation of His divinity, may He be blessed, cannot be revealed except through concealment, for in terms of His substance, may He be blessed, it is not manifested at all" (R. Aaron Ha-Levi, *Sha'arey ha-'Avodah,* II:12). On the teaching of "opposites" and its implications for Habad worship in its extreme spiritualist version, see R. Elior, *Torat ha-Elohut,* 244–88.

9. English: *Likutei Amarim,* part 4, trans. J. I. Schochet (Brooklyn, 1972) 186–87.

10. See R. Menahem Mendel, *Derekh Mizwotekha* (Poltava, 1911) 110.

11. On the kabbalistic sources of the Habad doctrine of the soul, see I. Tishby, *Mishnat ha-Zohar* (2 vols.; Jerusalem: Bialik, 1961) 2:3–67; idem, *Torat ha-Ra'weha-Qelipah be-Qabbalat ha-'Ari* (Jerusalem: Hebrew University Students Organization, 1965) part 4; M. Teitelbaum, *Ha-Rav mi-Ladi,* part 2 (Warsaw, 1910); and the introduction to Jacobs's edition of *Tract on Ecstasy.* The first fifteen chapters of *Tanya* concern the doctrine of the soul, and all Habad texts include detailed discussions of this subject. See, e.g., Menahem Mendel (Zemah Zedeq), *Derekh Mizwotekha* (Poltava, 1911) 1–38; R. Aaron Ha-Levi, *Sha'arey ha-'Avodah, Sha'ar Yihud ha-neshamot* (Sklow, 1821) etc.

12. See *Derekh Mizwotekha,* 15–16: "And this is a great rule, that the essential difference between the Side of Holiness and the Other Side (*sitra 'ahra*) is the attribute of *bittul,* that in holiness there is the negation of the finite . . . which is not the case in the Other Side. . . ." In scholarship on Habad, there are various different views concerning the Habad doctrine of evil; see further the sources mentioned above in n. 3.

13. For differing opinions concerning the spiritual and antispiritual characteristics of Habad

divine service, see R. Schatz, "Anti-Spiritualism in Hasidism"; Y. Tishby and J. Dan, "Hasidism"; and M. Halamish's dissertation "Mishnato ha-'Iyyunit."

14. On the concept of self-abnegation in Hasidism, see J. G. Weiss, "Via Passiva in Early Hasidism," *Journal of Jewish Studies* 11 (1960) 137–55; R. Schatz-Uffenheimer, *Ha-Hassidut ke-Mistiqah*, chaps. 1–3; idem, ed., critical edition of R. Dov Baer of Miedzyrzec *Maggid Devaraw le-Ya'aqov* (Jerusalem, 1976) index, s.v. *bittul;* Solomon Maimon, *An Autobiography* (New York, 1947) 49–55; R. Elior, *Torat ha-Elohut,* 178–243.

15. L. Jacobs, ed., *Tract on Ecstasy,* Introduction.

16. *Quntres ha-Hitbonenut* was first published in Kapost in 1820 as *Sha'ar ha-Yihud,* the second section of R. Dov Baer b. Shneur Zalman's *Ner Mizwah we-Torah Or.*

17. See G. Scholem, "Devekut, or Communion with God," *Review of Religion* 14 (1949–50) 115–39; also in *The Messianic Idea in Judaism and Other Essays* (New York: Schocken, 1971) 203–27.

18. See D. Z. Hillman, *Iggerot Ba'al ha-Tanya;* A. I. Brawer, "On the Dispute"; and R. Elior, "The Minsk Debate."

19. H. M. Heilman, *Bet Rabbi,* 87.

20. See L. Jacobs, ed., *Tract on Ecstasy,* Introduction; also R. Elior, "Dob Ber Schneersohn's 'Quntres ha-Hitpa'alut'" (Hebrew), *Kiryat Sefer* 54 (1979) 384–91.

21. See R. Elior, "The Controversy over the Leadership of the Habad Movement" (Hebrew), *Tarbiz* 49 (1980) 166–86. L. Jacobs, *Seeker of Unity;* H. J. T. C. Lowenthal, "The Concept of Mesirat Nefesh."

22. See n. 21; cf. Elior, *Torat ha-Elohut,* 189–326.

23. See R. Shneur Zalman, *Tanya,* 173; and compare the introduction to R. Yizhak Epstein of Homel, *Hanah Ariel* (Berdichev, 1912).
A comparison between the Habad concept of faith and that of Brastlav Hasidism should prove extremely instructive. On the complex meaning of faith in Brastlav, see A. Green, *Tormented Master: A Life of Rabbi Nahman of Bratslav* (University, AL: University of Alabama Press, 1979) 285–336; J. G. Weiss, *Mehqarim be-Hasidut Brastlav,* "The Question in the Thought of R. Nahman of Brastlav" (pp. 109–49), and "Mystical Hasidism and Hasidism of Faith" (pp. 87–95).

24. For a different interpretation of the Habad concept of *mesirat nefesh,* see Lowenthal, "The Concept of 'Mesirat-Nefesh.'"

25. See n. 21 above.

26. On the controversial role played by Torah study and the meaning of the *mizwot,* see R. Schatz-Uffenheimer, *Ha-Hassidut ke-Mistiqah,* 157–67; and J. G. Weiss, "Study of the Torah in Israel Baal Shem's Doctrine" (Hebrew), in *Essays Presented to Chief Rabbi Israel Brodie* (Hebrew volume; London: Soncino Press, 1967) 151–69. The understanding of Torah and *mizwot* in Habad is discussed in M. Teitelbaum, *Ha-Rav mi-Ladi,* 172–95; R. Schatz, "Anti-Spiritualism in Hasidism"; A. Steinsalz, "Habad," *Encyclopaedia Judaica,* 14:1436–40.

Bibliography

There is considerable bibliography in Hebrew concerning the Habad movement, including both that produced within Hasidic circles and the writings of European Jewish historians published between the beginning of this century and the Second World War. The general works on the history of Hasidism composed in the early twentieth century, such as those by Horodezky, Marcus, Bunim, et al. are of little value for the understanding of Habad and its thought. Orthodox historiography concentrated on the biography of R. Shneur Zalman of Lyady and his family and has preserved many important biographical details and interesting sociological and historical characteristics. These works include Heilman, Teitelbaum, Hillman. A brief biography in English appears in *Encyclopaedia Judaica* (14:1432–36). Noncritical "modern" biographies are Glitzenstein, Mindel. There is extensive bibliography on R. Shneur Zalman's central work, *Tanya*. The book has been translated into English (New York, 1962; London, 1973), and translations of its individual sections are available in updated editions. All references to *Tanya* in this essay are based on the photo-edition of the 1937 Vilna imprint, the standard Hebrew edition of the *Tanya*. Interesting evaluations of the place of the *Tanya* and its exoteric and esoteric aspects appear in the introductions to *Tanya*, to R. Aaron Ha-Levi's *Sha'arey ha-'avodah*, and to R. Dov Baer's *Torat Hayyim*; see also Tishby and Dan.

For descriptions of the spiritual characteristics of Habad, see Schatz, Tishby and Dan, Elior, Jacobs, Halamish, Lowenthal. On the spiritualist-quietistic background of Hasidism in general and that of the Maggid of Miedzyrzec in particular, which decisively influenced the teachings of Habad, see Schatz-Uffenheimer, Weiss ("Via Passiva"; "Contemplative Mysticism"; "Mystical Hasidism"). For a bibliographical survey of Habad literature, see Haberman ("Sha'arey Habad"; "Torat ha-Rav") and the most recent editions of *Tanya*, which contain much important bibliographical information. The appendixes to this book include listings of manuscripts, imprints, and various editions; see, for example, the 1982 Brooklyn edition.

Elior, R. *Torat ha-Elohut be-Dor ha-Sheni shel Hasidut Habad* [The Theory of Divinity of Hasidut Habad's Second Generation]. Jerusalem: Magnes Press, 1982.

Glitzenstein, A. H. *Sefer ha-Toldot RaSha Z mi-Lady.* Brooklyn: Otsar ha-Hasidim, 1967.

Habermann, A. M. "Sha'arey Habad." In *'Aley 'Ayin*, 293–370. S. Schocken Festschrift. Jerusalem, 1948–52.

———. "Torat ha-Rav." In *Sefer ha-Qe N*, 133–79. Jerusalem, 1969.

Halamish, M. "Mishnato ha-'Iyyunit shel R. Shneur Zalman mi-Lady we-yahasah le-Torat ha-Qabbalah we-reshit ha-Hassidut" [The Speculative Doctrine of R. Shneur Zalman of Lyady and Its Relationship to Kabbalistic Theory and to Early Hasidism]. Diss., Hebrew University, 1976.

Heilman, H. M. *Bet Rabbi.* Berdichev, 1903.

Hillman, D. Z. *Iggerot Ba'al ha-Tanya u-Veney Doro.* Jerusalem, 1953.

Jacobs, Louis. *Seeker of Unity.* New York: Basic Books, 1966.

Lowenthal, H. J. T. C. "The Concept of Mesirat Nefesh ('Self Sacrifice') in the Teaching of R. Dob Baer of Lubavich (1773–1827)." Diss., University of London, 1981.

Mindel, Nissen. *Rabbi Schneur Zalman.* Brooklyn: Habad Research Center, Kehot Publication Society, 1969.

Schatz, R. "Anti-Spiritualism in Hasidism: Studies in the Teachings of RaSha Z of Lyady" (Hebrew). *Molad* 20, no. 171 (1962) 513–28.

Schatz-Uffenheimer, R. *Ha-Hassidut ke-Mistiqah.* Jerusalem: Magnes Press, 1968.

Teitelbaum, M. *Ha-Rav mi-Ladi u-Mifleget HaBaD.* Warsaw, 1910.

Tishby, I., and J. Dan. "Hasidism." In *Ha-Enzeqlopedyah ha-'Ivrit*, 17:775–78. Jerusalem, 1969.

Weiss, J. G. "Contemplative Mysticism and 'Faith' in Hasidic Piety." *Journal of Jewish Studies* 4 (1953) 19–29.

———. "Mystical Hasidism and Hasidism of Faith" (Hebrew). In *Mehqarim be-Hasidut Brastlav*, 87–95. Edited by M. Piekarz. Jerusalem: Bialik, 1974.

———. "Via Passiva in Early Hasidism." *Journal of Jewish Studies* 11 (1960) 137–55.

Rabbi Israel Salanter and His Psychology of Mussar

IMMANUEL ETKES

Culture and Context

THE MUSSAR ("ETHICS") MOVEMENT first appeared in the mid-nineteenth century among the Jews of Lithuania. From its inception, this movement was associated with the name of Rabbi Israel Lipkin of Salant, known as R. Israel Salanter.[1] Indeed, the student of modern eastern European Jewish history will be hard put to identify another case of a new movement whose birth and initial dissemination may be directly attributed to the initiative and activity of a single individual—as is the case in that of R. Israel Salanter and the Mussar movement. R. Israel laid the theoretical groundwork for the new movement; he organized its first cells and fostered their growth; he led the movement until his death at the beginning of the 1880s; and his disciples, and their disciples in turn, led the movement thereafter.

The message R. Israel directed to his contemporaries involved three principal elements: the demand to grant higher priority to ethical education within Jewish life, a new understanding of the problematics of ethical education and the creation of an efficient system of education based on this understanding, and the identification of the ethical weak point of his contemporaries in the area of social relations.

Before discussing the details of his thought and his public activity, we must understand the cultural and social context within which he worked and grew, in order to define the character of Salanter's innovation from the point of view of his contemporaries.

R. Israel Salanter was born in the year 1810 to a rabbinical family in the town of Zagory, in northern Lithuania. His childhood and youth were spent studying Torah in the city of Salant under the tutelage of R. Zevi

Hirsch Broide. While still living in Salant, R. Israel encountered the extraordinary personality of the scholar-saint, R. Zundel, under whose influence he began to involve himself with questions of ethical perfection. Both in terms of his family background and of the cultural environment within which he was educated, R. Israel belonged to "Mitnaggedic" society in Lithuania. Moreover, through R. Zundel of Salant, R. Israel was connected with the school of the Gaon of Vilna and his outstanding disciple, R. Hayyim of Volozhin—two individuals who played a central role in determining the spiritual shape of Lithuanian Mitnaggedic Jewry of the nineteenth century.

The phenomenon of Mitnaggedism is generally depicted in historiography as bearing an exclusively negative message, that is, the repudiation of Hasidism. This image requires modification and completion. One may distinguish two principal stages in the history of Mitnaggedism. In the first stage, beginning in 1772 and continuing approximately until the end of the eighteenth century, Mitnaggedism was in fact essentially a negative reaction to Hasidism, expressed in the organized struggle carried out by the communal organization under the leadership of the Vilna Gaon. A discussion of the motivations of the Mitnaggedim during this stage is beyond the framework of this paper. It is sufficient for us to remember that they had no interest at this time in engaging in polemics with Hasidism, which, from their point of view, was a heretical "sect" to be publicly exposed and to be uprooted by any means available—at least within the borders of Lithuania.

At the beginning of the nineteenth century, it became clear that Mitnaggedism had suffered a serious defeat in its struggle with Hasidism. Not only was its hope of completely eliminating Hasidism disappointed, but in the course of the last third of the eighteenth century, Hasidism continued to expand and gain in strength. Moreover, many sons of the families of the learned elite were swept up by the influence of the new movement, so that the persecuted "sect" in fact itself threatened its pursuers. The transition to the second phase within the history of Mitnaggedism took place against the background of this development. In this stage, Lithuanian Mitnaggedism consolidated itself into a movement with a positive self-image; all-out war against Hasidism was replaced by ideological confrontation and social competition with the rival movement.

The figure who played a crucial role in the transformation of Mitnaggedism into a constructive and creative movement was Rabbi Hayyim of Volozhin—the leading disciple of the Gaon of Vilna. In his well-known book, *Nefesh ha-Hayyim*, R. Hayyim engaged in a serious, profound, and sharp polemic against Hasidism. But his ideological response to Hasidism went beyond polemics to the creation of a systematic doctrine which may be seen as a response and a counterbalance to the path of Hasidism. Together with his intellectual activity, at the beginning of the nineteenth century R. Hayyim founded a *yeshivah* (talmudic academy) in the town of Volozhin, which he headed until his death in 1821. Through this, he laid the groundwork for the rehabilitation and renascence of Torah institutions in Lithuania.

The most typical characteristic of Mitnaggedic society was its attitude to the study of Torah and to Torah scholars. Torah study was understood by this society as the supreme value and the primary focus of divine service. The centrality of Torah study was expressed not only in the acknowledgment of its value per se, but in the expectation that the bulk of one's time, one's spiritual resources, and one's economic means be devoted to it. In terms of this outlook, involvement in the world was perceived as lacking any intrinsic value, its sole justification being as a means of furthering the study of Torah. Greatness in Torah—that is, breadth and depth of knowledge of halakhic literature—was the primary source of authority in communal leadership. This had in fact been the traditional outlook in Europe for generations. However, the transformation wrought by Hasidism in the forms of religious worship and its rejection of the centrality heretofore enjoyed by Torah study, caused the emphasis on the supremacy of Torah study to be perceived as the distinctive mark of the Mitnaggedim. Moreover, in this period the traditional ideal of Torah study attained a level of realization among Lithuanian Mitnaggedic Jewry unprecedented both in power and scope. The admiration of scholarship was not restricted to the circles of scholars (*lomdim*) who engaged in study on a full-time basis, nor even to those of the "householders" (*ba'aley-batim*), many of whom had received extensive Torah educations and were accustomed to setting aside regular periods for Torah study, but also encompassed the masses of ordinary people. The image of the Torah sages—the *talmid-ḥakham*—exemplified the social ideal of Mitnaggedic Lithuanian Jewry. They were the subject of anecdotes and folk legends in this society and served as its source of inspiration and as an example to be emulated.

R. Israel Salanter saw himself as adhering to the accepted norm of his place and time regarding the centrality of Torah study. He was himself a scholar of considerable renown and had devoted years of intensive activity to the training of new generations of Torah scholars and the enhancement of their public position. Despite this, his call for reevaluation of the position of moral education was interpreted by many of his contemporaries as undermining the accepted view of the desired balance between Torah study and the cultivation of *yir'ah*.[2] We shall return to this subject after we survey the

principal elements of R. Israel's thought during the first phase of its development, that is, during the 1840s and 1850s.

A Retreat from Kabbalah

Study of Salanter's writings reveals that his underlying theological position
is not only lacking in any innovation but even entails a certain degree of
"retreat." Essentially, his approach marks a return to the classical rabbinic
thought of the Mishnah and the Talmud. The image of God in his writings
is strictly transcendent and personal: He is the God who reveals Himself
to humans in His Torah and His commandments; who is providential; who
rewards and punishes. Just as He is not the God of the philosophers, who
is the object of speculation and apprehension by the mind, so is He not, in
Salanter's thought, the God of the Kabbalah. The attempt to influence the
upper worlds, as well as the desire to cling to God in the mystical sense,
plays no role in his religious thought. Religious activity and meaning are
defined by the concepts of commandment and transgression, reward and
punishment, this world and the world to come. *The essence of divine worship
is in the very response to and obedience to the mizwot.*

In ignoring the entire complex of questions and solutions propounded by
the major theological movements in postrabbinic Judaism, Salanter retreats,
as it were, from the later and more sophisticated stages of Jewish thought
to an earlier and more basic stage. However, this "retreat" essentially reflects
a certain "theosophic apathy," to which curiosity and examination of
theosophic questions in themselves are of no interest. To the extent that he
does concern himself with questions of the nature of divine rule, as in that
of reward and punishment, he does so only because of its implications for
human moral education.

It is no surprise that medieval philosophical speculative literature did not
seriously influence Salanter's thought, since its influence within the social-
religious context from which he came was generally limited. Nevertheless,
his estranged attitude toward the Kabbalah is surprising, not only because
of the central role occupied by Kabbalah within Jewish thought from the
sixteenth century on but also because of the important place it occupied in
the thought of his teachers, the Vilna Gaon and R. Hayyim of Volozhin.
For this reason, R. Israel's position concerning the Kabbalah may properly
be described as a conscious retreat. We do not wish to argue here that
Salanter denied or even doubted the authority and authenticity of the Kabbalah. However, he did, so to speak, remove himself from its influence, so
that it no longer played a role in his religious outlook. Moreover, in the
light of Salanter's explicit statements concerning his relationship to

Kabbalah, it appears clear that his self-distancing from its sphere of influence was the result of a conscious and deliberate choice. When one of his acquaintances asked why he did not study Kabbalah, he replied: "What practical difference does it make in which heaven the Holy-One-Blessed-be-He sits? One thing is clear to me—that they will beat one with sticks! And that it will hurt very much! And the beatings will be fierce! This I know clearly—so what else do I need?" These comments indicate the connection between his "theosophic apathy" and his involvement in questions of yir'ah and mussar. R. Israel did not entirely repudiate the value of theosophic speculation, but he placed it on a low position in his scale of values. He argued that, from the viewpoint of an individual who is potentially subject to punishment in hell, theosophic speculation on esoteric matters is simply irrelevant!

Another statement of R. Israel indicative of his attitude toward the esoteric realm is the following: "The MaHaRaL of Prague (R. Judah Loeb, d. 1609) created a golem, and this was a great wonder. But how much more wonderful is it to transform a corporeal human being into a person (mentsh). . . ." In these words, a confrontation is created between involvement in the realm of the hidden, on the one hand, and the attempt to shape the patterns of human behavior, on the other. Between the two, R. Israel preferred moral education, not only as the more urgent of the two goals but also as a more significant and difficult religious challenge! A clear proof of R. Israel's position with regard to involvement in Kabbalah is found in a passage from his letter to a friend and disciple, R. Elijah of Cartinga: "Moses Hayyim Luzzatto's (1707–1746) work on the Kabbalah is not pertinent to me, because I do not study this subject and I do not know at all if the time for it is ripe."

There seems to be a relationship between R. Israel's self-imposed separation from the world of Kabbalah and his discussion concerning the structure of the human soul and the means of its moral improvement. In kabbalistic literature, the activities of the human soul are understood in terms of its contact with metaphysical forces. In Hasidic literature there is a tendency to psychologize certain concepts that are metaphysical in origin. However, Hasidic thought was molded by kabbalistic terminology and rooted in the theological assumptions of the Kabbalah, so that it was unable to cut itself off from the kabbalistic doctrine of the soul. R. Israel Salanter, on the other hand, because he separated himself both from the theological assumptions and the terminology of the Kabbalah, was prepared to accept and to develop an approach that saw the human soul as an autonomous unit, whose components and the mechanism of whose actions can be explained rationally.[3]

Ethics and the Problem
of Psychological Motivation

Salanter's "theosophic apathy" is expressed also in his understanding of the problem of Mussar. The uniqueness of his approach may be understood in contrast to the ethical thought of previous generations. Despite the wide spectrum of approaches to be found there, the majority of ethical works that enjoyed wide circulation and influence shared a common characteristic: a normative ethical-religious "message." That is, the authors of these books presented their readers with a framework of actions, behavioral norms, and "levels," themselves deserving of execution. Underlying this enterprise was the assumption that, by the very exposure of the reader to correct ethical norms, an important, if not the decisive, step was taken allowing the reader to progress toward ethical perfection. One need not add that many of the authors of ethical treatises also devoted attention, to a greater or lesser extent, to the problem of motivation in religious service and to the psychological pitfalls lying in the path. Nevertheless, their discussions of this aspect of Mussar were generally secondary and adjunct to their main concern of presenting the normative contents of Mussar.

In contrast to these characteristics of traditional Mussar literature, R. Israel Salanter's understanding of the problem of ethics is strikingly innovative. In essence, he moved the focus of the problem of Mussar from the theological to the psychological realm. The problem with which ethics must deal is not which ethical norms an individual ought to fulfill. These are explained and codified in halakhic literature, and there is no need to elaborate on them. The real problem of Mussar is that of the gap between cognitive knowledge, on the one hand, and psychological motivation, on the other. In other words, the fact that a given individual knows God's commandments, acknowledges their validity, and wishes to fulfill them, is no guarantee that the individual will in fact behave according to them in practice. This is because the behavior patterns and reactions of a human being are not guided and directed by his rational consciousness but by powerful, irrational emotional drives. In the light of this interpretation of the problem of Mussar, we may better understand Salanter's conception of the proper limits and subject matter of Mussar. It is needless to add that Mussar is not conceived here as an autonomous source of norms of religious behavior. Rather, its entire purpose is to create a connection between the normative demands of the halakhah and an individual's psychological capacity to fulfill them in actual life. The way toward accomplishing this task involves two stages: (1) the development of a psychological theory explaining the components and means of operation of the psychic mechanism;

(2) the development of educational methods based on this theory, through which one can gain control over one's emotional life and thus over one's behavior in general.

The starting point for Salanter's Mussar system is thus rooted in his understanding of the nature of the drives motivating human beings to ethically negative behavior. The most frequent and important concept in his discussions of this problem is "lust" or appetite (*ta'awah*). The meaning R. Israel gives to this term is based upon psychological reflection, in which it is liberated from the metaphysical burden that had been imposed on it in kabbalistic Mussar literature. "Appetite" is identified, quite simply, with the natural inclination toward the pleasurable implanted in humans from their birth. Its power is thus based upon one's cumulative experience. By means of the senses, the person experiences, on the one hand, painful and distressing experiences and, on the other, pleasurable and enjoyable ones. "Appetite" is the psychological drive to return to pleasurable experiences and to avoid painful ones, and it is characterized by attraction to immediate pleasures and the inability to weigh long-term consequences.

To the best of our knowledge, there is no statement in Salanter's writings categorically repudiating physical pleasures as such. R. Israel does not accept the polarization between matter and spirit common to the Neoplatonist stream of Mussar literature. His rejection of appetite is not based on the fact that it drives one to seek physical satisfactions, except insofar as this drive is in conflict with the commands of the halakhah—a conflict that is in many cases unavoidable, because of the limitations and restrictions it places on one's physical pleasures. R. Israel believes that appetite has a profound influence on all of one's activities and behavior. This influence is extremely dangerous, because worldly reality is filled with stimuli arousing one's appetites and bringing them into conflict with the halakhah, from which it follows that one's life in this world is filled with difficult tests and ceaseless struggle.

The main tool capable of breaking the appetite's control over human actions is "fear of God" (*yir'ah*). As is known, this concept played a central role in Mussar literature throughout the generations. Generally speaking, ethical writers drew a distinction between *yir'at ha-'onesh* ("fear of divine punishment") and *yir'at ha-romemut* ("fear of divine majesty"). We do not intend to discuss here the range of meanings that have been attached to the concept of *yir'at ha-romemut*. It is sufficient to note that by this concept the ethicists referred to a level in which the human being is motivated to serve God not by fear of divine punishment or by the anticipation of reward but by a positive spiritual relationship to the Creator. In ethical literature, there is a common view that "fear of divine majesty" is a far more sublime level than "fear of divine punishment." There were even those who completely rejected "fear of divine punishment" as a legitimate motivation for the service of God. Even those authors who did not go to that extreme saw it as a relatively low level.

Salanter seemingly ignored this tendency, primarily basing the struggle with appetite on the principle of "fear of divine punishment." This is because he believed that in a situation of actual ethical test—that is, when the irrational forces of appetite motivate one to act contrary to the demands of the halakhah—the only force capable of halting the appetite is the fear of anticipated punishment for sin. No doubt Salanter would agree that divine service motivated by love or by awe is far superior to that motivated by fear of punishment. However, he was convinced that these and similar motivations, as sublime as they may be, are not sufficiently powerful to influence behavior when one is overwhelmed by "appetite." In the light of this awareness, R. Israel reached the conclusion that we must distinguish between value motivations, bringing the person to serve God on the conscious level, and the psychological motivations that directly influence the person's actions. "Fear of divine punishment" is thus meant to serve as a psychological motivation for the service of God, but under no circumstance does Salanter see it as a value motivation. This distinction between "value motivations," that is, those that act on the conscious level, and psychological or emotional motivation is one of Salanter's outstanding innovations. This distinction is a further indication of the way in which the "Mussar system" transferred the emphasis from the theological to the psychological realm.

The expectation that "fear of divine punishment" would act as a curb upon the appetite is conditional upon the assistance of the intellect, as the mind is aware of the principle of reward and punishment and, unlike the appetite, which is a spontaneous instinct seeking immediate gratification, is capable of anticipating the future and weighing the consequences likely to follow from a given act in the present. However, one remains with the question of how one is to change "fear of divine punishment" from an abstract theological principle to a powerful emotional drive, capable of influencing one's actions and responses. Among the various means developed by Salanter to attain this end, particular importance is attached to the study of Mussar be-hitpa'alut, "in a state of excitement."

The nature of this form of study is implied by its name: hitpa'alut—that is, an experience of powerful emotional arousal. The ethical contents "studied" are not the subject of a process of intellectual knowledge and analysis but are rather the focus of an intense emotional experience through which they are internalized in the soul. Salanter suggested various methods of stimulating this "excitement." Voice and melody played an important role.

Mussar study *be-hitpa'alut* was performed aloud, the power of the voice, the special melody, and the rhythm all serving to arouse the emotions. From various accounts, we learn that this activity had a special melody which, unlike the traditional melody used for Talmud study, was characterized by sadness and brokenheartedness, mingled with groans and at times even with outbursts of tears. Despite the many differences, one cannot but be reminded here of the ecstatic prayer of early Hasidism, where strange movements and sounds were the target of much criticism and ridicule. The study of Mussar *be-hitpa'alut* was also at times an ecstatic experience. Another characteristic of this form of Mussar study was repetition: the student would read aloud a given sentence from Mussar work or a rabbinic saying expressing some ethical idea, which would then be repeated over and over again for a considerable period of time. In addition to learning out loud, the special melody, and repetition, Salanter recommended the arousal of "excitement" through parables. Each student would attempt to explain to himself the Mussar lessons that he was involved in by means of parables taken from his daily experience. These means of concretization were also intended to bring about the desired emotional state.

One cannot discuss the study of Mussar "with excitement" without referring to the institution of the Mussar House (*Mussar Shteibl*). The two were closely interrelated in Salanter's educational theory. The Mussar House was originally established to serve as an appropriate framework for Mussar study *be-hitpa'alut,* for two reasons: (1) the inappropriateness of the traditional Bet-Midrash (House of Study) for this purpose; and (2) the advantages offered by a Mussar House to the process of Mussar study. As is well known, the Bet-Midrash served as a place for the study of Torah by individuals and groups and was dominated by the air of sobriety characteristic of talmudic study. Even though this study was also customarily carried on out loud and to the accompaniment of a melody, the characteristic Talmud melody, which was a melodic expression of its dialectical patterns of thought, was totally unlike the melancholic chant of Mussar study. One who would attempt to study Mussar in this manner within the walls of the traditional Bet-Midrash would likely be subject to reactions of objection and ridicule, because of the peculiar nature of the sounds and motions that accompanied this study. In any event, the Mussar student needed to overcome deeper inhibitions in order to achieve the self-revelation and psychological stripping required by this method. Thus, the Mussar House was intended to guarantee a place in which one could engage in Mussar study *be-hitpa'alut* without fear or inhibition. Moreover, the special atmosphere existing in the Mussar House would also contribute to the study of Mussar.

In addition to the study of Mussar, which was intended to arouse the emotion of "fear of God," R. Israel described an entire path of activity for ethical perfection, which he referred to as "worldly wisdom." This wisdom was required because of the dangers involved in imposing the entire ethical burden upon fear alone, and this for two reasons: (1) it is very difficult to implant fear of God in the human heart; and (2) even when fear has found a place inside the human soul, there is no guarantee that in case of ethical trial one will succeed in overcoming the enormous power of the "appetite." Therefore, "worldly wisdom" is needed to assist "fear": whereas the purpose of "fear" is to restrain the appetite in times of ethical test, the purpose of "worldly wisdom" is to bypass the test, or at least to soften it, by means of advance preventative action.

"Worldly wisdom" is based on anticipation of the ethical trials that a person is likely to encounter in the future and the planning of future steps in order to overcome them. However, anticipation of the future is not enough. It is preceded by the demand for self-examination, in the course of which one discovers one's own weaknesses and faults. The obstacle standing in the way of this examination is one's tendency to deceive oneself and to cover up one's own sins. For this reason, penetrating self-criticism is a necessity.

Salanter deliberately avoided providing too many details of "worldly wisdom," which by its nature is a strictly personal wisdom, which each individual may acquire by penetrating examination of his own life experience. Nevertheless, Salanter's writings did include several points of advice and guidance to aid those engaged in this aspect of ethical self-correction. Thus, for example, he advises one to pursue modest goals, which are attainable, rather than grandiose goals whose fulfillment seems more doubtful. This advice is based, first of all, on his pessimistic assessment of the power of "appetite." To this, presumably, is added the fact that success in carrying out a relatively modest goal will encourage one to persist in the efforts, whereas failure in executing a more far-reaching plan is liable to conclude in despair. Against the background of these and similar considerations lies a basic fact: that R. Israel saw himself not as an ethical thinker but as an educator who devoted all his strength and talents to attempting to improve the ethical level of his contemporaries. Thus, he had no interest in preaching high "levels" whose accomplishment was doubtful. Unlike earlier ethical writers, who stressed the "desired" as against the "existing," R. Israel stressed the "desirable" which was also possible.

The Relationship between Torah and *Yir'ah*

Thus far we have outlined several of the main themes of R. Israel Salanter's thought in the first stage of its formation. The novelty of this approach expressed itself in two areas: on the theoretical level, in comparison with

Jewish ethical literature of earlier generations, R. Israel's innovation is expressed in his removal of the problem of ethics from the theological to the psychological plane. As we mentioned above, he proposed a naturalistic psychological theory of the evil inclination (*yezer ha-ra'*) and developed educational techniques based on it. His lack of interest in theosophical questions and his emphasis on existential experience seem to reflect certain general tendencies in modern European thought.

In social-cultural terms—that is, within the context of that Lithuanian Mitnaggedic Judaism to which R. Israel addressed himself—his thought may be seen as a call for reexamination of the relationship between Torah and fear of God (*yir'ah*). The problem of the relationship between these two— that is, between the values of Torah study and of ethical-religious perfection— has reappeared throughout the history of Jewish thought. The dialectical tension between them is rooted in classical rabbinic thought itself. The sages did not spare words in praise of the unique importance of Torah study but, on the other hand, they qualified this central value by declaring the impossibility of separating involvement in Torah from the desire for ethical perfection. This being the case, the question arises of the relative weight of these two values. In addition, there is the question of whether and in what sense there exists reciprocity between the effort invested in the study of Torah, on the one hand, and that devoted to ethical perfection, on the other.

The accepted view of the relationship between *Torah* and *yir'ah* among the learned elite in Lithuania was expressed in the writings and way of life of the Gaon of Vilna and R. Hayyim of Volozhin. Both argued that the study of Torah is infinitely more important than *yir'ah*. The Torah is the end, whereas *yir'ah* is essentially a means to its attainment. Nevertheless, *yir'ah* is an indispensable accompaniment to Torah study. Although both the Vilna Gaon and R. Hayyim left little doubt that the greater portion of one's time and energy is to be devoted to the study of Torah, they nevertheless did advise the dedication of a certain degree of effort to the cultivation of *yir'ah*. The preference of *Torah* over *yir'ah* was also expressed in the opinion of these two figures that study in and of itself is a central weapon in one's struggle with the *yezer ha-ra'* (evil urge).

Salanter did not challenge the axiom of the supremacy of Torah study per se, but he did ask his contemporaries to devote far more attention to the problem of *yir'ah*. His repeated criticisms of what seemed to him the relative neglect of *yir'ah* were based on his pessimistic view of the human person's emotional capacity to act in a moral way. The power of the appetite and the multitude of temptations encountered daily make it inevitable that spontaneous and unreflective behavior will lead to sin. Only continued and vigorous confrontation with the *yezer ha-ra'* is likely to save one from this lot.

Salanter's demand to devote more attention to the question of ethical perfection was expressed, among other things, in the distinction that he drew between the scope of the obligation to study Torah and that of Mussar study:

> Mussar study is unlike other forms of study, as no other kind of study is obligatory upon all people. Women are exempt from the obligation to study Torah; those suffering from mental handicaps or in severe distress also have reason to be exempted, each one in accordance with his situation. . . . But such is not the case with this subject; it is incumbent upon all people, bar none, for the battle is waged against all the living, namely, the battle of the *yezer* and its tricks. . . . (*Kitvey R. Yisrael Salanter,* 204–5)

Salanter's challenge to the view generally accepted among the learned elite in Lithuania concerning the relationship between *Torah* and *yir'ah* focused particularly upon the question of the value of Torah study as a means of ethical improvement. The assumption that involvement in Torah in and of itself would protect a person from the *yezer ha-ra'*, an assumption already found in classical talmudic literature, acquired great importance in the school of the Gaon of Vilna and R. Hayyim of Volozhin. While Salanter did not go so far as to deny the contribution of Torah study to the struggle against the *yezer,* he did claim that this contribution is limited and cannot serve as the exclusive or primary factor in the effort for moral improvement. Salanter explained this by means of a distinction he made between the respective functions of Torah study and of Mussar in the struggle against the *yezer ha-ra'*. One who studies Torah enjoys an influx of holiness which strengthens his powers of withstanding the *yezer,* but the connection between the study of a particular halakhic subject and the resultant influx of holiness as such are concealed from him. Thus, the study of Torah is a kind of supernatural cure. In contrast, ethical improvement based on Mussar study is, so to speak, a natural cure, based on an understanding of the psychological mechanism of the soul and a process of introspection in which the individual pinpoints his own weak points. This is thus a "natural" cure, in the sense that it is based on the identification of the relationship between cause and effect and that it seeks to prevent sin by dealing with its psychological roots. It follows that this approach must be more efficient and effective, as its use may be guided in accordance with the circumstances of each individual. On the basis of this distinction, R. Israel drew the conclusion that the primary effort toward moral improvement must be invested in the "natural" approach, while the contribution of Torah study will come by itself as the result of the *mizwah* of Torah study, which is a subject in and of itself.

Morality in the Social Realm

The new direction characterizing Salanter's Mussar message was expressed, among other things, in the statement that the ethical weak point of his generation lay in the area of social relationships. In both his written and his oral teachings, Salanter repeatedly protested against the gap between the widespread tendency toward meticulous observance of the "religious" commandments and the apathy and neglect displayed toward the *miẓwot* between a man and his fellow. Moreover, R. Israel argued, in many cases the meticulous observance of "religious" precepts took place at the expense of essential norms in the interpersonal realm. In order to emphasize how widespread this neglect was among his contemporaries, R. Israel pointed out that even the "scholars" and some of those who were considered "God-fearing" fell short in this area.

The presentation of the social realm as the focus of efforts toward moral improvement was something of a novelty. Salanter's predecessors, including the Gaon of Vilna and R. Hayyim, related to the problem of *yir'ah* from the point of view of the learned circles, while R. Israel removed it from the Bet-Midrash to the realms of economic and social activity. R. Israel expressed this demand in several ways. He devoted sermons to the subject, gave directions and advice to his students, and provided a personal example through his own behavior. This personal example was reflected in scores of legends circulated among his disciples and admirers. In the light of his sermons, the advice he gave to his students, and the stories concerning himself, R. Israel appears as an individual graced with unusual human and social sensitivity. This expressed itself in awareness and responsibility for the dignity, rights, and interests of others, combined with particular attention to the lot of the weaker elements within society.

It should be noted that the realization in practice of the responsibility for the interest of the other at times came into conflict with the view accepted among the "learned" that the major part of one's time should be devoted to the study of Torah. Indeed, his enthusiasm for doing good to others at times demanded the sacrifice of other norms of behavior whose importance R. Israel stressed. A typical example is found in the following anecdote: Once R. Israel was seen standing and speaking cheerfully and at great length with an acquaintance about "worldly matters." This incident seemed peculiar to his disciples, as it was his usual practice to take meticulous care against spending time in "frivolous speech," and to teach others to do the same. To the inquiry of one of his students concerning this behavior, R. Israel replied: "This man was feeling extremely bitter and depressed, and it was a great act of loving-kindness to cheer him and to make him forget his troubles and his worries. Could I have done this by lecturing him about *yir'ah* and Mussar? Surely, this could only be done by cheerful speech about down-to-earth matters" (*Sefer Or Yisra'el,* 112). This story reflects a clear tendency within R. Israel's personality: when there was a conflict between God-centered piety or kindness toward one's fellowman, R. Israel preferred the latter, even when it meant sacrificing the former.

R. Israel called the attention of his students to the fact that, at times, excessive piety may lead a person to improper behavior toward his fellowman. To illustrate this point, he related the following incident:

> Once, on the eve of Yom Kippur, while on his way towards the House of Study for the evening prayers, he encountered a man who was known for his "fear of God." His face reflected fear and awe of the Day of Judgment, and his cheeks were covered with tears. Rabbi Salanter stopped him to ask a question, but the man was so filled with fear of God that he did not answer him. Salanter, in relating this, said: "After I passed him, I thought to myself, 'Is it my fault that you are a God-fearing man and filled with trembling at the Day of Judgement? What has that to do with me? Are you not required to answer my question pleasantly and patiently, because such is the way of goodness and kindness?'" (*Or Yisra'el,* 118)

R. Israel also demanded of himself that he not be overly scrupulous in "religious" commandments when these conflicted with or caused neglect of obligations in the interhuman realm. Once Salanter was traveling together with a certain rabbi to the health-baths in Germany. Although the rabbi had supplied himself from the outset with a sufficient supply of bread for the entire journey, R. Israel did not hesitate to buy fresh rolls along the way. To the astonishment of his companion that he was not concerned about eating bread that was not strictly kosher, he replied that the funds for the trip had been given him by a friend who had stipulated that he refrain from any acts of superexemplary piety that might detract from his health. Thus, were he to refrain from eating non-Jewish bread, he would perform an act of piety but would thereby be deceiving and stealing from his benefactor. There is likewise a note of irony directed against the widespread tendency to piety in ritual matters, unaccompanied by similar care in human relations, in the following saying: "I am astounded by those people who wish to benefit their fellowman, and stand at the doors of the synagogues shouting '*Kedushah! Kedushah!* [i.e., the doxology prayers], please come in. . .' but do not stand at the doors to their homes when a rich repast is laid on the table and likewise cry out: 'A feast, a feast, please come in. . . .'"[4]

It must be stressed that R. Israel did not perceive these norms of inter-personal behavior as humanitarian gestures. As a talmudic scholar whose entire spiritual world was molded by the halakhah, he felt that these demands of himself and of others were rooted in and mandated by the halakhah. Thus, they were not gestures, but *mizwot*. The combination of sensitivity to the needs and rights of others and the profound conviction that the halakhah must guide all of the acts of the Jew led Salanter to new and unconventional interpretations and applications of the categories of Jewish civil law. R. Simhah Zissel Ziv, one of his closest disciples, gives testimony to this: "Our teacher innovated many new laws in torts and damages, which seemed strange to many people. Even some of the great scholars of the generation were among those who were astonished at his remarkable novellas, which had never been heard before"[5] (quoted by Dov Katz, I: 353).

There is good reason to assume that what sensitized Salanter to questions of social ethics were the economic poverty and social tension that oppressed Russian Jewry during the 1840s and 1850s. During that same period, the disparity between the natural rate of increase and the availability of means of livelihood widened considerably. The government of Nicholas I also imposed severe restrictions on the occupations of Jews, in addition to the already existing Pale of Settlement, which prohibited the settlement of Jews in the interior regions of Russia. These economic difficulties naturally exacerbated the social conflict. By the nature of things, the weaker strata of society were more exposed to the negative results of economic measures. Furthermore, the communal leadership, which was generally composed of the more prosperous elements, placed the main burden of taxes upon the shoulders of those of lesser means. The terrible law of conscription into the army also fell mostly upon this group.

These economic and social difficulties also, as is well known, lay in the background of the suggestions made by the Haskalah (Enlightenment) movement for radical change in the educational and economic patterns of the Jews. Salanter, who certainly disagreed with the contents of their proposals, apparently wished to deal with these same problems by means drawn from the Jewish tradition. While he did not pretend to alter the objective circumstances that caused these oppressive conditions, he did hope that, by introducing proper ethical norms into the life of society, it might be possible to reduce their weight and soften their sting.

The Mussar Movement

Thus far I have attempted to describe the new direction found in Salanter's "Mussar system." However, the novelty of his approach was not confined to the area of thought. He also introduced and established a new form of social organization, through which he attempted to disseminate and implement his ideas within the public. Through this organization, which over the course of time developed into what became known as the "Mussar movement," R. Israel hoped to catalyze an ethical-religious revival to encompass all of Lithuanian Jewry.

The local cells of Salanter's organization were the *havurot* of Mussar students, which gathered in the Mussar Houses. These *havurot* were mostly composed of individuals from the class of *ba'aley-batim* (householders), that is, individuals who had generally received a comprehensive Torah education, were economically established, and were active in the running of communal institutions. Salanter appealed to this group for two reasons. First, by its nature, R. Israel's system of ethical education demanded a certain minimal intellectual ability. Second, since this class was the backbone of Lithuanian Jewish society, he hoped through them to influence the entire society.

The *havurah* was based on the voluntary commitment of its members to engage in ethical self-improvement on the basis of Salanter's system. In practice, the members of the *havurah* gathered at fixed times—Salanter suggested that this be done daily, between the afternoon and evening prayers—and engage in Mussar study *be-hitpa'alut*. At the end of the study period, which lasted between half an hour and an hour, one of the members would read aloud a verse or rabbinic saying expressing the aspiration for ethical perfection, and all the members of the group would repeat it aloud after him. The repetition of the verse aloud and in a special melody served as an outlet for the spiritual tension which had accumulated during the study period. This was usually an experience of uplift, combined with feelings of guilt, regret, and longing for ethical improvement and spiritual purification. At times, when an appropriate person was present, a sermon would be given, the purpose of which was to inspire the participants and to guide them in their efforts toward ethical perfection.

Although Salanter emphasized the individual nature of the process of ethical education, he attached great importance to activity within the framework of the *havurah*. The advantage of this was its capacity to serve as a powerful incentive for each one of its members. On various occasions, Salanter advised the use of social pressure, to encourage the individual to persist in his efforts for ethical improvement despite difficulties and disappointments. He also attempted to use social pressure in order to disseminate his Mussar system within the broader public. In the detailed instructions that he gave to his students in Vilna, which was the first cell of the Mussar movement in Lithuania, he advised them first of all to approach the leaders of the community. If these would join the Mussar *havurot*, it would become fashionable and others would follow in their steps.

R. Israel's efforts to found *havurot* of Mussar students in various communities throughout Lithuania continued through the latter half of the 1840s and the 1850s. During the early years of his activity, he was full of hope, believing that the public would know how to assess properly the advantages of his system. This was the source of the pathos and persistence of his calls to carry out his Mussar system. However, despite his efforts and his hopes, the movement's growth was quite limited. We know with certainty of only six communities in Lithuania in which Mussar houses were established. Even if we assume that his ideas were accepted in a few other places, he was certainly not successful in establishing a broadly based movement encompassing the majority of Jewish communities of Lithuania, or even a significant number of them. We may assume that the failure of the attempt to spread the Mussar system to the entire householding class in Lithuania was related to the severity of the demands it placed upon the individual. The demands for scrupulously honest self-examination, for constant alertness to the temptations of the *yezer ha-ra'*, for advance planning of one's steps, and the use of various tricks in order to avoid ethical tests—all these demanded enormous emotional investment. It is not surprising that Lithuanian *ba'aley-batim* preferred the conventional approach, in which both emotional and intellectual satisfaction were derived from studying a page of Talmud.

Despite its limited growth, the Mussar movement aroused opposition. This was led by R. Leib Shapira, who served as rabbi of Kovno (Kaunas) during the 1850s. Shapira's role in the opposition to the Mussar movement stemmed from the fact that Salanter lived in Kovno during that period and that it served as a center for his public activity. However, he was not alone in his struggle against the new movement, but enjoyed the support of a number of prominent contemporary rabbis and scholars.

The fact that the opposition to the Mussar system was led by rabbis and scholars is indicative of the threat that it posed to their world view. From their point of view, Salanter's demand to place more emphasis on ethical education was a challenge to the centrality of Torah study, and to talmudic scholarship as the primary source of communal authority. However, the primary motivation underlying the opposition to the Mussar movement in the 1850s was the fear of a division within Lithuanian Jewry. This fear is alluded to in an exegetical wordplay attributed to R. Leib Shapira:

> In the Hallel prayer [Ps. 115], we read: "House of Israel, praise the Lord! House of Aaron, Praise the Lord!" and then, "Those who fear God, Praise the Lord!" It does not read, "*House* of the God-Fearers." From this, it follows that fear of God is a concern of each individual Jew, and not of a separate sect of people, who even have a special Bet-Midrash of their own.

It is thus clear that the opposition was not directed against Salanter's demand for cultivation of the quality of *yir'ah* as such, but against the fact that this had become a slogan around which a new social organization was formed. Their main concern was not the danger of social separation as such, but the fact that this separation was based on the cultivation of a religious value which, properly speaking, was the interest of all Jews. The very establishment of separate study-houses and *ḥavurot* under the banner of *mussar* and *yir'ah* implied that society in general did not fulfill its obligation in these matters.

There is no doubt that in the background of these rabbis' fears concerning the Mussar movement was the historical memory of the struggle against Hasidism. The failure of the Mitnaggedim to uproot this separatist "sect" and the transformation of the latter within a relatively short period of time into a mass movement prompted a suspicious attitude toward this new "sect" from the very beginning. Despite the great differences between Hasidism and the Mussar movement in terms of their contents and their inherent religious mentality, there was yet a definite similarity in the social dynamics caused by their establishment. In both cases, we speak of a group that claimed to act in the name of universally accepted values, but by their interpretation and execution of these values changed them considerably. In both cases, society interpreted the self-separation of the group as implying a stain upon the existing religious order, which drew its authority from its very continuity. Therefore, it blamed the innovators for arrogance and hypocrisy. Moreover, both Hasidism and the Mussar system introduced new norms for measuring an individual's religious stature, thereby challenging the authority of the existing religious leadership. Finally, both Hasidism and the Mussar movement were accompanied by new forms of externally visible religiosity, which by their very strangeness emphasized their departure from the accepted path.

The struggle against the Mussar movement during the 1850s was primarily conducted by means of propaganda. While it almost certainly seems that at times this struggle entailed the utilization of social pressure, in any event it never reached the stage of persecution and formal ostracism. It would seem that the relatively mild means used by the opponents of the Mussar movement stemmed from the great personal respect that they felt toward R. Israel Salanter. In any event, its opponents did not succeed in uprooting the new "sect," although it is possible that they contributed to the relative limitation of its spread.

The Kloiz

At the same time that certain Lithuanian rabbis attempted to halt the spread of the Mussar system, a new center was established for the dissemination of its ideas. This center was at the Nevyozer Kloiz in Kovno, where R. Israel had begun to teach Torah in the early 1850s. In retrospect, this *kloiz* (lit., "room," i.e., Bet-Midrash) may be seen as the kernel for the spread and influence of the Mussar movement after the death of its founder.

The *kloiz*, as an institution for the study of Torah, was a popular institution in the Lithuanian communities of that period. In general, it served as a center for young men who were capable of independent study. Nevertheless, there were those *kloiz* groups which enjoyed the leadership and inspiration of a scholarly personality. Thus, it is clear that the reputation of the Nevyozer Kloiz owed much to Salanter's prestige as a scholar. However, its uniqueness in comparison with other Torah institutions of the same period lay in its combination of ethical education in the spirit of the Mussar system with the study of Torah in the traditional sense. Salanter saw the balanced combination of these two elements as a necessary condition in the quest for the pursuit of wholeness in the service of God.

Furthermore, the inclusion of Mussar study in a Bet-Midrash devoted mainly to the cultivation of talmudic scholars reflected Salanter's view of the importance of ethical education in the training of "rabbi-judges." In a methodological discussion concerning the study of Torah, Salanter stated that one of the preconditions for the student's uncovering the truth of the Torah is "purity of thought." By this concept, taken from classical Mussar literature, he essentially meant what we refer to as "scientific objectivity." To be precise, R. Israel stated that the rabbi, in interpreting the halakhah, must attempt to be guided by pure thought, uninfluenced by emotional inclinations, which are subjective by nature.[6] This ability may only be acquired by appropriate ethical education during one's youth.

One may distinguish two complementary streams in the ethical educational activities conducted by Salanter in the *kloiz:* the first included those activities conducted within a group framework, that is, in the presence of all or some of the student body; the second involved the individual guidance Salanter gave to various students. At the focus of the group activity was the sermon. R. Yitzhak Blazer has reported the following concerning the nature of the sermons given by R. Israel:

> The basis of his sermons was not the exposition of Biblical verses or Midrashim, but ideas which he conceived and thought out inside himself: profound inquiries in the ways of Divine service; reward and punishment; and the way of various ethical traits. And when he would preach for several hours, he would occasionally embody a certain idea in a Biblical idiom or a Rabbinic saying. The power of his speech was awesome. In nearly all his sermons, he never failed to mention the matter of reward and punishment. (*Or Yisra'el,* 121)

The fact that at times Salanter's sermons continued for hours sheds light on their nature and purpose. It seems clear that he did not intend to develop new ideas during that time: their purpose, rather than the imparting of information, was to implant certain feelings and moods. The length of the sermons evidently grew out of Salanter's assumption that by the repetition of known ideas, and with the aid of appropriate rhetorical means, it is possible to change the hearts of one's listeners. He also believed in the effectiveness of examples and homilies taken from daily life. Through these, it was possible to concretize abstract ideas and rules and transform them into vital factors in a person's soul. Another rhetorical device he suggested was the use of *melizah*. In then-current usage, this term referred to a high-flown and even florid style of writing or oratory. Although such a style was totally inappropriate for halakhic discussions, in which the objective, intellectual consideration of the arguments must be protected against the involvement of the emotions, it played a positive role in the process of ethical education, because of its power to influence the feelings. R. Yitzhak Blazer reported that R. Israel's sermons incorporated "deep inquiries in the ways of divine service." It would appear that he refers here to Salanter's reflections on the nature of the human psyche, the *yezer ha-ra'* and its tricks, and the appropriate means of restraining the appetite and perfecting ethical qualities.

A subject that "he never failed to mention" in his sermons was reward and punishment. This reflected his understanding of the decisive role played by "fear of divine punishment" in shaping human behavior. His views on the subject may be inferred from his letters. He presumably repeated the substance of the "inquiries" pertaining to Divine Providence's policy of reward and punishment in his sermons. These "inquiries" were not motivated at all by theosophical curiosity, their only concern being to transform theoretical awareness of the principle of reward and punishment into a moving force within the human soul. Thus, he presumably repeated the "inquiry" leading to the conclusion that the magnitude of divine punishment a person might expect for a given sin would be greater than the pleasure originally given by that act. Likewise, he surely repeated the discussions concerning the interrelationship between the effort invested by an individual in the performance of a *mizwah* and the avoidance of transgression and his corresponding reward or punishment. His relativistic-individualistic understanding of reward and punishment was also intended to convert the fear of punishment into an effective force every time an individual encountered an ethical test.

By means of the sermons that he delivered to his students, R. Israel attempted to instill in them a mood of self-dissatisfaction, severe self-criticism, and ceaseless striving for ethical improvement and perfection. A typical expression of this tendency is found in the following quotation from Salanter, quoted by R. Simhah Zissel Ziv:

> It is certainly clear that a person is not considered human if he lives a life of pleasure and does not toil to acquire *yir'ah*, for the entire human task is to at least reach the level of, "Woe to me from my *yezer*, woe to me from my Creator." But as long as one lives a life of calmness and tranquility in the service of God it is clear that he is remote from true service. . . . For it is impossible that a person not encounter things which he desires and which the Torah prohibits. (*Kokhvey Or*, 187)

Peace, tranquility, and self-satisfaction are inconsistent with the service of God. By human nature itself, and that of the world in which he lives, it is impossible that there not be sharp conflicts between the "appetite" and the commandments of the Torah. It follows that peace and comfort are only possible for one who sinks further and further into sin and is not even aware of it.

From the accounts left by Salanter's various disciples, we know that his sermons always followed a fixed pattern. The first part was devoted to clarifying and examining various aspects of the service of God and was delivered in a relatively calm manner. The turning point came approximately in the middle of the sermon. when these inquiries were supplanted by "words of rebuke and inspiration." This entailed severe criticism of those present in terms of their religious service, including a detailed list of their most frequent shortcomings. The call to act immediately for ethical improvment came in the wake of this critical evaluation. During this part of the sermon, Salanter's listeners would become imbued with a mood of *yir'ah*, not only by the content of what he said but also by his raising of his voice, the use of a special melody, outbursts of weeping, etc. One of his students testifies to the power of this experience in saying that "the fear of God, so to speak, could be physically touched. . . ." The accumulated tension reached its climax, and also found its release, when in wake of these words of "inspiration" Salanter would cry out in a loud voice, in a heartbreaking, poignant melody, verses such as: "Return us to You, O Lord, as we shall return, renew our days as of old," which the group then repeated together in a loud voice. This "prayer," in the form of reciting and repeating verses, provided an avenue of expression for the turbulence created in the heart of those present.

As we said above, Salanter's educational activity was also expressed in personal instruction and guidance. One of the main focuses of this guidance was the perfection of one's character traits (*middot*). As we shall see below, R. Israel claimed that improvement of one's character was particularly appropriate for youth. This was especially true of the young men engaged in full-time *yeshivah* study who, as a result of their intellectual talents, were in great danger that their negative qualities would dominate their intellects and use them as tools to justify wicked ways. Moreover, as we explained above, character improvement was particularly important for one who was to serve in the future in the capacity of a rabbi-judge, since "purity of thought"—that is, the grounding of halakhic decision making in unbiased intellectual judgment, devoid of any emotional considerations—also came under the rubric of character improvement.

By the nature of things, the guidance Salanter gave to his students in these matters had an individual character, as "each person, and in particular every great man, is a world unto himself. . . ." For this reason, he took care not to dictate fixed or rigid formulas to his students in this area. When his disciple, R. Yitzhak Blazer, approached him for detailed guidance and instructions in these matters, Salanter answered: "There is no set path that can be placed before a great man such as him . . . and it would be dangerous to do so" (Or Yisra'el, 65). The means of ethical improvement and education of the middot must be set by each person, on the basis of life experience. Although in the healing of the body, for example, it is possible to extrapolate from our experience with one person's body to another, in the area of "healing the soul," that is, ethical improvement, this is impossible. For this reason, the fixing of set, rigid guidelines does more harm than good.

Among the techniques of character improvement utilized by Salanter's disciples, a central role was played by the study of Mussar be-hitpa'alut. It is interesting that, in terms of the nature and goal of this activity, there was no difference between what he told his students in the Nevyozer Kloiz and what he told the ba'aley-batim, although there was a difference in the framework of this study. As we have mentioned, Salanter attempted to institutionalize the Mussar study of the ba'aley-batim by setting a fixed time—between the afternoon and evening services—and a fixed place—the Mussar House—for it. From various accounts, it appears that this framework was intended only for the ba'aley-batim and not for those scholars who devoted most of their time to Torah study. The latter, who in any event spent most of their time in the Bet-Midrash, would presumably find no difficulty in devoting a short period of time to the regular study of Mussar. This being so, it seemed preferable not to impose a fixed time for this purpose, so that each individual could engage in the study of Mussar when his heart was ready for it and for the period of time that he felt was needed.

R. Israel was aware of the danger that the study of Mussar was liable to intrude, in terms of time, upon the time set aside for Torah study. For this reason, he warned his disciples, "Do not allow the study of Gemara and posqim to be disturbed by the study of Mussar, except during the Ten Days of Repentance. . ." (Or ha-Mussar, I:247). We may thus imagine that he instructed or advised his students to devote a limited amount of time to the study of Mussar, the rest of the day being devoted to the study of Torah.

The influence of the Mussar education Salanter introduced into the *kloiz* was expressed not only in those activities whose specific purpose this was, such as the sermon, formal Mussar study, etc., but also in the unique atmosphere created as the result of the sum of these activities, and even more so by the influence of R. Israel's personality per se. The spiritual tension and mood of striving for ethical perfection expressed themselves even in the discussions of *yir'ah* and *mussar* conducted by the young "scholars" among themselves, which had no fixed framework, but took place spontaneously. During these conversations, the young men exchanged with one another their own trials and experiences in seeking *yir'ah* and character improvement and inspired one another to added efforts in these matters. R. Israel himself claimed that it was desirable for a person to have a friend to help him in the process of ethical improvement, since an individual's capability of uncovering his own shortcomings is limited. The friend performs the task of critic and guide. Likewise, R. Israel taught that it is both possible and necessary for the *havurah* to serve as a stimulus for the ethical perfection of each individual within it, not only by the use of social pressure, which forces a person to act in accordance with the norms of society, but also through personal contacts in which each individual attempts by his own powers to influence those who have strayed. It is thus not surprising that discussions of *yir'ah* and *mussar* should have been a common phenomena among R. Israel's students.

It seems likely that, when Salanter established the Nevyozer Kloiz, shaping it into an institution combining Torah study with Mussar education, his main purpose was to cultivate God-fearing scholars. Nevertheless, he probably had an additional communal goal in mind: to train spiritual leaders who would be able to influence the broader public in the spirit of the Mussar system. Indeed, several of the future leaders of the Mussar movement came from among R. Israel's students in the Nevyozer Kloiz. Moreover, the Nevyozer Kloiz of the 1850s served as an archetypical model for the Mussar *yeshivot* to be established later by R. Israel's disciples, and by their disciples. Thus, for example, the Mussar sermon as developed by R. Israel, the study of Mussar *be-hitpa'alut,* and the discussions of *yir'ah* and *mussar* were among the salient characteristics of the Mussar *yeshivot.* However, as often happens in such movements, phenomena that bore an original and spontaneous character in the Nevyozer Kloiz became institutionalized and fixed in the later Mussar *yeshivot.* Even the institution of the *mashgiah,* the "spiritual guide," which played such a central role in the Mussar *yeshivot,* grew out of the image and role played by Salanter in the Nevyozer Kloiz.

Character Training

We have described above the early stages in the development of R. Israel Salanter's Mussar system—that is, during the 1840s and 1850s. We shall now discuss the further stages of his thought, from the end of the 1850s until his death in the early 1880s. This latter stage reflects a new dimension of depth and complexity, due both to his awareness of the phenomena of the subconscious and to his focus on the area of character training.

At the beginning of his discussion of character training, R. Israel attempts to disabuse his readers of the deterministic view of human nature, substituting for it an optimistic approach:

> Do not say that what God has made cannot be altered and that because He has planted within me an evil nature I cannot hope to uproot it. This is not the case, for the powers of a human being can be subdued, and even changed. Just as we see that man is able to tame animals and bend their will to his . . . and also to domesticate them . . . so does man have the power to subdue his own evil nature . . . and to change his nature toward the good through exercise and practice [from *Heshbon ha-Nefesh*].[7] (*Kitvey R. Yisrael Salanter*, 125)

The assumption that a person is able to alter his personality traits for the good lies at the basis of Salanter's doctrine of character training. The analogy with animal training, borrowed from R. Mendel Lefin's book *Heshbon ha-Nefesh*, is intended not only to demonstrate the truth of this axiom but also to provide a hint of the means that can be utilized in order to train character.

By removing the discussion from the area of *mizwah* and transgression to that of character training, Salanter transfers the focus from isolated external manifestations of behavior to the underlying psychological motivations. This change raises the question of the theological meaning attached by R. Israel to character training. That is, how did he envision the place and role of the training of character within the overall scheme of the service of God?

Although there is no explicit discussion of the religious meaning of character training in Salanter's writings, his views on the subject may be inferred from the overall context of his discussion of other subjects. First, it is clear that R. Israel did not see the "ethical good" as manifested in a harmony of the functions of the soul—as is found, for example, in R. Saadiah Gaon and Maimonides. Likewise, he does not believe that ethical perfection need be expressed in an attitude of apathy toward worldly things, which is the position of kabbalistic Mussar literature. In Salanter's writings generally, and in his discussions of character training in particular, there is no indication that normative meaning is attached to any ethical principle independent of the concepts of *mizwah* and transgression. This being so, what religious significance is there to *tiqqun ha-middot* ("transmutation of character traits")? How does he justify removing one's attention from acts of omission and commission—that is, the rubric of "commandment" and "transgression"—to the characteristics of the soul, which are not directly subject to the discussions and rulings of the halakhah? It seems to me that this is dealt with in two ways. First, there is a tendency within his writings to subsume various character traits under the categories of *mizwah* and *'averah*. Thus, for example, he writes, "A bad trait is a very great transgression, as the sages greatly stressed the punishment for it; and a good trait is a great *mizwah*, as the sages emphasized its value" (*Kitvey R. Yisrael Salanter*, 165). In referring to the position of the sages with regard to character traits, he quoted such sayings as: "Whoever is angry is subjected to all kinds of [punishment in] Gehinnom (Hell) . . ." (*Nedarim* 22a). This and similar sayings are not intended as categorical legal rulings but as ethical directives or advice. Thus, although it is doubtful that R. Israel would have included the various character traits within the formal enumeration of the 613 commandments, he nevertheless clearly wished to invoke the authority of the sages in this matter, to the extent of making it a subject of reward and punishment, like other *mizwot*.

But, while Salanter wished to give character traits the normative status of *mizwot* and *'averot*, there is no doubt that the significance attached to *tiqqun ha-middot* went beyond that, to shaping the personality in a manner appropriate to the commandments of the Torah. By creating harmony between the characteristics of the soul and the demands of the halakhah, the psychological obstacles hindering one from serving God are removed, and the way is paved for the maximal response to God's commandments. This view forms the background of the following statement by Salanter:

> There are two kinds of (character) improvement: one in which man turns the powers of his soul to the good, so that the power of evil is totally uprooted and not seen at all. To accomplish this, it is insufficient for man to improve his general will, to long for the good and to despise evil, but he must seek the means of correcting each individual trait of his soul. This is required in the case of the rational commandments, pertaining to man and his fellow. . . . The second way involves the "transmutation" of his general will, to love and to heed that which comes from the mouth of God in the a-rational *mizwot*, known to us by revelation, and to seek out and reduce the power of the appetite in each detail. (*Kitvey R. Yisrael Salanter*, 130)

It is clear from the distinction drawn between the "two kinds of transmutation" that correction of the *middot* relates to the realm of the *mizwot* between a man and his fellow, and not to those between humanity and God, since it is in the interpersonal realm that such traits as arrogance or modesty, anger or patience, are expressed. At the same time, it is clear that R. Israel does not wish to identify simply the *middot* with the realm of interpersonal *mizwot*. Rather, the relationship between these two distinct systems is one of interdependence. *Tiqqun ha-middot* creates the psychological framework that fosters and makes possible the observance of the *mizwot* between a man and his fellow. One might summarize by saying that, in Salanter's view, the theological significance of *tiqqun ha-middot* is anchored in the concepts of *mizwah* and transgression in two different ways: on the one hand, the tendency to define the *middot* themselves within the framework of these concepts; on the other hand, the ascription of instrumental significance to the *middot*—the transmutation of the traits prepares the soul to observe the entirety of the *mizwot* between a man and his fellow.

The special place occupied by *tiqqun ha-middot* within the overall framework of the effort toward ethical improvement is explained by R. Israel by means of a distinction between two concepts: *kibbush ha-yezer*, the "subjugation" of the evil impulse, and *tiqqun ha-yezer*, "correction" or "transmutation" of the evil impulse. The concept of "subjugation" of the *yezer* denotes the reining in and halting of the appetites by the power of will. The other concept, "transmutation" of the *yezer*, serves in a parallel sense to that of "correction" of the *middot*, that is, the reshaping of the personality by uprooting negative characteristics and introducing positive ones in their place.

At the beginning of his discussion of these two concepts, Salanter points out the superiority of *tiqqun ha-yezer*: while one who has succeeded in subjugating his *yezer* many times is still liable to fall into sin, one who has transmuted it is no longer exposed to the pull of appetite. It must be emphasized, nevertheless, that the preference given *tiqqun ha-yezer* over *kibbush ha-yezer* is not a value judgment, since Salanter does not see the presence of the appetites within the human personality as an ethical defect per se. The ethical-religious status of a person is not determined by the innate inclinations of the soul, but by the manner in which the person confronts them. R. Israel's preference for *tiqqun ha-yezer* is a functional, tactical one: one whose negative traits have been transmuted is stronger and more resistant to the temptations of the "appetite" and the *yezer*. Thus, the relationship between subjugation and transmutation of the *yezer* may be defined as that between two different ways of withstanding ethical tests. However, in addition to this functional judgment, Salanter places the two within a chronological framework. In the first stage of ethical growth, one is liable to struggle with the *yezer*, in the sense of "subjugating the *yezer*," while later on, one gradually advances to the stage of "transmutation" of the *yezer*.

At a later stage of his discussion, Salanter qualifies these earlier comments, so that the unqualified hierarchical structure described above becomes more complex. This new stage of the discussion opens with the warning that even one who has achieved the level of *tiqqun ha-yezer* cannot entirely forgo the need to "subjugate" the *yezer*. This warning is based on the possibility that the forces of the personality, hidden within the depths of the unconscious, will suddenly burst forth to the realm of the conscious in the wake of some external stimuli. In the light of this possibility, one may no longer see *tiqqun ha-yezer* as a final and permanent stage. Even one who has worked consistently and successfully to correct his character has no guarantee that he will not at some point find himself in the battleground of *kibbush ha-yezer*.

In the light of these considerations, R. Israel now suggests a new understanding of the interrelationship between "subjugation of the *yezer*" and "transmutation of the *yezer*." These are no longer thought of as two levels, to be acquired sequentially, but as two different approaches to the problem of ethical improvement, which are both necessary and complementary. Certainly, one must persist in *tiqqun ha-yezer*, since one whose character faults have been transmuted can conduct his life in an ethical manner without the enormous psychological effort demanded by "subjugation" of the *yezer*; but one may no longer rely exclusively upon *tiqqun ha-yezer*, so that one must continue to practice *kibbush ha-yezer* in order to assure an effective line of defense in case of emergency.

In his treatment of this problem, R. Israel encountered a new question: Which of these two methods is appropriate to each stage of human life? In answering this question, Salanter reverses the chronological order that had originally been suggested. Transmutation of the *middot*, which had at first been described as a later stage, is now seen as suitable to youth and adolescence, whereas "subjugation of the *yezer*" is now seen as more appropriate to maturity and old age. Salanter's argument for this is based on a number of factors. *Kibbush ha-yezer* involves a concentrated spiritual effort, demanding great powers of forbearance. As such, it is appropriate to more mature individuals, whose endurance and tolerance for suffering have been developed as a result of the trials of life and the struggle for survival. *Tiqqun ha-yezer*, on the other hand, is more suitable to young people, whose personalities are still flexible and capable of change. Moreover, the young man, who does not yet need to earn a living, enjoys a certain psychological calm and peace that allow for introspection and self-examination, careful planning of his actions, and the use of tricks and various other devices needed in order to transmute his traits. The older person, on the other hand, who must confront the pressures, temptations, and tests of practical life, lacks the emotional room necessary for serious work on his character.

In the course of his discussions of these problems, R. Israel observes a serious problem confronting the individual who is consistent in working on his character, a difficulty rooted in the demand to activate the identical traits in different and even contradictory ways, in a man's relationship to himself, on the one hand, and in his relationship to others, on the other. Can a person instill in himself an attitude of contempt and rejection toward any manifestation of honor and prestige and at the same time meticulously avoid doing any harm to the honor and dignity of his fellowman? Salanter's reply to this is in the affirmative. The psychological difficulty involved can be overcome by means of appropriate exercises. The student must learn to cultivate two separate sets of responses with regard to the same traits: one that guides and delimits the expressions of this trait in everything pertaining to himself and a second framework pertaining to others. He bases this assumption on an analogy from another realm of the emotional life:

> Do we not always find contradictory traits within a person's characteristics, which he nevertheless utilizes naturally (without any guide or ruler), each in its proper time and place, such as memory and forgetfulness, etc.? The same is true of the ability to expand the potentialities of one's personality and use them naturally in opposite ways. (*Kitvey R. Yisrael Salanter,* 132)

The selective utilization of contradictory psychological powers, such as memory and forgetfulness, are explained by R. Israel as being guided by a certain lawfulness rooted in the soul. It follows from this that, by means of properly directed exercise, it is possible to implant in the soul rules that will guide selective operation of the various character traits.

The mind plays an important role in the correction of the traits, according to Salanter. Decisions concerning the nature of both good and bad attributes are made by the mind. He refers here to "common sense" (*sekhel ha-yashar*), that is, reflection based on neither logical reasoning nor empirical evidence. He assumes an identity between the decisions of common sense and the ethical norms demanded by the Torah in the interpersonal realm. In addition to the distinction between good and evil traits, the mind fulfills an important function in the process of transmuting the *middot:* first, through the process of self-examination and introspection in order to locate and identify the negative traits. In this connection, Salanter again raises the demand for introspection, which we first encountered in his discussion of "worldly wisdom," but which here refers to a deeper and more penetrating kind of contemplation. The focus of this process is no longer the appetites, but rather the basic character traits. One must emphasize that this contemplation is directed not only toward the *middot* but also toward the various stimuli liable to awaken them.

The process of self-examination and identification of character faults is followed by the decisive and most difficult stage in the training of character: the attempt to "break" the negative traits and to implant and cultivate positive ones. The mind also has an important contribution to make at this stage—the "tricks of the mind." Before being surprised by the nature of these "tricks," we must remember the common view concerning habit as a means of correcting the *middot*. According to this view, first found in Greek ethics and appearing frequently in Jewish ethical literature, a given pattern of behavior may be turned into "second nature" by frequent repetition. But the authors of these Mussar works, who extolled habit as a tool of character training, did not give much thought to the problematics involved in the use of this technique in practice. For example, it is quite possible that one attempting to change his traits by means of habit will find it difficult to impose the decision of his will upon his actual behavior. How, then, will it be possible for him to repeat the desired behavior over and over again, sufficiently in order to transform it into "second nature"? It seems to me that the function of "tricks of the mind" may be understood in relation to this problem: they are designed to strengthen the will power, to enable it to overcome the negative traits, until they are uprooted from the personality.

We shall now examine the nature of these "tricks of the mind," through a number of examples from the testimony of R. Naphtali Amsterdam, one of Salanter's close disciples, who describes what he heard from his teacher:

> I once asked him for a cure for the trait of anger and short-temperedness, and he answered, "The cure is for a person to constantly bear in mind to be a good person, to do good to others. . . so that when a person awakens in his soul loving-kindness, and doing good with people, and becomes known as a good person who does good to all, this will make it easier for him to keep himself from anger and short-temper. . . ." (*Sefer Or ha-Mussar,* 1:76ff.)

At the basis of this trick lies a train of thought characteristic of Salanter as an educator, which we have already encountered during the course of our discussion—namely, the use of social pressure to motivate the individual to act as he should. In our case, R. Israel suggests awakening and directing social pressure by the deliberate development of a self-image that elicits certain definite expectations from society. The psychological tendency to respond to the expectations of society and to fulfill the "role" that it imposes on the individual in keeping with this image conflict with the negative trait and defeat it.

Another example of a "mental trick" that R. Naphtali Amsterdam heard from Salanter is directed against the trait of impatience or severity:

> . . . that a person should bear in mind three principles of the halakhah. . . . First, that the prohibition against stealing which appears in the Torah applies not only to actual theft, in which a person takes his fellow's money or belongings, but that anything which contradicts the civil law found in the section *Hoshen Mishpat* of the *Shulhan 'Arukh* is also theft. Second, that according to the law found there (in the *Hoshen Mishpat*) it makes no difference whether he takes from his neighbor a garment which had always been his, or if he gives his neighbor a garment as a gift . . . and afterwards takes away that same garment. This too is literally theft. The third principle is that a grudge against one's neighbor is also subject to the laws in the Talmud and in the *Shulhan 'Arukh*, and that one bears a grudge against his neighbor, where this is forbidden by law, is also culpable of theft. . . . On the basis of these principles, when a person is truly convinced in his heart that whenever another person does him wrong or goes against his will he may conquer his tendency to impatience by thinking in his heart that he forgives that person entirely (i.e., making him a "gift" of his forgiveness), and that it is thus forbidden by law to hold a grudge or complaint against that person, in this way he may conquer the hatred and severity that he bears in his heart. (*Sefer Or ha-Mussar,* 1:76ff.)

This "trick," which according to his own account Salanter himself used in his youth, is typical of a scholar. The familiarity with the halakhah and the speculative ability to manipulate a legal argument combine here to force upon the negative trait of severity the full seriousness and force of the laws of theft. In this manner, the deeply ingrained repugnance toward violating the prohibition on theft is marshaled in order to help the educator to overcome the trait of severity.

The common denominator of all of the various "tricks" described here is the attempt to awaken the forces and tendencies dormant within the soul, utilizing their hidden strength to foster the correction of the *middot*. The "trick" thus entails an element of guile, as it displaces a given psychological tendency to redirect it toward the realm in which it encounters and conquers an evil trait, or develops and strengthens a positive characteristic. In the background of these and similar "tricks" lies the analogy between animal training and the ethical education of human beings—an analogy that Salanter derived from the book *Heshbon ha-Nefesh,* by R. Menahem Mendel Lefin. According to this analogy, the soul, or personality, which is the object of moral education, is parallel to the animal to be trained, and the mind, which directs the process of moral training, is analogous to the animal trainer. Just as an animal trainer must ensnare his animals through guile, awakening their animal instincts and directing these toward the arena convenient for him, the mind of the human being who wishes to correct his own character traits must guide the impulses and tendencies of the personality toward the required framework for purposes of ethical education.

R. Israel's view of moral education as an individual process in which each person must act in accordance with his own personality and the circumstances dictated by his environment is even more true with regard to the transmutation of the *middot*. It would seem that this is the reason why R. Israel does not discuss the practical aspect of *tiqqun ha-middot* at length in his writings. By the nature of things, detailed instructions in these matters must be personal. As we mentioned above, even the "mental tricks" described above were based on verbal instructions given by R. Israel to one of his disciples. Likewise, the subject of *tiqqun ha-middot* was central to the personal guidance given by R. Israel to his students.

The "Conscious" and the "Unconscious"

The most striking development in R. Israel's psychological theory during this period related to the distinction drawn between "dark" forces and "bright" or "clear" forces within the human psyche—a distinction largely parallel to that made by modern psychology between the "conscious" and the "unconscious." This similarity has moved some authors to herald Salanter as having preceded Freud in discovering the unconscious. However, not only did he not claim such a distinction for himself, but he explicitly states that he borrowed this concept from "the researchers of the powers of the human soul." There were, in fact, a number of nineteenth-century thinkers who preceded Freud in discovering the unconscious life of the mind. Recently there has even been an interesting discovery relating to the exact source by which Salanter was apparently influenced, namely, Immanuel Kant, who in one of his tractates discusses the phenomenon of the unconscious, using the same terminology later used by Salanter. Whether Kant's influence was direct or indirect, his discussion seems to have been the source from which Salanter drew the distinction between "dark" and "bright" powers.[8] Of course, the denial of his "discovery" of the unconscious does not detract from the originality and creativity he displayed in his use of these new concepts and their incorporation within his thought.

How did Salanter understand the phenomenon of the unconscious and its significance for moral education? The division of psychological life into levels revealed to our consciousness and those concealed from it is present, according to Salanter, in both the emotional and intellectual realms. Indeed, insofar as this refers to the moral improvement of humanity, R. Israel's interest is concentrated on the emotional aspect of the unconscious. The example by which he chose to explain to his readers the phenomenon of the unconscious was that of the process of learning to read a new language. When he first begins, a student must invest considerable effort in order to combine the strange letters into words and the words into sentences—an effort that occurs on the conscious level. After he has practiced sufficiently, the student is able to read fluently without any special effort, because at this stage the entire process of combining the letters into words and the words into sentences takes place in the unconscious. In the light of this example, R. Israel states: "The same is true of the powers of arousal of the soul: there are bright powers (*klore*) and dark ones (*dunkele*). The dark forces are stronger and perform their functions powerfully and with little stimulus" (*Kitvey R. Yisrael Salanter,* 217).

In the final sentence, Salanter describes two traits which in his view characterize the feelings that belong to the realm of the unconscious: first, they are immeasurably stronger than the feelings in the realm of conscious: second, the emergence of these "dark" powers from their concealment in the depths of the soul into consciousness is the result of external stimuli, but a small stimulus is sufficient to release powerful "dark" forces. To illustrate this point, he uses a familiar example drawn from human experience: "A parent's love for his children is dark, and in most cases the person himself does not consciously feel it, but even a small stimulus awakens it to a burning passion" (*Kitvey R. Israel Salanter,* 217). What, then, are the external stimuli capable of making the "dark" forces emerge into the consciousness from the hidden recesses of the soul? In the case of a parent's love for his children, these feelings of love burst forth when he becomes aware of some danger threatening his offspring. Speaking in general, R. Israel describes the "awakening," or stimulus, as an event or phenomenon in a person's immediate environment, bearing some relation to a specific force hidden in the depths of the soul. In other words, the stimulus is a concrete point of contact between the hidden emotion and the realm of the conscious.

The significance of this phenomenon for ethical education is based on the fact that both the appetites and the *middot* are rooted in the unconscious realm of the soul. In practice, R. Israel understands the unconscious as a concealed storehouse of psychological forces, identical in content to those known to us from the consciousness. The same appetites and traits found in the conscious realm are permanently present in the hidden depths of the soul, until some external stimulus awakens them, causing them to be revealed.

A priori, it ought to be possible to recognize and identify the powers hidden in the depths of the soul by examination of the way in which they reveal themselves in the conscious realm. However, Salanter cautions against the delusion that one can reconstruct a picture of the unconscious by means of analogy with what is known to us of the psyche, since our picture of the unconscious, based upon what is reflected in the consciousness, is fragmentary and unbalanced. This is so because the degree and power of the appearance of the soul's various unconscious powers are not determined by their relative weight, but by "external reasons." Thus, examination on the conscious level of the soul can uncover no more than a portion of the unconscious.

In the light of this conclusion, the threat posed by the appetites and the negative traits to the possibility of one's ethical perfection becomes more real, since the process of self-examination advocated by Salanter as a preventive measure cannot possibly uncover and locate all of the possible dangers buried in the depths of the soul. Moreover, in some cases a serious disparity may exist between a given individual's overt behavior patterns and his hidden, unconscious personality. Salanter refers to this phenomenon, its causes, and its potential dangers, in the following passage:

> One must realize that man's internal and external powers are distinct from one another. A given person may have very good external forces, while his internal ones may be very evil; while at times, the opposite may be the case. For the basic foundation of the external forces is education: an individual who grew up and was educated by honest and pious parents and teachers, and among pious people, will be shaped in such a way that his external forces will reflect the path of ethics and justice, even though his internal forces may remain evil, as they were at birth. . . . At times the opposite may be true; the external forces will be evil, because he was educated by parents and teachers who rejected the ethical way, and because he associated with bad people, although his innate internal forces may be extremely good. Thus, we sometimes see a person renowned for piety who, in response to some powerful factor acting upon him at a certain time, is easily turned towards evil, because his inner nature is evil. This strong force arouses these evil forces within him, until they outweigh his good external forces, and so he moves from one extreme to the other. And at times the opposite may also take place. . . . (*Kitvey R. Yisrael Salanter,* 173)

The potential gap between the "inner" and "outer" forces of the soul is presented here in its full sharpness. In effect, Salanter describes two separate and distinct psychological systems, each with its own contents. The difference is rooted in the different origins of each of these systems: whereas the internal one is implanted in the soul from birth, the external one is the product of education and environment. We thus may even find an extreme situation in which education and environment act upon a person in a direction totally different from that of his natural inclination. R. Israel would seem to have chosen to emphasize this extreme possibility in order to illustrate a certain potential danger: that even one who has consolidated a regular, ethically positive way of life and whose behavior patterns seem to be the result of positive psychological traits may yet be subject to a radical transformation if changed circumstances bring about the liberation of those forces hitherto hidden in the depths of the soul. It seems that fixed habit and even the psychological "nature" formed by it are no guarantee of a person's sustained ethical level. In the light of this discovery, the aim or goal of ethical education becomes deeper and more complex, and the "inner" forces which dwell in the unconscious personality become the principal area of ethical self-confrontation.

In his writings, Salanter defines two ways of dealing with the appetites and negative traits concealed in the depths of the soul. The first method does not attempt to cause any change in these powers; its entire aim is to halt, or at least to diminish, the negative effects likely to incur from them. This goal may be accomplished thus:

> If [a person] sets his mind to penetrate to the depths of his heart to perceive the general forces within himself, which are likely to dominate his outer self as the result of a small stimulus, and to apply to them his understanding, to extinguish them somewhat so that they not go with quite such great rapidity, so that it will be possible for him to halt them by his will. (*Kitvey R. Yisrael Salanter*, 165)

Thus, despite the limitations of self-examination discussed above, Salanter continues to advise its practice. Although it does not have the capability of fully understanding the forces hidden in the depths of the soul, it is at least able to identify those forces which have on previous occasions broken through the threshold of consciousness. The identification of these forces and the location of the external "causes" that awaken them enable one to take appropriate preventive action. R. Israel returns here to the concept of the preventive act, which, as will be remembered, he advised in an earlier stage of development of his system. However, in the light of his awareness of the phenomenon of the unconscious and its implications, self-examination and preventive action lose the importance they earlier possessed.

The second method of dealing with the appetites and the negative traits found in the unconscious is more radical in that it attempts to convey a qualitative change within the soul. This is based on the assumption that, even if a man is unable to look into and act upon his unconscious directly, he is still able to affect it indirectly—that is, through appropriate actions in the realm of the conscious. One psychological action of this type is *hitpaʿalut*. The nature of *hitpaʿalut* and its advantages for ethical education are explained by Salanter by comparing it with intellectual activity:

The mind shall discover depths of wisdom . . . awakening both the knowledge and the initiative to search out and to ask, and clarifying those things
which are in doubt. The root of *hitpa'alut* is to open the closedness of the
heart, to fill it with the waters of understanding, which is known to man, but
has not penetrated to his innards. This is because the direct study of the way
of the traits and the purification of the potentialities of the soul is different
from the study of Torah or any other wisdom. In the latter, the object of
knowledge and the man who knows them are two separate entities, and
knowledge of them is merely stored away within man. . . . . This is not so with
regard to the *middot* and the purification of the powers of the soul, by which
man must live and conduct his actions. Knowledge of these is not enough,
if he does not acquire them in his heart and if they are not connected and
linked to him. This is the way of acquiring them by means of the doctrine
of *hitpa'alut,* whose path and might it is to bring blessing into the heart of
man, even after it has ceased. . . it will leave behind some gleanings in the
man. (*Kitvey R. Israel Salanter,* 148)

As mentioned previously, Salanter used the term *hitpa'alut* to refer to
intense emotional excitement. The comparison with intellectual knowledge
demonstrates the superiority of *hitpa'alut:* whereas the knowledge or insight gained by the intellect is stored in the consciousness or in the memory,
hitpa'alut leaves an impression upon the soul itself. Salanter explains the
distinction between the intellect and *hitpa'alut* as follows: By its very
nature, the process of intellectual awareness involves the dissipation of
spiritual energy, as the intellect examines the subject under discussion from
different angles, clarifying various possible solutions. *Hitpa'alut,* in contrast, is characterized by the maximum concentration of the powers of the
personality on one specific feeling. This focusing of emotional energy on
one point momentarily obscures all other feelings of the soul and weakens
their impression.

Thus far we have described the activity of *hitpa'alut* in the conscious
realm. However, R. Israel thought that, parallel to its influence upon the
conscious emotions, *hitpa'alut* also penetrates and leaves an impression on
the unconscious:

Also, in the inner-most, hidden recesses of the human soul, around whose
forces all of man's actions and feelings revolve . . . there, too, the power of
hitpa'alut comes to rest (albeit scarcely recognized or felt), to gather strength,
until the rest of man's powers are pushed aside by it, and nearly extinguished
(until the right time, when an arousing spirit shall come upon them that they
spread forth, to be seen and known). (*Kitvey R. Yisrael Salanter,* 149)

Thus we see that, insofar as we can speak about the influence of *hitpa'alut*
upon the personality, these processes are taking place simultaneously in
both the conscious and the unconscious realms. However, as is stated

explicitly in the last passage quoted, those powers pushed aside and weakened by *hitpaʿalut* may return and be restrengthened when and if one is exposed to the appropriate stimuli. How, then, is it possible to guarantee that this process of *hitpaʿalut* shall have the desired long-lasting results? One might say: by repeated experiences of *hitpaʿalut*, because, although the impression of a one-time experience of *hitpaʿalut* is liable to disappear with time, the quantitative impression of many experiences of this type combined together will bring about a qualitative difference in the soul. But the question of *hitpaʿalut* still needs to be explained from two points of view: First, what are the contents of this experience? Second, what are the means by which it may be aroused or used in a disciplined and controlled manner? R. Israel dealt with these questions in two different contexts, referring to the distinction between that variety of *hitpaʿalut* intended to correct the *middot* and that which is intended to deal with the "appetites." The latter is to be uprooted by means of the study of Mussar. Salanter had in fact repeatedly advised the study of Mussar by *hitpaʿalut*, but now its significance is explained in terms of the theory of the unconscious—that is, the experience of *hitpaʿalut* by Mussar study leaves an impression on the unconscious level of the personality. Thus, the accumulation of impressions which frequently comes in the wake of Mussar study implants in the depths of the soul "dark forces to aid in the struggle with the appetite." He refers here to subconscious positive forces which are able to halt, or even to submerge and uproot, unconscious appetites. Although he does not explain in this context what the content of these forces is, one may assume that he is referring here to the "dark forces" expressing the longing to fulfill God's commandments.

Whereas that form of *hitpaʿalut* which is intended to uproot the "appetite" is of a general character, that meant to effect *tiqqun ha-middot* is more specific, directed toward the specific trait that is to be uprooted or cultivated. Thus, for example, one who wishes to rid himself of the trait of pride and supplant it by modesty is instructed to bring about repeated states of *hitpaʿalut* concerning the meanness of his own personal traits in comparison with those of others. Such *hitpaʿalut* will gradually diminish his pride, until it ultimately completely disappears. The same holds true for the correction of other bad traits. In each case, the content of the *hitpaʿalut* must be suited to the particular quality being dealt with. This is done by the repetition of suitable rabbinic sayings, where the very act of repetition, the raising of the voice, and the special melody all contribute to the emotional excitement.

We have found that Salanter's becoming aware of the phenomenon of the unconscious did not bring about any radical change in the educational means that he advised, and all of those which he had already suggested at an earlier stage of his thought—self-examination, preventive actions, the study of Mussar through *hitpaʿalut*, and the repetition of rabbinic sayings— all continue to perform a significant task. However, in the light of his new understanding of the nature of the psyche, Salanter understood the significance and functioning of these techniques in a new light. From this it is possible to draw the conclusion that Salanter's system developed the practical insights prior to their theoretical justification. Thus, means which were developed through practical experience and which proved their effectiveness in practice were not displaced by the new theory, but were reinterpreted in its light.

In concluding this discussion, we may say that the inclusion of the theory of the unconscious in Salanter's Mussar system brought about a refining and sharpening of tendencies that were already present. The optimistic view that it is possible to bring about guided and controlled change in the human personality now takes on a new dimension of depth, because Salanter applies it even to the unconscious; on the other hand, the pessimism expressed in perpetual self-doubt apropos of the power of the appetite and the negative traits is also sharpened, since even one who has developed positive behavior patterns lives under the constant suspicion that evil forces hidden in the depths of his soul may suddenly break forth in response to some external "reason" and destroy the structure so painstakingly built up. From this it follows that a person cannot complete the process of ethical perfection through a concentrated, one-time effort. Ethical education is a process that one undergoes in all stages of one's life and through all one's transformations. In truth, R. Israel Salanter understood ethical education as a way of life.

Notes

1. This article is based upon my book *R. Yisrael Salanter we-reshitah shel Tenuʿat ha-Mussar* (Jerusalem: Magnes, 1982), which contains the detailed documentation upon which my statements and conclusions are based.

2. The concept *yirʾah* serves in several senses within the cultural context under discussion here. In its broadest sense, found extensively in literature of the period, the term denotes a high religious-ethical level, which constitutes a kind of social ideal. In this sense, *yirʾah* incorporates a number and variety of aspects of divine service, the emphasis being upon high quality. In R. Israel's writings, and all of the literature of the period, the term *yirʾah* also serves in a sense parallel to that of *mussar*. The more specific sense of the term *yirʾah* in Salanter's writings shall be explained below.

3. Hillel Goldberg, in his book *Israel Salanter: Text, Structure, Idea* (New York: Ktav, 1982) devotes several pages to a polemic with what I wrote elsewhere regarding the place of Kabbalah within R. Israel's thought. After a careful reading of his arguments, I continue to maintain my position as presented here. Most of Goldberg's arguments are concentrated on the question of

whether or not Salanter studied kabbalistic literature. His answer to this question is affirmative. However, this question, which was not discussed as such at all in the work that served as the target of Goldberg's criticisms, is of secondary importance. In my view, as one concerned with characterizing and analyzing Salanter's thought, the decisive question is to what extent this thought was influenced by that of the Kabbalah. I find nothing in Goldberg's book to contravene these conclusions.

4. Dov Katz, *Tenu'at ha-Mussar*, 1:371.

5. Ibid., 1:353.

6. In a profound discussion of this question, R. Israel expressed his opinion that intellectual analysis entirely free of the influence of the emotions is impossible and that, in the final analysis, the objectivity which students of Torah hope to achieve is relative. The conclusions of halakhic authorities receive the stamp of absolute "truth" only after the fact, on the basis of public recognition of their authority and their halakhic rulings.

7. The book *Heshbon ha-Nefesh*, by R. Menahem Mendel Lefin, one of the pioneers of the eastern European Haskalah, served as a vehicle through which R. Israel Salanter absorbed ideas and moods from European thought of the Enlightenment period. In the center of Lefin's book is a new and effective "trick" for the transformation of character traits, which he borrowed from the autobiography of the American thinker and statesman Benjamin Franklin. Lefin combined with this "trick" psychological discussions influenced by the writings of seventeenth- and eighteenth-century European philosophers. For a detailed discussion of Lefin's sources and of his influence on Salanter, see my *R. Israel Salanter*, 135–46.

8. This has been established by Yizhak Ahren in his article "Rabbi Israel Salanter und das Unbewusste," *Udim* 6 (1975–76).

Bibliography

Sources

Blazer, R. Yizhak. *Sefer Kokhve Or*. Jerusalem, 1974.
——, ed. and author. *Sefer Or Yisrael*. Vilna: Matz, 1900.
Pechter, Mordecai, ed. *Kitvey R. Yisrael Salanter*. Jerusalem: Bialik, 1972.
Sefer Or ha-Mussar. Bnai Brak, 1965.

Studies

Rabbi Dov Katz was the first one to devote a comprehensive work to the history of the Mussar movement. His five-volume work *Tenu'at ha-Mussar*, first published in 1945 and subsequently reprinted several times, contains detailed biographies of the leaders of the Mussar movement, their outlook on questions of ethical education, and their activities in this sphere. The first of the five volumes of Katz's work deals with R. Israel Salanter. One cannot exaggerate the importance of Rabbi Katz's contribution in locating and gathering together numerous sources which shed light upon the life of R. Israel Salanter. However, Rabbi Katz, himself a disciple of the Mussar movement and an enthusiastic devotee of its founder, tends toward idealization, which does not always stand up to criticism.

A more balanced and profound perspective is found in the articles concerning the Mussar movement by Rabbi Yehiel Ya'akov Weinberg. In his youth, Rabbi Weinberg was among the students at the celebrated Mussar yeshiva, "Kenesset Yizhak" of Slobodka, and he does not attempt to conceal his deep emotional connection to the heads of the Mussar movement who are the focus of his articles. Moreover, the articles include sections that are essentially personal reminiscences.

However, Rabbi Weinberg's migration from Lithuania to central Europe and the academic education he received there enabled him to look afresh at the Mussar movement with a certain distance and sobriety. His descriptions and analyses are thus the outcome of an interesting combination of direct experience, empathy, and critical examination.

Menahem G. Glenn wrote the earliest comprehensive work in English on Salanter and his work. The research on which the book was based was conducted parallel to and independent of Dov Katz's work, making Glenn one of the pioneers in the field. In this book, Glenn attempted to cover Salanter's biography as well as the principles of his Mussar system. His discussion is not characterized by excessive depth, and his knowledge both of the social-historical and the philosophical-spiritual context within which Salanter lived and worked is also quite superficial. Nevertheless, Glenn's book does provide an initial, if not always exact, acquaintance with the subject. The English reader will find particular interest in his translation of the "Mussar Epistle" (*Iggeret ha-Mussar*)—one of Salanter's better-known writings.

A comprehensive and penetrating discussion of the thought of R. Israel Salanter is found in Mordecai Pechter's introduction to his edition of Salanter's writings. As one trained in the discipline of history of ideas and as an expert in all aspects of Jewish ethical literature, Pechter was able to point out the typical and distinguishing features of Salanter's Mussar system. Even though the collection which he edited does not include all of Salanter's writings, it does contain many valuable points. The presentation of the text in "full" Hebrew orthography, utilizing a contemporary system of punctuation, and the addition of explanatory notes are of use to all who wish to study these involved and difficult texts.

Hillel Goldberg's book is devoted almost entirely to Salanter's thought. In his attempt to encompass the full scope of subjects touched on by Salanter in his writings, Goldberg did not restrict himself to the main lines of R. Israel's thought, but also included those of secondary or even marginal importance. Goldberg's discussions are characterized by particular attention to textual analysis. At the end of the book there is a detailed bibliographical survey.

In my own book I discussed three aspects of the subject: a reconstruction of Salanter's life history; a description of his communal activity and an evaluation of it against the background of the circumstances and events of the times; and a description and characterization of his thought in the realm of "Mussar," examining its roots and sources. The book thus includes biographical interpretation, discussion of the history of Jewish society in Russia, and discussions pertaining to the history of ideas. The combination of all these in one volume reflects the complexity of the subject and the assumption of the author that a fruitful discussion of a subject such as this requires attention to the reciprocal relationship between the personal, social-historical, and ideological factors.

Etkes, Immanuel. *R. Israel Salanter we-reshithah shel Tenu'at ha-Mussar.* Jerusalem: Magnes Press, 1982.

Glenn, Menahem G., *Israel Salanter: Religious-Ethical Thinker.* New York: Published for the Dropsie College for Hebrew and Cognate Learning by Bloch, 1953.

Goldberg, Hillel. *Israel Salanter: Text, Structure, Idea.* New York: Ktav, 1982.

Katz, Dov. *Tenu'at ha-Mussar, toldoteha isheha we-shitoteha.* 5 vols. Tel Aviv: Hotsa'at Bitan ha-Sefer, 1945.

Weinberg, Yehiel Ya'akov. *Seridey Esh,* 4:276–96. Jerusalem: Mossad Harav Kook, 1969.

———. *Yahadut Lita,* 1:320–36. Jerusalem, 1960.

8

The Traditional Piety of Ashkenazic Women

CHAVA WEISSLER

Shloymele's mother Sarah was frail and slight, with small, white hands crisscrossed with tiny purple veins, and the pale face and thin lips of a pious woman. She seemed to be pure spirit, to float rather than walk. She was a learned woman, who knew all kinds of prayers [*tkhines*], prayers of the Land of Israel and prayers of Sarah Bas Tovim; she was well-versed in the laws of *khala*, menstruation, and candle lighting, which are the particular province of women, and she read such books as *Tsena Urena, The Shining Candelabrum*, and the like. It was she who showed the women how to pray: what hymns to say, when to rise, when to stand on tip-toe in the *kedusha* prayer. In the women's gallery of the synagogue, she kept a lemon and other pungent remedies to revive herself or the other women whenever they felt faint. And in fact it was hardly possible to keep from fainting when Sarah read. She would read with great emotion, her melody melting the soul and pulling at the heart strings. When she wept, everyone wept with her; her tears would have melted a stone. . . .[1]

THE HISTORY OF JEWISH SPIRITUALITY as it has been written is chiefly the history of the religious life of the educated elite. Indeed, it must be, since the most important sources for this history are the written works produced by learned men. This has meant the comparative neglect of the religion of ordinary people, those who produced no works of religious philosophy, legal rulings, or mystical speculation. Yet ordinary Jews, too, rejoiced on the Sabbath and holidays, repented of their sins, hoped for redemption, and expressed their devotion to God in prayer. To understand the religious history of the Jewish people, we must understand these ordinary Jews as well.

Because so few women received more than the rudiments of Jewish education throughout the ages, the spiritual life of women, as a group, has been perhaps the most neglected area of the history of Jewish spirituality. Few

245

women learned Hebrew, the language of scholarly communication, and fewer still left any literary legacy, even in the vernacular.[2] Further, women were excluded from the arenas of public religious life: the talmudic academy, the rabbinical court, the kabbalistic conventicle, and the Hasidic gathering. Even in the synagogue, women did not count as one of the minimum number of ten adults required as a quorum for public prayer, could not lead the service, and sat behind a partition, in a balcony, or in a completely separate room.

Despite these problems, there does exist a rich array of sources for writing the religious history of Ashkenazic (central and eastern European) Jewish women. Beginning in the late sixteenth century, there began to appear in print a voluminous homiletical, ethical, and devotional literature in Yiddish, the vernacular of Ashkenazic Jews. It is clear from information on the title pages of these works and from contemporary accounts that women were the chief audience for these collections of pious tales, guides to the upright life, and paraphrases of the Bible.[3]

At the same time as these other genres began to appear, collections of Yiddish prayers also began to be published. Unlike the Hebrew liturgy, these prayers, called *tkhines*,[4] were voluntary. Women could recite them if and when they wished: there were *tkhines* for a wide variety of occasions.

Tkhines provide an excellent focus for the study of women's religious lives. Their use was widespread; collections of them were published and republished throughout the seventeenth, eighteenth, and nineteenth centuries. And in contrast to other Yiddish religious genres, a significant number of *tkhines* appear to have been written by women.[5] Further, as prayers, they express women's spiritual concerns in a more direct manner than the other types of Yiddish religious literature. Finally, since they are prayers, the *tkhines* may be compared to the Hebrew prayer literature, both the standard Hebrew liturgy and the voluntary mystical Hebrew devotional literature that arose at about the same time as the *tkhines*.

The *tkhine* literature reveals an intensely lived religious life, and a richly imagined spiritual world. This chapter explores some of the dimensions of that life and that world. A survey of the many occasions on which women recited *tkhines* will show us the important religious events of women's lives, and, in comparison with the occasions for Hebrew prayers, how men's and women's spiritual concerns differed. Further, an analysis of the content of the *tkhines* can reveal how women understood their religious activity. A *tkhine* for lighting the Sabbath candles which contains prayers for the protection of the woman's husband and children from evil, or images of the candelabrum in the ancient Temple, shows some of the meanings that kindling the lights might hold. There are also *tkhines* for customs not mandated by Jewish law, such as making memorial candles for the dead. Such *tkhines* reveal the significance of these folk religious practices to women. Finally, unlike Hebrew prayers, *tkhines* contain many references to the matriarchs, Sarah, Rebecca, Rachel, and Leah, and other women of the Bible. By analyzing their portrayal of these female figures, we can discern the images of women and women's religious lives that the *tkhine* literature presents.[6]

The Domains and Occasions of Women's Religious Lives

If prayers exist for an event, that event must have some religious significance. Prayers, then, whether required or voluntary, Hebrew or Yiddish, can show us how Jews organized their religious lives. The *siddur*, the Hebrew prayerbook, is organized by clock and calendar. Men prayed three times a day, reciting a fixed liturgy, which was expanded on Sabbaths and holidays. This liturgy marks the transitions at dusk and dawn, sanctifies the separation of the day of rest from the workaday week, and celebrates the turning of the seasons and the great events of Jewish history. In addition, prayer was essentially a communal event. Men prayed, preferably, with a congregation, and most prayers of the *siddur* are phrased in the plural.

Despite the fact that, according to some authorities, women were exempted from the duty of daily prayer—and by all accounts from communal prayer— many women daily recited the Hebrew liturgy and attended synagogue at least on Sabbaths and holidays. They thus participated in this overall rhythm of Jewish life. Yet, to the extent that they also recited *tkhines*, they defined for themselves an alternative rhythm as well. An inventory of the occasions for which *tkhines* exist shows us a world organized very differently from that of the *siddur*, a world structured by the private events of the woman's domestic life as much as by the communal events of the Jewish calendar.

Thus, before analyzing the contents of any particular *tkhine*, we begin with a survey of the table of contents of the *Seyder Tkhines [u-]Vakoshes*, (*Order of Supplications and Petitions*). This is one of the most comprehensive collections of *tkhines* published; it contains about 120 prayers. It was also very popular: numerous editions of it were issued throughout the eighteenth and nineteenth centuries.[7] All of the *tkhines* in this collection (and most other *tkhines* as well) are headed by notes that explain when they should be said and, often, by whom. For example, "Every woman should say this every day, morning and evening" (no. 38); or, "When a woman becomes pregnant, she should say this every day or when she is giving birth" (no. 95);

or "On the eve of the Day of Atonement at nightfall before *Kol nidre*[8] one should say this *tkhine* with devotion" (no. 85). Although *tkhines* were voluntary, it seems reasonable to assume that if a *tkhine* exists for a particular event, and especially if many *tkhines* exist for an event, that event had religious meaning for at least some women.

Some of the occasions for which we find *tkhines* are those we might expect from a general knowledge of Jewish life. This collection contains some thirty or forty prayers connected with the liturgy or the synagogue service.[9] In addition, there is a prayer for each day of the week and four for the Sabbath. About fifteen prayers are to be said "every day" or on no particular occasion. Fourteen *tkhines* concern the penitential season, from the beginning of the month of Elul, one month before the New Year, through the Day of Atonement. Three others are confessions of sins to be said throughout the year. There are only four prayers for the festivals, one for taking the Torah scroll out of the Ark on the festivals, two for luvav and ethrog, which are used on the holiday of Succoth, and one for Hoshana Rabba.[10] There are *tkhines* for each of the fast days, and several prayers for days on which one undertakes a private fast.

All these occasions were common to the religious lives of women and men. With *tkhines* for the special "women's commandments," three religious duties singled out as incumbent especially upon women, we enter the women's world. Thus, there is one *tkhine* for *ḥallah*, separating a small portion of the dough in memory of the priestly tithes; there are three for *niddah*, marital separation during menstruation and ritual immersion after menstruation; and four for *hadlaqah*, lighting candles on the eve of Sabbaths and festivals. Some *tkhines* are not connected with rituals at all. We find eleven *tkhines* concerned with pregnancy and childbirth, four concerning children and family (including two to be said while one's husband is away on a business trip), and one that "a widow should say with great devotion so that the dear God may once again give her what she asks of him" (no. 71). Several *tkhines* contain petitions for recovery from illness, rain during a drought, and sustenance and livelihood. There are eleven *tkhines* for what must have been a major event in women's religious lives, visiting the cemetery.[11] The new moon, *rosh ḥodesh*, was of special significance to women, who avoided heavy work on that day. This collection contains four prayers connected with *rosh ḥodesh*.[12]

It is clear from this inventory that the Hebrew liturgy was relevant to women's lives, but also that it was in need of amplification. A woman could recite a *tkhine* when she entered the synagogue (no. 1), while the cantor chanted the prayer "Grant Peace" (no. 6), or on the Days of Awe when the Torah scroll was taken out of the Ark (no. 31). Such *tkhines* must have been welcome to women for whom the Hebrew liturgy was largely incomprehensible. Indeed, a few of the prayers in this collection are Yiddish translations or paraphrases of Hebrew prayers, such as the *qaddish*, Psalm 119, or *Pereq shirah*.[13]

Yet, interestingly enough, the order of the *tkhines* in this collection does not follow the order of the service. This shows that the organizing principles of the *tkhine* literature differ from those of the liturgy. Prayers connected to the synagogue service are scattered among the other *tkhines*, which are grouped, roughly, according to themes such as fast days, the Days of Awe, pregnancy and childbirth, and visiting the cemetery.

From the list of nonliturgical *tkhines* there emerges a set of occasions of special importance to women. They were defined, whether biologically or culturally, as being in the women's domain: pregnancy and childbirth, the family, the new moon, the "women's commandments," and contact with and petitioning the dead. *Tkhines* hallowed women's biological lives and domestic routines. Menstruation, pregnancy, and childbirth were considered *religious* events, important subjects for prayer. By reciting *tkhines* women could also sanctify the ordinary events of home life: baking bread, preparing for the Sabbath, bringing up children.

Indeed, the *tkhines* give us the sense that women's religious life was more private than men's. We have already noted the public nature of men's prayer in Judaism. In general, men's domain in Ashkenazic life was, to a large extent, public and communal: the synagogue, the House of Study, the rabbinical court. According to cultural ideals, men prayed and studied with each other.[14] Women's domain was the home,[15] and most *tkhines* were clearly intended to be recited at home or privately in other settings, such as the bathhouse or cemetery.

Thus, the liturgy of the *siddur* and the literature of the *tkhines* contrast in many ways: the *siddur* is in Hebrew, the sacred and scholarly language, whereas the *tkhines* are in the vernacular Yiddish; the prayers of the *siddur* are fixed and obligatory, those of the *tkhine* collections voluntary and thus flexible,[16] and the prayers of the *siddur* were recited, by preference, in public, whereas the *tkhines* were recited in private. Yet there also existed a devotional literature which—although in Hebrew and thus intended for men—was also voluntary and, to some extent, private. Flowering in the wake of Lurianic Kabbalah, this mystical devotional literature provided an important channel for the popularization of hitherto esoteric kabbalistic ideas. Two important works of this genre are the devotional manuals *Sha'ar ha-Shamayim* and *Sha'arey Ziyyon*. Composed by the eminent halakhist and kabbalist Isaiah Horowitz (1565?–1630), the *Sha'ar ha-Shamayim* is an extensive kabbalistic commentary on the prayer book and includes prayers of

Horowitz's own composition. (It was first published in 1717 by the author's great grandson.)[17] The *Sha'arey Ziyyon*, written by Nathan Nata Hannover (d. 1683), was published in 1662 and reprinted numerous times. Its seven chapters contain prayers for a variety of liturgical and nonliturgical occasions.[18] These works provide an interesting point of comparison with the *tkhines*.

Thus, like the *tkhines*, this mystical devotional literature provides for prayer outside the framework of the fixed liturgy. And, like the *tkhines*, this literature flourished in the seventeenth and eighteenth centuries. There are, indeed, actual points of contact between the two literatures: Solomon Freehof has demonstrated that the *Sha'arey Ziyyon* and the *Sha'ar ha-Shamayim* both deeply influenced the *Seyder Tkhines u-Vakoshes*. Thus, the prayers for the days of the week found in this *tkhine* collection reflect the themes of the prayers for those days found in the *Sha'arey Ziyyon*, and some fifteen *tkhines* in all are translated or paraphrased from one or the other of these works.[19]

Nonetheless, despite the fact that certain *tkhines* originated in kabbalistic works, and despite Freehof's insistence that the *tkhines* contain what he calls "the usual Cabalistic ideas, the angels, the mysteries of God's name and the *Kawwanoth*," the spiritual world of the *tkhines* differs sharply from that of the *Sha'arey Ziyyon*, for example. Many of the prayers in the *Sha'arey Ziyyon* seek to affect the inner world of the Godhead by means of mystical concentration on permutations of divine names. These *kawwanot* ("intentions") are at the heart of the Lurianic conception of prayer. Such prayer disregards the literal meaning of the liturgy and seeks to transform and ultimately to redeem the cosmos by rearranging, as it were, relations among the *sefirot*, the ten emanations or aspects of the Godhead. Throughout the *Sha'arey Ziyyon*, the prayers are suffused with a consciousness of the sefirotic system and, often, a sense of their own theurgic efficacy.

These traits are entirely lacking in the *tkhine* literature. Although the *tkhines* do use material derived from kabbalistic sources, their approach is not kabbalistic. That is, although they contain references to demons and angels, and charms against the evil eye, the *tkhines* convey no sense that there exists a hidden level of meaning, an esoteric reality sharply at odds with the apparent reality of this world and the literal meaning of the words of prayer and sacred texts. Further, although, as Freehof points out, the *tkhines* do stress the importance of *kawwanah* (in the sense of the desirable state of devotion during prayer), they contain virtually no *kawwanot* (in the Lurianic sense described above). Even the very prayers for the days of the week, which Freehof points to as showing kabbalistic influence, are missing the Lurianic *kawwanot*. Further, I have as yet found no obvious references to the sefirot.[20] The only *tkhine* I have found that speaks of permutations of divine names specifically denies the ability of the reciter to engage in them:

> Lord of the whole world, you are an almighty and merciful God. You know well that we are only flesh and blood, and we have no power to be able to engage in mystical intentions, or to permute your holy names, or [concentrate on] all the intentions in all the prayers and all the blessings. . . . Yet the *tkhine* does not intend to assert that no one is able to pray mystically, for it concludes: May my prayer ascend before you, to make a crown for your head, with the other prayers of Jews who do know how to engage in mystical intentions, and to permute all the intentions and combinations of the holy names which are appropriate for each prayer and each blessing, which will bring together unity and holiness even unto the seventh heaven, Amen. (no. 3)

Thus it seems that it is the reciter of *tkhines*, in particular, who is unable to engage in mystical contemplation: the kabbalistic mysteries of prayer were not deemed appropriate for women.[21]

The kabbalistic and *tkhine* prayer literatures also differ in terms of their domains and occasions. First, although the *Sha'arey Ziyyon* contains some prayers intended to be recited privately, such as *tiqqun hazot*, the midnight service bewailing the destruction of the Temple and the exile of the *Shekhinah* (God's presence, the tenth *sefirah*), much of its contents are to be recited in a public setting, such as the synagogue or House of Study. For example, the confession of sins and declaration of faith while awaiting death and still of sound mind[22] is addressed by the man to a *bet din*, a rabbinical court. The same material, reworked in Yiddish, is addressed by the woman, privately, to Almighty God (no. 38).

In addition, and despite some similarities,[23] the occasions around which the prayers in the *Sha'arey Ziyyon* cluster are different from those of the *tkhine* collection. The *Sha'arey Ziyyon* reflects, naturally enough, the religious life of a man and a kabbalist. Perhaps the majority of the work is taken up by the Lurianic *kawwanot* of prayer, along with poems and songs based on the *sefirot* or permutations of divine names. The collection also includes prayers to be said before study and to retain what one has learned, before giving a sermon, before putting on phylacteries and prayer shawl, before setting out on a journey, and before intercourse. Since women did not study, give sermons, or wear phylacteries or prayer shawls, there are no *tkhines* for these activities. Despite the fact that women must sometimes have taken journeys, the *Seyder Tkhines u-Vakoshes* contains *tkhines* to be said while one's *husband* is on a journey. Although both women and men engaged in intercourse, the *tkhines* are in general less concerned with sexuality and more with the reproductive life.[24] Thus, even though material from the *Sha'arey Ziyyon* and other kabbalistic works reworked into Yiddish is found in the *Seyder Tkhines u-Vakoshes* (and some other *tkhine* collections as well), there are significant differences in the concerns of the two literatures.

The comparison of the domains and occasions for *tkhines,* and for Hebrew prayers, whether obligatory or voluntary, has shown that women participated in two religious worlds. Women, like men, prayed from the prayer book, observed Sabbaths, fasts, and holidays, were concerned with obtaining forgiveness for sin and maintaining a holy marital life. Yet women also had another set of religious concerns, focused around family life and events that took place in the home. On the one hand, then, the *tkhine* literature exhibits both the themes of general Jewish life and the more particular interests of women. On the other hand, however, the fact that women were situated in certain social roles influenced all of their religious life, even those observances shared with men. The two worlds were forged into one, rooted in women's social reality.

Thus, both women and men "remembered the Sabbath to keep it holy." But the burden of Sabbath preparations fell on women. And men greeted the Sabbath by praying at synagogue, while women greeted it by lighting candles at home. It is the women's observances for which there are *tkhines:* baking the Sabbath loaf, lighting the candles, even making kugel, the Sabbath pudding. Women's religion was centered on the domain in which women spent most of their time, the domestic.

It remains to describe, however, how women understood their participation in these religious acts, whether in the domestic domain or elsewhere. The *tkhines* provide rich data to interpret the meanings that lighting Sabbath candles, ritual immersion after menstruation, preparing for the Days of Awe, or greeting the new moon held for women. I have written "meanings" in the plural intentionally: An analysis of *tkhines* for the "women's commandments" will make it apparent that different women could understand the same act in different ways.

The Varieties of Women's Religious Expression: The Women's Commandments

From mishnaic times, the religious duties, *mizwot,* of separating a portion of dough in memory of the priestly tithes, maintaining sexual separation from one's spouse during menstruation, and lighting Sabbath candles were considered particularly incumbent upon women.[25] Thus, when preparing bread and certain other baked goods, the woman recited a Hebrew blessing, pinched off a small portion of the dough, and burned it in the oven (see

Num 15:19–21). Jewish law prescribes detailed menstrual avoidances between a woman and her husband (see Lev 15:19–24; 18:19). During menstruation and for seven days thereafter,[26] the married couple may not come into any physical contact whatsoever. After the menstrual period, the woman had to inspect herself twice daily for seven days to make certain the blood flow had entirely ceased. At the end of these seven "clean days," the woman immersed herself in a ritual bath, reciting a Hebrew blessing, after which she resumed physical contact and sexual relations with her husband. Finally, the woman kindled at least two lights on the eve of the Sabbaths and festivals, before sunset, reciting a Hebrew blessing as she did so. Since the Bible forbids lighting a fire on the Sabbath (see Exod 35:3), it was very important to kindle the lights before the sun set and the Sabbath began.[27]

These three *mizwot* were known by the Hebrew terms *hallah* (portion of dough); *niddah* (menstrual separation), and *hadlaqah* or *hadlaqat ha-ner* (kindling the light). The first letters of each word were combined to form a acrostic, *hanah*, which is the Hebrew for Hannah. For this reason, the biblical Hannah, the mother of the prophet Samuel, became associated with the women's commandments, and sometimes appears in *tkhines* for these acts.[28] Because of the long tradition that identified them with women and because of the intimate family setting of their observance, the women's commandments were a popular occasion for *tkhines*. Yet different *tkhine* authors approached this subject in different ways. To show this diversity, I shall analyze texts from three collections: the *Seyder Tkhines u-Vakoshes*, discussed above; the *Seyder Tkhines*, an earlier anonymous collection;[29] and the *Shloyshe she'orim* (*The Three Gates*), attributed to Sore (Sarah) bas Tovim.[30] This last in particular is a beautiful, erudite, and sophisticated document.

Part of the difference between these three collections is one of literary style. In his discussion of the *tkhine* literature, S. Niger makes much if its intimate, humble, feminine, tender quality. But although he is correct in characterising some *tkhines* in this way, other *tkhines* are far from humble or intimate. Further, even this intimate, tender tone may be achieved by a variety of literary means. *Tkhines* in the *Seyder Tkhines u-Vakoshes*, for example, invite the reader to project herself into the *tkhine*. Many of these texts have a slot for the woman to insert her own name as petitioner: "I, so-and-so, daughter of so-and-so, pray that you guard my husband and children. . . ." The *Shloyshe she'orim*, by contrast, allows the personality (or literary persona) of its author to emerge:

I, Sarah Bas-Tovim, do this for the sake of dear God, Blessed Be He, and Blessed Be his name. I arrange for a second time another beautiful new *tehinnah* in three gates. The first gate is based on the three commandments that were given to women: separation of dough, purification from menstrual uncleanness, and lighting of candles. Their name is *ḥallah, nidah,* and *hadlakat nerot.* The second gate is *tehinnah* to be prayed when the new moon is blessed, and the third gate is for the Days of Awe.

I take for my help the living God Blessed Be He, who lives forever and eternally and place this other beautiful new *tehinnah* in German with great love, with great fear, and with trembling, with affright, with broken limbs, with great supplication, with great . . . [word missing) May God have mercy on me and on all Israel, so that I may not have to be a wanderer long, through the merit of our mothers Sarah, Rebecca, Rachel, and Leah. And may my dear mother Leah also pray with me to God Blessed Be He, that my being a wanderer may be an atonement for all my sins. And may God forgive me for the fact that in my youth I talked in the synagogue when they were conducting the service and reading the dear Torah.[31]

Yet *tkhines* differ not only in style but also in substance. Indeed, to generalize about the tone of the *tkhines* is to imply that traditional Ashkenazic women's spirituality was monolithic. Yet it is obvious that one cannot speak of traditional Ashkenazic men's spirituality as if it were one entity. There were men of mystical bent and men of philosophical bent, men of keen halakhic insight and men of simple piety. At the most basic level, there were learned men and ignoramuses. So, too, there were learned women and unlettered women, although except in a few cases, women were learned only in the Yiddish devotional literature. There were women of varying spiritual gifts and varying literary powers. Because women wrote so much less than men, it is harder to delineate the varieties of their spiritual lives. Nonetheless, there exist *tkhines,* sometimes for the same act, which exhibit very different spiritual concerns and religious sensibilities. The *tkhines* for the women's *miẓwot* provide an excellent illustration of this.

Separating Ḥallah and Lighting Candles

The first "gate" (chapter) of the *Shloyshe she'orim* is devoted to the three women's commandments:

> This gate is founded on the three commandments for women:
> And my name Sarah is found [as an acrostic] at the beginnings of the verses.
> Women were commanded three commandments. The name of the three commandments is Hannah, which is [an acrostic for] *Ḥallah, Niddah, Hadlaqat ha-Ner.*[32]

This section of the *Shloyshe she'orim* includes a paragraph explaining the background and importance of each of the women's *miẓwot,* a brief summary (in rhymed Hebrew interspersed with Yiddish translation) promising easy childbirth to the woman who observes them scrupulously, a section

entitled "Laws of *Niddah*," a section entitled "Laws of *Hallah*," and the
Hebrew blessings for "taking *hallah*" (separating the portion of dough) and
lighting candles, each followed by a *tkhine*.[33] Hallmarks of the *Shloyshe
she'orim* are its erudition and its instructional character. The introductory
material concerning each commandment, including both historical background and laws of observance, prepares the woman who reads this book
to understand more deeply the religious acts themselves and even the allusions contained within the *tkhines* she recites. The *tkhines* for taking *hallah*
and lighting candles illustrate the wealth of information the *Shloyshe
she'orim* conveys and the thematic richness thereby created.

Thus, the introductory material concerning the taking of *hallah* begins by
quoting the biblical verse from which this *mizwah* is derived: "As the first
yield of your baking, you should set aside a loaf as a gift" (Num 15:20).[34]
The text continues by interpreting a paraphrase of Prov 8:21 ("By the merit
of this [commandment] God will fill your storehouses to satiety") as an
assurance that fulfilling the *mizwah* of *hallah* will ensure plentiful sustenance.[35] Next the author explains the biblical system of tithes and states that
since the destruction of the Temple, the *mizwah* of taking *hallah* is all that
remains of this system. In the quick transition between the historical and
the personal which is typical of the *Shloyshe she'orim*, the paragraph
continues:

> Therefore, Lord of the World, we pray that you accept the *mizwah* of *hallah*,
> and send great blessing on us wherever we turn. May our children not
> become strangers, and may we be able to provide for our children with a
> livelihood, I and my husband, by ourselves, during a long life.

A later section of the work, entitled "Laws of *Hallah*," explains that the
dough must be made with at least forty-three "eggs" (a rabbinic measure of
volume) or at least two "quarts" of flour (another edition specifies three
"quarts") in order for it to require that a portion be separated as *hallah*.[36]
This is followed by the blessing for separating *hallah* (in Hebrew), a little
paragraph asking that the performance of the commandment be acceptable
before God, and *yehi razon*, a brief Hebrew prayer of kabbalistic origin
asking God to rebuild the Temple. Next comes the *tkhine* for the act:

> May my *hallah* be accepted as the sacrifice on the altar was accepted. May my
> *mizwah* be accepted just as if I had performed it properly. In ancient times,
> the high priest came and caused the sins to be forgiven; so also may my sins
> be forgiven with this. May I be like a newborn child. May I be able to honor
> my dear Sabbaths and holidays. May God bestow upon me that I and my hus-
> band and my children be able to nourish ourselves. Thus may my *mizwah*
> of *hallah* be accepted: that my children may be fed by the dear God, be

blessed, with great mercy and great compassion. May this *mizwah* of *hallah* be accounted as if I had given the tithe. As I perform my *mizwah* of *hallah* with might and main, so may God, be blessed, guard me from anguish and pain. [The last line is in rhymed Yiddish: *Vi ikh tu mayn mitsve fun khale mit gantsn hartsn, zo zol Got botukh hu mikh hitn far payn un shmartsn.*]

This *tkhine* contains several themes: the desire to perform *mizwot* properly, the continued association of *hallah* with receiving adequate nourishment, the desire for forgiveness of sins. Perhaps most interesting, though, is the sense that by taking *hallah*, the woman is continuing the ancient system of sacrifices and tithes. In this *tkhine*, she identifies herself with those ancient Israelites who brought sin offerings and gave tithes to the poor and the Levites.

This identification is taken even further in the *tkhine* for candle lighting:

> Lord of the world, may my *mizwah* of kindling the lights be accepted like the *mizwah* of the high priest who kindled the lights in the dear Temple. "Your word is a lamp to my feet, a light to my path" [Ps 119:105; quoted in Hebrew]. That means, your words are a light to my feet. May the feet of my children walk on God's path, and may the *mizwah* of my candle lighting be acceptable, so that my children's eyes may be enlightened in the dear Torah. I also pray over the candles that the dear God may accept my *mizwah* of the lights as if my candles were the olive oil lamps which burned in the temple and were never extinguished.

Here the woman identifies not with the ordinary Israelite but with the high priest himself. This is an unexpected association: it seems to suggest, at the least, the woman's strong sense of the importance of her religious role: The reciter of the *tkhine* compares her own religious acts to those of the high priest, the highest religious functionary of ancient Israel.

These two *tkhines* contain a richness of historical and midrashic allusion. They also sustain a complex of associations: *hallah* and nourishment, Torah and light, and also, in material not quoted, light and health and livelihood. Yet not all *tkhines* are this sophisticated. The *Seyder Tkhines* contains a prayer for baking the Sabbath loaf which contrasts with the *Shloyshe she'orim* in style and substance.[37]

This she says as she puts the loaf into the oven:

> Lord of all the worlds, all blessing is in your hands. I come now to honor your holiness, and pray you to give your blessing on what I bake. Send an angel to guard the baking, so that everything will be well baked, will rise nicely, and will not burn. May this baking, over which we make the holy blessing, honor your holy Sabbath, which you have chosen that your people Israel may rest thereon. God, listen to my voice, for you are the one who

hears those who call upon you with the whole heart. May you be praised to eternity! (*Seyder Tkhines* [1666?] 6b)[38]

This text is perhaps closer to the humble, tender tone Niger describes. In its simplicity, this *tkhine* shows us how women could sanctify the most ordinary household chores. It also reminds us that women's spirituality was far from monolithic. While one woman was moved by envisioning herself as a participant in the ancient Temple worship, another found holiness in her own kitchen.

In oral tradition, it is possible to find even humbler expressions of women's attitudes toward Sabbath preparations. The folklorist N. Prylucki quotes three "Kugel songs" collected in Galicia. Kugel—a noodle, potato, or flour and fat pudding, often sweetened—was a highlight of the Sabbath meal. These songs are in rhymed dialectical Yiddish, including some Hebrew phrases. One of them begins thus:

> Leave me alone, I have no time,
> I have to go prepare for Sabbath
> If I had a bigger noodle pot
> You would not have to laugh at me.

Another runs:

> Kugel, kugel, I make you truly
> Truly will I make you
> So that no one will laugh at me.
> Into the oven you go,
> Then into the mouth just so.
> May you be as good as Jacob
> and as red as Esau.

The third example is particularly interesting because the lines alternate between Hebrew and Yiddish, as in some printed *tkhines*. In this case, however, the Hebrew phrases seem to be chosen chiefly for their rhymes rather than for their meaning, even though one of them faintly echoes the theme of regret for destroyed Temple and altar that we have found in the *Shloyshe she'orim*. To give some sense of the play of language, I give the text both in romanization and translation.[39]

Yehi rotsn milfonay (H)	May it be My will
Kigl zay mir qitray; (Y)	Kugel, be true to me;
Eyn lonu mizbeyakh (H)	We have no altar
Zolst mar zan fet in veyakh; (Y)	May you be rich and soft;
Mi-godl ve-ad kutn (H)	From the great to the small
Zolst may taki girutn. (Y)	May you come out well.[40]

As Prylucki points out, these are not really prayers. Nonetheless, they show Sabbath preparations—and, by implication the Sabbath itself—as matters of concern to the woman, who wishes the Sabbath meal to be memorable. The continuation of the first song quoted above apostrophizes the kugel, "May we remember you all week!" Further, the third example shows familiarity not only with a certain amount of Hebrew but also with a literary form in which Yiddish and Hebrew are interspersed.[41] This stylistic device had the effect of associating the down-to-earth activities of the woman in cooking for the Sabbath, which are described in Yiddish, with the world of holiness and tradition connoted by the Hebrew phrases.

Taken together, the *tkhines* for *ḥallah* and candle lighting in the *Shloyshe she'orim* and the *Seyder Tkhines,* and the oral material quoted by Prylucki, show that women differed in their levels of knowledge about Jewish tradition and found a variety of aspects of Sabbath preparation meaningful.

Tkhines for Niddah and Childbirth

With regard to the third of the women's *mizwot,* the observance of menstrual avoidances and ritual immersion after menstruation, I have yet to find songs or prayers collected from oral tradition. The printed *tkhines* for *niddah,* including menstrual inspection and ritual immersion, and for childbirth, once again exhibit a diversity of approaches to the *mizwah.* They vary in their emotional tone and in their attitude toward the traditional Jewish depiction of women's reproductive lives.

The *Shloyshe she'orim* contains no true *tkhine* for ritual immersion. Indeed, the subject of *niddah* seems not to have caught the author's imagination. She is at her driest and most didactic in her introductory and halakhic treatment of the subject. In contrast to the lengthy introductions to *ḥallah* and candle lighting, her introduction to the subject of *niddah* consists of only three, more or less unrelated, Hebrew sentences and their Yiddish paraphrases: "God searches all the chambers of the belly (cf. Prov 20:27). If you properly observe the commandments of *niddah,* God will protect your children [the Hebrew reads: protect you] from croup and dropsy. A locked garden is my sister the Daughter of Israel. I call her bride [the Hebrew quotes Song of Songs 4:12]."

Although the author picks up the image of the locked garden again in the section entitled "Laws of *Niddah,*" she is concerned with only one small detail of the observance of menstrual separation:

God takes pride in the daughters, that means the wives, of the children of Israel, because their garden is locked in the face of debauchery. Even from their own husbands do they also separate themselves 'onah ahat samukh le-wistah. That means: During the twenty-four hour period during which she expects to begin menstruating, the woman ought not to have intercourse with her husband.[42] For this reason, we have set out the law, in order to benefit the public, because the common people don't know about this. Thus many people stumble and, God forbid, suffer great punishment for it. Therefore, we have included the law in the tkhine, so that each woman will be warned about it. By the merit of observing this, they will have a good reward in this world: They will have good, pious and clever male children who will be rabbis. And in any case, they will have a great reward in the world to come.

May the merit of our mother Hannah defend their daughters, that they may keep their commandments properly; especially may they not take lightly the mizwah of niddah, for when they go to give birth, they may be judged, God forbid, but if they take proper care, they will give birth speedily and soon.

These paragraphs, while mentioning the rewards for meticulous observance, take an intellectual and halakhic approach to the matter. Perhaps assuming that most of the laws of menstrual separation and purification were well known to her readers, the author concentrates her attention on what may have been a more arcane detail. Further, her tone is didactic: her purpose is to educate the "common people" who lack her expert knowledge. Her lack of emotional involvement in the subject is apparent; perhaps this is because, she was, as the autobiographical information in the tkhine seems to indicate, an older woman and was long past her reproductive years.

This paucity of emotional and devotional material contrasts sharply with a cycle of tkhines for the various stages of observance of niddah as well as pregnancy and childbirth found in several tkhine collections. This cycle appears early on in Seyder Tkhines and is considerably amplified in Seyder Tkhines u-Vakoshes.[43] The original cycle includes five tkhines, to be recited (1) when putting on white underwear for self-inspection at the beginning of the seven "clean" days; (2) before ritual immersion; (3) after coming out of the ritual bath; (4) while in labor; and (5) on arising from childbed. The later version also includes tkhines for biting off the stem of the ethrog (citron used on the holiday of Succoth), thought to reduce pain in childbirth; for various stages of pregnancy; an additional tkhine for labor; for when the son is circumcised; for one woman to say for another pregnant woman; and for a woman who has a "difficult star" for children, that is, whose children are stillborn or die in infancy. Thus, by their very setting, the tkhines for the observance of niddah are connected to the whole of the woman's reproductive life. This is, of course, well in accord with tradition. Proper observance of niddah was thought to foster conception, easy childbirth, and male offspring. Further, the reproductive life has a religious dimension; it is a fit subject for prayer.

When we turn to the content of the *tkhines,* some specific themes emerge. One is first struck by the fact that, although self-inspection and immersion are very private acts, the *tkhines* exhibit a sense of community with the generations of Jewish women who have observed these laws. For example, the *tkhine* for putting on white underwear says, "I have waited until the time until which every pious woman in Israel waits, according to the commandment of our sages in accord with our holy Torah. Now comes the time that I must purify myself . . ." (*Seyder Tkhines u-Vakoshes,* no. 91). In other cases, the accent falls more strongly on the importance of purity, while still expressing connection to other Jewish women.

This she says when she goes to immerse herself.

> Lord of all the world, You have sanctified your people more than all peoples, and have commanded them to cleanse themselves of impurity, and to wash their flesh in water and be clean. Almighty God, today, the time has come for me to purify myself of my uncleanness. God, my Lord, may it be Your will that my uncleanness, and washing, and immersion, be accounted before You like all the purity of the pious women of Israel who purify themselves and immerse themselves at the proper time. God Almighty, listen to my prayer, for You are the One who hears the prayers of Israel Your children. May the words of my mouth and the thoughts of my heart be acceptable before You, God, my creator and redeemer. (*Seyder Tkhines* [1752] 9b)

In prayers such as these the importance of the cycle of purity and impurity to the woman is made particularly clear. In this case, it is connected to a sense of continuity with generations of Jewish women and the special holiness of the Jewish people.

This stress on holiness and purity is carried through in the *tkhine* to be recited after emerging from the ritual bath, which concerns itself with the resumption of sexual relations with the husband and the hoped-for conception of a child.

> God, my Lord, I, — — — daughter of — — — [the woman inserts her own name here] have kept Your commandment today with love, and have purified myself from my uncleanness, to come in purity to have intercourse with my husband, with great cleanliness, and with pure thoughts, so as to bring my husband in good will to fulfill your commandment to multiply the world and to fill it (cf. Gen 1:28). Merciful God, send me Your angels that they may meet me before I come to my husband, and that I may meet nothing unclean. Purify my heart and my thoughts that I may think no evil while he has intercourse with me, and may his whole deed be done in great cleanliness, not wantonly or brazenly. Send me the good angel to wait in the womb to bring the seed before You, Almighty God, that You may pronounce, from this seed

will come forth a righteous man, and a pious man, a fearer of Your Holy
Name, who will keep Your commandments, and find favor in Your eyes and
in the eyes of all people, and will study Torah day and night, and will never
be shamed in the rabbinical academy, and will not err in *halakhah*. And if it
is destined to be a daughter, grant me that she be tidy and not impudent, and
that she may learn to accept reproof from all who instruct her. . . . (*Seyder
Tkhines* [1752] 9b; *Seyder Tkhines u-Vakoshes*, no. 93)

In this example, there is a shift from the stress on the community of women
acting in purity. Here, the woman and her husband must be pure in their
sexual life so as to come in contact with the divine world, God and the
angels. The traditional Jewish idea that there are three partners in the
conception of every human being—mother, father, and God—is here made
concrete in the image of the angel standing by in the womb to convey the
incipient fetus to the Throne of Glory for God's pronouncement of its fate.[44]

In all of these examples, the woman, by reciting these *tkhines*, expresses
her acceptance of traditional Jewish conceptions of the desirability of male
offspring and of menstruation as a state of impurity. The *tkhines* give no
evidence that women questioned their social status, their role, and their fate
in the Jewish world. Yet they were concerned with understanding how their
physical suffering, in menstruation and childbirth, could be justified. The
tkhine for putting on white underwear[45] addresses this question:

God and my King, You are merciful. Who can tell or know Your justice or
Your judgment? They are as deep as brooks of water and the depths of
springs. You punished Eve, our old Mother, because she persuaded her husband Adam to trespass against Your commandment, and he ate from the tree
which was forbidden them. You spoke with anger that in sadness she would
give birth (cf. Gen 3:16). So we women must suffer each time, and have,
basely, (*gemeyniklekh*), our periods, with heavy hearts.[46] Thus, I have had my
period with a heavy heart and with sadness, and I thank Your Holy Name
and Your judgment, and I have received with great love from my great
Friend.[47] (*Seyder Tkhine u-Vakoshes*, no. 91)

Thus, God is just in punishing women, no matter how unfair it seems. Yet
there may be a muted protest here: Do we really all have to suffer for
something that happened so long ago? This is made more explicit in the
tkhine for biting off the end of the *ethrog*, the citron used along with palm,
myrtle, and willow branches in the ritual of the holiday of Succoth. For the
ethrog to be ritually fit, its stem and the protruberance on the blossom end
must be intact. There was a folk custom for women to bite off the end on
Hoshana Rabba, the last day of Succoth, after the *ethrog* was used ritually
for the last time. This was thought to reduce the pain of childbirth or to
promote conception.[48] This *tkhine* appears on the same page as the preceding one in *Seyder Tkhines u-Vakoshes*:

Lord of the World, because Eve ate of the apple, all of us women must suffer such great pangs as [almost] to die. Had I been there, I would not have had any enjoyment from [the fruit]. Just so, now I have not wanted to render the *ethrog* unfit during the whole seven days when it was used for a *miẓwah*. But now, on Hoshana Rabba, the *miẓwah* is no longer applicable, but I am [still] not in a hurry to eat it. And just as little enjoyment as I get from the stem of the *ethrog* would I have gotten from the apple which you forbade. (No. 89)[49]

In this *tkhine*, the woman repudiates Eve's sin, thus undermining the justification for her own suffering. Indeed, she tries to convince God that because she would not have participated in the sin, she ought not suffer the consequences.[50]

The *tkhines* associated with the observance of *niddah*, and with the reproductive life, show once again that women could approach the religious acts they performed in a variety of ways. The detached stance of the *Shloyshe she'orim*, with its stress on the details of observance might appeal to some, whereas others would wish to affirm more strongly the emotional centrality of a holy sexuality in their lives. Further, while accepting in general the *halakhah* regulating sexual behavior, women could still register a protest against the actual physical suffering, which was interpreted traditionally to mean that all women, from Eve on, were worthy of punishment.

Further, from the *tkhines* for all of the women's *miẓwot*, those acts characterized by tradition as central to women's religious lives, we can get a sense of the variety of meanings that a woman could find in these acts. Whether discovering holiness in the act of baking bread, imagining herself lighting the candelabrum in the ancient Temple, or picturing an angel within her very womb, the woman brought together the images of Jewish tradition and her everyday experience. Yet the expression of a distinctive woman's point of view emerges perhaps more clearly in *tkhines* unfettered by *halakhah*, *tkhines* for those customary practices which may have been created by the women themselves. Thus, it seems no accident that the strongest protest against women's condition that we have seen this far comes in a *tkhine* for biting off the end of the *ethrog*—a *tkhine* that may originate in oral tradition, for an act not prescribed by *halakhah*. An analysis of the *tkhine* for another women's custom, the making of candles for the Day of Atonement, will allow us to delineate more fully this women's point of view.

The Connection to Folk Religious Practice: Making Yom Kippur Candles

The history of the custom of making candles for Yom Kippur is shrouded in obscurity. Some time during the Middle Ages Jews began to *light* candles on the eve of the holiday. Authors living in Provence in the twelfth century and Bohemia in the thirteenth discuss the justification for this practice, which is not mandated in earlier Jewish law. They give a variety of reasons; the two that are related to the *making* of candles, as it is later documented, are these: Abraham ben Saul of Lunel states: "It is customary for every Jew to light [a candle] in the synagogue to obtain forgiveness for his parents" (presumably deceased).[51] By contrast, Abraham ben Nathan of Lunel connects the practice with a midrash which states that God asked the Israelites to kindle the lights of the tabernacle candelabrum in order to preserve their own souls, which are likened to candles.[52] Thus, from the twelfth century, Yom Kippur candles are connected to the ideas of commemorating the dead and preserving the living.

According to accounts dating from the nineteenth and the early twentieth centuries, women made these candles on the eve of Yom Kippur. (This was during an era when most candles were manufactured and purchased.) They went to the cemetery, measured the graves with candlewick, and later, at home or in the synagogue, rubbed the wicks with wax, reciting prayers over them. Each woman made two candles, a larger and thicker one for the souls of the living, or the "healthy," and a smaller, thinner one for the souls of the dead.

The *Shloyshe she'orim* contains a *tkhine* to be recited while making the candles. Although this is the only *tkhine* I have so far come across for this custom, both the making of the candles and the recitation of this particular *tkhine* were important enough to be independently documented. We possess a literary account of the recitation of the *tkhine* and literary and ethnographic accounts of the making of the candles.[53] These sources disagree about some of the details, such as whether the candles were made at home, privately, or in the synagogue, but in all accounts it is clear that the making of the candles had become a ritual. The *tkhine* refers to it repeatedly as a *mizwah*, a religious duty. Indeed, it begins thus:

> Lord of the world, I pray You, most merciful God, accept my *mizwah* of candles, which we will make for the sake of Your holy, dear Name and for the sake of the holy souls. . . .

And toward the end, it continues:

> Lord of the world, You have commanded us to make candles for the holy day. I beg You, kind Father, that You accept today the *mizwah* of my laying the wicks.

The clearest description of the actual process of making the candles is that by Bella Chagall. In her memoir of life in turn-of-the-century Vitebsk,

Chagall describes how, on the eve of Yom Kippur, she held the thread of the candlewicks for her mother. As her mother rubbed wax over one thread after the next, she prayed, weeping, for the life and health of each family member. Then she set aside the first group of threads and took up another. This time, each thread was for a family member who had died. She begged each of them to intercede before God for the family's welfare. Finally, she twisted the two groups of threads into two large candles, both of which were taken to burn in the synagogue. In this account, Chagall's mother composed her own prayers. Although these prayers do have a certain formulaic quality, they do not come from a printed book of *tkhines*.[54]

In contrast, Mendele refers directly to the text of the *Shloyshe she'orim*. His autobiographical novel, *Shloyme Reb Khayims* (*Ba-Yamim ha-Hem*), set in the 1840s, begins the description thus:

> It is worthwhile to quote here a little of the *tkhine* for the making of wicks for Yom Kippur candles: One candle for the synagogue, the memorial candle, and one candle to light at home, the candle of life.
>
> Sarah stands seriously, surrounded by women of the neighborhood. She takes up threads with which to make thick wicks, each thread corresponding to one of the patriarchs or matriarchs of Israel, so that they will give much light. Over each thread which she takes up and then lays down, she reads with tears, with a trembling voice, and with devotion, from the depths of her heart, these words.[55]

Mendele then quotes excerpts from a version that resembles, although not completely, the editions I have seen.[56] I translate here instead from the beginning of an edition of the *tkhine* from the first half of the nineteenth century:

> May it be Your will that we be remembered before God today on the eve of Yom Kippur with the *miẓwah* of the candles which we shall make in the synagogue. May we be remembered for good, and may we be worthy to give candles to the Temple, as it was of old. And may the prayers which are said by the light of these candles [or, while making these candles] be with great devotion, fear, and awe, so that Satan may not hinder our prayers. And the lights will be made for the holy, pure souls—may they awaken and each rouse the next all the way back to the holy patriarchs and matriarchs, who should further rouse each other all the way back to Adam and Eve, that they may repair the sin by which they brought death to the world. May they arise out of their graves and pray for us that this year may be a good year. For they caused death to enter the world, so it is fitting for them to plead for us that we may be rid of the Angel of Death.
>
> As I lay the next wick for the sake of our father Noah, it is appropriate for him, too, to pray for us, for he was in great need: Of him it is written, "For the waters have risen up to my neck" (Ps 69:2). May the God who helped

him, help us out of fire and water, and all evil which we fear, may it not come upon us.

The *tkhine* then continues with the laying of wicks for Abraham, Sarah, Isaac, Rebecca, Jacob, Rachel, Moses, Aaron, David, and Solomon, and one for "all the righteous and pious people who have ever lived," each accompanied by a short paragraph constructed on the model of the one for Noah.[57] In each case, some feature of the person as portrayed in the Bible or later legendary material is mentioned as making that person an especially appropriate intercessor, and the paragraph concludes with a prayer that is connected in some way with this feature. After the laying of all the wicks, the *tkhine* contains some further prayers. The *tkhine* asks for forgiveness of sins, sustenance, and good matches for one's children, but especially for redemption and the resurrection of the dead:

> May they [the patriarchs and matriarchs, and Adam and Eve] arise from their graves and pray for us, that this year, may it come for good, there may finally be the resurrection of the dead. May the Attribute of Justice become the Attribute of Mercy; may they be unified. May they pray for us that the resurrection of the dead be fulfilled. And may all the holy and pure angels pray that the dry bones may live again, speedily and soon. . . .
>
> . . . It is appropriate for us to pray for the dead, for those who died in our own generations, and for those who have died from the time of Adam and Eve on. Today we make candles for the sake of all the souls—for the sake of the souls who lie in the fields and the forests, and for all the saints, and for all those who have no children, and for all the little children. May they awake, may the dry bones live, speedily and soon. May we be worthy to see the resurrection of the dead this year, Amen, Selah.

Two features of this *tkhine* attract our attention. First, the author has created a liturgy in Yiddish for a religious act of folk origin. This practice is, of course, based on the idea that the dead can intercede for the living, an idea that was sometimes discouraged by rabbinical authorities.[58] Further, this act, the making of Yom Kippur candles, which was by all accounts practiced only by women, is raised to the dignity of a *mizwah*, by this liturgy. In addition, the performance of this ritual is given eschatological significance. Although most scholars writing about the *tkhines* have depicted them as almost exclusively devoted to petitions for the health and welfare of the woman's family, the woman who makes Yom Kippur candles and recites this *tkhine* asks God for purity of soul, deliverance from exile, the resurrection of the dead, and the restoration of Temple worship. (She also asks for a sufficient livelihood to keep the children in school and marry them off.)

This role for women as helping to bring about Israel's redemption is echoed in the *tkhine*'s second striking feature, the use the author makes of traditional source material. As in earlier sections of the *Shloyshe she'orim*, the author displays her erudition here. She was clearly familiar with a wealth of traditional material, from midrashic legends about biblical figures to biblical verses in Hebrew. Yet perhaps most interesting is the use to which she puts this material.

Thus, one aspect of this *tkhine* which leaps to the eye is the inclusion of the matriarchs, Sarah, Rebecca, and Rachel.[59] This contrasts with the Hebrew liturgy, where male figures only are mentioned.[60] Many *tkhines* (as well as other genres of women's literature) give an important place to the matriarchs, as well as to other, more obscure biblical women. It seems reasonable to assume that the reciter of the *tkhines* identified in some way with these biblical women. But what precisely was the content of the identification?

In this *tkhine* the matriarchs occupy a peculiar position: they are both subordinate and powerful.[61] This emerges most clearly when we compare the paragraphs concerning the patriarchs, Abraham, Isaac, and Jacob, with those for the matriarchs, Sarah, Rebecca, and Rachel. (The thematic treatment of the patriarchs is not carried through for those male figures who appear in the *tkhine* without female counterparts, except for Noah.) To begin with a brief example:

> As I lay the third thread of the wicks for our father Abraham, whom You saved from the fiery furnace, may You purify us of our sins and trespasses. May our souls return pure, just as they were given to us pure, without guilt, without any terror or fear, as [they] came into our bodies.[62]
>
> By the merit of my laying the thread for our mother Sarah, may God, be blessed, remember for us the merit of her pain when her beloved son Isaac was led to be bound on the altar. May she be an advocate for us before God, be blessed, that we may not this year be widowed, God forbid, nor our children taken away from the world during our lives.[63]

The prayers concerning the patriarchs (and also Noah) are all of one form: As you saved patriarch X from the danger of Y, so may you save or aid us. That is, the patriarchs are depicted as passive recipients of God's aid, and it is God, not the patriarchs, who will come to our aid as well. When we turn to the matriarchs, we note first that they are depicted exclusively within their enabling role—as mothers of their sons or offspring. Yet within this framework they are active. Thus, because Sarah suffered when her son Isaac was led away to be sacrificed, she will be an advocate for us. Because Rebecca took steps to ensure that Jacob received Isaac's blessing, that blessing will be fulfilled for us, and we will be redeemed from exile. And because Rachel has not let herself be comforted for the distress of her children in exile, the redeemer will eventually come, and God will bring us back to our land.

Thus, the *tkhine* affirms the value and power inherent in the traditional women's role of mothering. The children of Israel are aided by God—and by their mothers.

This assertion of the power of mothers may have been particularly important to women living in the uncertain conditions of Jewish eastern Europe, who were in fact powerless to protect their families from many of the dangers that beset them. Mendele depicts the women's response to the prayer that Sarah, whose son had been torn away from her, defend the reciter's husbands and children:

> As they said these words, the women broke into tears, thinking of how, at that time, sleeping children were snatched from their beds in their parents' houses and turned over to the army to live far from home among ignorant Gentiles, and to endure terrible evil and trouble. . . . The women wept mightily, and drenched the wick with their tears. Among them were impoverished widows, bereaved mothers, who remembered the dear ones stolen away from them, and wept a river of tears.[64]

Thus, this *tkhine* addresses, in a remarkably sophisticated way, the dilemmas in the religious lives of Ashkenazic Jewish women. It both asserts the importance of the woman's role, and provides solace for her deepest fears. It dignifies the woman's humble folk ritual by naming it a *mizwah*, a divine commandment, and by connecting it with powerful themes in Jewish tradition: forgiveness of sin, redemption from exile, restoration of Temple worship, and deliverance from mortality. Finally, in its description of the matriarchs, it portrays the inner strength available to the woman in her role as mother.

* * * * *

The *tkhines* we have analyzed, in the *Seyder Tkhines u-Vakoshes* and in the *Shloyshe she'orim*, show that not all women were cut off from the knowledge of traditional sources. Some *tkhines* are indeed rooted in popular religion and folk practice. Yet others exhibit familiarity with biblical texts, halakhah, midrash, and various sorts of kabbalistic literature. And sometimes, as in the *tkhine* for making Yom Kippur candles, a folk practice is combined with numerous references to midrashic material, though whether these derive directly from literary or oral sources is still an open question.

Even if women were not the authors of all of these texts, as *readers* they could acquire the knowledge the *tkhines* made available. The *tkhines*, along with the *Tsenerene*, the morality books, and the collections of pious tales, were thus a means of education, as well as a means of devotion or edification Yet, in many cases, such as the *tkhine* for making Yom Kippur candles, traditional material was transformed in the course of its transmission to women. The authors, male or female, selected and reworked what they took from the sources to make it conform to what they considered to be women's concerns.

An example of this is the significance of figures with whom the reader can identify in the *tkhines*. Despite the paucity of important women in Jewish, especially postbiblical, literature and their total absence from the liturgy, the women's devotional literature picks out well-known (and obscure) biblical women and selectively uses their midrashic characteristics to make them a focus for identification. In part, the *tkhine* literature grounds its portrayal of these figures in the concrete lives of Ashkenazic women, lives centered around the family and the home. Thus, in the *tkhine* for making Yom Kippur candles, Sarah, Rebecca, and Rachel are seen primarily as mothers, and their depiction articulates what being a mother means.[65]

Yet women's religious imagination was not fully circumscribed by their domestic realities. By comparing the separating of *hallah* to the bringing of tithes, women could picture themselves as participants in the Temple worship of the ancient Israelite kingdom. And in laying the wicks for Yom Kippur candles, women could see themselves as helping to bring about messianic salvation for all Israel. Further, the *tkhines* allowed women to identify with important *male* religious figures, such as the high priest. Thus, the *tkhines* do not speak with a single voice concerning women's religious lives.

In part this is because of the great diversity of authors and reciters of *tkhines;* but also, I think, it expresses a fundamental reality of the religious life. For while the specifics of this disparity between day-to-day experience and spiritual ideals are peculiar to this women's literature, the very fact of such a disparity is not. Indeed, as perhaps any religious literature must be, *tkhines* are both grounded in routine realities and in tension with them. They thus depict the holiness to be found in the mundane activities of a wife and mother and show women the angels, the high priest, and the ancient Temple worship. By reciting *tkhines,* generations of unknown Jewish women could both sanctify their daily acts and usual roles and transcend them. Thus, nurtured within the ritual structure of Jewish life, familiar with a limited array of Jewish sources, and hampered, perhaps, by the constraints of their social roles and lack of education, Ashkenazic Jewish women yet managed to create out of this tension between the mundane and the transcendent a rich array of visions of the religious life.

Notes

Acknowledgment: Many thanks to Martha Himmelfarb for her helpful comments on an earlier draft of this chapter.

1. Mendele Mokher Seforim, *Of Bygone Days,* in *A Shtetl and Other Yiddish Novellas,* comp. and trans. Ruth Wisse (New York: Behrman House, 1973) 300–301.

A note on the romanization. I have romanized words of Hebrew-Aramaic origin according to their Yiddish (or Ashkenazic) pronunciation (a) when they are used as Yiddish words, within Yiddish phrases or sentences; (b) when they occur in the titles of books the texts of which are entirely or almost entirely in Yiddish; or (c) when, for literary reasons (such as rhyme), the Ashkenazic pronunciation is important. In all other cases, I have used the standard (Sefardic) romanization system for Hebrew.

2. In many Jewish communities, throughout the ages, most women were probably illiterate. Ashkenazic women seem to have had a higher rate of literacy than Jewish women in many other communities; there are many more books in Yiddish, aimed at women, than in the other Jewish vernaculars.

3. Israel Zinberg, *Old Yiddish Literature from its Origins to the Haskalah Period,* chap. 5, esp. 124–26. S. Niger, "Di yidishe literatur un di lezerin," in his *Bleter Geshikhte fun der yidisher literatur* (New York: Sh. Niger Bukh-komitet baym alveltlekhn yidishn kultur-kongres, 1959) 35–107.

One Yiddish paraphrase of the Torah achieved tremendous popularity. The *Tsenerene,* by Jacob ben Isaac Ashkenazi of Yanov, first published around 1600 (Zinberg, *Old Yiddish Literature,* 130), became known as the "women's Torah." Rather than a literal translation of the Pentateuch into Yiddish, the *Tsenerene* contains rabbinic legends, ethical maxims, and exemplary tales interwoven with the biblical narrative.

4. From the Hebrew *tehinnah* ("supplication"; pl. *tehinnot*), the Yiddish word *tkhine* can refer either to an individual prayer or to a collection of such prayers.

5. Niger, "Yidishe literatur," 82–91 (includes a list of known female authors); Zinberg, *Old Yiddish Literature,* 250–59. Most of the early collections of *tkhines* are anonymous; of those which name their authors or compilers, some are attributed to men and others to women. Both Niger and Zinberg point out that, beginning in the 1860s, *maskilim,* "enlightened" Jews far from the world of traditional piety that the *tkhine* literature represents, fabricated *tkhines* in imitation of the traditional style in order to make money. (They often attached women's names to their productions.) For this reason, I have based this chapter only on *tkhines* that can be documented to have existed before 1860. Solomon Freehof ("Devotional Literature in the Vernacular," *CCAR Yearbook* 33 [1923] 375–415) seems to assume that authors of *tkhines* were male: "The books were written by humble men for humble men and women . . ." (p. 377).

It is not clear whether *tkhines* are primarily of literary or oral origin; see also note 40.

6. There are some difficulties complicating the use of this literature as a source for women's religious lives. First, there are important bibliographical problems that give rise to uncertainties about when and where particular collections of *tkhines* were first published. (I have not seen any discussion about whether or not *tkhine* collections existed in manuscript. The Jewish Theological Seminary Library does not appear to own any manuscripts of *tkhines.*) We know even less about when and where they were distributed and purchased. Second, since in most cases *tkhine authors* are unknown, we can only characterize the implied *reciter* of the *tkhines.* And we still need to know which women actually recited *tkhines.* They were probably upper- and middle-class, urban women, since these were more likely to be literate. However, illiterate women may have had an oral tradition that included *tkhines* or similar prayers. Finally, a few *tkhines* were intended for men; nonetheless, it is abundantly clear that most *tkhines* were intended for women and that most reciters of *tkhines* were women.

7. The edition I am using was published in Fürth in 1762. The title page of this edition actually reads *Seyder Tkhines bakoshes,* omitting the particle for "and"; however, most other editions of this work are entitled *Seyder Tkhines u-Vakoshes.* Both earlier and later editions, differing slightly or greatly, were published; cf. B. D. Friedberg, *Bet ʿeqed sefarim* (2nd rev. ed.; Tel Aviv: M. A. Bar-Juda, 1951) 1098. A later, somewhat different edition of this collection (Sulzbach; 1798) is discussed in detail by Freehof, "Devotional Literature." Some of the material in *Seyder Tkhines u-Vakoshes* appeared earlier in *Seyder Tkhines,* Venice? 1666? and other editions.

In the edition I am using, there are no page numbers; instead, the individual prayers are numbered.

8. The introduction to the evening service at the beginning of the Day of Atonement.

9. This count includes prayers for the holidays, which will also be enumerated separately below.

10. The holiday of Succoth, or Tabernacles (Booths), which falls in late September or early October, celebrates the autumn harvest and commemorates the Israelites' wandering in the desert. The holiday observance includes the use of the lulav and ethrog: during portions of the morning service on this holiday, each worshiper holds a palm frond, two willow twigs, and three myrtle twigs, together called the lulav, in his right hand, and a citron, the ethrog, in his left. This "festival bouquet" is waved to the four points of the compass, and up and down (see Lev 23:33–36, 39–44). After the morning service of the final day of Succoth, which became a minor holiday in its own right called Hoshana Rabba, the lulav and ethrog were no longer needed.

11. Men also visited the cemetery, and special collections of Hebrew prayers to be recited in the cemetery were published.

12. Under the influence of the kabbalists, men began to observe the new moon as a day of penitence; see below.

13. The *qaddish* is a prayer in Aramaic praising and glorifying God, which marks the divisions between the sections of a public worship service. *Pereq shirah* is "a short, anonymous tract containing a collection of hymnic sayings in praise of the Creator placed in the mouths of his creatures" (*Encyclopaedia Judaica,* s.v. Perek shirah).

14. There was also the tradition of the *parush,* the recluse, the lonely talmudic virtuoso or delver into mystical secrets.

15. And the marketplace. Although there were *tkhines* petitioning God for an adequate livelihood, they seem not to have been intended for recitation in the market or shop.

16 . At least in principle. In fact, once written, many *tkhines* were quite stable over several centuries, changing only linguistically and in minor details. However, new *tkhines* continued to be written and published into the twentieth century.

17. See *Encyclopaedia Judaica,* s.v. "Horowitz, Isaiah ben Abraham ha-Levi."

18. Nathan Nata Hannover, *Shaʿarey Ziyyon* (Israel: Hotsʾat Beney Yisrael). See also *Encyclopaedia Judaica,* s.v. "Hannover, Nathan Nata."

19. Freehof, "Devotional Literature," 405–15.

20. Occasionally the *tkhines* speak of making one's prayers a "crown" for God's holy head. However, this is probably not a reference to the *sefirah keter* ("crown") but rather a use of the motif of the coronation of God by prayers, used frequently in pre-kabbalistic *piyyut* (liturgical poetry).

21. Or nonlearned men.

22. Known as *mesirat modaʿah* (*Shaʿarey Ziyyon,* 350–53).

23. There are prayers in the *Shaʿarey Ziyyon,* and also *tkhines,* for recovery from illness, for rain in the time of drought, for offspring, and to be said on the new moon, on fast days, on Sabbaths, and on holidays.

24. See the section on *tkhines* for *niddah* (menstrual observances) below, for a discussion of themes concerning women's reproductive lives. Note 50 compares these themes to the kabbalistic devotional literature on male sexuality.

25. Mishnah *Shabbat* 2:6, phrased negatively: "Women die in childbirth for three transgressions: because they do not take care in observing marital separation, setting aside the portion of dough, and kindling the Sabbath light."

26. Or for twelve days in all, whichever is longer.

27. According to the Jewish calendar, the day begins at sunset. All of these commandments were also incumbent on men. Male bakers separated dough, husbands were, of course, obligated to avoid touching their wives during menstruation (although obviously they could not perform the inspection and immersion), and if there was no woman in the house, the man lit the Sabbath candles.

28. Hannah's prayer for a son (1 Sam 1:10–18) was taken by the rabbis to be the exemplar of proper prayer. In the course of talmudic discussion of Hannah's prayer, Rabbi Jose son of Rabbi Hanina states that Hannah repeated the phrase "your maidservant" three times in her prayer to remind God that she had never transgressed the commandments of menstrual separation, separating dough, and lighting Sabbath candles (*Berakhot* 31b). Here the commandments are not listed in the order that makes an acrostic of Hannah's name.

29. Venice? 1666? and Amsterdam, 1752.

30. There is some question about whether Sore bas Tovim was a historical or a legendary personage. See Zinberg, *Old Yiddish Literature,* 253–55; Niger, "Yidishe literatur," 83, 106n.

The publishing history of the *Shloyshe she'orim,* like that of so many *tkhines,* is obscure, to say the least. I used two slightly different editions, both found in the library of the Jewish Theological Seminary. One, printed with small type on bad paper, lacking a place and date of publication, seems to me to be from the first half of the nineteenth century, published in eastern Europe. The other, which on linguistic grounds seems somewhat later, was published in Vilna, by Romm, in 1864. Raphael Mahler quotes an Austrian censor's list from 1818 which mentions the *Shloyshe she'orim* (*ha-Hasidut weha-Haskalah* [Merhavyah: Sifriyat Po'alim, 1961] 139). In the *Encyclopaedia Judaica* Moshe Starkman states that "*Shloyshe Sheorim* was already popular in the 18th century" (*Encyclopaedia Judaica,* s.v. "Bas-Tovim, Sarah").

31. Trans. Bernard Martin, from Zinberg, *Old Yiddish Literature,* 255. (Except where noted, all other translations are my own.) Zinberg quotes from an edition of the *Shloyshe she'orim* which he attributed to the early nineteenth century, although it is undated. It differs slightly from both the editions I have seen.

32. The first two lines are in rhymed Hebrew. The next few sentences alternate between a Hebrew phrase and its Yiddish translation or paraphrase. To avoid repetition, I translate only the Yiddish. (If the Hebrew and Yiddish phrases differ substantially in meaning, or contrast in other relevant ways, I note the contrast.) The author of this *tkhine* uses a fair amount of Hebrew; clearly it was a language she knew. Many *tkhines* begin with Hebrew catchwords and include Hebrew phrases in the Yiddish text. An important textual aspect of the *tkhines* is the interplay between Hebrew and Yiddish. This is, of course, a big problem, for the translation into English. This interplay is a particularly prominent stylistic feature of the *Shloyshe she'orim.*

So far as I can determine, the name Sarah is not actually found as an acrostic in the text as we have it. I can find the *sin* and the *resh,* but the next paragraph begins with *het,* not *hey* as it should to complete the Hebrew spelling of the name.

33. As I shall discuss below, the *Shlyoshe she'orim* does not include the Hebrew blessing for ritual immersion or a *tkhine* for this religious act.

34. There is considerable scholarly disagreement as to the exact meaning of this verse. The *Shlyoshe she'orim,* however, translates the verse according to the rabbinic understanding of the *mizwah* of *hallah:* "The meaning of the verse is: The first part of your dough you shall separate as *hallah.*"

35. The source of the Hebrew phrases, including paraphrased and misquoted biblical verses and long sequences of rhyme, remains a puzzle. Did the author quote, mistakenly, from memory? Did she compose the many Hebrew sentences with no obvious source? Or was there some Hebrew

source on which she relied? Does the extensive use of Hebrew and familiarity with such esoteric sources as the *Zohar* indicate that the author was in fact a man? These questions remain to be answered.

36. The word *ḥallah* adds up to forty-three in Hebrew numerology.

37. In some varieties of eastern Yiddish, the Sabbath loaf is also called *ḥallah* (*khale*), because one must separate *ḥallah* in order to prepare it. The *Seyder Tkhines*, however, uses the western Yiddish term *berkhes*.

The *Seyder Tkhines* also contains a *tkhine* for taking *ḥallah* which recalls the sacrifices and the tithes, although it stops short of explicitly identifying the taking of *ḥallah* with the bringing of a sacrifice.

38. This translation corrects, in a few details, a translation of the same text that I published in my article "Voices from the Heart: Women's Devotional Prayers," in *The Jewish Almanac*, ed. Richard Siegel and Carl Rheins, 541–45.

39. I have romanized the Hebrew according to the Ashkenazic pronunciation, so as to make the rhymes apparent.

40. N. Prylucki, "Polemik: A tshuve eynem a retsenzent," in *Noyekh Prilutski's Zamelbikher far Yidishen Folklor, Filologye un Kulturgeshikhte* (Warsaw: Nayer Ferlag, 1912) 1:154–59. Prylucki quotes the kugel songs from an article in the journal *Mitteilungen zur jüdischen Volkskunde*, but he does not give a full citation.

Prylucki's article is a response to a review of his book by Sh. An-ski, which appeared (presumably in Russian) in *IEvreskaia Starina* (1911) 591. He quotes (in Yiddish) a passage from the review, part of which is of interest here: "Some of these [Yiddish women's] prayers are included in the women's prayer-books and [books of] *tkhines*, but the majority of them circulate in oral tradition, possessing a multitude of variants. . . ." Unfortunately, I have come across few recorded oral parallels to *tkhines*.

41. The Hebrew phrases in this song are not completely meaningless; many *tkhines* begin *Yehi razon milefanekha*, "May it be Your will." The song changes it to *milefanay* ("My [or my] will") for the sake of the rhyme.

42. The author gives the stricter halakhic interpretation of the matter. The Hebrew phrase that she quotes is usually understood to mean that women must separate themselves from their husbands "during the *twelve*-hour period during which they expect to begin menstruating," but the Yiddish translation specifies twenty-four hours (*eyn mesles*).

43. It is omitted entirely from a late edition of *Seyder Tkhines u-Vakoshes*, Vilna: Romm, 1863.

44. According to tradition, there are three partners in the creation of every human being: father, mother, and God (*Qiddushin* 30b). The idea that an angel carries the seed before God for a pronouncement of its fate is found in Midrash *Tanḥuma, Pequde,* 3 "and as an independent Midrash entitled Yezirat ha-Walad ('creation of the embryo') in *Avkat Rokhel* whence it was republished by" A. Jellinek in *Bet ha-Midrash* I, 153–55 (Louis Ginzberg, *The Legends of the Jews* [Philadelphia: Jewish Publication Society, 1968] 5:75). Cf. also *Niddah* 16b, *Zohar* 1:11a–11b.

45. To verify the cessation of the menstrual flow and thus begin counting the seven "clean" days.

46. The rabbis held that menstruation (as well as the pains of childbirth) was a punishment for Eve's sin. "In all the sources menstruation is regarded as a penalty for Eve's sin, and since sexual desire is considered the result of the eating of the forbidden fruit, the Gnostics, as well as the Kabbalists, maintain that menstruation came to Eve with the enjoyment of the fruit" (Ginzberg, *Legends,* 5:101; cf. '*Erubin* 100b; *Avot de-Rabbi Natan* 1, 7).

47. This is the way the text reads in *Seyder Tkhines u-Vakoshes*. *Seyder Tkhines* (Amsterdam, 1752) reads "and with great joy." The oldest text I have seen, *Seyder Tkhines* (Venice? 1666?) seems to contain a misprint. The phrase is *fun maynem groysn freyd* "from my great joy." It is not clear at this point what the correct reading should be.

48. "In Frankfort, according to Schudt, during the festival of *Sukkot, on Hosha'na Rabbah,*

women would bite off the petiole of an *etrog*, citron, at the time of delivery so as to reduce birth pangs" (Herman Pollack, *Jewish Folkways in Germanic Lands [1648–1806]* [Cambridge, MA: MIT Press, 1971] 17). The reference is to Johann Jacob Schudt, *Jüdische Merckwürdigkeiten* (4 vols. in two; Frankfort-Leipzig, 1714–1717) 2:8 (book 6, chap. 26)

49. This prayer is also found in *parashat Bere'shit* of the *Tsenerene*, the Yiddish paraphrase of the Torah for women, where it is introduced as follows: "Some sages say that [the Tree of Knowledge] was a citron tree. Therefore, the custom is that women take the ethrog and bite off the stem on Hoshana Rabba, and give charity, since charity saves from death, and they pray to God to be delivered from the sufferings of bearing the children they are carrying, that they may give birth easily. Had Eve not eaten from the Tree of Knowledge, each woman would give birth easily, as a hen lays an egg, without pain. The woman should pray and should say": [the prayer follows]. This paragraph and the following prayer are found in the Amsterdam (Kasper Shten, 1702–1703) and subsequent editions of the *Tsenerene*. I have not yet examined earlier editions to determine when this material entered the text, which has undergone a variety of changes since it was first published around 1600. The description of the custom and the prayer in the *Tsenerene* seem to point to an origin in oral tradition.

50. The prayers in the kabbalistic devotional literature having to do with male sexuality provide an interesting comparison to the *tkhines* for women's reproductive lives. Both sets of devotions are similar in showing a preference for sons, but differ in other ways. While the *tkhine* literature, as we have seen, contains a strong conception of menstruation as impure and stresses God's justice in causing the sufferings of childbirth, the kabbalistic devotional literature is pervaded by a sense of guilt for masturbation, a fear of sexual inadequacy, and a desire to suppress sexual thoughts. Thus, it is more directly concerned with sexuality than the *tkhines*.

In accordance with the kabbalistic idea that a man fathers demon offspring when he ejaculates because of masturbation or nocturnal emission, the *Sha'arey Ziyyon* contains a series of prayers designed to disown and nullify the influence of the demon children, as well as meditations to aid in avoiding inappropriate sexual arousal. It also contains prayers to be said before intercourse, asking God's aid in preventing impotence and expressing the hope for male offspring. In contrast to the *tkhine* quoted above, which prefers sons but will accept daughters, the *Sha'arey Ziyyon* actively seeks to prevent the possibility of female offspring: ". . . and do not forget your servant so-and-so son of your maidservant so-and-so, and grant your servant male offspring, and may the fetus now being created be a male child, and not female . . ." (pp. 230–31).

51. Abraham ben Saul of Lunel, *Sefer ha minhagot*, ed. Simhah Assaf, *Sifran shel Ri'shonim*, (Jerusalem: Mekizey Nirdamim, 1934–35) 152.

52. Abraham ben Nathan of Lunel, *Sefer ha-manhig*, ed. Yitzhak Raphael (Jerusalem: Mosad Harav Kook, 1978) 362–63 (*hilkot Zom Kippur*).

53. Mendele Mokher Seforim, *Ba-Yamin ha-Hem* in *Kol Kitvey Mendele Mokher Sefarim* (Tel Aviv: Devir, 1957–58) 272; also *Shloyme Reb Khayims*, vol. 2, *Ale Verk fun Mendele Mokher Sefarim* (Cracow, Warsaw, New York, Vilna: Farlag Mendele, 1910–11) 36–37; Bella Chagall, *Burning Lights*, 84–87; S. Weissenberg, "Das Feld- und das Kejwermessen," in *Mitteilungen zur jüdischen Volkskunde*, 7 (1906) 39–42. Although candles of this sort were most typically prepared for Yom Kippur, graves might also be measured and the candles donated to the synagogue or house of study in an effort to ameliorate some misfortune such as serious illness or difficult childbirth. See Joshua Trachtenberg, *Jewish Magic and Superstition* (Philadelphia: Jewish Publication Society, Meridian Books, 1961) 285 n. 6.

54. Chagall's account differs from Weissenberg's principally in the location of the candle making. According to Weissenberg, the candles were made in the synagogue, rather than the home, and one expert woman made candles for each women who wanted them.

55. Mendele, *Ba-Yamim ha-Hem*, 271. I have translated from the Hebrew rather than the Yiddish version because it contains a fuller explanation of the act.

56. Careful examination of Mendele's text, especially in Yiddish, leads one to the conclusion that he altered the text of the *tkhine* for his own programmatic reasons. I hope to discuss this more fully in a future study.

57. According to Weissenberg ("Das Feld- und das Kejwermessen"), after mentioning the patriarchs and matriarchs, the woman would go on to mention the dead members of her own family, asking them to intercede before God.

58. "The validity of the custom of visiting graves had already been questioned by R. Meir of Rothenburg (d. 1293) when he urged that 'the people pray directly to God as did Abraham'. . . . Apparently, the folk practice was not shaken by the critical viewpoint of this renowned scholar, but continued through the centuries" (Pollack, *Jewish Folkways*, 49).

59. Leah often received short shrift in *tkhines*.

60. *Tiqqun ḥazot*, the midnight prayer for the restoration of Zion from the *Sha'arey Ziyyon*, refers to Rachel and Leah, but clearly intends them as symbols of the tenth *sefirah*, rather than as personalities in their own right.

61. Only a thoroughgoing analysis of the depiction of female figures in the *tkhine* literature could show whether or not this pattern is widespread.

62. According to legend, when Abraham came to belief in the One God, he destroyed idols and refused to worship King Nimrod. Nimrod had him cast into a fiery furnace, from which he was rescued by divine intervention (*Sefer ha-Yashar*, Noah; *Bere'shit Rabba* 38:13). A woman would know this story from the *Tsenerene*.

63. Cf. Gen chap. 22. According to legend, Sarah wept when Abraham took Isaac away, although he did not tell her he was taking their son to be sacrificed. Later, Satan appeared to her, disguised as an old man, and told her that Abraham was sacrificing Isaac on the altar. In distress, she set forth seeking them. Satan met her again, this time telling her that Abraham had not sacrificed Isaac. Her joy was so great that she died on the spot (*Sefer ha-Yashar*, Wa-yera; *Pirqe de-Rabbi Eli'ezer*, 32).

64. Mendele, *Ba-Yamim ha-Hem*, 271. This passage does not occur in the Yiddish version. Mendele is referring to the Russian draft laws for Jews in force during the reign of Nicholas I (1825–1855). In order to coerce them to accept Christianity, Jewish boys were drafted for a period of twenty-five years, beginning at age eighteen. However, they could legally be drafted at age twelve, and were in fact often drafted as young as eight or nine, and were placed in special units where by threat of starvation, beating, and other brutalities they were "persuaded" to give up their allegiance to Judaism. Those who survived the terrible conditions were transferred to regular army units when they reached the age of eighteen, to begin a full twenty-five years of service.

The Jewish communities of the Pale of Settlement were required to furnish thirty recruits for every one thousand males. Since very few boys would enlist voluntarily, special Jewish communal officials, called *khapers* ("kidnappers") would seize young children and forcibly convey them to military service. These young recruits were known as "cantonists" (*Encyclopaedia Judaica*, s.v. "Cantonists").

65. The cycle of *tkhines* for visiting the cemetery also expresses, it seems to me, women's domestic role. After all, visiting the graves of relatives and asking them for aid is a way of keeping in touch with the family and reinforcing its solidarity.

The author of the *Shlyoshe she'orim* could also picture women in less traditional roles. In material not analyzed here, the women in paradise are depicted as engaging in prayer, contemplation, and Torah study. I plan to discuss this in a future study.

Bibliography

Two works available in English give an insider's view of the life of traditional Ashkenazic women: *The Memoirs of Glückel of Hameln* and the somewhat less abridged *Life of Glückel of Hameln*; and

Chagall. Glückel, who lived in Germany and France at the turn of the eighteenth century, wrote her memoirs to distract herself after the death of her first husband. In lively style, she describes her marriage (at age fourteen), Jewish community politics, her extensive business dealings, the matches she made for her children, and current events, and quotes extensively from the morality literature available to women. Chagall, who died in 1944, evokes the observance of Sabbaths and holidays in the home of her well-to-do Hasidic family.

Scholarly discussions of *tkhines* and other genres of Yiddish devotional literature are few. Zinberg has now been translated into English by Bernard Martin. This readable survey discusses both religious and profane literature and includes extensive bibliographical notes. Freehof contains translations of selected *tkhines* from *Seyder Tkhines u-Vakoshes*, a discussion of the themes of this literature, and a tracing of the origin of some of them in the kabbalistic devotional literature.

In addition to the texts found in Zinberg and Freehof, a small number of additional English translations of *tkhines* have been published. Glatzer, an anthology of Jewish prayers, includes about half a dozen translations from the Yiddish. Weissler includes two *tkhines* that are in the present chapter and also translations of *tkhines* for the new moon, the women's *mizwot*, visiting the cemetery, and private occasions. Klirs translates lengthy excerpts from seven collections of *tkhines* and includes some thematic analysis (and the original Yiddish texts). This work contains by far the largest number of *tkhines* in English translation yet to be made available; however, since it is an unpublished thesis, it may be difficult to obtain.

Finally, the *Tsenerene*, the Yiddish paraphrase of the Pentateuch and *Haftarot* known as the "women's Bible," is now appearing in English, translated by Miriam Stark Zakon. The translation is occasionally inaccurate or tendentious, but it is a readable version of the most popular volume in the library of the traditional Ashkenazic woman.

Chagall, Bella. *Burning Lights.* New York: Schocken, 1946.

Freehof, Solomon. "Devotional Literature in the Vernacular." *CCAR Yearbook* 33 (1923) 375–424.

Glatzer, Nahum N. *The Language of Faith.* New York: Schocken, 1967.

Klirs, Tracy Guren. "Bizkhus fun sore, Rivke, Rokhl un Leye: The *Tkhine* as the Jewish Woman's Self-Expression." Rabbinical thesis. Hebrew Union College, 1984.

Life of Glückel of Hameln, 1646–1724. Translated by Beth-Zion Abrahams. New York: T. Yoseloff, 1963.

The Memories of Glückel of Hameln. Translated by Marvin Lowenthal. New York: Schocken, 1977.

Tz'enah ur'enah: The Classic Anthology of Torah Lore and Midrashic Comment. Translated by Miriam Stark Zakon. New York: Mesorah Publications, 1983–1984.

Weissler, Chava. "Voices from the Heart: Women's Devotional Prayers." In *Jewish Almanac*, 541–45. Edited by Carl Rheins and Richard Siegel. New York: Bantam, 1980.

Zinberg, Israel. *A History of Jewish Literature.* Vol. 7, *Old Yiddish Literature from Its Origins to the Haskalah Period.* Translated by Bernard Martin. New York: Ktav; Cincinnati: Hebrew Union College Press, 1975.

Part Two

CHALLENGE
The Modern Age

On the Slaughter

Pity me sky.
If a god is within you
and a way to him
I have not found,
pray you for me.

My heart is dead.
My lips mouth no prayer.
Helpless. Hopeless.
How long, how long? how much more?

Hangman. Here's a throat. Slit it.
Cut my throat like a dog.
You've an arm and an axe
And the whole land for a block.
We are few.
No taboo on my blood
Crush the skull.
Let the murdered blood
of babes and crones
Spurt on your shirt
and never be blotted out.

If there is justice
Let it appear
after annihilation
Let his throne be razed
sky shrivel in evil
devils live in their filth
till their own blood cleanse them.

A curse on the crier for revenge.
Even Satan created no quittance
For a small child's blood.
Let the blood cleave the void
split the bottomless pit
eat away the dark
and rot the foundations
of the putrefying earth.

Hayyim Nahman Bialik

My Brother Refugee

I love my sad God,
my brother refugee.
I love to sit down on a stone with him
and tell him everything wordlessly
because when we sit like this, both perplexed,
our thoughts flow together
in silence.
A star lights up, a fiery letter.
His body longs for sleep.
The night leans like a sheep against our feet.

My poor God,
how many prayers I've profaned,
how many nights I've
blasphemed him
and warmed my frightened bones
at the furnace of the intellect.
And here he sits, my friend, his arm around me,
sharing his last crumb.

The God of my unbelief is magnificent,
how I love my unhappy God,
now that he's human and unjust.
How exalted is this proud pauper
now that the merest child rebels
against his word.

                              Jacob Glatstein

Guard Me, Oh God

Guard me, Oh God, from hating man my brother,
Guard me from recalling what, from my early youth, to me
    he did.
When all the stars in my sky are quenched, within me my
    soul's voice grows mute—
When I am overcome by disaster, let me not lay bare his
    guilt.

For he is my hidden dwelling-place, in him am I reflected
    again,
Like a wayfarer from the planets, beholding his face in a
    pool.
What use is all my struggle, to whom shall I wail out the
    pain—
If hollow, blemished is my distant night's moon?

When the gates are locked, darkness over the city reclining,
And emptied of love, rejected, I am bound to my rock:
Permit me to see in him a spark, only a spark still shining,
That I may know that in myself, in me, all is not yet
    snuffed out.

S. Sholom

7. Joseph Budko, *A Man Like Me Does Not Flee*, 1930.

8. Alice Lok Cahana, *Sabbath in Auschwitz*, 1985.

9. George Segal, *Abraham's Sacrifice*, 1973. The Mann Auditorium, Tel Aviv.

10. Anna Ticho, *Jerusalem from the Mount of Olives*, 1975.

Secularization, "Spirit," and the Strategies of Modern Jewish Faith

ARNOLD M. EISEN

> Why should she give her bounty to the dead?
> What is divinity if it can come
> Only in silent shadows and in dreams?
> ... Divinity must live within herself ...
> Wallace Stevens, *Sunday Morning*

FAITH IN THE MODERN WEST has been a commitment under siege. Institutions once controlled or swayed by religion have proceeded to rob it of its principal functions. Close-knit communities which once lent faith the supreme credibility of the self-evident have disintegrated in the face of urbanization, mobility, and centralized state power. Most important, perhaps, the sheer variety of beliefs and commitments available for the choosing has undermined the claim of any single commitment to ultimate truth—or lifelong loyalty. In response, the West's religions have adopted a series of defensive strategies designed to evade, disarm or even overpower their attackers, while strengthening the resistance of the faithful. Our concern here is the use made by Jewish thinkers of perhaps the most important defensive strategy of all: reliance on a notion of "spirituality" expanded, in this period, to fill the widening breach which called it forth.

That idea is not merely present in Jewish thought since Spinoza; it is pervasive, though we should note at the outset that it has not taken the form of a single concept, coherently employed. "Spirit" has rather connoted a *range* of ideas, set forth with varying rigor and drawn from a wide variety of sources. The Hebrew Bible, Spinoza, German Idealism, and Nietzsche all

283

contributed, along with popularizations that broadened and blurred the several conceptions. It was through this wide range of connotations that the idea of spirit assisted in the performance of the twin tasks that make up the burden of modern Jewish thought: depiction of a social/political order in which the Jews could find a place, and the formulation of a Judaism suited to that order. Those tasks have been carried out, as we shall see in the present essay and those that follow, with constant reference to "spirit," "spirituality," and (among Zionists) the "spiritual center." Cognate and dependent terms such as "religiosity" and "culture" have likewise figured centrally, while the more traditional vocabulary of "Torah," "revelation," "yoke of commandments," and—of course—"God," has largely ceded pride of place.

There are, I shall argue, three principal reasons for this shift. First, the several conceptions of "spirit" bequeathed to Western thought by German Idealism, principally Hegel, facilitated the Jews' adaptation to the new order in which they sought a place. Both the Jewish community and Jewish faith, it seemed, could take on new, universalist forms without discarding what had been essential—and distinctive—in the past. Second, that new vocabulary, once adopted, proved indispensable to the retention of Jewish commitment. Jews who had internalized the culture of their surroundings and as a result could no longer honestly commit themselves to their traditional belief or to God could not only speak, but wax enthusiastic, about "spirit," "history," or "culture." In the latter terms, authenticity appeared attainable, while the old vocabulary seemed to condemn such Jews to cant, apostasy, or silence. Third, Zionist thinkers such as Ahad Ha'am and A. D. Gordon likewise found the reigning notion of spirit essential to the formulation of a nationalist Jewish identity continuous with a religious Jewish past. Jews who did not desire or believe in a messianic ingathering of the exiles could nonetheless devote heart and soul to the quest for a "spiritual center," assured that it would carry on the spirit of their tradition—even as most Orthodox thinkers, observing the pioneers' brazen violation of the letter of the law, were convinced of precisely the opposite.

Contemporary Jewish thought continues to work with and within the vocabulary of "spirit" thus transmitted. The challenges first discerned by Spinoza, to faith in general and that of the Jews in particular, remain pressing; the response that he first suggested still serves. Following some further introductory remarks, I shall begin this survey with a sketch of the principal challenges raised by Spinoza followed by an outline of his own response to these. We will then observe the deployment of Spinoza's vocabulary and conceptualization of spirit, refined under the tutelage of German Idealism, in order to defend traditional faith (Nahman Krochmal and Abraham Isaac Kook), to overhaul and redefine it (Abraham Geiger and

Martin Buber) and to supplant it by a more or less secular nationalism (Aḥad Ha'am and A. D. Gordon). I will conclude with a survey of five contemporary strategies of "spirit," reflecting upon the price which such translations of tradition have exacted from Jewish faith—and from the currency of "spirituality" itself.

Modernization and the Jews

Sociological theory and research offer no clear or unitary definition of the other terminology crucial to our inquiry: that of "modernization" and "secularization." For our purposes, the obvious referents of the former are sufficient: such massive societal changes as urbanization, the growth of science and technology, and the centralization of political and economic decision making. Secularization—at once a component element of that larger process, a consequence of it, and one response to it—will be used here in the straightforward sense assigned the term by Peter Berger: the "process by which sectors of society and culture are removed from the domination of religious institutions and symbols."[1] Governments can and do set policy without significant regard for religious creeds or their organizational carriers. Individuals can be born, educated, married, divorced, and buried outside the jurisdiction of religious institutions. They can make crucial life decisions without (or against) the counsels of their churches. High and popular culture, finally, operate almost entirely outside the shrinking circle of significance that is centered on a transcendent God. Secularization has therefore occurred, even if the process has been uneven, and remains incomplete.

The institutional focus of Berger's definition is especially helpful if we wish to understand the impact of modernization upon Western Jewry. For centuries, we might summarize, Jews had passed their days, provided social services to their needy, taken each other to court, and developed the artifacts of their culture, inside the walls of relatively autonomous and self-contained communities or *kehillot*. Now, with emancipation, the *kehillot* disintegrated. In part, they were eliminated by absolutist states which refused to permit any corporate body or special grant of privilege to come between individual citizens and their governments. In part, the *kehillot* fell victim to economic pressures which overtook the larger societies on which they depended. In large measure, they simply collapsed under the weight of opportunity which now beckoned to Jews from outside. Whatever the reasons for this decline, its consequence was momentous. Jewish institutions and commitments would henceforth be voluntarist. Jews would regard themselves, and (at least in theory) be regarded by their governments, as individuals, whose allegiances were a matter of choice. The "plausibility structures" which had once lent prima facie credibility to the claims of Jewish tradition were seriously weakened, leaving Jews exposed to the prevailing winds. Despite residual loyalties, they would shop, along with Gentile neighbors, in the modern marketplace of commitments.

More than the model of Spinoza's *Tractatus Theologico-Politicus*, then, impelled Moses Mendelssohn to devote the first half of his essay *Jerusalem* (1783) to political theory. Mendelssohn carefully details a doctrine of church and state which separates the two powers absolutely, forbidding any attempt whatsoever to coerce religious loyalty. Only in the second half of the work does he turn to the redefinition of Jewish faith—a consequence, it is clear, of the new political realities that he has grasped. Education, rites of passage, social thought, communal gatherings, the arts—all that makes for a society, and a culture—could now take place outside the control or even the influence of Jewish religious institutions. Jewish faith could survive in such conditions, Mendelssohn reasoned, only if the nature of Jewish commitment were seriously reconceived.

For Western Jewry, then, modernization has meant emancipation first of all and only secondarily, as a result of that move "out of the ghetto," confrontation with what Berger has called the "secularization of consciousness." The phrase is overblown, the process not given to ready empirical confirmation. Yet it seems undeniable that, again in Berger's words, an increasing number of individuals in the west have come to "look upon the world and their own lives without the benefit of religious interpretations."[2] As a result, their outlook on both nature and the nature of the self has been radically transformed—two shifts especially relevant to the present inquiry.

Leo Strauss has termed the former change the modern project par excellence: mastery of the world, for the benefit of the human species. Enlightenment works such as the *Encyclopedia* articulated the project clearly; Karl Marx, too, embraced it with enthusiasm. Later social theorists, agreed on identification of the modern project, reacted to it with greater ambivalence. *Gesellschaft* had come at the price of *Gemeinschaft;* freedom of thought had perhaps exacted a cost in *anomie* and dislocation. Max Weber, whose investigations into "rationalization" lent the concept its greatest conceptual precision, was also the most ambivalent in assessing it. His findings are extremely helpful in understanding the challenges that modern Jewish defenders of faith have felt obliged to confront.

Weber's first masterpiece, *The Protestant Ethic and the Spirit of Capitalism,* sought to demonstrate that the West's unparalleled rationalization had received its primary impetus from the Puritans. "Rational conduct on the basis of the idea of the calling was born from the spirit of [Protestant] ascetism," Weber wrote, in particular from the robust and irrational fear of damnation that had sent Puritans scurrying for signs of this-worldly success. The process had then gone on to pervade every aspect of modern life and culture. Weber's evaluation of its result was somber. Where once the sense of calling had been borne lightly on the shoulders, like a cloak, it had since become an "iron cage" from which ultimate meaning had fled (pp. 180–181). Succeeding works, attempting to understand how this had occurred, surveyed the "economic ethics" of all the "major" religions, and only served to deepen Weber's initial pessimism. In the essay that stands as Weber's credo, "Science as a Vocation," he brooded on whether a vocation—that is, meaningful work—was even possible in a world which had come to believe that "principally there are no mysterious incalculable forces that come into play, but rather that one can, in principle, master all things by calculation." Science, "the most important fraction" of the process of rationalization that had accomplished that disenchantment, now stood unable to demonstrate that its own enterprise had any ultimate value (pp. 138–39).

The conclusion to Weber's essay is especially relevant to the present inquiry. "Grandiose" claims to absolute truth, whether metaphysical or ethical, would henceforth be relativized. Traditional authorities once able to pronounce "the one thing that is needful" would be undermined by a historical consciousness aware of development and ideology. Great art, in such a world, would be "intimate and not monumental." Only "within the smallest and intimate circles, in personal human situations, in *pianissimo*," could something "pulsate that corresponds to the prophetic *pneuma*, which in former times swept through the great communities like a firebrand, welding them together" (p. 155). Yet only the "bearing of man" had been disenchanted. Underneath, humanity continued to serve, and fight for, its many gods, a struggle over which "fate, and certainly not 'science,' holds sway" (p. 148).

The modern individual, Weber believed, had but two alternatives. He could "bear the fate of the times like a man," carrying on without ultimate meaning as best he could. Alternatively one could return to the fold of religion, one's "intellectual sacrifice" in hand (p. 155). "Spirit," however, has seemed to many Jewish thinkers in the modern period to offer a third alternative, of which they have decisively taken hold.

The second shift in "consciousness" relevant to our study concerns the nature of the individual self, the meaning of what Weber, following Immanuel Kant, called *personlichkeit*. Kant, of course, supplied the presiding vision of this self: an autonomous, integrated personality, who freely decides to conform his or her will to the rational demands of the "categorical imperative." The self attains to morality only by virtue of that free expression of its "good will," Kant insisted. Neither actions performed at the behest of coercive human authorities nor actions commanded by a living and present God could be considered at the court of ethics. G. Hegel, even while emphasizing that "nobility" and "baseness" were in large measure functions of a culturally given set of values, sought to retain the sense of individual ethical responsibility. F. Nietzsche, however, carried the historicization of values to a new extreme and often rejected the Kantian postulate of a free will—indeed, the very existence of a self divorceable from its driving "will to power." Autonomous and moral, he wrote in pointed criticism of Kant, were "mutually exclusive." The truly "emancipated individual—the master of a free will"—was beyond any definition of good and evil imposed, by a society, upon its far-from-emancipated "herd" (*Genealogy of Morals*, 2:2).

Even without accepting Nietzsche as the paradigmatic exponent of the modern self or equating that self with his *Ubermensch,* one recognizes that he articulates the themes of modern individualism with great clarity. Nietzsche would be his own man, the creation of his own artistry rather than the product of a traditional mold or the servant of a traditional order. Like his Zarathustra, he would be the prophet of a new truth, *his* truth. "Let me reveal my heart to you entirely, my friends. . . . If there were gods, how could I endure not to be a God? Hence there are no gods. . . . What could one create if gods existed?" (*Thus Spake Zarathustra*, 198). Weber, seeking a more nuanced description of this same craving for autonomy and originality, noted the cult of "personality" and "personal experience" which had penetrated even the practice of science. "People belabor themselves in trying to 'experience life'—for that befits a personality, conscious of its rank and station." In the defense of culture, Weber felt compelled to insist that "only he who is dedicated *solely* to the work at hand has 'personality' . . . inner devotion to the task, and that alone" ("Science," 137). Autonomous selves were bent rather on self-enlargement, through both vocation and "experience." In that way they sought to expand the interiority in which ultimate meaning—once communal and transcendent—would not have to dwell.

The imprecision of such an account is palpable. Equally important, the persistent combination of elegiac longing for lost faith with the conviction that the return to faith was impossible short of "intellectual sacrifice" suggests an analysis that falls short of "value-neutrality." Nonetheless, the analysis sketched so barely here is common to virtually all the theorists of modernization and is confirmed, in its general thrust if not in detail, by sociological and historical investigation. The passage from *Gemeinschaft* to *Gesellschaft,* the triumph of the project of rationalization spearheaded by science and technology, and the emergence of a self that seeks to be free of all "tutelage," can therefore serve us as a summary of the threefold challenge against which the Western faiths have sought to defend themselves. We shall now turn our attention to the use made by Jews of the principal defensive strategy: reliance on the concepts of "spirit" and "spirituality," understood in such a way as to ward off the modern assault.

Spinoza's Critique of Judaism

It was Spinoza who pioneered the first line of defense: faith was not untenable, but only misunderstood. The task of his *Tractatus Theologico-Politicus*, Spinoza announced at the outset, was to demonstrate that freedom of judgment and worship could "be granted without prejudice to the public peace," and indeed was a prerequisite of that peace. In order to prove the point, he had to "point out the misconceptions which, like scars of our former bondage, still disfigure our notion of religion" and to dispose, as well, of the "false views" which had distorted the true nature of civil authority (p. 6). The former task receives far more attention in the work than the latter. Faith had become "a mere compound of credulity and prejudices," religion a "tissue of ridiculous mysteries" (p. 7). The need for radical purification was therefore urgent.

A detailed analysis of the *Tractatus* is of course impossible here. We should note, however, that its very first chapter, "Of Prophecy," is designed to move the reader from the opening declaration that "prophecy, or revelation, is sure knowledge revealed by God to man," to the recognition that such knowledge is neither "sure" nor in any way extraordinary. In fact, we soon learn, "to suppose that knowledge of natural and spiritual phenomena can be gained from the prophetic books is an utter mistake" (p. 27). The vehicle for this antitraditional argument is highly traditional: the exegesis of Scripture, in particular of the "Hebrew word *ruah*, commonly translated 'spirit'" (p. 19). Maimonides, too, had analyzed the word in his *Guide for the Perplexed*, for precisely the opposite reason. Spirit was one of many "equivocal, derivative or amphibolous terms" examined in part 1 of the *Guide* in order to defend the authority of Scripture by dispelling the impression of divine anthropomorphism which such terms conveyed. Spirit, Maimonides explained, could mean simply "air" or the "blowing wind." The word could refer to "the animal spirit," or "the thing that remains of man after death and that does not undergo passing-away." Finally, it might signify the "divine intellectual overflow that overflows to the prophets and in virtue of which they prophesy," or "purpose and will." When applied to God, *ruah* was always used in the fifth sense, at times accompanied by the sixth (*Guide*, 5, 90–91).

Spinoza, for his part, discerns nine usages of *ruaḥ*—including "courage and strength," "virtue and fitness," "habit of mind," and "passions and faculties"—and follows this exegesis with another that elucidates "the way in which things are referred to God, and said to be of God." The "Temple of God," he reasons, was called such because it was "dedicated to him"—and not, by implication, because it was believed that God had caused his name, or a special part of himself, to dwell there. Amos had spoken of "the overthrow of the Lord [which] came upon Sodom and Gomorrah" because that "overthrow" had been "in the superlative degree," that is, very great—and not, by implication, because the text believed that God had accomplished it! Isaiah, asserting that "the flower fadeth because the Spirit of the Lord bloweth upon it," had meant only "a very strong, dry, and deadly wind." Finally, Scripture abounded in such references to God's spirit because "if the Jews were at a loss to understand any phenomenon, or were ignorant of its cause, they referred it to God" (*Tractatus*, 19–21).

The ground was now prepared for Spinoza's conclusion: the "spirit of the Lord" said to have imbued the prophets meant only that "the prophets were endowed with a peculiar and extraordinary power, and devoted themselves to piety with especial constancy." "God's spirit" signified only "God's mind or thought," and, equally, the laws that revealed his mind and thought to us. Thus, the prophetic imagination through which God's decrees were revealed could be called the mind of God only to the degree that every mind was God's mind. "On our minds also the mind of God and his external thoughts are impressed." Scripture contained or expressed God's spirit no more and no less than any other insight into divine law, including scientific knowledge of the laws of nature, which Spinoza calls "knowledge of God." If the Hebrews had failed to take all this into account and had made extravagant claims for their prophets and Scriptures, it was because they "claimed a preeminence, and despised other men and other men's knowledge" (p. 24).

We note that Spinoza's depiction of a religion compatible with the modern order requires a democratization of spirit, both "vertical" and "horizontal." Spirit no longer resided in a heavenly storehouse, awaiting transport to earth and the inspiration of chosen earthlings, whenever the God of Spirit gave the word. No such decree was possible, given the understanding of God set forth at length in Spinoza's *Ethics*. No special "purpose" or "divine intellectual overflow" could be conceived; Maimonides' exegesis of *ruaḥ*, therefore, was unfounded. By "the help of God," Spinoza summarizes in the *Tractatus*, "I mean the fixed and unchangeable order of nature or the chain of natural events." By "eternal decrees of God" he intends "eternal truth or necessity" (p. 44). Horizontally, too, possession of spirit has been democratized. Participation in God's mind was not the special gift of a chosen few, but was shared equally by (or at least was equally accessible to) all human beings who used their natural, rational gifts. Religions could proffer no unique truths and hold out hope of no unique salvation. The rites and symbols of faith, if they had any role at all in the modern state, served only to promote public piety among the masses whom philosophy could not hope to persuade rationally. Public piety, of course, was the proper concern of government, and so Spinoza's penultimate chapter argues that "the right over matters spiritual lies wholly with the Sovereign, and that outward forms of religion should be in accordance with Public Peace" (p. 245). Once such conformity has been assured, and, to the degree that it is not threatened by individual deviance, "every man may think what he likes and say what he thinks" (p. 257)—the point that the entire treatise, we recall, had been composed to demonstrate.

Subsequent Jewish thinkers could, of course, not accept *in toto* either Spinoza's theology or his politics. The former left no room for a personal and/or transcendent God and rendered the Torah an obsolete civil constitution for a state long since destroyed. The latter left no room for a Jewish people self-consciously set apart or for a religion that was more than mere ceremonial. Yet Spinoza could not be ignored. His philosophical challenge was too formidable, his inauguration of scientific biblical criticism all too prescient, his understanding of the new political realities too acute, and his response to those realities too compelling. When Moses Mendelssohn's own attempt at a re-definition of Judaism proved unsatisfactory, his heirs in the nineteenth century tried to get around Spinoza's challenge, in various ways, by employing the very vocabulary which he had introduced, with conceptual refinements introduced by German Idealism. Spirit—immanent, universal, and rational—would become the principal means of defending the Jewish community and the Jewish faith against both modernity's challenges and Spinoza's. We shall look briefly at three such defenses through "spirit" in the nineteenth century—Abraham Geiger's attempt to reform Jewish belief, Nahman Krochmal's attempt to reformulate it, and rabbinic sermons restructured to communicate both positions—before passing on to Asher Ginzburg (Ahad Ha'am)'s program for a "spiritual center" and the deployment of "spirit" by faith's defenders in our own century.

Geiger and the Spirit of Judaism

Abraham Geiger's practice of the "science of Judaism," like his program of reform, was pervaded by the Idealist vision of spirit as the moving force in national and world history. The two efforts were related. Geiger explained that his "General Introduction to the Science of Judaism," delivered as a series of lectures between 1872 and 1874, was intended to provide full understanding of "the religious thought and ideal content which pervades Judaism and which dwells within it as its unique life-giving force." Only when such understanding had been achieved, when the "spiritual motive behind Judaism" had been "traced inductively," would it be possible "to gain a true conception of its full content and its philosophical and religio-ethical trends." History, the history of spirit, was indispensable to theology. It ensured, through an account of how "the Idea" had "manifested itself in practice in the course of history," that nothing essential would be lost through the reform of contemporary manifestations (p. 149).

In Geiger's masterpiece, *Judaism and Its History*, the Idea is center stage. The Jewish religion had entered the world to present a new idea of God, to "illumine and ennoble all human relations and to teach the proper recognition and estimate of man" (p. 53). In order to initiate that effort, a nation had been necessary: "a numerous and united multitude raising high the banner of their idea, ready for victory or death." Once under way, however, Israel's "world-reforming idea" was not only protected but severely limited by the vessel of nationality. The idea, therefore, had to detach itself from the land and polity, going forth to what Geiger elsewhere called "a greater spirituality," which it then spread all over the world. The lesson for Geiger's own day was clear. Jews proud of their universalist mission should "look back with joy on our former life as a nation as being an essential transitional era in our history, and on our language, through which the life of that Jewish nation had taken root in spiritual soil" (*Judaism*, 68–69, 81; "Introduction," 150–51).

The concluding metaphor is more than a mere oxymoron, because Geiger takes seriously the notion of spirit which suffuses Hegel's own philosophy of history. He uses the idea to defy both Spinoza's challenge to Jewish particularity and Mendelssohn's insistence that this particularity retain its traditional form. Geiger, like Hegel, held that every people has a special talent, or genius, which confers a mission of enriching humanity with the truths that it has discovered. Unlike Hegel, however, he spoke of the Jewish mission in the present tense. "Is not the Jewish people, likewise, endowed with such a genius, a Religious Genius?" Judaism still "considers it its task to spread its blessings to all mankind . . . to become the religion of mankind" (*Judaism*, 46, 382). The world-historical Jewish mission continued, where that of the Greeks and Romans had long since been surrendered to other hands. The form of Judaism's Idea had changed, necessarily, with the times, but the Idea itself remained unaltered, and of utmost importance.

Geiger's conclusions are not straightforward. Spinoza had been correct in denying that spirit was the unique possession of Israel, in regarding much

of Jewish law as an anachronism, and in arguing the subservience of par-
ticularist ritual to universalist belief. He had erred, however, in seeing no
role for Jews and their Idea—Judaism— in the modern world. The messianic
kingdom had not yet arrived; the Jewish mission therefore had to continue.
Kant had made a similar mistake, treating Jewish faith only in its Old Testa-
ment form and ignoring all subsequent development. That development
had not been the product of a heteronomous God, but the creation of the
immanent Jewish spirit. Finally, the parties of extremism within the Jewish
community were also proven wrong—those "who would like to leave
everything as it is, because they deem it all to be sacred," no less than those
who declare that "there should be no Judaism at all . . . everything must be
cut down to the roots" (Introduction, 268–69). Only theologians trained in
Jewish history could advance the welfare of Israel, prudently changing what
had to be changed while preserving the essential Idea or spirit.

Krochmal and "The Spiritual"

A remarkably similar strategy, deployed for quite a different defense, a very
different Jewish commitment, can be found in Nahman Krochmal's *Guide
for the Perplexed of the Day*, written in the 1830s.[3] Krochmal, a Galician Jew
pious in his observance, sought to assuage the perplexity of Jews of similar
commitment whose belief had been undermined by challenges such as
Spinozism and historicism. Whereas in previous times the danger to faith
had consisted in revealing the concealed, he wrote, in the present time the
threat consisted in continuing to cover what had already been revealed.
Historical development could no longer be denied. It could, however, be
safely accommodated, and this, Krochmal insisted, was "holy work" attuned
to "the needs of the present time" (pp. 5, 143). Krochmal tried to accomplish
his task through unparalleled use of the Idealist vocabulary of spirit, terminology that enabled him to render traditional beliefs in contemporary
language at the same time as he demonstrated, in good Hegelian fashion,
that Jews had apprehended the truths of German Idealism long before
Christianity, let alone Hegel, had ever been born. Jewish faith had expressed
those truths, as religions do, in the form of symbolic representations, rather
than in the strictly logical concepts of philosophy. The truths thereby
apprehended and expressed, however, were the same.

Krochmal's strategy is already evident in the *Guide's* opening
philosophical discussions, where a rather traditional argument for God's
relation to humanity is couched in the traditional language of *ruḥaniyyim*,
spiritual beings or essences, and a similar term, *ruḥani sikhli*, is used to
render the study of the divine nature traditionally called *ma'aseh merkavah*

(pp. 10, 24). His intent is most obvious, however, in the better-known chapters (6–10), which trace the spiritual history of Israel or, in an equation derived directly from Hegel, the history of spirit in Israel. That history, Krochmal argues, had been unique, but he begins his discussion with comments on the nature of "general spirit" or spirit in general. Every religion participated in the *ruhani* or "spiritual," even the most primitive. Human beings were by nature spiritual creatures, whose very speech was proof that they alone could partake in spirit. Speech was a symbolic activity, not the mere ejaculation of sounds, and "only spirit can make symbols—for spirit." The Torah had expressed this attribute of humanity by distinguishing holy from profane—the *ruhani* from the *gufani* or corporeal. Purity and impurity, likewise, respectively symbolized the *ruhani*, which, for example, ascended to heaven in sacrifice, and the material or *homri*, unfit for sacrifice and ever earth-bound (pp. 29–32). As spirit was the animating force in the individual body, so too in the nation. Every people possessed a "spiritual treasure" which constituted its essence, holding the nation together and sustaining it. The Torah, recognizing the primacy of religion in such "general spirits," had even called these "first principles" of each collective consciousness (*tehillat ha-mahashava*) by the name *elohei ha'umah*, "gods of the people."

Note the concessions already made. First, holy and profane have been sociologized. They are not states of being imposed by divine fiat ("And the Lord blessed the seventh day and sanctified it") but divisions lodged in the "collective consciousness" of a particular group. Peoples made things holy, to rouse themselves to the quest for spirituality. Krochmal's position is distinguished from sociological reduction, however, by his belief that peoples are moved to divide sacred from profane by the indwelling Spirit which binds them together. We are spiritual beings, engaged in spiritual creation, and spirit is, in its very source and nature, divine. This conviction enables Krochmal to describe all of culture as a "spiritual inheritance," a "treasure of spiritual holiness." He can even make the striking assertion, in his own mini-exegesis of the word *ruah*, that in the Bible "God (*elohim*) comes mostly as an adjective and not as a noun" (p. 35). Krochmal, we might say, is able to use the adjective so literally because he never conflates it with the noun. The *ruhani* is of God, but not the same as God. Yet—a crucial shift, Krochmal's exegesis notwithstanding—the *Guide* speaks almost exclusively of spirit, whereas the Bible and the rabbis had spoken of God. The divine, for Krochmal, is to be apprehended in the history of spirit that he recounts—primarily, that is to say, in sacred texts.

The exceptionalism claimed for Israel by Geiger can in Krochmal be grounded in the workings of God, through spirit. While every civilization had flourished and later perished according to an ineluctable cycle of birth, maturity, and decline, Israel had survived that cycle, on more than one occasion, to start its creativity anew. This was because other nations had given themselves to one element of spirituality, one principal direction of culture, whereas Israel had learned early on that "the absolute *ruhani*, it and none beside it is the source of all spiritual existence, the sum total of them all . . . the absolute *ruhani*, The *Eyn Sof*" (p. 37). What had given Israel such a complete grasp of the nature of spirit by the time of its return from Babylonian exile? God's loving kindness, the *hesed elohim* "on the people which He chose, kindness that cannot be accounted for, not by us or any preceding generations" but had simply come by God's grace to the patriarchs (pp. 38–39). The secret of Israel's success, then, was not repeated divine intervention in its history but the inner workings of its own collective consciousness, which was in turn the product of a unique divine blessing to its founders.

Krochmal's work, while focusing on that immanent process of creation, does not ignore its transcendent source. Later in the *Guide*, for example, he ascribes the good fortune of the returning exiles to the "same divine providence that took the ancestors out of Egypt with signs and wonders." This time, however, God's hand had been invisible. "Indeed You are a hiding God, the Saving God of Israel." The passage, he explains, "teaches about the divine spiritual providence in this redemption (by hidden miracles)" (p. 53). The "Great Assembly," to which Krochmal assigns many of the biblical "writings," and which ingeniously serves him as a link between the prophets and the sages, likewise accomplished its great work "by the spirit that rested upon these holy men and by the hand of God that was strongly upon them. There is no doubt that without this holy spirit they would not have had the power or the chance at all to accomplish this great effort" (p. 64). God's providential workings through immanent spirit were providential nonetheless, and divine nonetheless.

Krochmal's overall project, then, is strictly Hegelian. He will trace the history of "religion and faith and good alterations and the general course of spirit" (p. 71). His vocabulary, including its biases, is also Hegelian: the opposition of spirit to slavery, the inferiority of the particular to the universal, the pejorative references to the merely material. Yet despite that vocabulary and the concessions made to biblical critics who argued for the late authorship of certain biblical texts, Krochmal can convincingly present his *Guide* as a defense of tradition. Challengers are disarmed, in large part, by their own weapons. Late authorship is used to prove that Spirit did not depart from Israel after the return from exile or the destruction of the Temple. The alleged superiority of nineteenth-century philosophical expositions over "primitive" scriptural "representations" is used to argue the prescience of the original. A medieval philosopher such as Ibn Ezra is interpreted at length to show that even in philosophical language the Jews and not the moderns had pioneered. Jewish history, finally, is ennobled by the *Guide*. That which was most important in any history—the creativity of spirit— had continued in defiance of exile and persecution. Moreover, it continued unabated, even in the present.

This is, of course, a clear message for Jewish critics of the tradition as well. Geiger's distinction between biblical insight and rabbinic stultification, essence and dross, was precluded by the conviction that every aspect of a people's national life bore the imprint of divine spirit. None could simply be cast off. All could, however, be translated—with the gain and loss attend- ant on any attempt to cast traditional commitments in contemporary words, and clearly evident in Krochmal's. Later strategists of spirit would learn this lesson well. Krochmal's location of divinity in nation and self, in history, culture, and text, would prove decisive for their own attempts to formulate Jewish tradition in terms more acceptable to modern Jewish sensibilities.

Preaching and Spirituality

Before turning to those developments, however, we should note that the vocabulary of spirit had a wider effect upon the Jewish community than in the works of historians and theologians alone, thanks to its diffusion through synagogue sermons. Alexander Altmann has shown how the change in both the form and substance of nineteenth-century sermons reflects the integration of Jews into German culture and, in particular, the impact of German philosophy. The traditional *derashah* gave way to, or was recast in accordance with, contemporary forms of address aimed at moral edification or theological explication. That synthesis of traditional homily with *Erbauungspredigt* was not seriously challenged, Altmann observes, throughout the century.

Michael Sachs, for example—a traditionalist rabbi who served in Prague and Berlin—made use of biblical, rabbinic, and even mystical materials in rationalist sermons shaped by Hegel's notion of the "Spirit of God in His community." Sachs sought, Altmann argues, "to revive the true 'spirit' of Judaism," which he believed had been "throttled by a nascent enlighten- ment." That spirit had not only infused all authentic Jewish texts of whatever period, but had also conferred on Sachs himself "the freedom of the Jewish spirit in any age to project itself into the past and to mold the past in the image of the present." Spirit, recognized in texts, provided freedom: "a free expression of the innermost life, as the free living movement within the circle of God's teaching" (p. 207).

Geiger, though he initially took a similar view of preaching, later insisted that edification was not sufficient. Synagogue ritual had to be part of a larger religious life and "spirituality." The preacher, however, could not draw upon this "veritable life of the spirit" in all domains of the Jew's existence unless he was guided by a comprehensive theology, based upon scholarship, that did not "confine itself to general moral and religious questions." In this, Altmann argues, Geiger followed Hegel, who had insisted that a unitary life of the spirit bound together each nation and all humanity. The task of the sermon, therefore, was to bind the individual worshiper to that eternal process by enabling him to "feel in himself the eternal, one Spirit which time cannot vanquish"—the "divine portion" in humanity (pp. 223–24).

Jewish preachers sought to perform that task by raising to consciousness the spirit at work in Jewish history, much as Geiger and Krochmal had done in their histories of spirit for more specialized audiences. Altmann notes that Hegel's description of revealed religion as "Spirit to spirit," which we observed earlier in Krochmal, can be found in the writings of such Jewish preachers as Isak Noa Mannheimer and Ludwig Philippson. It is even inscribed on the pulpit of the synagogue in Trier built in 1859. "Where Spirit addresses spirit let the word of God be thy soul's light" (pp. 226–27). Thousands of Jewish worshipers, Orthodox as well as Reform, were influenced weekly by such accounts of Jewish history and Jewish belief, rendered in a form and vocabulary borrowed directly from German Idealism.

The transformation, Altmann argues, was radical. Not only did the familiarity with Hebrew sources presumed by the traditional *derashah* no longer exist (p. 222). More important, "the type of piety it reflected had largely become defunct." The "halakhic ordering of the Jew's total existence" had given way to specified hours of devotional uplift. As the great preacher Siegmund Maybaum put it, once the traditional hallowing of the Sabbath was no longer practiced, rabbis sought "at least to regain a few hours of the Sabbath for edification." Yet, as Altmann reminds us, edification had become an end in itself. Religion was now located "in a state of soul" rather than a closeness to God founded on obedience to his law. Piety "now stood on its own, drawing its nourishment from the autonomy of moral Reason, the subjectivity of feeling, and the objectivity of the Idea to which the spirit was able to elevate itself" (pp. 233–34). This was a form of religious life appropriate to individuals who also now stood "on their own," defined by their exercise of "autonomous moral reason," and insisted on approaching divinity through the "subjectivity" of their own feeling.

Rebuilding the Spiritual Center

It is not surprising that this stress on subjective experience, coupled with the concept of a Diaspora mission to spread the Jewish "Idea" to all humanity, did not sit well with the Zionists. They argued the futility of Diaspora existence and the need for a return to the Jews' former homeland. More important, they tried to direct energy spent on culture and individual edification toward the objective, concrete, and national tasks involved in rebuilding Zion. Yet they too were forced to invoke the vocabulary of spirit. It served to unify a people dispersed among numerous nations and cultures as well as to unite that people with a past it had long since departed—two crucial preconditions of the Zionist enterprise. No less important, the idea of spirit helped to endow the Zionists' secular and political effort with the legitimation that came of perceived continuity with the Jewish religious tradition.

For political Zionists, of course, that tradition was not of central importance; indeed, the center into which the Diaspora poured did not have to be the Land of Israel, so long as it could serve the awesome need at hand. On this Leo Pinsker and Theodore Herzl were agreed. Among "cultural Zionists," however, the matter was very different, and in their thought—particularly that of their founding theorist, Ahad Ha'am—the role of spirit is pronounced. Several aspects of that role are examined by Ehud Luz elsewhere in this volume. Our focus here will be Ahad Ha'am's vision of renewed Diaspora communities radiating from the rebuilt homeland, which he called, significantly, the "spiritual center." That formulation, as we will see, enabled him to claim that his movement was saving Judaism at the very moment that he rejected the traditional faith and its commandments.

The theme of the spiritual center is apparent from the opening lines of Ahad Ha'am's introduction to his first collected set of essays, published in 1895. The idea of the Jewish mission, he complained, had been trumpeted in countless sermons, but had changed the lives of Jews not one iota. Now the Jewish people stood at a crossroads. One path, the status quo, could lead only to further anti-Semitism and assimilation. The path forward, to life and renewal, lay in the "concentration of the nation in Zion," lately undertaken by the movement called *Hibbat Ziyyon,* "Love of Zion." Redemption of the Land of Israel, however, had to begin with redemption of the soul of the people of Israel. Work on the soil would be fruitless, Ahad Ha'am contended, unless the nation's "spirit" had first been freed from its inner bonds, and this process involved a psychic "concentration of the spirit," the provision of a "center for the spirit" (*merkaz ha-ruah*), directly parallel to the larger project of building the "spiritual center" in Zion. Such concentration of the spirit was a known psychological phenomenon, he wrote. It consisted in "a particular spiritual matter in the depths of the soul gaining predominance over all other affairs, until it succeeds, imperceptibly, in uniting all of them around itself, in making them subservient to its purpose, and in changing the characters of all in accordance with its need." What was possible for one person was not impossible for the "spirit of the nation," but the "concentration of the people" in Zion had to be preceded by "concentration of the nation's spirit through *Hibbat Ziyyon*," which he, of course, urged (*Complete Writings*, 2).

Unequivocally, then, Ahad Ha'am linked the spiritual estate of the individual Jew with the spiritual well-being of the entire people. The former would be revived through a concentration of his or her spirit upon the single endeavor of national return to Zion—that is, upon the concentration of the people and *its* spirit in a single center. That connection was reemphasized in essays such as "The National Morality" (1899), which asserted, in Idealist terms by now familiar to us, that each people had a distinctive spirit which expressed itself in every aspect of national life—literature and language, morality and law—as well as in the heart of every healthy individual. In the West, Ahad Ha'am wrote, Jews mistakenly believed that this "spiritual inheritance" consisted of religion. In the East, however, they knew that the national spirit was not limited to faith, but extended to "spiritual obligations" such as the national renewal in Zion. Nationality was a law for life, he declared, not a leisure-time activity (pp. 159–61). The work of spirit was more pervasive than partisans of the Jewish "mission" such as Geiger could admit.

The development of the Jewish spirit, Ahad Ha'am contended, could not but be limited, even stunted, in exile. It could not import ideas from the outside, as any living culture did, lest it be overwhelmed by the foreign elements introduced. Surrounded by alien cultures, the Jewish spirit could not develop its own potential, nor could individual Jews be sure that what they did manage to create was authentically Jewish rather than mere mimicry of other cultures. "I at least know why I remain a Jew," he wrote in a polemic entitled "Slavery in the Midst of Freedom." "I am my own, and my opinions and feelings are my own. I have no reason for concealing or denying them, for deceiving others or myself." Ridiculing proponents of the Diaspora and its "mission," Ahad Ha'am concluded that he would not exchange his "spiritual freedom" for "all the emancipation in the world" (*Selected Writings*, 194).

Ahad Ha'am is "his own" because he belongs to his people. The Western Jew who looked for spirit in his own feelings or reason could not be sure that what he found there was truly Jewish—or himself. Aḥad Ha'am, who had received his spirit undiluted from the Jewish nation, could be sure of both. The self in his conception, we note, is not self-contained or self-possessing or inwardly directed. It is, rather, a national self, created in the image of Aḥad Ha'am's "godterm"—the national spirit.

The translation of religion (and the transfer of its authority) to that secular national spirit was crucial to Aḥad Ha'am's vision. In the "national morality," he sought an ideal that could provide a "guide to all the affairs of life," reach "to the depths of the heart," and "connect with all one's feelings and tendencies," as the Jewish religion had done in the age of belief now ending (*Complete Writings*, 160). Morality, along with the other elements of national culture, would no longer develop inside the framework of religion. Recognizing the centrality of faith in all of Jewish history, however, Aḥad Ha'am is provoked to ask a question that recurs in his writings. Could one be "a good atheist Jew" — "kosher" in one's nationalism but *aher* or "heretical" in "the rest of his being?" One could, he is convinced, if the national being were more than a "leisure-time activity," and this would be possible only in a national homeland (*Complete Writings*, 1160, 286, 292). Spiritual revival, we learned earlier, was a precondition for the spiritual center. The latter, conversely, was a precondition for the development and flowering of the Jewish spirit, which Aḥad Ha'am felt justified in calling *yahadut*—Judaism.

In the short term, he believed, no more than such a spiritual center was attainable. The hopes of the political Zionists for a sovereign state capable of absorbing the eastern European Jewish masses were unrealistic. Only a nucleus of settlement could be achieved, supporting the beginning of a spiritual revival and permitting the return to Palestine of the elite who would construct it. Aḥad Ha'am could simply not see the point of concentration on political goals rather than on "the lessening of, in Krochmal's term, the *ruhani*" (p. 298). All definitions of the Jewish homeland as a "center" were inherently spiritual rather than political, he argued, because such a center could not possibly exert political or economic influence on its Diaspora. He ridiculed those who claimed he had no interest in factories or commerce; the point was that Warsaw could never be an economic center of Poles around the world, no matter what its industrial output. Zion, likewise, could only strengthen the Jewish Diaspora's national consciousness, "purify" fallen spirits, and fill Jewish spiritual creativity with truly national content (pp. 393–94). The extent of the center's achievements could only be measured once it had been established. Aḥad Ha'am, paraphrasing Deuteronomy, expressed satisfaction at knowing what had already been revealed (pp. 426–28).

The concept of spirit, in sum, underlay Aḥad Ha'am's entire manifold vision. In essays that often bore the word in their titles— "The Way of Spirit," "Renewal of the Spirit," "Flesh and Spirit" —he asserted the dependence of individual on national spirit (the latter synonymous with culture, broadly understood); the need of national spirit for an environment suited to its growth; the possibility of a real connection, via spirit, among the various Jewish communities of the Diaspora, once they were centered on the national homeland; and, finally, the analogy between that shared conscious-ness—a national Jewish culture—and the faith that had sustained and united Jews for centuries. Love of Torah had been the "spiritual homeland" of the exile (p. 266). The renewed homeland would center on the spiritualized Torah of the return. We shall now turn to several twentieth-century thinkers who tried to synthesize the latter Torah with the original, Zionism with religious faith—again through conceptions of "spirit."

Gordon and Organic Nationhood

For A. D. Gordon (1856–1922), those conceptions were both indispensable and dangerous. As a man who had arrived in Palestine relatively late in life to work and wander the land, he found the priority given by some to revitalization of the Jewish spirit intolerable (though, as Ehud Luz points out in his essay, Gordon also opposed the attenuation of spirit through an exclusive emphasis on the material). At the opening of the Hebrew Univer-sity, Gordon declared that the problem of the Jewish people was not too much of either body or spirit, but the sickness of both caused by the spirit's exilic detachment from the body, its flight into the heavens. Return to the soil of Palestine offered Jews the opportunity for reunification, as well as renewed community and reconnection to the whole of being. But if life in Palestine only recreated the conditions and mentality of exile, it would be of no avail. Only if Jews returned to nature to "live more, to live nature," to "resurrect the 'I' of the nation, in nature," could the Jewish people and its individual members be saved (*Complete Writings*, 1:193–99; 348).

Gordon's experience of the Zionist Congress of 1913, he reported, was like that of a Jew at Kol Nidre—with all the ambivalence attached to "pour[ing] out his heart before God in a modern synagogue." The image is telling. For Gordon, immersion in nature was a religious act, and the enter-prise of restoring the Jews to nature a religious activity. The national awakening of Israel, he wrote, might in a former time have been called a *gillui Shekhinah*, a "revelation of God's presence." Biblical and kabbalistic language pervades Gordon's prose, lending force and a certain authenticity to his appeal. Yet Gordon is far removed from traditional faith, and he knows it. His assumptions are those of the same nineteenth-century commitment to spirit which he deplored when that commitment took the form of "galut individualism."

One sees this in his view of both nationalism and religion. The former possessed a "cosmic aspect, the spirit of nature of the nation's homeland, mixed with the spirit of the people. And this is its essence." Gordon went on to contrast true nations, which contained this cosmic dimension, with "mechanical societies" such as the United States, which possessed no independent spirit but rather drew on the national consciousness of others (p. 234). Philosophical terms such as materialism and idealism are derided for a similar reason. They are the products of "cold thought" rather than of "life" (p. 236). Gordon, connected with nature, spirit, and life, could look within himself for guidance. "I approach this collection," he wrote in the preface to a set of essays published in 1918, "not from the practical or conceptual aspect but according to the demands of the living soul" (p. 282). A similar passage, written the next year, insists that a people, like an individual, should take its direction not from mind or spirit but from *nefesh* ("soul"), immediate life which was national and vital, and should therefore "be our teacher at all times" (p. 447).

Such a statement is, of course, inconceivable in the Jewish religious tradition, which warns Jews to put fringes on their garments as a perpetual reminder of God's commandments lest they go astray by following their eyes or their heart (Num 15:39). Gordon's view of religion, predictably, is romantic. In an essay entitled "Essential and Peripheral in Religion," he writes that religion includes both the highest light of wisdom and the fruits of barbarity and wickedness. One therefore had to distinguish between the feeling of faith, the "religious relation" which precedes verbal expression, and the fixed forms of a particular tradition. The feeling was alive, eternal, in the soul, deeper than morality. The forms were too often antiquated, if only because groups were less capable of change than individuals. Gordon then observes that religious feelings, like nations (and *unlike* religious traditions, or "societies") were intrinsically connected to nature, affording access to the "tree of life" denied those who had eaten of the rational, technical "fruits" of the "tree of knowledge" (pp. 350–53).

Gordon, then, like his teacher Aḥad Haʿam, relied on the idea of spirit to revive a sick and "parasitic" Jewish people. He used the promise of spiritual vitality to entice Jews to physical rather than spiritual labor, and he emphasized the notion of a spiritual center, even while rejecting the term itself, to envision a renewed people focused on a rebuilt land. The nation as a whole could be healthy, Gordon wrote in 1920, even if only a minority returned to physical labor on the ancestral soil (p. 261); he took the metaphor of the national organism very seriously, and believed that the unifying and life-giving blood of spirit coursed through its veins. For all the Jewish elements in Gordon's lexicon, therefore, and all the declamation against foreign imports, it is Fichte and Toennies, Tolstoy and Durkheim, who prove decisive. Like Ahad Ha'am, Gordon hoped that the promise of revitalized existence through a renewed national spirit would draw Jews out of their privatism and their dispersion (the two were of course related) and pull them toward a collective effort at the center. However, enamored of romantic nationalism and romantic theology, he could confer a religious dimension on that national effort which Ahad Ha'am—far more sober and rationalist—could never claim.

Kook and the Coming of Redemption

For a traditionalist synthesis of Gordon's two vocabularies, drawing far more heavily on Jewish sources and only secondarily on German philosophy, one must turn to Rabbi Abraham Isaac Kook (1865-1935), the foremost theoretician of religious Zionism. That Kook could embrace the essentially secular Zionist project at all, let alone bless it as Palestine's chief rabbi, was only because of his kabbalistic conviction that holy Jewish "sparks" lay trapped in the Zionists' professedly atheist "husks," and awaited redemption. It was no coincidence, Kook believed, that such Jewish souls chose to rebel against tradition precisely by returning the people Israel to its holy land, thereby revitalizing the tradition. Jews were in their very essence inseparable from God. Divine Providence was at work, ever so cunningly, in their souls as in their history. God would, by means of such holy sparks in secular bodies, bring redemption in the very near future (e.g., *Hazon Ha-Ge'ulah*, 275).

It would be an exaggeration to claim that "spirit" is a prevalent motif in Kook's voluminous and lyrical writings. It is not; "holiness" and "light" are far more important. Yet the language of spirit figures centrally—and not only because the biblical phrase "holy spirit" well served Kook's purposes, as it had Spinoza's. The two vocabularies, poetically interwoven in Kook's prose, are mutually reinforcing. They make possible the legitimation in strictly traditional terms of a movement outside, and far beyond, the tradition's imagination. Kook hoped thereby to persuade the faithful that the Zionist movement deserved their support, while convincing the secular that the Jewish religious tradition was still relevant, and even compelling.

At the center of Kook's vision stands the people of Israel, once more rooted in its holy land. The unique sanctity of both the land and the people, Kook insists, is beyond rational understanding. Holiness descends to the world, to nature, via the blessed earth of Israel, thence to radiate outwards to the rest of the planet. Similarly, divine blessing spreads to all humanity from its concentration within God's "treasured people." "The spirit of the Lord and the spirit of Israel are one" (p. 70). Every aspect of the people's national life shares in the spirit: land, language, history, customs. An individual could "cut himself off" from the source of life, but the entire people could not. Nor could any other people attain to it. Israel's soul was unique. All other nations were founded on economic needs, the drive to sustain material life, and ascended from that base to their cultural achievements of order and beauty. Israel's soul, however, was founded on thirst for knowledge of God (*Orot [Lights]*, 20–22, 45, 88; *Hazon*, 76–78). No other nation required the divine idea for its very "completion." Others might participate in that idea, appearing to approach Israel's level of morality and religious devotion. Underneath, however, they remained pagan, essentially corporeal. Only Israel could receive the true faith, and therefore Jews could not survive on the "food of general culture" but had to exist as a people and a culture apart (*Orot*, 50, 58; *Hazon*, 36, 53).

Of late that survival—spiritual as well as material—had been threatened. Two thousand years of exile meant that the wells of spiritual creativity located in the Land of Israel had not been opened, because the people of Israel had not been living there. The people, without that nourishment, had seen its spiritual estate steadily decline. Moreover, in the "situation of galut," the spirit of God had departed from the nation; its penetration of the wholeness of life had been precluded. The divine had been hidden in the *miqdash me'at* ("small sanctuary") of "synagogues and study halls, family, religion and Torah" (*Orot*, 108). The world as a whole had suffered as well. Jewish law, restricted in its application to a narrow sphere, had tended to rigidify. Faith in general had turned brittle and was only now undergoing a cleansing impelled by rampant disbelief (*Orot*, 126). The secular *Zeitgeist* was attacking all humanity, Kook wrote, and had even claimed some Jewish souls. The latter, however, being closer to the light, to the fountain of life, had put up stronger resistance (*Orot*, 100). Jewish eyes would soon be opened to God's truth. Indeed, the secular Zionist movement had supplied the precondition for that awakening. When it occurred, Israel would produce a "spiritual center" which would reveal the divine idea to all the world, and in which all the nations of the world would rejoice (*Hazon*, 74, 113, 116).

Kook had no illusions about secular nationalism, no inclination to march under its banners of world-historical mission and national spirit. Nationalism, he asserted in a typically eclectic set of images, was wild, ugly, and materialist, sustained only by a spark of light of which nationalism itself was unaware because the spark was hidden under a surface of filth (*Orot*, 107). Yet because Kook believed in the providential ordering of history and the unique, irrevocable holiness of Israel, he could support the Jewish national movement and see positive elements in other nationalist movements, as part of a cosmic wholeness in which all opposites were reconciled. Kook was able to "embrace the Zionist project with an affection of soul that knows no bounds" (*Hazon*, 278), confident that its holy essence would soon overpower and break out of the secular vessel. German Idealist visions of spirit are similarly absorbed and made to serve, though at times the imports seem to get the upper hand: the exaltation of the First World War as leading to the deepening of national character and the coming of redemption; the assertion that once the Jewish people had been restored to wholeness on its land, its writers would be made holy—and know that this had occurred (*Orot*, 13–15, 82). Usually, however, the modern vocabulary is subsumed under the imagery of Nahmanides, Yehudah Halevi, and the Kabbalah generally, which permitted Kook to claim the triumph of the secular Zionist movement as a victory for God's spirit, the long-awaited arrival of redemption.

I believe that Kook's vision has proven so compelling to religious nationalists because of his union of the two vocabularies; to such a "marriage of true minds" one could not wish to "admit impediments." Kook's sociology of the modern world is far from superficial; his psychology of faith as deep as Kierkegaard's. His translation of both into theology therefore enjoys prima facie credibility. Kook, like Krochmal, wishes to save a tradition under historicist attack, by deploying a larger "historical" perspective which surrounds that attack, comprehending it. Like Ahad Ha'am, he seeks to discredit a vision of spirit limited to the private sphere of "synagogue and study hall, family and religion," by comparing it with the larger promise of wholeness achievable through nationalist commitment. Messianic energy is permitted to transfuse a secular project. Nonbelievers are to be disarmed by an ally who speaks their language and contains it within another, while the pious are to be reassured that religion remains an essential aspect of national spirit. In speaking the language of the latter, therefore, they discoursed in a tongue no less pleasing to God.

Buber and the Spirit of Israel

Jews not committed to either the Zionist project or the traditional faith have found the synthesis of vocabularies effected by Martin Buber (1878–1965) more inviting, even though Buber wrote as an ardent Zionist and a man who had experienced encounter with a personal God. Buber's religious Zionism, as we will see, excluded neither Diaspora Jews nor non-believers, and again the instrument of that appeal was "spirit" and "spirituality." Buber's early writings overflow with this terminology. Judaism is described as a spiritual process striving for elemental unity, as against the exilic predominance of barren intellect (*On Judaism*, 40). Spirit was one and indivisible; nations generally sought to avoid its commands, but could flourish only by subordinating themselves to it; in spirit lay the seed of true national life (p. 136). Spirit was the "prophetic teacher of faithfulness and renewal" (p. 146). Only if Jewish nationalism became a spiritual force would it endure (p. 141). Zionism represented the work of spirit insofar as it sought to restore wholeness to Jewish selves divided by the conditions of exile. The spirit "must determine, must command." Its laws were the laws of the soil (pp. 144–47).

In Buber's mature works, beginning with *I and Thou* (1923), "spirit" plays two roles. On the one hand, Buber continues to use the word liberally and conventionally. He speaks of the "history of spirit" and the "court of [one's own] spirit" (*Knowledge of Man*, 122, 126). He complains that Kant, unlike Plato, had lost faith in the spirit's ability to remain pure after achieving power (*Israel and the World*, 104). He features the word prominently in the titles of his essays: "Israel and the Command of the Spirit" (1958), "The Spirit of Israel and the World of Today" (1939). Yet as in the work of Buber's teacher Ahad Ha'am, the titles betray the importance of a conception of spirit which is both nuanced and taken with utmost seriousness. Thus, Buber defines spirit, in 1934, as follows:

> Man's totality that has become consciousness, the totality which comprises and integrates all his capacities, powers, qualities and urges. . . . Spiritual life is nothing but the existence of man, insofar as he possesses true human conscious totality which is not the result of development; it goes back to the origin of mankind, though it may unfold differently in different individuals.

In his own time, Buber adds, the word had come to mean something very different: that part of human thinking, the "greedy intellect," which had come to regard "totality as something alien," and to be removed from "organic vitality"; the "spirit turned into a homunculus" (*Israel*, 175).

Buber's definition incorporates human culture but is not restricted to it; as in Krochmal, and indeed in Hegel, culture points beyond itself to its own inspiriting force. That force remains eternally present in all that culture creates and animates every human being to strive for wholeness and his or her own fulfilment. In serving that which was "highest" in us, Buber wrote, we served spirit, and Jews, more than others, knew that spirit was not an activity of inner-directed contemplation or perfection but "that power which hallows the world" (*Israel,* 180).

This is the central point of Buber's entire vision. Like Kant, Buber divided the world into two worlds: the realm of space and time, of subject and object, in which we know what can be known about our world; and a second realm, in which true knowledge of others and God, as well as ourselves, can be found, and in which we relate to others as ends in themselves, through the wholeness of our beings. Buber's insistence that the latter "I-Thou" realm exists only in the present (not in memory, or hope) and only outside of all subject–object knowledge would seem to effect a radical disjunction between the two worlds. Yet he emphasized again and again that we emerge from the experience of "I-Thou" wholeness acutely sensitive to the demand that the "I-It" world be overhauled in keeping with the nature of that experience. The world as we know it through our minds, in other words, is not the world as we knew it in "I-Thou" experience, in large part because the former has not yet been penetrated by the latter, restructured so as to facilitate "I-Thou" encounters rather than to preclude them. The Bible is humanity's most profound text, Buber believed, because it "bears witness" with greater clarity than any other to the demand that all of life be transformed, insofar as this is possible for human creatures, into the "noumenal" self and world known only through I-Thou encounter.

Buber calls this demand the "spirit's will to perfection" (*Israel,* 241); it is, he writes elsewhere, "spirit in search of its own reality" (p. 180). Jews were more aware than others of this truth, more responsive to its commands, because their very existence as a nation was bound up in "religious" commitments born of a collective encounter with God, "the Eternal Thou," at Sinai. They had, in addition, recently approached realization of the biblical vision, in the Hasidic communities whose tales Buber sought to translate for a modern audience. Buber's Zionism, too, was founded on this understanding of the demands of the spirit. The Jewish people, restored to its soil in a renewed commitment to wholeness and community, would once again be able to serve "the spirit of Israel—that living truth which is not in our possession but by which we can be possessed, which is not dependent upon us but we upon it . . . the spirit of fulfilment (*Israel,* 185).

The Kantian dualism of phenomenal and noumenal, which underlies Buber's own depiction of a "twofold world," of course bears a strong resemblance to earlier dichotomies of temporal and eternal, material and spiritual. That similarity enables Buber to shift easily from talk of "the spirit," as in the sentence above, to his preferred language of dialogue and relation. The realm beyond space and time in which human beings are whole and relate to others as ends in themselves rather than as instruments of their ends or objects of their experience is the realm that other conceptions—and Buber himself—know as spirit. Buber was aware of the dangers of the latter vocabulary: the "use of this term [spirit] as a kind of metaphorical mask for our own egoism" (*Israel*, 193); the detachment of "spirit" from everyday life and institutions through a "spurious" idealism and realism (*Israel*, 90). Yet the conception was indispensable to him, for many of the same reasons that had rendered it essential to previous modern Jewish thinkers. It permitted him, as it had Geiger, to embrace the belief in revelation and the unique character of the Bible, without accepting the Bible as the content of revelation or its laws as binding. Like Ahad Ha'am and Gordon, Buber could denounce "religion" as the barrier to "religiosity" or "spirit" (*On Judaism*, 80–81) and believe that a "Hebrew Humanism" elevated above petty nationalism by the "spirit of Israel" could avoid the temptations of power and *Realpolitik*. At the very same moment, he could maintain, like Krochmal and Kook, that "Israel is not a nation like other nations, no matter how much its representatives have wished it during certain eras." Its chosenness was "not the mythical shape of a people's wishful dreams" (*Israel*, 248–250). Israel was uniquely constituted to serve—and transmit—the Spirit, because, as Krochmal had believed, its history had been uniquely (if indirectly) supervised by God.

Contemporary Strategies of "Spirit"

I have not, of course, attempted a comprehensive summary of the thinkers examined above, much less of modern Jewish thought as a whole, but only a survey designed to illustrate the centrality within that corpus of the conceptions and vocabulary of spirit. In its various connotations—as "culture" or "essence"; as a purposive force moving through individuals and nations, or the inspiration, in some sense divine, which raises each of us to the highest of which we are capable; as the soul or character unique to a given person or nation, or the defining preoccupations of an age; as the antinomy of "mere" form, or letter, or dross; as Reason in general, or a particular idea such as monotheism—"spirit" has proved malleable enough to serve both traditionalists and reformers, Zionists and partisans of a Diaspora "mission." It helped to integrate the Jews within larger cultures and political movements, as well as to preserve their distinctiveness as the special bearers and purveyors of an Idea destined for all. Spirit became the locus of a life beyond everyday concerns and above the reach of alienating institutions, even as it held out the hope that those institutions could be transformed according to its dictates—whether in Palestine or elsewhere. I would like, in conclusion, to turn to a discussion of contemporary strategies of Jewish commitment, derived from those already examined, which continue to rely to a greater or lesser degree on the conceptions of spirit encountered above. Those conceptions have been further refined, over the course of the century, to suit the needs of defenders of faith better acquainted than their predecessors with both modernity's challenges and its limitations.

One strategy, rarely employed as such by Jewish thinkers in our day, is the debunking of scientific claims to absolute truth, an effort Peter Berger has well dubbed "relativizing the relativizers." One could argue, following students of science such as Thomas Kuhn, that science too is merely one way of looking at things among others. Its account of creation or the solar system, therefore, is no more entitled to our prima facie assent than that of Genesis or its medieval interpreters.[5] Rather than resort to this extreme relativization, Jewish thinkers have generally opted for the strategy, pioneered by Kant, which we have already observed in Buber. Faith did not need to contest science, because it took place in an entirely separate realm. Space, time, objectivity, subject-object knowledge, all lay within the limits of the "I-It" world. Lived immediacy and relationships, including our relation to the Eternal You, occurred in the other world of "I-Thou." The Orthodox thinker Joseph Soloveitchik employs a similar strategy when he contrasts two aspects of human personhood called Adam I and Adam II after the Bible's two varying accounts of our creation. Adam I, characterized by "majesty" and "dignity," seeks to control and order the world. Adam II, who stands in wonder before the world, enters into convenantal relationship with other human beings (i.e., Eve) as well as with God. Both aspects are divinely willed, both a gift of God; indeed, we are commanded to use the knowledge gained through science for the improvement of God's world. Yet the two are in conflict, particularly in the modern era. If faith had atrophied in the face of scientific progress, it was because science had trespassed in a realm where it had no legitimate place. Kept within bounds it was not an enemy, but a necessary (if troublesome) ally (Soloveitchik, "The Lonely Man of Faith," 5–27, 55–65).

Such separation between the phenomenal and noumenal realms is commonplace in modern Jewish thought, a strategy that reasons from the premise that Genesis had never intended a "scientific" account of creation to the conclusion that Darwin, Einstein, and Freud could pose no threat to Jewish belief. The dichotomy on which such thinkers depend, as we have seen, derives from the older division of matter and spirit and is saved from the dualism of the latter conceptions by the idea that spirit pervades the entire life of any healthy body, individual or national. "Majesty" is redeemed by "covenant," secular nationalism by the "spark" of holiness, culture by its indwelling spirit. Such strategists of faith separate spirit from body, as it were, in order to save spirit from decomposition in a harsh climate. At the same time, however, they insist that we try to unite the two, in order to achieve a healthy human culture and/or carry out God's will. In this way the most obvious challenge posed by "modernization"—the scientific project to master the world for the benefit of the species—can be parried if not entirely neutralized.

A second and related strategy, likewise emerging in reaction to Kant, locates religion in another realm apparently immune to historical or philosophical analysis: the emotions. Schleiermacher's argument to faith's "cultured despisers" in 1799 has been of great use to Jewish thinkers throughout the modern period, as we have noted. Religion was to be protected by redefinition: it was not belief or ritual or even ethics, but a feeling of oneness with the whole of being or, as Schleiermacher later put it, a feeling of absolute dependence. Such emotion was prior to belief or practice devised to explain or recapture it; unlike the latter, therefore, it was invulnerable to philosophical critique or historicist reduction. Buber not surprisingly paraphrases entire passages of F. Schleiermacher's *Speeches* in *I and Thou.* Abraham Heschel, far more traditionalist, spends much of his work attempting to evoke in his readers the feelings of awe and wonder which he hoped would lead them beyond the bounds of reason to the "ineffable" domain of faith. We must "leave the shore of the known" because "our mind is like a fantastic seashell, and when applying our ear to its lips we hear a perpetual murmur from the waves beyond the shore." The problem, having been grasped by the demand of that mystery, was how to "tell it to our minds" (Heschel, *Man Is Not Alone,* 8, 71).

Berger has termed this the "inductive" approach to faith, which seeks to elicit belief by pointing to "signals of transcendence" which even nonbelievers recognize in the world. The underlying assumption of the approach is quite traditional: there is a faculty within the self that responds to stimuli provided by a corresponding faculty, the source of our own—the divine. Yet the focus of the conception has shifted in our period from a transcendent God or realm to the incarnation of spirit in a culture or an individual self. Jews were not bound to a set of obligations promulgated, for eternity, by the source of spirit, but bound themselves to temporal forms determined, as Altmann put it, by "the autonomy of moral Reason, the subjectivity of feeling." Soloveitchik and Heschel, like Krochmal, seek to justify the former commitment in terms acceptable to the latter sensibility.[6] Buber does not. The problem with this strategy is that the gap between wonder and "signals of trancendence," on the one side, and God and his commandments, on the other, cannot be bridged but only leaped. The sort of experience of God so basic to Heschel's belief, and even Buber's, derives from a world unavailable to most contemporary Jews, one not yet disturbed by the forces against which these defenders of the faith must contend.

A third strategy, adumbrated in Krochmal's *Guide,* refined by Ahad Ha'am, and brought to full articulation by Mordecai Kaplan in America, has attempted to fill that breach. The two halves of this strategy are both indebted to conceptions of spirit by now familiar to us: the substitution of culture for faith as the locus where spirit may be found, and the related acceptance of traditional beliefs and observances as symbolic representations, true and compelling in, and not despite, that very symbolism. Krochmal, we recall, had discerned the *ruhani* at work in the creation of Israel's sacred texts and thereby enabled his readers to find it there when they could no longer locate it in the world around them. Ahad Ha'am, disturbed that spirit in such a guise would become the mere object of leisure-time pursuit, sought a renewed national existence pervaded in its every aspect by a national culture removed from Jewish faith. Kaplan finally concluded that this rendering of *Judaism as a Civilization* could serve Diaspora communities as well as the spiritual center. Such communities would be held together precisely because they shared in the nourishment that such shared "civilization" could provide. Jews who lived among Gentiles could be Jews nonetheless, because of their participation in a Jewish culture. One notes how directly, and elegantly, this strategy responds to the three challenges which we identified. The *kehillah* could be recreated, even in America, animated by the national spirit which it would protect and develop through its institutions. Jews could accept, as that which most truly defined them, an identity that would necessarily remain fragmentary and be uninvolved in most of their daily activities. The challenge of science, second, could be neutralized. Judaism was whatever set of beliefs and practices a particular community of Jews defined as such, these beliefs and practices being symbolic vessels into which new meaning could be poured. Kaplan's "god-concept," he believed, captured the spirit of Jewish tradition without conflicting with any of the tenets of modern science. The autonomous self, finally, was to be embraced and persuaded to join in God's work of ordering the world. From here it was but one short step to the notion of civil religion which Kaplan advocated, or even the equation of spirit with a *conscience collective* that was entirely without divine origin or guidance—a viewpoint which Kaplan deplored.

As I have tried to show in a separate study,[7] an essential element of this strategy has been a shift in the language of religious thought, from a "theology" of rigorously formulated and interrelated concepts to an "ideology" composed of imagery, metaphor, hyperbole and even self-contradiction —all the normal devices of rhetoric. Rabbis invoked chosenness, exile,

Messiah and other traditional ideas as symbols meant to be grasped in their resonances, making sense of a situation otherwise incomprehensible rather than as logically expounded concepts to be believed in or denied. They thereby enabled their congregants to reach for affirmations that exceeded the grasp of their beliefs. This enterprise was conceptually possible, I believe, because nineteenth-century thinkers such as Geiger and even Krochmal had claimed in good faith, as had Hegel, that the two sorts of affirmation were essentially the same. Symbolic truth was truth; indeed, as many traditional thinkers had argued, it was the only truth that religion could supply. Images such as chosenness, then, were vessels for God's spirit, as were all the elements of culture. Knowing that, we could cleave through them to the source of spirit, especially when, as in the twentieth century, history seemed to confirm the truth to which the symbols pointed. Israel was chosen: this one knew, even if one did not accept the fact of Sinai. Jewish civilization and the community which it infused, one believed, were the location at which spirit now resided, the place where spirit could be found, even if the faith which had once defined both the civilization and the community had moved "beyond belief."

In particular—and a fourth and related strategy—the focus of spiritual life has shifted for many to the reading of sacred texts, along with others who are of similar mind. The subject of these texts, as discerned by such communal readings, is often (as it is in Buber) the nature of community itself. That which is most lacking in the modern *Gesellschaft,* according to the social theorists whose work Buber knew well, is precisely what he defines as the precondition of religious faith and the subject of sacred texts: relation, encounter, community. In the Land of Israel, one could seek to refashion an entire society in accordance with one's "I-Thou" experiences; in the Diaspora, one could seek refuge from "I-It" institutions in the "small and intimate circles" where, Weber predicted, spirit would now be sought. It is no coincidence, surely, that Buber's principal legacy is his selective reading of the two sets of Jewish texts where, he believed, spirit was now most discernible: the Bible and Hasidic tales. The traditional activity of scriptural exegesis becomes, in his reworking, the study of the words of human beings, who unlike most of their modern descendants, believed they had heard God's word directly. The antitraditional nature of such a reading becomes clear when we recall Buber's insistence that the divine "word" could only exist metaphorically. God communicated only presence and demand, not content. He left formulation of his word to the individual who had encountered him, leaving the individual safely in control of his or her experience. A wide variety of texts has been employed by other thinkers to similar purpose, no less repositories of the spirit than the Bible—precisely as Krochmal and Spinoza had maintained.

Small wonder that the Zionists and the Orthodox, for quite differing reasons, have found this understanding of Jewish faith unacceptable and inauthentic. Gordon argued that such notions of spirit were false, because ethereal, and needed literal grounding in labor upon the soil, the context of a complete national existence. His contemporary Israeli followers, making a similar point, "negate the diaspora" which, in their view, promotes the creativity of individual Jews at the expense of communal Jewish life and culture. Soloveitchik, for his part, has condemned the confinement of religious life to a "Temple," and devoted his energies to an account, in the vocabulary of modern philosophy, of life ordered according to halakhah ("The Man of Halakhah," 142–43). The two critiques merge in Kook's religious Zionism: a conceptual synthesis politically troublesome to those wary of its messianism, and religiously problematic to those who believe that the union of religion and state power has corrupted both, but especially the former. In theory, then, modern Jewish thinkers have called for the joining of "body" and "spirit," but in practice they have often preferred the degree of separation first urged, in our period, by Mendelssohn.

The final strategy that we shall examine here occupies a theological and political middle ground between the poles of separation and union of body and spirit which we have just noted. Spirit is not located in divine revelation on the one hand or culture on the other, but in the method and content of *tradition*. Geiger had erred, according to this view, in attempting to distill an essence of belief and practice from the sum total bequeathed to him by previous generations. No less had Orthodox thinkers erred in equating tradition with the particular, if extensive, set of texts and commandments which they held to be revealed or inspired. Rather, in keeping with the approach of Krochmal shared by the historian Heinrich Graetz and, more recently, by the philosopher Franz Rosenzweig, one should regard tradition as a process. Potential adaptations were to be judged according to whether they continued or disrupted that process; the theological question of whether a particular belief or observance was legitimate could be replaced by the essentially sociological question of whether or not it preserved the framework of Jewish life. That framework was composed by the history of what Jewish communities had said and done in the past—in other words, by Jewish tradition.

The clearest articulation of this strategy comes in an essay by Gershom Scholem entitled "Revelation and Tradition as Religious Categories in Judaism." Any tradition, Scholem writes, faces the problem of combining "spontaneity" with "that which is given."[8] Most traditions solved that problem by denying it: innovating—often radically—while pretending not to change a thing; deriving the authority for such alteration, or even the alteration itself, from the original revelation (in this case, from Sinai). Yet the sages of the Talmud had enough self-consciousness to tell the tale of Moses transported to the study hall of Rabbi Akiba, where Moses cannot understand a word. Only when Akiba traces his teaching to the Torah "given Moses at Sinai" is Moses' anxiety relieved. In another famous tale, a heavenly voice interrupts a rabbinic dispute to pronounce in favor of one of the parties and is declared out of order. God's Torah had already been given over to humanity. It was therefore subject to rational deliberation and decision. Kabbalists, similarly, sought to explain how two conflicting inter-pretations of God's law could both be accepted as flowing from the same divine fountain; "these and these are the words of the living God."

Recall Michael Sachs's explanation of his traditionalist innovations in nineteenth-century Germany: appropriation of the spirit which had animated one's ancestors conferred "the freedom of the Jewish spirit in any age to mold the past in the image of the present" and, presumably, vice versa. It was not so much a case of preserving the spirit by altering the letter as, in the words of Scholem's midrash, of adorning the existing letters without causing them to become blurred or confused with others. The historian or sociologist could argue more cogently than nineteenth-century opponents of Reform that the Jewish calendar and the Hebrew language were basic to the framework of Jewish tradition, and as such were non-negotiable. They could also, however, justify secular use of that language or changes in the observance marked by that calendar as consonant with the preservation of the framework. If the Jewish spirit that had created these cultural essentials was to remain vital, innovation within the bounds of tradition was not merely permissible but necessary. This was the first law of spirit, axiomatic to its historian or sociologist. Having accepted that law, the three challenges to faith which have concerned us could be accommodated, and so survived.

Conclusion: Spirit *"in pianissimo"*

Time will tell whether the proponents of these and similar strategies are correct or whether we must accept Weber's verdict that in a world dis-enchanted the options are limited to returning to the old faith, intellectual sacrifice in hand, or resolute perseverance without faith, perhaps while studying it or mourning its departure. Whatever the truth may be, dis-enchantment with the predicament that Weber so well described has given new impetus to the searches after spirit that we have recounted. The very difficulties posed to relation and commitment by the sovereign modern self have only increased the search for *Personlichkeit* and made its rare sightings seem all the more precious. "Other forces than science," including *Religionswissenschaft*, have their say in the outcome of such quests, as Weber observed; other factors than ideas have certainly played a part in forcing Jewish thinkers to join the search and defining what it is they have looked for.

Yet the single idea of spirit has played a remarkable role: facilitating Jewish adaptation to the modern order and helping Jews to defy or escape it, enriching vocabularies of faith overwhelmed by rationalization and suffering the inevitable trivialization that comes of such routine usage. The spirit which one contemporary observer has found in our churches ("You have the Spirit!")[9] is not Plato's or Spinoza's or Hegel's. Yet it serves, a symbolic reminder of its former self, "welding together" intimate circles, "*in pianissimo.*"

Notes

1. Peter Berger, *The Sacred Canopy* (Garden City, NY: Doubleday, 1969) 106.
2. Ibid., 108.
3. My analysis of Krochmal is greatly indebted to the dissertation in progress at Columbia by Jay Harris, "An Attempt at the Integration of Tradition and Modernity: Nachman Krochmal's *Guide to the Perplexed of the Time.*
4. A. Altmann, "The New Style of Preaching in Nineteenth-Century German Jewry," in *Essays in Jewish Intellectual History*, 190–92, 205.
5. Indeed, such an approach is precisely that taken in a paper circulated some years ago under the imprimatur of the Lubavitcher *rebbe.* — ED.
6. See Soloveitchik's statement of intention: "Whatever I am about to say is to be seen only as a modest attempt on the part of a man of faith to interpret his spiritual perceptions and emotions in modern theologico-philosophical categories" ("The Lonely Man of Faith," 10).
7. See the bibliography below for representative works of Kaplan and for my own study of American Jewish thought, the basis of the generalizations offered here.
8. G. Scholem, "Revelation and Tradition as Religious Categories in Judaism," in *The Messianic Idea in Judaism*, 282.
9. Richard Reeves, "America's Journey," *New Yorker* April 12, 1982, p. 54.

Bibliography

Ahad Ha'am, *Complete Writings* [Hebrew]. Jerusalem: Jewish Publishing House, Ltd., 1965.
Altmann, Alexander. "The New Style of Preaching in Nineteenth-Century German Jewry." Pp. 190–245 in *Essays in Jewish Intellectual History.* Hanover, NH: University Press of New England, 1981.
Berger, Peter. *The Sacred Canopy.* Garden City, NY: Doubleday, 1969.
Buber, Martin. *I and Thou.* Translated by Walter Kaufmann. New York: Scribners, 1970.
———. *Israel and the World.* New York: Schocken, 1963.
———. *Knowledge of Man.* New York: Harper Torchbooks, 1965.
———. *On Judaism.* Edited by Nahum Glatzer. New York: Schocken, 1972.

Geiger, Abraham. "A General Introduction to the Science of Judaism." In *Abraham Geiger and Liberal Judaism*, 149–54. Edited by Max Weiner. Philadelphia: Jewish Publication Society, 1962.
———. *Judaism and Its History.* Translated by Charles Newburgh. New York: Bloch, 1911.
Gordon, A. D. *Complete Writings, Vol. I.* [Hebrew] Jerusalem: World Zionist Organization, 1952.
Heschel, Abraham. *Man Is Not Alone.* New York: Harper and Row, 1966.
Kook, Abraham Isaac. *Hazon Ha-ge'ulah [The Vision of Redemption].* Jerusalem: Association for Publishing the Works of the Chief Rabbi A. I. Kook, 1941.
———. *Orot [Lights].* Jerusalem: Mossad Ha-rav Kook, 1975.
Krochmal, Nachman. *Guide for the Perplexed of the Time.* In *The Writings of Nachman Krochmal.* Edited by Simon Rawidowicz. [Hebrew] Waltham: Ararat Publishing Society, 1961.
Mendelssohn, Moses. *Jerusalem.* New York: Schocken, 1969.
Nietzsche, Friedrich. *Genealogy of Morals.* Translated by Walter Kaufmann. New York: Vintage, 1969.
———. *Thus Spake Zarathustra.* In *The Portable Nietzsche.* Edited and translated by Walter Kaufmann. New York: Vintage, 1969.
Reeves, Richard. "American Journey." In *The New Yorker,* April 12, 1982. Pp. 53–64.
Scholem, Gershom. "Revelation and Tradition as Religious Categories in Judaism." In *The Messianic Idea in Judaism,* 282–303. New York: Schocken, 1971.
Soloveitchik, Joseph B. *"Ish Ha-halakhah" [Halakhic Man].* In *Be-sod Ha-yahid Ve-ha-yahad,* 39–130. Edited by Pinchas Peli. Jerusalem: Orot, 1976.
———. "The Lonely Man of Faith." *Tradition* (Summer, 1965) 5–67.
Spinoza, Benedict de. *A Theologico-Political Treatise.* Translated by R. H. M. Elwes. New York: Dover, 1951.
Weber, Max. *The Protestant Ethic and the Spirit of Capitalism.* Translated by Talcott Parsons. New York: Scribners, 1958.
———. "Science as a Vocation." In *From Max Weber,* 129–56. Edited by Hans Gerth and C. Wright Mills. New York: Oxford University Press, 1969.

10

Law and Sacrament: Ritual Observance in Twentieth-Century Jewish Thought

PAUL MENDES-FLOHR

For Nathan Rotenstreich
Is wisdom in the aged
And understanding in the long-lived?
With him are wisdom and courage;
His are counsel and understanding.
Job 12:12–13 (JPS)

HEIR TO THE AGGRESSIVE HUMANISM of previous generations, twentieth-century Western culture is incontestably secular. God and the religiously sacred have been effectively banished from the most significant areas of public life.[1] Yet this culture that has lost the presence of the divine has witnessed ever since the turn of the century a markedly renewed interest in spirituality and, correspondingly, a quest for religious experience that is intensely personal, indeed often mystical.[2] In a culture where "religious experience is perhaps less available than ever before," as Louis Dupré has recently observed, "this inward trend" may seem paradoxical. But precisely because the public realm is bereft of the divine, as Dupré astutely explains, for the modern *homo religiosus* "there is nowhere to turn but inwardly," to the inner precincts of one's most personal experience.[3] Moreover, with the vastly diminished authority of positive religion in the lives of most denizens of Western culture, obedience to the external, formal aspects of religious faith is no longer self-evident;[4] the once indisputable authority of religious tradition has had to abdicate to personal, subjective "experience" — or at least an appreciation of the possibilities of such an experience[5]—as the ultimate arbiter of the existential (and thus *personal*) significance of any particular religious tradition.

Hence, the modern *homo religiosus* who desires to ground his spiritual quest in a positive religious tradition—and, we should add, who is not prepared to withdraw from the modern world and undergo a mental lobotomy, violently excising all traces of a modern sensibility—must perforce live with a certain and perhaps irresolvable tension between the need for spiritual interiority and the external requirements and practices of his "chosen" religious tradition.[6] For Jews, such a decision to ground their spiritual quest in the tradition of their ancestors entails an especially acute problem, specifically with respect to the nature of the *miẓwot,* or commandments, of Judaism. For many modern Jews, the problem has been largely defined by Kant's characterization of Judaism as a "heteronomous" religion of law and vapid ritualism and *ergo* a false faith that fails to promote not only true service to God but also human dignity.

The Onerous Legacy of Kant

Kant's critique of Judaism has its roots in Spinoza's depiction of the religion of Israel as a grand strategy to maintain through a quasi-legal structure of ritual obligations Jewish patriotism in exile.[7] At a deeper stratum of Western consciousness, Kant's conception of Judaism also seems to reflect the Pauline dichotomy between the Christian *kerygma* of love and the Hebrew Torah of law. In certain measure, the significance of Kant's conception of Judaism may be understood as giving a systematic, coherent articulation to these philosophical and theological antagonisms so basic to the Western perception of Judaism.[8] The ultimate impact of Kant's views, however, is undoubtedly to be explained by the prominent role his analysis of Judaism played in the development of his notion of a rational moral religion—a conception of religious faith and duty that captured the imagination of the emerging bourgeoisie and has since become until this very day a vital feature of the Western experience.[9]

Kant's view of religion was an extension of his analysis of moral consciousness. The key category for both his understanding of morality and religion was "autonomy"—the individual's ability and prerogative for "self-rule" through the exercise of reason and conscience. He conceived of autonomy as humankind's liberation from its millennial and demeaning bondage to "heteronomy"—the ultimately "self-incurred tutelage" of the individual to the arbitrary sanctions and authority of others.[10] One of the most insidious forms of heteronomy, in Kant's judgment, was evident in obedience to divine commandments simply because some external authority—Holy Writ, the church, tradition—demanded such obedience. Heteronomous obedience, Kant taught, vitiates and falsifies genuine service to God; the will of God can only be followed autonomously. Indeed, Kant insisted, properly conceived religion can only be an inward reality in which faith in God constitutes a trust in the ultimate efficacy and promise of the moral law. Because this faith is, he argued, consistent with the considerations of reason it is to be deemed a "rational faith."[11] Further, Kant averred, the only way to knowledge of God is through the autonomous realm of moral conscience or, as he preferred to call it, "practical reason." Thus, for Kant authentic divine service was synonymous with heeding the "rational" promptings of moral conscience, and "everything which apart from the moral way of life, man believes capable of doing to please God," such as prayer and ritual, must be regarded as mere "religious delusion," utterly irrelevant to genuine *devotio*.[12]

Following the pristine example of Christ's moral piety, the church, according to Kant, is beholden to a vision of a moral kingdom of God on earth. Kant further discerned a gradual but inexorable transition from a *visible* church, with a "statutory" liturgy and ritual to an *invisible* church in which obedience to God's moral laws will be "purely inward," that is, guided by the moral ideal of Jesus and the autonomous principles of practical reason, accessible to every rational person. In stark contrast to the church, Judaism exemplifies for Kant a heteronomous religion par excellence. Specifically, he held that, lacking a constitutive moral ideal analogous to Jesus, Judaism does not direct its members to serve God through moral duties but rather demands of them a tedious array of ritual and liturgical acts.[13] As a heteronomous religion that knows only ritual and prayer, according to Kant, Judaism is indeed no religion at all, but a pseudo-religion.[14]

Kant's indictment of Judaism was often repeated and in various formulations by any number of philosophers and theologians.[15] More significant, his critique of Judaism gained wide currency in educated discourse in general—and not simply, we must emphasize, as a pervasive bias. For notwithstanding the prejudices and misconceptions that inform his image of Judaism, the overall thrust of his critique was consistent with his conception of religion and morality. Thus for anyone accepting the premises of the critique it had prima facie a compelling validity: Judaism is, after all, in its classical expression undeniably a religion of rigorously prescribed—that is, heteronomous—religious practices (*miẓwot*). In this context it is perhaps apposite to note with Alasdair MacIntyre that in the light of Kant's decisive role in shaping the modern consciousness, for many "who have never heard of philosophy, let alone Kant, morality is roughly what Kant said it was."[16] Indeed, Kant's rejection of heteronomy in all its manifestations, especially moral and religious, has become a deeply ingrained aspect of the modern sensibility.

Ha'ol: A Jerusalem Circle of Religious Intellectuals

The abiding influence of the Kantian perspective on the sensibility of twentieth-century Jews, especially when considering the nature of their ancestral faith may be illustrated by a hitherto unpublished protocol of a group of young Zionist intellectuals who met in Jerusalem at the end of the thirties to discuss the possibilities of a "living" relationship to the tradition of Israel. Their meetings were initiated by a former American rabbi, Judah L. Magnes (1877-1948), who became in 1925 the first chancellor of the Hebrew University. Magnes envisioned the meetings as laying the foundation of a new religious society; in the proposed program, which he drafted in early 1939, Magnes suggested calling the society *mevaqshey panekha* ("those who seek Thy Face").[17] Explaining the name, an allusion to Psalm 24:6,[18] Magnes noted that he is referring to all those who seek the God of Israel, "those who have already found the path [to Him] and those, perhaps the great majority, who have not yet found the path—who knows if they ever will, although their search for the path is the deepest, most burning desire of their lives."[19] Magnes tellingly adds that the search is guided by "faith and theology but *not* religion." For "when one says 'religion,' one implies that the path has already been found, and you are already committed to the official articles and beliefs [of a given religious tradition]."[20] Rather, the society that Magnes had in mind would address the question: "Is there any possibility of knowing God's 'Face' either by direct communication or [by means of] an authoritative tradition, or by virtue of His deeds?"

Among those responding to Magnes's call were several colleagues at the Hebrew University, each of whom was to make a distinctive contribution to the renaissance of Jewish thought and scholarship in this century: Yitzhak Fritz Baer (1888-1979), Shmuel Hugo Bergman (1883-1975), Martin Buber (1878-1965), Julius Guttmann (1880-1950), Gershom Scholem (1897-1982), and Ernst Akiva Simon (b. 1899). The one extant protocol of their meetings is from a session of 13 July 1939 (or, according to the Hebrew date given in the protocol, 27 Tammuz 5699). This session was devoted to the following topic: "What is the Torah to us?" Scholem opened up with a brief statement which was then discussed by his colleagues. Given the uniqueness of this document and its significance for our discussion, we will cite it *in extenso.* Our translation from the Hebrew will by necessity reflect the truncated rhythms of the scribe's abridged transcription of the original proceedings.[21]

Scholem: The Torah is the sounding of a supernal voice that obliges one in an absolute manner. It does not acknowledge the autonomy (*autonomiah*) of the individual. To be sure, Jeremiah was promised a "Torah of the heart," but only at the end of days. The *hasidim,* in fact, did make an attempt to prepare the "Torah of the heart." A Hasidic work interprets a passage in Deuteronomy 17 [18f.] on the king of Israel—"and he shall write for himself in a book a copy of the Torah . . . , and it shall be with him, and he shall read in it all the days of his life . . ."—such that the king will read the Torah within him, that is, within himself.[22] This autonomous conception of the Torah, however, is not [at all] compatible with Traditional conception. Torah has two meanings: the designation of a path, and the transmission of something. Everything in the world, even a person, can be "Torah," but there *never* is Torah without supernal authority. The Torah is the Creator's dialogue with man, prayer is man's dialogue with the Creator. There is no Written Torah without the Oral Torah. Were we to desire to restrict the Torah to the Torah transmitted in writing, we would not be able to read even the pentateuch, but only the ten commandments. It follows that even the Torah [i.e., Scripture] is already Oral Torah. The Torah is understandable only as Oral Torah, only through its relativization. In itself it is the perfect Torah without a blemish, and only through its mediation, the Oral Torah, is it rendered intelligible.

From all this, however, it follows that [our understanding of] the Torah develops and changes, and according to its very nature it [i.e., the Torah as we understand it through the ever evolving Oral Torah] cannot be rendered a unified system. The Torah is rather a continuum of questions and answers. Nonetheless, in spite of this development, there is nothing arbitrary about it whatsoever. [Although] every generation wishes "its" Torah to be the divine voice of revelation, there is no place here for the individual's freedom of decision. In principle, therefore, Orthodoxy is correct.

But as regards ourselves, we are unable to accept the Oral Torah of Orthodoxy. Yet with respect to the Written Torah it is incumbent upon us to recall that nothing therein is in itself fixed without the exegesis of the Oral Torah. We must therefore wait for *our* own Oral Torah, which will have to be binding for us, leaving no room for free, non-authoritative decision. There is no Torah without revelation (*matan Torah*), and there is no Torah without heteronomy (*hetronomiah*), and there is no Torah without an authoritative tradition.

Buber: it is not necessary to assume that the source of Oral Torah must be in exegesis. The Oral Torah may have its source in a [single] word.

Guttmann: Scholem's position leads to utter subjectivism. According to him the Oral Torah is a function without a specific content. How can such a Torah be the possession of a collective? We must be beholden to the *content* of the [Written] Torah [i.e., the *mizwot*].

Simon: Scholem's view may be summarized thus: Had God brought us to Mount Sinai, but not given us the Torah [i.e., *miẓwot*], we should have been content (*dayyenu*).[23] [In my opinion, however], we must view the *miẓwot* as an echo of the Lord's words (*ke-hed devrey ha-gevurah*). [On the other hand], we cannot give up our autonomy. Were someone to demonstrate to me that the Oral Law understands the commandment "not to kill" as a prohibition against the killing of Jews by Jews alone, I would not accept this explanation of the commandment, and I would rely on my autonomy.

Baer: The theological question is of secondary importance. What is important is the responsibility of man before God and the organization of his life in accordance with this responsibility. This was the greatness of the Talmud. The Torah demands righteousness and justice. This is the task that lies before us: the creation of a social order that is in consonance with the Hebrew [conception of] justice. It is possible to *prepare* for the days of the Messiah. If we do not upbuild the Land [of Israel] with righteousness and justice, all is lost. This is the conclusion to be drawn from our history.

Buber: Indeed there is no messianic politics. It is impossible to say that this prepares the coming of the Messiah, and that this does not. Baer is right, however, when he implies that the deeds of men may elicit [a new] revelation—and revelation may also come from within a society. Revelation need not necessarily be transmitted through a voice; it can come by means of something, by an event.

Magnes: According to the accepted understanding, the Oral Torah is a fence around the Torah [i.e., the Written Torah and its *miẓwot*];[24] according to Scholem it is liberation from the Written Torah. This is the position of the Gospels. This position constitutes a negation of the Torah. The strength of Orthodoxy was in its commonly accepted exegesis. This is also the principle of Catholicism. Scholem's view is precisely the opposite.

Scholem: To a known degree we are all anarchists. But our anarchism is *transitional,* for we are the living example that this [our anarchism] does not remove us from Judaism. We are not a generation without *miẓwot,* but our *miẓwot* are without authority. I do not have a feeling of inferiority with respect to those who observe [the Law]. We are not less legitimate than our forefathers; they merely had a clearer text. Perhaps we are anarchists, but we oppose anarchy.

Addendum to the protocol submitted by Magnes: At the end of his lecture Scholem remarked: "I believe in God, this is the basis of my life and faith. All the rest [of Judaism] is in doubt and open to debate."

The Limits of Ethical Monotheism

It is significant that this group, which Magnes envisioned as a religious community in every respect,[25] eventually adopted the name *Ha'ol* ("The

Yoke")—an allusion to a rabbinic midrash: "Take upon yourselves the Yoke of the Kingdom of Heaven . . ." (*Sifre Deuteronomy* 32–29).[26] This consciously sententious name reflected the one, and perhaps most compelling, conviction unambiguously shared by the group, namely, that the founding moment of Judaism is the principle of ethical monotheism: that the Jewish consciousness of God is conterminous with a moral consciousness that charges Israel with the awesome and inescapable responsibility of serving as God's coworkers in the creation of a just and compassionate world order.[27] Although having its roots in classical rabbinic teachings, this particular conception of Israel's religious vocation was formulated in the nineteenth century in response to the Kantian critique of Judaism. It is not fortuitous that the conception of Judaism as a religion of ethical monotheism found its major exponents in two leading Kantian scholars, Moritz Lazarus (1824–1903) and Hermann Cohen (1842–1918).[28] At the turn of the century, the liberal German rabbi Leo Baeck (1873–1956) identified ethical monotheism as "the essence of Judaism," explaining that Judaism affirms "the relationship between man and the world in an ethical manner through the will and through the deed."[29] Such statements provided the *minimal* definition of Judaism accepted by virtually all modern Jews, from the neo-Orthodox to the non-observant.[30] The members of *Ha'ol* understood the charge, as Magnes put it, to be "servants of God,"[31] as a call to social and political activism, particularly on behalf of what they deemed to be the most exigent issue facing the Jewish community in Palestine: the need to promote Arab–Jewish rapprochement. It is not surprising that the energy was soon deflected from *Ha'ol* with its largely theological focus to more concretely political activities sponsored by other organizations, activities which in time led to the demise of Magnes's religious society.[32]

In any event, from the protocol of the meeting cited above, it is also clear that for most members of the short-lived *Ha'ol*, ethical monotheism in itself no longer provided an adequate synopsis of the Jew's duties before God. In his remarks, Scholem sought to clarify their predicament: How can the contemporary Jew estranged from Orthodoxy's conception of Torah and the duties of the Jew before God obtain a living relationship to God that is nonetheless grounded in Torah and the compelling word of God? The trouble with Orthodoxy's conception of Torah, however, is not heteronomy per se; for heteronomy, as he sternly reminded his colleagues, is inherent in the very notion of Torah *qua* the revealed word of God. The problem, which in the fragmented protocol he failed to spell out but was later to elaborate, is that the premises and teachings of the Oral Torah (i.e., the halakhic tradition) propounded by Orthodoxy were severely "undermined by historical criticism."[33] Because of our critical historical consciousness,

Orthodoxy's "system of coordinates," Scholem was convinced, must necessarily strike us as obscurantism and, indeed, as an untenable fundamentalism.[34] Orthodoxy's view of scripture as the absolute word of God that yields "an absolute system of reference, a common authoritative basis to which all further Jewish thinking can [and must] refer," could not in his judgment be uncritically accepted by the modern Jew.[35] But, alas, without Oral Torah (i.e., a tradition mediating the Written Torah) the word of God remains unintelligible. This situation, Scholem further observed, inevitably leads to a questioning of the very nature of Torah *qua* divine communication.[36] Again as he later put it, "The binding character of Revelation for a collective has disappeared. The Word of God no longer serves as a source for the definition of possible contents of a religious tradition. . . ."[37] For Jews who have lost their faith in Orthodoxy and are thus adrift without a clear understanding of what God's Torah demands of them, Scholem concluded, the halakhic regime of ritual commandments is effete. These commandments have ceased to elicit our obedience, he insisted, because they have lost for us their compelling basis as the word of God, and not primarily because we find heteronomy repugnant to our modern sensibility.[38]

Like the other members of *Ha'ol*, Scholem regarded himself as a religious person, believing firmly in the biblical God of creation, revelation (only the contents of which remained in doubt for him) and redemption.[39] In his personal practice there was, as may be anticipated from his theological position, little of traditional Jewish ritual. He said *kiddush* at the Friday night Sabbath meal, conducted a Passover *seder*, and, after a fashion, observed the Day of Atonement. He would occasionally pray; he had a great affection for the traditional prayer book (which he knew by heart), but he would do so irregularly and not necessarily at the appointed hour—and invariably alone in the privacy of his study.[40] Aside from a brief period in his youth,[41] he rarely and hesitantly attended synagogue. Yet he held Judaism to be a genuine, ongoing faith and, moreover, to be the matrix of his own struggling relationship with God. To capture this seeming paradox, he obliquely spoke of his Judaism as that of "the broken tablets" —which "still lie together with the holy tablets [of the Law] in the Ark of the Covenant. . . ."[42] These "broken tablets" are part of the "hidden" dialectic of Jewish spirituality.[43] It is this dialectic that determines the authentic shape of Jewish tradition or the oral law through which the Jew in each generation seeks to comprehend the word of God. To uncover this dialectic and quicken it anew was the true challenge Scholem saw facing his contemporaries, especially cultural Zionists, such as the members of *Ha'ol*, dedicated as they are to the renewal of Judaism.[44] In service of this, the true task of Zionism—which he counterpoised to the nihilism of the socialist *haluzim* (pioneers)[45] and the national romanticism of Ahad Ha'am (1856–1927) and his followers[46]—Scholem would dedicate his scholarship.[47]

Aside from Buber, the other members of Ha'ol did not share Scholem's resolute rejection of ritual observance. Indeed, as the protocol we have quoted indicates, they found Scholem's position, which he unapologetically called "religious anarchism," disturbing, perhaps even more so than Buber's more radical repudiation of mizwot. Scholem's anarchism was, as he emphasized, "transitional"; Buber's was not.[48] Scholem looked forward to a new Oral Torah, articulating God's authoritative, binding mizwot; for Buber, dialogue with God (and with one's fellow humans) must be unmediated, and thus it cannot countenance any form of heteronomy whatsoever. Ergo his peremptory rejection of liturgical prayer and ritual as legitimate forms of devotio. Buber's metanomian attitude, with its manifestly Kantian quality,[49] was undoubtedly more familiar and in a sense more understandable (although, to be sure, not necessarily acceptable) to his colleagues in Ha'ol than Scholem's dialectical, "transitional" anarchism.

Scholem's position clearly aroused the ire of his colleagues, who were evidently eager for a theological clarification of the nature of Torah and tradition that would allow them an affirmation, albeit qualified, of the mizwot. Magnes, the spiritus rector of Ha'ol, for instance, was a Reform rabbi who while still in America moved steadily to a position with respect to ritual observance that approximated that advocated by Conservative Judaism.[50] Theologically, however, he was decidedly uncomfortable with the pragmatic and sentimental-cum-cultural reasons marshaled by his American colleagues in support of a more traditional attitude toward the mizwot.[51] His diaries and a few published pronouncements reveal a Jew in deep struggle for a theology sanctioning a life of prayer and ritual devotion.[52] A similar inclination to tradition and theological quest was evinced by Julius Guttmann, professor of Jewish philosophy at the Hebrew University and a rabbi ordained by the famed Breslau Rabbinerseminar associated with the "historical school" of Judaism (i.e., what in contemporary America is known as the Conservative movement). Like Magnes he was deeply vexed by what he termed the "secularization of the mizwot," or the tendency to divorce the mizwot from their religious basis and to present them as a national patrimony worthy of the Jew's abiding affection and allegiance.[53] Guttmann had little patience for such a circumvention of the question of faith and the transcendent authority of the Torah. In a lecture he held before religious educators in 1943, Guttmann, however, suggested that our appreciation of the mizwot and their religious value need not await an adequate answer to these theological questions.[54] Clearly inspired by Rudolf Otto, he recommends a phenomenological approach, focusing on the quality of holiness manifest in the *miẓwot*. Accordingly, he observes, "There is a place for *miẓwot* even without a traditional belief in revelation (*torah min ha-shamayim*). For the principal reason for the *miẓwot*—the sacralization of life—remains valid": The performance of the *miẓwot*, even when their transcendent status is in doubt, endow one's life with a "feeling" of the Holy, of a sense of being in the presence of God. Guttmann conceived of the *miẓwot* as an act arousing "a religious feeling" of holiness, and he significantly adds that the *miẓwot*—at least those one might deem to be conducive to such a feeling—are freed of their "juridical dimension."[55] Shmuel Bergman and Ernst Simon, who otherwise regarded themselves as disciples of Buber, also affirmed the sacralizing quality of the *miẓwot*. They, however, were not satisfied with Guttmann's description of the feelings engendered by the *miẓwot* and adopted a more explicitly theocentric view, regarding ceremonial life of Jewish tradition as a revelatory, hierophonic reality in which God addresses the Jew. They were inspired by the saintly figure of Franz Rosenzweig and his unique understanding of the *miẓwot* as sacraments quickening one's relationship to God. It is to Rosenzweig's sacramental conception of ritual observance that we now turn.

Rosenzweig's Conception of Torah as Sacramental Piety

Rosenzweig's journey to Judaism is among the most edifying and inspiring chapters in the annals of twentieth-century religious spirituality: from the midst of assimilation and profound agnosticism to an affirmation of theistic faith which initially brought him to the portals of the church, and stopping just short of the baptismal font, he "returned" to his ancestral community and embraced the life of piety and ritual observance enjoined by Jewish tradition.[56] But his return, his *teshuvah* as rabbinic parlance has it, did not entail a rejection of the modern world, its culture and intellectual scruples. On the contrary, at least as he understood it, his affirmation of theistic faith and the life of traditional Jewish piety lent his culture—that is, Western culture in terms of most enduring and urgent concerns—a new depth.[57] His return to Judaism is thus best understood as post-traditional.[58]

Perhaps we should also add "post-liberal." Rosenzweig did not follow the patterns of religious life developed by nineteenth-century Jewry eager to adjust its ancestral religion to the modern, liberal age. In fact, in his religious practice and commitment to *talmud torah*, to the study of the sacred texts of Judaism, Rosenzweig resembled more of a traditional Jew than even most of his neo-Orthodox contemporaries. Theologically, however, the issues he faced and his approach to faith were generated by the experience of the Western liberal intellectual. With specific regard to positive religion as defined by an authoritative tradition and ceremonial life, his point of departure was a summary repudiation of heteronomy. As he once tersely commented, "faith based on authority is equal to unbelief" (*Autoritätsglaube ist gleich dem Ungläubigen*).[59] This declaration was in response to a Christian friend who derisively referred to the Jew as but "a paragraph of the Law. C'est tout."[60] Jewish faith, Rosenzweig sought to argue, did not in the deepest sense of its faith-reality rest in an acceptance of heteronomous authority. Kantian reverberations are clearly felt here as they are in virtually all of Rosenzweig's theological writings. On his road to faith, Kant's evaluation of religion and, specifically, of Judaism exercised him greatly. Indeed, *The Star of Redemption* (1921), his monumental and most systematic theological meditation, contains an implicit but sustained critique of Kant. In overcoming Kant, however, he absorbed much of the sage of Königsberg's thought, primarily his sensitivity to heteronomy and *mutatis mutandis,* his conviction that somehow moral and religious consciousness must be interrelated.[61] To be sure, in contrast to Kant, he maintained that religion is eminently more than morality: religion, or rather the faith-experience, as Rosenzweig understood it, is essentially an encounter with the divine presence and the ensuing knowledge of his love as manifest in what biblical theology calls creation, revelation, redemption. For the Jew, Rosenzweig explained, the bridge between this knowledge of God and morality is provided by the faith experience engendered by liturgical devotion and the *miẓwot.*

Rosenzweig's Debate with Buber

Rosenzweig's most elaborate consideration of the *miẓwot* was occasioned by a debate with Martin Buber. Having inspired assimilated German Jewry to appreciate anew the spiritual possibilities of Judaism, Buber sought to divorce Jewish spirituality from "the law" (*das Gesetz*), as he consistently referred to Jewish ritual observance. In fact, Buber adopted, as already noted, a metanomian attitude, pursuing with unbridled militancy his opposition to the law as a proper form of human-divine encounter. In an address in 1918 before Jewish youth—the reprinting of which in 1922 was the immediate cause prompting Rosenzweig to address to Buber an open letter challenging his position on the *miẓwot*—Buber decried the *miẓwot* as "unholy conditionalities."[62] He explained:

> [Religion] is detrimental to the unfolding of the people's energies where it concentrates ... on the enlargement of the *thou shalt not,* on the minute differentiation between the permitted and the forbidden. When this is the case, it neglects its true task, which is and remains: man's response to the

Divine, the response of the total being; hence, the unity of the spiritual and the worldly, [and] the spiritualization of the worldly; . . . that is, *freedom in God.*[63]

Later, in response to Rosenzweig, he would defiantly state: "God is not a law-giver (*Gesetzgeber*)."[64] Hence, the *miẓwot*—as all ritual precepts—do not stem from God. "I do not believe that revelation is ever a formulation of law (*Gesetzgebung*). . . . For this sentence I would hopefully be prepared to die at the hands of a Jewish World Church with inquisitorial powers."[65] To be sure, Buber concedes, the God of Israel is a Lord of Commandments, but his commandments are addressed to humankind—both as individuals and as a group—ever anew according to the exigencies of each unique situation; and these commandments demand a dialogical response—an unconditional, spontaneous response that involves a turning of the I to the Thou. For Buber this response to God's address, as already noted, is refracted through the unfolding life situation that almost invariably involves a human Thou; and hence the human-God encounter—and this is Buber's overarching message—is both homologous to and conterminous with human–human encounter. Ethics and devotion to God converge in the life of dialogue, or, as one commentator succinctly put it, Buber locates "the moral 'Ought' in dialogue."[66] Buber preferred to call the moral Ought "responsibility," and, emphasizing the etymology of this term (response-ability, *Ver-antwortung*)[67] he wove his dual conception of morality-*cum*-divine service into an elaborate ontology of responsibility.[68] Being, as he held, is an ever-renewed process that embraces all aspects of existence as well as God's relationship to the world. Spiritually, the renewal of being, however, requires the freedom of human response to God, the wellspring of being, who addresses the human person in the dynamic flux of being, that is, in the protean sphere of reality allotted to each individual and group. To effect the spiritual renewal of being, human response requires an utter freedom from all conditions that would lock one in a past reality: ontologically, the dialogical response (*qua* renewal of being) must then be free of all attitudes, acts, or institutions that would frustrate the requisite spontaneity and unconditionality. With these considerations in mind, Buber declared to Rosenzweig: "I cannot accept any [formalized principle as *miẓwot*] if I am to hold myself ready for the unmediated word of God directed to a specific hour of life."[69]

The Kantian inflections of Buber's view of religion are patent. Although his epistemological and ontological presuppositions differ from Kant's, Buber's identity of religious and moral consciousness clearly has its roots in Kant.[70] Further, his affinity to Kant is manifest in his categorical dismissal of the *mizwot,* which he deems to be a species of formalized laws, as a genuine expression of divine service.

In his open letter to Buber, which he entitled "The Builders" (1924), on the problem of ritual observance, Rosenzweig insisted that Buber erred in viewing the *mizwot* merely as legal constructs.[71] In fact, he accused Buber of yielding to the regnant prejudices with respect to the *mizwot.* Praising Buber for having in all other respects "removed us from the imminent danger of making our spiritual Judaism depend on whether or not it was possible for us to be followers of Kant,"[72] Rosenzweig intimates that Buber failed to free himself from the spell of the great prophet of autonomy when considering the *mizwot.*[73] Furthermore, Rosenzweig avers, Buber had been misled not only by Gentile traducers of Jewish spirituality but also by modern apologists of Orthodoxy, especially Samson Raphael Hirsch (1808–1888), who resolved to shore up loyalty to the Torah by proclaiming in sternly judicial terms the *mizwot* to be the immutable "*Law* of God," requiring Israel's unflinching obedience. Rosenzweig admits that so conceived the Torah is indeed a spiritually insipid legalism. But, he asks Buber:

> Is it really Jewish law with which you try to come to terms? . . . Is that really Jewish law, the law of millennia, studied and lived, analyzed and rhapsodized, the law of everyday and the day of death petty and yet sublime, sober and yet woven in legend; a law which knows both the fire of the Sabbath candle and that of the martyr's stake? . . . The law that always rises beyond itself, that can never be reached—and yet has always the possibility of becoming Jewish life, of being expressed in Jewish faces?[74]

Buber, alas, ignored the sacramental reality of "the law": the power of the Law to quicken the Jew's relationship to God. Had Buber maintained an open attitude to the inner, sacramental power of the law he would have ceased to view the *mizwot* as merely *Gesetze,* heteronomous laws and would have acknowledged that the law can in the living reality (*Heutigkeit*)[75] of Jewish piety be *Gebote,* divine commandments that address individuals directly and to the deepest core of their spiritual existence.

The *Mizwot* as Mediating Divine Love

Rosenzweig's appeal to Buber to reevaluate his position on the law is a nuanced phenomenological argument based on theological presuppositions regarding the nature of revelation which he developed in *The Star of Redemption* and which he believed he basically shared with Buber.[76] For Rosenzweig, revelation, which is the very fundament of his theology, is the experience of God—or, more precisely, the disclosure of divine love.[77] God, the Creator—that is, the ultimate ground of all being—turns to the individual and addresses him with a caring yes. Thus acknowledging his presence in the anonymous multitude of humanity, God affirms him in his unique (what philosophers are wont to call contingent) existence. So affirmed, the individual is freed from the existential anxiety attendant to his finitude and feeling of cosmic insignificance; beloved by God, he has become "ensouled" and thus capable of loving others, of reaching out to their Thou.[78] And noting that Kant's ethical formalism, while preserving autonomy, does not assure the successful fulfillment of the moral deed, Rosenzweig argued that only the actions originating in divine love are ethically efficacious. "Only the soul beloved of God can receive the commandment to love its neighbor *and* fulfill it. Ere man can turn himself over to God's will, God must first have turned to him."[79]

In order to tap the individual at the depths of his finitude and thus unique presence, as Rosenzweig explains in *The Star,* God's address must be wholly in the present. The ordinary forms of discourse—the past, indicative present, future tenses—are, however, bound to a rationalized grid of coordinates that perforce blur the uniqueness of the individual and reduce him to a comparative category. The only speech-act, Rosenzweig reasons, that is emphatically and unambiguously in the present is the imperative, the language of commandments. The commandment must then be the mode of divine address, the address of love; and the hearing of the commandment is the experience of divine love. Accordingly, Rosenzweig tells Buber in his open letter to him, the *mizwot* as God's commandments are experienced by the pious Jew as the address of divine love, as an encounter with the divine presence.

To appreciate the sacramental reality of the *mizwot,* however, one has to know them from *within.* "An outsider," as Rosenzweig explained in a gloss to "The Builders," "no matter how willing and sympathetic, can never be made to accept a single commandment as a 'religious' demand."[80] In the fulfillment of the *mizwot,* the Jew obtains the possibility of plummeting and experiencing their "inner power" (*Kraft*)—the power that transforms the *mizwot* from the statutory law of Jewish tradition to a living commandment and *ergo* experience of God's presence. Further, as living commandments, the *mizwot* cease to be the heteronomous dictates of tradition but become "our inner power," vouchsafing to the performance of the *mizwot* the "freedom" of a spontaneous deed.[81] The commandment we hear from *within* the *mizwot* addresses "not only our will but our ability to act." Hearing the commanding voice of God, the question of appropriating his commandment to our will is irrelevant, for his commandment has already been transformed into "our inner power"; his will already animates our actions.

Unlike "a general law [which] can address itself with its demands to the will" — an elliptical reference to the universal ethical law of Kant— "ability carries in itself its own law; there is only my, your, his ability, and built on them, ours; not everybody's. . . ." The *mizwot* are realized, Rosenzweig further explains "at the boundary of the merely do-able, where the voice of commandment causes the spark to leap from 'I must' to 'I can.'" The law, he assures Buber, "is built on such commandments, and only on them."[82] In that a particular *mizwah* becomes a question of *my* "inner ability," of *my* "inner must," as he had earlier written to a perplexed disciple, it is not a coercive but a free act.[83] Indeed, only as a free act enjoined by the commanding voice of God, engaging the individual at the deepest core of his being, does the performance of the *mizwot* obtain its religious fullness.

The sacramental power of the *mizwot* is not, if we may borrow from the lexicon of Roman Catholic doctrine, *ex opere operato,* that is, that the very act of performing the *mizwot* assures one of the "grace" of hearing the divine address.[84] To be sure, as Rosenzweig wrote several students eager for a clarification of this matter, "only in the commandment can the voice of Him who commands be heard. . . . Not that doing necessarily results in hearing and understanding. But one hears differently when one hears in doing."[85] The *mizwot* offer the Jew who embraces them in faith the possibility of experiencing through them God's commanding address of love. It is this hierophantic or sacramental possibility, according to Rosenzweig, that ultimately sanctifies the *miz*wot for the Jew, and not their origin at Mount Sinai per se. To be sure, he wrote Buber, a firm confidence in the historicity of the Sinaitic revelation "certainly plays a part" in inspiring traditional Jewry's fidelity to "the law." But as the Torah is *lived* by the Jew, he further explained, this consciousness of its venerable origins is hardly his most salient and compelling experience. It is rather the law's *Heutigkeit,* its living contemporary reality, that endows it with "authority" for the Jew. This *Heutigkeit,* more than the fact that God gave it to six hundred thousand Israelites at the foot of Mount Sinai, authenticates the law as the living word of God.[86]

Rosenzweig was even willing to concede that the traditional content of the law may not be truly divine,[87] for in essence revelation is but the disclosure of God's love.[88] What is crucial, however, is the experiential fact that the *mizwot* are heard as divine commandments.[89] Thus, "the problem of the Law," he tells Buber, "cannot be dispatched by merely affirming or denying the pseudo-historical theory of its origin, or the pseudo-juristic theory of its power to obligate."[90] These are "pseudo" questions because they falsify the sacramental faith-reality that "gave birth" to and continues to animate the law. These questions, which so burden the modern Jew (and

Gentile), begin, so to speak, at the wrong end and thus entertain the genetic fallacy of confounding the validity of the law with the question of its historical origins and logical or, in this case, juridical status. The validity of the law, Rosenzweig protests, rests in its *Heutigkeit*—the experiential realm in which the "external" objective status of the law is eclipsed by its living reality. Externally, the law clearly is a codified corpus that traces its authority to the Sinaitic revelation; but experientially, as Rosenzweig once somewhat enigmatically put it, "Judaism is not law, it creates law."[91] Initially and ideally the *mizwot* are performed not as heteronomous obligations, but as God's direct, personal address; as such they are a locus for the Jew's encounter with God. The *mizwot* are then recorded, so to speak, as a testimony to their revelatory power, serving as an invitation to all Jews in every generation. This invitation is not a guarantee but it points in faith to the *mizwot*'s revelatory possibility. The corpus of these invitations, the law of Moses, provides all of Jewry with a "common landscape."[92] Within this landscape traditional Jews tread upon a single, "obligatory" path encompassing all of the *mizwot*. The *ba'al teshuvah*, the modern Jew seeking to return to the tradition, as Rosenzweig taught and exemplified in his own life, finds within this landscape his own path—that set of *mizwot*—in which he *personally* hears the commanding voice of God.[93]

Rosenzweig: Jewish Spirituality as Sacred Time and Meta-history

Rosenzweig's sacramental conception of the *mizwot* restored for many modern Jews the dignity of ritual observance. In his generation and since, erstwhile non-observant Jews have been inspired to assume a life of ritual piety by his teaching that the *mizwot* not only need not violate the individual's autonomy but also can provide the matrix of a meaningful spiritual life—especially when they are viewed in their fuller context within Judaism's liturgical calendar.[94] The nuanced rhythms of traditional Jewish liturgical life, Rosenzweig held, is the genuine *Sitz im Leben* of Jewish ritual observance: here through a shared spiritual calendar, through a life of common prayer, celebration, commemoration, and ritual, the individual Jew joins the House of Israel in a covenental relationship to God. Torah, the Jew's life under "the law," thus, as Rosenzweig relates in nigh-rhapsodic terms, obtains its spiritual fullness by virtue of this relationship in which the Jews as one body affect "the heavens and the earth," establishing a special, sacralizing relationship to creation and history. As such, "the law," the life of Jewish prayer and ritual, is not at all irrelevant to the world; indeed, it bears on the very destiny of existence. With reference to an ancient Jewish mystical doctrine regarding the law as concealing within its hidden, inner-most meanings the mystery of creation, Rosenzweig observes:

> [The law] is not alienated from the world but the key to [its] enigma. For the Jew, the book of the law can thus, as it were, replace the book of nature or even the starry heavens. ... That is the basic idea of countless legends with which Judaism expands the apparently constricted world of its laws into the whole of the world, and ... precisely because it finds this world presaged in its laws see the world-to-come in it. ... [The] entire creation is interpolated between the Jewish God and the Jewish law, and that God and his law thereby both prove to be equally All embracing as — creation.[95]

Rediscovery of the spiritual mystery of the Torah and its sacramental qual-ity enabled Rosenzweig to lead modern Jewish thought beyond Kant and the stumbling block posed by the *mizwot* conceived as heteronomous ritualism. Yet although he may have overcome Kant, he did not negate him. For one thing, he yielded to Kantian scruples by insisting that the Torah need not deny the individual's autonomy. More significant, although he ascribes to the life of prayer and ritual an independent, ontological validity, Rosen-zweig nonetheless follows Kant in discerning an essential interrelationship between morality and religion. But whereas Kant gave primacy to moral consciousness on the ground of a genuine religious sensibility, Rosenzweig in effect reversed the interrelationship. For him, morality as a truly effica-cious and spontaneous act flows *from* religious consciousness: the individual's power to fulfill the root commandment of all morality, namely, to love one's neighbor, as we have seen, is deemed by Rosenzweig to be the gift of divine love made manifest for the Jews in the life of *mizwot* and prayer. Beloved by God, and thus free of metaphysical anxiety and the consequent mistrust of the world, one turns to others in love. It is only with this decisive moment that the moral drama truly begins. But Rosenzweig seems to stymie the Jew's full participation in this drama with his paradoxical teaching that the Jew obtains his special covenantal relationship with God through a withdrawal from the world and history: the life of the Law and, in particular, the liturgical calendar of the Jews — which engenders a sense of sacred time so utterly distinct from the profane rhythms of the world — isolate and detach the Jew from history, rendering him seemingly indifferent to the fate of other peoples.[96] This a-historical posture, however, has a meta-historical, dialectical virtue. Content with its unique relationship with the God of eternity and standing beyond history — namely, politics and war — the "synagogue" embodies the messianic promise and thereby prods the church enmeshed in history, to lead history beyond itself to the *eschaton*.[97] Meanwhile, the synagogue is to look inward in blissful seclusion from the world. Many of Rosenzweig's admirers and disciples, however, found his celebration of the synagogue's "divinely appointed" seclusion troubling and, accordingly, found his dialectical, eschatological justification for this seclusion morally inadequate, to say the least. Indeed, especially for Jews alert to the urgencies of both Jewish and world history, Rosenzweig's suggestion that Jewish spirituality required an indifference to history—at least as it unfolds in noneschatological times—was disquieting.

Buber, in striking contrast to Rosenzweig, evinced a sustained appreciation for what many of his contemporaries perceived as the moral imperative of social and political *engagement*. Moreover, in his central teachings, Buber acknowledged the profound spiritual, if not religious, nature of the passion that often animated a moral involvement in history. To be sure, Kant had already ascribed to the assumption of a moral responsibility for the shape of history—which, of course, goes above and beyond merely being morally upright—a religious value.[98] As the moral reconstruction of the world, according to Kant, history evokes "awe" and "elevates the spirit," for it bears so powerfully on "the sublimity of our destiny."[99] Buber's specific understanding of history as a moral-*cum*-religious task was most decisively shaped by his friend Gustav Landauer (1870–1919), one of the martyred heroes of the aborted socialist revolution in Bavaria in 1919. An individual of the most refined moral sensitivities, Landauer devoted his life to the poor urban masses of Germany, drawing intellectual inspiration from neo-Kantians who gave the doctrine of history as serving the highest good (*summum bonum*) even greater prominence and more systematic treatment than Kant.[100] Grounding these neo-Kantian presuppositions in a theological perspective, Buber spoke of biblical humanism:

> The men of the Bible are sinners like ourselves, but there is one sin they do not commit, our arch-sin: they do not dare confine God to a circumscribed space or division of life, to "religion." They have not the insolence to draw boundaries around God's commandments and say to Him: "Up to this point, you are sovereign, but beyond these bounds begins the sovereignty of science or society or the state."[101]

Biblical humanism, which obtained its most pristine expression in the teachings of the prophets, thus requires that faith be extended beyond the confines of the faith community to the "profane" spheres of public and political activity—provinces of life that in the contemporary world are all too often abandoned to instrumental considerations, if not cynicism. The healing of the division between the sacred and the profane, between faith and morality, and between morality and politics, Buber held, is the most urgent task facing humankind. He firmly believed that Judaism, specifically as enhanced by the Zionist endeavor, could play a crucial role in meeting this task. Guided by an ardent desire for the social and spiritual renewal of the Jewish people, he affirmed, Zionism would develop an ethos mending these divisions and thus herald the rebirth of biblical humanism—and Israel's mission to humanity to be a pristine exemplification of "the way of the Lord."[102]

Prayer and Ritual as the Ground of Prophetic Hope and Commitment

Buber tended to present the issues facing people of faith in a dichotomous fashion—indeed, as almost an intrinsic conflict between faith as ritual and liturgical piety, and faith as an active responsibility for the "secular" spheres of interpersonal relations and history.[103] Certainly at this critical hour, he declared, the command of God is to reach beyond the "narrow" precincts of the *ecclesia*—the corridors of prayer and ritual—and affirm the secular as the most meaningful arena of divine service. In this respect, he and Rosenzweig represented diametrically opposite poles of the spiritual possibilties for the modern Jew. But there were Jews who were drawn to both. Some like Shmuel Bergman and Ernst Simon, to whom we referred in our discussion of *Ha'ol*, sought to subsume both poles in their lives as pious, observant Jews, socialists and Zionists. Their Zionism and socialism were directly inspired by Buber—in Palestine and later in the State of Israel they joined him in various causes in the struggle for Arab–Jewish rapprochement, a struggle they regarded as not only to be the most urgent political issue but also the cardinal moral challenge facing Zionism.[104] And, like Buber, they viewed this struggle as a religious demand, as an expression of faith in God's benevolent sovereignty over all of creation. Yet Bergman and Simon parted with Buber in regarding prayer as the wellspring of faith and spiritual life in all its manifestations. They, moreover, learned from Rosenzweig that all of Jewish ritual life is essentially a form of prayer.[105] Thus, as Bergman observed, the Jew prefaces virtually every ritual act or deed with a benediction (*berakhah*): "Blessed art Thou our Lord. . . ."[106] This benediction, Bergman also explained, is an indication of the central feature of prayer as an existential quest to know God, to deepen one's faith in him and his world. "We pray out of belief, but believe out of prayer."[107] And in prayer, Bergman testified, echoing perhaps the most recurrent theme in Rosenzweig's writings,[108] "flows and rises the light of redemption."[109] But for Bergman prayer is not only the source of hope or, as Rosenzweig put it, the proleptic experience of the eschatological promise; prayer is the experience from which one derives the resolve to accept "the yoke of the Kingdom of

God" and its realization in the here and now of everyday existence. Behind this testimony of faith is a religious intuition which crystallized for Bergman even prior to his encounter with Rosenzweig's teachings.[110] While serving as a soldier at the front during World War I, in the midst of the horror and fury, Bergman wrote his parents:

> The basic thing [in life] is a belief in goodness, that man can do good. . . . The most difficult problem is the success of the good. I have to do good without being concerned about the results, and in spite of the fact that we know that often this is a trial—in the way Abraham was tried—and we are tempted to believe that we are laboring in vain, that the good will never triumph. This is where religious faith comes in: you have to do the good, not only because your conscience, "the Categorical Imperative" in your heart demands it, but because you believe that nevertheless in the end the good will triumph in the world. I therefore believe that there is a law in the universe by which no good deed ever gets lost, that there is a law of the conservation of the good, like that of the conservation of energy, in the world. My belief in this law is my belief in God. And it is also the basis of our Messianic belief.[111]

For Bergman—as for Simon—this faith and the sense of responsibility for the world issuing from it—were to be grounded in the sacramental reality of prayer and ritual.[112]

Notes

1. For a concise and illuminating analysis of this process, see Peter L. Berger, *The Social Reality of Reality* (London: Penguin University Books, 1973) 111–30.

2. For an excellent anthology of writings expressive of this trend, see *Rationalität und Mystik*, ed. H. D. Zimmermann (Frankfurt a/M: Insel, 1981). Also see my essay "Fin de siècle Orientalism, the *Ostjuden* and the Aesthetics of Jewish Self-Affirmation," in *Studies in Contemporary Jewry*, ed. Jonathan Frankel (Bloomington: Indiana University Press, 1984).

3. Louis Dupré, "Spiritual Life in a Secular Age." *Daedalus* 3/1 (Winter 1982) 25.

4. See my "Secular Religiosity" in *Approaches to Judaism in Modern Times*, ed. M. Raphael (Providence, RI: Brown University Press, 1983).

5. According to Dupré, "few of our contemporaries connect their faith with the kind of private or communal sacred experience described by Otto, Van der Leeuw, or Eliade. To be sure, intensive religious experiences continue to exist, but they have become the exception rather than the rule, and happen mostly to those who have already, and on different grounds, actively committed themselves to transcendent reality. Generally speaking, this new relation is marked more by personal reflections and deliberate choice than by direct experience" ("Spiritual Life," 23).

6. Again as Dupré notes, one usually "chooses" the religious tradition into which one is born, but since the affirmation of faith is an existential act, it is nonetheless appropriate to speak of "choice" ("Spiritual Life," 24–25).

7. "Kant obtained from Spinoza his knowledge and his judgment of Judaism" (Hermann Cohen, *Religion of Reason* [New York: Ungar, 1972] 331). See also Julius Guttmann, "Kant und das Judentum," in *Schriften der Gesellschaft zur Förderung der Wissenschaft des Judentums* (Leipzig, 1908), 50–51, 61 n.3.

8. When Kant first published his views on Judaism, the Jewish critic Saul Ascher (1769–1822) ironically observed that the philosopher's views were bound to lend popular prejudices about Judaism an "a priori status" (*Eisenmenger der Zweite* [Berlin, 1794] 78–79); cited in Jacob Katz, "Kant and Judaism: The Historical Context" (Hebrew), *Tarbiz* 41 (1970) 237.

9. For a recent statement on the enduring relevance of Kant to Western culture, see Norbert Hinske, *Kant als Herausforderung an die Gegenwart* (Freiburg: Alber, 1980).

10. Kant, "What is Enlightenment?" in Kant, *On History*, ed. L. W. Beck (Indianapolis, IN: Library of Liberal Arts, 1963) 3.

11. Kant, *Religion within the Limits of Reason Alone*, trans. Theodore M. Greene and Hoyt H. Hudson (New York: Harper Torchbooks, 1960) 79–84, 164–68.

12. Ibid., 156–58.

13. Ibid., 116–18.

14. For various perspectives on Kant's conception of Judaism, see E. L. Fackenheim, "Kant and Judaism," *Commentary* 36 (December 1963) 460–67; H. M. Graupe, "Kant und das Judentum," *Zeitschrift für Religions- und Geistesgeschichte* 13 (1961) 308–33; idem, *Die Entstehung des modernen Judentums* (Hamburg: Buske, 1977) 144–54; N. Rotenstreich, *The Recurring Pattern* (New York: Horizon Press, 1964) 23–47. See also the relevant works mentioned in nn. 7 and 8 above.

15. See N. Rotenstreich, *German Philosophy and the Jews* (New York: Schocken, 1984) part 1.

16. A. MacIntyre, *A Short History of Ethics: A History of Moral Philosophy from the Homeric Age to the Twentieth Century* (New York: Macmillan, 1966) 190.

17. Magnes's draft proposal is cited in full by S. H. Bergman, "J. L. Magnes Seeks His God: On the First Anniversary of his Death" (Hebrew), *Ha-aretz* [Tel Aviv daily newspaper] 2.

18. "Such is the generation of them that seek after Him, that seek Thy face. . . ." "Thy Face" (*panekha*) may also be translated as "Your Presence" (Mitchell Dahood, *Psalms I* [Anchor Bible 16; Garden City, NY: Doubleday, 1965] 153).

19. Cited in Bergman, "J. L. Magnes Seeks His God," 2.

20. Rejection of "religion," that is, the formal, institutional expression of religious faith, was rather fashionable in post-World War I theology, both Jewish and Christian. "God did not, after all, create religion: he created the world" (Franz Rosenzweig, "Das neue Denken," in *Kleinere Schriften* [Berlin, 1935] 389). *Mutatis mutandis*, Karl Barth also spoke of "religion" as "unbelief" (*The Epistle to the Romans* [New York: Oxford, 1960] 268). "[It] is surely significant that in our century 'religion' should have become almost a dirty word, not with atheists . . . , but with a certain brand of theologians" (R. J. Zwi Werblowsky, *Beyond Tradition and Modernity*, 35). Werblowsky's analysis of this flight from "religion" in the context of contemporary Christian and Jewish spirituality is particularly pertinent to our discussion. See Werblowsky, *Beyond Tradition*, 35–39, 53–60.

21. The protocol consists of two typewritten pages in Hebrew. The second page of the protocol was discovered several years ago by Professor Arthur Goren of the Hebrew University among the Judah Leib Magnes Papers, Central Archives for the History of the Jewish people, Mappe 2273 ("*Ha'ol*"). I wish to thank Professor Goren for bringing this document to my attention. The first page of the protocol was recently found among the papers of the late Professor Gershom Scholem by Dr. Avraham Shapira. I wish to express my gratitude to Dr. Shapira, who is currently editing a volume of Scholem's unpublished writings, and to Mrs. Fania Scholem for inviting me to examine and help them identify this fascinating document.

22. It is probably the comments by Kalonymos Kalman Epstein of Cracow that Scholem here had in mind; see his *Ma'or wa-Shemesh* ad loc. (ed. Breslau, 1841/42; reprint Tel Aviv, 1965) 220a.

23. Simon, of course, is here citing the famous thanksgiving hymn, "*Dayenu*," of the Passover *Haggadah*.

24. Cf. *Pirqe 'Avot* 3:13: "Tradition is a fence around the Torah." A standard rabbinic commentary explains this famous dictum from the Mishnah thus: "The Oral Torah—[the tradition] which

is passed from one generation to another—is a hedge or fence around the Written Torah, for without this tradition we would not understand the meaning of the [Written] Torah and its laws. And we should be like a vineyard without a fence, and everyone would do as he pleases, explaining and interpreting the Torah as he pleases" (Pinhas Kahtai, *Commentary to the Mishnah* [Hebrew] [9th ed.; Jerusalem: Keter, 1977] 2:359).

25. Among the various activities Magnes envisioned for the society was the acquisition of a cemetery for the members. See the early draft of the society from circa 1932, then tentatively called "A Hebrew moral-religious community" (*Judah Leib Magnes Papers*, Mappe 2436, document no. 143 [B of F]).

26. Cited on the front cover of a pamphlet containing letters by Magnes and Buber respectively to Mahatma Gandhi, published in English and Hebrew by *Ha'ol*, which called itself in English "The Bond," *Two Letters to Gandhi* (Jerusalem: Rubin Mass, 1939), pamphlet no. 1 of The Bond. Our information about *Ha'ol* is, unfortunately, rather fragmentary. Some material may be found in Bergman, "J. L. Magnes Seeks His God"; idem, *Faith and Reason*, 149–50; *Dissenter in Zion: From the Writings of Judah L. Magnes*, ed. A. Goren (Cambridge, MA: Harvard University Press, 1982) 50; *A Land of Two Peoples: Buber on Jews and Arabs*, ed. P. Mendes-Flohr (New York: Oxford University, 1983) 111–13; idem, "The Appeal of the Incorrigible Idealist: Judah L. Magnes and his Jerusalem Colleagues," in *Like All the Nations: The Life and Legacy of Judah L. Magnes*, ed. William Brinner and Moses Rischin (Albany: State University of New York Press, 1987).

27. The concept of "ethical monotheism" as characterizing the "radical innovation" of biblical faith, particularly of the prophets, was apparently first introduced by A. Kuenen, *Volksreligion und Weltreligion* (Berlin, 1883); cf. A. Altmann, *Leo Baeck and the Jewish Mystical Tradition* (Leo Baeck Memorial Lecture 17; New York: Leo Baeck Institute, 1973) 23 n. 7. In that such a view clearly served to improve the image of Judaism, it is not surprising that Jewish scholars and thinkers, especially those who "since Kant" had been seeking to emphasize the ethical character of Judaism, were quick to adopt it. On the tendency of German Jewish thinkers, from Reform to neo-Orthodox, to focus on the universal, ethical (metalegal) aspects of Judaism; see Max Wiener, "The Conception of Mission in Traditional and Modern Judaism," *YIVO Annual of Jewish Science* 2–3 (1947–48) 9–24.

28. M. Lazarus, *Ethik des Judenthums* (2 vols.; Frankfurt a/M, 1898, 1901) vol. 1, part 1, trans. Henrietta Szold as *Ethics of Judaism* (2 vols.; Philadelphia: Jewish Publication Society, 1900–1901); Hermann Cohen, *Religion der Vernunft* (Berlin, 1918), trans. from 2d ed. by Simon Kaplan as *Religion of Reason* (New York: Ungar, 1972). Cohen originally intended to subtitle his work "A Jewish philosophy of religion and a Jewish ethics." Despite their shared Kantian sensibilities and conception of Judaism as essentially an ethical system, Lazarus and Cohen seriously clashed on methodological grounds. See Cohen, "Das Problem der Jüdischen Sittenlehre: Eine Kritik von Lazarus 'Ethik des Judenthums,'" *Monatsschrift für Geschichte und Wissenschaft des Judenthums* 43 (1899) 385–90.

29. Baeck, *The Essence of Judaism*, ed. Irving Howe; trans. V. Grubenwiesser and L. Pearl (New York: Schocken, 1961) 41. First published in 1905, Baeck's *Das Wesen des Judenthums* was written as a reply to Adolf Harnack, *Das Wesen des Christenthums* (Leipzig, 1900). In his day, Harnack was regarded as the most distinguished liberal Protestant representative of the Kantian inspired school of "moral theology." In his book he contrasted the "essential" moral teachings of Jesus to the "essential" ritualism and legalism of the Pharisees. See Uriel Tal's incisive analysis of the "controversy" aroused by Harnack: *Christians and Jews in German: Religion, Politics, and Ideology in the Second Reich, 1870–1914*, trans. Noah J. Jacobs (Ithaca, NY: Cornell University Press, 1969) 160–222. See also U. Tal, "The Controversy about 'The Essence of Judaism' According to Jewish and Christian Sources of the Early 20th Century," in *Perspectives of German-Jewish History in the 19th and 20th Century* (Publications of the Leo Baeck Institute, Jerusalem; Jerusalem: Academic Press, 1971) 62–67. Parenthetically, much of Scholem's work may be viewed as a sustained critique

of Baeck's and others' attempt to reduce Judaism to a normative essence; he regarded this attempt as a modern analogue to Orthodoxy's imposition of a normative reading of the Torah. See Scholem, "Judaism," an unpublished essay to be included in *Contemporary Jewish Religious Thought*, ed. A. A. Cohen and P. Mendes-Flohr (New York: Scribner, 1985).

30. The neo-Orthodox, of course, would insist that the observance of the ritual commandments of the Torah was the normative core of Judaism. Nonetheless, the founder of neo-Orthodoxy, Samson Raphael Hirsch (1808–1888), offered a comprehensive ethical exegesis of the *miẕwot*, endeavoring to demonstrate that at root all the ritual commandments of the Torah have an ethical significance. See his *Choreb oder Versuche über Jissroels Pflichten in der Zerstreuung* (Frankfurt a/M, 1837). On the non-observant side of the ledger, see the testimony of Eduard Bernstein (1850–1932), who ascribed his socialist ethos to his youthful encounter with Liberal Judaism and the teachings of ethical monotheism: "Wie Ich als Jude in der Diaspora aufwuchs," *Der Jude* 2 (1917–18) 186–95. On the impact of the notion of Judaism as an elevated moral mission on Jews of widely varying religious inclinations, see Wiener, "The Conception of Mission," 9–24.

31. Cited in Bergman, "J. L. Magnes Seeks His God," 2.

32. *Ha'ol* did in fact contemplate some political activity, but largely confined these efforts to clarifying the ethical-religious issues involved in the political challenges that faced the Jewish people. See Bergman, "J. L. Magnes Seeks His God," 2; see also the one publication issued by *Ha'ol*, namely, *Two Letters to Gandhi*. Buber's letter is reprinted in *A Land of Two Peoples*, ed. Mendes-Flohr, 113–30. Most of the members of *Ha'ol* joined the League for Arab–Jewish Rapprochement, founded in April 1939, and the Ichud, a political association founded in August 1942 which promoted a humanistic conception of Arab–Jewish reconciliation. See *A Land of Two Peoples*, ed. Mendes-Flohr, 134–35, 137–38, 148–49.

33. Scholem, "Reflections on Jewish Theology," in Scholem, *On Jews and Judaism in Crisis*, 271. Scholem was, on the whole, rather reticent on these matters, leaving many of his commentators to conjecture regarding his personal theology. Ascribing Scholem's involvement in Kabbalah to a search for a "counter-tradition," David Biale, for instance, depending on Scholem's few and rather oblique published statements, fails to consider the relation of this search to his unbending conviction that the halakhah of Orthodoxy is not the word of God. See Biale, *Gershom Scholem: Kabbalah and Counter-History* (Cambridge, MA: Harvard University Press, 1979). The protocol of *Ha'ol*, if we have interpreted it correctly, points to such a relation. Only toward the end of his life did Scholem offer in print some (guarded) theological observations; see "With Gershom Scholem: An Interview" (1975), and "Reflections on Jewish Theology" (1973), in Scholem, *On Jews and Judaism in Crisis*, 1–48, 261–297; and "Irving Howe Interviews Gershom Scholem," *Present Tense* (Autumn 1980) 53–57.

34. Scholem, "Reflections on Jewish Theology," in *On Jews and Judaism in Crisis*, 262, 270, 271.

35. Ibid., 270.

36. Scholem treated these themes in 1962 in "Revelation and Tradition as Religious Categories in Judaism," in *The Messianic Idea in Judaism and Other Essays on Jewish Spirituality* (New York: Schocken, 1971) 282–303. Therein he observes: "As long as there is a living relationship between religious consciousness and revelation there is no danger to the tradition from within. But when this relationship dies tradition ceases to be a living force" (p. 292).

37. Scholem, "Reflection on Jewish Theology," in *On Jews and Judaism in Crisis*, 274.

38. It would be illuminating to compare Scholem's views on the nature of the decline of traditional Judaism in the modern are with those of Rosenzweig. Although he certainly felt that the problem of autonomy could not be gainsaid, Rosenzweig regarded the critical historical consciousness of moderns as the central factor undermining the dialectic of revelation and tradition, a dialectic that he, like Scholem, deemed to be the axis of a living theistic faith. See Rosenzweig, *The Star of Redemption*, trans. William Halle (New York: Holt, Rinehart & Winston, 1970) 93–102, esp. 99–100.

39. "The only thing in my life I have never doubted is the existence of God. I have been in doubt whether Orthodoxy is good. But I was never a secularist because I have never been in doubt about God" ("Irving Howe Interviews Gershom Scholem," 55). Also ". . . Without God there is no such thing as values or morality that carry any real, binding force. Faith in God—even if it doesn't have a positive expression in every generation—will reveal itself as a force, even by means of not manifesting itself. . . . The day may come when it will be forbidden to speak of God. But then the faith in Him will grow. A secular regime opens up more possibilities for the manifestation of those positive forces in man that are linked to something with a spark in it. I believe that God will then manifest Himself all the more strongly, though I'm not sure that that will be a world of the *Shulḥan 'Arukh*—though that is not out of the question" ("With Gershom Scholem: An Interview," in *On Jews and Judaism in Crisis,* 35). On Scholem's fundamental faith in "the theology of creation" and revelation, see "Reflections on Jewish Theology," in *On Jews and Judaism in Crisis,* 290–94.

40. Interview with G. Scholem's widow, Fania Scholem. August and October 1983.

41. "With Gershom Scholem: An Interview," in *On Jews and Judaism in Crisis,* 10.

42. Scholem, "Reflections on Jewish Theology," 297.

43. Biale aptly characterizes Scholem's quest for this hidden dialectic as "counter-history" (*Kabbalah and Counter-History,* 10–12, 114–15, 195–96, 201–5, 210).

44. On Scholem's cultural Zionism and that of other members of *Ha'ol,* see my "Appeal of the Incorrigible Idealist," in *Like All the Nations,* ed. Brinner and Rischin.

45. Scholem, "A Free Man: On J. L. Magnes" (Hebrew) in Scholem, *Devarim be-go: Writings on Jewish Heritage and Renaissance* (Tel Aviv: Am Oved, 1975) 489.

46. See Scholem, "Reflections on Jewish Theology," in *On Jews and Judaism in Crisis,* 275.

47. With respect to historical scholarship as serving the renewal of Judaism, see Scholem's essay of 1937 entitled "A Candid Word about the True Motives of My Kabbalistic Studies." Noting that his scholarship is prompted to tap anew the "secret," vital life of Judaism, he acknowledges the danger that he "will get stuck in the mist [of history]," and that he might "suffer a 'professorial death.'" But, he continues, "the necessity of historical criticism and critical history cannot be replaced by anything else even when it demands sacrifices. Certainly, history may seem to be fundamentally an illusion, but an illusion without which in temporal reality no insight into the essence of things is possible. For today's man, that mystical totality of 'truth' (*des Systems*), whose existence disappears particularly when it is projected into historical time, can only become visible in the purest way in the legitimate discipline of commentary and in the singular mirror of philological criticism. Today, as at the very beginning, my work lives in this paradox . . ." (published for the first time in Baile, *Kabbalah and Counter-History,* 75–76). It would be misleading to understand Scholem's interest in Kabbalah as a "counter-tradition" as implying that he regarded mysticism as an *alternative* tradition of halakhah. As Scholem repeatedly emphasized, the kabbalists were integrally part of the halakhic-rabbinic tradition; their theosophy and mystical doctrines perhaps provided them with a meta-nomian perspective, a perspective grounded in the fullness and paradoxical complexity of the "theo-human" encounter, which Scholem suggests instilled their observance of the law with a "dialectical tension" and sustaining power. The *Problemstellung* guiding Scholem's scholarship should then be understood as a desire to identify the metanomian dimension of Jewish ritual observance. On the relation of Kabbalah to halakhah, see Scholem's remarks in "With Gershom Scholem: An Interview," in *On Jews and Judaism in Crisis,* 19, 46–47.

48. See Scholem's somewhat opaque comparison of his position and that of Buber: "The fact, of course, is—to put it bluntly—that Buber is a religious anarchist (a term that is not meant to disparage him; I am an anarchist myself, though not one of Buber's persuasion)" ("Martin Buber's Hasidism," *Commentary* 32/4 [October 1961] 315).

49. Buber adopted the neo-Kantian distinction between religion (*qua* formal institutions,

beliefs, and practices) and religiosity (*qua* spontaneous experience and expression) developed by Georg Simmel, with whom he had studied at the University of Berlin. See my *Von der Mystik zum Dialog: Martin Bubers geistige Entwicklung bis hin zu 'Ich und Du'* (Königstein: Jüdischer Verlag im Athenäum Verlag, 1979) 288–97. In his early, so-called predialogical writings especially, Buber sought to promote a Jewish "religiosity" as a type of genuine spirituality unmediated by tradition. See "Jewish Religiosity" (1916), in Buber, *On Judaism*, trans. E. Jospe; ed. N. N. Glatzer (New York: Schocken, 1967) 79–94.

50. Already as a young student Magnes was called to serve as a rabbi to Temple Emmanuel, the citadel of Reform Judaism in New York City. His determined efforts to introduce a greater degree of tradition into the service, however, led to a severe conflict with the congregation, who obliged him to resign. He then became rabbi of B'nai Jeshurun (1911–1912), a Manhattan synagogue that became a charter member of the United Synagogue of America, the association of Conservative congregations founded in 1913. On Magnes's intention of transforming B'nai Jeshurun into a model Conservative congregation, see *Dissenter in Zion*, ed. Goren, 68, 123–25.

51. See Magnes's critique of Mordecai Kaplan in *Dissenter in Zion*, ed. Goren, 193–94.

52. Ibid., 222–25, 267–68; see also Magnes, *In the Perplexity of the Times: Addresses by the President of the Hebrew University* (Jerusalem: Hebrew University Press, 1946); and my "Appeal of the Incorrigible Idealist," in *Like All the Nations*, ed. Brinner and Rischin.

53. J. Guttmann, "On the Foundations of Judaism" (Hebrew) [protocol of a seminar on Religious Education held in Jerusalem 1934], reprinted in J. Guttmann, *Religion and Knowledge: Essays and Lectures*, ed. S. H. Bergman and N. Rotenstreich (Jerusalem: Magnes Press, 1955) 272.

54. Ibid., 274.

55. Ibid.

56. See *Franz Rosenzweig: His Life and Thought*, presented by Nahum N. Glatzer (New York: Schocken, 1953) 1–176; see also Mendes-Flohr and J. Reinharz, "From Relativism to Religious Faith: The Testimony of Franz Rosenzweig's Unpublished Diaries," *The Leo Baeck Institute Year Book* 22 (1977) 161–74.

57. This clearly is one way of reading his magnum opus, *The Star of Redemption* (1921), where Rosenzweig examines throughout the book the dialectic interplay between "paganism" (that is, all culture not informed by the principle of divine revelation) and theistic faith (that is, faith grounded in revelation).

58. For a fuller discussion of this concept and its applicability to Rosenzweig, see my "Secular Religiosity" in *Approaches to Judaism*, ed. Raphael.

59. F. Rosenzweig, *Briefe*, ed. Edith Rosenzweig (Berlin: Schocken, 1935) 717.

60. Ibid., 682.

61. See my "Rosenzweig and Kant: Two Views of Ritual and Religion," in *Mystics, Philosophers, and Politicians: Essays in Jewish Intellectual History in Honor of Alexander Altmann*, ed. J. Reinharz and D. Swetschinski (Duke Monographs in Medieval and Renaissance Studies 5; Durham, NC: Duke University Press, 1982) 315–41. In response to my aforementioned article on Rosenzweig and Kant, Professor Alexander Altmann elegantly summarized the relationship between the two: "What Kant describes is the moral act as such whereas Rosenzweig speaks about the mode of existence in which the moral act operates" (letter to author, dated 9 February 1982).

62. Buber, "Herut: On Youth and Religion" (1919), in Buber, *On Judaism*, 152.

63. Ibid., 158 [emphasis added].

64. M. Buber to F. Rosenzweig, letter dated 13 July 1924, in Franz Rosenzweig, *On Jewish Learning*, ed. N. N. Glatzer (New York: Schocken, 1955) 115.

65. M. Buber to F. Rosenzweig, letter dated 3 June 1925, in Buber, *Briefwechsel aus sieben Jahrzehnten*, ed. Grete Schaeder (3 vols.; Heidelberg: Lambert Scheinder, 1973) 2:222. For a fuller discussion of their exchange on the *mizwot*, see my "Rosenzweig and Kant," in *Mystics, Philosophers,*

and Politicians, ed. Reinharz and Swetschinski, 335–41, which provides a full bibliography of the scholarly discussion on the exchange (338 n. 150).

66. M. Friedman, "The Bases of Buber's Ethics," in *The Philosophy of Martin Buber,* ed. P. A. Schilpp and M. Friedman (Library of Living Philosophers 12; La Salle, IL: Open Court, 1967) 177.

67. "The idea of responsibility is to be brought back from the province of specialized ethics, of an 'ought' that swings free in the air, into the lived life. Genuine responsibility (*Verantwortung*) exists where there is real responding (*Antworten*)" (Buber, *Between Man and Man,* trans. R. G. Smith [New York: Macmillan, 1965] 16 [I have supplied the German.]).

68. See N. Rotenstreich, "The Right and Limitations of Buber's Dialogical Thought," in *The Philosophy of Martin Buber,* ed. Schilpp and Friedman, 99–100; Michael Theunissen, *Der Andere: Studien zur Sozialontologie der Gegenwart* (Berlin: de Gruyter, 1965) 243–373, passim; and Robert E. Wood, *Martin Buber's Ontology: An Analysis of 'I and Thou'* (Northwestern University Studies in Phenomenology and Existential Philosophy; Evanston, IL: Northwestern University Press, 1969) 57, 60–61.

69. M. Buber to F. Rosenzweig, letter dated 24 June 1924, cited in Rosenzweig, *On Jewish Learning,* 111. Upon his immigration to Jerusalem in 1938, Buber became increasingly demonstrative in his opposition to the *mizwot.* See the anecdote related by the Hebrew writer Yehuda Yaari, who assisted Buber in preparing the Hebrew edition of *Tales of the Hasidim* (*Or ha-Ganuz,* 1946/47): "During the year 1943, Buber would come to my home every afternoon in order to work on editing *Or ha-Ganuz.* Thus he came, to my great astonishment, also on the eve of *Yom Kippur.* I asked him: 'Do you not fast and pray on Yom Kippur?' And Buber replied with an emphatic no—but he added: 'Should I be disturbing you from going to pray, please let me know.' . . . He then rose and left" (Tzwi Tzameret, "Excerpts of My Talks with Yehuda Yaari" [Hebrew], *Shdemot: Forum of the Kibbutz Movement* [Tel Aviv] no. 85 [May 1983] 127).

70. On Buber's indebtedness to Kant's epistemology, see Steven Katz, "Eine kritische Wurdigung der Erkenntnistheorie des Ich-Du bei Martin Buber," in *Martin Buber: Bilanz seines Denkens,* ed. J. Bloch and H. Gordon (Freiburg: Herder, 1983) 107–37.

71. "The Builders" (*Die Bauleute*), in Rosenzweig, *On Jewish Learning,* 72–92.

72. Ibid., 77.

73. See my "Rosenzweig and Kant," in *Mystics, Philosophers, and Politicians,* ed. Reinharz and Swetschinski, 315–16, 336–38.

74. Rosenzweig, "The Builders," 77.

75. Ibid., 85. "*Heutigkeit*" is apparently Rosenzweig's coinage: ". . . dies imperativische Heute des Gebots," and "die Ganze Offenbarung tritt unter das grosse Heute" (*Stern der Erlösung* [Berlin: Schocken, 1930] 2 Teil, p. 115).

76. In fact, revelation is much more central to Rosenzweig's theology. See my "Rosenzweig and Kant," in *Mystics, Philosophers, and Politicians,* ed. Reinharz and Swetschinski, 323–24, 328–32; see also Emil L. Fackenheim, "Martin Buber's Concept of Revelation," in *The Philosophy of Martin Buber,* ed. Schilpp and Friedman, 273–96; G. Scholem, "Martin Buber's Conception of Judaism," in *On Jews and Judaism in Crisis,* 158–59; and Scholem, "Reflections on Jewish Theology," in *On Jews and Judaism in Crisis,* 272–74.

77. Rosenzweig, *The Star of Redemption,* 156–204.

78. Ibid., 199–201; cf. 274: "For what is redemption other than that the I learns to say Thou to the He?"

79. Ibid., 215 [emphasis added]. Indeed, Rosenzweig holds that sheer obedience to a formal moral law does not ensure a meaningful ethical life, a life that truly transforms the community of human beings into a fellowship. Only those actions, Rosenzweig averred, that originate in divine love are ethically efficacious. See n. 61 above.

80. Rosenzweig to Martin Goldner et al., letter dated "end of" November 1924, in *On Jewish Learning,* 121.

81. Rosenzweig, "The Builders," 85.

82. Ibid., 86.

83. Rosenzweig to Rudolf Hallo, letter dated 27 March 1922, in Rosenzweig, *Briefe*, 127.

84. To be sure, in contemporary Catholic theology the regnant tendency is to reject "the materialistic-sounding views of the sacraments suggested by the earlier declarations of the magisterium." Indeed, most Catholics prefer to understand the sacraments in their pristine sense as facilitating "the *gloriosa commercia* between God and man"; see *Sacramentum Mundi*, ed. Karl Rahner et al. (New York: Herder and Herder, 1968–70) 5:381. The latter conception of the sacraments approximates our use of the term. However, our use of the term to designate a ritual act or rite that serves to quicken one's relationship to God is more akin to Eliade's phenomenological definition of sacrament as "a communion with the sacred" (*The Sacred and the Profane: The Nature of Religion*, trans. W. R. Trask [New York: Harper Torchbooks, 1959] 14).

85. Rosenzweig to Martin Goldner et al., letter dated "end of" November 1924, in *On Jewish Learning*, 122.

86. Rosenzweig, "The Builders," 79.

87. "I, too, do not know whether the law 'is' God's law. I know that as little, and even less than I know that God 'is.' . . . Thus, revelation is certainly not Law-giving. It is only this: Revelation. The primary content of revelation is revelation itself. 'He came down' [on Sinai]—this already concludes the revelation; 'He spoke' is the beginning of interpretation, and certainly 'I am.'" Rosenzweig to Buber, letter dated 5 June 1925, in *On Jewish Learning*, 117.

88. "Gott offenbart in der Offenbarung eben nur immer—die Offenbarung. Anders gesagt: er offenbart immer nur sich selbst dem Menschen, dem Menschen sich selber. Dieser Akkusative und Dativ in seiner Verbindung ist der einzige Inhalt der Offenbarung" (Rozenzweig, *Jehuda Halevi: Zweiundneunzig Hymnen und Gedichte* [Berlin: Lambert Schneider, 1927] 174). Rosenzweig dedicated this volume to Martin Buber.

89. Rosenzweig to Martin Goldner et al., letter dated "end of" November 1924, in *On Jewish Learning*, 122.

90. Rosenzweig, "The Builders," 79–80.

91. Rosenzweig to Rudolf Hallo, letter dated 27 March 1922, in Rosenzweig, *Briefe*, 425.

92. Ibid., 426.

93. Ibid., 426–27.

94. See Rosenzweig, *The Star of Redemption*, 308–28.

95. Ibid., 409.

96. See A. Altmann, "Franz Rosenzweig on History," in *Between East and West: Essays Dedicated to the Memory of Bela Horovitz*, ed. Altmann (London: East and West Library, 1958) 194–214.

97. Rosenzweig, *The Star of Redemption*, 337–74, 413–17. See also *Judaism Despite Christianity: The 'Letters on Christianity and Judaism' between Eugen Rosenstock-Huessy and Franz Rosenzweig*, ed. E. Rosenstock-Huessy (New York: Schocken, 1971) passim.

98. See Y. Yovel, *Kant and the Philosophy of History* (Princeton, NJ: Princeton University Press, 1980) 209–11.

99. Cited in Yovel, *Kant*, 209.

100. See Mendes-Flohr, "Glaube und Politik im Werk Martin Bubers," in *Dialog mit Martin Buber*, ed. W. Licharz (Frankfurt a/M: Haag & Herchen, 1982) 96–98. See also Eugene Lunn, *Prophet of Community: The Romantic Socialism of Gustav Landauer* (Berkeley: University of California Press, 1973) 102–4.

101. Buber, "Hebrew Humanism" (1941), in Buber, *Israel and the World: Essays in a Time of Crisis* (2nd ed.; New York: Schocken, 1963) 247.

102. See Buber, "Zionism—True and False," in *Unease in Zion*, ed. E. ben Ezer (New York: Quadrangle, 1974) 114–18; see also Buber, "Politics and Morality" (1945), in *A Land of Two Peoples*, ed. Mendes-Flohr, 169–72; and my introduction to *A Land of Two Peoples*, 3–33.

103. See Scholem, "Martin Buber's Conception of Judaism," in *The Philosophy of Martin Buber*, ed. Schilpp and Friedman, 133–35, 164–65; and Baruch Kurzweil, "Three Views on Revelation and Law," *Judaism* 9/4 (Fall 1960) 292–98.

104. See E. Simon, "The Arab Question as a Jewish Question," in *Unease in Zion*, ed. E. ben Ezer, 297–320. Bergman was among the first Zionist intellectuals to recognize the importance of the Arab question as a moral touchstone of Zionism; see "Notes on the Arab Question" (1911), in Bergman, *Be-mesh'ol* (Essays) (Hebrew), ed. N. Rotenstreich (Tel Aviv: Am Oved, 1976) 81–83. See also his somewhat more elliptical remarks in "Hallowing the Divine Name," trans. A. Schwartz, in *Shefa' Quarterly* 2/2 (1980) 46–47.

105. See Bergman, "Revelation, Prayer, and Redemption in Franz Rosenzweig's Teachings" (Hebrew), in Bergman, *'Anashim u-Derakhim: Philosophical Essays* (Jerusalem: Bialik, 1967) 308–17.

106. Bergman, "On the Benediction" (*'al ha-brakhah*), in *'Anashim*, 387–91.

107. Bergman, "Philosophy and Religion," *Judaism* 4/1 (Winter 1955) 65. In this context Bergman quotes Eugen Rosenstock-Huessy: "He who has never prayed, to him the meaning of the name God is closed even if he would search through all the dictionaries." The citation is apparently from Rosenstock-Huessy, *Der Atem des Geistes* (Frankfurt a/M: Verlag der Frankfurter Hefte, 1951).

108. Rosenzweig, *The Star of Redemption*, 265–98.

109. Bergman, "The Hope of Israel," in *The Quality of Faith: Essays on Judaism and Morality*, trans. Y. Hanegbi (Jerusalem: The Youth and Hechalutz Department of the World Zionist Organization, 1970) 62.

110. Unlike Simon, Bergman did not know Rosenzweig personally and never quite considered himself a disciple of this great *ba'al teshuvah*. Although he drew profound inspiration from Rosenzweig, the sources of his spirituality and way to faith were rather eclectic; he had a pronounced inclination for mysticism and even the occult. He remained until his death at the age of ninety-two a "religious seeker," forever questioning and exploring. It is not surprising that his attitude to Jewish religious practice was relatively fluid. His ritual observance was, accordingly, less disciplined than Simon's; he would pray when so moved and not always at the set schedule of the liturgy; and he performed the other *mizwot* (that is, those that had a sacramental power for him—at an advanced age he once requested Simon to remind him how to perform the rite of donning the phylacteries) also in an irregular pattern. Appropriately, he once referred to his approach to Judaism as one of "nonorthodox religiosity" (interviews with Nathan Rotenstreich, the executor of S. H. Bergman's literary estate, August 1983; and with Ernst Akiva Simon, September 1983. Also see the proceedings of a symposium devoted to the life and thought of Bergman, *Schmuel Hugo Bergman: In Memoriam*, *'Iyyun [A Hebrew Philosophical Quarterly: Separatum* (80 pp.) issued with vol. 26 [1977]).

111. Bergman to parents, letter dated 14 August 1914. Cited by him in *The Quality of Faith*, ed. A. Shapira, 42.

112. See Simon, "Law and Observance in Jewish Experience," in *Tradition and Contemporary Experience*, ed. A. Jospe (New York: Schocken, 1970) 221–38.

Bibliography

Various aspects of the challenge to theistic faith and spirituality posed by the secular sensibility are discussed in Berger, Dupré, MacIntyre. The impact of the secular sensibility on Jewish spiritual expression is considered by Mendes-Flohr, Werblowsky. An insightful analysis of the strains that modern secular culture and consciousness have placed on tradition as the cognitive and devotional ground of faith is provided by Rotenstreich (*Tradition*). The ramified implications and effects of Kant's critique of Judaism as a heteronomous, pseudoreligion are traced and analyzed in Fackenheim, Graupe, Rotenstreich (*Jews and German Philosophy*). For a systematic delineation of the varied conceptions of *mizwot* in modern Jewish thought since Mendelssohn, Heinemann's compendious study is indispensable. A comparable study in English is a desideratum. For various perspectives on the *mizwot* as "law and sacrament," see Bergman, Borowitz, Simon. These aforementioned essays explore the issue from a "post-traditional" perspective; for the perspective of an Orthodox Jew, see Calebach. A synoptic presentation of the extensive issues raised in this article is to be found in Scholem's magisterial essay "Reflections on Jewish Theology."

Berger, Peter. *The Heretical Imperative.* Garden City, NY: Doubleday, 1979.

Bergman, S. H. *Faith and Reason: An Introduction to Modern Jewish Thought,* chap. 1. Translated by A. Jospe. New York: Schocken, 1961.

Borowitz, E. B. *A New Jewish Theology in the Making.* Philadelphia: Westminster, 1968. Chapter 9, "Autonomy Versus Tradition."

Calebach, A. "Autonomy, Heteronomy, and Theonomy." In *A Treasury of Tradition,* 28–51. Edited by N. Lamm and W. S. Wurzberger. New York: Hebrew Publishing Co., 1967.

Dupré, Louis. *Transcendent Selfhood.* New York: Seabury, 1979.

Fackenheim, E. L. *Encounters between Judaism and Modern Philosophy.* Philadelphia: Jewish Publication Society, 1973. Chapter 2, "Abraham and the Kantians: Moral Duties and Divine Commandments."

Graupe, H. M. *The Rise of Modern Judaism.* Translated by J. Robinson. Huntington, NY: Robert K. Krieger, 1979. Chapter 11.

Heinemann, I. *Ta'amei ha-mizwot be-sifrut yisrael* [*Reasons for the Commandments in Jewish Literature*], vol. 2. Jerusalem: World Zionist Organization, 1954.

MacIntyre, A. C. *Secularization and Moral Change.* London: Oxford University Press, 1967.

Mendes-Flohr, P. "Secular Religiosity: Reflections on Post-Traditional Jewish Spirituality and Community." In *Approaches to Judaism in Modern Times,* 19–31. Edited by M. L. Raphael. Brown Judaic Studies 49. Chico, CA: Scholars Press, 1983.

Rotenstreich, N. *Jews and German Philosophy.* New York: Schocken, 1984. Part 1, "On the Authority of Religious Conviction."

———. *Tradition and Reality: The Impact of History on Modern Jewish Thought,* chap. 1. New York: Random House, 1972.

Scholem, Gershom. "Reflections on Jewish Theology." In *On Jews amd Judaism in Crisis: Selected Essays,* 261–97. Edited by W. J. Dannhauser. New York: Schocken, 1976.

Simon, E. "Law and Observance in Jewish Experience." In *Tradition and Contemporary Experience: Essays on Jewish Thought and Life,* 221–39. Edited by A. Jospe. New York: Schocken, 1970.

Werblowsky, R. J. Z. *Beyond Tradition and Modernity: Changing Religions in a Changing World.* London: Athlone Press, 1976. Chapter 3, "Sacral Particularity: The Jewish Case. . . ."

11

Revelation and the Bible according to Twentieth-Century Jewish Philosophy

R I V K A   H O R W I T Z

The Problem of Revelation in Our Time

MARTIN BUBER, in one of his articles on the Bible, wrote "man of today resists the Scriptures because he cannot endure revelation."[1] Human beings of our age have great difficulties in accepting revelation; they approach the Bible as a book like other books and not as the *Biblia* which is "an encounter between a group of people and the Lord of the world in the course of history." There is a chasm between the human being and the Bible and one does not bear witness to the "Word." Today the Bible is studied by many scientific approaches, from the points of view of anthropology, history, archaeology, linguistics, etc., yet we remain detached from its main spirit. As Buber said, we lock ourselves away "in one of the unholy compartments and feel relieved."[2] Buber, who rejected this attitude, wished to awaken his reader to the message of the Bible.

Buber had devoted many years of his life to showing that the books of the Bible are holy Scriptures and that their revelation is the revelation of God. He wished to help moderns to regain an openness that they had lost and to be able to "hear the Word." However, some of the problems of modern times are also those of Buber. Hence, his description of revelation differs drastically from the description found in classical Judaism or in later premodern periods.

It is our task in this paper to study not only Buber but also Hermann Cohen, Franz Rosenzweig, and other modern Jewish authors in regard to their views of revelation, which include innovations or motifs rarely found

346

before. What are the characteristics that these modern thinkers ascribe to revelation and how are they determined? Modern thinkers are no doubt influenced by the formidable *historical* criticism of Bible since the Enlightenment, but in the end it is rather their own *philosophical* understanding that is their primary concern.

Modern Interpretations versus Classical Views

The direction of Hermann Cohen in his interpretation of revelation is an extreme rational spiritualization and an antimythical approach, whereas the direction of Buber and Rosenzweig is based on the mythical. Buber and Rosenzweig explain revelation in terms of a mutual dialogue between God and humanity, the meaning of which in the end remains problematic. The direction of Hermann Cohen could be considered more consistent than that of Buber and Rosenzweig because their views vascillate between a mystical view which denies divine speech and a more biblical approach which affirms it. We shall pay special attention to their interpretation of "Torah from Sinai" and their way of coping with the problem of Torah and biblical criticism.

The first major difference between the traditional view and those of these three modern thinkers is their optimistic understanding of revelation: they all claim that revelation is *present.* They widen the concept of revelation and disregard the traditional distinction between prophecy and later inspiration to a degree rarely found in our tradition. Revelation for Hermann Cohen, Martin Buber, and Franz Rosenzweig exists in the present; for Cohen and Buber it is also definitely universal.[3] This optimism stands in contrast to much of the religious despair and the Kafka-like inability to "find the key" or the feeling of "facing an iron wall," so common in our time.

The understanding that revelation is present is, as Rosenstock-Huessy explained, a demand for the vitality and dynamism of religion; it is a return to the Bible and a rejection of the humility and despair expressed in the midrash and other later writings that claimed that prophecy has ended.[4] In this spirit, Isaac Breuer asks whether it is just because God revealed himself in the past that he must reveal himself today? Rosenstock-Huessy thought that if one accepts the view that revelation has ceased, religion would lose its strength and become obsolete. The rabbis, on the other hand, thought that their period differed from the golden age, when a direct relation between God and humanity existed; in their period a subdued holy spirit was believed to continue, then as always. The rabbinic saying "If our predecessors were human beings we are as donkeys" expresses not only their historical view but also their attitude to authority and to prophecy. The sages attempted to magnify the past and see the revelation of Mount Sinai as a cosmic event in which all of nature had participated; in this light their own period is dwarfed. They definitely recognized a hierarchy of moments and thought that they lived in an age of decline.

Yet these three philosophers, Cohen, Buber, and Rosenzweig, each in his own way claims that revelation is present. This should not be understood only in the negative sense of questioning the authenticity of past events; it is also a positive statement of enormous importance. One must also mention here that, although this view draws parallels between the ancient prophet and the modern person, the examples given by these philosophers are more humble: they speak of revelation in relation to one's ability to pray, to confess one's sins before God, or to repent and to find one's mission in life after return.

Revelation as an Ongoing Phenomenon

Hermann Cohen, the great rationalist and founder of the Marburg school, considered in his last book *Religion of Reason out of the Sources of Judaism* (1918) that revelation means God revealing to humanity ethical reason. Revelation is the sign of reason, which comes from God and relates humanity to God. For Cohen, *God always reveals himself to humanity.* Cohen says that the Torah does not contain any mystery, any unveiling.[5] In prayer God is called *"noten ha-Torah,"* the "Giver of the Torah," in the present; this giving by God is, as Cohen explains, no secret giving. God gives the Torah as he gives everything: life, bread, and also death. Hence, revelation is universal, rational, and present; there is nothing supernatural related to it. But this interpretation of Cohen's is brought along with quotations from the Bible, the Talmud, Maimonides, and Ibn Ezra. He gives this rationalistic view a traditional Jewish setting; one feels through every page of his work an enormous concern for his fellow Jews and an emotional weight, as though he were standing before martyrdom.

For Buber, too, revelation is universal; this idea, which has sources in the Bible, midrash, and in medieval philosophy appears more central in our generation than in earlier periods. Cohen quotes a midrash that calls heaven and earth as witness that the holy spirit may rest "on an Israelite or on a pagan, a man or a woman, a slave or a maidservant."[6] Buber, however, who does not feel the need to quote sources, speaks directly to the reader and says that revelation is present and universal; it is I and Thou. He explains that it is "absolute present which can never become past and must therefore become present and be present in every time and for every time."[7]

This is one of his most important demands, whereas for Cohen the present is not a moment in time but a rational revealing of reason which is *always;* for Rosenzweig and for Buber it is a *moment* in time, an event here and now. Buber thinks that revelation, the dialogue between God and humanity, is an event that happens to humans today, and was the foundation of the great communities at the turning points of human time.[8] However, for Buber as well as for Rosenzweig, human life here and now is of central interest. The present is not seen by them as an end of an "elapsed time" but as actual fulfilled present. Buber wrote "what is essential is lived in the present," on which Walter Kaufmann commented that this is not a single outrageous statement—in fact, it is the central motif of Buber's *I and Thou.*[9] For Buber and Rosenzweig, the biblical events are similar to experiences in the present. For Buber, the great biblical revelations are not the central events; he claims that Judaism does not set a past event as a midpoint between origin and goal, between creation and redemption. In the course of history, the Jew experiences revelation, a revelation "I experience as if I am there."[10] The emphasis is on the present witness of the biblical prophecy.

One could argue that the emphasis on the witness *is on account of the disbelief in the past event* whose reliability has been undermined by higher criticism, a move amply attested in recent religious thinking. In Buber, however, the emphasis is rather on a Kierkegaardian type of seriousness, demanding that revelation is either present or it is nothing. In fact, only because God reveals himself today, Rosenzweig and Buber argue, can we believe that he revealed himself in the past. This idea is based on the assumption that human nature has not changed, nor has God's relation to the world: "What happened once happens now and always."[11] Though there are qualitative differences in historical ages and there are periods of eclipse of God, time is not developing in simple progression; rather God "never ceases in accordance with His nature to be You for us."[12] All depends on whether it is a "moment of grace" and on whether we are present to it. Rosenzweig's *Star of Redemption,* which precedes *I and Thou,* already contains the idea of revelation as present; it is the center of Rosenzweig's book, his philosophy, and his life. He wrote: "Revelation is of the present, indeed it is being present in itself;" the dialogue between God and humans is "purely the present."

This idea is quite fantastic. We rarely meet people who claim that they were addressed by God, yet the implication that the past events *depend* on that present revelation is found in their writings. I think one must assume that these philosophers are speaking of an experience of revelation, of receiving a presence, or hearing a voice. In Buber's writings, however, we do not find reports on divine revelation; in Rosenzweig's case there are at least some hints of a real experience. There is one in a letter to Gritli, the wife of Eugen Rosenstock-Huessy, with whom he was very friendly, describing his return to Judaism as follows:

> From July to September, 1913 I was quite willing to die, to let everything within myself die. . . . It is extraordinary in us that God, in our case, has not only spoken to us through our lives; in addition, He has made the life around us fall down like the wings of a theatrical decoration, and on the empty stage *He has spoken to us.*[13]

At the end of *The Star* he also wrote explaining the biblical verse "May he make his countenance to shine upon you": the countenance of God is shining so we may recognize Him.[14]

> God, who is the last and the first—He unlocked to me doors of the sanctuary which is built in the innermost middle. He allowed Himself to be seen. He led me to the border of life where seeing is vouchsafed. "For no man shall see Him and live." Thus that sanctuary where He granted me to see Him had to be a segment of the hypercosmos in the world itself, a life beyond life.

Rabbi Abraham Isaac Kook also believed in the present possibility of revelation, but not in that universal sense, not everywhere, and not without conditions.[15] For him there is a connection between the Land of Israel, the Torah, and revelation: this land is the center of revelation. The possibility of revelation exists even now, according to Rav Kook, but the present revelation (which he even calls prophecy) appears to him of a somewhat lower type than ancient prophecy. The present one is irregular, whereas the ancient one was constant; Rav Kook even considered that the present revelation stems from a different source in the divine. He composed mystical poetry, but kept the distinction that was the basis of classical halakhah. He believed that the messianic age was approaching, and this belief was certainly related to his understanding of divine inspiration.

The idea that revelation still continues is found in talmudic literature. For example, Deuteronomy 5:19, *qol gadol we-lo' yasaf* (" The Lord spoke those words—those and no more . . . with a mighty voice . . ." [JPS]) is interpreted in two different ways: either as "stopped" or as "going on," the subject of the verb being the great voice of Sinai. Thus, one finds the Talmud and the Targum also saying that the "voice of Sinai goes on forever," a matter later quoted in Rashi and recently discussed in the writings of Abraham Joshua Heschel.[16] Rabbi Isaiah Horowitz, in his famous kabbalistic ethical work *Shney Luḥot ha-Berit* (*The Two Tablets of the Covenant*) considers that matter, saying that God is "the One who gives the Torah"; he adds: "He is still giving it and He will never stop giving it."[17] Horowitz also says that the authority of the mystics who know the secret is the authority of that voice. Revelation appears to Horowitz like a fountain that gushes forth forever. A very daring thought is expressed by him in interpreting the morning prayer "Give us a share in Thy Torah," on which he says: "Give us a share in the Torah which God Himself studies, or else may we become worthy of having Him say a teaching in our name." Horowitz's interpretation is an example of how gates open in mystical interpretation of revelation.

But Buber and Rosenzweig diverge from Horowitz in their awareness and acceptance of higher criticism and in the thought that the Bible or, more precisely, the text of the Torah may be corrupt. Given that point of view, how can moderns, even those who accept revelation, relate to the Bible? Yet Buber and Rosenzweig translated the Bible. They made an extraordinary effort to bring back the oral word as it had been before it was written down. However, the undertaking sometimes seemed impossible to them, when either the tradition or the text appeared unreliable. On 29 January 1925 Rosenzweig wrote to his cousin Hans Ehrenberg:

> I perhaps believe in any miracle, but I would believe, when I am forced to believe, or where it comes to me all by itself. Thus I do not even believe in the splitting of the Red Sea, nor even in Sinai as I believe in the whole. That miracles occurred in relation with those events is for me a strong conviction, but those which we find in the Bible may be falsely reported. Scriptures are poison, even holy ones.[18]

Authenticity of the Sinaitic Revelation

In the Middle Ages an appeal was made to the historical proof developed by Saadiah Gaon, who said that the Torah must be divine revelation because the children of Israel saw it and it is hardly likely that they would have agreed to a lie.[19] Exodus 20:19 says "you yourselves have seen that I have spoken to you from heaven." It became, so Saadiah thought, incumbent upon us to accept the religion, because its authenticity had been proved by the senses, the ear and the eye. Rational consideration of this fact would preserve that standpoint through the course of time. There exists, according to Saadiah, an authentic historical tradition, a truth that our minds cannot deny. The revelation of Sinai was thus a historical truth that had developed into a rational one. In the Middle Ages an appeal was often made to the enormous number of witnesses, the six hundred thousand Israelites who heard the voice at Sinai. This argument seemed very appealing and was used in disputations with Christians, one form being the claim that since the number of witnesses to the Israelite revelation was far greater than those who attested to Jesus, their religion was the more reliable.

An appeal to the historical argument can still be found in the writings of

Moses Mendelssohn, who wrote in the late eighteenth century. He distinguished between an eternal, rational truth and a historical truth. Judaism, being a revealed legislation, is a historical truth. Mendelssohn's exegesis of Genesis starts uncritically with Adam; and in his philosophical writings, he states that the Torah is binding because of the covenant at Mount Sinai, where God, the absolute Sovereign, made his laws known to us through Moses.[20]

About 150 years later, in the writings of Hermann Cohen or those of his disciple Franz Rosenzweig, Judaism is no longer considered a historical truth. The doubt in the historical proof is expressed by Rosenzweig, who says that his relationship to Judaism does not depend on the fact that six hundred thousand heard the divine voice at Sinai.[21] If the Samaritan recension of the Torah text turned out to be superior, this would not diminish his belief in revelation. Revelation does not, as we have seen, depend on the Torah. He explains to Jacob Rosenheim that whereas for Samson Raphael Hirsch the oral Torah is a parallel stream to the written one, the two having started at the same fountain, for him the oral one is the completion of the written one and "both unities are equally miraculous."

Cohen accepted theories of higher criticism; he was also a great believer in progress and his eye was toward the future. He had great hopes for the messianic universal peace that he thought was not far away. Not relying on the historical, he considered Judaism to be eternal. He quotes Deuteronomy 5:3: "The Eternal made this covenant not with our fathers, but with us, even with us, who are all of us here alive today."[22] The whole historical thread is rejected with the strongest emphasis, and yet it is not abolished, but rather it is immediately attached to the present, living people. Cohen then goes one step farther and thinks that the eternal is removed from historical experience altogether. He concludes that the eternal is the warrant of the spirit of history and precedes it. Reason precedes history; the beginning is the eternal originative principle. In the end, his Judaism does not depend on the past but on reason.

Rosenzweig also develops his thought on Judaism in relation to eternity and history, but he gives them a different meaning. With regard to the same verse, Deuteronomy 5:3, he writes: "Our independence from history or, to put it positively, our eternity gives simultaneity to all moments of our history. Turning back, recapturing what has remained behind, is here a permanent necessity. For we must be able to live in our eternity."[23] The Jew who lives here and now identifies with the Bible, the Talmud, and Rashi, Alfasi, and other commentaries, all of which constitute for him the eternal present. The historical facts of where and how our ancestors lived are put in shadow in comparison to their writings, which are part of the edifice of the present. He quotes "blessed be He who implanted eternal life into our midst." The convenant God made, as he cites Deuteronomy, "not with you alone but with those who are not yet standing here with us this day . . . and with those who are with us this day."[24] The emphasis in Rosenzweig is on the living present rather than on the past. The presentness of the miracle of revelation is and remains its content. He wrote: "Its historicity, however, is its ground and its warrant."[25]

Although the emphasis is really not on the past, the past must have occurred. Rosenzweig quotes the saying from the haggadah that every individual Jew is bound to regard the exodus from Egypt as if he himself has been one of those to go.[26] The historicity is, in Rosenzweig's opinion, a necessity; yet he had a high opinion of higher criticism, and the biblical past appears vague, perhaps on account of Hegelian or Christian influences. Judaism as we know it is the foundation of Jewish life, and it is such primarily from the time of Rabbi Yohanan ben Zakkai or Rabbi Akiba. Rosenzweig admired Heinrich Graetz for starting his *History of the Jews* from that period.[27] In an article in 1928, Rosenzweig complained that only Jewish orthodoxy feels obliged to retain the dogma of "Torah from Heaven" literally, as if the Torah had been given in words or even in letters.[28] He argues against those who accept the midrash and the medieval interpretations without considering modern criticism; the separation between the old and the new is a mistake.

In his description of the Jewish law in *The Star*, Rosenzweig does not mention Torah from Sinai at all. In comparing Judaism and Christianity, he states that the Jews do not count their years from any event in history—unlike the Christians, who count from the birth of Christ—and he concludes that no event in our history is absolute, alluding to Mount Sinai. In comparison with Christianity this is correct; there is no before or after in the Jewish calender, which starts with the creation of the world. Sinai is less central in some of the prophetic books, though in the Song of Deborah (Judges 5) already it has taken on the cosmic dimensions found later in the rabbis' description of the event at Sinai where "heavens bent, the earth moved, kings trembled, the inhabitants of all the earth were alarmed." Buber, in his *Prophetic Faith*, starts with that very ancient Song of Deborah to prove the historicity of Sinai. Rosenzweig, like Psalm 136, which recounts the past without mentioning Sinai at all, puts the emphasis on the present Jew and the Torah. Yet one must see that there is an attempt in his writings to reinterpret the past in a way that the truth of the Torah and that of higher criticism do not contradict each other.[29]

Hermann Cohen

Hermann Cohen, discussing the revelation at Mount Sinai, writes: "Revelation is first of all a singular event in the history of the people: the revelation on Sinai."[30] The version of the story of the revelation in Deuteronomy appears to Cohen preferable to that in Exodus because it broke the "early naïveté"; Deuteronomy's account appears to Cohen more spiritual and more abstract. As for the question of how the incorporeal God could communicate a revelation to finite beings, Cohen answers by saying that there was an event at Sinai, but there was no audible voice. Cohen speaks of a "spiritual hearing."[31] He is of the opinion that there was no theophany at Sinai, and he quotes Deuteronomy 4:15–16: "Take ye therefore good heed for your souls for you saw no manner of form on the day that the Eternal spoke unto you in Horeb out of the midst of fire." And in 4:12 it says "ye heard the voice of words but ye saw no form." Cohen wishes to exclude any relation to the physical or to the senses; he claims that hearing is just as sensual as seeing and neither one is meant in the revelation at Sinai, because "all materiality was to be kept away from that revelation."[32] He explains that the words "Ye heard" imply no voice but the hearing of words, which is interpreted by him to mean understanding, obeying, or doing. Each one, Cohen says, following Maimonides and an early midrash, understood the revelation on Mount Sinai according to his own level. Moses had, according to Cohen, no special task in transmitting the revelation; the whole people received it.[33] His special talents were those of a leader; he took them out of slavery in Egypt and he was the teacher who explained the ethical teachings to them, as described in the fifth book of Moses. The anthropomorphic expression of Deuteronomy 5:4 that God spoke to the people "face to face" is explained by Ibn Ezra to mean that the revelation was direct and without a mediator.[34] Cohen considers the whole Bible to be the national literature of the Jews. Deuteronomy is important because it teaches social and political institutions, courts of justice in theory and practice, especially in chapters 12–28. His interests in social justice and in compassion for the neighbor are well known. In Deuteronomy Cohen also pays specific attention to the verse "Hear Israel," which is significant because monotheism is founded, as he says, in the national consciousness on Mount Sinai.

Cohen then asks:

> Is revelation unique to Sinai? Is not the whole Torah revelation? And was the Torah in the entire fullness of its content revealed on Sinai? The rabbis did not shrink from the conclusion that . . . the whole content of the Torah was included in the revelation of Sinai. They even went so far as to explain their own exposition as oral Torah, an exposition they based on those laws which

they designated as given to "Moses at Sinai." Despite all this, the Decalogue, as the revelation proper on Sinai retained special place. Thereby, however, the content and concept of revelation fluctuate.[35]

An attempt to show that revelation has a multiple content is found in innumerable traditional interpretations, including, for example, the Introduction of Naḥmanides to the Torah.

Given these assumptions, it is not surprising to find in Cohen's writings that "the notion of the sons of Noah is based on the presupposition that revelation, that religion, did not begin only with the revelation on Sinai."[36] Cohen speaks also of the patriarchs in that regard. It is interesting to note that Rav Kook, more than a decade before Cohen, thought that the ethics of the ancient Near East must have been of an extremely high standard if Abraham came from there.[37] There were, in his view, ancient ethical laws in the Near East that could be the foundation for the ethics of the world and these were incorporated into our Torah; in this sense Kook considers the Torah as a source of universal ethical law.

In his evolving view, Cohen then considered the Torah as an ancient memory upon which prophets like Jeremiah and Ezekial built their individual theories. For Cohen the individual is superior to the nation. Did not Ezekiel, the prophet of the Diaspora, speak of personal and not collective guilt? Did he not speak of a "new heart" and a "new covenant" between God and humanity? The real conclusion of Cohen is that "man, and not the people and not Moses, man as a rational being is the correlate of the God of revelation."[38] Cohen's line of thinking is close not only to Kant but also to Maimonides, who considers the Torah in *The Guide of the Perplexed* 3 as a foundation of human ethical behavior. The highest stage is then described by Cohen as transferring Sinai into the human heart.[39] Gershom Scholem has noted parallels to this extreme spiritualized ahistorical concept of Mount Sinai in the Kabbalah. He comments that Cohen's interpretation may be related to Deuteronomy 30:14. Sinai in the heart appears to Scholem to be a mystical expression, seemingly extraordinary as the climax of a rationalistic theory based on ethics and the fear of God.[40]

Martin Buber

Buber and Cohen are in many ways opposites, especially in their understanding of myth. For Buber myth was important not only early in his development when he tended toward mysticism but also throughout his life, even in his dialogic thinking. He saw the greatness of Judaism in the fact that it was not occidental rationalism, but used stories in a mythical way;

for the Jew "an event is worth telling only when it has been grasped in its divine significance."[41] All story-telling books of the Bible have but one subject matter: the account of God's encounters with his people. Whereas for Cohen the events of Sinai were spiritualized and based on reason, for Buber they were understood by the senses. Buber asks: "What are we to find in the statement that God came down in fire, to the sound of thunder and the horn, to the mountain that smoked like a furnace, and spoke to His people?"[42] He rejects Cohen's type of interpretation that explains the event in "figurative language," which is used to express a "spiritual" process, and he equally rejects an allegorical interpretation that argues that the Bible does not recall actual events. Buber goes in a third direction: he thinks that the event is a verbal record of a natural event that took place in the world of senses common to all human beings. The assemblage experienced this event as a revelation vouchsafed to them by God and preserved it as such in the memory of generations, an enthusiastic, spontaneous, formative memory. The witnesses related what they saw; they listened and communicated that which the voice sounding forth from this event wished to communicate to them.

Natural events, says Buber, are the carriers of revelation, implying that it is not carried by the supernatural. There is, however, a voice that comes out of the event and communicates to the hearers. Buber thinks that what occurred is an "otherness," the touch of the other. He explains revelation, both old and new, by using Nietzsche's phrase, "You take, you do not ask who it is that gives."[43] "But," Buber continues, "when we do find the Giver, we find out that revelation exists."[44] Revelation is, for Buber, not an experience of a mystic;[45] in *I and Thou* Buber rejects the mystic who wishes to remain with God and has no interest in the world. The mystic thinks that revelation is a goal in itself, but for Buber revelation is a demand by God that one act in the world and help to bring closer its redemption. All human beings have their own ways by which they fulfill this mission, by which they act in the world with God in their hearts.

Revelation for Buber is not formal, but is rather the personal address of God to humanity. The biblical verse "In all thy ways know him" (Prov 3:6) fits Buber; he quotes the Hasidic saying to the effect that there is no way in which God cannot be worshiped. The Lurianic Kabbalah speaks of six hundred thousand aspects of the Torah, implying that there are as many ways of worshiping God as there are Jews. This thought, as quoted in Buber's writings, also has a humanistic contemporary aspect as it stresses the individuality of every person. Buber laid extremely little weight on the divine rules; hence revelation is not prescribed on two tablets that could be held over Israel's head.[46] The meaning we receive can be put into action only by each person in the uniqueness of his or her being. "No prescription can lead us to the encounter and none leads from it." Thus, there are no preparations that may help us to reach revelation, and a general rule cannot be an outcome of revelation. It seems then that the Torah has a different message.

In his works on prophecy, Buber describes the outcome of revelation in a different manner. With regard to the *navi*,[47] the prophet, Buber speaks of *pneuma* and *logos, ruah* and *davar.* He explains that the spirit, the presence that overcomes the prophet, is the spirit of God, and this is prior to the word, the *logos.* The word, however, does not displace the *logos,* but joins with it. The *pneuma* is the stimulus and the *logos* the content, so that in prophecy human words are a creation of both God and the human being.

The Torah, Buber explains elsewhere, speaks, as the sages said "in the language of man";[48] this hides, according to Buber, a deep seriousness— namely, that the unutterable can only be uttered in the language of humans. In a letter to Rosenzweig, Buber said: "I do not believe that revelation is ever formulation of law. It is only through man in his self-contradiction that revelation becomes legislation."[49] Buber demands that each person stand alone before God. He saw no value in habits or customs; he wished, if one may say so, that we should face God without the crutch of tradition, or the ways of our fathers. Ernst Simon, in an important study on Buber, has shown that Buber not only rejects the idea of the priest, which appears to him as the personification of formalism, but also that of the patriarch.[50] For this reason he calls Abraham by the unusual name "the Seer." The ideal man for Buber is the prophet who does not begin a line of succession or hierarchy. Buber believed that there should always be a renewal; institutions lead to inertia, yet they continue to rule. Buber demanded that decisions ever be made anew.

Buber's thoughts on revelation contain two versions, one that ascribes no content to revelation and the other that relates some content to it. Scholem considered only the first interpretation.[51] In commenting on it, he said that Buber's thought, although it appears in the form of dialogue, is in fact mystical. To prove his point he quotes *I and Thou,* where Buber says:

> This is the eternal revelation which is present here and now. I neither know nor believe in any revelation that is not the same in this primal phenomenon. . . . Revelation is: "I am there as whoever I am there." That which reveals is that which reveals. The eternal source of strength flows, the eternal touch is waiting, the eternal voice sounds, nothing more.[52]

Side by side with this, however, Buber also has a biblical view of revelation, based on the dialogue between God and humanity, in which God acts for the sake of humanity. Buber wrote: "Man is addressed by God in his life" and "God never ceases instructing man."[53] Even the Decalogue and the injunctions supplementing it are, according to Buber, God's address to us, "God addressed Himself to a 'thou' that is certainly the 'thou' of each individual in each generation of the people." According to Buber, the human being is not a blind tool in the dialogue, but rather a created being who stands vis-à-vis God, free to surrender or to refuse Him. To God's sovereign address, the human being gives the autonomous answer. Buber's theory takes its cue from the Bible, where the dialogue between heaven and earth is found. The Bible has given, according to Buber, a decisive form of expression to that ever-recurring event.

Buber's understanding of dialogue rejects any attempt at being taken as psychologized religion—considering revelation merely as an event in the human soul. At times he similarly opposes a view that the dialogue is without any content, a line of thought that would annihilate the dialogue and lead to pantheism or monism and to the consideration of the dialogue as one within the human soul. For him the work of the prophet is joined with that of the divine, and it is filled with his spirit.

There thus appear to be two directions in Buber's understanding of the dialogue, one more in agreement with a mystical view, where revelation is a speechless presence; the other containing an address of God to humanity. In both cases Buber considers revelation as a pure event in time that bursts into the world in a moment without depending on any prior process. Buber also accepts the idea, one he shares with Rosenzweig, that the moment of presence is broadened so as to include a biblical understanding of time and place: the before and the after, the above and the below.

Franz Rosenzweig

Rosenzweig's understanding of the dialogue is also problematic: here too one can find a lack of consistency, sometimes tending more toward a mystical type of speechless encounter and at other times emphasizing speech. In *The Star* one can read, on the one hand, that "in the world of revelation everything must become word and what cannot become word is either prior or posterior to the word," and, on the other hand, that "revelation is nothing more than revelation."[54] Years later he explained: "All that God reveals is Himself."

Rosenzweig, unlike Buber, makes a strong point of ascribing speech to God. This is the basis of his philosophy of language or his speech-thinking, which he probably developed, as E. Freund has shown, out of E. Rosenstock-Huessy's writings.[55] Rosenzweig is not afraid of anthropomorphism. He calls his theory theomorphism, which refers to the idea that God had made human beings in His image.[56] This notion he thinks is necessary for divine-human dialogue and does not lead to crude pagan anthropomorphism. Pagans ascribe to their deity permanent attributes or characteristics, describing a god with a beard or curls, or being cruel, etc. In the Bible the emphasis is not on the description of God, but on momentary events. The Bible does not mean to say that God has eyes or ears, etc. but that in a certain moment God's eyes are watching human beings, or that God's ears hear people's prayer. The descriptions of God in the Bible do not include many human characteristics simultaneously, but *one* at a time, and these characteristics are always related to a *meeting* between God and the human person. There is no interest in the Bible in a description of the divine per se. In this context Rosenzweig also rejects theories such as Kabbalah, which are preoccupied with the hidden God. They appear to Rosenzweig to lead to a universe filled with multiple intermediary forces, a view that he rejects and for which he finds no justification in the Bible.

Since revelation is primarily present, the cardinal example of a dialogue in the biblical sense is God's question to Adam, the question of God to every human being here and now: "Where art thou?"[57] A person can hide, as did Adam, who could not face God to confess his sins; he did not dare to stand before God as the righteous Abraham did, when he said to God "here I am." The confession of sin through repentance in shame and guilt, as David did after he sinned with Bathsheba, is an important example for Buber and Hermann Cohen, each of whom also developed this direction of thought.[58] All sins are before God, and only He can purify human beings.

"Love me!" is then the command of love to the human soul, according to Rosenzweig's theory.[59] This commandment of God is only momentary. It can grow or diminish, and it is never a general law (there is a distinction in Rosenzweig's thought between law and commandment, a fact that is then carried over to his understanding of halakhah). The command of God is always to a particular human being in a particular moment; it can never be a universal rule. That command is, according to *The Star*, linked with the biblical comand *we-ahavta* ("You shall love"), which is important for both Christians and Jews. It is the principal command, from which all others are derived. Hermann Cohen's theory is concerned with the ethical and social aspects of life, while Rosenzweig's emphasis is on the theological, the love of God.

In an extremely daring line of thought, Rosenzweig explains how we find in the Bible the prophet saying in the name of God "I am."[60] He argues that the prophet neither mediates between God and humans, nor does he receive a revelation and then pass it on. Instead he becomes a vessel of God, and "the voice of God sounds forth directly from within him, God speaks directly as 'I' from within him." Therefore the prophet cannot use the third person, speaking of God merely as He.

Johann Georg Hammann's understanding of language, his view of the name as *energia*, and his recognition of the power of the language as divine come close to the thought of Rosenzweig, who claims that both love and speech cannot be simply human. They are for Rosenzweig "sensual and super-sensual." He rejects the interpretation of the Song of Songs, since the time of Herder, as a beautiful shepherd love song. What is, in effect, implied by this interpretation, he says, is that God cannot love. This is in line with Rosenzweig's rejection of the philosophy of Spinoza and his followers in the Enlightenment; on the contrary, he said, only because God loves can humans love.[61]

A different line of thought appears in Rosenzweig's writing after his close friendship with Buber was established, namely, the view that revelation has no content and that God cannot give any commandment to humans. Rosenzweig then ignored what he himself had written on the subject and used language closer to those passages in *I and Thou* where Buber had said that revelation had no content. (The cross-fertilization of ideas between Buber and Rosenzweig in the years of their friendship was tremendous and demands a separate study.) In a private letter after publishing "The Builders," an open address to Buber in which he had thought to bring Buber closer to halakhah, he wrote: "Revelation is certainly not law-giving."[62] "The primary content of revelation is revelation itself. . . . 'He came down [on Mount Sinai]' concludes the revelation: 'He spoke' is the beginning of human interpretation and certainly *'anokhi*, 'I am.'" Rosenzweig nowhere explained why "I am" must be human interpretation and why he changed his view. Is the rejection of attributing speech to God related to an acceptance of higher criticism, or a rejection of ascribing general rules to God? For him, as he said, God was "certainly not a Lawgiver." Does this imply that revelation is "just" revelation, in a speechless (mystical) sense?[63] Did he change his view because of his dialogue with Buber? Earlier he had written in *The Star* that God speaks to humans and commands them to love Him, this being the command from which the rest are derived.

Nahum Glatzer, who was Rosenzweig's disciple in those years, understood Rosenzweig's statement to Buber to mean that only "the election of Israel is of divine origin, but the Torah in all its details is from man alone." Rosenzweig, upon hearing Glatzer's interpretation of his own thinking was shocked and tried to reformulate it, because he then felt strongly that "election and Torah belong together." Is the Torah divine or human? To answer this Rosenzweig applies his earlier philosophy, his distinction between experience and objective data. The first election must be that of

God and the second that of Israel, who, in responding, elect God. Rosenzweig wishes to give to the covenant of Sinai the character of a dialogue. First, God elects the people: "Our people [is] the only one that did not originate from the womb of nature that bears nations, but—and this is unheard of!—'was led forth' a nation from the midst of another nation'" (Deut 4:34). The people, even before it was born, was chosen by Him. When the people became aware of their election they become active. Rosenzweig then distinguishes between relating to the commandments or to the Torah as to an "I and Thou" or an objective datum. At the moment in which one fulfills a commandment one cannot report on it or give a rational account of it; it is between the human being and his father in heaven; no outsider can share in it. To explain this matter Rosenzweig gives the example of a marriage in which moments of intimacy, if reported to an outsider, would appear as ugly gossip. Similarly, in the time of prayer one puts aside the sociological study of Max Weber or the psychological study of Sigmund Freud. This does not mean that these studies are unimportant or untrue, but that one has to distinguish between the realm of knowledge, which can be only a foundation of the commandment but not part of it, and the commandment itself. The scientific study of the Bible must be put aside in the moment of relating to it in religious terms, such as, for example, the time when one hears the portion of the week being read in the synagogue.[64] "It" is the theo-human reality of the commandment that permits us to pray "Blessed are Thou." The whole year the story of Balaam's talking ass may be a mere fairy tale, says Rosenzweig, using an ill-chosen example, but on that Sabbath wherein this portion is read, one hears it differently. When studying it objectively we say "He"; when performing a commandment we say "Thou." One may perhaps compare it to the distinction between learning the *Shema*ʿ and praying it; the learning of this chapter as part of the Bible does not suffice to the performance of the commandment.

What then is the divine element and what is the human? This is not a distinction between the whole and the part, but between that which can be expressed and that which we know but cannot express. Using a biblical simile, Rosenzweig says that God appeared to Abraham and then he lifted his eyes and saw three human beings; with God's help Abraham or the human person can see another dimension of the terrestial life.[65]

The recognition of moments that purge the soul from the darkening elements found in daily life is a motif in Judah Halevi's *Kuzari*, a text that was certainly known to Rosenzweig.[66] In his discussion of prayer and holidays he contrasts them with the weekdays at the market; the holy moments are, for Halevi, "the heart and the fruit of time." For Rosenzweig too these moments are central; it is our choice whether to increase the number of such moments in our lives or to diminish them.

The understanding of the divine commandments in Rosenzweig's thought differs from that in Buber's. Both agree that one has to act in accordance with what God commands, but the two mean two different things. They agree that action refers to the here and now; it means an answer to a personal address by God. For Buber this demands a responsible act of the human in the world, whereas for Rosenzweig it is specifically the fulfilling of halakhah. They disagree on the role of halakhah in present life. Rosenzweig asked of Buber to apply that which he had advocated regarding Jewish learning to the commandments as well.[67] Buber continued to reject this view of Rosenzweig, in accord with his distrust of religious institutions, including the synagogue.[68] Rosenzweig, in contrast to Buber, yearned for a life within the frame of Jewish law. Rosenzweig's way was considered by Hugo Bergman, who was in this matter his disciple, to be a "tremendous revolution": giving the decision over the commandments into the free hands of the individual Jew, thus rescuing the freedom of the individual.[69] It is common knowledge, of course, that every Jew decides by free choice what to accept and what not to accept of halakhah. This fact is not theoretically accepted, however, by the tradition. Rosenzweig gave this practice a theoretical justification and foundation; he saw in it an individual existential act. He says, "Nobody should be allowed to tell us what belongs to its sphere" — no rabbi, no teacher, and no friend.[70] For the old-fashioned Jews, according to Rosenzweig's thought, the law is static; they keep it because it was revealed in the past. Rosenzweig wished to give it actuality, hence, he quotes Deuteronomy 5:3: "The Lord made this covenant not with our fathers, but with us . . . here alive this day." Thus in the end he considers revelation dynamic, given to each individual "today." In this he comes close to Hermann Cohen's understanding of revelation, which has been described earlier.

There is an important contemporary message in Rosenzweig's interpretation of halakhah. Jews who live today in an open society, whether in the United States, Europe, or in non-orthodox circles in Erez Israel have to decide on their relation to halakhah. Rosenzweig said, "I am a Jew, Therefore nothing Jewish should be alien to me" and demanded of his followers that they learn Judaism, not as additional objective information but as modernized *yeshiva*-type learning, where the learner joins himself in the learning as the newest link in the chain of the generations, a learning that leads to action. The choice one makes in accepting halakhah has to be based on one's inner truth, on one's ability to accept. The criterion cannot be a light utilitarian one; it is based on the existential truth of one's life, as if one were to say: "If I fulfill this commandment, it will be a lie," and a lie in action is one of the worst lies. Rosenzweig had a deep understanding of Judaism; he felt that his return came from the roots of his soul and was an expression of his being a part of the community of Israel. For him Judaism is a dynamic and living organism within which even the present "sons" can again become "builders,"[71] "Judaism *is* not law but it creates law."

Rosenzweig's understanding of the law differs from both the Reform and the Orthodox. Whereas the Reform decide publicly which laws are important and which can be discarded, Rosenzweig thinks that this decision should be private and individual. He himself accepted only parts of halakhah, but he did not wish to publicize the details. Rosenzweig thought that Orthodox Jews did not need his reform; they would find their own way out of the present crisis. He differs from the Orthodox in speaking of personal choice, objecting to the acceptance of halakhah on the basis of obedience. His return was to the whole, but he continued to struggle with the details, a distinction that orthodoxy does not accept.

Rosenzweig offers many interpretations of "Torah from Sinai" using *midrashim* to show that the Torah is both halakhah and aggadah, custom and law, old and new. He wrote:

No doubt the Torah, both written and oral, was given to Moses on Sinai, but was it not created before the creation of the world? Written against a background of shining fire in letters of somber flame?[72] And was not the world created for its sake? And did not Adam's son Seth found the first House of Study for teaching Torah? And did not the Patriarchs keep the Law for half a millennium before Sinai? And—when it was finally given on Sinai—was it not given in all the seventy languages spoken in the world? It has 613 commandments, a number which, to begin with, mocks all endeavor to count what is countless, but a number which in itself (plus the two commandments heard directly from the lips of the Almighty) represents the numerical value of the word Torah and the sum of the days of the year and the joints in the body of man. Did not these 613 commandments of the Torah include everything that the scrutiny and penetration of later scholars, who "put to shame" our teacher Moses himself, discovered in the crownlets and tips of the letters? And everything that the industrious student could ever hope to discover there in all future time? The Torah, which God himself learns day after day![73]

Special attention should be given to a mystical-mythical inclination that shines through in his use of quotations such as "the Torah preceded the creation of the world" or "the Torah of fire." In Kabbalah this mythical and suprahistorical aspect of rabbinic thought is much expanded. Here we see that one of the solutions to the twentieth-century problem of Torah and revelation is found in the attempt to strengthen the historical Torah by *midrashim* on the mythical Torah taken from the realm of Kabbalah and related sources.

Myth and Mysticism in the Twentieth Century

The tendency toward myth and mysticism has become part of the twentieth-century self-understanding; the writings of Heschel, Breuer, Soloveitchik, and Rav Kook all include material from the Kabbalah. The artificial fence that existed in Jewish thinking in the nineteenth century between East and West, between the rational philosophy of Judaism that was acceptable in Germany and the Kabbalah and Hasidism, which belonged to eastern Europe, has no more meaning in the twentieth century. Two examples will be given: Isaac Breuer, who devoted much of his energy to his dream of establishing a Torah state in Erez Israel and the rule of divine law on earth, was an ardent admirer of the Jewish law. As a Kantian, however, he admitted that "Torah from Sinai" cannot be proved any more than one can prove the existence of God. Breuer had a disdain for higher criticism; he found no room for it in his point of view. The Bible of modern scholarship appeared to him a lowly type, cut off from its divine roots.[74] Breuer thought that just as the *phenomena* would be a dream without the *numina,* so the Torah of higher criticism is a fantasy because it is unrelated to the Torah in itself; the real Torah is "the Torah in itself." Breuer formed that kind of interpretation so that he could strengthen the position of "Torah from Sinai" against external attacks. To do this he used the highly unusual combination of Kant and such kabbalistic sources as Nahmanides, the *Zohar,* and *Shney Luhot ha-Berit* of Isaiah Horowitz. Breuer considered the Torah to be an aspect of God, meaning that it is one of the *sefirot* (*Hokhmah* or divine wisdom). Considering the apparent Torah, he said[75] that behind the Torah there broods a mystery. The real Torah, the Torah in itself, cannot be reached by human reason, and of it one can say very little. Alluding to Nahmanides' introduction to his Torah commentary, Breuer said that in God's Torah the letters exist in different combination than in ours. What that heavenly Torah is like is hard to say, though Breuer certainly thought that the divine or preexistent Torah helps the rule of the present Torah on earth. Sometimes Breuer uses the simile of a garb, also very popular in kabbalistic writings; he speaks of the primal Torah that has to be covered with robes so that it can be comprehended. Alluding to Kant, he argues that just as there cannot be a world of objects without a world in itself, so there cannot be a Torah of objects without the primal Torah. In the Torah that we have, God availed Himself of human language. The Jewish people are Knesset Israel, and there exists a unity between Knesset Israel, the Torah, and God. The Torah, according to Breuer precedes *'am ha-torah,* meaning the Jewish people.[76] This statement, which appears in numerous places in his writings, implies a preexistence of the Torah. One can see that in his interpretation he founds the historical ground of "Torah from Sinai" on a higher level. Breuer is here quite remote from his grandfather Samson Raphael Hirsch.

Breuer's line of thinking may be compared with that of Abraham Joshua Heschel, who also dealt with the problem in a metaphysical manner and who also did not struggle with the real dilemma of higher criticism and "Torah from Sinai." He also created a *midrash* of two Torahs, or two views of Torah—the one of Sinai, a this-worldly Torah, and the other of a heavenly character, the "Torah from heaven." He relates the Torah of Sinai to the saying of Rabbi Ishmael, "the Torah speaks in the language of man," while the heavenly Torah is associated by him with Rabbi Akiba's approach.

According with Rabbi Ishmael's approach, one can find in the Torah expressions that are a result of literary form or repetitions, which need not have additional superimposed meaning. The Torah was given at Sinai: it has a *peshat;* it has a human garb; it depends on time and place. To this school of thought Heschel also ascribes a certain mild protocritical approach. Certain parts of the Torah were decisions and statements of Moses, not God's decrees. Heschel interpreted Rabbi Ishmael's thirteen rules for expounding the Torah as implying that there are logical rules of exegesis that were given together with the Torah. He also quotes Y. N. Epstein, who said that Rabbi Ishmael realized that laws have no explicit source and even contradict the literal meaning of the Torah.

On the other hand, Heschel saw in Rabbi Akiba the root of future Jewish mysticism. Rabbi Akiba does not consider the Torah in its historical dimension, but in mythic and transhistorical terms. The Torah has a preexistence, before the creation of the world. Torah includes everything; the saying of Ben Bag-Bag ("Turn it over and turn it over, for all is therein") is brought out by Heschel as belonging to this school. All wisdom is in the Torah. Deuteronomy 32:47, "for it is not an empty matter for you," Rabbi Akiba explained thus:, "If it is empty to you, it is only because you do not know how to interpret the Torah." Rabbi Akiba widened the Torah to an enormous hypostasy. Heschel claimed that Rabbi Akiba's approach was novel in his time. Rabbi Akiba also assumed that Moses ascended not to Sinai but to heaven to receive the Torah. Moses was the only human being who ever ascended to heaven and came down again. On the question of who wrote the Torah, Heschel mentions a rabbinic saying that God Himself is the author, as the Torah itself says (Exod 24:12), "which I have written."

* * * * *

In conclusion, we have seen that revelation and Torah are understood in our time through a much broader spectrum of thought than in the previous century. Today both the rational and mystical aspects of the tradition play a role; the growth of the mystical element is due to a number of factors, both positive and negative. We saw that higher criticism destroyed the classic interpretation of the revelation of Mount Sinai, which saw in this divine event the establishment of Jewish law. Revelation and halakhah became separated and halakhah lost its divine source. However, halakhah may find a way to be reestablished by the way of Rosenzweig, who considers the modern learner to be a link in the chain of the generations who learn the Torah in order to receive it. The Torah *is* divine for us, but one who tries to concretize it tries the impossible.

Notes

1. Martin Buber, "The Man of Today and the Jewish Bible," in *Israel and the World*, 95.

2. Ibid, 92.

3. Franz Rosenzweig in *The Star of Redemption* ascribes revelation only to Judaism and Christianity.

4. This was part of a conversation held with Rosenstock in Spring 1961 in his home in Norwich, Vermont.

5. Hermann Cohen, *Religion of Reason out of the Sources of Judaism*, trans. S. Kaplan (New York: Ungar, 1972) 83–84.

6. Cohen, *Religion of Reason*, 107, citing *Tana Dve Eliyahu*, chap. 8.

7. Rivka Horwitz, *Buber's Way to 'I and Thou'* (A historical analysis and the first publication of Martin Buber's lectures *Religion als Gegenwart;* Heidelberg: Lambert Schneider, 1978) 48.

8. M. Buber, *I and Thou*, with prologue and notes by W. Kaufmann (Edinburgh: T. & T. Clark, 1970) 166.

9. Ibid, 66, and Kaufmann's note on p. 64.

10. Buber, *Israel and the World*, 94–96.

11. Buber "The Dialogue between Heaven and Earth," in *On Judaism*, 215. A. Heschel rejects that view of Buber through attacks on Leopold von Ranke; see *God in Search of Man*, 129, 205, 251.

12. Buber, *I and Thou*, 147.

13. Letter of 15 June 1920; see F. Rosenzweig, *Briefe und Tagebuecher* (The Hague: Nijhoff, 1979) 2:675.

14. Rosenzweig, *The Star of Redemption*, 418, 423ff.

15. Rav A. Y. Kook, *Orot ha-Qodesh* (Hebrew), ed. D. Cohen (Jerusalem: Mosad Harav Kook, 1959) 1:274.

16. Heschel, *God in Search of Man*, 138, 143.

17. Isaiah Horowitz, *Shney Luhot ha-Berit* (photocopy of Amsterdam edition of 1689; New York, 1946) 24-25; see also G. Scholem, *The Messianic Idea in Judaism and Other Essays* (New York: Schocken, 1972) 298, 301. In *Theology of Judaism* (Hebrew) (London: Soncino, 1962) 1:240, Heschel quotes Menahem Azariah of Fano and the *Zohar* as sources; see *Zohar*, 4b.

18. Rosenzweig, *Briefe und Tagebuecher*, 2:1022. Scriptures are poison because they are the written word and not the oral word.

19. Saadiah Gaon, *The Book of Beliefs and Opinion*, trans. S. Rosenblatt (New Haven, CT: Yale University Press) 31ff.

20. Moses Mendelssohn, *Jerusalem and Other Jewish Writings* (New York: Schocken, 1969) 154.

21. Rosenzweig, "Die Einheit der Bibel," in *Kleinere Schriften*, 128.

22. Cohen, *Religion of Reason*, 76, 84.

23. Rosenzweig, "The Builders," in *On Jewish Learning*, ed. N. N. Glatzer, 90.

24. Rosenzweig, *The Star of Redemption*, 298.

25. Ibid, 183.

26. Ibid, 304. The emphasis on the experience of the past is found in many contemporaries. See, e.g., Heschel, *God in Search of Man*, 14; and J. Soloveitchick, *Ish Ha-Halakhah* (Jerusalem: World Zionist Organization, Department of Religious Education in the Diaspora, 1979) 148.

27. Rosenzweig, "Geist und Epochen der juedischen Geschichte," in *Kleinere Schriften*, 17.

28. Rosenzweig, "Zur Encyclopedia Judaica," in *Kleinere Schriften*, 523.

29. Shalom Rosenberg, "Bible Research in Modern Religious Thinking" (Hebrew), in *The Bible and Us*, ed. Uriel Simon (Tel Aviv: Dvir, 1979) 86–119. Rosenberg relies heavily on Rav Kook, and in conclusion he says: "Science means freedom; no limitation should be put on this freedom" (p. 119).

30. Cohen, *Religion of Reason*, 73.

31. Ibid, 74.

32. Ibid.

33. Ibid, 75. In the writings of Mendelssohn, Samuel David Luzzatto, and S. R. Hirsch, one can also see an outlook that the children of Israel were the receivers of the Torah. Hirsch even played down the greatness of Moses; see Mendelssohn, *Jerusalem*, 69; Luzzatto's *Perush al ha-Torah* (*Exegesis on the Torah*) Exodus 20:1; and Hirsch's exegesis on the Torah, Exodus 24:1; 6:26; and 32:15.

34. Cohen, *Religion of Reason*, 75.

35. Ibid, 73.

36. Ibid, 327.

37. A. Y. Kook, *Eder Ha-Yegar*, 42.

38. Cohen, *Religion of Reason*, 82, 79.

39. Ibid, 84.

40. Gershom Scholem, "Some Fundamental Observations on an Ancient Tradition in our Secularized and Technological Modern World," *The Center Magazine* 7 (1974) 62.

41. M. Buber, *On Judaism*, 105.

42. Buber, *Israel and the World*, 97.

43. Ibid, 98.

44. Buber, *I and Thou*, 158.

45. Ibid, 155; Buber calls the mystic "religious" in quotation marks.

46. Ibid, 159.

47. Buber, *The Prophetic Faith*, 64.

48. Buber, *Israel and the World*, 99.

49. Letter of Buber of 24 June 1924; see F. Rosenzweig, *On Jewish Learning*, 111.

50. Ernst Simon, "Martin Buber and Judaism," '*Iyyun: A Hebrew Philosophical Quarterly*, 9 (1958) 18. Soloveitchick rejects Buber and Ahad Ha'am's dichotomy between prophecy and legalism. He shows that Judaism is both prophecy and law (*Ish Ha-Halakhah*, 225, 216). Heschel (*God in Search of Man*, 344) also rejects this view; he speaks of the value of habits.

51. Scholem, "Some Fundamental Observations," 62.

52. Buber, *I and Thou*, 160.

53. Buber, *On Judaism*, 218.

54. Rosenzweig, *The Star of Redemption*, 178, 161. The second quotation is from Rosenzweig's comments on Judah Halevi. See N. N. Glatzer, *F. Rosenzweig, His Life and Thought*, 285. The more

traditional view is found in Heschel's writings, where he does not speak of God's self-revelation, but of the revelation of his ways; see *God in Search of Man*, 261.

55. Else Freund, *Die Existenzphilosophie Franz Rosenzweigs* (Hamburg: Felix Meiner, 1959) 144ff.

56. Rosenzweig, *Kleinere Schriften*, 525–33.

57. Rosenzweig, *The Star of Redemption*, 175; and M. Buber, *Between Man and Man* (New York: Macmillan, 1967) 166.

58. Cohen, *Religion of Reason*, 102ff.

59. Rosenzweig, *The Star of Redemption*, 176.

60. Ibid, 178.

61. Ibid, 199.

62. Letter of 5 June 1925; see Rosenzweig, *On Jewish Learning*, 118.

63. Gershom Scholem comments that this understanding of Sinai as a revelation without words is mystical in meaning, and he compares it with a statement by Rabbi Mendel of Rymanov that all that Israel heard at Sinai was the *aleph* of '*anokhi, aleph* being a silent letter (Scholem, *On the Kabbalah and Its Symbolism* [New York: Schocken, 1973] 30).

64. Rosenzweig, *On Jewish Learning*, 122.

65. Ibid, 124. Rosenzweig quotes a sermon of Rabbi Nobel that he had heard.

66. *The Kuzari*, 3:5, p. 135. On Halevi and Rosenzweig, see Rivka Horwitz, "Rosenzweig's Understanding of Jewish History" (Hebrew), *Proceedings of American Academy for Jewish Research* 37 (1969) 1–25.

67. Rosenzweig, *On Jewish Learning*, 75.

68. See Ernst Simon, "Martin Buber and Judaism," 13; also Rosenzweig, *On Jewish Learning*, 114–15.

69. Hugo Bergman, introduction to Rosenzweig's "The Builder."

70. Rosenzweig, *On Jewish Learning*, ed. N. N. Glatzer (New York: Schocken, 1955).

71. Letter to R. Hallo of 27 March 1922; see Rosenzweig, *Briefe und Tagebuecher*, 2:762.

72. That the Torah of fire has mystical character is based on Deut 33:2, "At His right hand was a fiery law."

73. Rosenzweig, *On Jewish Learning*, 78–79.

74. Isaac Breuer, *Der neue Kuzari* (Frankfurt: Rabbiner Hirsch Gesellschaft, 1934) 337; see also 244, 249.

75. Ibid, 329.

76. Isaac Breuer, *Moriah* (Hebrew) (Jerusalem: Mosad Harav Kook, 1982) 62.

Bibliography

For introductory works, see Guttmann's *Philosophies of Judaism*, which is a good introduction to Cohen and Rosenzweig by a disciple of Cohen. However, both Guttmann and Rotenstreich in *Jewish Philosophy in Modern Times* are useful references, though difficult to read. The books by Bergman and A. A. Cohen are relatively easy introductions. In Hebrew, Schweid is good for background but does not deal with the twentieth century.

For a primary source on Hermann Cohen, see his *Religion of Reason*, translated by S. Kaplan. This edition includes two introductory essays, one by the translator and one by the brilliant Leo Strauss. Another useful work on Cohen is Melber. Franz Rosenzweig's excellent essay on Hermann Cohen has not yet appeared in English; in Hebrew it is to be found in *Naharayim* (Jerusalem, 1960) pp. 109–53; the German original is in *Kleinere Schriften*, pp. 299–350. One should also consult the interesting volume of Hermann Cohen's *Briefe*. There is no Hermann Cohen archive; his wife, Martha, was killed in the Holocaust and his papers were lost.

On Buber the literature is very extensive. The best introduction to Buber is Kohn, in spite of the fact that it is old. Other important sources include Schaeder, and the volume from the Library of Living Philosophers, *The Philosophy of Martin Buber,* edited by P. A. Schilpp and M. Friedman, in which see especially Fackenheim. A more recent collection of essays on Buber is *Martin Buber: A Centenary Volume,* edited by H. Gordon and J. Bloch, in which see especially Uffenheimer. From Rivka Horwitz's book *Buber's Way to I and Thou,* one can learn Buber's way from the mystic unity to the dialogue, his early friendship with Rosenzweig, and the debates on the dialogue and idealism. For both Buber and Rosenzweig dialogue meant also revelation. Among the important primary sources by Buber, we note first *I and Thou,* especially part 3; *Israel and the World; On Judaism,* especially "The Dialogue between Heaven and Earth"; *Moses, The Prophetic Faith;* and finally the anthology of Glatzer, *Martin Buber on the Bible.*

Introductory material on Franz Rosenzweig can be found in the anthology of Glatzer, *Franz Rosenzweig, His Life and Thought,* which includes also some useful bibliography. See also Rosenstock-Huessy, which presents the exchange of letters between Rosenzweig and Rosenstock-Huessy on Christianity and Judaism. In the collection of essays edited by Glatzer, *Franz Rosenzweig, On Jewish Learning,* see especially "The Builders." Rosenzweig's major book, *The Star of Redemption,* is a difficult work, but one of the greatest books in modern Jewish thought; see especially the chapters on revelation and on Judaism.

Heschel's most important works for our study are *God in Search of Man* and *The Prophets.*

On Rav Kook, see Agus, and, in Hebrew, Yaron. Primary sources for Rav Kook, all in Hebrew, include *Orot ha-Kodesh* and *Eder Ha-Yekar.*

For Isaac Breuer, a useful English introduction is Levinger. Breuer wrote many books, most of which have not yet been translated from their original German or Hebrew; see especially *Moriah.*

Agus, J. B. *The Banner of Jerusalem.* New York: Bloch, 1946.
Bergman, Hugo. *Faith and Reason: An Introduction to Modern Jewish Thought.* Translated by A. Jospe. New York: Schocken, 1961.
Breuer, Isaac. *Moriah.* Jerusalem: Mosad Harav Kook, 1982.
———. *Der neue Kuzari.* Frankfurt: Rabbiner Hirsch Gesellschaft, 1934.
Buber, Martin. *I and Thou.* With Prologue and Notes by W. Kaufmann. Edinburgh: T. & T. Clark, 1970.
———. *Israel and the World.* New York: Schocken, 1963.
———. *Moses.* New York: Harper, 1946.
———. *On Judaism.* New York: Schocken, 1967.
———. *The Prophetic Faith.* New York: Harper & Row, 1960.
Cohen. A. A. *The Natural and Supernatural Jew.* New York: Behrman House, 1979.
Cohen, Hermann. *Briefe.* Edited by Bertha Strauss and Bruno Strauss. Berlin: Schocken Verlag, 1939.
Fackenheim, E. "Martin Buber's Concept of Revelation." In *The Philosophy of Martin Buber.* Edited by A. Schilpp and M. Friedmann. Library of Living Philosophers 12. La Salle, IL: Open Court, 1967.
Glatzer, N. N., ed. *Franz Rosenzweig, His Life and Thought.* New York: Schocken, 1961.
———. *Martin Buber on the Bible.* New York, 1968.
Gordon, Haim, and Johanan Bloch, eds. *Martin Buber: A Centenary Volume.* New York: Ktav, 1984.
Guttmann, Julius. *Philosophies of Judaism.* Translated by David W. Silverman. New York: Holt, Rinehart and Winston, 1964.
Heschel, A. *God in Search of Man.* New York: Jewish Publication Society, 1964.
———. *The Prophets.* Philadelphia: Jewish Publication Society, 1955.
Horwitz, Rivka. *Buber's Way to I and Thou.* Heidelberg: Lambert Schneider, 1978.

Jewish Philosophy in Modern Times. Edited by Nathan Rotenstreich. New York: Holt, Rinehart and Winston, 1968.

Kohn, Hans. *Martin Buber, sein Werk und seine Zeit.* Cologne: Melzer, 1961.

Kook, Rav. *Orot ha-kodesh.* Edited by D. Cohen. Jerusalem: Mosad Harav Kook, 1959.

———. *Eder Ha-Yeqar.* Jerusalem: Mosad Harav Kook, 1967.

Levinger, Jacob, ed. *Isaac Breuer, Concepts of Judaism.* Jerusalem: Israel Universities Press, 1974.

Melber, Jehuda. *Hermann Cohen's Philosophy of Judaism.* New York: J. David, 1968.

Rosenstock-Huessy, Eugen. *Judaism despite Christianity.* University, AL: University of Alabama Press, 1969.

Rosenzweig, Franz. *The Star of Redemption.* Translated by W. Hallo. New York: Holt, Rinehart and Winston, 1970.

———. *Kleinere Schriften.* Berlin: Schocken, 1937.

Schaeder, Grete. *The Hebrew Humanism of Martin Buber.* Translated by Noah J. Jacobs. Detroit: Wayne State University Press, 1984.

Schweid, Eliezer. *Toledot Ha-hagut Ha-yehudit* (*A History of Jewish Thought in Modern Times*). Jerusalem: Keter, 1977.

Uffenheimer, Benyamin. "Buber and Modern Biblical Scholarship." In *Martin Buber: A Centenary Volume.* Edited by Haim Gordon and Johanan Bloch. New York: Ktav, 1981.

Yaron, Z. *Mishnato shel Ha-Rav Kook* (*The Philosophy of Rabbi Kook*). Jerusalem: World Zionist Organization, 1974.

Spiritual and Anti-Spiritual Trends in Zionism

EHUD LUZ

Dialectics of "Earthliness" and "Spirituality" in Zionism

HAGSHAMAH ("fulfillment" or "concretization") is among the fundamental concepts in Zionist literature and thought. The term originates in medieval Jewish philosophy,[1] in which it signifies the attribution of physical characteristics or material images, derived from natural reality, to the divine reality, which is spiritual-transcendent in nature. In this sense, *hagshamah* is a negative term; a good deal of intellectual effort was invested by medieval rationalistic philosophers in the purification of the God-concept from all traces of *hagshamah* ("corporealization"). In Zionist thought, on the other hand, the term *hagshamah* has an extremely positive connotation, serving as a slogan expressing the very essence of the Zionist idea. There, *hagshamah* signifies the active effort to realize the spirit within life, to embody what had until then been a centuries-old dream in an earthly, concrete reality. The term thus embodies a dialectical tension between the two extremes it is meant to bridge: dream and realization, spirit and life. To use the language of the philosophical school, *hagshamah* wishes to overcome the opposition between *vita contemplativa* and *vita activa:* through it, *speculation* on reality is connected in an unmediated manner with the practical formation of that reality. From this point of view, there is a clear similarity between the Zionist concept of *hagshamah* and the Marxist idea of "praxis." In Marx's thought, revolutionary activity unites the speculative and critical aspects— the examination or analysis of reality in the light of the idea—with the practical aspect—the concretization of the idea in the creation of a new reality. In Zionist *hagshamah* there is the same dialectic as is found in

Marxist praxis: it measures reality in relation to a certain vision, discovering that the realization of that vision demands a revolution in Jewish existence. At the same time, reality requires the dream, since without it there is no content for it to fulfill.

Authentic concretization entails a situation of constant tension: while dedication to the ideal may deplete the enormous energies required for concrete building, excessive involvement in practical work is likely to make one forget that the structure itself was only created to serve as a dwelling place for the spirit and the vision. This dialectic between spirit and life, between "spirituality" and "earthliness," occupies Zionism ceaselessly. It is reflected not only in its thought, but also in its belles lettres—in the Hebrew prose, poetry, and drama that were part of the movement of national renewal from its very inception. Any discussion of the spiritual tendencies within Zionism must necessarily relate to the entire gamut of literary creativity and not restrict itself to thought. This paper, which discusses the Zionist concept of *hagshamah,* will concentrate primarily on thought, but from time to time we shall draw upon expressions of these ideas in the belles lettres of the period.

In order to understand the source of the tension between "earthliness" and "spirituality," which existed in the Zionist movement from its very inception, I shall begin with a letter written by Moses Mendelssohn. In 1770, a German nobleman approached Mendelssohn with a plan for establishing a Jewish state in Palestine. In his reply, Mendelssohn praised the author for his daring and nobility, but totally rejected the idea. In enumerating the difficulties facing realization of the plan, he wrote:

> The greatest difficulty which seems to me to stand in the way of the project is the character of my people [*Nation*]. It is not adequately equipped to undertake anything great. The pressure under which we have lived for so many centuries has deprived our spirit of all *vigueur*. It is not our fault; but we cannot deny that *the natural urge to freedom* has completely ceased to be active in us. It has transformed itself into a monkish virtue and expresses itself *in prayer and patience, not in action.*[2]

These words, written about one hundred years before the emergence of Zionism, remind us of the famous passage in the *Theologico-Political Treatise* in which Spinoza discusses in an "aside" the possibility of the rebuilding of a Jewish state.[3] They present the problem which I wish to discuss here in the sharpest terms. The exile, as has been observed by the historian Yitzhak Baer, is not only a reality imposed from without, but "one of the decisive political realities of the structure of religious thought" of our predecessors.[4] Over the course of many generations, the Jewish people saw itself as a people living outside of historical time, so that its existence was not dependent on the same "earthly" historical factors that determined the being and destiny of other nations. The messianic view of history, coupled with the sufferings and trials of the Jewish people, destroyed "the natural impulse toward freedom" almost completely and silenced the will to seek a political solution to the problem of exile by active and daring efforts on the part of the entire nation. The main concern was directed toward insuring the fulfill-ment of the Torah and *mizwot* in the present, while questions of the future and active planning toward it were utterly remote from their collective consciousness. For this reason, the renewed conquest by the Jewish people of the "earthly" within history was impossible without first breaking through the barrier of the traditional world view, which removed Judaism from the flow of time, and without questioning the totally "spiritual" character of Jewish existence in *galut* (exile). This was in fact one of the principal goals of modern Hebrew literature in eastern Europe, as we shall explain below, and it is not surprising that this literature served as a decisive factor in the birth of Zionism. However, in so doing, it confronted the Zionist movement with the following question: to what extent can the earthly-secular elements be reinstated within the national existence of the Jewish people, without destroying their unique spiritual identity, which was formed primarily under the conditions of exile? One may say that this is the principal spiritual question that has occupied Zionist thought and literature from that time through the present day.

Spiritualization of the Land of Israel in Exile

One of the consequences of the *galut*, which uprooted the Jewish people from its homeland for such a long period of time, was that the Land of Israel more and more became a spiritual and symbolic element in the national consciousness. The "Heavenly Jerusalem," found in the center of the messi-anic vision, displaced the "earthly Jerusalem," the concrete, tangible piece of earth. The various kinds of Jewish literature—prayer, liturgical poetry, homiletics and thought—fostered this process, whether deliberately or not. During the course of time, *Erez Yisra'el* (the Land of Israel) completely ceased, in the mind of many Jews, to represent an earthly reality, with which one could enter into tangible contact in this world. From this viewpoint, Rabbi Naḥman of Bratslav's account of what he heard from "important people" in the Land of Israel who had come there shortly before his own visit there (1798) is highly instructive. They stated that, before they had come to the land, they could not imagine that *Erez Yisra'el* actually existed in this world. On the basis of everything written in the books about its holiness, they had imagined that the Land was "in an entirely different world." Only after they came to the Land were they certain that it really exists in this world and that, in external appearance, it was no different from the lands from which they had come, and nevertheless that it was holy (*Liqqutey MoHaRan*, 2:16).[5]

It was actually at the beginning of the modern period that the process of spiritualization of the Land of Israel reached its peak, both in eastern and western Europe. One of the paradoxes of Jewish history is that on this point the position of ultraconservative movements coincides with that of modernistic movements. In eastern Europe, Hasidic thought made a decisive contribution to what Rivka Schatz calls the process of "spiritualistic internalization" of such concepts as exile, redemption, "outside of the Land," and *Erez Yisra'el*. The religious intimacy cultivated by Hasidism was acquired at the price of apathy and passivity toward the real historical life in exile. The concrete reality of *galut* no longer constitutes an obstacle to spiritual attainments or to an intimate connection with God, because of the central role assigned by Hasidism to attachment to the *Zaddiq*. Exile lost much of its concrete historical significance and became a symbol of a psychological-existential situation, similar to its transformation in several modern existential approaches, in which exile becomes the symbol of human alienation within the world. The *Zaddiq* himself symbolizes the age of redemption in microcosm, a redemption with which one may for the present be satisfied. This is a highly significant turn in the history of Jewish thought, one that may be described as having a "Christian" coloration, transferring the focus of redemption as it does from the national, historical plane to the spiritual plane of the individual's inner life.[6]

There is an extremely interesting parallel between the mystical-symbolic understanding of *Erez Yisra'el* and *galut* in Hasidism and the rationalistic understanding of these concepts by western European liberal Judaism of the nineteenth century! Through deliberate distortion of the texts, reminiscent of Christian allegorical interpretation, such figures as Abraham Geiger and Hermann Cohen argued that the return to Zion anticipated by the prophets is a symbol for the "spiritual" redemption of humanity, requiring the dispersion of the Jewish people throughout the world. "For mankind," wrote Hermann Cohen, "the prophets discovered the world, the 'new heavens' and the 'new earth.' To them, Palestine is nothing more than a *symbol* of this land to come in the future." In his polemics with both anti-Semites and Zionists, Cohen argued that Jerusalem for which we yearn is not only the earthly Jerusalem, "a finite piece of soil upon which a certain modern movement wishes us to be confined," but primarily that upon which the Holy One blessed be he, according to the Talmud, wishes to renew his world.[7]

It should be noted here that it was not only the longing for emancipation and for incorporation within non-Jewish society that drove Jewish intellectuals to remove from Judaism any vestige of its concrete historical characteristics. This was also assisted by the philosophy of the period, particularly the Idealistic-Hegelian school, which presented philosophical reflection as the highest stage in the development of human history. The *Wissenschaft des Judentums,* which set for itself the goal of scientifically studying the historical development of Judaism, interpreted Jewish history as a spiritual process in the course of which the religious idea of Judaism attains self-consciousness: with the Enlightenment ended the spontaneous, innocent creativity of the Jewish people and the higher stage—that of reflective contemplation—began. Thus, we find a clear turn from the historical, concrete realm to the spiritual one.

Materialistic Tendencies in Eastern Haskalah

In the light of what we have described thus far, the obvious question is: How were *Erez Yisra'el* and the "return to Zion" transformed from strictly spiritual concepts into concrete reality? How did it happen that, specifically at the end of the nineteenth century, this revolution achieved historical expression, and why specifically in eastern Europe? The answer to this is to be found in a combination of two factors: the social character of the Jewish collectivity in the East and the nature of the Hebrew *Haskalah,* which differed from the Jewish Enlightenment in western Europe.

Because of the political and demographic conditions in the Jewish "Pale of Settlement" in Russia, Jewish national consciousness existed there far more intensely than in the West. The vacillation between romantic-nationalist and rational-universalistic tendencies within the Hebrew Haskalah was thus far greater. Both of these tendencies, however, tended in practice to transform Judaism into a national "culture" in the full sense of the word. Rationalistic criticism, which questioned the foundations of traditional Jewish society and its world view in order to break the confining boundaries of Judaism and adapt it to the spirit of the times, tended to restore the realm of the "earthly" to the Jewish people and to give them, in the words of Moses L. Lilienblum (1843–1910), a "materialistic outlook" upon life. *Maskilim* ("enlighteners") such as Judah Leib Gordon (1830–1892)—the outstanding figure of the eastern European Haskalah—Peretz Smolenskin, or M. L. Lilienblum questioned the old educational ideal of the *talmid-ḥakham* (talmudic scholar), who studies Torah for its own sake. This type now became a synonym for a layabout, an "obscurantist" and a parasite. Against it was posed the ideal of the enlightened *maskil,* who is involved in the reality of the world and knows how to conduct himself among people.

The romantic tendencies, on the other hand, expressed longings for a full Jewish life through the renewal of Jewish creativity and its extension into those aesthetic, ethical, and intellectual realms which had until then been closed to the Jew. The commitment to Hebrew as the language of creativity—at a time when most of the Jewish public did not speak it—was itself a kind of protest against the artificial, self-imposed confinement to the realm of religious beliefs or ritual observance of western emancipated Jewry, one which led to an obfuscation of their own uniqueness.

Despite the clear-cut differences between the romantic and the rationalistic streams within the Haskalah, they shared the assumption that traditional Judaism—that embodied in the world of sacred books and of halakhah, with all its strictures—contained a distorted spiritual image. They protested against the exaggerated rule of "the book" over life and the enslavement to the "written" word: a subjugation that led to stagnation of Jewish cultural creativity and its isolation from real life. "Religion" and "life"—whether "life" is understood in the rational sense of the supremacy of understanding, or in the romantic sense of the longing for spontaneous and full expression of the inner world of feelings and impulses—were now seen more and more as conflicting concepts. The more the *maskilim* failed to realize their longings, because of the opposition of the Orthodox leadership, the more deeply rooted became the idea in Hebrew literature that there was an unbridgeable gap between "religion" and "life." Although there was a certain one-sidedness to this view, its sources were in the longing for human breadth and scope, for "culture" in the broadest sense. This mood prepared the soil for the appearance of "earthly" nationalism as the basis of a new culture, and it was this that motivated Jews who had been uprooted from their homes—as the result of political and economic circumstances—to wish to return to the "earthly" Zion.[8]

The earliest Zionist thinkers—L. Pinsker, M. L. Lilienblum, T. Herzl, and Ahad Ha'am—did not yet clearly see the necessary reciprocity between the "earthly" element and the development of national culture. The ideological dispute that accompanied the shaping of the Zionist idea followed from this. At the center of this debate were the views of Ahad Ha'am (1856–1927), who strongly protested against the path of the Zionist leadership of his day. As against those who placed the emphasis upon practical activity in *Erez Yisra'el* (Lilienblum) or political activity (Herzl), Ahad Ha'am saw the central aim of Zionism as the revival of Jewish culture. He thought that, in the wake of secularism and modernization, the Jewish spirit in *galut* was in danger of extinction and that, by cultivating attachment to the national, historical treasures of the Jewish people, it would be saved from this danger and there would be an awakening and continuation of creativity. The Land of Israel was to play a central role in this process. His continuous call to act for the "revival of hearts" and for the dissemination of Hebrew national culture in the Diaspora elicited a broad response within the religious and secular Hebrew intelligentsia in the Diaspora. However, among that group which was actively realizing Zionism, his influence was relatively weak, since Aḥad Ha'am did not see what the Palestinian Labor movement first saw—namely, the organic connection between the renascence of Hebrew culture and the renewal of social and economic life in Erez Yisra'el.

Zionism and "Lebensphilosophie"

One of the human types commonly portrayed in the literature of the transitional generation between Haskalah and Zionism was that of the "uprooted" (talush)—the maskil, uprooted from the traditional Jewish community in the wake of the ideas of the Haskalah, who is nevertheless unable to put down roots anywhere else. In the short story "Menahem," by Micha Josef Berdyczewski (1865–1921), published in 1900, he portrays a yeshiva student from a small town in eastern Europe who has come to study in the capital of Germany, where his world is turned totally upside down:

> He has no people and no folk-ways, neither parents nor relatives. . . . There he sits, remote away from everything he had, in a strange land which has become his own, and which is nevertheless strange. . . . Shall he perhaps return to whence he came? But that place is no longer a place for him, and its air is not his air. . . . He is unable to rebuild what he has destroyed, and he does not wish to build it; he is unable to strangle the freedom which is in his soul, but his heart will not be at peace with the freedom in his soul.[9]

The type described here by Berdyczewski is typical of the psychological-social situation of a large segment of the Hebrew intelligentsia in eastern Europe, who, in the wake of the rapid spiritual revolution that passed over it, found itself in a social and cultural void. Berdyczewski does not speak in vain of the "rent in the heart." In terms of their values and beliefs, these intellectuals had become alienated from the Jewish masses in the East who still lived within the traditional framework, while they were emotionally connected to this community by the deepest ties. Thus, to an uprooted individual such as Menahem, the need for national-social redemption was at the same time a powerful personal-existential need. The "uprooted" transformed their own existential dilemma into a source of strength directed toward the creation of a new culture and a new society, redeeming them from loneliness and granting them a feeling of belonging and of historical continuity. In this manner, Zionism became a movement of "realization" (*hagshamah*).

Several of the dominant spiritual movements in Europe at the end of the nineteenth century played a role in the ideological formulation of the impulse toward *hagshamah*. As we have already suggested above, nineteenth-century Jewish philosophy was decisively influenced by the rationalistic-idealistic stream in European philosophy. Zionist thought and literature in the late nineteenth and early twentieth century drew upon entirely different non-Jewish sources: the *Lebensphilosophie* with its romantic elevation of vitality, the various schools of modern sociology, and the great "realistic" school in Russian literature. This seemingly strange combination of divergent and contradictory ideas was what gave Zionisn its peculiar coloration: the combination of the impulse toward personal liberation with the vision of national-social redemption. The sociological perspective gave Zionism a new understanding of the connection between ideas and reality, as well as the tools to analyze the actual factors determining Jewish existence, an analysis that led it to the Zionist conclusion; whereas romanticism, in combination with Russian realism, contributed to its idealism and the impulse toward radical personal fulfillment.

No non-Jewish thinker had so decisive an impact on modern Hebrew literature—that which catalyzed Zionist *hagshamah*—as F. Nietzsche.[10] Under his influence, the rebellion against historical Jewish "spirituality"—which had begun with the Hebrew Haskalah—reached its peak. It will suffice to quote one well-known passage from his writings to understand his role in the process described here:

> I beseech you, my brothers, *remain faithful to the earth,* and do not believe those who speak to you of otherworldly hopes! Poison-makers are they, whether they know it or not. Despisers of life are they, decaying and poisoned themselves, of whom the earth is weary: so let them go.
>
> Once the sin against God was the greatest sin; but God died, and these sinners died with him. To sin against the earth is now the most dreadful thing, and to esteem the entrails of the unknowable higher than the meaning of the earth.[11]

What is significant for our discussion is the unequivocal identification Nietzsche makes between the healthy life and its earthly basis—one with far-reaching consequences for Zionist *hagshamah*. This healthy life is opposed to the old world of values, which weakens humanity, and against which Nietzsche had declared war. These views—which this is not the place to discuss in detail—were very appealing to the mood of rebellious youths who felt the sharp opposition between their earthly longings and the excessively spiritual character of traditional Judaism. No Hebrew author gave this opposition so profound, nor so tragic, an expression as did Berdyczewski. In his writings, the conflict between the "earthly" and the "spiritual" appears in its full severity. The struggle between them is not only unavoidable, but leaves no room for compromise. Traditional Judaism is unable to reform or to alter itself, it is an obstacle that must be overcome by destroying it from within: "I have concluded: to dismantle the domain of the *spirit* and to enthrone the *material,* to restore to us strength and power, to make us into human beings who know *life* and not only Levites, guardians of the Law."[12]

This rebellious mood was based upon a revolutionary philosophy of history. Berdyczewski gives a radical reinterpretation of the phrase from the Prayer Book "because of our sins we were exiled from our land," namely, that the sin which caused *galut* came from within historical Judaism itself. The exile, in all its negative meaning, is not the consequence of a political disaster, but is the immanent result of Judaism itself. Thus, the way was paved for a total transvaluation of the past and of Jewish culture. Berdyczewski distinguishes between two contradictory tendencies—an earthly and a spiritual—which have battled with one another since the genesis of Jewish history. These two tendencies are symbolized by Jerusalem and Yavneh. Jerusalem symbolizes the period preceding the "rule of the book," during which the Jewish people still celebrated explicitly secular values: natural beauty, spontaneity, unqualified acceptance of the forces of life, closeness to nature, and active strength. To use Berdyczewski's term, this was the "culture of the sword." Yavneh, on the other hand, symbolizes the domination of life by the written word, abstraction, and enslavement to law, which resulted in suppression of the vital strength of the people and the cultivation of a passive mood and the suppression of vital forces. This is the "culture of the book." The struggle between these two cultures began even before the revelation on Mount Sinai. The original, natural inclination of the people, at the beginning of its history, was toward the "culture of the sword," but the people's leaders succeeded in imposing on them the "culture of the book," which was alien to its true spirit. The victory of monotheism caused the degeneration of the Jewish people, which in the final analysis brought about the exile.[13] We find, then, that in Berdyczewski's opinion there is no possibility of redemption from Exile without redemption from Judaism itself. The slogan of "negation of the Exile" (*shelilat ha-galut*) found here its most radical expression.

More than any other Hebrew author, Berdyczewski laid the foundations of a very powerful Zionist myth—the myth of "the new Hebrew" (the use of the term "Hebrew" rather than "Jew" emphasizes the motif of departure from the past), which forms the most substantial element of his teaching. Although its lines are not absolutely clear-cut, its conflict with historical

Judaism is clear, as is its relation to the Nietzschean idea of the "super-man." All of Berdyczewski's scholarly, literary, and philosophical creations are dedicated to uncovering this myth, both in the distant past and in the present Jewish exilic existence. His attraction towards those types who embody irrational, healthy life, remote from any exaggerated spirituality, stems from this. The desire for Jewish national revival is connected in a natural way to the vital sources of Jewish experience and being as a basis for the establishment of a new myth: the myth of strength and earthliness. Various figures from the Jewish past rejected by the rabbinic tradition, such as the Zealots or the *biryonim* at the end of the Second Temple period—here reappear to assume a primary role in the generation's historic consciousness. Zionist activism, which strives for the realization of "renew our days as of old," is profoundly opposed to the passivity of the *galut*. Its use of these figures for its own self-awareness is a concrete example of what Nietzsche called "monumental history."[14]

The dream of the creation of the "new Hebrew" was naturally connected to the longing for the soil of the Land of Israel and the renewal of Jewish independence, since only upon the ancient homeland could this be fulfilled. The experience of revolution and of rebellion was a kind of messianic one, embracing a religious pathos and a romantic longing for inner integrity and holiness stemming from life here and now *within* nature and *within* the world. The great charm of this teaching was in its dialectic of revolution and continuity at one and the same time: in the yearning to return to the ancient foundation which had been distorted by history and in the daring to begin everything from the present, to take upon oneself the absolute responsibility to stand by oneself in the world, without any reliance upon the tradition. By this, Berdyczewski expressed one of the deepest underlying impulses of Zionism.

However, Berdyczewski himself remained doubtful about the possibilities of renewal, and it is not surprising that he himself never came to *Erez Yisra'el*. He was well aware of the price of realizing the myth which he himself had encouraged—that is, severance from the spiritual sources of Judaism—and precisely for this reason he saw the great potential danger in Zionism and was full of fears lest this severance bring about not a renascence but total destruction. However, those he influenced were far less ambivalent. His great negation was transformed for them into a creative force, which brought about the fulfillment of Zionism. Romantic rebellion was translated into social and national deeds; the total negation of both the "earthly" and "spiritual" *galut* spurred individual Jews to a transformation of their own values and to the building of a new society radically different from *galut* Judaism. This is the great importance of Berdyczewski's work for the formation of the Zionist-pioneering ethic. It is not surprising that he and, in his wake, J. H. Brenner, who carried the negation of traditional Judaism to its extreme, had such great influence over the same portion of the Zionist movement which carried upon its shoulders the main burden of Zionist fulfillment.

The same ideas expressed by Berdyczewski in a lyrical, spontaneous manner, full of contradictions, were crystallized into a systematic, consistent system by the philosopher Ya'akov Klatzkin (1882-1948). In his book *Sheqi'at ha-Ḥayyim* (*The Setting of Life*, 1925), Klatzkin presented his philosophic system, which served as a basis for his Zionist world view. Its starting point is the Nietzschean dichotomy between knowledge and what Klatzkin calls "the lust for life." The drive for consciousness—which is in itself a manifestation of the life force—brings about, by a process of dialectic development, the weakening and defeat of these very forces. Life is a closed system, which is destroyed by looking outside of itself. The mind cannot answer the principal question of existence: Why? The domination of the human being by the *ratio* causes the freezing of life.[15]

On the basis of these assumptions, Klatzkin begins his evaluation of Zionism. Since the rationalistic Haskalah began to be victorious within Judaism, it has caused a progressive deterioration among the Jews of the *galut*. Secularism questions the integrity of natural Jewish life. Judaism loses its vital powers—which existed so long as religion dominated life—and becomes a disembodied spiritual entity. There is no solution but to return to the concrete, earthly basis of national life, which will assure its natural existence. Zionism, in Klatzkin's eyes, is thus an expression of the sense of natural existence. Any question about the purpose of the existence of the Jewish people is totally invalid and is itself a sign of the deterioration of its sense of national existence, allowing abstract thought to thrust the poison of its doubt upon it. Making Judaism dependent on any idea or *Weltanschauung* is "the first form of national degeneration." The will for "earthly life" is for its own sake and not for the sake of heaven. It is "a renewal of a simple, honest and innocent instinct."[16]

Klatzkin is the outstanding spokesman of the idea of normalization. One of the meanings of this idea is that a people does not need any norm to justify its existence, outside of itself. Consistent secular thinking eliminates the need to justify the existence of the nation, whether on metaphysical or theological grounds. From this follows also the surrendering, at times the explicit negation, of the idea of *election*. This is one of the manifestations of protest against *abstraction: will* is the decisive factor in life.

The Ḥalutz as the Ideal of Concretization

The new evaluation of life, stressing the importance of vital, irrational forces, lies at the root of a broad current within Hebrew literature of the early twentieth century. Outstanding in it are the motif of the opposition between "earth" and "heaven" and the absolute affirmation of the earthly and the immediate.[17] For example, the poem by Saul Tchernichowsky (1875–1943), "Visions of the False Prophets,"[18] expresses in capsule form that generation's feelings of new life, containing elements of longing for archaic myth and fullness of earthly life in the here and now. These longings stand in total opposition to the "heavenliness" of traditional Judaism, which is seen as the source of the loss of spontaneity and human freedom.[19]

Yaakov Cohen wrote a song of praise (1903) to the "brigands" (biryonim – zealots who declared a rebellion against the Romans in 66 C.E. and who in Cohen symbolize the rebellion against exile and against acceptance of the Jewish destiny), and Zalman Schneour (1886–1959), praises the 'amey ha-arez in "A Song of Praise to the Unlearned." The 'amey ha-arez, the coarse, Jewishly ignorant class is the antithesis of the nonproductive talmid-ḥakham. Their earthly vitality and primitiveness are the healthy basis of Jewish existence, the only cure for a people ill with the degenerative disease of over-spiritualitzation.[20]

In his short story "The Sermon," Hayyim Hazaz (1898–1973) places in the mouth of his protagonist—a pioneer of the Third Aliyah—the thesis that the Jewish people in exile did not create its own history but that it was made for them by the Gentiles. This idea caught on among other writers and thinkers who shaped the consciousness of pioneering Zionism: thus, the galut Jew became the symbol of passivity and submission to fate.[21]

This anti-galut mood originated the new social ideal of Zionism—the ideal of the pioneer (ḥaluz). As opposed to the spiritual, contemplative ideal of the bookish talmid-ḥakham, who saw as his main task the preservation of the tradition and its transmission to future generations, the ḥaluz ideal is an activist one, directed toward the regeneration of life on the soil of the homeland and drawing its inspiration from the emotional connection with the land.

In 1919, the author Joseph Hayyim Brenner (1881–1921)—one of the outstanding figures of the Second Aliyah—created a new literary forum, Ha-Adamah ("The Land"—itself a typical name). In the introduction to the first issue, he explained the significance of this name as follows:

> "The Land!"—This means not only soil (agriculture) and not only a country (political state), but something more. "The land" is the longing for

fundamentals in all aspects of life, a vision of things as they are, recognition of the basis of reality. The "land" — is the attraction towards the source of life and of growth, to the source of renewal, to the source of human truth.[22]

What is significant about these comments is the combination of two different elements, both of which draw upon the connection to the land: on the one hand, the land enables those who live on it to evaluate realistically reality as it is, without illusions; on the other hand, it serves as a source of renewal for the Jew. This combination of clearheaded realism with utopian longing for renewal and growth characterizes the spirit of pioneering Zionism. The realistic Zionist vision does not lead to a narrow, cynically materialistic outlook, but to the most elevated idealism, the elevation of humanity over reality.

A unique combination of realism and idealism is found in a letter written by Brenner in 1900 to the friend of his youth, the author Uri Nissan Gennesin (1881-1913). In the letter, Brenner opposed the aesthetic idea of "literature for its own sake" advocated by Gennesin:

> My outlook on life is entirely different. In brief: we must sacrifice ourselves to reduce the evil in the world, the evils of hunger, slavery, unemployment, hypocrisy and the like. One must *understand* everything, understand and avoid *mystifications* and imaginary things; one must increase *realism and holiness* in the world.[23]

What is the connection between "realism" and "holiness"? Perhaps that it is precisely through a realistic, clear, and cruel understanding of reality, liable to lead one to skepticism, disappointment, and confusion, that one may draw the strength to ascend. The Jew's longing for life, which is stronger than any rational arguments, carries him from negation to liberation from his yoke. Realism implies self-understanding, recognition of that which is lacking and blemished in our lives and of the need for a radical alternative, implying the human's self-elevation — in which there is an element of *holiness*.[24] It is the bond with *the land* which creates the connection between realism and holiness.

Holiness now no longer dwells in heaven, but on earth. The Jew longs for a complete and natural life in the world, in all its fullness, of which he had been deprived in the exile. This sense of longing, which is usually expressed in religious experience as a vision of being lifted from earth to heaven, here reverses its *direction*, to move from the heavenly to the earthly. The Jewish youth who is rebelling against the Torah in the name of "life" seeks his inspiration in the earthly realm: in the field and in manual labor. This impulse toward full regeneration of the person and of life is what gave to Zionism,

even in its most extreme expressions, the meaning of a redemptive movement in the original religious sense.[25]

The turning toward the "soil" is the extreme opposite pole from exile. The
connection to the soil not only redeems the Jew from his earthly
uprootedness but also from his cosmic alienation. This feeling is expressed
both in the writings of A. D. Gordon—who coined the phrase, "cosmic or-
phancy"—and in the new *Erez Yisra'el* poetry. A short poem by Rahel
Bluwstein (1980–1931), the poetess of the Second Aliyah, is one of the most
authentic expressions of this mood:

> Here on the earth—not in high clouds—
> On this mother earth that is close:
> To sorrow in her sadness, exult in her meager joy
> That knows, so well, how to console.
> Not nebulous tomorrow but today: solid, warm, mighty,
> Today materialized in the hand:
> Of this single, short day to drink deep
> Here in our own land.
> Before night falls—come, oh come all!
> A unified, stubborn effort, awake
> With a thousand arms. Is it impossible to roll
> The stone from the mouth of the well?
> (*Kan 'al peney ha-adamah,* 1927)[26]

It is not surprising that the land acquires here a cultic significance. The
land is *the holy land* in the full sense of the word, and it demands of one
heavy sacrifices—spiritual and physical—in order for one to work it and to
become connected with it in a renewed "covenant." The religious-cultic
significance of work in general, and of working the land in particular, is a
powerful motif in the new Hebrew poetry and drama of the Land of
Israel.[27] This motif reflects the general spirit of the period, which can be
described by the term "earthly holiness" (or, to use the language of Rabbi
Kook, the sanctification of the profane).

Sanctification of the Profane

Does the sanctification of the "earthly" totally contradict Jewish exilic
"spirituality" and require a total break with it, or does it complete it? This
was one of the great questions that divided Zionism. Unlike Berdyczewski
and Brenner, who saw an unbridgeable gap between the need for renewal
of the Jew and the spirit of Judaism, another branch of Zionism saw its very
"earthliness" as a fulfillment of the authentic spirit of Judaism. According to
this view, *hagshamah* is immanent in the way of life and the world view of

Judaism. In order to prove this claim, various Zionist thinkers analyzed the difference between Judaism and Christianity, albeit from a perspective totally different from that of medieval and early modern Jewish philosophy: here the critique of Christianity becomes, in essence, one of the entire "ethos" of modern Western civilization.

The Russian thinker Vladimir Soloviev (1853–1900), who had deep admiration for Judaism, cites among the outstanding characteristics of the Jewish people what he describes a their "extreme materialism." But this materialism is religious in nature and as such differs from two other kinds of materialism—practical-sensual and scientific-philosophical (i.e., Marxism)—both of which are atheistic. The Jew "believes in the spirit, but only in a spirit which penetrates all that is material, which uses matter as its envelope and as its instrument." This is why he nevertheless becomes a partner of God in the world, "for in the depth of its soul this people desires more strongly and more fully than any other people for the fullest incarnation of the Divine idea." Since in the eyes of the Jew God is the ideal of perfection, he demands uncompromisingly that this ideal be realized in the world in a concrete and visible way.[28]

Soloviev's words shed light on the problem under discussion: to what extent was Zionist *hagshamah* an expression of an inner drive characteristic of Jewish culture itself? The question of course does not relate to specific theological principles, but to underlying structures that form the framework for its world view.

It is agreed that the most typical element of the Jewish world view is halakhah (Jewish law). One might describe halakhah as the realm in which the transcendent enters into the immanent. The material world, as such, is the arena within which holiness is realized. From this, it follows that in practice there is no absolute separation in Judaism between the holy and the profane—unlike Christianity. A distinction does exist, but not a separation, the profane being the "matter" upon which holiness impresses its "form." The organic connection between "study" and "action," between aggadah (legend, theology, homiletics, thought, etc.) and halakhah—a pairing well described by Hayyim Nahman Bialik in his classic essay, "Halakhah and Agadah"—follows from this. Jewish messianism expresses the longing for the time when holiness will embrace all of the life of this world and the transcendent will become fully unified with the immanent—the world of *tiqqun* ("repair"), in Kabbalistic language.

In contrast to rationalistic Jewish thinkers, from Mendelssohn on, who stressed Judaism's supremacy over Christianity in its *rationalism*, several Zionist thinkers stressed Judaism's superiority because of its *concreteness*.

Here we find one of the most interesting aspects of the dialectical development of Zionist thought, which places itself in double opposition to traditional *galut* Judaism, on the one hand, and to the Christian European ethos, on the other. The idea of *hagshamah* serves as a yardstick for criticism of the exaggerated spiritualization of both the Jewish people in exile and of Christianity; however, while the *galut*, which distorted the original spirit of Judaism, was forced upon it by historical circumstance, Christianity from its founding was a spiritualistic religion, whose ethos was opposed to concrete, real life. Christianity—so it was argued—creates a total separation between faith and life, and thereby also creates a separation between the individual and the collectivity. On the other hand, in Judaism there is no separation between faith and human ethical action, for which reason there is not and cannot be any conflict within it between the individual and the collective. In other words: Judaism is not satisfied with shaping the private faith of the individual, but wishes to shape the concrete way of life both of the individual and of the community as a whole. Zionism is a manifestation of this spirit of *hagshamah*, which typifies Judaism in the modern period.

This emphasis upon the "concreteness" present in Judaism—in contrast to the spiritualizing of Christianity—is a new motif in the Jewish-Christian polemic, revealing the new direction implicit within Zionism that I defined as "sanctification of the profane." This tendency breaks out of the traditional realm of sanctity—as crystallized during the long period of exile—by sanctifying new areas of life which until now had not been under the authority of the halakhah. This breakthrough was to be realized in two contrasting ways: one way was that of, for example, Rabbi Kook, in which the halakhah itself expanded until it contained within itself all of those areas of worldly existence that were conquered by Zionist *hagshamah*. In another path—that represented by such figures as Moses Hess, A. D. Gordon, and Martin Buber—the sanctification of life is dependent on the liberation of the individual Jew from the absolute authority of traditional halakhah and by granting freedom of expression to human ethical spontaneity in relation to the absolute, in response to the renewed flow of national life. As distinguished from the first way, in which there is a certain fixed harmony between Zionism and the halakhah, the latter path is based on an inner tension—if not actual opposition—between *hagshamah* and halakhah. Whereas *hagshamah* takes note of the perpetual dynamic of the Jew who is actively involved in the historical-social process, the halakhah is characterized by attention to the routine of daily life.

The argument based on the dualism of Christianity—as opposed to Judaism's tendency toward monism—is a central theme in the Zionist thought of Moses Hess (1812–1875). In his opinion, Christianity introduced dualism, the separation between the ideal and real life, into the human soul.[29] This dualism is the source of the separation of spirituality and materialism into two antagonistic world views, which is the clear sign of the modern spirit. Modern individualism, beginning with Protestantism, is also the consequence of this dualism. The antagonism between the individual and the group is the other aspect of the hostile opposition between idealism and materialism:

> Christianity was able to isolate man from disintegrating society, and to extend to him, in compensation for the loss of *earthliness, heavenly* possessions which would bring about the redemption of the individual soul and aid in its liberation from the rule of society; but it never was and never will be able to connect him to his family, his homeland and to human society without first restoring its roots in Judaism.[30]

The egoistic redemption of the individual soul in and of itself—which is the main way that religion is perceived in the modern age—is totally foreign to the spirit of Judaism. Judaism sees an organic connection between the individual and the family, between the family and the nation, and between the nation and humanity. Thus, it does not have a division between "religious" and "lay": "Jewish life is unitary, like its ideal of God, and this life and unity stand as a defence against modern materialism, which is none other than the reverse side of Christian spiritualizing."[31]

Judaism's strength stems from its being a *social* religion, which does not distinguish between faith and social law. It stands on the basis of an organized society and a common *soil*—the holy land. Hess sees the basis of Zionism in this: the Jewish people needs a land of its own in order to create upon it *social* institutions, through which the socialistic law can be realized in full. Only in its own land can the Jewish people realize its messianic ideal of "the rule of God *upon earth*."[32] Taking into account the fact that Hess came to Zionism via European socialism, we would not be mistaken if we saw a relationship between his ideas and the Marxian concept of "praxis." One might say that he gave praxis a religious-nationalist interpretation, thereby creating a unique combination of traditional Judaism, Zionism, and socialism.

In his essay "Flesh and Spirit," Ahad Ha-'am (1856–1927) follows Hess's line of thought, despite the great difference between them. In his opinion, Judaism, as opposed to Christianity, did not draw a sharp division between flesh and spirit, and thus avoided the two extremes of materialism and of one-sided spirituality. This was also why there is no opposition in Judaism between the individual and the group. The relationship between spirit and matter, like that between the individual and the collectivity, is one of complementarity and the union of opposites:

> [Unlike Christianity, the Jewish people did not] turn its gaze upward to create *in Heaven* an eternal habitation for the souls of men. It offered eternal life *here on earth.* This it did by emphasizing the *sense of collectivity,* by teaching the individual to regard himself not as an isolated unit, with an existence bounded by his own birth and death, but as part of a larger and more important whole, as a member of the social body."[33]

Yaakov Klatzkin also saw the principal shortcoming of Christianity in its essential dualism, in that it is a religion which in its innermost self rejects concretization. Its essence is abstraction, so that its entire being is outside of reality. From this follows also its poetic enthusiasm: it is the enthusiasm of longing for an idea whose fulfillment has not come, reflecting the distance between teaching and life.

As opposed to this, Judaism is a religion that has been fulfilled. Its essence is truthfulness, "the truth of practical realization." Faith is realized in deed and in law. For that reason the Oral Torah—the halakhah, with all of its strictures and rules—is the immanent expression of the Jewish demand for *hagshamah* of religion.

However, precisely because the existence of Judaism has until now been dependent on deeds and laws whose authority has become diminished in our own time, it cannot continue its existence unless it rebuilds itself in new, secularized national forms. For Klatzkin, the meaning of holding onto the earthly forms of Jewish existence is a consequence of the tendency toward concretization found in Judaism itself.[34]

A. D. Gordon: Concretization of Spirit in Life

The concept of *hagshamah* acquired a central position in Zionist thought during the period of the Second Aliyah (1904–1914). This wave of immigration was the first to achieve a clear recognition that Zionism must be a synthesis of "spirit" and "matter," of idealism and materialism. Labor, social creativity, is the link connecting the two. The *haluz* who builds the land simultaneously realizes his own self, as in the words of the famous song, "We have come up to the land, to build and to be built by it."

The thinker who expressed this idea most profoundly was A. D. Gordon (1856–1922). Gordon's teaching, like Hess's, will be more understandable to us if we examine it not only from the point of view of his critique of *galut* Judaism but also in terms of his critique of modern European culture, based upon Christianity. Gordon also takes as his starting point the duality in the process of human development. The sign of this duality is the intense development of the consciousness and of the rational element within the human being, at the expense of the irrational, spiritual element, which he designates by the term "experience." Since these two elements are interdependent, the lack of balance in their respective development is an important factor contributing to the contradictions in modern society: between matter and spirit, between the individual and the collective, etc. The constriction of experience means the isolation of humanity from nature and from cosmic life, from which grow exaggerated individualism, on the one hand, and materialism, on the other. Materialism and idealism are, in Gordon's opinion, concepts that may play a role in the cold, abstract speculations of the mind, but have no place in life:

> In life there is no matter without spirit, and no spirit without matter. This is so in the life of every living body, and so it is in collective life.... This is life's criterion: for every atom of matter, a drop of spirit; and to the contrary: for every drop of spirit, an atom of matter. Any favoring of one side or the other is an anomaly in life, and this is ... the criterion of all morality as well.[35]

Gordon also explains the failure of all the attempts to renew life and to regenerate the human spirit—including modern socialism—from this point of view. All of these movements tended too much toward either spirit or matter. They expressed ideas or spiritual longings, but they did not require their adherents to change their practical way of life—they did not demand personal *hagshamah*.[36] The way to human renewal is only by the overcoming of contradictions and the dualism between spirit and matter, that is, through *general* renewal. This is, in Gordon's opinion, the crucial element in Zionism. Gordon is therefore very critical of his friends working in the Land of Israel who opposed the creation of the Hebrew University on the grounds that the Jewish people needed workers and not intellectuals. Gordon saw in this another sign of the grave disease besetting humanity in general and the Jewish people in particular, the disease of separation between matter and spirit. The Jewish people is sick in both mind and in body, and therefore their cure must also involve both body and spirit.[37]

Because of the physical separation of the Jewish people from the nature of its land, an excessive inclination toward the spirit was developed. The spirit became isolated from real life, harming the people's creativity. In any event, Gordon thought that this damage was not equivalent to the harm that would be caused by exclusive emphasis on the material, as certain Zionist thinkers wished. For this reason, he fiercely opposed the struggle of that stream within Zionism—of which Berdyczewski and Brenner were the

spokesmen—against the spiritual tendencies of the people. Gordon saw in
their rejection of the past an act of suicide and a total distortion of the
meaning of Zionism. Zionism does not need to mean a struggle against the
spiritual tendency, but its purification through work within nature: "Our
entire desire in work here, the essence of the idea of labour, is to renew the
human spirit, to purify and refine it of both artificial spirituality and of
empty materialism, and to base it upon life, upon work and creativity. . . ."[38]

How does work create a connection between spirit and life? Gordon
thought of work not only as a means of supplying economic needs, but first
and foremost as an activity by means of which one expresses a connection
to both the human world and to the world of nature; that is, an area in
which the individual "I" expands itself until it merges with the nation,
humanity, and the entire cosmos (Gordon referred to this process, borrow-
ing from Hasidic terminology, as *hitpashtut*, "spreading forth"). This is the
religious significance of work in Gordon. Through creativity and labor, one
realizes the authentic self, the image of God within. He rejected the traditional distinction between sacred and profane, identifying the holy with the
spirit and the profane with matter. In authentic life, there are no holy and
profane apart from each other. True holiness is precisely that area in which
spirit becomes integrated with life.[39] Thus, whereas Hess saw the area in
which this integration was to take place as the social act, Gordon sees it
occurring in the relationship between humanity and nature.

Unity of Earth and Heaven

Gordon's concept of *hagshamah*, which strives toward the unification of the
spirit of Judaism with the renewal of life in the land, represents one branch
of Zionist utopianism, opposed to that of Berdyczewski and his followers.
A dramatic expression of this longing was given by the poet Shin Shalom
(who came to Palestine in 1922), in a play written in 1942 entitled *Adamah*
(*Land*). This play portrays the vacillation between the two elements in the
vision of the return to Zion: the spirit and the land. Shalom observes:
"There are times when the spirit is unable to make peace with the four ells
of the soil, and it returns to its uprootedness . . . and there are times when
the land threatens to dominate the spirit and to subjugate it entirely. What
is desired is the mixture of both elements together." The pioneer, working
the land and laying the foundation for the building of a new, ideal society,
performs a ritual act mixing together the "heaven" and the "earth": the
spirituality and idealism of the Jewish people in *galut* are mixed in an erotic
covenant with the bodily sensuousness of the soil of the homeland, to give
birth to a new people.[40]

This vision of unity is also at the basis of Martin Buber's Zionist thought. In Buber's understanding, the concept of *hagshamah* expressed the essence of the spirit of Israel from its inception, and it is the most valuable possession Israel inherited from classical Judaism. "The spirit of Israel is the spirit of fulfilment. Fulfilment of what? Fulfilment of the simple truth, that man has been created for a purpose."[41] *Hagshamah* is, according to Buber, "the basis of the covenant between God and man." Like Gordon—and also like Hess—he sees the concept of realization as the antithesis of European dualism, which divides human existence into separate compartments among which there is no connection: ethics and religion, the national realm and the social realm. This separation between faith and action, between the truth of the sprit and the reality of life, is totally foreign to Judaism. Judaism demands that humans live with God *within* this world and not outside of it. The human person must build a dwelling-place for God within the world: therefore, the area of true realization is society, and authentic society is that in which the divine principle is realized.[42] What is unique to the Jewish people is that it accepted that truth which demands fulfillment as a *people,* that is, as a *community* who are commanded to govern their lives by holiness. According to Buber's definition, holiness is true union with God and true union with the world as one—that is, a dialogic relation.

The exile was a period of "sterile spirituality . . . which distanced itself greatly from life and from living desires for unity."[43] Zionism is thus a return to the original idea of Judaism, the idea of unity, meaning the realization of spirit within life:

> Our revolution, the revolutionary settlement, signifies the elective fulfillment of a task with which our tradition has charged us. We must choose in this tradition the elements that constitute closeness to the soil, hallowed worldliness, and absorption of the Divine in nature; and reject in this tradition the elements that constitute remoteness from the soil, detached rationality, and nature's banishment from the presence of God.[44]

On the basis of this approach, Buber arrived at the idea of "sanctification of the profane," an idea which was developed also in the thought of Rabbi Kook, as we shall see below. Buber drew this idea from Hasidism, and particularly from the idea of "the service of God through material things." In Hasidism, this idea expresses the demand to serve God not only within the realm of holiness defined by the tradition—that of *mizwot* and Torah study—but also in the satisfaction of daily, routine needs, such as eating and drinking or ordinary concourse with other people (*'avodat Ha-Shem begashmi'ut*). In this view, it is precisely the realm of "neutral" acts (that is, those which involve neither *mizwot* nor transgressions) which opens to

human beings an infinite number of opportunities to serve God and to cling
to him, all depending on the *intention* that one invests in the deed that one
performs and not in its content per se.

According to Buber's interpretation, Hasidism is characterized by the
demand to sanctify all areas and activities of life. For him, the "profane"
designates a borderline dynamic concept: "The Holy strives to include
within itself the whole of life. The Law differentiates between the holy and
the profane, but the Law desires to lead the way towards the messianic
removal of the differentiation, to the all-sanctification." To Hasidism, the
profane is nothing more than "a designation for the not yet sanctified, for
that which is to be sanctified."[45]

Buber transferred this idea from the ritual realm to that of social life: the
life of society is the profane realm waiting to be reshaped by the holy, that
is, by the realization of the religious-ethical command, which signifies a life
of justice and of brotherhood both within and without, toward other
nations. The people of Israel will fulfill its destiny as a chosen people by
living "absolute life," that is, a life of union between religion and ethics,
between faith and deed, between heaven and earth.

Rabbi Kook and G. Scholem:
Zionism as a Dialectical Movement

> Time is the place in which we live, while place is the place where the other
> nations live. . . . And that's the whole basic might and power of Judaism, and
> the difference between Israel and the other peoples. . . . Now we have
> mistaken time for place, the great entirety for one abject little detail, the
> world of the spirit for this turbid and troublesome matter, the earthly and
> everyday with all its trifling physical desires and longings. . . . And thence
> comes danger to Israel, the peril of decline, of decadence. . . .[46]

In these words, Hazaz warns against the danger confronting Zionism as
the result of its very attachment to the "earthly," a danger to which we
referred at the beginning of our discussion. The deep transformation in the
life of the nation is likely to harm its spiritual identity, to obliterate its
uniqueness among the nations and thereby cause its decline and disappearance. Nathan Birnbaum (1864–1936), among the early Zionists in Austria,
who subsequently abandoned Zionism and embraced Orthodoxy, also clearly
felt the dangerous disturbance of the balance between "religious" and
"secular" tendencies within Judaism caused by Zionism. While Birnbaum
recognized the fact that, as a result of its overwhelming longing for spiritual
existence, the Jewish people was pushed away entirely from the secular path,
he was also convinced that *thousands of years were required in order to*

overcome the stress upon one side. For this reason, he attacked the tendency of nationalistic *maskilim* who longed to bring about a revolution and lay in wait "to deprive the Jewish people of its sanctity, its God and its unique Divine Presence." In his opinion, they endangered Judaism far more than the "constriction" against which they protested.[47]

Birnbaum's pessimistic evaluation of Zionism stemmed from a one-sided perception of it, for, as I have demonstrated above, there were—and still are—antagonistic streams struggling within Zionism. A more optimistic and far deeper interpretation is found in the writings of the most significant thinker of religious Zionism—Rabbi A. I. Kook (1865–1935). His optimism was rooted in a dialectic understanding of reality, whose sources were, on the one hand, the Kabbalah and, on the other, modern dialectical philosophies. In his approach, we find some of the same ideas that are present in such thinkers as Hess, Gordon, and Buber. The people of Israel, more than any other people, is unable to tolerate contradiction and spiritual division: "Peace and union in their ideal form are an external feature of us." The people of Israel express through their lives the unity of the ethical, spiritual, and intellectual world with the practical, technical, and social world of action. Life in *Erez Yisra'el* is intended to establish this unity, which gives a new aspect to all of human culture.[48]

Rabbi Kook agrees with the principal claim of secular Zionism: that exile forced the Jewish people to abandon responsibility for its physical existence, so that it lost the fundamental balance underlying its national life and its existence became too "spiritual": "Israel in Exile abandoned its concern with worldly things on the part of the nation as a whole. It put its heart and mind only *towards heaven* above, and it no longer went out to acquire armies of chariots and horses, like any nation on its soil, and the nation as a whole was no longer involved in material things."[49] While this restraint from material and political involvements for such a long period of time brought many blessings to the nation, in our own time it endangers its continued existence. As a result of this imbalance, not only was the "natural" strength of the nation weakened, but the spirit of the nation also began to degenerate. The people Israel feels that "separation between matter and spirit brought deep and profound troubles upon it, and it seeks a way to return to unity."[50] This unity is, in the eyes of Rabbi Kook, the fulfillment of holiness.

The nation's unhealthy situation in *galut* demands a temporary re-emphasis of the material side, as a cure to this disease. Rabbi Kook explains the pioneer's rebellion against the tradition in these terms: "The need for this rebellion derives from the tendency towards materialism, which must be carried within the entirety of the nation in an intensive way, after so many years during which the need and the possibility of material occupations was totally lacking to them."[51]

Thus, Rabbi Kook saw secularism as a necessary transitional stage in the nation's process of development, which he believed to be in itself a harbinger of the approaching messianic redemption. Just as Israel is unable to tolerate falsified spirituality, so can it not bear empty materialism. After the pioneers complete their labor of destroying imaginary spirituality, they will come to break the "idol of materialism."[52] Thus, in the future, the national movement shall then bring about a new and healthy balance between the elements, so that there will be no longer any antagonism between holy and profane:

> The first step away from exaggerated spirituality towards materialism must be somewhat exaggerated towards the other side—and this is the source of the arrogance of the birthpangs of Messiah (based upon the Talmudic tradition that, during the time of the birthpangs of Messiah, arrogance will increase. See Mishnah Sotah 9:15). In any event, this exaggerated tendency will not last long, as there is a fundamental balance in the basis of the nation.[53]

Rabbi Kook believed that the renascence of the Jewish people will tend toward a unification of prophecy—the utopian-revolutionary element in Judaism—and halakhah—the static element, giving a fixed shape to human life. In this manner, the dialectic inherent within the Zionist concept of *hagshamah* will bring about its complete negation.

The scholar Gershom Scholem (1897–1982) held a similar historical-philosophical perception of Zionism. Even though his starting point was totally different, like Rabbi Kook he understood Zionism as a dialectical movement vacillating between two contradictory tendencies: the revolutionary tendency toward a break with the past and the tendency toward historical continuity. The tension between these two is an extremely fruitful one, and any one-sided decision in favor of one or the other is likely to bear weighty consequences for the Jewish people. The decisive question confronting Zionism is thus: Can a true and fruitful synthesis be created between the two tendencies, without their negating or denying each other?[54] Scholem believes that the process of secularization is necessary from the standpoint of Judaism and is, in any event, unavoidable, but that it contains many dangers. Zionist *hagshamah* was directed, first and foremost, toward the resolution of practical problems, resulting from the actual needs of the period, so that, without being aware of this, it emptied the concept of *galut* of the hints of redemption contained within it. In this way, there was created a fundamental lack of balance that has not yet been corrected.[55] In any event, Scholem believed that Judaism will survive this crisis of changing form. It is impossible to see secularization as a final point, but only as a transitional stage. This is a period of "hiddenness of God's face," but God will be revealed even more strongly through the crisis confronting Zionism. The Jews cannot exist without theology, without the meta-historical dimension;[56] hence, the slogan of normalization, "a nation like other nations," cannot succeed. Scholem reminds us—as did Gordon and Buber—that "the demand to sanctify the profane (one raised by several Zionist thinkers) by the fulfillment of the Torah as the divine commandment, a demand anchored in the purely religious concept of holiness, is diametrically opposed to true secularization. . . ."[57]

Despite the similarity between the ideas of Scholem and of Rabbi Kook, one must not forget the decisive difference between them in their relationship to halakhah: whereas for Kook the national renascence will bring about an extension of the authority of traditional halakhah to all areas of political and social life, Scholem sees the future renascence in terms of a decisive change in both the status and the form of halakhah.

Victory of "Earthliness" and Its Price

Was Rabbi Kook correct in his optimistic prognosis? The future will tell. The spiritual-dialectical development of Zionism during the past two generations contains much that confirms Kook's vision. Without doubt, the trend that enjoyed the greatest influence during the "formative period" of the Yishuv (the Jewish community in *Erez Yisra'el*) was that which demanded a nearly total break with the *galut* and with historical Judaism. Thus, the "earthly" tendency shaped the first generation of native Israelis.

One of the consequences of the victory of this "earthly" trend was the emergence of the movement of Young Hebrews (popularly known by the name Canaanites) in the 1940s. This movement encompassed a small group of young intellectuals—poets, writers and scientists—most of whom were born in the Land of Israel. The movement's founder and spiritual leader was the poet Yonatan Ratosh. Its members shared the consciousness of a new identity, which made them different from the generation of *haluzim* who had been born in *galut*. This identity was no longer determined by an unmitigated connection to the Jewish people and to Jewish history, but was the spontaneous expression of the relationship of the young Israelis to their native land. They believed that a new people was coming into existence in the Land of Israel, with nothing in common with the Jewish people in exile or with what that people created during the period of its subjugation. On the other hand, they stressed their connection to the pre-biblical Canaanite period and to the Semitic region to which *Ereẓ Yisra'el* belongs. Thus, they drew daring and unequivocal conclusions from the rebellion declared by such writers as Berdyczewski and Tchernichowsky. Moreover, while the pioneering generation remained emotionally connected to the Jewish people, despite their rebellion against tradition, the Young Hebrews declared a break not only with the exilic past but also with the living Jewish people. Despite the fact that the movement attracted very few actual supporters, their ideas reflected a mood that was quite widespread among Israeli youth at that time. Its disappearance from the public stage at the end of the 1950s reflected not its failure but its success in expressing a broad sector of the younger generation.[58]

Already in 1933 Berl Katzenelson, the spiritual leader of the workers movement in *Ereẓ Yisra'el,* foresaw with a nearly prophetic sense the price that Zionism would have to pay during the next generation for the complete dedication of the pioneering generation to concrete action, to the building of the land:

> We are now engaged in a period of primary building of the land. We are involved in nothing but gathering pitch and tar and erecting skeletal structures, and have not yet put our minds to the furnishings of the building, to its internal arrangement. . . . We have not yet the freedom for a profound spiritual life. The only thing which justifies the life of our generation, that gives it taste and lasting value is the effort to build itself. Apart from that we are poor and impoverished, like saplings that have not yet been properly absorbed in the ground. The danger of a life of riff-raff surrounds us on all sides. We have not yet given thought to anything but the provisions of basic needs. . . .
>
> But we shall yet see days when many Jews shall dwell in this land, and our cultural impoverishment will give them no rest. And what we see today in contempt, whether because of difficult work or blunting of the spirit, will be seen by those who come after us as a great travail of the soul.[59]

Berl's words here again reveal the dialectic of *hagshamah:* that exclusive dedication to "earthliness" required in order to establish the Yishuv in Palestine does not allow "freedom for a profound spiritual life," that is, for the development of culture and its propogation. This situation is likely to lead, in coming generations, to a "great travail of the soul." Hebrew literature written in Israel, beginning with the end of the 1960s, clearly reveals this "travail of the soul," one characterized by increasing cynicism and doubt concerning the goals of Zionism, or pain concerning their means of realization. The great question hovering over much of this literature is that of the price that the Jewish people must pay for its "earthly" existence. The protracted military struggle for the state's survival—a struggle that harms the social fabric—and the immersion in the pursuit of material things place a grave question mark over certain Zionist ideals.[60]

Israel's constant battle for survival raised radical existential questions, which had until now largely been repressed from consciousness, such as the question of the meaning of Jewish existence and that of the special connection between the people and its land. The slogan of normalization was no longer accepted as self-evident in light of the fact that, despite Zionism's great efforts, the Jewish people does not enjoy a "normal" existence even in its own homeland, and its fortune is substantially different from that of other nations. Together with this, there occurred an awakening from the myth of the "New Hebrew" as symbolized by the image of the *sabra* (native Israeli). This myth, which was cultivated by the younger generation of Hebrew authors, saw the *sabra* as the antithesis of the *galut* Jew. An anti-intellectual type, he or she finds self-realization primarily through intensive concrete activity—whether through physical labor or by acts of courage and adventure expressing a spontaneous relation to the soil of the homeland. On the other hand, this type almost completely negates any interest in the historical destiny of the Jewish people or its cultural heritage. Awakening from this myth meant a certain skepticism regarding the purely "earthly" ideal expressed by the Young Hebrews movement, at the same time that it reopened a renewed interest in the historical roots of Zionism.

The Six-Day War sharpened the spiritual conflicts within Israeli society even more. The contrast between the feeling of fear and annihilation that preceded the war and the great victory it brought, as well as the renewed encounter with historical dimensions of the Land of Israel— particularly the Old City of Jerusalem—populated by Arab inhabitants, brought about a profound spiritual shock and confronted Israeli society with severe moral dilemmas. These dilemmas all focused around the debate concerning the meaning of Zionism and Israel's cultural-social image: What is our right to the Land of Israel? What are the legitimate limits of the use of military power to achieve of the aims of Zionism? What is the relationship of Zionism to the Jewish heritage, on the one hand, and to humanistic ideas, on the other? These questions today divide Israeli society to its depths, creating severe political and social polarization. This polarization is by no means coterminus with that between "religious" and "secular" Israelis, as these questions divide both the religious and secular camps.

In any event, there is no doubt that since the Six-Day War there has been a devaluation of certain "secular" ideals of Zionism, ones that had previously been almost totally unquestioned. Against the background of this loss of faith in secular Zionist ideals, there grew within Israeli society certain traditionalist trends, some of them very extreme, whether in the religious-nationalist or in the fundamentalist direction. This process was fostered in no small measure by the decisive change in the sociological makeup of Israeli society, in wake of the increase in the political and social significance of Jews of Middle Eastern origin. The latter had undergone a process of modernization different in character from that undergone by Western Jewry, one that was lacking in those "anti-*galut*" and "anti-traditionalist" sentiments found among the pioneers of European origin. On the other hand, it was not involved in the organic absorption of the ideas of modern humanism and socialism. Thus, both the problematics and the various ideologies that developed during the "formative period" of Israeli society remained foreign to this community. The growing importance of this element is likely to change the direction of development of the spiritual conflict in the future.

In the light of the spiritual-political crisis in which secular Zionism was involved, the phenomenon of return to Orthodox Judaism (popularly referred to as *ḥazarah bi-teshuvah,* "repentance") has become far more common than in the past. This phenomenon is accompanied by nearly total rejection of the secular ideals of Zionism and a return to the bosom of premodern Orthodoxy. For this very reason, it points up the power of the tensions between old and new. On the other hand, in other circles of Israeli society, a new approach to Judaism, flowing from existential motivations, is taking shape. This approach recognizes the necessity for the historical break made by the founding fathers of Zionism, but wishes to overcome it by discovering a renewed, spontaneous, and open connection to the sources of traditional Jewish culture, in a deliberate effort to find within them the hidden paths that led to the original Zionist ideals. This approach brings out the dynamic and utopian traits within the various layers of Jewish culture, traits that always allowed Judaism— both in its homeland and in *galut*—to preserve its eternal principles while confronting a new and changing reality. There is no doubt that the destiny of Zionism will also be decided by its degree of success in creating a synthesis between two elements that struggled within it from the very beginning: the attachment to a "spiritual" tradition and the longing for renewal on an "earthly" basis. The Zionist ideal of *hagshamah* has thus been a profound revolution in the consciousness and in the life of the Jewish people, one that signified the refusal to be satisfied with the dream and the supreme effort to realize it, out of responsibility for the historical life of a people on its land. This involved great daring and danger. The prospects for the future of this revolution to a great extent depend on its ability to preserve its connection with the dream out of which it was born.

Notes

1. J. Klatzkin, *Ozar ha-Munahim ha-Filosofiyim* (Berlin: Eshkol, 1928) 1:121–22.

2. Moses Mendelssohn, *Gesammelte Schriften* (1844) 5:494 (all emphasis added); English translation in Ben Halpern, *The Idea of the Jewish State* (Cambridge, MA: Harvard University Press, 1967) 67.

3. "Nay, I would go so far as to believe that if the foundations of their religion have not emasculated their minds they may even, if occasion offers, so changeable are human affairs, raise up their empire afresh, and that God may a second time elect them" (B. Spinoza, *Theologico-Political Treatise,* trans. R. H. M. Elwes [New York: Dover, 1951] 56).

4. Y. Baer, "The Land of Israel and the Exile in the eyes of the Medieval Generations" (Hebrew), *Zion* 6 (1934) 159; idem, "The Educational Value of Jewish History" (Hebrew), *Gilyonot* 12 (1941) 129–30.

5. Compare M. Buber, *On Zion. The History of an Idea* (London: East and West Library, 1972) 89–108, esp. 94–96.

6. R. Schatz-Uffenheimer, *Ha-Hassidut ke-Mistiqah* (Jerusalem: Magnes, 1968) 168–77; Y. Jacobson, "Exile and Redemption in Gur Hasidim" (Hebrew), *Da'at* 2–3 (1978–79) 175–216; see esp. the summary on pp. 214–15.

7. H. Cohen, *Jüdische Schriften* (Berlin: B. Strauss, 1924) 2:328–40.

8. S. Zemah, "Literature and Alienation" (Hebrew), *Shedemot* 30 (1968) 17–37.

9. M. J. Berdyczewski, "Menahem," *Mi-bayit umi-huz* (Warsaw: Ze'irim, 1900).

10. On this influence, see B. Kurzweil, "The Influence of the Philosophy of Vitalism upon Hebrew Literature at the Beginning of the 20th Century" (Hebrew) in his *Sifrutenu Ha-hadashah, Hemshekh O Mahapekhah?* 225–69.

11. F. Nietzsche, *Thus Spoke Zarathustra*, trans. W. Kaufmann, in his *The Portable Nietzsche* (New York: Viking Press, 1954) 125.

12. M. J. Berdyczewski, introduction to the collection "Ba-derekh," in *Kol ma' amerei* (Tel-Aviv: Devir, 1952) 375.

13. M. J. Berdyczewski, *Nemoshot* (Warsaw: Ze'irim, 1900) 18–23, 89–95.

14. F. Nietzsche, *The Use and Abuse of History* (New York: Liberal Arts Press, 1949) 20–25.

15. Y. Klatzkin, *Sheqi'at ha-Hayyim* (Berlin: Devir, 1925) 167–69, 177–79.

16. Klatzkin, *Tehumim,* 12–16.

17. B. Kurzweil, *Sifrutenu Ha-hadashah,* 260.

18. S. Tchernichowsky, *Kol Shiraw* (Jerusalem and Tel-Aviv: Schocken, 1957) 95–101.

19. B. Kurzweil, *Bailik we-Tchernihovski–Mehqarim be-Shiratam* (Jerusalem and Tel-Aviv: Schocken, 1961) 229–31.

20. Z. Schneour, "Shir Mizmor le-'Amey ha-Arazot," *Pandrey ha-Gibor* (Tel Aviv: Yavneh, 1958) 3–6.

21. H. Hazaz, "The Sermon" (Hebrew), *Avanim Rothot* (Tel Aviv: Am Oved, 1958; English translation in R. Alter, ed., *Modern Hebrew Literature* [New York: Behrman House, 1975] 271–87).

22. Y. H. Brenner, *Kol Kitvey . . .* (Tel Aviv: Ha-Kibbutz ha Meuhad, 1967) 3:481.

23. Ibid, 222.

24. M. Meged, "Reality against Holiness" (Hebrew), in *'Al shirah we-sifrut,* ed. Z. Malachi (Tel Aviv: Haifa University Press, 1977) 111–17.

25. E. Schweid, *Ha-Yahid–'Olamo shel A. D. Gordon* (Tel Aviv: Am Oved, 1970) 172.

26. *Shirat Rahel* (Tel Aviv: Davar, 1954) 62, English translation from Ruth Finer Mintz, *Modern Hebrew Poetry* (Berkeley, CA, and Los Angeles: University of California Press, 1966) 110–12.

27. On the importance of this motif in Israeli drama, see G. Ofrat, *Adamah, Adam, Dam.*

28. Vladimir Soloviev, quoted by Nicholas O. Lossky, *History of Russian Philosophy* (New York: International Universities Press, 1952) 120–21. As an example of the Jew's impatience with the

idea, Soloviev mentions the well-known poem from the Passover Haggadah, "God Almighty, now build your temple near and soon . . . now build, now build, now build your temple near."

29. M. Hess, *Ketavim Yehudi'im we-Zioniyyim* (Jerusalem: Zionist Library, 1954) 222–23.

30. Ibid., 198.

31. Ibid., 52.

32. Ibid., 223, 231; cf. M. Buber, *On Zion*, 117.

33. Ahad Ha'am (pseud.), *Kol Kitvey Ahad ha-Am* (Jerusalem: Devir, 1953) 350; English: "Flesh and Spirit," in *The Zionist Idea*, ed. A. Hertzberg, 256.

34. Y. Klatzkin, *Tehumim*, 185–87. Klatzkin's definition of Judaism as a "realized religion" is parallel to the general idea expressed by Bialik in his famous essay, "Halakhah and Aggadah" (Hebrew).

35. A. D. Gordon, *Ha-Umah weha-'Avodah* (Tel Aviv: Haifa Labour Council, 1957) 236.

36. Ibid., 312, 418.

37. A. D. Gordon, "A Hebrew University" (Hebrew), in *Ha-Umah weha-'Avodah*, 167–79.

38. Ibid., 464.

39. Ibid., 418.

40. Quoted by G. Ofrat, *Adamah, Adam, Dam*, 82–83.

41. M. Buber, *Israel and the World*, 185–86.

42. M. Buber, *Te'udah we-yi'ud* (Jerusalem: Zionist Library, 1960) 1:89–92.

43. Ibid., 35.

44. M. Buber, "The Holy Way," in *On Judaism*, 145.

45. Buber, "The Two Foci of the Jewish Soul," in *Israel and the World*, 34.

46. H. Hazaz, "Drabkin," *Avanim Rothot* (Tel Aviv: Am Oved, 1965) 181–82; English in *Israel Argosy* 4 (1956) 107.

47. N. Birnbaum, "Yeqizat ha-Neshamah ha-Yehudit," in *he-'Atid*, ed. S. Horowitz (Berlin, 1912) 4:98–99. This article was published in German in the collection *Vom Judentum* (Prague, 1913).

48. Rabbi A. I. Kook, *Orot*, 169–70.

49. A. I. Kook, *Hazon Ha-Ge'ulah*, 53.

50. A. I. Kook, "Ahdut u-Sheneyut," in *ha-Nir* (Jerusalem, 1929) 45–47.

51. Kook, *Orot*, 84.

52. Kook, *ha-Nir*, 45–47.

53. Kook, *Orot*, 159.

54. G. Scholem, *Devarim Be-Go*, 135–36.

55. Ibid., 221.

56. Ibid., 41–42.

57. Ibid., 585.

58. On the Young Hebrews movement, see B. Kurzweil, "The Nature and Sources of the Young Hebrews movement" (Hebrew), in *Sifrutenu Ha-Hadasha*, 270–300.

59. B. Katzenelson, *Ketavim* (Tel Aviv: Mapai, 1947) 6:337–38.

60. Examples of this trend are found in the novels of Binyamin Tamuz, one of the outstanding members of the Young Hebrews, and in the novels of Amos Oz. On tendencies in the Hebrew theater, see the final chapter of G. Ofrat's *Adamah, Adam, Dam*.

Bibliography

Texts

Berdyczewski, M. J. *Kol ma'marei*. Tel Aviv: Devir, 1952.
Buber, M. *Israel and the World*. New York: Schocken, 1963.

――――. *On Judaism*. New York: Schocken, 1967

Gordon, A. D. *Kol Kitvei*. Tel Aviv and Haifa, 1957.

Hess, M. *Rome and Jerusalem*. Translated by Meyer Waxman. New York: Bloch, 1943.

Klatzkin, J. *Tehumim*. Berlin: Devir, 1925.

Kook, Rabbi A. I. *Orot*. Jerusalem: Mossad Harav Kook, 1963.

Kook, Rabbi A. I. *Hazon Ha-Ge'ulah*. Jerusalem: Association for Publishing the Works of Chief Rabbi A. I. Kook, 1941.

Scholem, G. *Devarim Be-Go*. 2 vols. Tel Aviv: Am Oved, 1976.

Studies

Hertzberg, A. (ed.) *The Zionist Idea*. New York: Atheneum, 1973.

Kurzweil, B. *Sifrutenu Ha-hadashah, Hemshekh O Mahapekha?* Jerusalem and Tel Aviv: Schocken, 1960.

Ofrat, G. *Adamah, Adam, Dam*. Tel Aviv: Tcherikover, 1980.

Rotenstreich, N. *Ha-mahshavah Ha-Yehudit Ba-et Ha-hadashah*, vol. 1. Tel Aviv, 1945.

Schweid, E. *Ha-yahadut Ve-hatarbut Ha-hilonit*. Tel Aviv: Am Oved, 1966.

Yaron, Z. *Mishnato shel Ha-rav Kook*. Jerusalem: World Zionist Organization, 1974.

13

The Renewal of Jewish Spirituality: Two Views

LAURENCE J. SILBERSTEIN

TO MANY PHILOSOPHERS and social theorists, modern life is characterized by the alienation of large numbers of people from the goals, norms, and ends that had constituted the framework of meaning in traditional societies. In such a situation, "the goals, norms, and ends which define the common practices or institutions begin to seem irrelevant or even monstrous, or . . . the norms are redefined so that the practices appear a travesty of them."[1] Such alienation is particularly evident in the realm of religious faith.

Giants of the modernist mentality like Nietzsche, Marx, and Freud, held religion to be especially responsible for the alienation of the modern individual. Fostering an illusory system of meaning, religion stifles the creative actualization of the individual and perpetuates conditions of sociopolitical oppression. Accordingly, religion constitutes a major impediment to human psychological growth.

While the intellectuals aimed their barbs at religion, religious interpretations of everyday events and relationships increasingly lost their force for large numbers of people. As the pragmatic, rational ethos grew in strength, people increasingly found theological interpretations of reality obsolete and replaced them with rational goal-oriented frameworks of meaning. Estranged from the divine, from nature, and from the intimate ties of community, the modern person grew skeptical of, or hostile to, metaphysical and theological systems. Religious symbols, which had once provided the basic paradigms for organizing and structuring ideas and experiences, were now viewed as alien or, at best, ineffectual.

This loss of religious meaning has been accomplished by a growing sense of loneliness, isolation, and meaninglessness. One of the most poignant descriptions of this condition is the famous passage from Nietzsche's *The Gay Science:*

> Whither are we moving? Away from all suns? Are we not plunging continually? Backward, forward, in all directions? Is there still an up or down? Are we not straying through an infinite nothing? Do we not feel the breath of empty space? Has it not become colder? Is not night continually closing in on us? Do we not need to light lanterns in the morning? Do we hear nothing as yet of the noise of the grave diggers who are burying God? Do we smell nothing as yet of the divine decomposition? Gods too, decompose. God is dead. God remains dead. And we have killed him.[2]

Nietzsche was not elated by his cultural vision. Although the death of God might ultimately contribute to the liberation of the individual, its immediate effect was to remove the foundations upon which Western views of reality had been grounded for centuries.

According to Nietzsche, individuals, to develop fully as persons, must turn away from all traditional systems, philosophical as well as theological, and focus on their inner being, their instincts and their physical selves. Traditional religious and philosophical systems not only fail to provide the meaning and comfort we so desperately seek, they actually prevent us from acquiring a genuine understanding of the psychological processes that constitute the basis of our lives. So long as we retain outmoded theological and metaphysical beliefs, we are doomed to remain alienated from ourselves and the world around us.

In contrast to Nietzsche, S. Kierkegaard insisted that the problem of human alienation could only be overcome through religious commitment in the face of uncertainty. Without a personal relationship to the divine, one's existence lacks true meaning. However, Kierkegaard did not advocate a return to traditional religion. Highly critical of institutionalized religious forms and structures, he distinguished these forms, which he labeled "Christendom," from genuine faith, which he referred to as "Christianity."

For modern persons to overcome their alienation, a renewal of genuine faith was essential:

> Without risk, there is no faith. Faith is precisely the contradiction between the infinite passion of the individual's inwardness and the objective uncertainty. If I am capable of grasping God objectively, I do not believe, but precisely because I cannot do this I must believe.[3]

Kierkegaard, like Nietzsche, considered philosophical and religious systems to be a primary source of alienation. Endeavoring to strip away the illusions that block individuals from their authentic selves, Kierkegaard reflected on the anxiety that results from the precarious, unstable, threatening quality of modern existence: "Deep within every human being there still lives the anxiety over the possibility of being alone in the world, forgotten by God, overlooked among the millions and millions in this enormous household."[4]

Kierkegaard endeavored to revise the prevailing, established conception of Christianity and replace it with an existential one. Criticizing the established church in Denmark, he accused it of contradicting the principles of genuine Christianity: "Christendom has done away with Christianity without being quite aware of it. The consequence is that, if anything, one must try again to introduce Christianity into Christendom."[5]

According to Kierkegaard, the specific content of faith was far less important than the way in which one lived that faith:

> In the ethico-religious sphere, the accent is again on the "how." But this is not to be understood as referring to demeanor, expression, delivery or the like; rather it refers to the relationship sustained by the existing individual, in his own existence, to the content of his utterance.
>
> Objectively the interest is focussed only on the thought-content, subjectively on the inwardness.[6]

From the Nietzschean perspective, Kierkegaard's leap of faith is but another example of alienation. According to Nietzsche, to be liberated from the condition of alienation, one had to unmask the illusion of all religious faith, trust one's own instincts and drives and nurture one's creative impulses. However, in one important sense Nietzsche and Kierkegaard were in agreement. To each, the true starting point of all genuine thought is the inner life of the individual, a fact that traditional philosophical and theological systems ignored. Subordinating the personal experiences of the individual to abstract systems, philosophy and theology suppress the deepest drives of human existence. Accordingly, both Kierkegaard and Nietzsche undertook to deconstruct the presuppositions of current philosophical systems and to focus our attention on the inner life and experience of the individual. For them, the starting point of philosophy is the immediate experience of the individual, prior to all language and concepts: "Two ways, in general, are open for an existing individual: either he can do his utmost to forget that he is an existing individual . . . or he can concentrate his entire energy upon the fact that he is an existing individual."[7]

Eschewing the categories of science, rational philosophy, and historical inquiry, Nietzsche and Kierkegaard engaged in in-depth, psychological analyses of the inner life. Penetrating the façade of philosophical systems and rational constructs, they introduced a radically new way of philosophizing about the human condition, thereby precipitating the emergence of existentialism. At the same time, stripping away the illusions that ensnare the life of the individual, they revealed the abyss over which that life hung precariously.

The processes of alienation and loss of meaning that characterize Western culture in general have also eroded the foundations of traditional Jewish religious faith. Modern Jews, immersed in Western culture, have increasingly found that religious forms and beliefs no longer provide an effective framework of meaning. Finding religious symbols to be ineffective in ordering life and structuring their relation to other persons and to the world in general, modern Jews have enthusiastically embraced the values of modern society.

Buber and Heschel: Jewish Responses to Alienation

The writings of Martin Buber and Abraham Joshua Heschel make up two of the most articulate and powerful responses to the processes of alienation and secularization in modern Jewish thought. Rejecting Nietzsche's vision of the death of God, both men sought to formulate an approach to religious faith that would enhance rather than constrict the humanity of the individual. Repelled by the spreading dehumanization that characterizes the modern technological society, each decried the growing tendency to reduce human beings to objects to be manipulated for the ends of society. To both Buber and Heschel, Judaism offered a viable, necessary alternative to the rationalized ethos of modern life.

Both men recognized that the modern Jew feels alienated from the religious forms and structures of Jewish tradition. In contrast to the secular nationalists, however, Buber and Heschel insisted that religious faith is essential to Judaism. Thus, they each endeavored to formulate a way of thinking and talking about Judaism that would reveal its spiritual power and existential force. Each sought to develop categories and concepts that would help modern Jews overcome their alienation from Judaism and recover its hidden spiritual resources.

While focusing on the inner life of the individual and the existential foundations of religious life, Buber and Heschel differed in their conceptions of religious faith and their attitudes toward tradition. Breaking with the rabbinic framework, Buber rooted his philosophy of Judaism in the realm of interhuman relations. In his relational philosophy of religion, the divine is met through everyday encounters with other beings, particularly other persons. Although he did not deny the possibility of direct divine–human encounters, Buber focused his attention on meetings between persons.

To Buber, religion is not a distinct realm of human culture or experience.

One lives religiously by acting and relating to others in a hallowing manner. From his existential perspective, institutionalized forms stifle spontaneity and impede the nurturing, confirming relations essential to human growth. Criticizing the destructive effect that institutionalized religion exercises on genuine faith experience, Buber showed a marked antipathy to rabbinic Judaism. In its place, he advocated a revisionistic interpretation of Judaism that simultaneously emphasized the actualization of the individual self and the responsibility to others.

In marked contrast to Buber's revisionistic stance, Abraham Joshua Heschel defended the religious power of rabbinic tradition. In Heschel's view, the force and power of Judaism derive from its capacity to shape the thought and the actions of the individual. Through a dialectical system of halakhah (normative, legally binding patterns of behavior) and aggadah (nonlegal teachings including ethics, legendary anecdotes, and homiletical passages), rabbinic Judaism provides the Jew with a framework of thinking and living that is a distinct alternative to the dehumanizing structure of modern society.

In contrast to Buber's emphasis on the actualization of the divine in inter-human relations, Heschel focused on the manifestation of the divine in the consciousness of the individual. Seeking to reveal the constitutive elements of religious consciousness, Heschel grounded his philosophy of religion in such concepts as awe, wonder, mystery, and radical amazement. Focusing on the experiential dimension of religious faith, Heschel sought to relate that faith to the existential situation of the individual. In his discussions of the Bible and *mizwot,* Heschel endeavored to help the contemporary Jew experience and understand their spiritual power and existential significance. However, apart from the pragmatic value of *mizwot,* Heschel considered them to be divine commandments incumbent upon all Jews. In the spirit of Kabbalah, Heschel viewed *mizwot* as actions that fulfill a divine need.

Both Heschel and Buber argued that God needs the human being. Revising Hasidic teachings, Buber insisted that any action performed with the proper attitude has the power to free the divine sparks and unify God. Heschel, faithful to traditional Kabbalah, linked the liberation of the sparks to the performance of the *mizwot.*

Martin Buber: The Revisioning of Judaism

Attracted by Buber's emphasis on inwardness and the interhuman, Jews and non-Jews alike have found his writings to be a source of enlightenment and inspiration. However, many readers have difficulty in finding the uniquely Jewish elements in Buber's major philosophical work, *I and Thou,* or even in his writings on Hasidism. His basic categories, such as "religiosity," "hallowing the everyday," and "I-You relation" do not seem to be distinctively Jewish.[8] A question frequently raised by students encountering his writings for the first time is What is Jewish about Buber's thought? Or, Is what he is talking about really Judaism.?

This puzzlement over the Jewishness of Buber's writings is exacerbated by his negative attitude to the forms and structures of rabbinic Judaism, including the Sabbath, the festivals, and synagogue worship. To many Jews, Buber ignores or rejects the very elements that distinguish Judaism as a unique way of life. The confusion regarding Buber's works is largely the result of the fact that, unlike most writers on Judaism, he approaches his task as a revisionist. Whereas conventional writings on Judaism strive to preserve or reinterpret traditional forms of Jewish belief and worship, Buber sought to formulate a new way of talking and thinking about Judaism. Rather than interpret traditional forms and structures, he wished to alter the way in which we conceptualize Judaism. The resulting conception of Judaism significantly differs from conventional conceptions, liberal as well as traditional.

One may best understand Buber's intellectual orientation to Judaism and to philosophy in general by recognizing that, like Nietzsche and Kierkegaard, he is an edifying rather than a normal, systematic philosopher. Mainstream or normal philosophers develop systems of thought in order to describe reality accurately. These systems are validated by their degree of correspondence to the objective reality under discussion. Edifying philosophers, on the other hand, eschew all efforts to describe objective reality systematically. Instead, the edifying philosopher engages in a conversation in an effort to help free people from obsolete, alienating ways of thinking, speaking, and acting. Such philosophers, and Buber is one of them, write to liberate the individual from all illusions that keep decisions from being made in a free and responsible manner.[9]

To the edifying philosopher, conventional ways of thinking and speaking alienate the individual from the authentic self, other persons, and the natural world. Thus, rather than perpetuate conventional categories and concepts, they unmask the alienating forms of conventional discourse and replace them with alternative ways of talking. Ultimately, the edifying philosopher wants not only to change the way in which people think but also to help change the way in which they live.

All of Buber's writings were efforts to liberate readers from the alienating conditions of life and thought and educate them to alternative forms. Whether writing about religion or society, Buber endeavored to unmask the sources of alienation that estrange persons from themselves, from others, and from their community. In his writings on Judaism, he endeavored to free Jews from outmoded categories and forms of life and to indicate a new direction in Jewish life and thought compatible with existential freedom and individual responsibility.

Buber's revisionist stance is reflected in his writings on Judaism and on Hasidism in particular. Departing from conventional interpretations, he read the Hasidic sources in the light of his existential and edifying concerns. The result was a conception of Judaism and Hasidism that differed significantly from the conventional conceptions.[10]

The revisionist character of Buber's thought is evident in his earliest lectures on Judaism. Addressing young Jewish intellectuals dissatisfied with the existing forms of Jewish life, Buber, eschewing the prevailing ideologies, focused on the inner experience of the individual:

> The question I put before you, as well as before myself is the question of the meaning of Judaism for the Jews.
> Why do we call ourselves Jews? I want to speak to you not of an abstraction, but of your own life, of our own life; and not of life's outer hustle and bustle, but of its authenticity and essence. (*On Judaism*, 11)

Urging his audience to abandon inherited formulas and trust their own experience,[11] Buber insisted that concepts like Judaism, religion, and nation must directly express the individual Jew's inner, existential reality. While these concepts are commonly used to define the nature of Judaism, they are themselves in need of explanation and depend for their meaning on the personal experience of the individual. Like his precursor, Kierkegaard, Buber emphasized the "inner reality" of a person's life over the inherited forms and teachings of tradition.

Buber was a nationalist deeply committed to the survival of the Jewish people. However, in his discussion of Jewish nationalism, Buber rejected conventional views and focused on the existential foundations of nationhood. Although Buber did not deny the importance of such elements as land, language, and literature, his primary concern was the inner, existential dimension of nationhood. This existential dimension emerges when, in the course of his life, an individual recognizes that his own individual self is rooted in qualities inherited from past generations.

In keeping with the prevailing nationalist thought of the time, Buber, in his pre–World War I writings, utilized the concept of "blood," to refer to a combination of genetic and psychological factors, "that something which is implanted within us by the chain of fathers and mothers, by their nature and by their fate, by their deeds and by their sufferings; it is times great heritage that we bring with us into the world" (*On Judaism*, 17).[12]

Buber refused either to subordinate the individual to the group or to elevate the nation above humanity in general. To him, a nation provides individuals with the means to actualize their innate humanity. To be a Jew, a member of the Jewish nation, is to act out one's destiny through the Jewish people and its culture. Buber valued the survival of the Jewish nation, but he focused on the spiritual renewal of the individual and, ultimately, of all humanity.

Unlike the secular nationalist, Buber believed that in Judaism, nation and faith are intertwined. However, like the concept "nation," the concept "religion" often masks the existential grounds of genuine faith. Contrasting religion and religiosity, Buber endeavored to revise the prevailing conception of religious belief. While religion is oriented to institutionalized forms, religiosity refers to the existential dimension of faith, to "the longing to establish a living communion with the unconditioned" (*On Judaism*, 80). Whereas religion, "the sum total of the customs and teachings of a certain epoch in a people's life," has the tendency to stagnate, religiosity, dynamic and creative, resists all efforts to channel it into fixed forms or intellectual formulations. In religion, symbols and structures, detached from the basic event that generated them, are objectified and reified in rules and dogmas which stifle the original, creative, spontaneous divine–human encounter. "Once religious rites and dogmas have become so rigid that religiosity cannot move them or no longer wants to comply with them, religion becomes uncreative and therefore untrue" (*On Judaism*, 80).

The dichotomy between the creative, spontaneous moment of lived experience and the stifling, objectifying process of institutionalization or routinization is a recurring theme in Buber's writings. Like his teacher, Georg Simmel, he believed that form and content, structure and lived experience are locked in perennial combat.[13] In the spirit of radical mysticism, existentialism and *Lebensphilosophie*,[14] Buber protested the stifling effect of forms and structures.

In the light of this, Buber's negative attitude toward halakhah and rabbinic Judaism in general is understandable. Halakhah, like any system of norms and behavior, is epiphenomenal to the immediate moment of divine–human encounter. Impeding and suppressing the immediate divine–human encounter, all systems, including the rabbinic system, serve as a refuge from choice and responsibility. Buber acknowledged that "to exist as a religion, religiosity needs form; for a continuous religious community, perpetuated from generation to generation, is possible only where a common way of life is maintained." Nevertheless, he continually criticized halakhah for stifling creativity and freedom and substituting casuistry for the free exercise of ethical decision (*On Judaism*, 91–92).

Like Nietzsche, another of his early mentors, Buber utilized a conflict model of history. Reversing conventional interpretations of Jewish history, he identified rabbinic Judaism as "official," establishment Judaism, which was locked in perennial conflict with genuine, authentic, underground Judaism.[15] Subsuming priestly and rabbinic Judaism under the category of religion, Buber identified the creative forces in Jewish life with such movements as prophecy, the Essenes, pre-Pauline Christianity, and Hasidism.

Unlike nineteenth-century Jewish rationalists, who identified myth with paganism, Buber considered myth to be an authentic, immediate expression of the divine–human encounter. Viewing rational conceptualization as distorting the immediate moment of divine–human encounter, he saw myth as a creative expression of a community's response to its encounter with God. Utilizing the rhetoric of *Lebensphilosophie*, which he subsequently rejected, Buber contrasted myth to institutionalized, formalized religion: "All myth, in contrast, is the expression of the fullness of existence, its image, its sign; it drinks incessantly from the gushing fountains of life. . . . The history of the Jewish religion is in great part the history of its fight against myth" (*Legends of the Baal Shem Tov*, 11).[16]

Buber's revisionist orientation is clearly reflected in his writings on Hasidism. In this eighteenth-century movement of religious renewal, Buber discovered an indigenous form of Jewish spiritual renewal and creative expression. To Buber, Hasidism embodied the creative forces of Judaism. "No renewal of Judaism is possible that does not bear in itself the elements of Hasidism" (*Legends*, 12–13).

Far too westernized to affiliate with the Hasidic movement, Buber undertook to recover its spiritual power and life-force by retelling its myths and legends. Rejecting the prevailing modes of rationalistic philosophizing and historical inquiry, Buber set out to generate a renewal of Jewish mythos: "I bear in me the blood and the spirit of those who created it, and out of my blood and spirit it has become new. I stand in the chain of narrators, a link between links. . . . My narration stands on the earth of Jewish myth, and the heaven of Jewish myth is over it" (*Legends*, 10–11).

To Buber, Hasidism offered an alternative to the rational liberalism of the reformers, the secular nationalism of the Zionists and the rationalistic ethos of European culture. In the teachings of Hasidism, he saw an alternative to what Weber had called "the iron cage" of rationalized, bureaucratized Western society.

Eschewing the path of historical inquiry, Buber sought to uncover Hasidism's spiritual, mythic power. Contrasting his approach to that of conventional historiography, he endeavored "to convey to our own time the force of a former life of faith, and to help our age renew its ruptured bond with the absolute" ("Interpreting Hasidism," 218).

In his efforts to make Hasidism's original spiritual power available to the modern Jew, he revised and extended these teachings. However, far from distorting them, he insisted that he was simply making manifest that which was already implicit in them: "I tell once again the old stories, and if they sound new, it is because the new already lay dormant in them when they were told for the first time" (*Legends,* 10).

If Hasidism was to serve the modern Jew as a source of spiritual power, it first had to be liberated from its rabbinic framework. So long as it remained within the institutionalized structure of rabbinic Judaism, Hasidism would only perpetuate religion's stifling effect. Accordingly, Buber drew out the existential, individualistic tendencies within Hasidism and elevated them to a position of prominence.

Judaism and the Philosophy of Relation

Buber's conception of religion and, consequently, his interpretation of Judaism, took a decisive turn in 1918. Whereas he had previously viewed religious faith in terms of the individual's communion with the divine, he now shifted the focus to the interhuman:

> The Divine may come to life in individual man, may reveal itself within individual man; but it attains its earthly fulness only where, having awakened to an awareness of their universal being, individual beings open themselves to one another, disclose themselves to one another, help one another; where immediacy is established between one human being and another . . . where the eternal rise in the Between, the seemingly empty space; that true space is community, and true community is that relationship in which the Divine comes to its actualization between person and person. (*On Judaism,* 110)

The Lurianic myth of the "breaking of the vessels" provided the mythic underpinning for Buber's understanding of life and religious faith. In the Lurianic myth, creation is depicted as a cataclysmic event in which the primordial divine unity is shattered. Divine sparks, falling to earth, become trapped in shells. The shattering of the primordial divine unity and the separation of the sparks from their divine source precipitated a condition of cosmic exile.[17]

Lurianic Kabbalah assigned the individual Jew a major role in the process of redemption (*tiqqun*). By performing the traditional *mizwot* with the proper attitude and intention, the Jew helps to liberate the sparks from the shells and reunite them with the divine source. In Hasidism, *tiqqun* was broadened to include other actions as well and was given a decidedly ethical thrust. However, Hasidism never broke with the traditional rabbinic framework.[18] Buber, however, broke through the parameters of the rabbinic framework. In his reading of Hasidism, no realm of existence was considered to lie outside of the sphere of the holy. All spheres of life, like all actions, are potentially sacred. Consequently, the traditional *mizwot* are no longer necessary to the process of redemption. A Jew fulfills his obligations by hallowing the everyday, that is, by performing all acts in the proper spirit and with the proper intention. "For no thing can exist without a divine spark, and each person can uncover and redeem this spark at each time and through each action, even the most ordinary, if only he performs them in purity, wholly directed to God and concentrated in Him" ("My Way to Hasidism," in *Hasidism and Modern Man*, 49).

Like Kierkegaard, Buber insisted that the substance of our actions was less important than the manner in which they are carried out. In religion, as in all of life, the "how" is far more important than the "what." Insofar as all acts of hallowing serve to actualize the divine in human life, the specific modes of sanctification prescribed by rabbinic Judaism are no longer necessary. Buber endorsed a pluralistic conception of religious life. Each individual is unique and must find his or her own distinct path to God. Insofar as each person is responsible to choose and to act, no one may prescribe specific norms and principles of behavior for another. Although viewed by his critics as a religious anarchist, Buber did not advocate a total abandonment of principles of behavior.[19] To him, the myth of the sparks provides a definite sense of direction and limits. First of all, insofar as each person embodies a divine spark, he is responsible to nurture and cultivate his own uniqueness:

> Every person born into this world represents something new, something that never existed before, something original and unique. It is the duty of every person in Israel to know and consider that he is unique in the world in his particular character and that there has never been anyone like him in the world. (*Hasidism*, 139–40)

Moreover, besides actualizing one's own potential, each person is obligated to help others to actualize their unique qualities. We actualize our own uniqueness only by confining the uniqueness of others. By relating to others in this way, we help to actualize the divine as a real presence in our world. Thus, to live religiously is to live in relation to others.

> The Baal Shem teaches that no encounter with a being or a thing in the course of our life lacks a hidden significance. The people we live with or meet with, the animals that help us with our farm work, the soil we till, the tools we use, they all contain a mysterious spiritual substance which depends on

us for helping it toward its pure form, its perfection. If we neglect this spiritual substance sent across our path, if we think only in terms of momentary purposes, without developing a genuine relationship to the beings and things in whose life we ought to take part, as they in ours, then shall ourselves be barred from true, fulfilled existence. (*Hasidism*, 173)

This succinct statement of Buber's understanding of religious life and Judaism reveals another basic motif he derived from the myth of the sparks: the unity of creation. Insofar as each spark was originally a part of the primordial divine unity, each person embodies a part of the divine. Moreover, all beings are linked by means of their divine sparks. "As the primal source of the divine is bound with all His soul-sparks scattered in the world, so what we do to our fellow men is bound with what we do to God" (*Hasidism*, 241).

The separation of the sparks from their divine source and from one another represents alienation on a cosmic scale.[20] Similarly, the separation of one person from another, the unnatural separation of beings from that to which they are naturally joined, also constitutes alienation. Thus, when we relate to other beings, human and nonhuman, in a hallowing manner, we help to restore the primordial unity and to reduce the degree of alienation in the world. Thus, Buber succeeded in synthesizing his existentialist concern for the individual self with his social concern for community and his religious concern for the divine.

In Buber's interpretation, Hasidism speaks to the condition of all persons: "The central example of the Hasidic overcoming of the distance between the sacred and the profane points to an explanation of what is to be understood by the fact that Hasidism has its word to speak to the crisis of western man" (*Hasidism*, 38). Buber thus bridged the gap between his particular Jewish commitments and his universal human commitments. Hasidism not only teaches one how to be Jewish; it also teaches how to be human: "Man cannot approach the Divine by reaching beyond the human; he can approach Him through becoming human. To become human is what he, this individual person, has been created for. This, so it seems to me, is the eternal core of Hasidic life and of Hasidic teaching" (*Hasidism*, 42–43).

Thus, Buber's integration of Hasidism, existentialism, and community produced a radically revised conception of Judaism. No longer is Jewish life defined by a specific set of actions or principles. Like all persons, the Jew reaches the divine by hallowing the everyday. Religion is no longer predicated on the division between the sacred and the profane. All of life is potentially sacred.

Just as Hasidism, transforming Kabbalah into ethos, expanded the parameters of religious existence to encompass the individual's relationship to others and to the community, Buber universalized that ethos by severing its connection to rabbinic Judaism. Convinced that the teachings of Hasidism spoke to the general condition of alienation permeating modern life, Buber undertook to make them accessible to the world at large through translations and interpretations of the Hasidic tales. However, Buber felt that to make the teachings of Hasidism universally accessible, he had to translate them into philosophical discourse.[21] Accordingly, in *I and Thou*, Buber sought to formulate philosophical categories to convey effectively the teachings of Hasidism. Embarking on an existential-phenomenological inquiry into the realm of the interhuman, he transposed such concepts as "hallowing the everyday," into a social key. In response to Nietzsche, Buber insisted that life was ultimately grounded in the human being's relation to the divine. Unlike Kierkegaard, however, Buber insisted that not the individual, but the individual in relation to the other, the I in relation to the You, is the starting point of religious faith.[22]

In *I and Thou*, Buber set forth a philosophical critique of the prevailing instrumentalist, rationalized ethos of Western society. Describing human existence in terms of our relation to other persons, the natural world, and the divine, he revised prevailing notions of person, community, and religion. Like Nietzsche and Kierkegaard, Buber considered the modern individual to be estranged from his authentic self. The rationalized, technological structure of modern life, graphically depicted by social thinkers like F. Tonnies, Simmel, and Weber, provides little opportunity to cultivate our own uniqueness or that of others. Viewing others through the objectivistic categories of the modern consciousness, we relate to them as "its" whose primary purpose is to serve our ends: "One sees the other beings around one as centers of productivity which need to be recognized and employed in their specific capacities as bundles of experienceable, influenceable, manageable, usable properties" ("The Task," in *A Believing Humanism*, 99).

Judaism, particularly Hasidism, provides a viable alternative to the modern Western vision of society. In contrast to the prevailing dehumanizing instrumentalist ethos, Hasidism offers a model of direct, need-free, loving relationships between persons. In contrast to the pessimistic, deterministic view of Western social thinkers, Hasidism emphasizes the possibility of *teshuvah*, interpreted by Buber as a complete reversal in the existential stance of the individual:

> The life of a human being does not exist merely in the sphere of goal directed verbs. It does not consist merely of activities that have something for their object.

I perceive something, I feel something, I imagine something, I want something, I sense something, I think something. The life of a human being does not consist of all this and its like. (*I and Thou*, 54)

Without the structured, goal-oriented activities that constitute the realm of the It, society cannot survive. However, by itself, the It does not contribute to the actualization of the self. One actualizes one's humanity only by being fully present to others and by relating to them as "Yous" rather than "Its." In modern society, dominated by the objectivistic ethos of science and the instrumental ethos of modern technology, it is increasingly difficult to attain this relationship. In the modern world, the ethos of utility, efficiency and profit pervades all relationships:

In sick ages, it happens that the It world, no longer irrigated and fertilized by the living currents of the You world, severed and stagnant, becomes a gigantic swamp phantom and overpowers man. As he accommodates himself to the world of objects that no longer achieve any presence for him, he succumbs to it. The common causality grows into an oppressive and crushing doom. (*I and Thou*, 102)

Unless the everyday pattern of functional relationships and activities is broken by the incursion of genuine I-You relationships, life, according to Buber, remains dehumanizing: "in all seriousness of truth listen: without It a human being cannot live. But whoever lives only with that is not human" (*I and Thou*, 85).

The Philosophy of Relation and the Renewal of Judaism

Buber believed that young Jews, alienated by the rationalized, intellectualized ethos of modern society, suffer, like their European counterparts, from existential loneliness. Besides the general alienation of Western society, Jews also experience a peculiarly Jewish form of alienation—exile. However, the anxiety and depression produced by this loneliness provide the seeds of spiritual renewal: "Out of the anxiety and depression of such a state of mind, modern Europe's youth longs for community, longs for it so powerfully that it is ready to surrender to any phantom of community" (*On Judaism*, 159).

While deeply concerned over the plight of humanity, Buber was not only a universalistic humanitarian. As he indicated in the lectures discussed earlier, a people plays an essential role in shaping individuals, providing them with an indefinable substratum of their being. Moreover, the people provides the historic framework through which one acts out the human drama. Thus, in his writings, the community of Israel is the social vehicle through which Jews fulfill their obligations to humanity.

By separating themselves from their people, Jews deprive themselves of the primary group through which to actualize their human potential. The history and culture of Israel provide unique opportunities for a life of relation and dialogue. The historic career of Israel reflects a unique consciousness of duality and a continual drive to overcome that duality. In the teachings of the prophets and the writings of Hasidism, young Jews can find ways to further their quest for authentic human existence.

Buber also believed that one's people provides the symbols that shape and nurture one's basic orientation to reality. Without the bond to a people, one remains amorphous and adrift. In the Bible and Hasidic tales, Jew find a record of the people's ongoing dialogue with the divine, a paradigm of interhuman relation and a vision of community (*On Judaism*, 154). Seen in this light, the conventional Jewish nationalist vision of renewal is inadequate. Although a Jewish homeland could have an "invigorating and cohesive influence on Jewish life in the diaspora," it could not bring about the radical upheaval necessary to overcome "the great ambivalence, the boundless despair, the infinite longing and pathetic inner chaos of many of today's Jews" (*On Judaism*, 39). Only a renewal originating "in the deeper regions of the people's spirit" could succeed in the current crisis.

To Buber, the Jew is heir to a unique task which the Jewish people accepted upon itself at its very inception. As described in the Bible, the vocation of Israel is to actualize genuine community and foster genuine relations:

> The human world is meant to become a single body through the actions of men themselves. We men are charged to perfect our own portion of the universe—the human world. There is one nation which once upon a time heard this charge so loudly that the charge penetrated to the very depths of its soul. (*Israel and the World*, 186)

Like any other nation, Israel's task is to form communities that engender genuine relations. In such communities, people are able to relate in a way that confirms the uniqueness of each. To live as a Jew, therefore, is to live a genuine human existence in the midst of the people of Israel. This, in turn, entails being committed to establishing genuine relation at all levels of life:

> And how is it given to us to fulfill this truth if not by building the social pattern of our own people in Palestine all the way, from the pattern of family, neighborhood and settlement to that of the whole community? For it is no real community (true community) if it is not composed of real families and real neighborhoods and real settlements, and it is not a real nation if it does not maintain its truthfulness in true relations as well, the relationships of a fruitful and creative peace with its neighbors. (*Israel and the World*, 193)

For Buber, Jewish living is a comprehensive mode of life encompassing national consciousness and responsibility to the historic vocation of the nation. In quest of this mode of life, the Jew engages in a dialogue with the teachings of Judaism.[23] However, responsibility to God stands above one's responsibility to one's people. Although the national framework of Jewish life is a given, the actual content of that life demands ongoing choice and responsibility:

> It is only a question of the right line of demarcation that has to be drawn ever anew—the thousandfold system of demarcation between the spheres which must of necessity be centralized and those which can operate in freedom; between the degree of government and the degree of autonomy; between the law of unity and the claim of community. . . . The realization of community, like the realization of any idea, cannot occur once and for all time; always it must be the moment's answer to the moment's question, and nothing more. (*Paths in Utopia*, 134)

The Bible, a unique expression of Jewish faith and life, provides the basic foundation for Jewish life and thought. However, under the influence of modern thought, the Jew has become estranged from the Bible, viewing it either as distorted history or as mere poetry. Properly understood, however, the Bible provides the modern Jew with access to genuine sources of revelation. Yet, unwilling "to endure this moment full of possible decisions, to respond to and be responsible for every moment," the modern Jew seeks to control the biblical text, reducing it to poetry or legend (*Israel and the World*, 95). Consequently, an abyss separates him from the Hebrew Bible. Buber's many works of interpretation and the translation effort undertaken jointly with Franz Rosenzweig were efforts to help bridge this gap.

Buber considered the Bible to be an authentic record of Israel's encounter with God. The biblical tales record events as experienced by the community and preserved through its "formative, myth-creating" memory. If modern readers, divested of all prejudices, can approach the Bible in total openness, they can recover the original situation and once again hear the address:

> [The modern reader] must face the book with a new attitude as something new. He must yield to it, withhold nothing of his being, and let whatever will occur between himself and it. He does not know which of its sayings and images will overwhelm him and mold him, from where the spirit will ferment and enter into him, to incorporate itself anew in his body. But he holds himself open. (*Israel and the World*, 93)

Although he viewed the Bible as an outcome of divine revelation, Buber rejected the traditional rabbinic conception of the "giving of the Torah." In keeping with his existentialist perspective, he denied that revelation entailed prescribed commandments. Instead, in the moment of revelation, the individual experiences a presence and feels a heightened sense of the meaningfulness of existence. Feeling addressed, one is moved to act. However, the precise content of these actions depends upon the unique response of each individual.

Abraham Joshua Heschel: The Renewal of Jewish Tradition

In a work completed shortly before his death, Abraham Joshua Heschel wrote: "When, long ago, I began to read the works of Kierkegaard, the father of modern Existentialism, I was surprised to find that most of his thoughts were familiar to me" (*A Passion for Truth*, 85). In the writings of Kierkegaard, Heschel, like Buber, discovered ideas that confirmed the basic views of life and faith learned from the teachings of Hasidism. Kierkegaard's emphasis on the inner life of the individual, his critique of established institutions, his recognition of the paradoxes of faith, and his impatience with dishonesty all coincided with the orientation to life that emerged from the sources of Judaism.

Like Kierkegaard, Heschel believed that religious faith entails alienation. To be religious is to stand apart from society and engage in an ongoing "fight against spiritual inertia, indolence and callousness" (*Passion*, 183). Heschel, too, believed that a recovery of religious faith is essential if the individual is to recover the roots of authentic being.

The scion of a prestigious Hasidic family, Heschel had been raised and educated in a traditional religious environment. In contrast to Buber, he never entirely rejected that environment. Instead, he considered traditional Judaism to be a unique, viable alternative to the moral and intellectual ethos of modern Western society.

For Heschel, in contrast to Buber, the traditional forms of rabbinic Judaism are essential to a Jewish renewal. Denying that form and structure stifle genuine religious faith, Heschel argued that traditional Judaism was directly related to the existential situation of the individual believer. Accordingly, rather than revise rabbinic tradition, he endeavored to formulate categories that reveal its force and power to the modern Jew.

Heschel was deeply disturbed by the extent to which Judaism had, from his point of view, been distorted. Drawing from the teachings of the Bible, the Talmud, Hasidism, and Kabbalah on the one hand, and existentialism and phenomenology on the other, Heschel sought to correct the prevailing misconceptions. Although he, like Buber, drew heavily from the teachings of Kabbalah and Hasidism, he considered them to be inexorably linked to the rabbinic tradition. Fully aware of the dangers of stagnation and perversion, Heschel nevertheless accepted the rabbinic framework as a given. The rabbinic system, incorporating both halakhah and aggadah, constitutes a uniquely Jewish bridge to the sacred. What was required was a spiritual interpretation of halakhah that could show its grounding in the inwardness of personal faith.

Unlike Buber, who addressed Jewish communities in Europe and Israel, Heschel, although raised and educated in Europe, directed his writings to American Jewish life. Furthermore, whereas Buber taught in universities, Heschel, an ordained rabbi, spent most of his years teaching in rabbinical seminaries. Whereas Buber spent his life outside of the pale of organized religion, Heschel lived within it, addressing himself to the excesses in American Jewish institutional life, particularly the American synagogue.[24] In contrast to Buber, Heschel stood squarely within traditional Jewish life and institutions. Deeply committed to traditional Judaism, he was pained by the modern Jew's inability to perceive its spiritual depth and beauty. Through his writings, he endeavored to ensure Judaism's survival as a meaningful mode of life.

The Crisis In Contemporary Life

Heschel, like Buber, was critical of the modern rationalist ethos, with its emphasis on individual needs and its making priorities of the tangible, the material, and the verifiable. His philosophy of religion and his philosophy of Judaism proceed from a critique of modernity. Like Buber, he believed that the modern ethos suppressed the existential concerns of the individual. In words reminiscent of Buber, Heschel denounced the destructiveness of this ethos: "What is the spirit of the age? It is, I believe, the instrumentalization of the world, the instrumentalization of man, the instrumentalization of all values" (*The Insecurity of Freedom*, 40).

In the modern age, the category of "thing" prevails. In religious life, God is reduced to a thing that can be manipulated and cajoled: "Thing is a category that lies heavy on our minds, tyrannizing all our thoughts. . . . Reality is thinghood, consisting of substances that occupy space; even God is conceived by most of us as a thing" (*Insecurity*, 80). Relating to himself and others as things, the modern individual is primarily concerned with satisfying his basic needs. In the social sciences and in education, personal needs serve as the starting point. The instrumentalist ethos of modern society is destructive to both the individual and the community: "In reducing the world to an instrument, man himself becomes an instrument. Man is the tool, and the machine is the consumer. The instrumentalization of the world leads to the disintegration of man" (*Insecurity*, 41). Viewing life in terms of the satisfaction of our personal needs, we see others as objects whose sole function is to satisfy those needs. As a result, deceit and suspicion prevail in human relations. Only by altering our way of seeing and thinking can we hope to recover the humanity of the individual. Besides needing to feel that life is meaningful, a person needs to feel that his existence is significant to others. Whereas animals need only satisfy their basic physical needs, the human being has the need to be needed. As long as this need is not satisfied, we are plagued by anxiety: "Personal needs come and go, but one anxiety remains. Am I needed? There is no man that has not been moved by that anxiety" (*Man Is Not Alone*, 193).

The modern person's existential quest for meaning is blocked on two levels. Under the impact of science, philosophy challenges the meaning and validity of all metaphysical and theological concepts, including the idea of ultimate meaning. Moreover, in our society, dominated by a calculating, means–end orientation, anything unrelated to practical, goal-oriented pursuits is held to be irrelevant. The modern individual, estranged from other persons and from the world around him, is beset by a terrible loneliness: "Day after day a question goes up desperately in our minds: Are we alone in the wilderness of the self, alone in this silent universe, of which we are a part, and in which we feel at the same time like strangers?" (*God in Search of Man*, 101).

On the existential level, the destructive effect of the instrumentalist ethos is evident. Viewing ourselves primarily as need-fulfilling, satisfaction-seeking beings, we are estranged from our authentic selves. Sooner or later, however, we must confront the question of the ultimate meaning of life. Our alienation eventually drives us to reflect on the ultimate meaning and significance of our lives. To this question, instrumentalism has no answer (*Insecurity*, 59). At this point, we turn to religious faith. Religious faith offers the beleaguered individual an alternative attitude toward life and a new way of thinking about the world. Modern culture, viewing the fundamental questions of religion as practically and philosophically invalid, considers religion obsolete (*Search*, 3; see also *Insecurity*, 59). For religion to be renewed, we must "rediscover the questions to which religion is an answer" (*Search*, 3). This is the primary task of philosophy of religion.

While recognizing that the plight of religion derives, in part, from events in the nonreligious realm, Heschel preferred to focus responsibility on religion itself: "Religion declined not because it was refuted, but because it became irrelevant, dull, oppressive, insipid. . . . Faith is completely replaced by creed, worship by discipline, love by habit. . . . The crisis of today is ignored because of the splendor of the past" (*Insecurity*, 3–4; see also *Search*, 3ff.).

Heschel, like Buber, was concerned with repairing the individual's broken bond with the divine. To that end, he sought to correct the prevailing misconceptions and distortions about religion. To a great extent, these distortions are the result of the way that religion is studied. Modern thinkers, reducing religion to an expression of psychological and social needs, have mistaken its latent functions for its essence (*Alone*, 275). Applying objective scholarship to the origin and development of religious forms, scholars overlook the essential nature of piety and religious faith.

Like Buber, Heschel was skeptical of language's capacity to mirror reality. In science, where language is used to provide an accurate description of reality, it functions "descriptively." In the realm of religion, however, language functions in a totally different way. Unlike science, religion deals with a dimension of reality that eludes direct description.

In the tradition of mysticism, Heschel viewed religious experience as ineffable. Thus, in a religious context, words can only be used to point to or indicate a reality that is not directly visible. However, contemporary thinkers ignore this indicative function of religious language and read religious texts as literal, descriptive statements. This results in a distorted conception of religion. Heschel agreed with Buber that the detached orientation of the sciences is inappropriate to the field of religion. To understand religion we must employ a phenomenological approach, which views philosophizing as an act of radical self-understanding: "Radical self-understanding must embrace not only the fruits of thinking, namely the concepts and symbols, but the roots of thinking, the depths of insight, the moments of immediacy in the communion of the self with reality" (*Search*, 6). But scientists and social scientists are not the only ones responsible for the prevailing misconception of religion. Theologians, too, contribute to the confusion. Focusing on religious dogmas, symbols, rituals, or institutions, conventional theologians lose sight of the existential core of religion. However, any valid inquiry into religious faith must begin with the existential situation of the believer. Accordingly, Heschel advocated a phenomenological mode of religious inquiry which he called, "depth-theology": "The theme of theology is the content of believing; the theme of depth theology is the act of believing, its purpose being to explore the depth of faith, the substratum out of which belief arises. It deals with acts which precede articulation and defy definition" (*Insecurity*, 117–18).

Protesting that "religion has been reduced to institution, symbol, theology," Heschel argued that the theologian must recover "the situations which both precede and correspond to the theological formulations" (*Insecurity*, 115–16). In contrast to conventional theologians, depth theologians look behind the content and structures, in an effort to recover the experiential foundation or situation out of which religion emerges.

Whereas Buber had focused his phenomenological inquiry on the sphere of interhuman relations, Heschel focused on the consciousness of the individual believer. In particular, he sought to describe the forms, structures, and categories through which the religious person experiences reality. To this end, he inquired into the religious believer's attitudes toward God, the world, and life:

> Our purpose is to direct our attention to those essential, constitutive elements that are common to different types of piety, disregarding accidental colorings and the unimportant accompanying circumstances which may differ in different cases. Our task will be to describe piety as it is, without claiming to explain it or to suggest its derivation from other phenomena. (*Alone*, 276)

Heschel wished to isolate the invariant elements of religious faith and recover the experiential substratum common to all manifestations of faith.[25] Viewing religious faith as a universal phenomenon rooted in human consciousness, he considered individual religions to be particular expressions of universal faith. The basic foundations of religious faith are preconceptual, antecedent to language: "The living encounter with reality takes place on a level that precedes conceptualization, on a level that is responsive, immediate, preconceptual, presymbolic" (*Search*, 115).[26] Consequently, any effort to translate the preconceptual moment into rational concepts distorts the original moment. Instead, we must read religious statements indicatively, as pointing toward rather than describing reality. Like poetry, religious language is indicative or metaphorical. The objectified forms of religious life, such as symbols, rituals, or sacred writings, are attempts by religious believers to point to a situation or experience that transcends language.

In inquiring into the experiential substratum of religious faith, Heschel utilized the categories of awe, wonder, mystery, and radical amazement. These, he believed, provide the most direct access to the consciousness of the believer. Moreover, they refer to universal experience accessible to all people (*Insecurity*, 20–21). Awe and wonder are the starting point for all knowledge, including philosophy and science. Although reason is valuable, insight and intuition yield the deepest meaning of life. Knowledge originates in moments of insight that are prior to conceptualization. Religious faith, however, is a unique mode of thought and experience that embodies a distinct attitude and orientation to reality.

The scientist, endeavoring to explain the world and harness its power, views it in terms of cause and effect. The artist, on the other hand, perceiving the beauty of the world, seeks to express his appreciation. In contrast to both, the religious believer sees the world liminally, with everything pointing to a transcendent reality: "Everything hints at something that transcends it; the detail indicates the whole, the whole its idea, the idea its mysterious root. . . . To be means to stand for, because every being is representative of something that is more than itself; because the seen, the known, stands for the unknown" (*Alone*, 31).[27]

To religious believers, every experience is allusive. This sense of transcendent mystery differentiates religious believers from all who deny the transcendent nature of existence outright, as well as those who seek to explain all events in terms of natural processes. Besides seeing the world differently, religious believers also respond differently. Awed by the mystery of transcendence, they seek to determine what is asked of them: The root of religion is the question, what to do with the feeling for the mystery of living, what to do with the awe, wonder, or fear. Religion, the end of isolation, begins with a consciousness that something is asked of us (*Alone*, 69).

Unfortunately, people have lost sight of the existential quality of religion. Cut off from the experiential, existential, situational roots of religious faith, modern persons find religion dull and irrelevant to their ultimate concerns. Forms and structures, detached from their existential roots, acquire an independent life of their own.

Although recognizing the dangers of reification and alienation, Heschel insisted that traditional teachings, rituals, and institutions are indispensable to religious and, therefore, Jewish life: "The vitality of religion depends upon keeping alive the polarity of doctrine and insight, of dogma and faith, of ritual and response, of institution and individual person" (*Insecurity*, 121). Unlike Buber, who willingly relinquished structure in his quest for authentic faith, Heschel insisted that religion requires form as well as spontaneity.

The Crisis in Modern Judaism: Toward a Spiritual Renewal

While addressing himself to the general philosophical issues relating to religion, Heschel's primary concern was to formulate a philosophy of Judaism. His inquiry into religious faith was a prelude to his inquiry into Judaism. In his view, the distorted conception of religion that prevails in modern society is also evident in Jewish life. Endeavoring to correct these distortions and misconceptions, Heschel wished to replace them with a dynamic conception of Judaism. Deeply troubled by the extent to which externalization and reification prevail in Jewish life and distressed by the modern Jew's alienation from traditional Judaism, he became an eloquent advocate of Jewish spiritual renewal.

For a genuine renewal of Judaism to occur, the individual Jew must be convinced that the teachings of Judaism relate to the very core of his or her existence:

> Every human being is beset by personal problems. He is involved in perplexities and embarrassments, in loneliness and frustrations. There is a question which is uppermost in his mind: what comfort and guidance do I receive from belonging to the community of Israel? What does it mean to me personally? He will not affirm and appreciate that belonging unless he is convinced that Judaism does bestow upon him the sort of guidance which no other source is capable of giving him; that living as a Jew will raise him to a plane which cannot otherwise be reached. (*Insecurity*, 194–95)

Jews seeking to recover their connection with Judaism can find intimations of the divine in nature, in the Bible, and in the traditional patterns of Jewish life. Through worship, learning, and action, Jews can find a way back to God. However, these paths are blocked by misinterpretations and misconceptions. Only by surrendering preconceived notions will Jews be able to experience the awe and wonder that is the starting point of genuine faith (*Alone*, 5).

Awareness of the ineffable dimension of reality does not necessarily lead to faith in the God of Israel. Such faith is not the outcome of thought processes. All efforts to prove the existence of God or to deduce it from other givens are impediments on the path to genuine faith. Opposing inductive theologizing, Heschel posited the idea of an "ontological presupposition":

> The certainty of the realness of God does not come about as a corollary of logical premises, as a leap from the realm of logic to the realm of ontology, from an assumption to a fact. It is, on the contrary, a transition from an immediate apprehension to a thought, from a preconceptual awareness to a definite assurance, from being overwhelmed by the presence of God to an awareness of His existence. . . . It is an ontological presupposition (*Search*, 121)

The Bible and the *mizwot* are unique sources of insight and faith. The writings of the prophets provide norms through which one can test one's private insights. By penetrating beyond the biblical text to the underlying religious situations, we can confirm private moments of faith and experience the holy dimension of existence. In contrast to the prevailing functional, exploitative orientation to reality, the Bible teaches the grandeur of the universe. However, the modern reader, imbued with a functional orientation, sees the Bible either as a body of obsolete doctrines and teachings or as a work of art and a source of aesthetic delight. What is needed is a hermeneutical approach that can unlock the sacredness of the Bible.

Like all religious language, the language of the Bible must not be read as descriptive of external reality. Responding to unique, nonrecurring revelatory events, the biblical writers utilized the language of poetry (*Alone*, 37).[28] In reading the Bible, the cardinal sin is literal-mindedness: "We must not try to read chapters in the Bible dealing with the event at Sinai as if they were texts in systematic theology. Its intention is to celebrate the mystery, to introduce us to it rather than to penetrate or to explain it. As a report about revelation, the Bible itself is a midrash" (*Search*, 185).

Insisting on the distinctiveness of biblical thought, Heschel criticized efforts to reconcile the Bible and philosophy: "The problem is no longer how to reconcile the Bible with Aristotle's view of the universe and of man, but rather: How should we understand ourselves in terms of Biblical thinking" (*Search*, 22). To truly understand the Bible, one must approach it with reverence and awe. If we are not willing to take the prophets' claim to revelation seriously, their words have no claim on us. Like religious faith in general, reading the Bible presupposes a basic act of faith. Only by first accepting the Bible's authority can we sense its authority. "This, indeed, is the paradox of faith, the paradox of existence" (*Search*, 253).

While a correct reading of the Bible requires a prior commitment, the very act of reading the Bible can inspire this commitment. According to Heschel, the reader's attitude interacts dialectically with the text to facilitate the recovery of the sacred. Through a phenomenological inquiry into the reading of sacred texts, this dialectical process is revealed.

In addition to the Bible, prayer and *mizwot* offer to Jews the experience of the holiness of life. However, just as they are estranged from God and the Bible, modern Jews are also estranged from the *mizwot*. This is the inner Jewish ailment which resulted from the "collapse of communication between the realm of tradition and the inner world of the individual" and the "loss of understanding for the relevance of that tradition."

> There is also the inner Jewish ailment. The detachment from tradition, the loss of memory. . . . The daily observance of countless rituals ceased to convey any meaning; they ceased to hold any answer to the countless problems of the individual soul, just as the ancient teachings seemed to be totally unrelated to the modern situation. Ritual had become a routine. . . . Study was superintellectualized. (*Insecurity*, 214)

Whereas Buber led his readers away from rabbinic Judaism to a faith rooted in the unique experiences and response of the individual, Heschel sought to lead his readers back to tradition.[29] He recognized, however, that in order to retain their power, traditional forms and structures must be linked to and expressive of the existential situation of the individual. In his writings on prayer and the Sabbath, Heschel sought to disclose their religious power.[30] In *The Sabbath*, Heschel offered a phenomenological inquiry into the meaning of the Sabbath in the life of the ideal Sabbath observer. Analyzing rituals and prayers, he depicted the Sabbath as a uniquely Jewish way to combat the dehumanizing effects of rational, technological civilization.

In contrast to Buber, Heschel insisted that Judaism demands specific patterns of behavior. Translating ideas into deeds and metaphysical insights into patterns of action, Judaism imbues all dimensions of life with holiness: "By enacting the holy on the stage of concrete living, we perceive our kinship with the divine, the presence of the divine. What cannot be grasped in reflection, we comprehend in deeds" (*Search*, 296). By providing form and stability, by systematizing and rationalizing, by delimiting and measuring, halakhah creates a sacred order of living. However, in the spirit of Hasidism, Heschel criticized those who would reduce Judaism to halakhah. To elevate action above meaning and intention is to distort the authentic character of Judaism. Both traditionalists who emphasize halakhah to the exclusion of all else and liberals who reject halakhah perpetuate this distortion.

Like all reality, Judaism embodies "tension, contrast and contradiction" (*Search*, 341). As a "polar phenomenon," Judaism is a dialectical pattern containing opposite properties like halakhah and aggadah. Whereas halakhah deals with behavior, aggadah deals with experience and the intellect. If either is eliminated, one no longer has authentic Judaism. "Halacha deals with the law; agada with the meaning of the law. . . . Halacha gives us norms for action; agada, the vision of the ends of living. Halacha prescribes, agada suggests; halacha decrees, agada inspires; halacha is definite; agada is illusive. . . . Halacha thinks in the category of quantity; agada is the category of quality" (*Search*, 336–37).

To properly understand halakhah, we must juxtapose it to aggadah, which "deals with man's ineffable relations to God, to other men, and to the world" (*Search*, 336). Criticizing "pan-halakhism," Heschel insisted that "the law is the means, not the end; the way, not the goal. . . . Halacha is neither the ultimate nor the all-embracing term for Jewish learning and living" (*Search*, 323). The ultimate end of Jewish living is to sanctify persons and train them in the art of love of God. However, this can occur only if individuals are mindful of the meaning and significance of their actions. Thus, like Hasidism, Heschel emphasized *kawwanah*, alternatively translated as "meaning," "purpose," "motive," and "intention." "Halacha must not be observed for its own sake, but for the sake of God. The law must not be idolized. It is a part, not all, of the Torah. We live and die for the sake of God rather than for the sake of the law" (*Search*, 326).[31]

Although halakhah is essential, Judaism's center of gravity lies in personal experience and inner consciousness. It is important to ask what to do with awe, wonder, and mystery, but it is no less essential to ask what the experience of awe, wonder, and mystery means in our lives. The function of mizwot is not to satisfy our individual needs, but to subordinate them to transcendent meaning:

> All Mitzvot are means of evoking in us the awareness of living in the neighborhood of God, of living in the holy dimension. They call to mind the inconspicuous mystery of things and acts, and are reminders of our being the stewards rather than the landlords of the universe; reminders of the fact that man does not live in a spiritual wilderness, that every act of man is an encounter of the human and the holy. (*Search*, 356)

Seeking to understand the significance of mizwot, the modern Jew should ask: "Are they spiritually meaningful?" (*Search*, 351). Heschel eschewed all efforts to explain mizwot rationally. Like art and music, mizwot comprise a distinct framework of meaning and can only be understood through the categories that are peculiar to that framework: "The order of Jewish living is a spiritual one; it has a spiritual logic of its own which cannot be apprehended unless its basic terms are lived and appreciated" (*Search*, 349).

Above and beyond their practical and spiritual effects, mizwot, to Heschel, are divine commandments. Unlike humanly constructed symbols, they are actions that the human being and God have in common. While medieval philosophers sought to remove from God any vestige of need, Heschel, in the tradition of Kabbalah, believed that God was in need of the human being. We satisfy this divine need when we carry out mizwot: "We are not only in need of God, but also in need of serving his ends, and these ends are in need of us" (*Search*, 291).

Here, the neo-orthodox dimension of Heschel's thought is evident. While emphasizing the existential situation of the individual as the locus of religious faith, Heschel, in the final analysis, affirmed the claim of rabbinic tradition to divine authority. The traditional forms and structures of rabbinic Judaism have a prior claim. In contrast to Buber, for whom the individual's existential response was primary, Heschel subordinated the individual to tradition:

> The individual's insight alone is unable to cope with all the problems of living. It is the guidance of tradition on which we must rely, and whose norms we must learn to interpret and to apply. We must learn not only the ends, but also the means by which to realize the ends; not only the general laws but also the particular forms. (*Search*, 298)

Yet, given the alienated condition of the modern Jew, a policy of "all or nothing" was inappropriate. Rather than make halakhah the starting point for the contemporary Jew's return to Judaism, one must build a bridge between the modern Jew and the divine. "In the spiritual crisis of the modern Jew, the problem of faith takes precedence over the problem of law" (*Search*, 339).

Today, matters of the spirit demand priority. Accordingly, Heschel advocated a "ladder of observances," by means of which the individual can approach the divine gradually. The task of the religious teacher is not to induct persons into a system of observances and teachings, but to awaken their sense of awe and wonder.

* * * * *

Buber and Heschel, while emphasizing the existential nature of religious faith, formulated two distinct approaches to Judaism. Their writings offer the modern Jew alternative conceptions of Jewish life and thought. Buber forsook the rabbinic system and revised Judaism in a radically new way, and Heschel preserved rabbinic Judaism while imbuing it with emotional force and relating it to the existential situation of the individual.

Although both men grounded their philosophy of Judaism in an existential foundation, they offer the contemporary Jew a definitive choice. For those who choose Buber's way, the value of rabbinic tradition is greatly diminished. Jewish life is based on an existential bond with the Jewish people and an abiding concern for interhuman relations. For those who are drawn to Heschel, observance of the traditional *mizwot* remains central. While rabbinic Judaism must be imbued with the spiritual focus derived from Kabbalah and Hasidism, Judaism is unthinkable outside of the rabbinic framework.

Heschel and Buber differed decidedly in the views of religious faith and in their attitudes toward tradition. Buber, focusing on the sphere of the "between," as manifested in interhuman relations, insisted that persons actualize themselves through relations to others. While not denying the possibility of direct divine–human encounters, Buber focused his attention on the manifestation of the divine in the encounters between persons. Accordingly, relation is the key concept in his philosophy of religion. One encounters the divine through everyday encounters with other beings, particularly other persons. From his perspective, religion is no longer perceived as a distinct realm of human culture. One is religious by carrying out all acts and entering into all relations in a hallowing manner. The precise nature of these acts and relations are spelled out in *I and Thou*.

For Buber, institutionalized forms stifle spontaneity and impede the nurturing, confirming relations essential to human growth. In the context of religious faith, institutions and systems of beliefs pose a great danger to the individual's relation to the divine. Consequently, Buber showed a marked antipathy to rabbinic Judaism, especially halakhah. Rebelling against halakhah, Buber advocated a pluralistic, individualistic conception of religion which focused on relations with others. In Heschel's view, the force and power of Judaism derive from its capacity to shape both the thought and the actions of the individual. As a polar system encompassing both halakhah and aggadah, rabbinic Judaism provides the modern Jew a framework of thinking and living which is a distinct alternative to the dehumanizing frameworks of modern society.

To Heschel, God needs the human being. The Jew satisfies this need by observing *mizwot*. While Buber considered all actions to have the potential to free the divine sparks and unify God, Heschel, faithful in this expanded sense to the Lurianic system, linked the liberation of the sparks to the performance of the traditional *mizwot*.

Significantly, both Buber and Heschel viewed human society as the ultimate testing ground of religious faith. For each of them, the truth of one's faith is determined by one's readiness to apply it to the fundamental moral issues of our time. Throughout his life, Buber stood out as a minority voice insisting that the faith of Israel is tested in the everyday social and political situations of the State of Israel. Working untiringly for a just solution to the conflict between Jews and Arabs in Israel, Buber emulated the prophets in applying faith to life. In addition, dedicated to ensuring the future of humanity in general, Buber spoke out on issues of international peace and justice, acquiring a reputation as one of the outstanding moral voices of the age.[32]

For most of his life, Heschel limited his activities to scholarship and teaching. However, beginning around 1960, Heschel began to speak out on fundamental social issues. Addressing himself to the problems of the aged, juvenile delinquency, health care, and race, he sought, like Buber, to apply the teachings of the prophets to current realities.[33] His burning moral concern, articulated in his study of the prophets, found its ultimate expression in his activities in support of Martin Luther King and in his protest over the Vietnam War. In spite of the negative reactions from his scholarly colleagues, Heschel became one of the few representatives of the traditional Jewish community to march in behalf of civil rights and peace.[34]

Although they disagreed sharply over the nature of Judaism, Buber and Heschel, deeply influenced by the prophets of Israel, agreed that religious Jews are commanded to act out their faith in actual political and social situations. Like the prophets, each of these scholars, in spite of the disapprobation of colleagues and the community at large, applied his beliefs to social and political issues. In spite of their differences, both Buber and Heschel agreed that, to be viable and genuine, Judaism must motivate people to speak out and act in the face of injustice.

Notes

1. Charles Taylor, *Hegel and Modern Society* (New York: Cambridge University Press, 1979) 90.
2. F. Nietzsche, *The Gay Science*, p. 181, #125.
3. S. Kierkegaard, *Concluding Unscientific Postscript*, 182.
4. Kierkegaard, *Journals and Papers*, P, I, 100; quoted in *The Concept of Anxiety* Supplement, 171.
5. Kierkegaard, *Training in Christianity*, in *A Kierkegaard Anthology*, ed. Robert Bretall (Princeton, NJ: Princeton University Press, 1946) 397.
6. Kierkegaard, in *Kierkegaard Anthology*, ed. Bretall, 214.
7. Kierkegaard, *Concluding Unscientific Postscript*, 179.
8. The most formidable examples of this critique are two essays by Gershom Scholem: "Martin Buber's Interpretation of Hasidism," in *The Messianic Idea in Judaism* (New York: Schocken, 1971) 227–50; and "Martin Buber's Conception of Judaism," in *Jews and Judaism in Crisis* (New York: Schocken, 1976) 126–71. For a more sympathetic critique, see Akiba Ernst Simon, "Mordecai Martin Buber and the Faith of Israel" (Hebrew), in *Divre Iyyun Mukdashim le-Mordekhai Martin Buber bi-Melot Lo Shemonim Shanah* (Jerusalem, 1958) 19–56.
9. The distinction between edifying and normal philosophizing is drawn from Richard Rorty, *Philosophy and the Mirror of Nature* (Princeton, NJ: Princeton University Press, 1979).
10. On the concept of revisionism, see Harold Bloom, *Agon: Towards a Theory of Revisionism* (New York: Oxford University Press, 1982); Rorty, *Philosophy and the Mirror of Nature*, especially Introduction and chap. 8; see also idem, *Consequences of Pragmatism* (Minneapolis: University of Minnesota Press, 1982) chaps. 6 and 8.
11. The views of the Bar Kokhba group before whom Buber delivered his early lectures are reflected in *Vom Judentum: Ein Sammelbuch herausgegeben vom Verein Jüdischer Hochschüler Bar Kochba in Prag* (Leipzig: Kurt Wolff, 1913). See also Maurice Friedman, *Martin Buber's Life and Work: The Early Years, 1878-1923* (New York: E. P. Dutton, 1981) chap. 7; Hans Kohn, *Living in a World Revolution* (New York: Pocket Books, 1964); Nahum Glatzer, "Editor's Postscript" in Buber, *On Judaism*; and Robert Weltsch, "Introduction," in Buber, *Te'dah we-Ye'ud*, vol. 1 (Jerusalem: HaSifriah HaZionit, 1959) 7–14.
12. Buber's relationship to German Volkist ideology is discussed in George Mosse, *Germans and Jews* (New York: Grosset & Dunlap, 1970) chap. 4. For a different interpretation, see Robert Lunn, *Prophet of Community* (Berkeley: University of California Press, 1973). Lunn's subject is Buber's close friend Gustav Landauer, but the views of the two men were very close.
13. See Georg Simmel, "The Conflict in Modern Culture," in *The Conflict in Modern Culture and Other Essays*, trans. K. Peter Etzkorn (New York: Teachers College Press, 1968). Alienation and social theory are discussed by Arthur Mitzman in *The Iron Cage: An Historical Interpretation of Max Weber* (New York: Grosset & Dunlap, 1969), and *Sociology and Estrangement* (New York: Knopf, 1973). See also Robert Nisbet, *The Sociological Tradition* (New York: Basic Books, 1966) chap. 7.
14. The term *Lebensphilosophie* refers to a loosely constructed school of thought that flourished at the turn of the century, which adhered to the teachings, among others, of Nietzsche and Simmel. See Nicholas Gier, *Wittgenstein and Phenomenology* (Albany: State University of New York Press, 1981) chap. 3.

15. This distinction between official and underground Judaism parallels Kierkegaard's distinction between Christendom and Christianity (see *Training in Christianity* in *A Kierkegaard Anthology*, ed. Bretall, 1946) 397. Buber's conflict model of Jewish history is similar to Nietzsche's Apollonian/Dionysian distinction, developed for the first time in *The Birth of Tragedy*. On Nietzsche's views, see Hayden White, *Metahistory: The Historical Imagination in Nineteenth Century Europe* (Baltimore, MD: Johns Hopkins University Press, 1973) chap. 9.

16. For Nietzsche's views on myth as fundamental to cultural renewal, see *Birth of Tragedy*, trans. Francis Golffing (Garden City, NY: Doubleday, 1956) esp. 136–40. Nineteenth-century Jewish attitudes to myth are discussed by Moshe Schwartz, *Language, Myth, Art: Studies in Modern Jewish Thought* (Hebrew) (Jerusalem: Schocken, 1966) 15–53, 143–252.

17. For a summary of the Lurianic Kabbalah, see Gershom Scholem, *On the Kabbalah and Its Symbolism* (New York: New American Library, 1978) 128–44.

18. For the Hasidic interpretation of the Lurianic myth, see *Encyclopaedia Judaica* 7:1403–13; Scholem, *Messianic Idea*, 176–227; and Louis Jacob, *Hasidic Prayer* (New York: Schocken, 1972) esp. chap. 9.

19. The charge of "religious anarchism" is leveled by Scholem in "Martin Buber's Interpretation of Hasidism," in *Messianic Idea*, 227–50.

20. Alienation has been defined as referring to "different kinds of dissociation, break or rupture between human beings and their objects, whether the latter be other persons, or the natural world, or their own creations in art, science and society" (see F. H. Heinemann, *Existentialism and the Human Predicament* [New York: Harper & Brothers, 1958] 9).

21. See *I and Thou*, 171; and *The Philosophy of Martin Buber*, ed. P. Schilpp and M. Friedman (La Salle, IL: Open Court, 1967) 689–91.

22. Buber's specific critique of Kierkegaard is found in *Between Man and Man* (New York: Macmillan, 1964) 40–82, 161–63, 171–205; on Nietzsche, see pp. 148–56.

23. See "Herut," in *On Judaism*, 154–64; and *Israel and the World*, 137–63, 240–52.

24. See the essays in *The Insecurity of Freedom*.

25. The phenomenologist's concern for invariant forms and structures of consciousness is discussed in *Phenomenology: The Philosophy of Edmund Husserl and Its Interpretations*, ed. Joseph Kockelmans (Garden City, NY: Doubleday, 1967) esp. 24–36.

26. The existentialists' orientation to language is discussed by John MacQuarrie, *Existentialism* (New York: Penguin, 1972) chap. 7. For critical views of this orientation, see Steven Katz, "Language, Epistemology and Mysticism," in *Mysticism and Philosophical Analysis*, ed. Steven T. Katz (New York: Oxford, 1978) 22–74; and Ian Barbour, *Myths, Models, and Paradigms* (New York: Harper & Row, 1974) esp. chap. 4.

27. See Philip Wheelwright, *The Burning Fountain: A Study in the Language of Symbolism* (Bloomington: IN: Indiana University Press, 1968). This work is cited by Heschel in *Search*, 124 n. 1.

28. On the role of poetry in Heschel's philosophy, see Edward Kaplan, "Language and Philosophy in Abraham Heschel's Philosophy of Religion," *Journal of the American Academy of Religion* 41 (1973) 94–113; idem, "Three Dimensions of Human Fullness: Poetry, Love and Prayer," *Judaism* 22 (1973) 309–15. For a similar view of the creative power of poetic language, see Buber, *Israel and the World*, 89–102.

29. Heschel devoted two volumes to the thought of the talmudic sages, endeavoring to demonstrate the deep spiritual currents that infuse rabbinic literature. See *Theology of Ancient Judaism* (Hebrew). Just as Buber was criticized by scholars for distorting Hasidism, Heschel's interpretation of rabbinic thought was sharply criticized by E. E. Urbach; see *The Sages: Their Concepts and Beliefs* (Hebrew) (Jerusalem: Magnes Press, 1969) 14, 26.

30. For Heschel's phenomenological analysis of prayer, see *Man's Quest for God*.

31. The tension between the existential experience of the individual and the demands of tradition is a basic theme in the writings of Franz Rosenzweig; see *On Jewish Learning*, ed. N. N.

Glatzer (New York: Schocken, 1955) 72–92, 116–18. For the debate between Buber and Rosenzweig, see pp. 109–18.

32. Buber was one of the leaders of *Ihud,* an organization devoted to fostering Arab–Jewish rapprochement. For his views on this subject, see *A Land of Two Peoples: Martin Buber on Jews and Arabs,* edited with commentary by Paul R. Mendes-Flohr (New York: Oxford University Press, 1983). Essays on the world situation can be found in *Pointing the Way* (New York: Harper & Row, 1957) 109–239. Dag Hammarskjöld, the late Secretary General of the United Nations, discussed the implications of Buber's writings for world peace in a speech delivered at Cambridge University on 5 June 1958. At the time of his death, Hammarskjöld was engaged in translating *I and Thou* into Swedish.

33. See *Insecurity of Freedom,* 3–111.

34. See Edward Kaplan, "The Spiritual Radicalism of Abraham Joshua Heschel," *Conservative Judaism* 28 (1973) 40–49. Heschel discussed the radical implications of faith in *A Passion for Truth,* section 4, "Radicalism."

Bibliography

For Buber's conception of Judaism see *On Judaism* and *Israel and the World.* On the national idea in Judaism, see *On Zion. Paths in Utopia* contains Buber's views on utopian socialism and the kibbutz. On Hasidism, see *Hasidism and Modern Man, The Origin and Meaning of Hasidism,* and *Tales of the Hasidim.* A convenient selection of his views on the Bible is found in *On the Bible. I and Thou* is best read together with the first two essays in *The Knowledge of Man* and "The Way of Man According to the Teachings of Hasidism," in *Hasidism and Modern Man* (pp. 126–76). For a recent biography, see Friedman.

On Heschel, see *Man Is Not Alone* and *God in Search of Man.* A convenient anthology is *Between God and Man,* edited by Fritz A. Rothschild. For Heschel's theological premises, see "Depth Theology," in *The Insecurity of Freedom.* Heschel's last work, *A Passion for Truth,* contains fascinating glimpses of his feelings toward the end of his life and his reactions to the tragedy of the Holocaust; see also "Reflections on Death."

Buber, M. *A Believing Humanism.*
———. *Hasidism and Modern Man.* New York: Horizon Press, 1958.
———. *I and Thou.* Translated by Walter Kaufmann. New York: Scribner, 1970.
———. "Interpreting Hasidism."
———. *Israel and the World.* New York: Schocken, 1963.
———. *The Knowledge of Man.* Edited by M. Friedman. New York: Harper & Row, 1965.
———. *Legends of the Baal Shem Tov.*
———. *On Judaism.* Edited by N. N. Glatzer. New York: Schocken, 1967.
———. *On the Bible.* New York: Schocken, 1982.
———. *On Zion: The History of an Idea.* Translated by Stanley Goldman with a new foreword by N. N. Glatzer. New York: Schocken, 1973.
———. *The Origin and Meaning of Hasidism.* New York: Horizon Press, 1960.
———. *Paths in Utopia.* Boston: Beacon Press, 1958.
———. *Tales of the Hasidim.* 2 vols. New York: Schocken, 1957.
Friedman, Maurice. *Martin Buber's Life and Work.* 3 vols. New York: E. P. Dutton, 1981–84.
Heschel, A. J. *God in Search of Man.* Philadelphia: Jewish Publication Society, 1959.
———. *The Insecurity of Freedom.* New York: Farrar, Straus & Giroux, 1966.
———. *Man Is Not Alone.* New York: Farrar, Straus & Young, 1951.
———. *Man's Quest for God.*
———. *A Passion for Truth.* New York: Farrar, Straus & Giroux, 1973.
———. "Reflections on Death." Reprint. *Conservative Judaism* 38 (1973) 3–9.
Rothschild, Fritz A., ed. *Between God and Man: An Interpretation of Judaism.* New York: Harper & Brothers, 1959.

Contributors

ARTHUR GREEN, editor of this volume, is President of the Reconstructionist Rabbinical College and Adjunct Associate Professor of Religious Studies at the University of Pennsylvania. He is the author of *Tormented Master: A Life of Rabbi Nahman of Bratslav* (1981).

JONATHAN CHIPMAN, translator of several essays in these volumes, is Rabbi, Assistant Editor of *Immanuel: A Journal of Religious Thought and Research in Israel*, and editor of the English edition of the Kehati Mishnah.

ARNOLD M. EISEN is Associate Professor in the Department of Religion at Stanford University. He is the author of *The Chosen People in America: A Study in Jewish Religious Ideology* (1983).

RACHEL ELIOR is Senior Lecturer of Kabbalah and Hasidut at the Hebrew University. She is the author of *The Theory of Divinity of Hasidut Habad* (1982).

IMMANUEL ETKES is Senior Lecturer in the Departments of Jewish History and Education at the Hebrew University. He is the author of *Rabbi Israel Salanter and the Beginning of the Mussar Movement* (1982).

LAWRENCE FINE is Associate Professor of Religious Studies at Indiana University. He is the author of *Safed Spirituality* (1984).

RIVKA HORWITZ is Associate Professor in Jewish Thought at Ben-Gurion University and the author of *Buber's Way to 'I and Thou'* (1978).

LOUIS JACOBS is Rabbi of the New London Synagogue, England. He is the author of *A Jewish Theology* (1973) and works on Jewish Theology, the Talmud, and Jewish Mysticism.

JACOB KATZ is Professor Emeritus of Sociology and Jewish History at the Hebrew University. He is the author of numerous works including *Halakhah and Kabbalah Studies in the History of Jewish Religion, its Various Faces and Social Relevance* (1984).

EHUD LUZ is Senior Lecturer in the Department of Jewish Thought at Haifa University and in the Oranim School of Education. He is the author of *Parallels Meet: Religion and Nationalism in the Early Zionist Movement* (1985).

PAUL MENDES-FLOHR is Senior Lecturer in Modern Jewish Thought at the Hebrew University. He is the author of *Contemporary Jewish Religious Thought* (1986).

LAURENCE J. SILBERSTEIN is Philip and Muriel Berman Professor of Judaica at Lehigh University. He has recently completed the book *Alienation and the Quest for Meaning: The Social and Religious Philosophy of Martin Buber.*

CHAVA WEISSLER is Assistant Professor and Mellon Preceptor in Modern Judaism in the Department of Religion at Princeton University. She is the author of the forthcoming *Making Judaism Meaningful: Ambivalence and Tradition in a Havurah Community* and is currently writing a book on Jewish women's spirituality.

R. J. Z. WERBLOWSKY is Martin Buber Professor of Comparative Religion at the Hebrew University. He is the author of *Joseph Karo, Lawyer and Mystic* (1962).

Photographic Credits

The editor and publisher wish to thank the custodians of the works of art for supplying photographs and granting permission to use them. In particular, the art editor wishes to acknowledge the research assistance of Linda Altshuler, Director, B'nai B'rith Klutznick Museum; and Susan Morgenstein, Curator, United States Holocaust Memorial Museum.

1. Israel Museum, Jerusalem.

2. Gift of Evelyn and Bob Roberts, JM 85-79. Jewish Museum/Art Resource, New York.

3. The Ivan F. and Seema Boesky Family Library, The Jewish Theological Seminary of America, New York.

4. The H. Ephraim and Mordecai Benquiat Family Collection, S256. Jewish Museum/Art Resource, New York.

5. Jewish Museum/Art Resource, New York.

6. Jewish Museum/Art Resource, New York.

7. Israel Museum, Jerusalem.

8. Collection of Edward Victor. Photograph by David Crosseley.

9. Photograph by George Segal. Courtesy of Jane Dillenberger.

10. Israel Museum, Jerusalem.

Indexes

Subjects

'*Adam Qadmon:* and *sefirot,* 102–3; and tetra-grammaton, 83–85; and *yihudim,* 66–67, 69
Abgeschiedenheit (Azikri), 19
acosmism: and divinity, 163, 166; doctrine of, 160–61; and finite versus infinite, 175; and self-abnegation, 181–82, 190
activism, 158
aggadah: definition of, 35; and halakhah, 34–36, 426; and Kabbalah, 36–37; and philosophy, 36–37
alienation: and Buber, 405–6, 415; and faith, 402; and Heschel, 405–6, 418, 422; and Jewish spirituality, 402, 405–6; and Judaism, 405–6; and Kierkegaard, 403–4; and Nietzsche, 402–3
anger, 71
anti-Semitism, 9–10, 30
appetite, 212, 239–40
asceticism, 12, 115–16
Ashkenazic Jews, 10, 54
Ashkenazic women: and childbirth, 258–62; domains of religious life of, 247–52; and *hadlaqah,* 253–58; and *hallah,* separating, 254–58; and humble expressions, 267–68; and lighting candles, 254–58; *mizwot* of, 252–54; and *niddah,* 253, 258–62; occasions of religious life of, 247–52; spiritual history of, 245–47; and *tkhines* for *niddah,* 258–62; varieties of religious expression of, 252–54; and Yom Kippur candles, making, 262–67
'*Avodat ha-Shem,* 178–81

"Baraitha of Rabbi Pinhas ben Yair," 17
Bible. *See* Scripture
biblical humanism, 334–35
bittul. See self-abnegation
"breaking the vessels," 66–68

character training: basis of, 229; and mind, 233–36; and Mussar movement, 227, 229–36; Salanter's views of, 229–30, 236; and subjugation, 230–33; and transmutation, 230–33
childbirth, 258–62
Chmielnicki massacres, 9
coincidentia oppositorum, 164–67
communion. *See devequt;* soul
conscious: and gap between unconscious, 238–40; and intellectual awareness, 240–41; and Mussar movement, 236–42; Salanter's views of, 236–38; and spirit, 287–88
contemplation: and *devequt,* 18–20, 22; of divine names, 83–85; of emanation, 183–84; and faith, 196–97; of greatness of God, 183–84; in Habad thought, 159, 182–86; and kabbalists, 70; and Luria, 65; and mystical illumination, 26–29; and self-abnegation, 182–86; Vital's theory of, 22–27. *See also* Habad thought; *yihudim*
Cossack massacres of 1648, 10, 30
creation: and divinity, 163, 166–67; in Habad thought, 178; and worship of God, 178–79

devequt: and contemplation, 18–20, 22; and Hasidism, 123; and inspiration, 24–25; and kabbalists, 17, 22; and *kawwanot,* 123; and mystical illumination, 22–24; and mystical tradition, 23; and prophetic tradition, 22–23; and solitude, 19, 21–22
dialectical reciprocity, 164
Diaspora mission, 298–301
divine love, 329–32
divine names, 251
divine perfection, 166–68
divinity: and acosmism, 163, 166; and creation, 163, 166–67; duality of perception of, 173–75; and existence, 161–62, 165; in

Habad thought, 160–73; immanence of, 163, 172; and leadership, 129–30; in *mizwot*, 200; names of, 83–85; perfection of, 166–68; relationship of, with world, 163–68; and substance versus manifestation, 168–73; in Torah, 200–202; unification of male and female within, 83–85. *See also* God

divrey Torah, 35

earthliness: dialectics of, in Zionism, 371–73; victory of, in Zionism, 395–98
Eastern Haskalah, 375–77
ecstasy, 197–98
emanation, 183–84
emotional arousal, 213–15, 240–42
Epistle on Repentance (Gerona), 12
equalization, 165
esoteric teachings, 53, 55, 57
ethical monotheism, 322–26
ethical perfection, 214–15
ethics, 211–215. *See also* Mussar movement
European Enlightenment, 11
European Jews, 11–12, 206
existence, 161–62, 165, 178
exoteric teachings, 53, 55, 57
Expulsion, 7, 9–10
Eyn Sof, 65–66, 101–2, 108

faith: and alienation, 402; and Berger, 310; and Bergman, 335–36; and Buber, 309–13; and contemplation, 196–97; and ecstasy of heart and mind, 197–98; and Geiger, 291–93, 312; and Hasidism, 313; and Hegel, 312; and Heschel, 418, 422; and Kant, 319; and Kaplan, 311; and Kochmal, 293–96, 312; and *mizwot*, 424–25; modern, 283–85; paradox of, 192–93, 195; and Schleiermacher, 310; and Scholem, 313–14; and Scripture, 424–25; and self-abnegation, 191–92, 195–96; Spinoza's critique of, 289–91; transrational, 193–94; and Zionism, 313
fasting, 77–78
finite: and acosmism, 175; perception of, 195–96; and self–abnegation, 186–88
First Crusade, 10
"Flesh and Spirit" (Aḥad Ha'am), 387–88
"Four Travelers," 23

galut, 202, 373, 390, 395
gnosis, 16

gnostic mythology, 29–30
God: communion with, 17–18; fear of, 212–13; love of, 17–18; and world, relationship between, 163–68; worship of, 178–81. *See also devequt;* divinity
gravesite visiting, 82–83
Great Awakening, 11
Guide for the Perplexed of the Day (Krochmal), 293–96

Ha-Adamah (Brenner), 382–83
HaBaD movement. *See* Habad thought
Habad thought: and acosmism, 160–61, 163, 166; and activism, 158; and coincidentia oppositorum, 164–67; concerns of, 157–58, 160; contemplation in, 159, 182–86; and divinity, 160–73; and duality of perception, 173–75; evil in, 177; and existence, 161–63, 165; and Hasidism, 122; innovation of, 158–59; literature of, 157–58, 160; and manifestation of divinity, 168–73; and *mizwot*, 198–203; and mysticism of divinity, 168–73; opposition to, 159; origins of, 157; positive and negative spiritual forces in, 176–77; and relationship of divinity, with world, 163–68; and self-abnegation, 181–91; and soul, 175–78; and spiritualism, 158; and substance of divinity, 168–73; teaching of, 159–60; term of, 157; and theory of divinity, 160–63; and Torah, 198–203; and transrational perception, 191–98; and worship of God, 178–81
hadlaqah, 253–58
hadlaqat ha-ner, 253–58
hagshamah: Buber's concept of, 391; connotation of, 371–72; Gordon's concept of, 388–92; and halakhah, 386; and spiritual movements in Europe, 378
halakhah: and aggadah, 34–36, 426; in Bohemia-Moravia, 56; and Buber, 409, 429; and competition with Kabbalah, 46; definition of, 35; expansion of, 46–47; and *hagshamah,* 386; in Hasidism, 57; and ibn Gabbai, 44; and Judaism, 385, 427–28; and Kabbalah, 42–46, 53–56; and kabbalists, 39–40; and Meir, 42–45; and motivation, psychological, 211–12; in Poland-Lithuania, 56; primacy of, 35–36; and revelation, 366; and Rosenzweig, 362–63; in Safed, 45–49; and *yihudim,* 73; and *zaddiq,* 57; and *Zohar,* 37–38

hallah, 253–58
halutz, 382–84
Ha'ol. See Jerusalem circle
hashba'ot, 27–28
hashwa'ah, 164–67
hasid. See zaddiq
Hasidism: and asceticism, 115–16; and Buber, 392, 410–11, 413–14; and devequt, 123; egalitarianism in, 116–17; and European Enlightenment, 11; and faith, 313; first published work of, 128; and Habad thought, 122; halakhah in, 57; and holy sparks, 115–25; and Kabbalah, 147; and kabbalists, 32; and kawwanot, 123; and leadership, 127–30, 138; and Mitnagdim, 56–59; movement of, 128–129; and mysticism, 8, 15, 115–25; opposition to, 115, 159; phenomenon of, 157; rise of, 31–32; and Sabbatian heresy, 115–16; spirituality of, 12; and Talmud, 56–57; teaching of, 115; tiqqun in, 411–12; and yeshivot, 57. See also zaddiq
havurot, 221–22
Hebrew Haskalah, 375
Hibbat Ziyyon, 298–99
hilluqim, 54–55
Hitbonenut. See contemplation
hitpa'alut. See emotional arousal
holiness, 383–84
holy sparks: development of, 124–25; and eve of new moon festival, 110; and Hasidism, 115–25; and kabbalists, 124–25; and kawwanot, 109, 111–13; and Lurianic Kabbalah, 106–9, 115–16; origin of, 124; and prayer, 110–13; rescue of, from qelipot, 106, 112; restoring fallen, 109–10; and Sabbatian heresy, 125; and Shekhinah, 109–10; and tiqqun, 107–8; and zaddiq, 117, 125
Holy Spirit, 72–73
humanity, 415–16

Iberian Jews, 7, 9, 74
idealism, 383, 388–89
idle conversation, 72–73
immanence, 163, 172
individualism, 387
inspiration, prophetic: attainment of, 70, 86–87; and devequt, 24–25. See also yihudim
intellectual awareness, 240–41
Israel: spirit of, 305–8; spirituality of, 373–75
Italian Jews, 7–8

Jerusalem (Mendelssohn), 286
Jerusalem circle: and ethical monotheism, 323–26; and Jewish thought, 320–22; name of, 322–23; organizing of, 320; and Torah, 320–22; and Zionism, 320–22
Jewish Middle Ages, 7, 9
Jewish spirituality: and alienation, 402, 405–6; and Buber, 405–18, 428–30; crisis of, modern, 419–23; and Heschel, 405–6, 418–30; as meta-history, 332–35; and relation, 411–18; renewal of, 402–11, 423–28; revisioning, 406–11; as sacred time, 332–35; women's history in, 245–46. See also spirituality
Jewish thought: and ethical monotheism, 322–26; and Jerusalem circle, 320–22; and Kant, 318–20; and mizwot, 329–32; and ritual observances, 335–36; and Rosenzweig, 326–29, 332–35; and Western culture, 317–18
Jews. See specific groups of
joyfulness, 71
Judaism: and alienation, 405–6; approaches to, 428–30; and Buber, 305–8, 355–56, 405–18, 428–30; and commandments, 35; concreteness of, 385–86; crisis in, modern, 423–28; and Diaspora mission, 298–301; doctrines of, 8–9; and ethical monotheism, 323; in future, 314–15, 388; and Geiger, 291–93; and Gordon, 301–3, 388–90; and halakhah, 385, 427–28; and Heschel, 405–6, 418–30, 423–24, 426, 428–30; and individualism, 387; and Israel, spirit of, 305–8; Kant's critique of, 318–20; and Kook, 303–5; and Krochmal, 293–96; and messianism, 30–31; and mizwot, 427; modernization of, 285–89; and oral tradition, 34–36; and organic nationhood, 301–3; Orthodox, 398; and philosophy, 36–37; and preaching, 296–97; and quotations, 8; and redemption, 303–5; and relation, philosophy of, 411–18; science of, 291–92; and secularization, 285, 305–8; socialness of, 387; and Soloviev, 385; Spinoza's critique of, 289–91; and spirit, 283–85; spirit of, 291–93, 308–15; and spiritual center, rebuilding, 298–301; and spirituality, 296–98; spread of, 10; and Western culture, 414–15; and written tradition, 34–35. See also Hasidism
Judaism and Its History, 292

Kabbalah: and aggadah, 36–37; and Ashke-
    nazic Jews, 54; and competition with
    halakhah, 46; and Cordovero, 47, 49; and
    halakhah, 42–46, 53–56; and Hasidism, 147;
    and Hayyat, 41–42; and Hayyim, 58; and
    Horowitz, 54–56; and ibn Gabbai, 45; and
    Luria, 49–51; and Meir, 44–45; and mes-
    sianism, 31; and Mussar movement, 209–10;
    primacy of, 39–42; and Ramak, 47–49; in
    Safed, 45–49, 53–56; and Safed Revival,
    10–11; and Salanter, 209–10; spread of,
    53–56; study of, 47–48; and Talmud, 40–41;
    and Torah, 56; and Vital, 51–53; and zaddiq,
    133; and Zohar, 37–39. See also kabbalists;
    Lurianic Kabbalah
kabbalists: and contemplation, 70; and devequt,
    17, 22; and halakhah, 39–40; and Hasidism,
    32; and holy sparks, 124–25; in Karo's house,
    13–14; and light, 99–101; and messianism,
    31; and moral qualities, 72; mystical expe-
    rience of, 16–17; mystical knowledge of,
    93–94; and mysticism, 16–17; and prayer,
    110; pre-Lurianic, 13; and prophets, 146–47;
    Safed, 74; and sefirot, 83, 101–4, 107; and
    sexuality, 77; sexual symbolism of, 107;
    spirituality of, 15; and spiritual qualities, 72;
    types of, 47; writings of, 12. See also
    Kabbalah
kairos, 16
kawwanah, 250, 426
kawwanot: and devequt, 123; and Hasidism,
    123; and holy sparks, 109, 111–13; and
    Lurianic Kabbalah, 112–13, 123–24; and
    yihudim, 79
kehillot, 285
kibbush ha-yezer, 230–33
king, 142–46
kloiz, 223–28
knowledge, revelatory, 93–94

law. See ritual observances
leadership: and divinity, 129–30; in early rab-
    binic times, 137–38; and Hasidism, 127–30,
    138; in late Second Temple times, 137–38;
    paradigms of, 136–38; and Polonnoye, 128;
    and prophetic tradition, 146–49; and rab-
    binate, 127–30; in Scripture, 137. See also
    zaddiq
Lebensphilosophie, 377–81, 409
le-gabaw, 174

legabei didey, 174
le-gabey didan, 174
light, symbol of, 99–101
lighting candles, 254–58
Lithuanian Jews, 206, 208
love, divine, 329–32
Lurianic idea, 64
Lurianic Kabbalah: and holy sparks, 106–9,
    115–16; and kawwanot, 112–13, 123–24; and
    messianism, 109; mythological themes in,
    65–70; and redemption, 411–12; and Sab-
    batian heresy, 114–15; and sefirot, 101–2,
    106–7; and Shekhinah, 109–10; and sinful-
    ness, 74; understanding of, 64–65; and Vital,
    51–53; and worlds without number, 104. See
    also yihudim
Lurianic myth: shevirat ha-kelim, 66-68;
    tiqqun, 68–70; zimzum, 65–66
lust, 212

Maggid, 147–48
Maggid Mesharim (Karo), 14
materialism, 385, 388–89
meditation. See contemplation
mental tricks, 234–36
mesirat nefesh, 194
messianism: and asceticism, 12; and Judaism,
    30–31; and Kabbalah, 31; and kabbalists, 31;
    and Lurianic Kabbalah, 109; and mysticism,
    11; outburst of, 30–31; and Sabbatian heresy,
    11, 114–15, 125; and Safed Revival, 13–16;
    and spirituality, 13–15
mevaqshey panekha. See Jerusalem circle
Middle Ages, 7, 10, 351
middot, 231–37
midnight vigil, 72–73
Minor Day of Atonement, 110
Mitnagdim, 56–59
Mitnaggedism, 207–8
mizwot: of Ashkenazic women, 252–54; and
    Buber, 327–28; and divine love, 329–32;
    divinity in, 200; and faith, 424–25; and galut,
    202; and Habad thought, 198–203; and
    Heschel, 427, 429; humanity in, 199–200,
    202; and Jewish thought, 329–32; and
    Judaism, 427; and Otto, 325–26; and Rosen-
    zweig, 327–28, 332–35; and Spanish Jews,
    10; and Torah, 198–203
modernization, 285–89
modesty, 72

morality: and Kant, 318–20, 334; and Mussar movement, 218–20; and *yihudim*, 71–72
moral qualities, 71–72
motivation, psychological, 211–15
mussar, 32–33
Mussar House, 214
Mussar movement: and character training, 227, 229–36; and consciousness, 236–42; cultural context of, 206–9; and ethics, 211–15; *havurot* of, 221–22; and Kabbalah, 209–10; and *kloiz*, 223–28; and morality, 218–20; and motivation, psychological, 211–15; occurrence of, 206; opposition to, 222–23; organization of, 220–22; and Salanter, 206–9; and social realm, 218–20; teaching of, 223–28; and Torah, 215–17; and unconscious, 236–42; and *yir'ah*, 215–17
mystical illumination: and contemplation, 26–29; and *devequt*, 22–24
mystical tradition, 23, 64
mysticism: and divinity, 168–70; and Hasidism, 8, 15, 115–25; and holy sparks, 106–13; and kabbalists, 16–17; and light, 99–101; and messianism, 11; and *parzufim*, 104; and revelation in modern times, 364–66; and Sabbatian heresy, 113–15; and *sefirot*, 101–4; and tetragrammaton, 105; and worlds without number, 104
myth: and Buber, 355–56; and revelation in modern times, 364–66

names, divine, 83–85
nationalism, 301–5. *See also* Zionism
Nefesh ha-Hayyim (Hayyim), 207–8
Nevyozer Kloiz, 223–24, 227–28
New Hebrew, 379–80, 397
niddah, 253, 258–62
normalization, 381

ontological presupposition, 424
oral tradition, 35–36, 257
organic nationhood, 301–3. *See also* Zionism

pantheism, 163
parzufim, 68–70, 104, 108
Path of the Upright (Luzzatto), 12
penitance: and redemption, 17; and *tiqqun*, 76–77; and *yihudim*, 74–78
perception: duality of, 173–75; transrational, 191–98

perfection. *See* divine perfection; ethical perfection
periodization of history, 7
philosophy, 36–37
physical ecstasy, 197–98
physical pleasures, 212
piety: and Torah, 326–27; and *yihudim*, 72–74. *See also* Ashkenazic women
pilpul, 50, 55
prayer: and Bergman, 335–36; and Buber, 335; and holy sparks, 110–13; and kabbalists, 110; and ritual observances, 335–36; as spiritual sacrifice, 140; and *tiqqun*, 111; weekday, 113. *See also* *tkhines*
preachers. *See* priests; rabbis
preaching, 296–98
priests, 138–42
"Primordial Man," 66–67, 69
prophets, 146–49
Prophetic Faith (Buber), 353
prophetic inspiration. *See* inspiration
prophetic tradition: and *devequt*, 22–23; and leadership, 146–49; Maimonides's theory of, 25; revival of, 147; Vital's theory of, 22–25
Protestant Ethic and the Spirit of Capitalism, The (Weber), 286–87
purification, of soul, 72
Puritans, 286–87

qelipot, 67, 69, 106, 112
Quntres ha-Hitpa'alut (Baer) 197

Ra'aya Meheimna, 38–40
rabbinate, 127–30
rabbis, 136, 149–52
rav, 150
realism, 383
reconstruction, 68–70
redemption, 303–5, 374, 411–12
relation, philosophy of: and Judaism, 411–15; and renewal of Judaism, 415–18
Religion of Reason out of the Sources of Judaism (Cohen), 348
Reshit Hokhmah (de Vidas), 15, 74
revelation: and Buber, 348–49, 355–58; classical views of, 347–48; and Cohen, 352, 354–55; and halakhah, 366; and Kook, 350; modern interpretation of, 347–48; and mysticism, 364–66; and myth, 364–66; as ongoing phenomenon, 348–51; problem of,

in modern times, 346–47; and Rosenzweig, 352–53, 358–64; Sinaitic, authenticity of, 351–53; and Torah, 366

revelations, 92–94

ritual observances: and commitment, 335–36; and Jewish thought, 335–36; and Otto, 325–26; and prayer, 335–36; and prophetic hope, 335–36; and Rosenzweig, 326–29; and Scholem, 323–25; and *yihudim*, 72–74

royalty. *See* king

Russian Jews, 220

Sabbath, The (Heschel), 426

Sabbatian heresy: description of, 114–15; and Hasidism, 115–16; and holy sparks, 125; and leadership, 136; and Lurianic Kabbalah, 114–15; and messianism, 11, 114–15, 125; and modern Jews, 8; origin of, 113–14

sabra, 397

sacrament. *See* ritual observances

sadness, 71

Safed: halakhah in, 45–49; Kabbalah in, 45–49, 53–56; and Luria, 49–51; revelations in, 92–94. *See also* Safed Revival

Safed Revival: achievement of, 11; beginning of, 13; dating of, 9; and Kabbalah, 10–11; and mysticism, 13–16; period of, 7–9. *See also* kabbalists; Safed

salvation, 30. *See also* tiqqun

sanctification, of profane, 384–88

science, 287, 309, 425

Scripture: and Buber, 346, 417–18; and faith, 424–25; and Heschel, 425; and leadership, 137; study of, 346

secularization: and Buber, 305–8; and Kook, 394; and modernization, 285, 305–8

sefirot: and *'Adam Qadmon*, 102–3; and kabbalists, 83, 101–4, 107; and Lurianic Kabbalah, 101–2, 106–7; and mysticism, 101–4; and *parzufim*, 104; and tetragrammaton, 105; and *zimzum*, 65–67

self-abnegation: achievement of perfect, 191; and acosmism, 181–82, 190; categories of service of, 187–89; and contemplation, 182–86; and faith, 191–92, 195–96; and finite, 186–88; and Habad thought, 181–91; highest level of, 191–92; significance of, 182, 189; and *zimzum*, 184, 186

self-limitation, 65–66

separating *hallah*, 254–58

Sephardic Jews, 10, 13

"Sermon, The" (Hazaz), 382

Seyder Tkhines u-Vakoshes, 247, 250–53

Sha'arey Ziyyon (Hannover), 249–52

Sha'ar ha-Shamayim (Horowitz), 249–52

Shekhinah, 13–15, 18, 108–10

Sheney Luhot ha-Berit (Horowitz), 55–56, 350–51

Sheqi'at ha-Hayyim (Klatzkin), 381

shevirat ha-kelim, 66–68

Shivhey ha-BeSHT, 128–29

Shloyshe she'orim (Tovim), 253–57

siddur, 247, 249

sin, 74–77

Sinaitic revelation, 351–53

Six-Day War, 397

solitude, 19–21. *See also* contemplation

"Song of Praise to the Unlearned, A" (Schneur), 382

soul: animal, 175–78; communion of, 79–83; divine, 175–78; and existence, 178; in Habad thought, 175–78; Lurianic teaching of, 80–82; and penitance, 74–78; purification of, 72; Vital's teaching of, 79–80

Spanish Jews, 10, 41

spirit: and Ahad Ha'am, 298–301; and Buber, 305–8; concretization of, in life, 388–90; and consciousness, 287–88; expansion of, 283–85; in future, 314–15; and Gordon, 302–3; idealist vision of, 291–93; of Israel, 305–8; of Judaism, 291–93, 308–15; and Kook, 303–5; and preaching, 296–98; and Sachs, 296–97; strategies of, 308–14; and Zionism, 284, 390–91

spiritual, 293–96

spiritual center, 298–301

spiritual ecstasy, 197–98

spiritualism, 158

spirituality: and asceticism, 12; and earthliness, 372; expansion of, 283; Hasidic, 12; and Judaism, 296–98; kabbalistic, 15; and messianism, 13–15; and *mussar*, 32–33; study of, 12; term of, 9; in Zionism, 371–73. *See also* Jewish spirituality

spiritual qualities, 71–72

Star of Redemption (Rosenzweig), 327, 349, 353, 358–59

subjugation, 230–33

Talmud: and Berab, 46; and Kabbalah, 40–41; and *zaddiq*, 131–32 *tehiru,* 66–67

tetragrammaton, 83–84, 105, 108

tiqqun: in Hasidism, 411–12; and holy sparks, 107–8; in Lurianic myth, 68–70; and penitance, 76–77; and prayer, 111

tiqquney 'awonot, 74–78

Tiqquney Zohar, 38–40, 42–43

tiqqun ha-middot. See character training

tiqqun ha-yezer, 230–33

tkhines: differences in, 253–54; and divine names, 251; for *hallah,* separating, 254–56; and kabbalistic prayers, 250–52; for lighting candles, 254–58; literature of, 249–50; and matriarchs, 266–67; for *niddah,* 258–62; occasions of, 247–49; origination of, 250; and patriarchs, 266; study of, 246, 267–68; women's saying of, 246–47

Tola'at Ya'aqov, 43–44

Toledot Ya'aqov Yosef, 128

Torah: and Baer, 322; and Breuer, 364–65; and Buber, 321–22; and divine names, 83; divinity in, 200–202; and *galut,* 202; and Guttmann, 321; and Habad thought, 198–203; and Heschel, 365; humanity in, 199–200, 202; and Jerusalem circle, 320–22; and Kabbalah, 56; and Magnes, 322; and Mitnaggedism, 208; and *mizwot,* 198–203; and Mussar movement, 215–17; Orthodoxy's conception of, 323–24; and piety, 326–27; and revelation, 366; and Rosenzweig, 326–27, 332–33; and Scholem, 320–22; and Simon, 322; study of, 34; and tetragrammaton, 105; and *yir'ah,* 215–17; and *zaddiq,* 130–31, 151–52; and *Zohar,* 38–39

Tractatus Theologico-Politicus (Spinoza), 286, 289–291, 372

transgression. *See* sin

transmutation, 230–33

transrational dimension, 191–98

tricks of the mind, 234–36

unconscious: and gap between conscious, 238–40; and intellectual awareness, 240–41; and Mussar movement, 236–42; Salanter's view of, 236–37

unification: of earth and heaven, 390–92; of male and female, 107–8; of tetragrammaton, 108

"Visions of the False Prophets" (Tchernichowsky), 382

Western culture, 317–18, 414–15

Western Jews, 286, 398

women: commandments of, 252–54; in Jewish spirituality, 245–46. *See also* Ashkenazic women

worldly wisdom, 215

worship: Habad approach to, 178–81; and self-abnegation, 181–91

written tradition, 34–36

yeshivot, 53–54, 56–58

yezer, 230–33

YHWH, 84–85

yihudim, and *'Adam Qadmon,* 66–67, 69; definition of, 65; and divine names, contemplation of, 83–85; and halakhah, 73; and *hashba'ot,* 27–29; and inspiration, prophetic, 86–87; and *kawwanot,* 79; and knowledge, new mystical, 93–94; and Luria, 51, 87–88; and moral qualities, 71–72; and penitance, 74–78; and piety, ritual, 72–74; place for practice of, 78–79; qualifying for practice of, 70–71; and revelations, heavenly, 92–93; and ritual observances, 72–74; and soul, communion of, 79–83; and spiritual qualities, 71–72; time for practice of, 78–79; and Vital, 51, 88–92; and *Zohar,* 73

yir'ah, 212–13, 215–17

Yom Kippur, 262–63

Yom Kippur candles, making, 262–67

Yom Kippur Qatan, 110

zaddiq: authority of, 117, 130; communion with, 79–83; as healer, 140–41; and halakhah, 57; and holy sparks, 117, 125; and Kabbalah, 133; as king, 142–46; and literature of seventeenth and eighteenth centuries, 133–34; and models of leadership, 138; and Moses, 148; as priest, 138–42; as prophet, 146–49; as rabbi, 149–52; and *rav,* 150; and redemption, 374; and Talmud, 131–32; and teachers of Hasidism, 134; term of, 134–35; and Torah, 130–31, 151–52; and tradition, 135–36; and Vital, 92

zimzum, 65–66, 184, 186

Zionism: and Arab-Jewish struggle, 335; and Berdyczewski, 379–81; and biblical humanism, 334–35; and Birnbaum, 392–93; and Buber, 305–8; as dialectical movement, 392–95; and Diaspora mission, 298–99;

earthliness in, 371–73, 395–98; and Eastern Haskalah, 375–77; and faith, 313; and *galut*, 373; and Gordon, 388–90, 389–90; and *hagshamah*, 371–72, 378, 388; and *halutz*, 382–84; and idealism, 383; and Israel, spiritualization of, 373–75; and Jerusalem circle, 320–22; and Katzenelson, 396–97; and Klatzin, 381; and Kook, 303, 392–95; and *Lebensphilosophie*, 377–81; and Nietzsche, 378–79; and Orthodox Judaism, 398; and realism, 383; and religious, 392–93; and sanctification of profane, 384–88; and Scholem, 392–395; and secular, 392–93; and Six-Day War, 397; and spirit, 284, 388–91; spirituality in, 371–73; and Torah, 320–22; and unity of heaven and earth, 390–92; and victory of earthliness, 395–98

Zionist Congress of 1913, 301

Zohar: and halakhah, 37–38; and Kabbalah, 37–39; and light, 100; and mystical knowledge, 94; printing of, 16; and Torah, 38–39; and *yihudim*, 73

Names

Aaron of Karlin, 145
Abraham ben Eliezer ha-Levi Berukhim, 73, 96
Abraham ben Nathan of Lunel, 263
Abraham ben Saul of Lunel, 263
Abulafia, Abraham, 26, 28
Ahad Ha'am, 284, 285, 291, 298–303, 305–6, 308, 311, 325, 376–77, 387
Akiba, 37, 88, 91, 314, 353, 365
Alkabez, Solomon, 13–16, 64, 82, 92
Alsheikh, Moses, 51
Amsterdam, Naphtali, 234–35
Aqavyah ben Mahalalel, 91, 97
Ashvili, Yom Tov, 42
Ashkenazi, Bezalel, 49
Azikri, Eliezar, 17–19, 21–22, 51, 82
Azriel of Gerona, 38

Ba'al Shem Tov, Israel (BeSHT), 8, 32, 115, 118, 121–22, 128–29, 131, 144, 150, 153–54
Baeck, Leo, 323, 338–39
Baer, Yitzhak Fritz, 320, 322, 372
Bag-Bag, Ben, 365
Baruch of Miedzhybozh, 118, 144
Benjamin of Zalozhtsy, 148
Berab, Jacob, 46
Berdyczewski, Micha Josef, 377, 379–81, 384, 389–90, 396
Bergman, Hugo, 320, 326, 335–36, 362
Bernstein, Eduard, 339
Berukhim, Abraham Halevi, 14
Bialik, Hayim Nahman, 279, 385
Birnbaum, Nathan, 392–93
Blazer, Yitzhak, 224–25, 227
Bluwstein, Rahel, 384
Brenner, Joseph Hayyim, 381–84, 389
Breuer, Isaac, 347, 364–65
Broide, Zevi Hirsch, 206–7
Buber, Martin, 8, 285, 305–10, 312, 320–22, 325–31, 334–35, 346–49, 351, 353, 355–60, 362, 386, 391–93, 395, 405–30

Cohen, Hermann, 323, 346–48, 352, 354–56, 359, 362, 374
Cohen, Yaakov, 382
Cordovero, Moses, 13, 15–16, 47–49, 64, 82, 92, 95, 97

David ha-Re'ubeni, 14
David of Makarov, 144
Delattes, Isaac, of Mantua, 16, 94
Dov Baer, of Miedzyrzec, 157, 159, 182–83, 185, 196–97
Duran, Profiat, 40–41

Ehrenberg, Hans, 351
Elijah de Vidas, 15, 74, 95
Elijah Gaon of Vilna, 130, 207, 209, 216–18
Elijah of Cartinga, 210
Elimelech of Lizensk, 120, 123–24
Epstein, Kalonymos Kalman, of Cracow, 123
Ergas, Joseph, 100–101
Ezra of Gerona, 38

Frankel, Baruch Teomim, 57
Freud, Sigmund, 309, 361, 402

Galante, Abraham, 82, 95
Galante, Moses, 95
Geiger, Abraham, 284, 291–92, 294, 296–97, 299, 308, 312–13, 374
Gennesin, Uri Nissan, 383
Gerondi, Nissim, 40
Gershon of Kuty, 129
Ginzburg, Asher, 291
Gordon, A. D., 284–85, 301–3, 308, 313, 384, 386, 388–91, 393, 395
Gordon, Judah Leib, 375
Gottlober, Abraham Baer, 144
Graetz, Heinrich, 313, 353
Guttmann, Julius, 320–21, 325–26

Ha-Levi, Aaron, 161–63, 165, 167–68, 170–72, 174, 179, 185–92, 194, 197, 199, 201–2
Halevi, Judah, 18, 305, 361
Hammann, Johann Georg, 360
Hamon, Ovadiah, 97
Hanina ben Dosa, 131–32
Hannover, Nathan Nata, 250–51
Hayyat, Judah, 41–42
Hayyim of Sanz, 57, 145
Hayyim of Volozhin, 57–58, 207–9, 216–18
Hayyon, Gedaliah, 112
Hazaz, Hayyim, 382, 392
Hegel, G. F. W., 284, 288, 292–97, 306, 312, 315

Herzl, Theodore, 298, 376
Heschel, Abraham Joshua, of Apt, 118, 119, 140, 310, 350, 364–65, 405–30
Hess, Moses, 386–88, 393
Hirsch, Samson Raphael, 329, 339, 352, 365
Horowitz, Isaiah, 54–56, 58, 132, 249–50, 350–51, 364

Ibn Adret, Solomon, 40, 42
Ibn Ezra, Abraham, 36, 296, 348, 354
Ibn Ezra, Moses, 18,
Ibn Gabbai, Meir, 42–45
Ibn Paquda, Bahya, 17, 21–22
Ibn Tabul, Joseph, 82, 96
Ibn Zimra, David, 44, 49
Isaac of Acre, 21
Isaac the Blind, 38
Israel of Ruzhyn, 144–45

Jacob Joseph of Polonnoye, 117, 128, 134, 154
Jonah of Gerona, 12, 20, 22
Joseph della Reyna, 27
Joseph of Sagis, 21
Joseph of Yokrat, 16

Kant, Immanuel, 236, 287–88, 293, 306–7, 309–10, 318–20, 323, 325, 327–31, 333–34, 355, 364
Kaplan, Mordecai, 311
Karo, Joseph, 13–14, 44, 49–51, 82, 92, 157
Katzenelson, Berl, 396
Kierkegaard, S., 305, 403–4, 407, 414, 418
Klatzkin, J. (Yaakov), 381, 388
Kook, Abraham Isaac, 284, 303–5, 308, 313, 350, 355, 364, 384, 386, 391–95
Krochmal, Nahman, 284, 291, 293–97, 300, 305–6, 308, 310–13

Landau, Ezekiel, in Prague, 130
Landauer, Gustav, 334
Lazarus, Moritz, 323
Lefin, Menahem Mendel, 229, 235
Leon, Moses de, 38
Levi Yizhak, of Berdichev, 150
Lilienblum, Moses L., 375–76
Lipkin, Israel, of Salant, 206–44
Loeb, Judah, 210
Loew of Prague, 12
Luria, Isaac, 13–14, 29–32, 49–51, 64–98, 101, 117–18, 120–22

Luzzatto, Moses Hayyim, 12, 17, 33, 210

Magnes, Judah L., 320, 322–23, 325
Maimonides, 7, 10–11, 17, 22, 25, 36, 42, 50, 229, 289–90, 348, 354–55
Mannheimer, Isak Noa, 297
Marx, Karl, 286, 371, 402
Maybaum, Siegmund, 297
Menahem Mendel of Kossov, 185
Menahem Nahum of Chernobyl, 132
Mendelssohn, M., 286, 291, 313, 352, 372, 385
Mizrahi, Elijah, 37
Molkho, Solomon, 14, 27
Mordecai of Chernobyl, 144

Nagara, Israel, 18
Nahman of Bratslav, 151, 373
Nahmanides, 22, 37–38, 305, 355, 364
Nathan of Gaza, 30, 113, 114
Nathan of Nemirov, 151
Nietzsche, F., 283, 288, 356, 378, 380, 402–5, 407, 410, 414

Philippson, Ludwig, 297
Pinsker, Leo, 298, 376
Plato, 306, 315

Rashi, 140, 143, 350, 52
Ratosh, Yonatan, 395
Rosenheim, Jacob, 352
Rosenzweig, Franz, 313, 326–36, 346–49, 351–53, 357–64, 366, 417

Saadiah Gaon, 7, 229, 351
Sachs, Michael, 296, 314
Sagis, Jonathan, 73
Schleiermacher, F., 310
Schneur Zalman of Lyady, 157, 161–63, 155–67, 172–73, 175, 177–78, 180–85, 192, 197, 382
Scholem, Gershom, 7, 11, 15, 30–32, 39, 64, 67–69, 117, 313–14, 320–25, 355, 357, 392–95
Sevi, Sabbatai, 8, 11, 30–32, 113–14, 125
Shalom, Shin, 390
Shapira, Leib, 222
Shar'abi, Shalom, 112–13
Shlomiel, Solomon, 94
Simmel, Georg, 409, 414

Simon, Ernst Akiva, 320, 322, 326, 335–36, 357

Simon bar Yohai, 16, 18, 20, 48, 82–83

Smolenskin, Peretz, 375

Soloviev, Vladimir, 385

Spinoza, B., 8, 283–84, 286, 289–92, 303, 313, 315, 318, 360, 372

Taytazak, Joseph, of Salonica, 14

Tchernichowsky, Saul, 382, 396

Teitelbaum, Moses, of Ujhely, 125

Vital, Hayyim, 22–28, 50–55, 70–77, 79, 82, 86–89, 91–92, 94–97

Vital, Shmuel, 74

Weber, Max, 286–88, 312, 314–15, 361, 410, 414

Yavetz, Joseph, 41–42

Yitzhak Eisik of Komarno, 121

Yohanan ben Zakkai, 36, 353

Ze'ev Wolf of Zhitomir, 119–20, 147

Ziv, Simhah Zissel, 220, 225